W. Somerset Maugham

W. Somerset Maugham

30 Great
Short Stories

A selection from *The Complete Short Stories* first
published in three volumes in Great Britain in 1951
by William Heinemann Limited

This edition first published in 1984 by arrangement with
Doubleday & Company, Inc

by

Octopus Books Limited
59 Grosvenor Street
London W1

ISBN 0 7064 2198 1

Printed in the United States of America by
Kingsport Press

W. Somerset Maugham

Contents

Rain	13
The Fall of Edward Barnard	40
Honolulu	62
The Art and the Grasshopper	78
The Pool	81
Mackintosh	106
The Three Fat Women of Antibes	128
The Facts of Life	138
Gigolo and Gigolette	151
The Voice of the Turtle	163
The Unconquered	174
The Escape	192
Mr Know-all	195
The Romantic Young Lady	200
A Man From Glasgow	207

Before the Party   214
The Vessel of Wrath   231
Louise   256
The Promise   261
The Yellow Streak   266
The Force of Circumstance   284
Flotsam and Jetsam   301
The Alien Corn   317
The Creative Impulse   342
Virtue   365
The Closed Shop   389
The Dream   395
The Colonel's Lady   398
Miss King   410
The Hairless Mexican   432

Many writers seem to me not to observe at all, but to create their characters in stock sizes from images in their own fancy . . . . I have taken living people and put them into the situations, tragic or comic, that their characters suggested. I might well say that they invented their own stories.

W. SOMERSET MAUGHAM: *The Summing Up*

Rain

♦

It was nearly bed-time and when they awoke next morning land would be in sight. Dr Macphail lit his pipe and, leaning over the rail, searched the heavens for the Southern Cross. After two years at the front and a wound that had taken longer to heal than it should, he was glad to settle down quietly at Apia for twelve months at least, and he felt already better for the journey. Since some of the passengers were leaving the ship next day at Pago-Pago they had had a little dance that evening and in his ears hammered still the harsh notes of the mechanical piano. But the deck was quiet at last. A little way off he saw his wife in a long chair talking with the Davidsons, and he strolled over to her. When he sat down under the light and took off his hat you saw that he had very red hair, with a bald patch on the crown, and the red, freckled skin which accompanies red hair; he was a man of forty, thin, with a pinched face, precise and rather pedantic; and he spoke with a Scots accent in a very low, quiet voice.

Between the Macphails and the Davidsons, who were missionaries, there had arisen the intimacy of shipboard, which is due to propinquity rather than to any community of taste. Their chief tie was the disapproval they shared of the men who spent their days and nights in the smoking-room playing poker or bridge and drinking. Mrs Macphail was not a little flattered to think that she and her husband were the only people on board with whom the Davidsons were willing to associate, and even the doctor, shy but no fool, half unconsciously acknowledged the compliment. It was only because he was of an argumentative mind that in their cabin at night he permitted himself to carp.

'Mrs Davidson was saying she didn't know how they'd have got through the journey if it hadn't been for us,' said Mrs Macphail, as she neatly brushed out her transformation. 'She said we were really the only people on the ship they cared to know.'

'I shouldn't have thought a missionary was such a big bug that he could afford to put on frills.'

'It's not frills. I quite understand what she means. It wouldn't have been very nice for the Davidsons to have to mix with all that rough lot in the smoking-room.'

'The founder of their religion wasn't so exclusive,' said Dr Macphail with a chuckle.

'I've asked you over and over again not to joke about religion,' answered his wife. 'I shouldn't like to have a nature like yours, Alec. You never look for the best in people.'

He gave her a sidelong glance with his pale, blue eyes, but did not reply. After many years of married life he had learned that it was more conducive to peace to leave his wife with the last word. He was undressed before she was, and climbing into the upper bunk he settled down to read himself to sleep.

When he came on deck next morning they were close to land. He looked at it with greedy eyes. There was a thin strip of silver beach rising quickly to hills covered to the top with luxuriant vegetation. The coconut trees, thick and green, came nearly to the water's edge, and among them you saw the grass houses of the Samoans; and here and there, gleaming white, a little church. Mrs Davidson came and stood beside him. She was dressed in black and wore round her neck a gold chain, from which dangled a small cross. She was a little woman, with brown, dull hair very elaborately arranged, and she had prominent blue eyes behind invisible pince-nez. Her face was long, like a sheep's, but she gave no impression of foolishness, rather of extreme alertness; she had the quick movements of a bird. The most remarkable thing about her was her voice, high, metallic, and without inflexion; it fell on the ear with a hard monotony, irritating to the nerves like the pitiless clamour of the pneumatic drill.

'This must seem like home to you,' said Dr Macphail, with his thin, difficult smile.

'Ours are low islands, you know, not like these. Coral. These are volcanic. We've got another ten days' journey to reach them.'

'In these parts that's almost like being in the next street at home,' said Dr Macphail facetiously.

'Well, that's rather an exaggerated way of putting it, but one does look at distances differently in the South Seas. So far you're right.'

Dr Macphail sighed faintly.

'I'm glad we're not stationed here,' she went on. 'They say this is a terribly difficult place to work in. The steamers' touching makes the people unsettled; and then there's the naval station; that's bad for the natives. In our district we don't have difficulties like that to contend with. There are one or two traders, of course, but we take care to make them behave, and if they don't we make the place so hot for them they're glad to go.'

Fixing the glasses on her nose she looked at the green island with a ruthless stare.

'It's almost a hopeless task for the missionaries here. I can never be sufficiently thankful to God that we are at least spared that.'

Davidson's district consisted of a group of islands to the North of Samoa; they were widely separated and he had frequently to go long distances by canoe. At these times his wife remained at their headquarters and managed the mission. Dr Macphail felt his heart sink when he considered the efficiency with which she certainly managed it. She spoke of the depravity of the natives in a voice which nothing could hush, but with a vehemently unctuous horror. Her sense of delicacy was singular. Early in their acquaintance she had said to him:

'You know, their marriage customs when we first settled in the islands were so shocking that I couldn't possibly describe them to you. But I'll tell Mrs Macphail and she'll tell you.'

Then he had seen his wife and Mrs Davidson, their deck-chairs close together, in earnest conversation for about two hours. As he walked past them backwards and forwards for the sake of exercise, he had heard Mrs Davidson's agitated whisper, like the distant flow of a mountain torrent, and he saw by his wife's open mouth and pale face that she was enjoying an alarming experience. At night in their cabin she repeated to him with bated breath all she had heard.

'Well, what did I say to you?' cried Mrs Davidson, exultant next morning. 'Did you ever hear anything more dreadful? You don't wonder that I couldn't tell you myself, do you? Even though you are a doctor.'

Mrs Davidson scanned his face. She had a dramatic eagerness to see that she had achieved the desired effect.

'Can you wonder that when we first went there our hearts sank? You'll hardly believe me when I tell you it was impossible to find a single good girl in any of the villages.'

She used the word *good* in a severely technical manner.

'Mr Davidson and I talked it over, and we made up our minds the first thing to do was to put down the dancing. The natives were crazy about dancing.'

'I was not averse to it myself when I was a young man,' said Dr Macphail.

'I guessed as much when I heard you ask Mrs Macphail to have a turn with you last night. I don't think there's any real harm if a man dances with his wife, but I was relieved that she wouldn't. Under the circumstances I thought it better that we should keep ourselves to ourselves.'

'Under what circumstances?'

Mrs Davidson gave him a quick look through her pince-nez, but did not answer his question.

'But among white people it's not quite the same,' she went on, 'though I must say I agree with Mr Davidson, who says he can't understand how a husband can stand by and see his wife in another man's arms, and as far as I'm concerned I've never danced a step since I married. But the native dancing is quite another matter. It's not only immoral in itself, but it distinctly leads to immorality. However, I'm thankful to God that we stamped it out, and I don't think I'm wrong in saying that no one has danced in our district for eight years.'

But now they came to the mouth of the harbour and Mrs Macphail joined them. The ship turned sharply and steamed slowly in. It was a great land-locked harbour big enough to hold a fleet of battleships; and all around it rose, high and steep, the green hills. Near the entrance, getting such breeze as blew from the sea, stood the governor's house in a garden. The Stars and Stripes dangled languidly from a flagstaff. They passed two or three trim bungalows, and a tennis court, and then they came to the quay with its warehouses. Mrs Davidson pointed out the schooner, moored two or three hundred yards from the side, which was to take them to Apia. There was a crowd of eager, noisy, and good-humoured natives come from all parts of the island, some from curiosity, others to barter with the travellers on their way to Sydney; and they brought pineapples and huge bunches of bananas, tapa cloths, necklaces of shells or sharks' teeth, *kava*-bowls, and models of war canoes. American sailors, neat and trim, clean-shaven and frank of face, sauntered among them, and there was a little group of officials. While their luggage was being landed the Macphails and Mrs Davidson watched the crowd. Dr Macphail looked at the yaws from which most of the children and the young boys seemed to suffer, disfiguring sores like torpid ulcers, and his professional eyes glistened when he saw for the first time in his experience cases of elephantiasis, men going about with a huge, heavy arm or dragging along a grossly disfigured leg. Men and women wore the lava-lava.

'It's a very indecent costume,' said Mrs Davidson. 'Mr Davidson thinks it should be prohibited by law. How can you expect people to be moral when they wear nothing but a strip of red cotton round their loins?'

'It's suitable enough to the climate,' said the doctor, wiping the sweat off his head.

Now that they were on land the heat, though it was so early in the morning, was already oppressive. Closed in by its hills, not a breath of air came in to Pago-Pago.

'In our islands,' Mrs Davidson went on in her high-pitched tones, 'we've practically eradicated the lava-lava. A few old men still continue to wear it, but that's all. The women have all taken to the Mother Hubbard, and the men wear trousers and singlets. At the beginning of our stay Mr Davidson said in one of his reports: the inhabitants of these islands will never be thoroughly Christianized till every boy of more than ten years is made to wear a pair of trousers.'

But Mrs Davidson had given two or three of her birdlike glances at heavy grey clouds that came floating over the mouth of the harbour. A few drops began to fall.

'We'd better take shelter,' she said.

They made their way with all the crowd to a great shed of corrugated iron, and the rain began to fall in torrents. They stood there for some time and then were joined by Mr Davidson. He had been polite enough to the Macphails during the journey, but he had not his wife's sociability, and had spent much of his time reading. He was a silent, rather sullen man, and you felt that his affability was a duty that he imposed upon himself Christianly; he was by nature reserved and even morose. His appearance was singular. He was very tall and thin, with long limbs loosely jointed; hollow cheeks, and curiously high cheek-bones; he had so cadaverous an air that it surprised you to notice how full and sensual were his lips. He wore his hair very long. His dark eyes, set deep in their sockets, were large and tragic; and his hands with their big, long fingers, were finely shaped; they gave him a look of great strength. But the most striking thing about him was the feeling he gave you of suppressed fire. It was impressive and vaguely troubling. He was not a man with whom any intimacy was possible.

He brought now unwelcome news. There was an epidemic of measles, a serious and often fatal disease among the Kanakas, on the island, and a case had developed among the crew of the schooner which was to take them on their journey. The sick man had been brought ashore and put in hospital on the quarantine station, but telegraphic instructions had been sent from Apia to say that the schooner would not be allowed to enter the harbour till it was certain no other member of the crew was affected.

'It means we shall have to stay here for ten days at least.'

'But I'm urgently needed at Apia,' said Dr Macphail.

'That can't be helped. If no more cases develop on board, the schooner will be allowed to sail with white passengers, but all native traffic is prohibited for three months.'

'Is there a hotel here?' asked Mrs Macphail.

Davidson gave a low chuckle.

'There's not.'

'What shall we do then?'

'I've been talking to the governor. There's a trader along the front who has rooms that he rents, and my proposition is that as soon as the rain lets up we should go along there and see what we can do. Don't expect comfort. You've just got to be thankful if we get a bed to sleep on and a roof over our heads.'

But the rain showed no signs of stopping, and at length with umbrellas and waterproofs they set out. There was no town, but merely a group of official buildings, a store or two, and at the back, among the coconut trees and plantains, a few native dwellings. The house they sought was about five minutes' walk from the wharf. It was a frame house of two storeys, with broad verandas on both floors and a roof of corrugated iron. The owner was a half-caste named Horn, with a native wife surrounded by little brown children, and on the ground-floor he had a store where he sold canned goods and cottons. The rooms he showed them were almost bare of furniture. In the Macphails' there was nothing but a poor, worn bed with a ragged mosquito net, a rickety chair, and a washstand. They looked round with dismay. The rain poured down without ceasing.

'I'm not going to unpack more than we actually need,' said Mrs Macphail.

Mrs Davidson came into the room as she was unlocking a portmanteau. She was very brisk and alert. The cheerless surroundings had no effect on her.

'If you'll take my advice you'll get a needle and cotton and start right in to mend the mosquito net,' she said, 'or you'll not be able to get a wink of sleep tonight.'

'Will they be very bad?' asked Dr Macphail.

'This is the season for them. When you're asked to a party at Government House at Apia you'll notice that all the ladies are given a pillowslip to put their–their lower extremities in.'

'I wish the rain would stop for a moment,' said Mrs Macphail. 'I could try to make the place comfortable with more heart if the sun were shining.'

'Oh, if you wait for that, you'll wait a long time. Pago-Pago is about the rainiest place in the Pacific. You see, the hills, and that bay, they attract the water, and one expects rain at this time of year anyway.'

She looked from Macphail to his wife, standing helplessly in different parts of the room, like lost souls, and she pursed her lips. She saw that she must take them in hand. Feckless people like that made her impatient, but her hands itched to put everything in the order which came so naturally to her.

'Here, you give me a needle and cotton and I'll mend that net of yours, while you go on with your unpacking. Dinner's at one. Dr Macphail, you'd better go down to the wharf and see that your heavy luggage has been put in a dry place. You know what these natives are, they're quite capable of storing it where the rain will beat in on it all the time.'

The doctor put on his waterproof again and went downstairs. At the door Mr Horn was standing in conversation with the quartermaster of the ship they had just arrived in and a second-class passenger whom Dr Macphail had seen several times on board. The quartermaster, a little, shrivelled man, extremely dirty, nodded to him as he passed.

'This is a bad job about the measles, doc,' he said. 'I see you've fixed yourself up already.'

Dr Macphail thought he was rather familiar, but he was a timid man and he did not take offence easily.

'Yes, we've got a room upstairs.'

'Miss Thompson was sailing with you to Apia, so I've brought her along here.'

The quartermaster pointed with his thumb to the woman standing by his side. She was twenty-seven perhaps, plump, and in a coarse fashion pretty. She wore a white dress and a large white hat. Her fat calves in white cotton stockings bulged over the tops of long white boots in glacé kid. She gave Macphail an ingratiating smile.

'The feller's tryin' to soak me a dollar and a half a day for the meanest-sized room,' she said in a hoarse voice.

'I tell you she's a friend of mine, Jo,' said the quartermaster. 'She can't pay more than a dollar, and you've sure got to take her for that.'

The trader was fat and smooth and quietly smiling.

'Well, if you put it like that, Mr Swan, I'll see what I can do about it. I'll talk to Mrs Horn and if we think we can make a reduction we will.'

'Don't try to pull that stuff with me,' said Miss Thompson. 'We'll settle this right now. You get a dollar a day for the room and not one bean more.'

Dr Macphail smiled. He admired the effrontery with which she bargained. He was the sort of man who always paid what he was asked. He preferred to be over-charged than to haggle. The trader sighed.

'Well, to oblige Mr Swan I'll take it.'

'That's the goods,' said Miss Thompson. 'Come right in and have a shot of hooch. I've got some real good rye in that grip if you'll bring it along, Mr Swan. You come along too, doctor.'

'Oh, I don't think I will, thank you,' he answered. 'I'm just going down to see that our luggage is all right.'

He stepped out into the rain. It swept in from the opening of the harbour in sheets and the opposite shore was all blurred. He passed two or three natives clad in nothing but the lava-lava, with huge umbrellas over them. They walked finely, with leisurely movements, very upright; and they smiled and greeted him in a strange tongue as they went by.

It was nearly dinner-time when he got back, and their meal was laid in the trader's parlour. It was a room designed not to live in but for purposes of prestige, and it had a musty, melancholy air. A suite of stamped plush was arranged neatly round the walls, and from the middle of the ceiling, protected from the flies by yellow tissue-paper, hung a gilt chandelier. Davidson did not come.

'I know he went to call on the governor,' said Mrs Davidson, 'and I guess he's kept him to dinner.'

A little native girl brought them a dish of Hamburger steak, and after a while the trader came up to see that they had everything they wanted.

'I see we have a fellow lodger, Mr Horn,' said Dr Macphail.

'She's taken a room, that's all,' answered the trader. 'She's getting her own board.'

He looked at the two ladies with an obsequious air.

'I put her downstairs so she shouldn't be in the way. She won't be any trouble to you.'

'Is it someone who was on the boat?' asked Mrs Macphail.

'Yes, ma'am, she was in the second cabin. She was going to Apia. She has a position as cashier waiting for her.'

'Oh!'

When the trader was gone Macphail said:

'I shouldn't think she'd find it exactly cheerful having her meals in her room.'

'If she was in the second cabin I guess she'd rather,' answered Mrs Davidson. 'I don't exactly know who it can be.'

'I happened to be there when the quartermaster brought her along. Her name's Thompson.'

'It's not the woman who was dancing with the quartermaster last night?' asked Mrs Davidson.

'That's who it must be,' said Mrs Macphail. 'I wondered at the time what she was. She looked rather fast to me.'

'Not good style at all,' said Mrs Davidson.

They began to talk of other things, and after dinner, tired with their early rise, they separated and slept. When they awoke, though the sky was still grey and the clouds hung low, it was not raining and they went for a walk on the high road which the Americans had built along the bay.

On their return they found that Davidson had just come in.

'We may be here for a fortnight,' he said irritably. 'I've argued it out with the governor, but he says there is nothing to be done.'

'Mr Davidson's just longing to get back to his work,' said his wife, with an anxious glance at him.

'We've been away for a year,' he said, walking up and down the veranda. 'The mission has been in charge of native missionaries and I'm terribly nervous that they've let things slide. They're good men, I'm not saying a word against them, God-fearing, devout, and truly Christian men–their Christianity would put many so-called Christians at home to the blush–but they're pitifully lacking in energy. They can make a stand once, they can make a stand twice, but they can't make a stand all the time. If you leave a mission in charge of a native missionary, no matter how trustworthy he seems, in course of time you'll find he's let abuses creep in.'

Mr Davidson stood still. With his tall, spare form, and his great eyes flashing out of his pale face, he was an impressive figure. His sincerity was obvious in the fire of his gestures and in his deep, ringing voice.

'I expect to have my work cut out for me. I shall act and I shall act promptly. If the tree is rotten it shall be cut down and cast into the flames.'

And in the evening after the high tea which was their last meal, while they sat in the stiff parlour, the ladies working and Dr Macphail smoking his pipe, the missionary told them of his work in the islands.

'When we went there they had no sense of sin at all,' he said. 'They broke the commandments one after the other and never knew they were doing wrong. And I think that was the most difficult part of my work, to instil into the natives the sense of sin.'

The Macphails knew already that Davidson had worked in the Solomons for five years before he met his wife. She had been a missionary in China, and they had become acquainted in Boston, where they were both spending part of their leave to attend a missionary congress. On their marriage they had been appointed to the islands in which they had laboured ever since.

In the course of all the conversations they had had with Mr Davidson one thing had shone out clearly and that was the man's unflinching courage. He was a medical missionary, and he was liable to be called at any time to one or other of the islands in the group. Even the whaleboat is not so very safe a conveyance in the stormy Pacific of the wet season, but often he would be sent for in a canoe, and then the danger was great. In cases of illness or accident he never hesitated. A dozen times he had spent the whole night baling for his life, and more than once Mrs Davidson had given him up for lost.

'I'd beg him not to go sometimes,' she said, 'or at least to wait till the weather was more settled, but he'd never listen. He's obstinate, and when he's once made up his mind, nothing can move him.'

'How can I ask the natives to put their trust in the Lord if I am afraid to do so myself?' cried Davidson. 'And I'm not, I'm not. They know that if they send for me in their trouble I'll come if it's humanly possible. And do you think the Lord is going to abandon me when I am on his business? The wind blows at his bidding and the waves toss and rage at his word.'

Dr Macphail was a timid man. He had never been able to get used to the hurtling of the shells over the trenches, and when he was operating in an advanced dressing-station the sweat poured from his brow and dimmed his spectacles in the effort he made to control his unsteady hand. He shuddered a little as he looked at the missionary.

'I wish I could say that I've never been afraid,' he said.

'I wish you could say that you believed in God,' retorted the other.

But for some reason, that evening the missionary's thoughts travelled back to the early days he and his wife had spent on the islands.

'Sometimes Mrs Davidson and I would look at one another and the tears would stream down our cheeks. We worked without ceasing, day and night, and we seemed to make no progress. I don't know what I should have done without her then. When I felt my heart sink, when I was very near despair, she gave me courage and hope.'

Mrs Davidson looked down at her work, and a slight colour rose to her thin cheeks. Her hands trembled a little. She did not trust herself to speak.

'We had no one to help us. We were alone, thousands of miles from any of our own people, surrounded by darkness. When I was broken and weary she would put her work aside and take the Bible and read to me till peace came and settled upon me like sleep upon the eyelids of a child, and when at last she closed the book she'd say: "We'll save them in spite of themselves." And I felt strong again in the Lord, and I answered: "Yes, with God's help I'll save them. I must save them."'

He came over to the table and stood in front of it as though it were a lectern.

'You see, they were so naturally depraved that they couldn't be brought to see their wickedness. We had to make sins out of what they thought were natural actions. We had to make it a sin, not only to commit adultery and to lie and thieve, but to expose their bodies, and to dance and not to come to church. I made it a sin for a girl to show her bosom and a sin for a man not to wear trousers.'

'How?' asked Dr Macphail, not without surprise.

'I instituted fines. Obviously the only way to make people realize that an action is sinful is to punish them if they commit it. I fined them if they didn't come to church, and I fined them if they danced. I fined them if they were improperly dressed. I had a tariff, and every sin had to be paid for either in money or work. And at last I made them understand.'

'But did they never refuse to pay?'

'How could they?' asked the missionary.

'It would be a brave man who tried to stand up against Mr Davidson,' said his wife, tightening her lips.

Dr Macphail looked at Davidson with troubled eyes. What he heard shocked him, but he hesitated to express his disapproval.

'You must remember that in the last resort I could expel them from their church membership.'

'Did they mind that?'

Davidson smiled a little and gently rubbed his hands.

'They couldn't sell their copra. When the men fished they got no share of the catch. It meant something very like starvation. Yes, they minded quite a lot.'

'Tell him about Fred Ohlson,' said Mrs Davidson.

The missionary fixed his fiery eyes on Dr Macphail.

'Fred Ohlson was a Danish trader who had been in the islands a good many years. He was a pretty rich man as traders go and he wasn't very pleased when we came. You see, he'd had things very much his own way. He paid the natives what he liked for their copra, and he paid in goods and whisky. He had a native wife, but he was flagrantly unfaithful to her. He was a drunkard. I gave him a chance to mend his ways, but he wouldn't take it. He laughed at me.'

Davidson's voice fell to a deep bass as he said the last words, and he was silent for a minute or two. The silence was heavy with menace.

'In two years he was a ruined man. He'd lost everything he'd saved in a quarter of a century. I broke him, and at last he was forced to come to me like a beggar and beseech me to give him a passage back to Sydney.'

'I wish you could have seen him when he came to see Mr Davidson,' said the missionary's wife. 'He had been a fine, powerful man, with a lot of fat on him, and he had a great big voice, but now he was half the size, and he was shaking all over. He'd suddenly become an old man.'

With abstracted gaze Davidson looked out into the night. The rain was falling again.

Suddenly from below came a sound, and Davidson turned and looked questioningly at his wife. It was the sound of a gramophone, harsh and loud, wheezing out a syncopated tune.

'What's that?' he asked.

Mrs Davidson fixed her pince-nez more firmly on her nose.

'One of the second-class passengers has a room in the house. I guess it comes from there.'

They listened in silence, and presently they heard the sound of dancing. Then the music stopped, and they heard the popping of corks and voices raised in animated conversation.

'I daresay she's giving a farewell party to her friends on board,' said Dr Macphail. 'The ship sails at twelve, doesn't it?'

Davidson made no remark, but he looked at his watch.

'Are you ready?' he asked his wife.

She got up and folded her work.

'Yes, I guess I am,' she answered.

'It's early to go to bed yet, isn't it?' said the doctor.

'We have a good deal of reading to do,' explained Mrs Davidson. 'Wherever we are, we read a chapter of the Bible before retiring for the night and we study it with the commentaries, you know, and discuss it thoroughly. It's a wonderful training for the mind.'

The two couples bade one another good night. Dr and Mrs Macphail were left alone. For two or three minutes they did not speak.

'I think I'll go and fetch the cards,' the doctor said at last.

Mrs Macphail looked at him doubtfully. Her conversation with the Davidsons had left her a little uneasy, but she did not like to say that she thought they had better not play cards when the Davidsons might come in at any moment. Dr Macphail brought them and she watched him, though with a vague sense of guilt, while he laid out his patience. Below the sound of revelry continued.

It was fine enough next day, and the Macphails, condemned to spend a fortnight of idleness at Pago-Pago, set about making the best of things. They went down to the quay and got out of their boxes a number of books. The doctor called on the chief surgeon of the naval hospital and went round the beds with him. They left cards on the governor. They passed Miss Thompson on the road. The doctor took off his hat, and she gave him a 'Good morning doc,' in a loud, cheerful voice. She was dressed as on the day before, in a white frock, and her shiny white boots with their high heels, her fat legs bulging over the tops of them, were strange things on that exotic scene.

'I don't think she's very suitably dressed, I must say,' said Mrs Macphail. 'She looks extremely common to me.'

When they got back to their house, she was on the veranda playing with one of the trader's dark children.

'Say a word to her,' Dr Macphail whispered to his wife. 'She's all alone here, and it seems rather unkind to ignore her.'

Mrs Macphail was shy, but she was in the habit of doing what her husband bade her.

'I think we're fellow lodgers here,' she said, rather foolishly.

'Terrible, ain't it, bein' cooped up in a one-horse burg like this?' answered Miss Thompson. 'And they tell me I'm lucky to have gotten a room. I don't see myself livin' in a native house, and that's what some have to do. I don't know why they don't have a hotel.'

They exchanged a few more words. Miss Thompson, loud-voiced and garrulous, was evidently quite willing to gossip, but Mrs Macphail had a poor stock of small talk and presently she said:

'Well, I think we must go upstairs.'

In the evening when they sat down to their high tea, Davidson on coming in said:

'I see that woman downstairs has a couple of sailors sitting there. I wonder how she's gotten acquainted with them.'

'She can't be very particular,' said Mrs Davidson.

They were all rather tired after the idle, aimless day.

'If there's going to be a fortnight of this I don't know what we shall feel like at the end of it,' said Dr Macphail.

'The only thing to do is to portion out the day to different activities,' answered the missionary. 'I shall set aside a certain number of hours to study and a certain number to exercise, rain or fine—in the wet season you can't afford to pay any attention to the rain—and a certain number to recreation.'

Dr Macphail looked at his companion with misgiving. Davidson's programme oppressed him. They were eating Hamburger steak again. It seemed the only dish the cook knew how to make. Then below the gramophone began. Davidson started nervously when he heard it, but said nothing. Men's voices floated up. Miss Thompson's guests were joining in a well-known song and presently they heard her voice too, hoarse and loud. There was a good deal of shouting and laughing. The four people upstairs, trying to make conversation, listened despite themselves to the clink of glasses and the scrape of chairs. More people had evidently come. Miss Thompson was giving a party.

'I wonder how she gets them all in,' said Mrs Macphail suddenly breaking into a medical conversation between the missionary and her husband.

It showed whither her thoughts were wandering. The twitch of Davidson's face proved that, though he spoke of scientific things, his mind was busy in the same direction. Suddenly, while the doctor was giving some experience of practice on the Flanders front, rather prosily, he sprang to his feet with a cry.

'What's the matter, Alfred?' asked Mrs Davidson.

'Of course! It never occurred to me. She's out of Iwelei.'

'She can't be.'

'She came on board at Honolulu. It's obvious. And she's carrying on her trade here. Here.'

He uttered the last word with a passion of indignation.

'What's Iwelei?' asked Mrs Macphail.

He turned his gloomy eyes on her and his voice trembled with horror.

'The plague spot of Honolulu. The Red Light district. It was a blot on our civilization.'

Iwelei was on the edge of the city. You went down side streets by the harbour, in the darkness, across a rickety bridge, till you came to a deserted road, all ruts and holes, and then suddenly you came out into the light. There was parking room for motors on each side of the road, and there were saloons, tawdry and bright, each one noisy with its mechanical piano, and there were barbers' shops and tobacconists. There was a stir in the air and a sense of expectant gaiety. You turned down a narrow alley, either to the right or to the left, for the road divided Iwelei into two parts, and you found yourself in the district. There were rows of little bungalows, trim and neatly painted in green, and the pathway between them was broad and straight. It was laid out like a garden-city. In its respectable regularity, its order and spruceness, it gave an impression of sardonic horror; for never can the search for love have been so systematized and ordered. The pathways were lit by a rare lamp, but they would have been dark except for the lights that came from the open windows of the bungalows. Men wandered about, looking at the women who sat at their windows, reading or sewing, for the most part taking no notice of the passers-by; and like the women they were of all nationalities. There were Americans, sailors from the ships in port, enlisted men off the gunboats, sombrely drunk, and soldiers from the regiments, white and black, quartered on the island; there were Japanese, walking in twos and threes; Hawaiians, Chinese in long robes, and Filipinos in preposterous hats. They were silent and as it were oppressed. Desire is sad.

'It was the most crying scandal of the Pacific,' exclaimed Davidson vehemently. 'The missionaries had been agitating against it for years, and at last the local press took it up. The police refused to stir. You know their argument. They say that vice is inevitable and consequently the best thing is to localize and control it. The truth is, they were paid. Paid. They were paid by the saloon-keepers, paid by the bullies, paid by the women themselves. At last they were forced to move.'

'I read about it in the papers that came on board in Honolulu,' said Dr Macphail.

'Iwelei, with its sin and shame, ceased to exist on the very day we arrived. The whole population was brought before the justices. I don't know why I didn't understand at once what that woman was.'

'Now you come to speak of it,' said Mrs Macphail, 'I remember seeing her come on board only a few minutes before the boat sailed. I remember thinking at the time she was cutting it rather fine.'

'How dare she come here!' cried Davidson indignantly. 'I'm not going to allow it.'

He strode towards the door.

'What are you going to do?' asked Macphail.

'What do you expect me to? I'm going to stop it. I'm not going to have this house turned into—into . . .'

He sought for a word that should not offend the ladies' ears. His eyes were flashing and his pale face was paler still in his emotion.

'It sounds as though there were three or four men down there,' said the doctor. 'Don't you think it's rather rash to go in just now?'

The missionary gave him a contemptuous look and without a word flung out of the room.

'You know Mr Davidson very little if you think the fear of personal danger can stop him in the performance of his duty,' said his wife.

She sat with her hands nervously clasped, a spot of colour on her high cheek-bones, listening to what was about to happen below. They all listened. They heard him clatter down the wooden stairs and throw open the door. The singing stopped suddenly, but the gramophone continued to bray out its vulgar tune. They heard Davidson's voice and then the noise of something heavy falling. The music stopped. He had hurled the gramophone on the floor. Then again they heard Davidson's voice, they could not make out the words, then Miss Thompson's, loud and shrill, then a confused clamour as though several people were shouting together at the top of their lungs. Mrs Davidson gave a little gasp, and she clenched her hands more tightly. Dr Macphail looked uncertainly from her to his wife. He did not want to go down, but he wondered if they expected him to. Then there was something that sounded like a scuffle. The noise now was more distinct. It might be that Davidson was being thrown out of the room. The door was slammed. There was a moment's silence and they heard Davidson come up the stairs again. He went to his room.

'I think I'll go to him,' said Mrs Davidson.

She got up and went out.

'If you want me, just call,' said Mrs Macphail, and then when the other was gone: 'I hope he isn't hurt.'

'Why couldn't he mind his own business?' said Dr Macphail.

They sat in silence for a minute or two and then they both started, for the gramophone began to play once more, defiantly, and mocking voices shouted hoarsely the words of an obscene song.

Next day Mrs Davidson was pale and tired. She complained of headache, and she looked old and wizened. She told Mrs Macphail that the missionary had not slept at all; he had passed the night in a state of frightful agitation and at five had got up and gone out. A glass of beer had been thrown over him and his clothes were stained and stinking. But a sombre fire glowed in Mrs Davidson's eyes when she spoke of Miss Thompson.

'She'll bitterly rue the day when she flouted Mr Davidson,' she said. 'Mr Davidson has a wonderful heart and no one who is in trouble has ever gone to him without being comforted, but he has no mercy for sin, and when his righteous wrath is excited he's terrible.'

'Why, what will he do?' asked Mrs Macphail.

'I don't know, but I wouldn't stand in that creature's shoes for anything in the world.'

Mrs Macphail shuddered. There was something positively alarming in the triumphant assurance of the little woman's manner. They were going out together that morning, and they went down the stairs side by side. Miss Thompson's door was open, and they saw her in a bedraggled dressing-gown, cooking something in a chafing-dish.

'Good morning,' she called. 'Is Mr Davidson better this morning?'

They passed her in silence, with their noses in the air, as if she did not exist. They flushed, however, when she burst into a shout of derisive laughter. Mrs Davidson turned on her suddenly.

'Don't you dare to speak to me,' she screamed. 'If you insult me I shall have you turned out of here.'

'Say, did I ask Mr Davidson to visit with me?'

'Don't answer her,' whispered Mrs Macphail hurriedly.

They walked on till they were out of earshot.

'She's brazen, brazen,' burst from Mrs Davidson.

Her anger almost suffocated her.

And on their way home they met her strolling towards the quay. She had all her finery on. Her great white hat with its vulgar, showy flowers was an affront. She called out cheerily to them as she went by, and a couple of American sailors who were standing there grinned as the ladies set their faces to an icy stare. They got in just before the rain began to fall again.

'I guess she'll get her fine clothes spoilt,' said Mrs Davidson with a bitter sneer.

Davidson did not come in till they were half-way through dinner. He was wet through, but he would not change. He sat, morose and silent, refusing to eat more than a mouthful, and he stared at the slanting rain. When Mrs Davidson told him of their two encounters with Miss Thompson he did not answer. His deepening frown alone showed that he had heard.

'Don't you think we ought to make Mr Horn turn her out of here?' asked Mrs Davidson. 'We can't allow her to insult us.'

'There doesn't seem to be any other place for her to go,' said Macphail.

'She can live with one of the natives.'

'In weather like this a native hut must be a rather uncomfortable place to live in.'

'I lived in one for years,' said the missionary.

When the little native girl brought in the fried bananas which formed the sweet they had every day, Davidson turned to her.

'Ask Miss Thompson when it would be convenient for me to see her,' he said.

The girl nodded shyly and went out.

'What do you want to see her for, Alfred?' asked his wife.

'It's my duty to see her. I won't act till I've given her every chance.'

'You don't know what she is. She'll insult you.'

'Let her insult me. Let her spit on me. She has an immortal soul, and I must do all that is in my power to save it.'

Mrs Davidson's ears rang still with the harlot's mocking laughter.

'She's gone too far.'

'Too far for the mercy of God?' His eyes lit up suddenly and his voice grew mellow and soft. 'Never. The sinner may be deeper in sin than the depth of hell itself, but the love of the Lord Jesus can reach him still.'

The girl came back with the message.

'Miss Thompson's compliments and as long as Rev Davidson don't come in business hours she'll be glad to see him any time.'

The party received it in stony silence, and Dr Macphail quickly effaced from his lips the smile which had come upon them. He knew his wife would be vexed with him if he found Miss Thompson's effrontery amusing.

They finished the meal in silence. When it was over the two ladies got up and took their work. Mrs Macphail was making another of the innumerable comforters which she had turned out since the beginning of the war, and the doctor lit his pipe. But Davidson remained in his chair and with abstracted eyes stared at the table. At last he got up and without a word went out of the room. They heard him go down and they heard Miss Thompson's defiant 'Come in' when he knocked at the door. He remained with her for an hour. And Dr Macphail watched the rain. It was beginning to get on his nerves. It was not like soft English rain that drops gently on the earth; it was unmerciful and somehow terrible; you felt in it the malignancy of the primitive powers of nature. It did not pour, it flowed. It was like a deluge from heaven, and it rattled on the roof of corrugated iron with a steady persistence that was maddening. It seemed to have a fury of its own. And sometimes you felt that you must scream if it did not stop, and then suddenly you felt powerless, as though your bones had suddenly become soft; and you were miserable and hopeless.

Macphail turned his head when the missionary came back. The two women looked up.

'I've given her every chance. I have exhorted her to repent. She is an evil woman.'

He paused, and Dr Macphail saw his eyes darken and his pale face grow hard and stern.

'Now I shall take the whips with which the Lord Jesus drove the usurers and the money changers out of the Temple of the Most High.'

He walked up and down the room. His mouth was close set, and his black brows were frowning.

'If she fled to the uttermost parts of the earth I should pursue her.'

With a sudden movement he turned round and strode out of the room. They heard him go downstairs again.

'What is he going to do?' asked Mrs Macphail.

'I don't know.' Mrs Davidson took off her pince-nez and wiped them. 'When he is on the Lord's work I never ask him questions.'

She sighed a little.

'What is the matter?'

'He'll wear himself out. He doesn't know what it is to spare himself.'

Dr Macphail learnt the first results of the missionary's activity from the half-caste trader in whose house they lodged. He stopped the doctor when he passed the store and came out to speak to him on the stoop. His fat face was worried.

'The Rev Davidson has been at me for letting Miss Thompson have a room here,' he said, 'but I didn't know what she was when I rented it to her. When people come and ask if I can rent them a room all I want to know is if they've the money to pay for it. And she paid me for hers a week in advance.'

Dr Macphail did not want to commit himself.

'When all's said and done it's your house. We're very much obliged to you for taking us in at all.'

Horn looked at him doubtfully. He was not certain yet how definitely Macphail stood on the missionary's side.

'The missionaries are in with one another,' he said, hesitatingly. 'If they get it in for a trader he may just as well shut up his store and quit.'

'Did he want you to turn her out?'

'No, he said so long as she behaved herself he couldn't ask me to do that. He said he wanted to be just to me. I promised she shouldn't have no more visitors. I've just been and told her.'

'How did she take it?'

'She gave me Hell.'

The trader squirmed in his old ducks. He had found Miss Thompson a rough customer.

'Oh, well, I daresay she'll get out. I don't suppose she wants to stay here if she can't have anyone in.'

'There's nowhere she can go, only a native house, and no native'll take her now, not now that the missionaries have got their knife in her.'

Dr Macphail looked at the falling rain.

'Well, I don't suppose it's any good waiting for it to clear up.'

In the evening when they sat in the parlour Davidson talked to them of his early days at college. He had had no means and had worked his way through by doing odd jobs during the vacations. There was silence downstairs. Miss Thompson was sitting in her little room alone. But suddenly the gramophone began to play. She had set it on in defiance, to cheat her loneliness, but there was no one to sing, and it had a melancholy note. It was like a cry for help. Davidson took no notice. He was in the middle of a long anecdote and without change of expression went on. The gramophone continued. Miss Thompson put on one reel after another. It looked as though the silence of the night were getting on her nerves. It was breathless and sultry. When the Macphails went to bed they could not sleep. They lay side by side with their eyes wide open, listening to the cruel singing of the mosquitoes outside their curtain.

'What's that?' whispered Mrs Macphail at last.

They heard a voice, Davidson's voice, through the wooden partition. It went on with a monotonous, earnest insistence. He was praying aloud. He was praying for the soul of Miss Thompson.

Two or three days went by. Now when they passed Miss Thompson on the road she did not greet them with ironic cordiality or smile; she passed with her nose in the air, a sulky look on her painted face, frowning, as though she did not see them. The trader told Macphail that she had tried to get lodging elsewhere, but had failed. In the evening she played through the various reels of her gramophone, but the pretence of mirth was obvious now. The ragtime had a cracked, heart-broken rhythm as though it were a one-step of despair. When she began to play on Sunday Davidson sent Horn to beg her to stop at once since it was the Lord's day. The reel was taken off and the house was silent except for the steady pattering of the rain on the iron roof.

'I think she's getting a bit worked up,' said the trader next day to Macphail. 'She don't know what Mr Davidson's up to and it makes her scared.'

Macphail had caught a glimpse of her that morning and it struck him that her arrogant expression had changed. There was in her face a hunted look. The half-caste gave him a sidelong glance.

'I suppose you don't know what Mr Davidson is doing about it?' he hazarded.

'No, I don't.'

It was singular that Horn should ask him that question, for he also had the idea that the missionary was mysteriously at work.

He had an impression that he was weaving a net around the woman, carefully, systematically, and suddenly, when everything was ready, would pull the strings tight.

'He told me to tell her,' said the trader, 'that if at any time she wanted him she only had to send and he'd come.'

'What did she say when you told her that?'

'She didn't say nothing. I didn't stop. I just said what he said I was to and then I beat it. I thought she might be going to start weepin'.'

'I have no doubt the loneliness is getting on her nerves,' said the doctor. 'And the rain—that's enough to make anyone jumpy,' he continued irritably. 'Doesn't it ever stop in this confounded place?'

'It goes on pretty steady in the rainy season. We have three hundred inches in the year. You see, it's the shape of the bay. It seems to attract the rain from all over the Pacific.'

'Damn the shape of the bay,' said the doctor.

He scratched his mosquito bites. He felt very short-tempered. When the rain stopped and the sun shone, it was like a hot-house, seething, humid, sultry, breathless, and you had a strange feeling that everything was growing with a savage violence. The natives, blithe and childlike by reputation, seemed then, with their tattooing and their dyed hair, to have something sinister in their appearance; and when they pattered along at your heels with their naked feet you looked back instinctively. You felt they might at any moment come behind you swiftly and thrust a long knife between your shoulder-blades. You could not tell what dark thought lurked behind their wide-set eyes. They had a little the look of ancient Egyptians painted on a temple wall, and there was about them the terror of what is immeasurably old.

The missionary came and went. He was busy, but the Macphails did not know what he was doing. Horn told the doctor that he saw the governor every day, and once Davidson mentioned him.

'He looks as if he had plenty of determination,' he said, 'but when you come down to brass tacks he has no backbone.'

'I suppose that means he won't do exactly what you want,' suggested the doctor facetiously.

The missionary did not smile.

'I want him to do what's right. It shouldn't be necessary to persuade a man to do that.'

'But there may be differences of opinion about what is right.'

'If a man had a gangrenous foot would you have patience with anyone who hesitated to amputate it?'

'Gangrene is a matter of fact.'

'And Evil?'

What Davidson had done soon appeared. The four of them had just finished their midday meal, and they had not yet separated for the siesta which the heat imposed on the ladies and on the doctor. Davidson had little patience with the slothful habit. The door was suddenly flung open and Miss Thompson came in. She looked round the room and then went up to Davidson.

'You low-down skunk, what have you been saying about me to the governor?'

She was spluttering with rage. There was a moment's pause. Then the missionary drew forward a chair.

'Won't you be seated, Miss Thompson? I've been hoping to have another talk with you.'

'You poor low-life bastard.'

She burst into a torrent of insult, foul and insolent. Davidson kept his grave eyes on her.

'I'm indifferent to the abuse you think fit to heap on me, Miss Thompson,' he said, 'but I must beg you to remember that ladies are present.'

Tears by now were struggling with her anger. Her face was red and swollen as though she were choking.

'What has happened?' asked Dr Macphail.

'A feller's just been in here and he says I gotter beat it on the next boat.'

Was there a gleam in the missionary's eyes? His face remained impassive.

'You could hardly expect the governor to let you stay here under the circumstances.'

'You done it,' she shrieked. 'You can't kid me. You done it.'

'I don't want to deceive you. I urged the governor to take the only possible step consistent with his obligations.'

'Why couldn't you leave me be? I wasn't doin' you no harm.'

'You may be sure that if you had I should be the last man to resent it.'

'Do you think I want to stay on in this poor imitation of a burg? I don't look no busher, do I?'

'In that case I don't see what cause of complaint you have,' he answered.

She gave an inarticulate cry of rage and flung out of the room. There was a short silence.

'It's a relief to know that the governor has acted at last,' said Davidson finally. 'He's a weak man and he shilly-shallied. He said she was only here for a fortnight anyway, and if she went on to Apia, that was under British jurisdiction and had nothing to do with him.'

The missionary sprang to his feet and strode across the room.

'It's terrible the way the men who are in authority seek to evade their responsibility. They speak as though evil that was out of sight ceased to be evil. The very existence of that woman is a scandal and it does not help matters to shift it to another of the islands. In the end I had to speak straight from the shoulder.'

Davidson's brow lowered, and he protruded his firm chin. He looked fierce and determined.

'What do you mean by that?'

'Our mission is not entirely without influence at Washington. I pointed out to the governor that it wouldn't do him any good if there was a complaint about the way he managed things here.'

'When has she got to go?' asked the doctor, after a pause.

'The San Francisco boat is due here from Sydney next Tuesday. She's to sail on that.'

That was in five days' time. It was next day, when he was coming back from the hospital where for want of something better to do Macphail spent most of his mornings, that the half-caste stopped him as he was going upstairs.

'Excuse me, Dr Macphail, Miss Thompson's sick. Will you have a look at her?'

'Certainly.'

Horn led him to her room. She was sitting in a chair idly, neither reading nor sewing, staring in front of her. She wore her white dress and the large hat with the flowers on it. Macphail noticed that her skin was yellow and muddy under her powder, and her eyes were heavy.

'I'm sorry to hear you're not well,' he said.

'Oh, I ain't sick really. I just said that, because I just had to see you. I've got to clear on a boat that's going to 'Frisco.'

She looked at him and he saw that her eyes were suddenly startled. She opened and clenched her hands spasmodically. The trader stood at the door, listening.

'So I understand,' said the doctor.

She gave a little gulp.

'I guess it ain't very convenient for me to go to 'Frisco just now. I went to see the governor yesterday afternoon, but I couldn't get to him. I saw the secretary, and he told me I'd got to take that boat and that was all there was to it. I just had to see the governor, so I waited outside his house this morning, and when he came out I spoke to him. He didn't want to speak to me, I'll say, but I wouldn't let him shake me off, and at last he said he hadn't no objection to my staying here till the next boat to Sydney if the Rev Davidson will stand for it.'

She stopped and looked at Dr Macphail anxiously.

'I don't know exactly what I can do,' he said.

'Well, I thought maybe you wouldn't mind asking him. I swear to God I won't start anything here if he'll just only let me stay. I won't go out of the house if that'll suit him. It's no more'n a fortnight.'

'I'll ask him.'

'He won't stand for it,' said Horn. 'He'll have you out on Tuesday, so you may as well make up your mind to it.'

'Tell him I can get work in Sydney, straight stuff, I mean. 'Tain't asking very much.'

'I'll do what I can.'

'And come and tell me right away, will you? I can't set down to a thing till I get the dope one way or the other.'

It was not an errand that much pleased the doctor, and, characteristically perhaps, he went about it indirectly. He told his wife what Miss Thompson had said to him and asked her to speak to Mrs Davidson. The missionary's attitude seemed rather arbitrary and it could do no harm if the girl were allowed to stay in Pago-Pago another fortnight. But he was not prepared for the result of his diplomacy. The missionary came to him straightway.

'Mrs Davidson tells me that Thompson has been speaking to you.'

Dr Macphail, thus directly tackled, had the shy man's resentment at being forced out into the open. He felt his temper rising, and he flushed.

'I don't see that it can make any difference if she goes to Sydney rather than to San Francisco, and so long as she promises to behave while she's here it's dashed hard to persecute her.'

The missionary fixed him with his stern eyes.

'Why is she unwilling to go back to San Francisco?'

'I didn't inquire,' answered the doctor with some asperity. 'And I think one does better to mind one's own business.'

Perhaps it was not a very tactful answer.

'The governor has ordered her to be deported by the first boat that leaves the island. He's only done his duty and I will not interfere. Her presence is a peril here.'

'I think you're very harsh and tyrannical.'

The two ladies looked up at the doctor with some alarm, but they need not have feared a quarrel, for the missionary smiled gently.

'I'm terribly sorry you should think that of me, Dr Macphail. Believe me, my heart bleeds for that unfortunate woman, but I'm only trying to do my duty.'

The doctor made no answer. He looked out of the window sullenly. For once it was not raining and across the bay you saw nestling among the trees the huts of a native village.

'I think I'll take advantage of the rain stopping to go out,' he said.

'Please don't bear me malice because I can't accede to your wish,' said Davidson, with a melancholy smile. 'I respect you very much, doctor, and I should be sorry if you thought ill of me.'

'I have no doubt you have a sufficiently good opinion of yourself to bear mine with equanimity,' he retorted.

'That's one on me,' chuckled Davidson.

When Dr Macphail, vexed with himself because he had been uncivil to no purpose, went downstairs, Miss Thompson was waiting for him with her door ajar.

'Well,' she said, 'have you spoken to him?'

'Yes, I'm sorry, he won't do anything,' he answered, not looking at her in his embarrassment.

But then he gave her a quick glance, for a sob broke from her. He saw that her face was white with fear. It gave him a shock of dismay. And suddenly he had an idea.

'But don't give up hope yet. I think it's a shame the way they're treating you and I'm going to see the governor myself.'

'Now?'

He nodded. Her face brightened.

'Say, that's real good of you. I'm sure he'll let me stay if you speak for me. I just won't do a thing I didn't ought all the time I'm here.'

Dr Macphail hardly knew why he had made up his mind to appeal to the governor. He was perfectly indifferent to Miss Thompson's affairs, but the missionary had irritated him, and with him temper was a smouldering thing. He found the governor at home. He was a large, handsome man, a sailor, with a grey toothbrush moustache; and he wore a spotless uniform of white drill.

'I've come to see you about a woman who's lodging in the same house as we are,' he said. 'Her name's Thompson.'

'I guess I've heard nearly enough about her, Dr Macphail,' said the governor, smiling. 'I've given her the order to get out next Tuesday and that's all I can do.'

'I wanted to ask you if you couldn't stretch a point and let her stay here till the boat comes in from San Francisco so that she can go to Sydney. I will guarantee her good behaviour.'

The governor continued to smile, but his eyes grew small and serious.

'I'd be very glad to oblige you, Dr Macphail, but I've given the order and it must stand.'

The doctor put the case as reasonably as he could, but now the governor ceased to smile at all. He listened sullenly, with averted gaze. Macphail saw that he was making no impression.

'I'm sorry to cause any lady inconvenience, but she'll have to sail on Tuesday and that's all there is to it.'

'But what difference can it make?'

'Pardon me, doctor, but I don't feel called upon to explain my official actions except to the proper authorities.'

Macphail looked at him shrewdly. He remembered Davidson's hint that he had used threats, and in the governor's attitude he read a singular embarrassment.

'Davidson's a damned busybody,' he said hotly.

'Between ourselves, Dr Macphail, I don't say that I have formed a very favourable opinion of Mr Davidson, but I am bound to confess that he was within his rights in pointing out to me the danger that the presence of a woman of Miss Thompson's character was to a place like this where a number of enlisted men are stationed among a native population.'

He got up and Dr Macphail was obliged to do so too.

'I must ask you to excuse me. I have an engagement. Please give my respects to Mrs Macphail.'

The doctor left him crestfallen. He knew that Miss Thompson would be waiting for him, and unwilling to tell her himself that he had failed, he went into the house by the back door and sneaked up the stairs as though he had something to hide.

At supper he was silent and ill-at-ease, but the missionary was jovial and animated. Dr Macphail thought his eyes rested on him now and then with triumphant good-humour. It struck him suddenly that Davidson knew of his visit to the governor and of its ill success. But how on earth could he have heard of it? There was something sinister about the power of that man. After supper he saw Horn on the veranda and, as though to have a casual word with him, went out.

'She wants to know if you've seen the governor,' the trader whispered.

'Yes. He wouldn't do anything. I'm awfully sorry, I can't do anything more.'

'I knew he wouldn't. They daren't go against the missionaries.'

'What are you talking about?' said Davidson affably, coming out to join them.

'I was just saying there was no chance of your getting over to Apia for at least another week,' said the trader glibly.

He left them, and the two men returned into the parlour. Mr Davidson devoted one hour after each meal to recreation. Presently a timid knock was heard at the door.

'Come in,' said Mrs Davidson, in her sharp voice.

The door was not opened. She got up and opened it. They saw Miss Thompson standing at the threshold. But the change in her appearance was extraordinary. This was no longer the flaunting hussy who had jeered at them in the road, but a broken, frightened woman. Her hair, as a rule so elaborately arranged, was tumbling untidily over her neck. She wore bedroom slippers and a skirt and blouse. They were unfresh and bedraggled. She stood at the door with the tears streaming down her face and did not dare to enter.

'What do you want?' said Mrs Davidson harshly.

'May I speak to Mr Davidson?' she said in a choking voice.

The missionary rose and went towards her.

'Come right in, Miss Thompson,' he said in cordial tones. 'What can I do for you?'

She entered the room.

'Say, I'm sorry for what I said to you the other day an' for—for everythin' else. I guess I was a bit lit up. I beg pardon.'

'Oh, it was nothing. I guess my back's broad enough to bear a few hard words.'

She stepped towards him with a movement that was horribly cringing.

'You've got me beat. I'm all in. You won't make me go back to 'Frisco?'

His genial manner vanished and his voice grew on a sudden hard and stern.

'Why don't you want to go back there?'

She cowered before him.

'I guess my people live there. I don't want them to see me like this. I'll go anywhere else you say.'

'Why don't you want to go back to San Francisco?'

'I've told you.'

He leaned forward, staring at her, and his great, shining eyes seemed to try to bore into her soul. He gave a sudden gasp.

'The penitentiary.'

She screamed, and then she fell at his feet, clasping his legs.

'Don't send me back there. I swear to you before God I'll be a good woman. I'll give all this up.'

She burst into a torrent of confused supplication and the tears coursed down her painted cheeks. He leaned over her and, lifting her face, forced her to look at him.

'Is that it, the penitentiary?'

'I beat it before they could get me,' she gasped. 'If the bulls grab me it's three years for me.'

He let go his hold of her and she fell in a heap on the floor, sobbing bitterly. Dr Macphail stood up.

'This alters the whole thing,' he said. 'You can't make her go back when you know this. Give her another chance. She wants to turn over a new leaf.'

'I'm going to give her the finest chance she's ever had. If she repents let her accept her punishment.'

She misunderstood the words and looked up. There was a gleam of hope in her heavy eyes.

'You'll let me go?'

'No. You shall sail for San Francisco on Tuesday.'

She gave a groan of horror and then burst into low, hoarse shrieks which sounded hardly human, and she beat her head passionately on the ground. Dr Macphail sprang to her and lifted her up.

'Come on, you mustn't do that. You'd better go to your room and lie down. I'll get you something.'

He raised her to her feet and partly dragging her, partly carrying her, got her downstairs. He was furious with Mrs Davidson and with his wife because they made no effort to help. The half-caste was standing on the landing and with his assistance he managed to get her on the bed. She was moaning and crying. She was almost insensible. He gave her a hypodermic injection. He was hot and exhausted when he went upstairs again.

'I've got her to lie down.'

The two women and Davidson were in the same positions as when he had left them. They could not have moved or spoken since he went.

'I was waiting for you,' said Davidson, in a strange, distant voice. 'I want you all to pray with me for the soul of our erring sister.'

He took the Bible off a shelf, and sat down at the table at which they had supped. It had not been cleared, and he pushed the tea-pot out of the way. In a powerful voice, resonant and deep, he read to them the chapter in which is narrated the meeting of Jesus Christ with the woman taken in adultery.

'Now kneel with me and let us pray for the soul of our dear sister, Sadie Thompson.'

He burst into a long, passionate prayer in which he implored God to have mercy on the sinful woman. Mrs Macphail and Mrs Davidson knelt with covered eyes. The doctor, taken by surprise, awkward and sheepish, knelt too. The missionary's prayer had a savage eloquence. He was extraordinarily moved, and as he spoke the tears ran down his cheeks. Outside, the pitiless rain fell, fell steadily, with a fierce malignity that was all too human.

At last he stopped. He paused for a moment and said:

'We will now repeat the Lord's prayer.'

They said it and then, following him, they rose from their knees. Mrs Davidson's face was pale and restful. She was comforted and at peace, but the Macphails felt suddenly bashful. They did not know which way to look.

'I'll just go down and see how she is now,' said Dr Macphail.

When he knocked at her door it was opened for him by Horn. Miss Thompson was in a rocking-chair, sobbing quietly.

'What are you doing there?' exclaimed Macphail. 'I told you to lie down.'

'I can't lie down. I want to see Mr Davidson.'

'My poor child, what do you think is the good of it? You'll never move him.'

'He said he'd come if I sent for him.'

Macphail motioned to the trader.

'Go and fetch him.'

He waited with her in silence while the trader went upstairs. Davidson came in.

'Excuse me for asking you to come here,' she said, looking at him sombrely.

'I was expecting you to send for me. I knew the Lord would answer my prayer.'

They stared at one another for a moment and then she looked away. She kept her eyes averted when she spoke.

'I've been a bad woman. I want to repent.'

'Thank God! Thank God! He has heard our prayers.'

He turned to the two men.

'Leave me alone with her. Tell Mrs Davidson that our prayers have been answered.'

They went out and closed the door behind them.

'Gee whizz,' said the trader.

That night Dr Macphail could not get to sleep till late, and when he heard the missionary come upstairs he looked at his watch. It was two o'clock. But even then he did not go to bed at once, for through the wooden partition that separated their rooms he heard him praying aloud, till he himself, exhausted, fell asleep.

When he saw him next morning he was surprised at his appearance. He was paler than ever, tired, but his eyes shone with inhuman fire. It looked as though he were filled with an overwhelming joy.

'I want you to go down presently and see Sadie,' he said. 'I can't hope that her body is better, but her soul—her soul is transformed.'

The doctor was feeling wan and nervous.

'You were with her very late last night,' he said.

'Yes, she couldn't bear to have me leave her.'

'You look as pleased as Punch,' the doctor said irritably.

Davidson's eyes shone with ecstasy.

'A great mercy has been vouchsafed me. Last night I was privileged to bring a lost soul to the loving arms of Jesus.'

Miss Thompson was again in the rocking-chair. The bed had not been made. The room was in disorder. She had not troubled to dress herself, but wore a dirty dressing-gown, and her hair was tied in a sluttish knot. She had given her face a dab with a wet towel, but it was all swollen and creased with crying. She looked a drab.

She raised her eyes dully when the doctor came in. She was cowed and broken.

'Where's Mr Davidson?' she asked.

'He'll come presently if you want him,' answered Macphail acidly. 'I came here to see how you were.'

'Oh, I guess I'm O.K. You needn't worry about that.'

'Have you had anything to eat?'

'Horn brought me some coffee.'

She looked anxiously at the door.

'D'you think he'll come down soon? I feel as if it wasn't so terrible when he's with me.'

'Are you still going on Tuesday?'

'Yes, he says I've got to go. Please tell him to come right along. You can't do me any good. He's the only one as can help me now.'

'Very well,' said Dr Macphail.

During the next three days the missionary spent almost all his time with Sadie Thompson. He joined the others only to have his meals. Dr Macphail noticed that he hardly ate.

'He's wearing himself out,' said Mrs Davidson pitifully. 'He'll have a breakdown if he doesn't take care, but he won't spare himself.'

She herself was white and pale. She told Mrs Macphail that she had no sleep. When the missionary came upstairs from Miss Thompson he prayed till he was exhausted, but even then he did not sleep for long. After an hour or two he got up and dressed himself, and went for a tramp along the bay. He had strange dreams.

'This morning he told me that he'd been dreaming about the mountains of Nebraska,' said Mrs Davidson.

'That's curious,' said Dr Macphail.

He remembered seeing them from the windows of the train when he crossed America. They were like huge mole-hills, rounded and smooth, and they rose from the plain abruptly. Dr Macphail remembered how it struck him that they were like a woman's breasts.

Davidson's restlessness was intolerable even to himself. But he was buoyed up by a wonderful exhilaration. He was tearing out by the roots the last vestiges of sin that lurked in the hidden corners of that poor woman's heart. He read with her and prayed with her.

'It's wonderful,' he said to them one day at supper. 'It's a true rebirth. Her soul, which was black as night, is now pure and white like the new-fallen snow. I am humble and afraid. Her remorse for all her sins is beautiful. I am not worthy to touch the hem of her garment.'

'Have you the heart to send her back to San Francisco?' said the doctor. 'Three years in an American prison. I should have thought you might have saved her from that.'

'Ah, but don't you see? It's necessary. Do you think my heart doesn't bleed for her? I love her as I love my wife and my sister. All the time that she is in prison I shall suffer all the pain that she suffers.'

'Bunkum,' cried the doctor impatiently.

'You don't understand because you're blind. She's sinned, and she must suffer. I know what she'll endure. She'll be starved and tortured and humiliated. I want her to accept the punishment of man as a sacrifice to God. I want her to accept it joyfully. She has an opportunity which is offered to very few of us. God is very good and very merciful.'

Davidson's voice trembled with excitement. He could hardly articulate the words that tumbled passionately from his lips.

'All day I pray with her and when I leave her I pray again, I pray with all my might and main, so that Jesus may grant her this great mercy. I want to put in her heart the passionate desire to be punished so that at the end, even if I offered to let her go, she would refuse. I want her to feel that the bitter punishment of prison is the thank-offering that she places at the feet of our Blessed Lord, who gave his life for her.'

The days passed slowly. The whole household, intent on the wretched, tortured woman downstairs, lived in a state of unnatural excitement. She was like a victim that was being prepared for the savage rites of a bloody idolatry. Her terror numbed her. She could not bear to let Davidson out of her sight; it was only when he was with her that she had courage, and she hung upon him with a slavish dependence. She cried a great deal, and she read the Bible, and prayed. Sometimes she was exhausted and apathetic. Then she did indeed look forward to her ordeal, for it seemed to offer an escape, direct and concrete, from the anguish she was enduring. She could not bear much longer the vague terrors which now assailed her. With her sins she had put aside all personal vanity, and she slopped about her room, unkempt and dishevelled, in her tawdry dressing-gown. She had not taken off her night-dress for four days, nor put on stockings. Her room was littered and untidy. Meanwhile the rain fell with a cruel persistence. You felt that the heavens must at last be empty of water, but still it poured down, straight and heavy, with a maddening iteration, on the iron roof. Everything was damp and clammy. There was mildew on the walls and on the boots that stood on the floor. Through the sleepless nights the mosquitoes droned their angry chant.

'If it would only stop raining for a single day it wouldn't be so bad,' said Dr Macphail.

They all looked forward to the Tuesday when the boat for San Francisco was to arrive from Sydney. The strain was intolerable. So far as Dr Macphail was concerned, his pity and his resentment were alike extinguished by his desire to be rid of the unfortunate woman. The inevitable must be accepted. He felt he would breathe more freely when the ship had sailed. Sadie Thompson was to be escorted on board by a clerk in the governor's office. This person called on the Monday evening and told Miss Thompson to be prepared at eleven in the morning. Davidson was with her.

'I'll see that everything is ready. I mean to come on board with her myself.'

Miss Thompson did not speak.

When Dr Macphail blew out his candle and crawled cautiously under his mosquito curtains, he gave a sigh of relief.

'Well, thank God that's over. By this time tomorrow she'll be gone.'

'Mrs Davidson will be glad too. She says he's wearing himself to a shadow,' said Mrs Macphail. 'She's a different woman.'

'Who?'

'Sadie. I should never have thought it possible. It makes one humble.'

Dr Macphail did not answer, and presently he fell asleep. He was tired out, and he slept more soundly than usual.

He was awakened in the morning by a hand placed on his arm, and, starting up, saw Horn by the side of his bed. The trader put his finger on his mouth to prevent any exclamation from Dr Macphail and beckoned to him to come. As a rule he wore shabby ducks, but now he was barefoot and wore only the lava-lava of the natives. He looked suddenly savage, and Dr Macphail, getting out of bed, saw that he was heavily tattooed. Horn made him a sign to come on to the veranda. Dr Macphail got out of bed and followed the trader out.

'Don't make a noise,' he whispered. 'You're wanted. Put on a coat and some shoes. Quick.'

Dr Macphail's first thought was that something had happened to Miss Thompson.

'What is it? Shall I bring my instruments?'

'Hurry, please, hurry.'

Dr Macphail crept back into the bedroom, put on a waterproof over his pyjamas, and a pair of rubber-soled shoes. He rejoined the trader, and together they tiptoed down the stairs. The door leading out to the road was open and at it were standing half a dozen natives.

'What is it?' repeated the doctor.

'Come along with me,' said Horn.

He walked out and the doctor followed him. The natives came after them in a little bunch. They crossed the road and came on to the beach. The doctor saw a group of natives standing round some object at the water's edge. They hurried along, a couple of dozen yards perhaps, and the natives opened out as the doctor came up. The trader pushed him forwards. Then he saw, lying half in the water and half out, a dreadful object, the body of Davidson. Dr Macphail bent down—he was not a man to lose his head in an emergency—and turned the body over. The throat was cut from ear to ear, and in the right hand was still the razor with which the deed was done.

'He's quite cold,' said the doctor. 'He must have been dead some time.'

'One of the boys saw him lying there on his way to work just now and came and told me. Do you think he did it himself?'

'Yes. Someone ought to go for the police.'

Horn said something in the native tongue, and two youths started off.

'We must leave him here till they come,' said the doctor.

'They mustn't take him into my house. I won't have him in my house.'

'You'll do what the authorities say,' replied the doctor sharply. 'In point of fact I expect they'll take him to the mortuary.'

They stood waiting where they were. The trader took a cigarette from a fold in his lava-lava and gave one to Dr Macphail. They smoked while they stared at the corpse. Dr Macphail could not understand.

'Why do you think he did it?' asked Horn.

The doctor shrugged his shoulders. In a little while native police came along, under the charge of a marine, with a stretcher, and immediately afterwards a couple of naval officers and a naval doctor. They managed everything in a businesslike manner.

'What about the wife?' said one of the officers.

'Now that you've come I'll go back to the house and get some things on. I'll see that it's broken to her. She'd better not see him till he's been fixed up a little.'

'I guess that's right,' said the naval doctor.

When Dr Macphail went back he found his wife nearly dressed.

'Mrs Davidson's in a dreadful state about her husband,' she said to him as soon as he appeared. 'He hasn't been to bed all night. She heard him leave Miss Thompson's room at two, but he went out. If he's been walking about since then he'll be absolutely dead.'

Dr Macphail told her what had happened and asked her to break the news to Mrs Davidson.

'But why did he do it?' she asked, horror-stricken.

'I don't know.'

'But I can't. I can't.'

'You must.'

She gave him a frightened look and went out. He heard her go into Mrs Davidson's room. He waited a minute to gather himself together and then began to shave and wash. When he was dressed he sat down on the bed and waited for his wife. At last she came.

'She wants to see him,' she said.

'They've taken him to the mortuary. We'd better go down with her. How did she take it?'

'I think she's stunned. She didn't cry. But she's trembling like a leaf.'

'We'd better go at once.'

When they knocked at her door Mrs Davidson came out. She was very pale, but dry-eyed. To the doctor she seemed unnaturally composed. No word was exchanged, and they set out in silence down the road. When they arrived at the mortuary Mrs Davidson spoke.

'Let me go in and see him alone.'

They stood aside. A native opened a door for her and closed it behind her. They sat down and waited. One or two white men came and talked to them in undertones. Dr Macphail told them again what he knew of the tragedy. At last the door was quietly opened and Mrs Davidson came out. Silence fell upon them.

'I'm ready to go back now,' she said.

Her voice was hard and steady. Dr Macphail could not understand the look in her eyes. Her pale face was very stern. They walked back slowly, never saying a word, and at last they came round the bend on the other side of which stood their house. Mrs Davidson gave a gasp, and for a moment they stopped still. An incredible sound assaulted their ears. The gramophone which had been silent for so long was playing, playing ragtime loud and harsh.

'What's that?' cried Mrs Macphail with horror.

'Let's go on,' said Mrs Davidson.

They walked up the steps and entered the hall. Miss Thompson was standing at her door, chatting with a sailor. A sudden change had taken place in her. She was no longer the cowed drudge of the last days. She was dressed in all her finery, in her white dress, with the high shiny boots over which her fat legs bulged in their cotton stockings; her hair was elaborately arranged; and she wore that enormous hat covered with gaudy flowers. Her face was painted, her eyebrows were boldly black, and her lips were scarlet. She held herself erect. She was the flaunting queen that they had known at first. As they came in she broke into a loud, jeering laugh; and then, when Mrs Davidson involuntarily stopped, she collected the spittle in her mouth and spat. Mrs Davidson cowered back, and two red spots rose suddenly to her cheeks. Then, covering her face with her hands, she broke away and ran quickly up the stairs. Dr Macphail was outraged. He pushed past the woman into her room.

'What the devil are you doing?' he cried. 'Stop that damned machine.'

He went up to it and tore the record off. She turned on him.

'Say, doc, you can that stuff with me. What the hell are you doin' in my room?'

'What do you mean?' he cried. 'What d'you mean?'

She gathered herself together. No one could describe the scorn of her expression or the contemptuous hatred she put into her answer.

'You men! You filthy, dirty pigs! You're all the same, all of you. Pigs! Pigs!'

Dr Macphail gasped. He understood.

The Fall of Edward Barnard

◆

Bateman Hunter slept badly. For a fortnight on the boat that brought him from Tahiti to San Francisco he had been thinking of the story he had to tell, and for three days on the train he had repeated to himself the words in which he meant to tell it. But in a few hours now he would be in Chicago, and doubts assailed him. His conscience, always very sensitive, was not at ease. He was uncertain that he had done all that was possible, it was on his honour to do much more than the possible, and the thought was disturbing that, in a matter which so nearly touched his own interest, he had allowed his interest to prevail over his quixotry. Self-sacrifice appealed so keenly to his imagination that the inability to exercise it gave him a sense of disillusion. He was like the philanthropist who with altruistic motives builds model dwellings for the poor and finds that he has made a lucrative investment. He cannot prevent the satisfaction he feels in the ten per cent which rewards the bread he had cast upon the waters, but he has an awkward feeling that it detracts somewhat from the savour of his virtue. Bateman Hunter knew that his heart was pure, but he was not quite sure how steadfastly, when he told her his story, he would endure the scrutiny of Isabel Longstaffe's cool grey eyes. They were far-seeing and wise. She measured the standards of others by her own meticulous uprightness and there could be no greater censure than the cold silence with which she expressed her disapproval of a conduct that did not satisfy her exacting code. There was no appeal from her judgement, for, having made up her mind, she never changed it. But Bateman would not have had her different. He loved not only the beauty of her person, slim and straight, with the proud carriage of her head, but still more the beauty of her soul. With her truthfulness, her rigid sense of honour, her fearless outlook, she seemed to him to collect in herself all that was most admirable in his country-women. But he saw in her something more than the perfect type of the American girl, he felt that her exquisiteness was peculiar in a way to her environment, and he was assured that no city in the world could have produced her but Chicago. A pang seized him when he remembered that he must deal so bitter a blow to her pride, and anger flamed up in his heart when he thought of Edward Barnard.

But at last the train steamed in to Chicago and he exulted when he saw the long streets of grey houses. He could hardly bear his impatience at the thought of State and Wabash with their crowded pavements, their hustling traffic, and their noise. He was at home. And he was glad that he had been born in the most important city in the United States. San Francisco was provincial, New York was effete; the future of America lay in the development of its economic possibilities, and Chicago, by its position and by the energy of its citizens, was destined to become the real capital of the country.

'I guess I shall live long enough to see it the biggest city in the world,' Bateman said to himself as he stepped down to the platform.

His father had come to meet him, and after a hearty handshake, the pair of them, tall, slender, and well-made, with the same fine, ascetic features and thin lips, walked out of the station. Mr Hunter's automobile was waiting for them and they got in. Mr Hunter caught his son's proud and happy glance as he looked at the street.

'Glad to be back, son?' he asked.

'I should just think I was,' said Bateman.

His eyes devoured the restless scene.

'I guess there's a bit more traffic here than in your South Sea island,' laughed Mr Hunter. 'Did you like it there?'

'Give me Chicago, dad,' answered Bateman.

'You haven't brought Edward Barnard back with you.'

'No.'

'How was he?'

Bateman was silent for a moment, and his handsome, sensitive face darkened.

'I'd sooner not speak about him, dad,' he said at last.

'That's all right, my son. I guess your mother will be a happy woman today.'

They passed out of the crowded streets in the Loop and drove along the lake till they came to the imposing house, an exact copy of a château on the Loire, which Mr Hunter had built himself some years before. As soon as Bateman was alone in his room he asked for a number on the telephone. His heart leaped when he heard the voice that answered him.

'Good morning, Isabel,' he said gaily.

'Good morning, Bateman.'

'How did you recognize my voice?'

'It is not so long since I heard it last. Besides, I was expecting you.'

'When may I see you?'

'Unless you have anything better to do perhaps you'll dine with us tonight.'

'You know very well that I couldn't possibly have anything better to do.'

'I suppose that you're full of news?'

He thought he detected in her voice a note of apprehension.

'Yes,' he answered.

'Well, you must tell me tonight. Good-bye.'

She rang off. It was characteristic of her that she should be able to wait so many unnecessary hours to know what so immensely concerned her. To Bateman there was an admirable fortitude in her restraint.

At dinner, at which beside himself and Isabel no one was present but her father and mother, he watched her guide the conversation into the channels of an urbane small-talk, and it occurred to him that in just such a manner would a marquise under the shadow of the guillotine toy with the affairs of a day that would know no morrow. Her delicate features, the aristocratic shortness of her upper lip, and her wealth of fair hair suggested the marquise again, and it must have been obvious, even if it were not notorious, that in her veins flowed the best blood in Chicago. The dining-room was a fitting frame to her fragile beauty, for Isabel had caused the house, a replica of a palace on the Grand Canal at Venice, to be furnished by an English expert in the style of Louis XV; and the graceful decoration linked with the name of that amorous monarch enhanced her loveliness and at the same time acquired from it a more profound significance. For Isabel's mind was richly stored, and her conversation, however light, was never flippant. She spoke now of the Musicale to which she and her mother had been in the afternoon, of the lectures which an English poet was giving at the Auditorium, of the political situation, and of the Old Master which her father had recently bought for fifty thousand dollars in New York. It comforted Bateman to hear her. He felt that he was once more in the civilized world, at the centre of culture and distinction; and certain voices, troubling and yet against his will refusing to still their clamour, were at last silent in his heart.

'Gee, but it's good to be back in Chicago,' he said.

At last dinner was over, and when they went out of the dining-room Isabel said to her mother:

'I'm going to take Bateman along to my den. We have various things to talk about.'

'Very well, my dear,' said Mrs Longstaffe. 'You'll find your father and me in the Madame du Barry room when you're through.'

Isabel led the young man upstairs and showed him into the room of which he had so many charming memories. Though he knew it so well he could not repress the exclamation of delight which it always wrung from him. She looked round with a smile.

'I think it's a success,' she said. 'The main thing is that it's right. There's not even an ash-tray that isn't of the period.'

'I suppose that's what makes it so wonderful. Like all you do it's so superlatively right.'

They sat down in front of a log fire and Isabel looked at him with calm grave eyes.

'Now what have you to say to me?' she asked.

'I hardly know how to begin.'

'Is Edward Barnard coming back?'

'No.'

There was a long silence before Bateman spoke again, and with each of them it was filled with many thoughts. It was a difficult story he had to tell, for there were things in it which were so offensive to her sensitive ears that he could not bear to tell them, and yet in justice to her, no less than in justice to himself, he must tell her the whole truth.

It had all begun long ago when he and Edward Barnard, still at college, had met Isabel Longstaffe at the tea-party given to introduce her to society. They had both known her when she was a child and they long-legged boys, but for two years she had been in Europe to finish her education and it was with a surprised delight that they renewed acquaintance with the lovely girl who returned. Both of them fell desperately in love with her, but Bateman saw quickly that she had eyes only for Edward, and, devoted to his friend, he resigned himself to the role of confidant. He passed bitter moments, but he could not deny that Edward was worthy of his good fortune, and, anxious that nothing should impair the friendship he so greatly valued, he took care never by a hint to disclose his own feelings. In six months the young couple were engaged. But they were very young and Isabel's father decided that they should not marry at least till Edward graduated. They had to wait a year. Bateman remembered the winter at the end of which Isabel and Edward were to be married, a winter of dances and theatre-parties and of informal gaieties at which he, the constant third, was always present. He loved her no less because she would shortly be his friend's wife; her smile, a gay word she flung him, the confidence of her affection, never ceased to delight him; and he congratulated himself, somewhat complacently, because he did not envy them their happiness. Then an accident happened. A great bank failed, there was a panic on the exchange, and Edward Barnard's father found himself a ruined man. He came home one night, told his wife he was penniless, and after dinner, going into his study, shot himself.

A week later, Edward Barnard, with a tired, white face, went to Isabel and asked her to release him. Her only answer was to throw her arms round his neck and burst into tears.

'Don't make it harder for me, sweet,' he said.

'Do you think I can let you go now? I love you.'

'How can I ask you to marry me? The whole thing's hopeless. Your father would never let you. I haven't a cent.'

'What do I care? I love you.'

He told her his plans. He had to earn money at once, and George Braunschmidt, an old friend of his family, had offered to take him into his own business. He was a South Sea merchant, and he had agencies in many of the islands of the Pacific. He had suggested that Edward should go to Tahiti for a year or two, where under the best of his managers he could learn the details of that varied trade, and at the end of that time he promised the young man a position in Chicago. It was a wonderful opportunity, and when he had finished his explanations Isabel was once more all smiles.

'You foolish boy, why have you been trying to make me miserable?'

His face lit up at her words and his eyes flashed.

'Isabel, you don't mean to say you'll wait for me?'

'Don't you think you're worth it?' she smiled.

'Ah, don't laugh at me now. I beseech you to be serious. It may be for two years.'

'Have no fear. I love you, Edward. When you come back I will marry you.'

Edward's employer was a man who did not like delay and he had told him that if he took the post he offered he must sail that day week from San Francisco. Edward spent his last evening with Isabel. It was after dinner that Mr Longstaffe, saying he wanted a word with Edward, took him into the smoking-room. Mr Longstaffe had accepted good-naturedly the arrangement which his daughter had told him of and Edward could not imagine what mysterious communication he had now to make. He was not a little perplexed to see that his host was embarrassed. He faltered. He talked of trivial things. At last he blurted it out.

'I guess you've heard of Arnold Jackson,' he said, looking at Edward with a frown.

Edward hesitated. His natural truthfulness obliged him to admit a knowledge he would gladly have been able to deny.

'Yes, I have. But it's a long time ago. I guess I didn't pay very much attention.'

'There are not many people in Chicago who haven't heard of Arnold Jackson,' said Mr Longstaffe bitterly, 'and if there are they'll have no difficulty in finding someone who'll be glad to tell them. Did you know he was Mrs Longstaffe's brother?'

'Yes, I knew that.'

'Of course we've had no communication with him for many years. He left the country as soon as he was able to, and I guess the country wasn't sorry to see the last of him. We understand he lives in Tahiti. My advice to you is to give him a wide berth, but if you do hear anything about him Mrs Longstaffe and I would be very glad if you'd let us know.'

'Sure.'

'That was all I wanted to say to you. Now I daresay you'd like to join the ladies.'

There are few families that have not among their members one whom, if their neighbours permitted, they would willingly forget, and they are fortunate when the lapse of a generation or two has invested his vagaries with a romantic glamour. But when he is actually alive, if his peculiarities are not of the kind that can be condoned by the phrase, 'he is nobody's enemy but his own', a safe one when the culprit has no worse to answer for than alcoholism or wandering affections, the only possible course is silence. And it was this which the Longstaffes had adopted towards Arnold Jackson. They never talked of him. They would not even pass through the street in which he had lived. Too kind to make his wife and children suffer for his misdeeds, they had supported them for years, but on the understanding that they should live in Europe. They did everything they could to blot out all recollection of Arnold Jackson and yet were conscious that the story was as fresh in the public mind as when first the scandal burst upon a gaping world. Arnold Jackson was as black a sheep as any family could suffer from. A wealthy banker, prominent in his church, a philanthropist, a man respected by all, not only for his connexions (in his veins ran the blue blood of Chicago), but also for his upright character, he was arrested one day on a charge of fraud; and the dishonesty which the trial brought to light was not the sort which could be explained by a sudden temptation; it was deliberate and systematic. Arnold Jackson was a rogue. When he was sent to the penitentiary for seven years there were few who did not think he had escaped lightly.

When at the end of this last evening the lovers separated it was with many protestations of devotion. Isabel, all tears, was consoled a little by her certainty of Edward's passionate love. It was a strange feeling that she had. It made her wretched to part from him and yet she was happy because he adored her.

This was more than two years ago.

He had written to her by every mail since then, twenty-four letters in all, for the mail went but once a month, and his letters had been all that a lover's letters should be. They were intimate and charming, humorous sometimes, especially of late, and tender. At first they suggested that he was homesick, they were full of his desire to get back to Chicago and Isabel; and, a little anxiously, she wrote begging him to persevere. She was afraid that he might throw up his opportunity and come racing back. She did not want her lover to lack endurance and she quoted to him the lines:

> I could not love thee, dear, so much,
> Loved I not honour more.

But presently he seemed to settle down and it made Isabel very happy to observe his growing enthusiasm to introduce American methods into that forgotten corner of the world. But she knew him, and at the end of the year, which was the shortest time he could possibly stay in Tahiti, she expected to have to use all her influence to dissuade him from coming home. It was much better that he should learn the business thoroughly, and if they had been able to wait a year there seemed no reason why they should not wait another. She talked it over with Bateman Hunter, always the most generous of friends (during those first few days after Edward went she did not know what she would have done without him), and they decided that Edward's future must stand before everything. It was with relief that she found as the time passed that he made no suggestion of returning.

'He's splendid, isn't he?' she exclaimed to Bateman.

'He's white, through and through.'

'Reading between the lines of his letter I know he hates it over there, but he's sticking it out because . . .'

She blushed a little and Bateman, with the grave smile which was so attractive in him, finished the sentence for her.

'Because he loves you.'

'It makes me feel so humble,' she said.

'You're wonderful, Isabel, you're perfectly wonderful.'

But the second year passed and every month Isabel continued to receive a letter from Edward, and presently it began to seem a little strange that he did not speak of coming back. He wrote as though he were settled definitely in Tahiti, and what was more, comfortably settled. She was surprised. Then she read his letters again, all of them, several times; and now, reading between the lines indeed, she was puzzled to notice a change which had escaped her. The later letters were as tender and as delightful as the first, but the tone was different. She was vaguely suspicious of their humour, she had the instinctive mistrust of her sex for that unaccountable quality, and she discerned in them now a flippancy which perplexed her. She was not quite certain that the Edward who wrote to her now was the same Edward that she had known. One afternoon, the day after a mail had arrived from Tahiti, when she was driving with Bateman he said to her:

'Did Edward tell you when he was sailing?'

'No, he didn't mention it. I thought he might have said something to you about it.'

'Not a word.'

'You know what Edward is,' she laughed in reply, 'he has no sense of time. If it occurs to you next time you write you might ask him when he's thinking of coming.'

Her manner was so unconcerned that only Bateman's acute sensitiveness could have discerned in her request a very urgent desire. He laughed lightly.

'Yes. I'll ask him. I can't imagine what he's thinking about.'

A few days later, meeting him again, she noticed that something troubled him. They had been much together since Edward left Chicago; they were both devoted to him and each in his desire to talk of the absent one found a willing listener; the consequence was that Isabel knew every expression of Bateman's face, and his denials now were useless against her keen instinct. Something told her that his harassed look had to do with Edward and she did not rest till she had made him confess.

'The fact is,' he said at last, 'I heard in a roundabout way that Edward was no longer working for Braunschmidt and Co., and yesterday I took the opportunity to ask Mr Braunschmidt himself.'

'Well?'

'Edward left his employment with them nearly a year ago.'

'How strange he should have said nothing about it!'

Bateman hesitated, but he had gone so far now that he was obliged to tell the rest. It made him feel dreadfully embarrassed.

'He was fired.'

'In heaven's name what for?'

'It appears they warned him once or twice, and at last they told him to get out. They say he was lazy and incompetent.'

'Edward?'

They were silent for a while, and then he saw that Isabel was crying. Instinctively he seized her hand.

'Oh, my dear, don't, don't,' he said. 'I can't bear to see it.'

She was so unstrung that she let her hand rest in his. He tried to console her.

'It's incomprehensible, isn't it? It's so unlike Edward. I can't help feeling there must be some mistake.'

She did not say anything for a while, and when she spoke it was hesitatingly.

'Has it struck you that there was anything queer in his letters lately?' she asked, looking away, her eyes all bright with tears.

He did not quite know how to answer.

'I have noticed a change in them,' he admitted. 'He seems to have lost that high seriousness which I admired so much in him. One would almost think that the things that matter—well, don't matter.'

Isabel did not reply. She was vaguely uneasy.

'Perhaps in his answer to your letter he'll say when he's coming home. All we can do is to wait for that.'

Another letter came from Edward for each of them, and still he made no mention of his return; but when he wrote he could not have received Bateman's inquiry. The next mail would bring them an answer to that. The next mail came, and Bateman brought Isabel the letter he had just received; but the first glance of his face was enough to tell her that he was disconcerted. She read it through carefully and then, with slightly tightened lips, read it again.

'It's a very strange letter,' she said. 'I don't quite understand it.'

'One might almost think that he was joshing me,' said Bateman, flushing.

'It reads like that, but it must be unintentional. That's so unlike Edward.'

'He says nothing about coming back.'

'If I weren't so confident of his love I should think . . . I hardly know what I should think.'

It was then that Bateman had broached the scheme which during the afternoon had formed itself in his brain. The firm, founded by his father, in which he was now a partner, a firm which manufactured all manner of motor vehicles, was about to establish agencies in Honolulu, Sydney, and Wellington; and Bateman proposed that himself should go instead of the manager, who had been suggested. He could return by Tahiti; in fact, travelling from Wellington, it was inevitable to do so; and he could see Edward.

'There's some mystery and I'm going to clear it up. That's the only way to do it.'

'Oh, Bateman, how can you be so good and kind?' she exclaimed.

'You know there's nothing in the world I want more than your happiness, Isabel.'

She looked at him and she gave him her hands.

'You're wonderful, Bateman. I didn't know there was anyone in the world like you. How can I ever thank you?'

'I don't want your thanks. I only want to be allowed to help you.'

She dropped her eyes and flushed a little. She was so used to him that she had forgotten how handsome he was. He was as tall as Edward and as well made, but he was dark and pale of face, while Edward was ruddy. Of course she knew he loved her. It touched her. She felt very tenderly towards him.

It was from this journey that Bateman Hunter was now returned.

The business part of it took him somewhat longer than he expected and he had much time to think of his two friends. He had come to the conclusion that it could be nothing serious that prevented Edward from coming home, a pride, perhaps, which made him determined to make good before he claimed the bride he adored; but it was a pride that must be reasoned with. Isabel was unhappy. Edward must come back to Chicago with him and marry her at once. A position could be found for him in the works of the Hunter Motor Traction and Automobile Company. Bateman, with a bleeding heart, exulted at the prospect of giving happiness to the two persons he loved best in the world at the cost of his own. He would never marry. He would be godfather to the children of Edward and Isabel, and many years later when they were both dead he would tell Isabel's daughter how long, long ago he had loved her mother. Bateman's eyes were veiled with tears when he pictured this scene to himself.

Meaning to take Edward by surprise he had not cabled to announce his arrival, and when at last he landed at Tahiti he allowed a youth, who said he was the son of the house, to lead him to the Hôtel de la Fleur. He chuckled when he thought of his friend's amazement on seeing him, the most unexpected of visitors, walk into his office.

'By the way,' he asked, as they went along, 'can you tell me where I shall find Mr Edward Barnard?'

'Barnard?' said the youth. 'I seem to know the name.'

'He's an American. A tall fellow with light brown hair and blue eyes. He's been here over two years.'

'Of course. Now I know who you mean. You mean Mr Jackson's nephew.'

'Whose nephew?'

'Mr Arnold Jackson.'

'I don't think we're speaking of the same person,' answered Bateman, frigidly.

He was startled. It was queer that Arnold Jackson, known apparently to all and sundry, should live here under the disgraceful name in which he had been convicted. But Bateman could not imagine whom it was that he passed off as his nephew. Mrs Longstaffe was his only sister and he had never had a brother. The young man by his side talked volubly in an English that had something in it of the intonation of a foreign tongue, and Bateman, with a sidelong glance, saw, what he had not noticed before, that there was in him a good deal of native blood. A touch of hauteur involuntarily entered into his manner. They reached the hotel. When he had arranged about his room Bateman asked to be directed to the premises of Braunschmidt and Co. They were on the front, facing the lagoon, and, glad to feel the solid earth under his feet after eight days at sea, he sauntered down the sunny road to the water's edge. Having found the place he sought, Bateman sent in his card to the manager and was led through a lofty barn-like room, half store and half warehouse, to an office in which sat a stout, spectacled, bald-headed man.

'Can you tell me where I shall find Mr Edward Barnard? I understand he was in this office for some time.'

'That is so. I don't know just where he is.'

'But I thought he came here with a particular recommendation from Mr Braunschmidt. I know Mr Braunschmidt very well.'

The fat man looked at Bateman with shrewd, suspicious eyes. He called to one of the boys in the warehouse.

'Say, Henry, where's Barnard now, d'you know?'

'He's working at Cameron's, I think,' came the answer from someone who did not trouble to move.

The fat man nodded.

'If you turn to your left when you get out of here you'll come to Cameron's in about three minutes.'

Bateman hesitated.

'I think I should tell you that Edward Barnard is my greatest friend. I was very much surprised when I heard he'd left Braunschmidt and Co.'

The fat man's eyes contracted till they seemed like pin-points, and their scrutiny made Bateman so uncomfortable that he felt himself blushing.

'I guess Braunschmidt and Co. and Edward Barnard didn't see eye to eye on certain matters,' he replied.

Bateman did not quite like the fellow's manner, so he got up, not without dignity, and with an apology for troubling him bade him good day. He left the place with a singular feeling that the man he had just interviewed had much to tell him, but no intention of telling it. He walked in the direction indicated and soon found himself at Cameron's. It was a trader's store, such as he had passed half a dozen of on his way, and when he entered the first person he saw, in his shirt-sleeves, measuring out a length of trade cotton, was Edward. It gave him a start to see him engaged in so humble an occupation. But he had scarcely appeared when Edward, looking up, caught sight of him, and gave a joyful cry of surprise.

'Bateman! Who ever thought of seeing you here?'

He stretched his arm across the counter and wrung Bateman's hand. There was no self-consciousness in his manner and the embarrassment was all on Bateman's side.

'Just wait till I've wrapped this package.'

With perfect assurance he ran his scissors across the stuff, folded it, made it into a parcel, and handed it to the dark-skinned customer.

'Pay at the desk, please.'

Then, smiling, with bright eyes, he turned to Bateman.

'How did you show up here? Gee, I am delighted to see you. Sit down, old man. Make yourself at home.'

'We can't talk here. Come along to my hotel. I suppose you can get away?'
This he added with some apprehension.

'Of course I can get away. We're not so business-like as all that in Tahiti.' He
called out to a Chinese who was standing behind the opposite counter. 'Ah-
Ling, when the boss comes tell him a friend of mine's just arrived from America
and I've gone out to have a dram with him.'

'All-light,' said the Chinese, with a grin.

Edward slipped on a coat and, putting on his hat, accompanied Bateman out
of the store. Bateman attempted to put the matter facetiously.

'I didn't expect to find you selling three and a half yards of rotten cotton to a
greasy nigger,' he laughed.

'Braunschmidt fired me, you know, and I thought that would do as well as
anything else.'

Edward's candour seemed to Bateman very surprising, but he thought it
indiscreet to pursue the subject.

'I guess you won't make a fortune where you are,' he answered, somewhat
dryly.

'I guess not. But I earn enough to keep body and soul together, and I'm quite
satisfied with that.'

'You wouldn't have been two years ago.'

'We grow wiser as we grow older,' retorted Edward, gaily.

Bateman took a glance at him. Edward was dressed in a suit of shabby white
ducks, none too clean, and a large straw hat of native make. He was thinner than
he had been, deeply burned by the sun, and he was certainly better-looking
than ever. But there was something in his appearance that disconcerted
Bateman. He walked with a new jauntiness; there was a carelessness in his
demeanour, a gaiety about nothing in particular, which Bateman could not
precisely blame, but which exceedingly puzzled him.

'I'm blest if I can see what he's got to be so darned cheerful about,' he said to
himself.

They arrived at the hotel and sat on the terrace. A Chinese boy brought them
cocktails. Edward was most anxious to hear all the news of Chicago and
bombarded his friend with eager questions. His interest was natural and
sincere. But the odd thing was that it seemed equally divided among a
multitude of subjects. He was as eager to know how Bateman's father was as
what Isabel was doing. He talked of her without a shade of embarrassment, but
she might just as well have been his sister as his promised wife; and before
Bateman had done analysing the exact meaning of Edward's remarks he found
that the conversation had drifted to his own work and the buildings his father
had lately erected. He was determined to bring the conversation back to Isabel
and was looking for the occasion when he saw Edward wave his hand cordially.
A man was advancing towards them on the terrace, but Bateman's back was
turned to him and he could not see him.

'Come and sit down,' said Edward gaily.

The new-comer approached. He was a very tall, thin man, in white ducks,
with a fine head of curly white hair. His face was thin too, long, with a large,
hooked nose and a beautiful, expressive mouth.

'This is my old friend Bateman Hunter. I've told you about him,' said
Edward, his constant smile breaking on his lips.

'I'm pleased to meet you, Mr Hunter. I used to know your father.'

The stranger held out his hand and took the young man's in a strong, friendly grasp. It was not till then that Edward mentioned the other's name.

'Mr Arnold Jackson.'

Bateman turned white and he felt his hands grow cold. This was the forger, the convict, this was Isabel's uncle. He did not know what to say. He tried to conceal his confusion. Arnold Jackson looked at him with twinkling eyes.

'I daresay my name is familiar to you.'

Bateman did not know whether to say yes or no, and what made it more awkward was that both Jackson and Edward seemed to be amused. It was bad enough to have forced on him the acquaintance of the one man on the island he would rather have avoided, but worse to discern that he was being made a fool of. Perhaps, however, he had reached this conclusion too quickly, for Jackson, without a pause, added:

'I understand you're very friendly with the Longstaffes. Mary Longstaffe is my sister.'

Now Bateman asked himself if Arnold Jackson could think him ignorant of the most terrible scandal that Chicago had ever known. But Jackson put his hand on Edward's shoulder.

'I can't sit down, Teddie,' he said. 'I'm busy. But you two boys had better come up and dine tonight.'

'That'll be fine,' said Edward.

'It's very kind of you, Mr Jackson,' said Bateman, frigidly, 'but I'm here for so short a time; my boat sails tomorrow, you know; I think if you'll forgive me, I won't come.'

'Oh, nonsense. I'll give you a native dinner. My wife's a wonderful cook. Teddie will show you the way. Come early so as to see the sunset. I can give you both a shake-down if you like.'

'Of course we'll come,' said Edward. 'There's always the devil of a row in the hotel on the night a boat arrives and we can have a good yarn up at the bungalow.'

'I can't let you off, Mr Hunter,' Jackson continued with the utmost cordiality. 'I want to hear all about Chicago and Mary.'

He nodded and walked away before Bateman could say another word.

'We don't take refusals in Tahiti,' laughed Edward. 'Besides, you'll get the best dinner on the island.'

'What did he mean by saying his wife was a good cook? I happen to know his wife's in Geneva.'

'That's a long way off for a wife, isn't it?' said Edward. 'And it's a long time since he saw her. I guess it's another wife he's talking about.'

For some time Bateman was silent. His face was set in grave lines. But looking up he caught the amused look in Edward's eyes, and he flushed darkly.

'Arnold Jackson is a despicable rogue,' he said.

'I greatly fear he is,' answered Edward, smiling.

'I don't see how any decent man can have anything to do with him.'

'Perhaps I'm not a decent man.'

'Do you see much of him, Edward?'

'Yes, quite a lot. He's adopted me as his nephew.'

Bateman leaned forward and fixed Edward with his searching eyes.

'Do you like him?'

'Very much.'

'But don't you know, doesn't everyone here know, that he's a forger and that he's been a convict? He ought to be hounded out of civilized society.'

Edward watched a ring of smoke that floated from his cigar into the still, scented air.

'I suppose he is a pretty unmitigated rascal,' he said at last. 'And I can't flatter myself that any repentance for his misdeeds offers one an excuse for condoning them. He was a swindler and a hypocrite. You can't get away from it. I never met a more agreeable companion. He's taught me everything I know.'

'What has he taught you?' cried Bateman in amazement.

'How to live.'

Bateman broke into ironical laughter.

'A fine master. Is it owing to his lessons that you lost the chance of making a fortune and earn your living now by serving behind a counter in a ten-cent store?'

'He has a wonderful personality,' said Edward, smiling good-naturedly. 'Perhaps you'll see what I mean tonight.'

'I'm not going to dine with him if that's what you mean. Nothing would induce me to set foot within that man's house.'

'Come to oblige me, Bateman. We've been friends for so many years, you won't refuse me a favour when I ask it.'

Edward's tone had in it a quality new to Bateman. Its gentleness was singularly persuasive.

'If you put it like that, Edward, I'm bound to come,' he smiled.

Bateman reflected, moreover, that it would be as well to learn what he could about Arnold Jackson. It was plain that he had a great ascendancy over Edward, and if it was to be combated it was necessary to discover in what exactly it consisted. The more he talked with Edward the more conscious he became that a change had taken place in him. He had an instinct that it behoved him to walk warily, and he made up his mind not to broach the real purport of his visit till he saw his way more clearly. He began to talk of one thing and another, of his journey and what he had achieved by it, of politics in Chicago, of this common friend and that, of their days together at college.

At last Edward said he must get back to his work and proposed that he should fetch Bateman at five so that they could drive out together to Arnold Jackson's house.

'By the way, I rather thought you'd be living at this hotel,' said Bateman, as he strolled out of the garden with Edward. 'I understand it's the only decent one here.'

'Not I,' laughed Edward. 'It's a deal too grand for me. I rent a room just outside the town. It's cheap and clean.'

'If I remember right those weren't the points that seemed most important to you when you lived in Chicago.'

'Chicago!'

'I don't know what you mean by that, Edward. It's the greatest city in the world.'

'I know,' said Edward.

Bateman glanced at him quickly, but his face was inscrutable.

'When are you coming back to it?'

'I often wonder,' smiled Edward.

This answer, and the manner of it, staggered Bateman, but before he could ask for an explanation Edward waved to a half-caste who was driving a passing motor.

'Give us a ride down, Charlie,' he said.

He nodded to Bateman, and ran after the machine that had pulled up a few yards in front. Bateman was left to piece together a mass of perplexing impressions.

Edward called for him in a rickety trap drawn by an old mare, and they drove along a road that ran by the sea. On each side of it were plantations, coconut and vanilla; and now and then they saw a great mango, its fruit yellow and red and purple among the massy green of the leaves, now and then they had a glimpse of the lagoon, smooth and blue, with here and there a tiny islet graceful with tall palms. Arnold Jackson's house stood on a little hill and only a path led to it, so they unharnessed the mare and tied her to a tree, leaving the trap by the side of the road. To Bateman it seemed a happy-go-lucky way of doing things. But when they went up to the house they were met by a tall, handsome native woman, no longer young, with whom Edward cordially shook hands. He introduced Bateman to her.

'This is my friend Mr Hunter. We're going to dine with you, Lavina.'

'All right,' she said, with a quick smile. 'Arnold ain't back yet.'

'We'll go down and bathe. Let us have a couple of pareos.'

The woman nodded and went into the house.

'Who is that?' asked Bateman.

'Oh, that's Lavina. She's Arnold's wife.'

Bateman tightened his lips, but said nothing. In a moment the woman returned with a bundle, which she gave to Edward; and the two men, scrambling down a steep path, made their way to a grove of coconut trees on the beach. They undressed and Edward showed his friend how to make the strip of red trade cotton which is called a pareo into a very neat pair of bathing-drawers. Soon they were splashing in the warm, shallow water. Edward was in great spirits. He laughed and shouted and sang. He might have been fifteen. Bateman had never seen him so gay, and afterwards when they lay on the beach, smoking cigarettes, in the limpid air, there was such an irresistible light-heartedness in him that Bateman was taken aback.

'You seem to find life mighty pleasant,' said he.

'I do.'

They heard a soft movement and looking round saw that Arnold Jackson was coming towards them.

'I thought I'd come down and fetch you two boys back,' he said. 'Did you enjoy your bathe, Mr Hunter?'

'Very much,' said Bateman.

Arnold Jackson, no longer in spruce ducks, wore nothing but a pareo round his loins and walked barefoot. His body was deeply browned by the sun. With his long, curling white hair and his ascetic face he made a fantastic figure in the native dress, but he bore himself without a trace of self-consciousness.

'If you're ready we'll go right up,' said Jackson.

'I'll just put on my clothes,' said Bateman.

'Why, Teddie, didn't you bring a pareo for your friend?'

'I guess he'd rather wear clothes,' smiled Edward.

'I certainly would,' answered Bateman, grimly, as he saw Edward gird himself in the loincloth and stand ready to start before he himself had got his shirt on.

'Won't you find it rough walking without your shoes?' he asked Edward. 'It struck me the path was a trifle rocky.'

'Oh, I'm used to it.'

'It's a comfort to get into a pareo when one gets back from town,' said Jackson. 'If you were going to stay here I should strongly recommend you to adopt it. It's one of the most sensible costumes I have ever come across. It's cool, convenient, and inexpensive.'

They walked up to the house, and Jackson took them into a large room with white-washed walls and an open ceiling in which a table was laid for dinner. Bateman noticed that it was set for five.

'Eva, come and show yourself to Teddie's friend, and then shake us a cocktail,' called Jackson.

Then he led Bateman to a long low window.

'Look at that,' he said, with a dramatic gesture. 'Look well.'

Below them coconut trees tumbled down steeply to the lagoon, and the lagoon in the evening light had the colour, tender and varied, of a dove's breast. On a creek, at a little distance, were the clustered huts of a native village, and towards the reef was a canoe, sharply silhouetted, in which were a couple of natives fishing. Then, beyond, you saw the vast calmness of the Pacific and twenty miles away, airy and unsubstantial like the fabric of a poet's fancy, the unimaginable beauty of the island which is called Murea. It was all so lovely that Bateman stood abashed.

'I've never seen anything like it,' he said at last.

Arnold Jackson stood staring in front of him, and in his eyes was a dreamy softness. His thin, thoughtful face was very grave. Bateman, glancing at it, was once more conscious of its intense spirituality.

'Beauty,' murmured Arnold Jackson. 'You seldom see beauty face to face. Look at it well, Mr Hunter, for what you see now you will never see again, since the moment is transitory, but it will be an imperishable memory in your heart. You touch eternity.'

His voice was deep and resonant. He seemed to breathe forth the purest idealism, and Bateman had to urge himself to remember that the man who spoke was a criminal and a cruel cheat. But Edward, as though he heard a sound, turned round quickly.

'Here is my daughter, Mr Hunter.'

Bateman shook hands with her. She had dark, splendid eyes and a red mouth tremulous with laughter; but her skin was brown, and her curling hair, rippling down her shoulders, was coal-black. She wore but one garment, a Mother Hubbard of pink cotton, her feet were bare, and she was crowned with a wreath of white scented flowers. She was a lovely creature. She was like a goddess of the Polynesian spring.

She was a little shy, but not more shy than Bateman, to whom the whole situation was highly embarrassing, and it did not put him at ease to see this sylph-like thing take a shaker and with a practised hand mix three cocktails.

'Let us have a kick in them, child,' said Jackson.

She poured them out and smiling delightfully handed one to each of the men. Bateman flattered himself on his skill in the subtle art of shaking cocktails and he was not a little astonished, on tasting this one, to find that it was excellent. Jackson laughed proudly when he saw his guest's involuntary look of appreciation.

'Not bad, is it? I taught the child myself, and in the old days in Chicago I considered that there wasn't a bar-tender in the city that could hold a candle to me. When I had nothing better to do in the penitentiary I used to amuse myself by thinking out new cocktails, but when you come down to brass tacks there's nothing to beat a dry Martini.'

Bateman felt as though someone had given him a violent blow on the funny-bone and he was conscious that he turned red and then white. But before he could think of anything to say a native boy brought in a great bowl of soup and the whole party sat down to dinner. Arnold Jackson's remark seemed to have aroused in him a train of recollections, for he began to talk of his prison days. He talked quite naturally, without malice, as though he were relating his experiences at a foreign university. He addressed himself to Bateman and Bateman was confused and then confounded. He saw Edward's eyes fixed on him and there was in them a flicker of amusement. He blushed scarlet, for it struck him that Jackson was making a fool of him, and then because he felt absurd—and knew there was no reason why he should—he grew angry. Arnold Jackson was impudent—there was no other word for it—and his callousness, whether assumed or not, was outrageous. The dinner proceeded. Bateman was asked to eat sundry messes, raw fish and he knew not what, which only his civility induced him to swallow, but which he was amazed to find very good eating. Then an incident happened which to Bateman was the most mortifying experience of the evening. There was a little circlet of flowers in front of him, and for the sake of conversation he hazarded a remark about it.

'It's a wreath that Eva made for you,' said Jackson, 'but I guess she was too shy to give it to you.'

Bateman took it up in his hand and made a polite little speech of thanks to the girl.

'You must put it on,' she said, with a smile and a blush.

'I? I don't think I'll do that.'

'It's the charming custom of the country,' said Arnold Jackson.

There was one in front of him and he placed it on his hair. Edward did the same.

'I guess I'm not dressed for the part,' said Bateman, uneasily.

'Would you like a pareo?' said Eva quickly. 'I'll get you one in a minute.'

'No, thank you. I'm quite comfortable as I am.'

'Show him how to put it on, Eva,' said Edward.

At that moment Bateman hated his greatest friend. Eva got up from the table and with much laughter placed the wreath on his black hair.

'It suits you very well,' said Mrs Jackson. 'Don't it suit him, Arnold?'

'Of course it does.'

Bateman sweated at every pore.

'Isn't it a pity it's dark?' said Eva. 'We could photograph you all three together.'

Bateman thanked his stars it was. He felt that he must look prodigiously foolish in his blue serge suit and high collar—very neat and gentlemanly—with that ridiculous wreath of flowers on his head. He was seething with indignation, and he had never in his life exercised more self-control than now when he presented an affable exterior. He was furious with that old man, sitting at the head of the table, half-naked, with his saintly face and the flowers on his handsome white locks. The whole position was monstrous.

Then dinner came to an end, and Eva and her mother remained to clear away while the three men sat on the veranda. It was very warm and the air was scented with the white flowers of the night. The full moon, sailing across an unclouded sky, made a pathway on the broad sea that led to the boundless realms of Forever. Arnold Jackson began to talk. His voice was rich and musical. He talked now of the natives and of the old legends of the country. He told strange stories of the past, stories of hazardous expeditions into the unknown, of love and death, of hatred and revenge. He told of the adventurers who had discovered those distant islands, of the sailors who, settling in them, had married the daughters of great chieftains, and of the beach-combers who had led their varied lives on those silvery shores. Bateman, mortified and exasperated, at first listened sullenly, but presently some magic in the words possessed him and he sat entranced. The mirage of romance obscured the light of common day. Had he forgotten that Arnold Jackson had a tongue of silver, a tongue by which he had charmed vast sums out of the credulous public, a tongue which very nearly enabled him to escape the penalty of his crimes? No one had a sweeter eloquence, and no one had a more acute sense of climax. Suddenly he rose.

'Well, you two boys haven't seen one another for a long time. I shall leave you to have a yarn. Teddie will show you your quarters when you want to go to bed.'

'Oh, but I wasn't thinking of spending the night, Mr Jackson,' said Bateman.

'You'll find it more comfortable. We'll see that you're called in good time.'

Then with a courteous shake of the hand, stately as though he were a bishop in canonicals, Arnold Jackson took leave of his guest.

'Of course I'll drive you back to Papeete if you like,' said Edward, 'but I advise you to stay. It's bully driving in the early morning.'

For a few minutes neither of them spoke. Bateman wondered how he should begin on the conversation which all the events of the day made him think more urgent.

'When are you coming back to Chicago?' he asked, suddenly.

For a moment Edward did not answer. Then he turned rather lazily to look at his friend and smiled.

'I don't know. Perhaps never.'

'What in heaven's name do you mean?' cried Bateman.

'I'm very happy here. Wouldn't it be folly to make a change?'

'Man alive, you can't live here all your life. This is no life for a man. It's a living death. Oh, Edward, come away at once, before it's too late. I've felt that something was wrong. You're infatuated with the place, you've succumbed to evil influences, but it only requires a wrench, and when you're free from these surroundings you'll thank all the gods there be. You'll be like a dope-fiend when he's broken from his drug. You'll see then that for two years you've been breathing poisoned air. You can't imagine what a relief it will be when you fill your lungs once more with the fresh pure air of your native country.'

He spoke quickly, the words tumbling over one another in his excitement, and there was in his voice sincere and affectionate emotion. Edward was touched.

'It is good of you to care so much, old friend.'

'Come with me tomorrow, Edward. It was a mistake that you ever came to this place. This is no life for you.'

'You talk of this sort of life and that. How do you think a man gets the best out of life?'

'Why, I should have thought there could be no two answers to that. By doing his duty, by hard work, by meeting all the obligations of his state and station.'

'And what is his reward?'

'His reward is the consciousness of having achieved what he set out to do.'

'It all sounds a little portentous to me,' said Edward, and in the lightness of the night Bateman could see that he was smiling. 'I'm afraid you'll think I've degenerated sadly. There are several things I think now which I daresay would have seemed outrageous to me three years ago.'

'Have you learnt them from Arnold Jackson?' asked Bateman, scornfully.

'You don't like him? Perhaps you couldn't be expected to. I didn't when I first came. I had just the same prejudice as you. He's a very extraordinary man. You saw for yourself that he makes no secret of the fact that he was in a penitentiary. I do not know that he regrets it or the crimes that led him there. The only complaint he ever made in my hearing was that when he came out his health was impaired. I think he does not know what remorse is. He is completely unmoral. He accepts everything and he accepts himself as well. He's generous and kind.'

'He always was,' interrupted Bateman, 'on other people's money.'

'I've found him a very good friend. Is it unnatural that I should take a man as I find him?'

'The result is that you lose the distinction between right and wrong.'

'No, they remain just as clearly divided in my mind as before, but what has become a little confused in me is the distinction between the bad man and the good one. Is Arnold Jackson a bad man who does good things or a good man who does bad things? It's a difficult question to answer. Perhaps we make too much of the difference between one man and another. Perhaps even the best of us are sinners and the worst of us are saints. Who knows?'

'You will never persuade me that white is black and that black is white,' said Bateman.

'I'm sure I shan't, Bateman.'

Bateman could not understand why the flicker of a smile crossed Edward's lips when he thus agreed with him. Edward was silent for a minute.

'When I saw you this morning, Bateman,' he said then, 'I seemed to see myself as I was two years ago. The same collar, and the same shoes, the same blue suit, the same energy. The same determination. By God, I was energetic. The sleepy methods of this place made my blood tingle. I went about and everywhere I saw possibilities for development and enterprise. There were fortunes to be made here. It seemed to me absurd that the copra should be taken away from here in sacks and the oil extracted in America. It would be far more economical to do all that on the spot, with cheap labour, and save freight, and I saw already the vast factories springing up on the island. Then the way they extracted it from the coconut seemed to me hopelessly inadequate and I invented a machine which divided the nut and scooped out the meat at the rate of two hundred and forty an hour. The harbour was not large enough. I made plans to enlarge it, then to form a syndicate to buy land, put up two or three large hotels, and bungalows for occasional residents; I had a scheme for improving the steamer service in order to attract visitors from California. In twenty years, instead of this half-French, lazy little town of Papeete I saw a great American city with ten-storey buildings and street-cars, a theatre and an opera house, a stock exchange and a mayor.'

'But go ahead, Edward,' cried Bateman, springing up from the chair in excitement. 'You've got the ideas and the capacity. Why, you'll become the richest man between Australia and the States.'

Edward chuckled softly.

'But I don't want to,' he said.

'Do you mean to say you don't want money, big money, money running into millions? Do you know what you can do with it? Do you know the power it brings? And if you don't care about it for yourself think what you can do, opening new channels for human enterprise, giving occupation to thousands. My brain reels at the visions your words have conjured up.'

'Sit down, then, my dear Bateman,' laughed Edward. 'My machine for cutting the coconuts will always remain unused, and so far as I'm concerned street-cars shall never run in the idle streets of Papeete.'

Bateman sank heavily into his chair.

'I don't understand you,' he said.

'It came upon me little by little. I came to like the life here, with its ease and its leisure, and the people, with their good nature and their happy smiling faces. I began to think. I'd never had time to do that before. I began to read.'

'You always read.'

'I read for examinations. I read in order to be able to hold my own in conversation. I read for instruction. Here I learned to read for pleasure. I learned to talk. Do you know that conversation is one of the greatest pleasures in life? But it wants leisure. I'd always been too busy before. And gradually all the life that had seemed so important to me began to seem rather trivial and vulgar. What is the use of all this hustle and this constant striving? I think of Chicago now and I see a dark, grey city, all stone—it is like a prison—and a ceaseless turmoil. And what does all that activity amount to? Does one get there the best out of life? Is that what we come into the world for, to hurry to an office, and work hour after hour till night, then hurry home and dine and go to a theatre? Is that how I must spend my youth? Youth lasts so short a time, Bateman. And when I am old, what have I to look forward to? To hurry from my home in the morning to my office and work hour after hour till night, and then hurry home again, and dine and go to a theatre? That may be worth while if you make a fortune; I don't know, it depends on your nature; but if you don't, is it worth while then? I want to make more out of my life than that, Bateman.'

'What do you value in life then?'

'I'm afraid you'll laugh at me. Beauty, truth, and goodness.'

'Don't you think you can have those in Chicago?'

'Some men can, perhaps, but not I.' Edward sprang up now. 'I tell you when I think of the life I led in the old days I am filled with horror,' he cried violently. 'I tremble with fear when I think of the danger I have escaped. I never knew I had a soul till I found it here. If I had remained a rich man I might have lost it for good and all.'

'I don't know how you can say that,' cried Bateman indignantly. 'We often used to have discussions about it.'

'Yes, I know. They were about as effectual as the discussions of deaf mutes about harmony. I shall never come back to Chicago, Bateman.'

'And what about Isabel?'

Edward walked to the edge of the veranda and leaning over looked intently at the blue magic of the night. There was a slight smile on his face when he turned back to Bateman.

'Isabel is infinitely too good for me. I admire her more than any woman I have ever known. She has a wonderful brain and she's as good as she's beautiful. I respect her energy and her ambition. She was born to make a success of life. I am entirely unworthy of her.'

'She doesn't think so.'

'But you must tell her so, Bateman.'

'I?' cried Bateman. 'I'm the last person who could ever do that.'

Edward had his back to the vivid light of the moon and his face could not be seen. Is it possible that he smiled again?

'It's no good your trying to conceal anything from her, Bateman. With her quick intelligence she'll turn you inside out in five minutes. You'd better make a clean breast of it right away.'

'I don't know what you mean. Of course I shall tell her I've seen you.' Bateman spoke in some agitation. 'Honestly I don't know what to say to her.'

'Tell her that I haven't made good. Tell her that I'm not only poor, but that I'm content to be poor. Tell her I was fired from my job because I was idle and inattentive. Tell her all you've seen tonight and all I've told you.'

The idea which on a sudden flashed through Bateman's brain brought him to his feet and in uncontrollable perturbation he faced Edward.

'Man alive, don't you want to marry her?'

Edward looked at him gravely.

'I can never ask her to release me. If she wishes to hold me to my word I will do my best to make her a good and loving husband.'

'Do you wish me to give her that message, Edward? Oh, I can't. It's terrible. It's never dawned on her for a moment that you don't want to marry her. She loves you. How can I inflict such a mortification on her?'

Edward smiled again.

'Why don't you marry her yourself, Bateman? You've been in love with her for ages. You're perfectly suited to one another. You'll make her very happy.'

'Don't talk to me like that. I can't bear it.'

'I resign in your favour, Bateman. You are the better man.'

There was something in Edward's tone that made Bateman look up quickly, but Edward's eyes were grave and unsmiling. Bateman did not know what to say. He was disconcerted. He wondered whether Edward could possibly suspect that he had come to Tahiti on a special errand. And though he knew it was horrible he could not prevent the exultation in his heart.

'What will you do if Isabel writes and puts an end to her engagement with you?' he said, slowly.

'Survive,' said Edward.

Bateman was so agitated that he did not hear the answer.

'I wish you had ordinary clothes on,' he said, somewhat irritably. 'It's such a tremendously serious decision you're taking. That fantastic costume of yours makes it seem terribly casual.'

'I assure you, I can be just as solemn in a pareo and a wreath of roses, as in a high hat and a cut-away coat.'

Then another thought struck Bateman.

'Edward, it's not for my sake you're doing this? I don't know, but perhaps this is going to make a tremendous difference to my future. You're not sacrificing yourself for me? I couldn't stand for that, you know.'

'No, Bateman, I have learnt not to be silly and sentimental here. I should like you and Isabel to be happy, but I have not the least wish to be unhappy myself.'

The answer somewhat chilled Bateman. It seemed to him a little cynical. He would not have been sorry to act a noble part.

'Do you mean to say you're content to waste your life here? It's nothing less than suicide. When I think of the great hopes you had when we left college it seems terrible that you should be content to be no more than a salesman in a cheap-John store.'

'Oh, I'm only doing that for the present, and I'm gaining a great deal of valuable experience. I have another plan in my head. Arnold Jackson has a small island in the Paumotas, about a thousand miles from here, a ring of land round a lagoon. He's planted coconut there. He's offered to give it me.'

'Why should he do that?' asked Bateman.

'Because if Isabel releases me I shall marry his daughter.'

'You?' Bateman was thunderstruck. 'You can't marry a half-caste. You wouldn't be so crazy as that.'

'She's a good girl, and she has a sweet and gentle nature. I think she would make me very happy.'

'Are you in love with her?'

'I don't know,' answered Edward reflectively. 'I'm not in love with her as I was in love with Isabel. I worshipped Isabel. I thought she was the most wonderful creature I had ever seen. I was not half good enough for her. I don't feel like that with Eva. She's like a beautiful exotic flower that must be sheltered from bitter winds. I want to protect her. No one ever thought of protecting Isabel. I think she loves me for myself and not for what I may become. Whatever happens to me I shall never disappoint her. She suits me.'

Bateman was silent.

'We must turn out early in the morning,' said Edward at last. 'It's really about time we went to bed.'

Then Bateman spoke and his voice had in it a genuine distress.

'I'm so bewildered, I don't know what to say. I came here because I thought something was wrong. I thought you hadn't succeeded in what you set out to do and were ashamed to come back when you'd failed. I never guessed I should be faced with this. I'm so desperately sorry, Edward. I'm so disappointed. I hoped you would do great things. It's almost more than I can bear to think of you wasting your talents and your youth and your chance in this lamentable way.'

'Don't be grieved, old friend,' said Edward. 'I haven't failed. I've succeeded. You can't think with what zest I look forward to life, how full it seems to me and how significant. Sometimes, when you are married to Isabel, you will think of me. I shall build myself a house on my coral island and I shall live there, looking after my trees—getting the fruit out of the nuts in the same old way that they have done for unnumbered years—I shall grow all sorts of things in my garden, and I shall fish. There will be enough work to keep me busy and not enough to make me dull. I shall have my books and Eva, children, I hope, and above all, the infinite variety of the sea and the sky, the freshness of the dawn and the beauty of the sunset, and the rich magnificence of the night. I shall make a garden out of what so short a while ago was a wilderness. I shall have created something. The years will pass insensibly, and when I am an old man I hope I shall be able to look back on a happy, simple, peaceful life. In my small way I too shall have lived in beauty. Do you think it is so little to have enjoyed contentment? We know that it will profit a man little if he gain the whole world and lose his soul. I think I have won mine.'

Edward led him to a room in which there were two beds and he threw himself on one of them. In ten minutes Bateman knew by his regular breathing, peaceful as a child's, that Edward was asleep. But for his part he had no rest, he was disturbed in mind, and it was not till the dawn crept into the room, ghostlike and silent, that he fell asleep.

Bateman finished telling Isabel his long story. He had hidden nothing from her except what he thought would wound her or what made himself ridiculous. He did not tell her that he had been forced to sit at dinner with a wreath of flowers round his head and he did not tell her that Edward was prepared to marry her uncle's half-caste daughter the moment she set him free. But perhaps Isabel had keener intuitions than he knew, for as he went on with his tale her eyes grew colder and her lips closed upon one another more tightly. Now and then she looked at him closely, and if he had been less intent on his narrative he might have wondered at her expression.

'What was this girl like?' she asked when he finished. 'Uncle Arnold's daughter. Would you say there was any resemblance between her and me?'

Bateman was surprised at the question.

'It never struck me. You know I've never had eyes for anyone but you and I could never think that anyone was like you. Who could resemble you?'

'Was she pretty?' said Isabel, smiling slightly at his words.

'I suppose so. I daresay some men would say she was very beautiful.'

'Well, it's of no consequence. I don't think we need give her any more of our attention.'

'What are you going to do, Isabel?' he asked then.

Isabel looked down at the hand which still bore the ring Edward had given her on their betrothal.

'I wouldn't let Edward break our engagement because I thought it would be an incentive to him. I wanted to be an inspiration to him. I thought if anything could enable him to achieve success it was the thought that I loved him. I have done all I could. It's hopeless. It would only be weakness on my part not to recognize the facts. Poor Edward, he's nobody's enemy but his own. He was a dear, nice fellow, but there was something lacking in him, I suppose it was backbone. I hope he'll be happy.'

She slipped the ring off her finger and placed it on the table. Bateman watched her with a heart beating so rapidly that he could hardly breathe.

'You're wonderful, Isabel, you're simply wonderful.'

She smiled, and, standing up, held out her hand to him.

'How can I ever thank you for what you've done for me?' she said. 'You have done me a great service. I knew I could trust you.'

He took her hand and held it. She had never looked more beautiful.

'Oh, Isabel, I would do so much more for you than that. You know that I only ask to be allowed to love and serve you.'

'You're so strong, Bateman,' she sighed. 'It gives me such a delicious feeling of confidence.'

'Isabel, I adore you.'

He hardly knew how the inspiration had come to him, but suddenly he clasped her in his arms; she, all unresisting, smiled into his eyes.

'Isabel, you know I wanted to marry you the very first day I saw you,' he cried passionately.

'Then why on earth didn't you ask me?' she replied.

She loved him. He could hardly believe it was true. She gave him her lovely lips to kiss. And as he held her in his arms he had a vision of the works of the Hunter Motor Traction and Automobile Company growing in size and importance till they covered a hundred acres, and of the millions of motors they would turn out, and of the great collection of pictures he would form which should beat anything they had in New York. He would wear horn spectacles.

And she, with the delicious pressure of his arms about her, sighed with happiness, for she thought of the exquisite house she would have, full of antique furniture, and of the concerts she would give, and of the *thés dansants*, and the dinners to which only the most cultured people would come.

'Poor Edward,' she sighed.

Honolulu

◆

The wise traveller travels only in imagination. An old Frenchman (he was really a Savoyard) once wrote a book called *Voyage autour de ma Chambre*. I have not read it and do not even know what it is about, but the title stimulates my fancy. In such a journey I could circumnavigate the globe. An eikon by the chimneypiece can take me to Russia with its great forests of birch and its white, domed churches. The Volga is wide, and at the end of a straggling village, in the wine-shop, bearded men in rough sheepskin coats sit drinking. I stand on the little hill from which Napoleon first saw Moscow and I look upon the vastness of the city. I will go down and see the people whom I know more intimately than so many of my friends, Alyosha, and Vronsky, and a dozen more. But my eyes fall on a piece of porcelain and I smell the acrid odours of China. I am borne in a chair along a narrow causeway between the padi fields, or else I skirt a tree-clad mountain. My bearers chat gaily as they trudge along in the bright morning and every now and then, distant and mysterious, I hear the deep sound of a monastery bell. In the streets of Peking there is a motley crowd and it scatters to allow passage to a string of camels, stepping delicately, that bring skins and strange drugs from the stony deserts of Mongolia. In England, in London, there are certain afternoons in winter when the clouds hang heavy and low and the light is so bleak that your heart sinks, but then you can look out of your window, and you see the coconut trees crowded upon the beach of a coral island. The strand is silvery and when you walk along in the sunshine it is so dazzling that you can hardly bear to look at it. Overhead the mynah birds are making a great to-do, and the surf beats ceaselessly against the reef. Those are the best journeys, the journeys that you take at your own fireside, for then you lose none of your illusions.

But there are people who take salt in their coffee. They say it gives it a tang, a savour, which is peculiar and fascinating. In the same way there are certain places, surrounded by a halo of romance, to which the inevitable disillusionment which you must experience on seeing them gives a singular spice. You had expected something wholly beautiful and you get an impression which is infintely more complicated than any that beauty can give you. It is like the weakness in the character of a great man which may make him less admirable but certainly makes him more interesting.

Nothing had prepared me for Honolulu. It is so far away from Europe, it is reached after so long a journey from San Francisco, so strange and so charming associations are attached to the name, that at first I could hardly believe my eyes. I do not know that I had formed in my mind any very exact picture of what I expected, but what I found caused me a great surprise. It is a typical western city. Shacks are cheek by jowl with stone mansions: dilapidated frame houses stand next door to smart stores with plate-glass windows; electric cars rumble noisily along the streets; and motors, Fords, Buicks, Packards, line the pavement. The shops are filled with all the necessities of American civilization. Every third house is a bank and every fifth the agency of a steamship company.

Along the streets crowd an unimaginable assortment of people. The Americans, ignoring the climate, wear black coats and high, starched collars, straw hats, soft hats, and bowlers. The Kanakas, pale brown, with crisp hair, have nothing on but a shirt and a pair of trousers; but the half-breeds are very smart with flaring ties and patent-leather boots. The Japanese, with their obsequious smile, are neat and trim in white duck, while their women walk a step or two behind them, in native dress, with a baby on their backs. The Japanese children, in bright coloured frocks, their little heads shaven, look like quaint dolls. Then there are the Chinese. The men, fat and prosperous, wear their American clothes oddly, but the women are enchanting with their tightly-dressed black hair, so neat that you feel it can never be disarranged, and they are very clean in their tunics and trousers, white, or powder-blue, or black. Lastly there are the Filipinos, the men in huge straw hats, the women in bright yellow muslin with great puffed sleeves.

It is the meeting-place of East and West. The very new rubs shoulders with the immeasurably old. And if you have not found the romance you expected you have come upon something singularly intriguing. All these strange people live close to each other, with different languages and different thoughts; they believe in different gods and they have different values; two passions alone they share, love and hunger. And somehow as you watch them you have an impression of extraordinary vitality. Though the air is so soft and the sky so blue, you have, I know not why, a feeling of something hotly passionate that beats like a throbbing pulse through the crowd. Though the native policeman at the corner, standing on a platform, with a white club to direct the traffic, gives the scene an air of respectability, you cannot but feel that it is a respectability only of the surface; a little below there is darkness and mystery. It gives you just that thrill, with a little catch at the heart, that you have when at night in the forest the silence trembles on a sudden with the low, insistent beating of a drum. You are all expectant of I know not what.

If I have dwelt on the incongruity of Honolulu, it is because just this, to my mind, gives its point to the story I want to tell. It is a story of primitive superstition, and it startles me that anything of the sort should survive in a civilization which, if not very distinguished, is certainly very elaborate. I cannot get over the fact that such incredible things should happen, or at least be thought to happen, right in the middle, so to speak, of telephones, tramcars, and daily papers. And the friend who showed me Honolulu had the same incongruity which I felt from the beginning was its most striking characteristic.

He was an American named Winter and I had brought a letter of introduction to him from an acquaintance in New York. He was a man between forty and fifty, with scanty black hair, grey at the temples, and a sharp-featured, thin face. His eyes had a twinkle in them and his large horn spectacles gave him a demureness which was not a little diverting. He was tall rather than otherwise and very spare. He was born in Honolulu and his father had a large store which sold hosiery and all such goods, from tennis racquets to tarpaulins, as a man of fashion could require. It was a prosperous business and I could well understand the indignation of Winter *père* when his son, refusing to go into it, had announced his determination to be an actor. My friend spent twenty years on the stage, sometimes in New York, but more often on the road, for his gifts were small; but at last, being no fool, he came to the conclusion that it was better to sell sock-suspenders in Honolulu than to play small parts in Cleveland, Ohio. He left the stage and went into the business. I think after the hazardous existence he had lived so long, he thoroughly enjoyed the luxury of driving a large car and living in a beautiful house near the golf-course, and I am quite sure, since he was a man of parts. he managed the business competently. But he could not bring himself entirely to break his connexion with the arts and since he might no longer act he began to paint. He took me to his studio and showed me his work. It was not at all bad, but not what I should have expected from him. He painted nothing but still life, very small pictures, perhaps eight by ten; and he painted very delicately, with the utmost finish. He had evidently a passion for detail. His fruit pieces reminded you of the fruit in a picture by Ghirlandajo. While you marvelled a little at his patience, you could not help being impressed by his dexterity. I imagine that he failed as an actor because his effects, carefully studied, were neither bold nor broad enough to get across the footlights.

I was entertained by the proprietary, yet ironical air with which he showed me the city. He thought in his heart that there was none in the United States to equal it, but he saw quite clearly that his attitude was comic. He drove me round to the various buildings and swelled with satisfaction when I expressed a proper admiration for their architecture. He showed me the houses of rich men.

'That's the Stubbses' house,' he said. 'It cost a hundred thousand dollars to build. The Stubbses are one of our best families. Old man Stubbs came here as a missionary more than seventy years ago.'

He hesitated a little and looked at me with twinkling eyes through his big round spectacles.

'All our best families are missionary families,' he said. 'You're not very much in Honolulu unless your father or your grandfather converted the heathen.'

'Is that so?'

'Do you know your Bible?'

'Fairly,' I answered.

'There is a text which says: The fathers have eaten sour grapes and the children's teeth are set on edge. I guess it runs differently in Honolulu. The fathers brought Christianity to the Kanaka and the children jumped his land.'

'Heaven helps those who help themselves,' I murmured.

'It surely does. By the time the natives of this island had embraced Christianity they had nothing else they could afford to embrace. The kings gave the missionaries land as a mark of esteem, and the missionaries bought land by way of laying up treasure in heaven. It surely was a good investment. One missionary left the business—I think one may call it a business without offence—and became a land agent, but that is an exception. Mostly it was their sons who looked after the commercial side of the concern. Oh, it's a fine thing to have a father who came here fifty years ago to spread the faith.'

But he looked at his watch.

'Gee, it's stopped. That means it's time to have a cocktail.'

We sped along an excellent road, bordered with red hibiscus, and came back into the town.

'Have you been to the Union Saloon?'

'Not yet.'

'We'll go there.'

I knew it was the most famous spot in Honolulu and I entered it with a lively curiosity. You get to it by a narrow passage from King Street, and in the passage are offices, so that thirsty souls may be supposed bound for one of these just as well as for the saloon. It is a large square room, with three entrances, and opposite the bar, which runs the length of it, two corners have been partitioned off into little cubicles. Legend states that they were built so that King Kalakaua might drink there without being seen by his subjects, and it is pleasant to think that in one or other of these he may have sat over his bottle, a coal-black potentate, with Robert Louis Stevenson. There is a portrait of him, in oils, in a rich gold frame; but there are also two prints of Queen Victoria. On the walls, besides, are old line engravings of the eighteenth century, one of which, and heaven knows how it got there, is after a theatrical picture by De Wilde; and there are oleographs from the Christmas supplements of the *Graphic* and the *Illustrated London News* of twenty years ago. Then there are advertisements of whisky, gin, champagne, and beer; and photographs of baseball teams and of native orchestras.

The place seemed to belong not to the modern, hustling world that I had left in the bright street outside, but to one that was dying. It had the savour of the day before yesterday. Dingy and dimly lit, it had a vaguely mysterious air and you could imagine that it would be a fit scene for shady transactions. It suggested a more lurid time, when ruthless men carried their lives in their hands, and violent deeds diapered the monotony of life.

When I went in, the saloon was fairly full. A group of business men stood together at the bar, discussing affairs, and in a corner two Kanakas were drinking. Two or three men who might have been store-keepers were shaking dice. The rest of the company plainly followed the sea; they were captains of tramps, first mates, and engineers. Behind the bar, busily making the Honolulu cocktail for which the place was famous, served two large half-castes, in white, fat, clean-shaven and dark-skinned, with thick, curly hair and large bright eyes.

Winter seemed to know more than half the company, and when we made our way to the bar a little fat man in spectacles, who was standing by himself, offered him a drink.

'No, you have one with me, Captain,' said Winter.

He turned to me.

'I want you to know Captain Butler.'

The little man shook hands with me. We began to talk, but, my attention distracted by my surroundings, took small notice of him, and after we had each ordered a cocktail we separated. When we had got into the motor again and were driving away, Winter said to me:

'I'm glad we ran up against Butler. I wanted you to meet him. What did you think of him?'

'I don't know that I thought very much of him at all,' I answered.

'Do you believe in the supernatural?'

'I don't exactly know that I do,' I smiled.

'A very queer thing happened to him a year or two ago. You ought to have him tell you about it.'

'What sort of thing?'

Winter did not answer my question.

'I have no explanation of it myself,' he said. 'But there's no doubt about the facts. Are you interested in things like that?'

'Things like what?'

'Spells and magic and all that.'

'I've never met anyone who wasn't.'

Winter paused for a moment.

'I guess I won't tell you myself. You ought to hear it from his own lips so that you can judge. How are you fixed up for tonight?'

'I've got nothing on at all.'

'Well, I'll get hold of him between now and then and see if we can't go down to his ship.'

Winter told me something about him. Captain Butler had spent all his life on the Pacific. He had been in much better circumstances than he was now, for he had been first officer and then captain of a passenger-boat plying along the coast of California, but he had lost his ship and a number of passengers had been drowned.

'Drink, I guess,' said Winter.

Of course there had been an inquiry, which had cost him his certificate, and then he drifted further afield. For some years he had knocked about the South Seas, but he was now in command of a small schooner which sailed between Honolulu and the various islands of the group. It belonged to a Chinese to whom the fact that his skipper had no certificate meant only that he could be had for lower wages, and to have a white man in charge was always an advantage.

And now that I had heard this about him I took the trouble to remember more exactly what he was like. I recalled his round spectacles and the round blue eyes behind them, and so gradually reconstructed him before my mind. He was a little man, without angles, plump, with a round face like the full moon and a little fat round nose. He had fair short hair, and he was red-faced and clean-shaven. He had plump hands, dimpled on the knuckles, and short fat legs. He was a jolly soul, and the tragic experience he had gone through seemed to have left him unscarred. Though he must have been thirty-four or thirty-five he looked much younger. But after all I had given him but a superficial attention, and now that I knew of this catastrophe, which had obviously ruined his life, I promised myself that when I saw him again I would take more careful note of him. It is very curious to observe the differences of emotional response that you find in different people. Some can go through terrible battles, the fear of imminent death and unimaginable horrors, and preserve their soul unscathed, while with others the trembling of the moon on a solitary sea or the song of a bird in a thicket will cause a convulsion great enough to transform their entire being. Is it due to strength or weakness, want of imagination or instability of character? I do not know. When I called up in my fancy that scene of shipwreck, with the shrieks of the drowning and the terror, and then later, the ordeal of the inquiry, the bitter grief of those who sorrowed for the lost, and the harsh things he must have read of himself in the papers, the shame and the disgrace, it came to me with a shock to remember that Captain Butler had talked with the frank obscenity of a schoolboy of the Hawaiian girls and of Iwelei, the Red Light district, and of his successful adventures. He laughed readily, and one would have thought he could never laugh again. I remembered his shining, white teeth; they were his best feature. He began to interest me, and thinking of him and of his gay insouciance I forgot the particular story, to hear which I was to see him again. I wanted to see him rather to find out if I could a little more what sort of man he was.

Winter made the necessary arrangements and after dinner we went down to the water front. The ship's boat was waiting for us and we rowed out. The schooner was anchored some way across the harbour, not far from the breakwater. We came alongside, and I heard the sound of a ukulele. We clambered up the ladder.

'I guess he's in the cabin,' said Winter, leading the way.

It was a small cabin, bedraggled and dirty, with a table against one side and a broad bench all round upon which slept, I supposed, such passengers as were ill-advised enough to travel in such a ship. A petroleum lamp gave a dim light. The ukulele was being played by a native girl and Butler was lolling on the seat, half lying, with his head on her shoulder and an arm round her waist.

'Don't let us disturb you, Captain,' said Winter, facetiously.

'Come right in,' said Butler, getting up and shaking hands with us. 'What'll you have?'

It was a warm night, and through the open door you saw countless stars in a heaven that was still almost blue. Captain Butler wore a sleeveless undershirt, showing his fat white arms, and a pair of incredibly dirty trousers. His feet were bare, but on his curly head he wore a very old, a very shapeless felt hat.

'Let me introduce you to my girl. Ain't she a peach?'

We shook hands with a very pretty person. She was a good deal taller than the captain, and even the Mother Hubbard, which the missionaries of a past generation had, in the interests of decency, forced on the unwilling natives, could not conceal the beauty of her form. One could not but suspect that age would burden her with a certain corpulence, but now she was graceful and alert. Her brown skin had an exquisite translucency and her eyes were magnificent. Her black hair, very thick and rich, was coiled round her head in a massive plait. When she smiled in a greeting that was charmingly natural, she showed teeth that were small, even, and white. She was certainly a most attractive creature. It was easy to see that the captain was madly in love with her. He could not take his eyes off her; he wanted to touch her all the time. That was very easy to understand; but what seemed to me stranger was that the girl was apparently in love with him. There was a light in her eyes that was unmistakable, and her lips were slightly parted as though in a sigh of desire. It was thrilling. It was even a little moving, and I could not help feeling somewhat in the way. What had a stranger to do with this lovesick pair? I wished that Winter had not brought me. And it seemed to me that the dingy cabin was transfigured and now it seemed a fit and proper scene for such an extremity of passion. I thought I should never forget that schooner in the harbour of Honolulu, crowded with shipping, and yet, under the immensity of the starry sky, remote from all the world. I liked to think of those lovers sailing off together in the night over the empty spaces of the Pacific from one green, hilly island to another. A faint breeze of romance softly fanned my cheek.

And yet Butler was the last man in the world with whom you would have associated romance, and it was hard to see what there was in him to arouse love. In the clothes he wore now he looked podgier than ever, and his round spectacles gave his round face the look of a prim cherub. He suggested rather a curate who had gone to the dogs. His conversation was peppered with the quaintest Americanisms, and it is because I despair of reproducing these that, at whatever loss of vividness, I mean to narrate the story he told me a little later in my own words. Moreover he was unable to frame a sentence without an oath, though a good-natured one, and his speech, albeit offensive only to prudish ears, in print would seem coarse. He was a mirth-loving man, and perhaps that accounted not a little for his successful amours; since women, for the most part frivolous creatures, are excessively bored by the seriousness with which men treat them, and they can seldom resist the buffoon who makes them laugh. Their sense of humour is crude, Diana of Ephesus is always prepared to fling prudence to the winds for the red-nosed comedian who sits on his hat. I realized that Captain Butler had charm. If I had not known the tragic story of the shipwreck I should have thought he had never had a care in his life.

Our host had rung the bell on our entrance and now a Chinese cook came in with more glasses and several bottles of soda. The whisky and the captain's empty glass stood already on the table. But when I saw the Chinese I positively started, for he was certainly the ugliest man I had ever seen. He was very short, but thick-set, and he had a bad limp. He wore a singlet and a pair of trousers that had been white, but were now filthy, and, perched on a shock of bristly, grey hair, an old tweed deer-stalker. It would have been grotesque on any Chinese, but on him it was outrageous. His broad, square face was very flat as though it had been bashed in by a mighty fist, and it was deeply pitted with smallpox; but the most revolting thing in him was a very pronounced harelip which had never been operated on, so that his upper lip, cleft, went up in an angle to his nose, and in the opening was a huge yellow fang. It was horrible. He came in with the end of a cigarette at the corner of his mouth and this, I do not know why, gave him a devilish expression.

He poured out the whisky and opened a bottle of soda.

'Don't drown it, John,' said the captain.

He said nothing, but handed a glass to each of us. Then he went out.

'I saw you lookin' at my Chink,' said Butler, with a grin on his fat, shining face.

'I should hate to meet him on a dark night,' I said.

'He sure is homely,' said the captain, and for some reason he seemed to say it with a peculiar satisfaction. 'But he's fine for one thing, I'll tell the world; you just have to have a drink every time you look at him.'

But my eyes fell on a calabash that hung against the wall over the table, and I got up to look at it. I had been hunting for an old one and this was better than any I had seen outside the museum.

'It was given me by a chief over on one of the islands,' said the captain, watching me. 'I done him a good turn and he wanted to give me something good.'

'He certainly did,' I answered.

I was wondering whether I could discreetly make Captain Butler an offer for it, I could not imagine that he set any store on such an article, when, as though he read my thoughts, he said:

'I wouldn't sell that for ten thousand dollars.'

'I guess not,' said Winter. 'It would be a crime to sell it.'

'Why?' I asked.

'That comes into the story,' returned Winter. 'Doesn't it, Captain?'

'It surely does.'

'Let's hear it then.'

'The night's young yet,' he answered.

The night distinctly lost its youth before he satisfied my curiosity, and meanwhile we drank a great deal too much whisky while Captain Butler narrated his experiences of San Francisco in the old days and of the South Seas. At last the girl fell asleep. She lay curled up on the seat, with her face on her brown arm, and her bosom rose and fell gently with her breathing. In sleep she looked sullen, but darkly beautiful.

He had found her on one of the islands in the group among which, whenever there was cargo to be got, he wandered with his crazy old schooner. The Kanakas have little love for work, and the laborious Chinese, the cunning Japs, have taken the trade out of their hands. Her father had a strip of land on which he grew taro and bananas and he had a boat in which he went fishing. He was vaguely related to the mate of the schooner, and it was he who took Captain Butler up to the shabby little frame house to spend an idle evening. They took a bottle of whisky with them and the ukulele. The captain was not a shy man and when he saw a pretty girl he made love to her. He could speak the native language fluently and it was not long before he had overcome the girl's timidity. They spent the evening singing and dancing, and by the end of it she was sitting by his side and he had his arm round her waist. It happened that they were delayed on the island for several days and the captain, at no time a man to hurry, made no effort to shorten his stay. He was very comfortable in the snug little harbour and life was long. He had a swim round his ship in the morning and another in the evening. There was a chandler's shop on the water front where sailormen could get a drink of whisky, and he spent the best part of the day there, playing cribbage with the half-caste who owned it. At night the mate and he went up to the house where the pretty girl lived and they sang a song or two and told stories. It was the girl's father who suggested that he should take her away with him. They discussed the matter in a friendly fashion, while the girl, nestling against the captain, urged him by the pressure of her hands and her soft smiling glances. He had taken a fancy to her and he was a domestic man. He was a little dull sometimes at sea and it would be very pleasant to have a pretty little creature like that about the old ship. He was of a practical turn too, and he recognized that it would be useful to have someone around to darn his socks and look after his linen. He was tired of having his things washed by a Chink who tore everything to pieces; the natives washed much better, and now and then when the captain went ashore at Honolulu he liked to cut a dash in a smart duck suit. It was only a matter of arranging a price. The father wanted two hundred and fifty dollars, and the captain, never a thrifty man, could not put his hand on such a sum. But he was a generous one, and with the girl's soft face against his, he was not inclined to haggle. He offered to give a hundred and fifty dollars there and then and another hundred in three months. There was a good deal of argument and the parties could not come to any agreement that night, but the idea had fired the captain, and he could not sleep as well as usual. He kept dreaming of the lovely girl and each time he awoke it was with the pressure of her soft, sensual lips on his. He cursed himself in the morning, because a bad night at poker the last time he was at Honolulu had left him so short of ready money. And if the night before he had been in love with the girl, this morning he was crazy about her.

'See here, Bananas,' he said to the mate, 'I've got to have that girl. You go and tell the old man I'll bring the dough up tonight and she can get fixed up. I figure we'll be ready to sail at dawn.'

I have no idea why the mate was known by that eccentric name. He was called Wheeler, but though he had that English surname there was not a drop of white blood in him. He was a tall man, and well-made though inclined to stoutness, but much darker than is usual in Hawaii. He was no longer young, and his crisply curling, thick hair was grey. His upper front teeth were cased in gold. He was very proud of them. He had a marked squint and this gave him a saturnine expression. The captain, who was fond of a joke, found in it a constant source of humour and hesitated the less to rally him on the defect because he realized that the mate was sensitive about it. Bananas, unlike most of the natives, was a taciturn fellow and Captain Butler would have disliked him if it had been possible for a man of his good nature to dislike anyone. He liked to be at sea with someone he could talk to, he was a chatty, sociable creature, and it was enough to drive a missionary to drink to live there day after day with a chap who never opened his mouth. He did his best to wake the mate up, that is to say, he chaffed him without mercy, but it was poor fun to laugh by oneself, and he came to the conclusion that, drunk or sober, Bananas was no fit companion for a white man. But he was a good seaman and the captain was shrewd enough to know the value of a mate he could trust. It was not rare for him to come aboard, when they were sailing, fit for nothing but to fall into his bunk, and it was worth something to know that he could stay there till he had slept his liquor off, since Bananas could be relied on. But he was an unsociable devil, and it would be a treat to have someone he could talk to. That girl would be fine. Besides, he wouldn't be so likely to get drunk when he went ashore if he knew there was a little girl waiting for him when he came on board again.

He went to his friend the chandler and over a peg of gin asked him for a loan. There were one or two useful things a ship's captain could do for a ship's chandler, and after a quarter of an hour's conversation in low tones (there is no object in letting all and sundry know your business), the captain crammed a wad of notes in his hip-pocket, and that night, when he went back to his ship the girl went with him.

What Captain Butler, seeking for reasons to do what he had already made up his mind to, had anticipated, actually came to pass. He did not give up drinking, but he ceased to drink to excess. An evening with the boys, when he had been away from town two or three weeks, was pleasant enough, but it was pleasant too to get back to his little girl; he thought of her, sleeping so softly, and how, when he got into his cabin and leaned over her, she would open her eyes lazily and stretch out her arms for him: it was as good as a full hand. He found he was saving money, and since he was a generous man he did the right thing by the little girl: he gave her some silver-backed brushes for her long hair, and a gold chain, and a reconstructed ruby for her finger. Gee, but it was good to be alive.

A year went by, a whole year, and he was not tired of her yet. He was not a man who analysed his feelings, but this was so surprising that it forced itself upon his attention. There must be something very wonderful about that girl.

He couldn't help seeing that he was more wrapped up in her than ever, and sometimes the thought entered his mind that it might not be a bad thing if he married her.

Then, one day the mate did not come in to dinner or to tea. Butler did not bother himself about his absence at the first meal, but at the second he asked the Chinese cook:

'Where's the mate? He no come tea?'

'No wantchee,' said the Chink.

'He ain't sick?'

'No savvy.'

Next day Bananas turned up again, but he was more sullen than ever, and after dinner the captain asked the girl what was the matter with him. She smiled and shrugged her pretty shoulders. She told the captain that Bananas had taken a fancy to her and he was sore because she had told him off. The captain was a good-humoured man and he was not of a jealous nature; it struck him as exceeding funny that Bananas should be in love. A man who had a squint like that had a precious poor chance. When tea came round he chaffed him gaily. He pretended to speak in the air, so that the mate should not be certain that he knew anything, but he dealt him some pretty shrewd blows. The girl did not think him as funny as he thought himself, and afterwards she begged him to say nothing more. He was surprised at her seriousness. She told him he did not know her people. When their passion was aroused they were capable of anything. She was a little frightened. This was so absurd to him that he laughed heartily.

'If he comes bothering round you, you just threaten to tell me. That'll fix him.'

'Better fire him, I think.'

'Not on your sweet life. I know a good sailor when I see one. But if he don't leave you alone I'll give him the worst licking he's ever had.'

Perhaps the girl had a wisdom unusual in her sex. She knew that it was useless to argue with a man when his mind was made up, for it only increased his stubbornness, and she held her peace. And now on the shabby schooner, threading her way across the silent sea, among those lovely islands, was enacted a dark, tense drama of which the fat little captain remained entirely ignorant. The girl's resistance fired Bananas so that he ceased to be a man, but was simply blind desire. He did not make love to her gently or gaily, but with a black and savage ferocity. Her contempt now was changed to hatred and when he besought her she answered him with bitter, angry taunts. But the struggle went on silently, and when the captain asked her after a little while whether Bananas was bothering her, she lied.

But one night, when they were in Honolulu, he came on board only just in time. They were sailing at dawn. Bananas had been ashore, drinking some native spirit, and he was drunk. The captain, rowing up, heard sounds that surprised him. He scrambled up the ladder. He saw Bananas, beside himself, trying to wrench open the cabin door. He was shouting at the girl. He swore he would kill her if she did not let him in.

'What in hell are you up to?' cried Butler.

The mate let go the handle, gave the captain a look of savage hate, and without a word turned away.

'Stop here. What are you doing with that door?'

The mate still did not answer. He looked at him with sullen, bootless rage.

'I'll teach you not to pull any of your queer stuff with me, you dirty, cross-eyed nigger,' said the captain.

He was a good foot shorter than the mate and no match for him, but he was used to dealing with native crews, and he had his knuckle-duster handy. Perhaps it was not an instrument that a gentleman would use, but then Captain Butler was not a gentleman. Nor was he in the habit of dealing with gentlemen. Before Bananas knew what the captain was at, his right arm had shot out and his fist, with its ring of steel, caught him fair and square on the jaw. He fell like a bull under the pole-axe.

'That'll learn him,' said the captain.

Bananas did not stir. The girl unlocked the cabin door and came out.

'Is he dead?'

'He ain't.'

He called a couple of men and told them to carry the mate to his bunk. He rubbed his hands with satisfaction and his round blue eyes gleamed behind his spectacles. But the girl was strangely silent. She put her arms round him as though to protect him from invisible harm.

It was two or three days before Bananas was on his feet again, and when he came out of his cabin his face was torn and swollen. Through the darkness of his skin you saw the livid bruise. Butler saw him slinking along the deck and called him. The mate went to him without a word.

'See here, Bananas,' he said to him, fixing his spectacles on his slippery nose, for it was very hot. 'I ain't going to fire you for this, but you know now that when I hit, I hit hard. Don't forget it and don't let me have any more funny business.'

Then he held out his hand and gave the mate that good-humoured, flashing smile of his which was his greatest charm. The mate took the outstretched hand and twitched his swollen lips into a devilish grin. The incident in the captain's mind was so completely finished that when the three of them sat at dinner he chaffed Bananas on his appearance. He was eating with difficulty and, his swollen face still more distorted by pain, he looked truly a repulsive object.

That evening, when he was sitting on the upper deck, smoking his pipe, a shiver passed through the captain.

'I don't know what I should be shiverin' for on a night like this,' he grumbled. 'Maybe I've gotten a dose of fever. I've been feelin' a bit queer all day.'

When he went to bed he took some quinine, and next morning he felt better, but a little washed out, as though he were recovering from a debauch.

'I guess my liver's out of order,' he said, and he took a pill.

He had not much appetite that day and towards evening he began to feel very unwell. He tried the next remedy he knew, which was to drink two or three hot whiskies, but that did not seem to help him much, and when in the morning he surveyed himself in the glass he thought he was not looking quite the thing.

'If I ain't right by the time we get back to Honolulu I'll just give Dr Denby a call. He'll sure fix me up.'

He could not eat. He felt a great lassitude in all his limbs. He slept soundly enough, but he awoke with no sense of refreshment; on the contrary he felt a peculiar exhaustion. And the energetic little man, who could not bear the thought of lying in bed, had to make an effort to force himself out of his bunk. After a few days he found it impossible to resist the languor that oppressed him, and he made up his mind not to get up.

'Bananas can look after the ship,' he said. 'He has before now.'

He laughed a little to himself as he thought how often he had lain speechless in his bunk after a night with the boys. That was before he had his girl. He smiled at her and pressed her hand. She was puzzled and anxious. He saw that she was concerned about him and tried to reassure her. He had never had a day's illness in his life and in a week at the outside he would be as right as rain.

'I wish you'd fired Bananas,' she said. 'I've got a feeling that he's at the bottom of this.'

'Damned good thing I didn't, or there'd be no one to sail the ship. I know a good sailor when I see one.' His blue eyes, rather pale now, with the whites all yellow, twinkled. 'You don't think he's trying to poison me, little girl?'

She did not answer, but she had one or two talks with the Chinese cook, and she took great care with the captain's food. But he ate little enough now, and it was only with the greatest difficulty that she persuaded him to drink a cup of soup two or three times a day. It was clear that he was very ill, he was losing weight quickly, and his chubby face was pale and drawn. He suffered no pain, but merely grew every day weaker and more languid. He was wasting away. The round trip on this occasion lasted about four weeks and by the time they came to Honolulu the captain was a little anxious about himself. He had not been out of his bed for more than a fortnight and really he felt too weak to get up and go to the doctor. He sent a message asking him to come on board. The doctor examined him, but could find nothing to account for his condition. His temperature was normal.

'See here, Captain,' he said, 'I'll be perfectly frank with you. I don't know what's the matter with you, and just seeing you like this don't give me a chance. You come into the hospital so that we can keep you under observation. There's nothing organically wrong with you, I know that, and my impression is that a few weeks in hospital ought to put you to rights.'

'I ain't going to leave my ship.'

Chinese owners were queer customers, he said; if he left his ship because he was sick, his owner might fire him, and he couldn't afford to lose his job. So long as he stayed where he was his contract safeguarded him, and he had a first-rate mate. Besides, he couldn't leave his girl. No man could want a better nurse; if anyone could pull him through she would. Every man had to die once and he only wished to be left in peace. He would not listen to the doctor's expostulations, and finally the doctor gave in.

'I'll write you a prescription,' he said doubtfully, 'and see if it does you any good. You'd better stay in bed for a while.'

'There ain't much fear of my getting up, doc,' answered the captain. 'I feel as weak as a cat.'

But he believed in the doctor's prescription as little as did the doctor himself, and when he was alone amused himself by lighting his cigar with it. He had to get amusement out of something, for his cigar tasted like nothing on earth, and he smoked only to persuade himself that he was not too ill to. That evening a couple of friends of his, masters of tramp steamers, hearing he was sick came to see him. They discussed his case over a bottle of whisky and a box of Philippine cigars. One of them remembered how a mate of his had been taken queer just like that and not a doctor in the United States had been able to cure him. He had seen in the paper an advertisement of a patent medicine, and thought there'd be no harm in trying it. That man was as strong as ever he'd been in his life after two bottles. But his illness had given Captain Butler a lucidity which was new and strange, and while they talked he seemed to read their minds. They thought he was dying. And when they left him he was afraid.

The girl saw his weakness. This was her opportunity. She had been urging him to let a native doctor see him, and he had stoutly refused; but now she entreated him. He listened with harassed eyes. He wavered. It was very funny that the American doctor could not tell what was the matter with him. But he did not want her to think that he was scared. If he let a damned nigger come along and look at him, it was to comfort *her*. He told her to do what she liked.

The native doctor came the next night. The captain was lying alone, half awake, and the cabin was dimly lit by an oil lamp. The door was softly opened and the girl came in on tip-toe. She held the door open and someone slipped in silently behind her. The captain smiled at this mystery, but he was so weak now, the smile was no more than a glimmer in his eyes. The doctor was a little, old man, very thin and very wrinkled, with a completely bald head, and the face of a monkey. He was bowed and gnarled like an old tree. He looked hardly human, but his eyes were very bright, and in the half darkness they seemed to glow with a reddish light. He was dressed filthily in a pair of ragged dungarees, and the upper part of his body was naked. He sat down on his haunches and for ten minutes looked at the captain. Then he felt the palms of his hands and the soles of his feet. The girl watched him with frightened eyes. No word was spoken. Then he asked for something that the captain had worn. The girl gave him the old felt hat which the captain used constantly and taking it he sat down again on the floor, clasping it firmly with both hands; and rocking backwards and forwards slowly he muttered some gibberish in a very low tone.

At last he gave a little sigh and dropped the hat. He took an old pipe out of his trouser pocket and lit it. The girl went over to him and sat by his side. He whispered something to her, and she started violently. For a few minutes they talked in hurried undertones, and then they stood up. She gave him money and opened the door for him. He slid out as silently as he had come in. Then she went over to the captain and leaned over him so that she could speak into his ear.

'It's an enemy praying you to death.'

'Don't talk fool stuff, girlie,' he said impatiently.

'It's truth. It's God's truth. That's why the American doctor couldn't do anything. Our people can do that. I've seen it done. I thought you were safe because you were a white man.'

'I haven't an enemy.'

'Bananas.'

'What's he want to pray me to death for?'

'You ought to have fired him before he had a chance.'

'I guess if I ain't got nothing more the matter with me than Bananas' hoodoo I shall be sitting up and taking nourishment in a very few days.'

She was silent for a while and she looked at him intently.

'Don't you know you're dying?' she said to him at last.

That was what the two skippers had thought, but they hadn't said it. A shiver passed across the captain's wan face.

'The doctor says there ain't nothing really the matter with me. I've only to lie quiet for a bit and I shall be all right.'

She put her lips to his ear as if she were afraid that the air itself might hear.

'You're dying, dying, dying. You'll pass out with the old moon.'

'That's something to know.'

'You'll pass out with the old moon unless Bananas dies before.'

He was not a timid man and he had recovered already from the shock her words, and still more her vehement, silent manner, had given him. Once more a smile flickered in his eyes.

'I guess I'll take my chance, girlie.'

'There's twelve days before the new moon.'

There was something in her tone that gave him an idea.

'See here, my girl, this is all bunk. I don't believe a word of it. But I don't want you to try any of your monkey tricks with Bananas. He ain't a beauty, but he's a first-rate mate.'

He would have said a good deal more, but he was tired out. He suddenly felt very weak and faint. It was always at that hour that he felt worse. He closed his eyes. The girl watched him for a minute and then slipped out of the cabin. The moon, nearly full, made a silver pathway over the dark sea. It shone from an unclouded sky. She looked at it with terror, for she knew that with its death the man she loved would die. His life was in her hands. She could save him, she alone could save him, but the enemy was cunning, and she must be cunning too. She felt that someone was looking at her, and without turning, by the sudden fear that seized her, knew that from the shadow the burning eyes of the mate were fixed upon her. She did not know what he could do; if he could read her thoughts she was defeated already, and with a desperate effort she emptied her mind of all content. His death alone could save her lover, and she could bring his death about. She knew that if he could be brought to look into a calabash in which was water so that a reflection of him was made, and the reflection were broken by hurtling the water, he would die as though he had been struck by lightning; for the reflection was his soul. But none knew better than he the danger, and he could be made to look only by a guile which had lulled his least suspicion. He must never think that he had an enemy who was on the watch to cause his destruction. She knew what she had to do. But the time was short, the time was terribly short. Presently she realized that the mate had gone. She breathed more freely.

Two days later they sailed, and there were ten now before the new moon. Captain Butler was terrible to see. He was nothing but skin and bone, and he could not move without help. He could hardly speak. But she dared do nothing yet. She knew that she must be patient. The mate was cunning, cunning. They went to one of the smaller islands of the group and discharged cargo, and now there were only seven days more. The moment had come to start. She brought some things out of the cabin she shared with the captain and made them into a bundle. She put the bundle in the deck cabin where she and Bananas ate their meals, and at dinner time, when she went in, he turned quickly and she saw that he had been looking at it. Neither of them spoke, but she knew what he suspected. She was making her preparations to leave the ship. He looked at her mockingly. Gradually, as though to prevent the captain from knowing what she was about, she brought everything she owned into the cabin, and some of the captain's clothes, and made them all into bundles. At last Bananas could keep silence no longer. He pointed to a suit of ducks.

'What are you going to do with that?' he asked.

She shrugged her shoulders.

'I'm going back to my island.'

He gave a laugh that distorted his grim face. The captain was dying and she meant to get away with all she could lay hands on.

'What'll you do if I say you can't take those things? They're the captain's.'
'They're no use to you,' she said.

There was a calabash hanging on the wall. It was the very calabash I had seen when I came into the cabin and which we had talked about. She took it down. It was all dusty, so she poured water into it from the water-bottle, and rinsed it with her fingers.

'What are you doing with that?'
'I can sell it for fifty dollars,' she said.
'If you want to take it you'll have to pay me.'
'What d'you want?'
'You know what I want.'

She allowed a fleeting smile to play on her lips. She flashed a quick look at him and quickly turned away. He gave a gasp of desire. She raised her shoulders in a little shrug. With a savage bound he sprang upon her and seized her in his arms. Then she laughed. She put her arms, her soft, round arms, about his neck, and surrendered herself to him voluptuously.

When the morning came she roused him out of a deep sleep. The early rays of the sun slanted into the cabin. He pressed her to his heart. Then he told her that the captain could not last more than a day or two, and the owner wouldn't so easily find another white man to command the ship. If Bananas offered to take less money he would get the job and the girl could stay with him. He looked at her with love-sick eyes. She nestled up against him. She kissed his lips, in the foreign way, in the way the captain had taught her to kiss. And she promised to stay. Bananas was drunk with happiness.

It was now or never.

She got up and went to the table to arrange her hair. There was no mirror and she looked into the calabash, seeking for her reflection. She tidied her beautiful hair. Then she beckoned to Bananas to come to her. She pointed to the calabash.

'There's something in the bottom of it,' she said.

Instinctively, without suspecting anything, Bananas looked full into the water. His face was reflected in it. In a flash she beat upon it violently, with both her hands, so that they pounded on the bottom and the water splashed up. The reflection was broken in pieces. Bananas started back with a sudden hoarse cry and he looked at the girl. She was standing there with a look of triumphant hatred on her face. A horror came into his eyes. His heavy features were twisted in agony, and with a thud, as though he had taken a violent poison, he crumpled up on the ground. A great shudder passed through his body and he was still. She leaned over him callously. She put her hand on his heart and then she pulled down his lower eye-lid. He was quite dead.

She went into the cabin in which lay Captain Butler. There was a faint colour in his cheeks and he looked at her in a startled way.

'What's happened?' he whispered.

They were the first words he had spoken for forty-eight hours.

'Nothing's happened,' she said.

'I feel all funny.'

Then his eyes closed and he fell asleep. He slept for a day and a night, and when he awoke he asked for food. In a fortnight he was well.

It was past midnight when Winter and I rowed back to shore and we had drunk innumerable whiskies and sodas.

'What do you think of it all?' asked Winter.

'What a question! If you mean, have I any explanation to suggest, I haven't.'

'The captain believes every word of it.'

'That's obvious; but, you know, that's not the part that interests me most: whether it's true or not, and what it all means; the part that interests me is that such things should happen to such people. I wonder what there is in that common-place little man to arouse such a passion in that lovely creature. As I watched her, asleep there, while he was telling the story I had some fantastic idea about the power of love being able to work miracles.'

'But that's not the girl,' said Winter.

'What on earth do you mean?'

'Didn't you notice the cook?'

'Of course I did. He's the ugliest man I ever saw.'

'That's why Butler took him. The girl ran away with the Chinese cook last year. This is a new one. He's only had her there about two months.'

'Well, I'm hanged.'

'He thinks this cook is safe. But I wouldn't be too sure in his place. There's something about a Chink, when he lays himself out to please a woman she can't resist him.'

The Ant and the Grasshopper

♦

When I was a very small boy I was made to learn by heart certain of the fables of La Fontaine, and the moral of each was carefully explained to me. Among those I learnt was *The Ant and The Grasshopper*, which is devised to bring home to the young the useful lesson that in an imperfect world industry is rewarded and giddiness punished. In this admirable fable (I apologize for telling something which everyone is politely, but inexactly, supposed to know) the ant spends a laborious summer gathering its winter store, while the grasshopper sits on a blade of grass singing to the sun. Winter comes and the ant is comfortably provided for, but the grasshopper has an empty larder: he goes to the ant and begs for a little food. Then the ant gives him her classic answer:

'What were you doing in the summer time?'

'Saving your presence, I sang, I sang all day, all night.'

'You sang. Why, then go and dance.'

I do not ascribe it to perversity on my part, but rather to the inconsequence of childhood, which is deficient in moral sense, that I could never quite reconcile myself to the lesson. My sympathies were with the grasshopper and for some time I never saw an ant without putting my foot on it. In this summary (and as I have discovered since, entirely human) fashion I sought to express my disapproval of prudence and common sense.

I could not help thinking of this fable when the other day I saw George Ramsay lunching by himself in a restaurant. I never saw anyone wear an expression of such deep gloom. He was staring into space. He looked as though the burden of the whole world sat on his shoulders. I was sorry for him: I suspected at once that his unfortunate brother had been causing trouble again. I went up to him and held out my hand.

'How are you?' I asked.

'I'm not in hilarious spirits,' he answered.

'Is it Tom again?'

He sighed.

'Yes, it's Tom again.'

'Why don't you chuck him? You've done everything in the world for him. You must know by now that he's quite hopeless.'

I suppose every family has a black sheep. Tom had been a sore trial to his for twenty years. He had begun life decently enough: he went into business, married, and had two children. The Ramsays were perfectly respectable people and there was every reason to suppose that Tom Ramsay would have a useful and honourable career. But one day, without warning, he announced that he didn't like work and that he wasn't suited for marriage. He wanted to enjoy himself. He would listen to no expostulations. He left his wife and his office. He had a little money and he spent two happy years in the various capitals of Europe. Rumours of his doings reached his relations from time to time and they were profoundly shocked. He certainly had a very good time. They shook their heads and asked what would happen when his money was spent. They soon found out: he borrowed. He was charming and unscrupulous. I have never met anyone to whom it was more difficult to refuse a loan. He made a steady income from his friends and he made friends easily. But he always said that the money you spent on necessities was boring; the money that was amusing to spend was the money you spent on luxuries. For this he depended on his brother George. He did not waste his charm on him. George was a serious man and insensible to such enticements. George was respectable. Once or twice he fell to Tom's promises of amendment and gave him considerable sums in order that he might make a fresh start. On these Tom bought a motor-car and some very nice jewellery. But when circumstances forced George to realize that his brother would never settle down and he washed his hands of him, Tom, without a qualm, began to blackmail him. It was not very nice for a respectable lawyer to find his brother shaking cocktails behind the bar of his favourite restaurant or to see him waiting on the box-seat of a taxi outside his club. Tom said that to serve in a bar or to drive a taxi was a perfectly decent occupation, but if George could oblige him with a couple of hundred pounds he didn't mind for the honour of the family giving it up. George paid.

Once Tom nearly went to prison. George was terribly upset. He went into the whole discreditable affair. Really Tom had gone too far. He had been wild, thoughtless, and selfish, but he had never before done anything dishonest, by which George meant illegal; and if he were prosecuted he would assuredly be convicted. But you cannot allow your only brother to go to gaol. The man Tom had cheated, a man called Cronshaw, was vindictive. He was determined to take the matter into court; he said Tom was a scoundrel and should be punished. It cost George an infinite deal of trouble and five hundred pounds to settle the affair. I have never seen him in such a rage as when he heard that Tom and Cronshaw had gone off together to Monte Carlo the moment they cashed the cheque. They spent a happy month there.

For twenty years Tom raced and gambled, philandered with the prettiest girls, danced, ate in the most expensive restaurants, and dressed beautifully. He always looked as if he had just stepped out of a bandbox. Though he was forty-six you would never have taken him for more than thirty-five. He was a most amusing companion and though you knew he was perfectly worthless you could not but enjoy his society. He had high spirits, an unfailing gaiety, and incredible charm. I never grudged the contributions he regularly levied on me for the necessities of his existence. I never lent him fifty pounds without feeling that I was in his debt. Tom Ramsay knew everyone and everyone knew Tom Ramsay. You could not approve of him, but you could not help liking him.

Poor George, only a year older than his scapegrace brother, looked sixty. He had never taken more than a fortnight's holiday in the year for a quarter of a century. He was in his office every morning at nine-thirty and never left it till six. He was honest, industrious, and worthy. He had a good wife, to whom he had never been unfaithful even in thought, and four daughters to whom he was the best of fathers. He made a point of saving a third of his income and his plan was to retire at fifty-five to a little house in the country where he proposed to cultivate his garden and play golf. His life was blameless. He was glad that he was growing old because Tom was growing old too. He rubbed his hands and said:

'It was all very well when Tom was young and good-looking, but he's only a year younger than I am. In four years he'll be fifty. He won't find life so easy then. I shall have thirty thousand pounds by the time I'm fifty. For twenty-five years I've said that Tom would end in the gutter. And we shall see how he likes that. We shall see if it really pays best to work or be idle.'

Poor George! I sympathized with him. I wondered now as I sat down beside him what infamous thing Tom had done. George was evidently very much upset.

'Do you know what's happened now?' he asked me.

I was prepared for the worst. I wondered if Tom had got into the hands of the police at last. George could hardly bring himself to speak.

'You're not going to deny that all my life I've been hardworking, decent, respectable, and straightforward. After a life of industry and thrift I can look forward to retiring on a small income in gilt-edged securities. I've always done my duty in that state of life in which it has pleased Providence to place me.'

'True.'

'And you can't deny that Tom has been an idle, worthless, dissolute, and dishonourable rogue. If there were any justice he'd be in the workhouse.'

'True.'

George grew red in the face.

'A few weeks ago he became engaged to a woman old enough to be his mother. And now she's died and left him everything she had. Half a million pounds, a yacht, a house in London, and a house in the country.'

George Ramsay beat his clenched fist on the table.

'It's not fair, I tell you, it's not fair. Damn it, it's not fair.'

I could not help it. I burst into a shout of laughter as I looked at George's wrathful face, I rolled in my chair, I very nearly fell on the floor. George never forgave me. But Tom often asks me to excellent dinners in his charming house in Mayfair, and if he occasionally borrows a trifle from me, that is merely from force of habit. It is never more than a sovereign.

The Pool

◆

When I was introduced to Lawson by Chaplin, the owner of the Hotel Metropole at Apia, I paid no particular attention to him. We were sitting in the lounge over an early cocktail and I was listening with amusement to the gossip of the island.

Chaplin entertained me. He was by profession a mining engineer and perhaps it was characteristic of him that he had settled in a place where his professional attainments were of no possible value. It was, however, generally reported that he was an extremely clever mining engineer. He was a small man, neither fat nor thin, with black hair, scanty on the crown, turning grey, and a small, untidy moustache; his face, partly from the sun and partly from liquor, was very red. He was but a figurehead, for the hotel, though so grandly named but a frame building of two storeys, was managed by his wife, a tall, gaunt Australian of five-and-forty, with an imposing presence and a determined air. The little man, excitable and often tipsy, was terrified of her, and the stranger soon heard of domestic quarrels in which she used her fist and her foot in order to keep him in subjection. She had been known after a night of drunkenness to confine him for twenty-four hours to his own room, and then he could be seen, afraid to leave his prison, talking somewhat pathetically from his veranda to people in the street below.

He was a character, and his reminiscences of a varied life, whether true or not, made him worth listening to, so that when Lawson strolled in I was inclined to resent the interruption. Although not midday, it was clear that he had had enough to drink, and it was without enthusiasm that I yielded to his persistence and accepted his offer of another cocktail. I knew already that Chaplin's head was weak. The next round which in common politeness I should be forced to order would be enough to make him lively, and then Mrs

Chaplin would give me black looks.

Nor was there anything attractive in Lawson's appearance. He was a little thin man, with a long, sallow face and a narrow, weak chin, a prominent nose, large and bony, and great shaggy black eyebrows. They gave him a peculiar look. His eyes, very large and very dark, were magnificent. He was jolly, but his jollity did not seem to me sincere; it was on the surface, a mask which he wore to deceive the world, and I suspected that it concealed a mean nature. He was plainly anxious to be thought a 'good sport' and he was hail-fellow-well-met; but, I do not know why, I felt that he was cunning and shifty. He talked a great deal in a raucous voice, and he and Chaplin capped one another's stories of beanos which had become legendary, stories of 'wet' nights at the English Club, of shooting expeditions where an incredible amount of whisky had been consumed, and of jaunts to Sydney of which their pride was that they could remember nothing from the time they landed till the time they sailed. A pair of drunken swine. But even in their intoxication, for by now, after four cocktails each, neither was sober, there was a great difference between Chaplin, rough and vulgar, and Lawson: Lawson might be drunk, but he was certainly a gentleman.

At last he got out of his chair, a little unsteadily.

'Well, I'll be getting along home,' he said. 'See you before dinner.'

'Missus all right?' said Chaplin.

'Yes.'

He went out. There was a peculiar note in the monosyllable of his answer which made me look up.

'Good chap,' said Chaplin flatly, as Lawson went out of the door into the sunshine. 'One of the best. Pity he drinks.'

This from Chaplin was an observation not without humour.

'And when he's drunk he wants to fight people.'

'Is he often drunk?'

'Dead drunk, three or four days a week. It's the island done it, and Ethel.'

'Who's Ethel?'

'Ethel's his wife. Married a half-caste. Old Brevald's daughter. Took her away from here. Only thing to do. But she couldn't stand it, and now they're back again. He'll hang himself one of these days, if he don't drink himself to death. Good chap. Nasty when he's drunk.'

Chaplin belched loudly.

'I'll go and put my head under the shower. I oughtn't to have had that last cocktail. It's always the last one that does you in.'

He looked uncertainly at the staircase as he made up his mind to go to the cubby hole in which was the shower, and then with unnatural seriousness got up.

'Pay you to cultivate Lawson,' he said. 'A well-read chap. You'd be surprised when he's sober. Clever too. Worth talking to.'

Chaplin had told me the whole story in these few speeches.

When I came in towards evening from a ride along the seashore Lawson was again in the hotel. He was heavily sunk in one of the cane chairs in the lounge and he looked at me with glassy eyes. It was plain that he had been drinking all the afternoon. He was torpid, and the look on his face was sullen and vindictive. His glance rested on me for a moment, but I could see that he did not recognize me. Two or three other men were sitting there, shaking dice, and they took no notice of him. His condition was evidently too usual to attract attention. I sat down and began to play.

'You're a damned sociable lot,' said Lawson suddenly.

He got out of his chair and waddled with bent knees towards the door. I do not know whether the spectacle was more ridiculous than revolting. When he had gone one of the men sniggered.

'Lawson's fairly soused today,' he said.

'If I couldn't carry my liquor better than that,' said another, 'I'd climb on the waggon and stay there.'

Who would have thought that this wretched object was in his way a romantic figure or that his life had in it those elements of pity and terror which the theorist tells us are necessary to achieve the effect of tragedy?

I did not see him again for two or three days.

I was sitting one evening on the first floor of the hotel on a veranda that overlooked the street when Lawson came up and sank into a chair beside me. He was quite sober. He made a casual remark and then, when I had replied somewhat indifferently, added with a laugh which had in it an apologetic tone:

'I was devilish soused the other day.'

I did not answer. There was really nothing to say. I pulled away at my pipe in the vain hope of keeping the mosquitoes away, and looked at the natives going home from their work. They walked with long steps, slowly, with care and dignity, and the soft patter of their naked feet was strange to hear. Their dark hair, curling or straight, was often white with lime, and then they had a look of extraordinary distinction. They were tall and finely built. Then a gang of Solomon Islanders, indentured labourers, passed by, singing; they were shorter and slighter than the Samoans, coal-black, with great heads of fuzzy hair dyed red. Now and then a white man drove past in his buggy or rode into the hotel yard. In the lagoon two or three schooners reflected their grace in the tranquil water.

'I don't know what there is to do in a place like this except to get soused,' said Lawson at last.

'Don't you like Samoa?' I asked casually, for something to say.

'It's pretty, isn't it?'

The word he chose seemed so inadequate to describe the unimaginable beauty of the island that I smiled, and smiling I turned to look at him. I was startled by the expression in those fine sombre eyes of his, an expression of intolerable anguish; they betrayed a tragic depth of emotion of which I should never have thought him capable. But the expression passed away and he smiled. His smile was simple and a little naïve. It changed his face so that I wavered in my first feeling of aversion from him.

'I was all over the place when I first came out,' he said.

He was silent for a moment.

'I went away for good about three years ago, but I came back.' He hesitated. 'My wife wanted to come back. She was born here, you know.'

'Oh yes.'

He was silent again, and then hazarded a remark about Robert Louis Stevenson. He asked me if I had been up to Vailima. For some reason he was making an effort to be agreeable to me. He began to talk of Stevenson's books, and presently the conversation drifted to London.

'I suppose Covent Garden's still going strong,' he said. 'I think I miss the opera as much as anything here. Have you seen *Tristan and Isolde*?'

He asked me the question as though the answer was really important to him, and when I said, a little casually I daresay, that I had, he seemed pleased. He began to speak of Wagner, not as a musician, but as the plain man who received from him an emotional satisfaction that he could not analyse.

'I suppose Bayreuth was the place to go really,' he said. 'I never had the money, worse luck. But of course one might do worse than Covent Garden, all the lights and the women dressed up to the nines, and the music. The first act of the *Walküre*'s all right, isn't it? And the end of *Tristan.* Golly!'

His eyes were flashing now and his face was lit up so that he hardly seemed the same man. There was a flush on his sallow, thin cheeks, and I forgot that his voice was harsh and unpleasant. There was even a certain charm about him.

'By George, I'd like to be in London tonight. Do you know the Pall Mall restaurant? I used to go there a lot. Piccadilly Circus with the shops all lit up, and the crowd. I think it's stunning to stand there and watch the buses and taxis streaming along as though they'd never stop. And I like the Strand too. What are those lines about God and Charing Cross?'

I was taken aback.

'Thompson's, d'you mean?' I asked.

I quoted them:

> 'But when so sad, thou canst not sadder,
> Cry, and upon thy so sore loss
> Shall shine the traffic of Jacob's ladder
> Pitched between Heaven and Charing Cross.'

He gave a faint sigh.

'I've read *The Hound of Heaven*. It's a bit of all right.'

'It's generally thought so,' I murmured.

'You don't meet anybody here who's read anything. They think it's swank.'

There was a wistful look on his face, and I thought I divined the feeling that made him come to me. I was a link with the world he regretted and a life that he would know no more. Because not so very long before I had been in the London which he loved, he looked upon me with awe and envy. He had not spoken for five minutes perhaps when he broke out with words that startled me by their intensity.

'I'm fed up,' he said. 'I'm fed up.'

'Then why don't you clear out?' I asked.

His face grew sullen.

'My lungs are a bit dicky. I couldn't stand an English winter now.'

At that moment another man joined us on the veranda and Lawson sank into a moody silence.

'It's about time for a dram,' said the newcomer. 'Who'll have a drop of Scotch with me? Lawson?'

Lawson seemed to arise from a distant world. He got up.

'Let's go down to the bar,' he said.

When he left me I remained with a more kindly feeling towards him than I should have expected. He puzzled and interested me. And a few days later I met his wife. I knew they had been married for five or six years, and I was surprised to see that she was still extremely young. When he married her she could not have been more than sixteen. She was adorably pretty. She was no darker than a Spaniard, small and very beautifully made, with tiny hands and feet, and a slight, lithe figure. Her features were lovely; but I think what struck

me most was the delicacy of her appearance; the half-castes as a rule have a
certain coarseness, they seem a little roughly formed, but she had an exquisite
daintiness which took your breath away. There was something extremely
civilized about her, so that it surprised you to see her in those surroundings,
and you thought of those famous beauties who had set all the world talking at
the Court of the Emperor Napoleon III. Though she wore but a muslin frock
and a straw hat she wore them with an elegance that suggested the woman of
fashion. She must have been ravishing when Lawson first saw her.

He had but lately come out from England to manage the local branch of an
English bank, and, reaching Samoa at the beginning of the dry season, he had
taken a room at the hotel. He quickly made the acquaintance of all and sundry.
The life of the island is pleasant and easy. He enjoyed the long idle talks in the
lounge of the hotel and the gay evenings at the English Club when a group of
fellows would play pool. He liked Apia straggling along the edge of the lagoon,
with its stores and bungalows, and its native village. Then there were week-
ends when he would ride over to the house of one planter or another and spend
a couple of nights on the hills. He had never before known freedom or leisure.
And he was intoxicated by the sunshine. When he rode through the bush his
head reeled a little at the beauty that surrounded him. The country was
indescribably fertile. In parts the forest was still virgin, a tangle of strange
trees, luxuriant undergrowth, and vine; it gave an impression that was
mysterious and troubling.

But the spot that entranced him was a pool a mile or two away from Apia to
which in the evenings he often went to bathe. There was a little river that
bubbled over the rocks in a swift stream, and then, after forming the deep pool,
ran on, shallow and crystalline, past a ford made by great stones where the
natives came sometimes to bathe or to wash their clothes. The coconut trees,
with their frivolous elegance, grew thickly on the banks, all clad with trailing
plants, and they were reflected in the green water. It was just such a scene as
you might see in Devonshire among the hills and yet with a difference, for it
had a tropical richness, a passion, a scented languor which seemed to melt the
heart. The water was fresh, but not cold; and it was delicious after the heat of
the day. To bathe there refreshed not only the body but the soul.

At the hour when Lawson went, there was not a soul and he lingered for a
long time, now floating idly in the water, now drying himself in the evening
sun, enjoying the solitude and the friendly silence. He did not regret London
then, nor the life that he had abandoned, for life as it was seemed complete and
exquisite.

It was here that he first saw Ethel.

Occupied till late by letters which had to be finished for the monthly sailing
of the boat next day, he rode down one evening to the pool when the light was
almost failing. He tied up his horse and sauntered to the bank. A girl was sitting
there. She glanced round as he came and noiselessly slid into the water. She
vanished like a naiad startled by the approach of a mortal. He was surprised and
amused. He wondered where she had hidden herself. He swam downstream
and presently saw her sitting on a rock. She looked at him with uncurious eyes.
He called out a greeting in Samoan.

'*Talofa.*'

She answered him, suddenly smiling, and then let herself into the water
again. She swam easily and her hair spread out behind her. He watched her
cross the pool and climb out on the bank. Like all the natives she bathed in a

Mother Hubbard, and the water had made it cling to her slight body. She wrung out her hair, and as she stood there, unconcerned, she looked more than ever like a wild creature of the water or the woods. He saw now that she was half-caste. He swam towards her and, getting out, addressed her in English.

'You're having a late swim.'

She shook back her hair and then let it spread over her shoulders in luxuriant curls.

'I like it when I'm alone,' she said.

'So do I.'

She laughed with the childlike frankness of the native. She slipped a dry Mother Hubbard over her head and, letting down the wet one, stepped out of it. She wrung it out and was ready to go. She paused a moment irresolutely and then sauntered off. The night fell suddenly.

Lawson went back to the hotel and, describing her to the men who were in the lounge shaking dice for drinks, soon discovered who she was. Her father was a Norwegian called Brevald who was often to be seen in the bar of the Hotel Metropole drinking rum and water. He was a little old man, knotted and gnarled like an ancient tree, who had come out to the islands forty years before as mate of a sailing vessel. He had been a blacksmith, a trader, a planter, and at one time fairly well-to-do; but, ruined by the great hurricane of the nineties, he had now nothing to live on but a small plantation of coconut trees. He had had four native wives and, as he told you with a cracked chuckle, more children than he could count. But some had died and some had gone out into the world, so that now the only one left at home was Ethel.

'She's a peach,' said Nelson, the super-cargo of the *Moana*. 'I've given her the glad eye once or twice, but I guess there's nothing doing.'

'Old Brevald's not that sort of a fool, sonny,' put in another, a man called Miller. 'He wants a son-in-law who's prepared to keep him in comfort for the rest of his life.'

It was distasteful to Lawson that they should speak of the girl in that fashion. He made a remark about the departing mail and so distracted their attention. But next evening he went again to the pool. Ethel was there; and the mystery of the sunset, the deep silence of the water, the lithe grace of the coconut trees, added to her beauty, giving it a profoundity, a magic, which stirred the heart to unknown emotions. For some reason that time he had the whim not to speak to her. She took no notice of him. She did not even glance in his direction. She swam about the green pool. She dived, she rested on the bank, as though she were quite alone: he had a queer feeling that he was invisible. Scraps of poetry, half forgotten, floated across his memory, and vague recollections of the Greece he had negligently studied in his school days. When she had changed her wet clothes for dry ones and sauntered away he found a scarlet hibiscus where she had been. It was a flower that she had worn in her hair when she came to bathe and, having taken it out on getting into the water, had forgotten or not cared to put in again. He took it in his hands and looked at it with a singular emotion. He had an instinct to keep it, but his sentimentality irritated him, and he flung it away. It gave him quite a little pang to see it float down the stream.

He wondered what strangeness it was in her nature that urged her to go down to this hidden pool when there was no likelihood that anyone should be there. The natives of the islands are devoted to the water. They bathe, somewhere or other, every day, once always, and often twice; but they bathe in bands, laughing and joyous, a whole family together; and you often saw a group of girls, dappled by the sun shining through the trees, with the half-castes among them, splashing about the shallows of the stream. It looked as though there were in this pool some secret which attracted Ethel against her will.

Now the night had fallen, mysterious and silent, and he let himself down in the water softly, in order to make no sound, and swam lazily in the warm darkness. The water seemed fragrant still from her slender body. He rode back to the town under the starry sky. He felt at peace with the world.

Now he went every evening to the pool and every evening he saw Ethel. Presently he overcame her timidity. She became playful and friendly. They sat together on the rocks above the pool, where the water ran fast, and they lay side by side on the ledge that overlooked it, watching the gathering dusk envelop it with mystery. It was inevitable that their meetings should become known—in the South Seas everyone seems to know everyone's business—and he was subjected to much rude chaff by the men at the hotel. He smiled and let them talk. It was not even worth while to deny their coarse suggestions. His feelings were absolutely pure. He loved Ethel as a poet might love the moon. He thought of her not as a woman but as something not of this earth. She was the spirit of the pool.

One day at the hotel, passing through the bar, he saw that old Brevald, as ever in his shabby blue overalls, was standing there. Because he was Ethel's father he had a desire to speak to him, so he went in, nodded and, ordering his own drink, casually turned and invited the old man to have one with him. They chatted for a few minutes of local affairs, and Lawson was uneasily conscious that the Norwegian was scrutinizing him with sly blue eyes. His manner was not agreeable. It was sycophantic, and yet behind the cringing air of an old man who had been worsted in his struggle with fate was a shadow of old truculence. Lawson remembered that he had once been captain of a schooner engaged in the slave trade, a blackbirder they call it in the Pacific, and he had a large hernia in the chest which was the result of a wound received in a scrap with Solomon Islanders. The bell rang for luncheon.

'Well, I must be off,' said Lawson.

'Why don't you come along to my place one time?' said Brevald, in his wheezy voice. 'It's not very grand, but you'll be welcome. You know Ethel.'

'I'll come with pleasure.'

'Sunday afternoon's the best time.'

Brevald's bungalow, shabby and bedraggled, stood among the coconut trees of the plantation, a little away from the main road that ran up to Vailima. Immediately around it grew huge plantains. With their tattered leaves they had the tragic beauty of a lovely woman in rags. Everything was slovenly and neglected. Little black pigs, thin and high-backed, rooted about, and chickens clucked noisily as they picked at the refuse scattered here and there. Three or four natives were lounging about the veranda. When Lawson asked for Brevald the old man's cracked voice called out to him, and he found him in the sitting-room smoking an old briar pipe.

'Sit down and make yerself at home,' he said. 'Ethel's just titivating.'

She came in. She wore a blouse and skirt and her hair was done in the European fashion. Although she had not the wild, timid grace of the girl who came down every evening to the pool, she seemed now more usual and consequently more approachable. She shook hands with Lawson. It was the first time he had touched her hand.

'I hope you'll have a cup of tea with us,' she said.

He knew she had been at a mission school, and he was amused, and at the same time touched, by the company manners she was putting on for his benefit. Tea was already set out on the table and in a minute old Brevald's fourth wife brought in the tea-pot. She was a handsome native, no longer very young, and she spoke but a few words of English. She smiled and smiled. Tea was rather a solemn meal, with a great deal of bread and butter and a variety of very sweet cakes, and the conversation was formal. Then a wrinkled old woman came in softly.

'That's Ethel's granny,' said old Brevald, noisily spitting on the floor.

She sat on the edge of a chair, uncomfortably, so that you saw it was unusual for her and she would have been more at ease on the ground, and remained silently staring at Lawson with fixed, shining eyes. In the kitchen behind the bungalow someone began to play the concertina and two or three voices were raised in a hymn. But they sang for the pleasure of the sounds rather than from piety.

When Lawson walked back to the hotel he was strangely happy. He was touched by the higgledy-piggledy way in which those people lived; and in the smiling good-nature of Mrs Brevald, in the little Norwegian's fantastic career, and in the shining mysterious eyes of the old grandmother he found something unusual and fascinating. It was a more natural life than any he had known, it was nearer to the friendly, fertile earth; civilization repelled him at that moment, and by mere contact with these creatures of a more primitive nature he felt a greater freedom.

He saw himself rid of the hotel which already was beginning to irk him, settled in a little bungalow of his own, trim and white, in front of the sea so that he had before his eyes always the multi-coloured variety of the lagoon. He loved the beautiful island. London and England meant nothing to him any more, he was content to spend the rest of his days in that forgotten spot, rich in the best of the world's goods, love and happiness. He made up his mind that whatever the obstacles nothing should prevent him from marrying Ethel.

But there were no obstacles. He was always welcome at the Brevalds' house. The old man was ingratiating and Mrs Brevald smiled without ceasing. He had brief glimpses of natives who seemed somehow to belong to the establishment, and once he found a tall youth in a lava-lava, his body tattooed, his hair white with lime, sitting with Brevald, and was told he was Mrs Brevald's brother's son; but for the most part they kept out of his way. Ethel was delightful with him. The light in her eyes when she saw him filled him with ecstasy. She was charming and naïve. He listened enraptured when she told him of the mission school at which she was educated, and of the sisters. He went with her to the cinema which was given once a fortnight and danced with her at the dance which followed it. They came from all parts of the island for this, since gaieties are few in Upolu; and you saw there all the society of the place, the white ladies keeping a good deal to themselves, the half-castes very elegant in American clothes, the natives, strings of dark girls in white Mother Hubbards and young men in unaccustomed ducks and white shoes. It was all very smart and gay. Ethel was pleased to show her friends the white admirer who did not leave her side. The rumour was soon spread that he meant to marry her and her friends looked at her with envy. It was a great thing for a half-caste to get a white man to marry her, even the less regular relation was better than nothing, but one could never tell what it would lead to; and Lawson's position as manager of the bank made him one of the catches of the island. If he had not been so absorbed in

Ethel he would have noticed that many eyes were fixed on him curiously, and he would have seen the glances of the white ladies and noticed how they put their heads together and gossiped.

Afterwards, when the men who lived at the hotel were having a whisky before turning in, Nelson burst out with:

'Say, they say Lawson's going to marry that girl.'

'He's a damned fool then,' said Miller.

Miller was a German-American who had changed his name from Müller, a big man, fat and bald-headed, with a round, clean-shaven face. He wore large gold-rimmed spectacles, which gave him a benign look, and his ducks were always clean and white. He was a heavy drinker, invariably ready to stay up all night with the 'boys', but he never got drunk; he was jolly and affable, but very shrewd. Nothing interfered with his business; he represented a firm in San Francisco, jobbers of the goods sold in the islands, calico, machinery and what not; and his good-fellowship was part of his stock-in-trade.

'He don't know what he's up against,' said Nelson. 'Someone ought to put him wise.'

'If you'll take my advice you won't interfere in what don't concern you,' said Miller. 'When a man's made up his mind to make a fool of himself, there's nothing like letting him.'

'I'm all for having a good time with the girls out here, but when it comes to marrying them—this child ain't taking any, I'll tell the world.'

Chaplin was there, and now he had his say.

'I've seen a lot of fellows do it, and it's no good.'

'You ought to have a talk with him, Chaplin,' said Nelson. 'You know him better than anyone else does.'

'My advice to Chaplin is to leave it alone,' said Miller.

Even in those days Lawson was not popular and really no one took enough interest in him to bother. Mrs Chaplin talked it over with two or three of the white ladies, but they contented themselves with saying that it was a pity; and when he told her definitely that he was going to be married it seemed too late to do anything.

For a year Lawson was happy. He took a bungalow at the point of the bay round which Apia is built, on the borders of a native village. It nestled charmingly among the coconut trees and faced the passionate blue of the Pacific. Ethel was lovely as she went about the little house, lithe and graceful like some young animal of the woods, and she was gay. They laughed a great deal. They talked nonsense. Sometimes one or two of the men at the hotel would come over and spend the evening, and often on a Sunday they would go for a day to some planter who had married a native; now and then one or other of the half-caste traders who had a store in Apia would give a party and they went to it. The half-castes treated Lawson quite differently now. His marriage had made him one of themselves and they called him Bertie. They put their arms through his and smacked him on the back. He liked to see Ethel at these gatherings. Her eyes shone and she laughed. It did him good to see her radiant happiness. Sometimes Ethel's relations would come to the bungalow, Old Brevald of course, and her mother, but cousins too, vague native women in Mother Hubbards and men and boys in lava-lavas, with their hair dyed red and their bodies elaborately tattooed. He would find them sitting there when he got back from the bank. He laughed indulgently.

'Don't let them eat us out of hearth and home,' he said.

'They're my own family. I can't help doing something for them when they ask me.'

He knew that when a white man marries a native or a half-caste he must expect her relations to look upon him as a gold mine. He took Ethel's face in his hands and kissed her red lips. Perhaps he could not expect her to understand that the salary which had amply sufficed for a bachelor must be managed with some care when it had to support a wife and a house. Then Ethel was delivered of a son.

It was when Lawson first held the child in his arms that a sudden pang shot through his heart. He had not expected it to be so dark. After all it had but a fourth part of native blood, and there was no reason really why it should not look just like an English baby; but, huddled together in his arms, sallow, its head covered already with black hair, with huge black eyes, it might have been a native child. Since his marriage he had been ignored by the white ladies of the colony. When he came across men in whose houses he had been accustomed to dine as a bachelor, they were a little self-conscious with him; and they sought to cover their embarrassment by an exaggerated cordiality.

'Mrs Lawson well?' they would say. 'You're a lucky fellow. Damned pretty girl.'

But if they were with their wives and met him and Ethel they would feel it awkward when their wives gave Ethel a patronizing nod. Lawson had laughed.

'They're as dull as ditchwater, the whole gang of them,' he said. 'It's not going to disturb my night's rest if they don't ask me to their dirty parties.'

But now it irked him a little.

The little dark baby screwed up its face. That was his son. He thought of the half-caste children in Apia. They had an unhealthy look, sallow and pale, and they were odiously precocious. He had seen them on the boat going to school in New Zealand, and a school had to be chosen which took children with native blood in them; they were huddled together, brazen and yet timid, with traits which set them apart strangely from white people. They spoke the native language among themselves. And when they grew up the men accepted smaller salaries because of their native blood; girls might marry a white man, but boys had no chance; they must marry a half-caste like themselves, or a native. Lawson made up his mind passionately that he would take his son away from the humiliation of such a life. At whatever cost he must get back to Europe. And when he went in to see Ethel, frail and lovely in her bed, surrounded by native women, his determination was strengthened. If he took her away among his own people she would belong more completely to him. He loved her so passionately he wanted her to be one soul and one body with him; and he was conscious that here, with those deep roots attaching her to the native life, she would always keep something from him.

He went to work quietly, urged by an obscure instinct of secrecy, and wrote to a cousin who was a partner in a shipping firm in Aberdeen, saying that his health (on account of which like so many more he had come out to the islands) was so much better, there seemed no reason why he should not return to Europe. He asked him to use what influence he could to get him a job, no matter how poorly paid, on Deeside, where the climate was particularly suitable to such as suffered from diseases of the lungs. It takes five or six weeks for letters to get from Aberdeen to Samoa, and several had to be exchanged. He had plenty of time to prepare Ethel. She was as delighted as a child. He was amused to see how she boasted to her friends that she was going to England; it was a step

up for her; she would be quite English there; and she was excited at the interest
the approaching departure gave her. When at length a cable came offering him
a post in a bank in Kincardineshire she was beside herself with joy.

When, their long journey over, they were settled in the little Scots town with
its granite houses Lawson realized how much it meant to him to live once more
among his own people. He looked back on the three years he had spent in Apia
as exile, and returned to the life that seemed the only normal one with a sigh of
relief. It was good to play golf once more, and to fish–to fish properly, that was
poor fun in the Pacific when you just threw in your line and pulled out one big
sluggish fish after another from the crowded sea–and it was good to see a paper
every day with that day's news, and to meet men and women of your own sort,
people you could talk to; and it was good to eat meat that was not frozen and to
drink milk that was not canned. They were thrown upon their own resources
much more than in the Pacific, and he was glad to have Ethel exclusively to
himself. After two years of marriage he loved her more devotedly than ever, he
could hardly bear her out of his sight, and the need in him grew urgent for a
more intimate communion between them. But it was strange that after the first
excitement of arrival she seemed to take less interest in the new life than he had
expected. She did not accustom herself to her surroundings. She was a little
lethargic. As the fine autumn darkened into winter she complained of the cold.
She lay half the morning in bed and the rest of the day on a sofa, reading novels
sometimes, but more often doing nothing. She looked pinched.

'Never mind, darling,' he said. 'You'll get used to it very soon. And wait till
the summer comes. It can be almost as hot as in Apia.'

He felt better and stronger than he had done for years.

The carelessness with which she managed her house had not mattered in
Samoa, but here it was out of place. When anyone came he did not want the
place to look untidy; and, laughing, chaffing Ethel a little, he set about putting
things in order. Ethel watched him indolently. She spent long hours playing
with her son. She talked to him in the baby language of her own country. To
distract her, Lawson bestirred himself to make friends among the neighbours,
and now and then they went to little parties where the ladies sang drawing-
room ballads and the men beamed in silent good nature. Ethel was shy. She
seemed to sit apart. Sometimes Lawson, seized with a sudden anxiety, would
ask her if she was happy.

'Yes, I'm quite happy,' she answered.

But her eyes were veiled by some thought he could not guess. She seemed to
withdraw into herself so that he was conscious that he knew no more of her than
when he had first seen her bathing in the pool. He had an uneasy feeling that she
was concealing something from him, and because he adored her it tortured
him.

'You don't regret Apia, do you?' he asked her once.

'Oh, no–I think it's very nice here.'

An obscure misgiving drove him to make disparaging remarks about the
island and the people there. She smiled and did not answer. Very rarely she
received a bundle of letters from Samoa and then she went about for a day or
two with a set, pale face.

'Nothing would induce me ever to go back there,' he said once. 'It's no place
for a white man.'

But he grew conscious that sometimes, when he was away, Ethel cried. In
Apia she had been talkative, chatting volubly about all the little details of their

common life, the gossip of the place; but now she gradually became silent, and, though he increased his efforts to amuse her, she remained listless. It seemed to him that her recollections of the old life were drawing her away from him, and he was madly jealous of the island and of the sea, of Brevald, and all the dark-skinned people whom he remembered now with horror. When she spoke of Samoa he was bitter and satirical. One evening late in the spring when the birch trees were bursting into leaf, coming home from a round of golf, he found her not as usual lying on the sofa, but at the window, standing. She had evidently been waiting for his return. She addressed him the moment he came into the room. To his amazement she spoke in Samoan.

'I can't stand it. I can't live here any more. I hate it. I hate it.'

'For God's sake speak in a civilized language,' he said irritably.

She went up to him and clasped her arms around his body awkwardly, with a gesture that had in it something barbaric.

'Let's go away from here. Let's go back to Samoa. If you make me stay here I shall die. I want to go home.'

Her passion broke suddenly and she burst into tears. His anger vanished and he drew her down on his knees. He explained to her that it was impossible for him to throw up his job, which after all meant his bread and butter. His place in Apia was long since filled. He had nothing to go back to there. He tried to put it to her reasonably, the inconveniences of life there, the humiliation to which they must be exposed, and the bitterness it must cause their son.

'Scotland's wonderful for education and that sort of thing. Schools are good and cheap, and he can go to the University at Aberdeen. I'll make a real Scot of him.'

They had called him Andrew. Lawson wanted him to become a doctor. He would marry a white woman.

'I'm not ashamed of being half native,' Ethel said sullenly.

'Of course not, darling. There's nothing to be ashamed of.'

With her soft cheek against his he felt incredibly weak.

'You don't know how much I love you,' he said. 'I'd give anything in the world to be able to tell you what I've got in my heart.'

He sought her lips.

The summer came. The highland valley was green and fragrant and the hills were gay with the heather. One sunny day followed another in that sheltered spot, and the shade of the birch trees was grateful after the glare of the high road. Ethel spoke no more of Samoa and Lawson grew less nervous. He thought that she was resigned to her surroundings, and he felt that his love for her was so passionate that it could leave no room in her heart for any longing. One day the local doctor stopped him in the street.

'I say, Lawson, your missus ought to be careful how she bathes in our highland streams. It's not like the Pacific, you know.'

Lawson was surprised, and had not the presence of mind to conceal the fact.

'I didn't know she was bathing.'

The doctor laughed.

'A good many people have seen her. It makes them talk a bit, you know, because it seems a rum place to choose, the pool up above the bridge, and bathing isn't allowed there, but there's no harm in that. I don't know how she can stand the water.'

Lawson knew the pool the doctor spoke of, and suddenly it occurred to him that in a way it was just like that pool at Upolu where Ethel had been in the habit of bathing every evening. A clear highland stream ran down a sinuous course, rocky, splashing gaily, and then formed a deep, smooth pool, with a little sandy beach. Trees overshadowed it thickly, not coconut trees, but beeches, and the sun played fitfully through the leaves on the sparkling water. It gave him a shock. With his imagination he saw Ethel go there every day and undress on the bank and slip into the water, cold, colder than that of the pool she loved at home, and for a moment regain the feeling of the past. He saw her once more as the strange, wild spirit of the stream, and it seemed to him fantastically that the running water called her. That afternoon he went along to the river. He made his way cautiously among the trees and the grassy path deadened the sound of his steps. Presently he came to a spot from which he could see the pool. Ethel was sitting on the bank, looking down at the water. She sat quite still. It seemed as though the water drew her irresistibly. He wondered what strange thoughts wandered through her head. At last she got up, and for a minute or two she was hidden from his gaze; then he saw her again, wearing a Mother Hubbard, and with her little bare feet she stepped delicately over the mossy bank. She came to the water's edge, and softly, without a splash, let herself down. She swam about quietly, and there was something not quite of a human being in the way she swam. He did not know why it affected him so queerly. He waited till she clambered out. She stood for a moment with the wet folds of her dress clinging to her body, so that its shape was outlined, and then, passing her hands slowly over her breasts, gave a little sigh of delight. Then she disappeared. Lawson turned away and walked back to the village. He had a bitter pain in his heart, for he knew that she was still a stranger to him and his hungry love was destined ever to remain unsatisfied.

He did not make any mention of what he had seen. He ignored the incident completely, but he looked at her curiously, trying to divine what was in her mind. He redoubled the tenderness with which he used her. He sought to make her forget the deep longing of her soul by the passion of his love.

Then one day, when he came home, he was astonished to find her not in the house.

'Where's Mrs Lawson?' he asked the maid.

'She went into Aberdeen, Sir, with the baby,' the maid answered, a little surprised at the question. 'She said she would not be back till the last train.'

'Oh, all right.'

He was vexed that Ethel had said nothing to him about the excursion, but he was not disturbed, since of late she had been in now and again to Aberdeen, and he was glad that she should look at the shops and perhaps visit a cinema. He went to meet the last train, but when she did not come he grew suddenly frightened. He went up to the bedroom and saw at once that her toilet things were no longer in their place. He opened the wardrobe and the drawers. They were half empty. She had bolted.

He was seized with a passion of anger. It was too late that night to telephone to Aberdeen and make inquiries, but he knew already all that his inquiries might have taught him. With fiendish cunning she had chosen a time when they were making up their periodical accounts at the bank and there was no chance that he could follow her. He was imprisoned by his work. He took up a paper and saw that there was a boat sailing for Australia next morning. She must be now well on the way to London. He could not prevent the sobs that were wrung painfully from him.

'I've done everything in the world for her,' he cried, 'and she had the heart to treat me like this. How cruel, how monstrously cruel!'

After two days of misery he received a letter from her. It was written in her school-girl hand. She had always written with difficulty:

Dear Bertie

I couldn't stand it any more. I'm going home. Good-bye.

Ethel

She did not say a single word of regret. She did not even ask him to come too. Lawson was prostrated. He found out where the ship made its first stop, and, though he knew very well she would not come, sent a cable beseeching her to return. He waited with pitiful anxiety. He wanted her to send him just one word of love; she did not even answer. He passed through one violent phase after another. At one moment he told himself that he was well rid of her, and at the next that he would force her to return by withholding money. He was lonely and wretched. He wanted his boy and he wanted her. He knew that, whatever he pretended to himself, there was only one thing to do and that was to follow her. He could never live without her now. All his plans for the future were like a house of cards and he scattered them with angry impatience. He did not care whether he threw away his chances for the future, for nothing in the world mattered but that he should get Ethel back again. As soon as he could he went into Aberdeen and told the manager of his bank that he meant to leave at once. The manager remonstrated. The short notice was inconvenient. Lawson would not listen to reason. He was determined to be free before the next boat sailed; and it was not until he was on board of her, having sold everything he possessed, that in some measure he regained his calm. Till then to those who had come in contact with him he seemed hardly sane. His last action in England was to cable to Ethel at Apia that he was joining her.

He sent another cable from Sydney, and when at last with the dawn his boat crossed the bar at Apia and he saw once more the white houses straggling along the bay he felt an immense relief. The doctor came on board, and the agent. They were both old acquaintances and he felt kindly towards their familiar faces. He had a drink or two with them for old times' sake, and also because he was desperately nervous. He was not sure if Ethel would be glad to see him. When he got into the launch and approached the wharf he scanned anxiously the little crowd that waited. She was not there and his heart sank, but then he saw Brevald, in his old blue clothes, and his heart warmed towards him.

'Where's Ethel?' he said, as he jumped on shore.

'She's down at the bungalow. She's living with us.'

Lawson was dismayed, but he put on a jovial air.

'Well, have you got room for me? I daresay it'll take a week or two to fix ourselves up.'

'Oh, yes, I guess we can make room for you.'

After passing through the custom-house they went to the hotel and there Lawson was greeted by several of his old friends. There were a good many rounds of drinks before it seemed possible to get away and when they did go at last to Brevald's house they were both rather gay. He clasped Ethel in his arms. He had forgotten all his bitter thoughts in the joy of beholding her once more. His mother-in-law was pleased to see him, and so was the old, wrinkled beldame, her mother; natives and half-castes came in, and they all sat round, beaming on him. Brevald had a bottle of whisky and everyone who came was given a nip. Lawson sat with his little dark-skinned boy on his knees, they had taken his English clothes off him and he was stark, with Ethel by his side in a Mother Hubbard. He felt like a returning prodigal. In the afternoon he went down to the hotel again and when he got back he was more than gay, he was drunk. Ethel and her mother knew that white men got drunk now and then, it was what you expected of them, and they laughed good-naturedly as they helped him to bed.

But in a day or two he set about looking for a job. He knew that he could not hope for such a position as that which he had thrown away to go to England; but with his training he could not fail to be useful to one of the trading firms, and perhaps in the end he would not lose by the change.

'After all, you can't make money in a bank,' he said. 'Trade's the thing.'

He had hopes that he would soon make himself so indispensable that he would get someone to take him into partnership, and there was no reason why in a few years he should not be a rich man.

'As soon as I'm fixed up we'll find ourselves a shack,' he told Ethel. 'We can't go on living here.'

Brevald's bungalow was so small that they were all piled on one another, and there was no chance of ever being alone. There was neither peace nor privacy.

'Well, there's no hurry. We shall be all right here till we find just what we want.'

It took him a week to get settled and then he entered the firm of a man called Bain. But when he talked to Ethel about moving she said she wanted to stay where she was till her baby was born, for she was expecting another child. Lawson tried to argue with her.

'If you don't like it,' she said, 'go and live at the hotel.'

He grew suddenly pale.

'Ethel, how can you suggest that!'

She shrugged her shoulders.

'What's the good of having a house of our own when we can live here.'

He yielded.

When Lawson, after his work, went back to the bungalow he found it crowded with natives. They lay about smoking, sleeping, drinking *kava*; and they talked incessantly. The place was grubby and untidy. His child crawled about, playing with native children, and it heard nothing spoken but Samoan. He fell into the habit of dropping into the hotel on his way home to have a few cocktails, for he could only face the evening and the crowd of friendly natives when he was fortified with liquor. And all the time, though he loved her more passionately than ever, he felt that Ethel was slipping away from him. When the baby was born he suggested that they should get into a house of their own, but Ethel refused. Her stay in Scotland seemed to have thrown her back on her own people, now that she was once more among them, with a passionate zest, and she turned to her native ways with abandon. Lawson began to drink more. Every Saturday night he went to the English Club and got blind drunk.

He had the peculiarity that as he grew drunk he grew quarrelsome and once he had a violent dispute with Bain, his employer. Bain dismissed him, and he had to look out for another job. He was idle for two or three weeks and during these, sooner than sit in the bungalow, he lounged about in the hotel or at the English Club, and drank. It was more out of pity than anything else that Miller, the German–American, took him into his office; but he was a businessman, and though Lawson's financial skill made him valuable, the circumstances were such that he could hardly refuse a smaller salary than he had had before, and Miller did not hesitate to offer it to him. Ethel and Brevald blamed him for taking it, since Pedersen, the half-caste, offered him more. But he resented bitterly the thought of being under the orders of a half-caste. When Ethel nagged him he burst out furiously:

'I'll see myself dead before I work for a nigger.'

'You may have to,' she said.

And in six months he found himself forced to this final humiliation. The passion for liquor had been gaining on him, he was often heavy with drink, and he did his work badly. Miller warned him once or twice and Lawson was not the man to accept remonstrance easily. One day in the midst of an altercation he put on his hat and walked out. But by now his reputation was well known and he could find no one to engage him. For a while he idled, and then he had an attack of delirium tremens. When he recovered, shameful and weak, he could no longer resist the constant pressure and he went to Pedersen and asked him for a job. Pedersen was glad to have a white man in his store and Lawson's skill at figures made him useful.

From that time his degeneration was rapid. The white people gave him the cold shoulder. They were only prevented from cutting him completely by disdainful pity and by a certain dread of his angry violence when he was drunk. He became extremely susceptible and was always on the lookout for affront.

He lived entirely among the natives and half-castes, but he had no longer the prestige of the white man. They felt his loathing for them and they resented his attitude of superiority. He was one of themselves now and they did not see why he should put on airs. Brevald, who had been ingratiating and obsequious, now treated him with contempt. Ethel had made a bad bargain. There were disgraceful scenes and once or twice the two men came to blows. When there was a quarrel Ethel took the part of her family. They found he was better drunk than sober, for when he was drunk he would lie on the bed or on the floor, sleeping heavily.

Then he became aware that something was being hidden from him.

When he got back to the bungalow for the wretched, half-native supper which was his evening meal, often Ethel was not in. If he asked where she was Brevald told him she had gone to spend the evening with one or other of her friends. Once he followed her to the house Brevald had mentioned and found she was not there. On her return he asked her where she had been and she told him her father had make a mistake; she had been to so-and-so's. But he knew that she was lying. She was in her best clothes; her eyes were shining, and she looked lovely.

'Don't try any monkey tricks on me, my girl,' he said, 'or I'll break every bone in your body.'

'You drunken beast,' she said, scornfully.

He fancied that Mrs Brevald and the old grandmother looked at him maliciously and he ascribed Brevald's good humour with him, so unusual those days, to his satisfaction at having something up his sleeve against his son-in-law. And then, his suspicions aroused, he imagined that the white men gave him curious glances. When he came into the lounge of the hotel the sudden silence which fell upon the company convinced him that he had been the subject of the conversation. Something was going on and everyone knew it but himself. He was seized with furious jealousy. He believed that Ethel was carrying on with one of the white men, and he looked at one after the other with scrutinizing eyes; but there was nothing to give him even a hint. He was helpless. Because he could find no one on whom definitely to fix his suspicions, he went about like a raving maniac, looking for someone on whom to vent his wrath. Chance caused him in the end to hit upon the man who of all others least deserved to suffer from his violence. One afternoon, when he was sitting in the hotel by himself, moodily, Chaplin came in and sat down beside him. Perhaps Chaplin was the only man on the island who had any sympathy for him. They ordered drinks and chatted a few minutes about the races that were shortly to be run. Then Chaplin said:

'I guess we shall all have to fork out money for new dresses.'

Lawson sniggered. Since Mrs Chaplin held the purse-strings, if she wanted a new frock for the occasion she would certainly not ask her husband for the money.

'How is your missus?' asked Chaplin, desiring to be friendly.

'What the hell's that got to do with you?' said Lawson, knitting his dark brows.

'I was only asking a civil question.'

'Well, keep your civil questions to yourself.'

Chaplin was not a patient man; his long residence in the tropics, the whisky bottle, and his domestic affairs had given him a temper hardly more under control than Lawson's.

'Look here, my boy, when you're in my hotel you behave like a gentleman or you'll find yourself in the street before you can say knife.'

Lawson's lowering face grew dark and red.

'Let me just tell you once for all and you can pass it on to the others,' he said, panting with rage. 'If any of you fellows come messing round with my wife he'd better look out.'

'Who do you think wants to mess around with your wife?'

'I'm not such a fool as you think. I can see a stone wall in front of me as well as most men, and I warn you straight, that's all. I'm not going to put up with any hanky-panky, not on your life.'

'Look here, you'd better clear out of here, and come back when you're sober.'

'I shall clear out when I choose and not a minute before,' said Lawson.

It was an unfortunate boast, for Chaplin in the course of his experience as a hotel-keeper had acquired a peculiar skill in dealing with gentlemen whose room he preferred to their company, and the words were hardly out of Lawson's mouth before he found himself caught by the collar and arm and hustled not without force into the street. He stumbled down the steps into the blinding glare of the sun.

It was in consequence of this that he had his first violent scene with Ethel. Smarting with humiliation and unwilling to go back to the hotel, he went home that afternoon earlier than usual. He found Ethel dressing to go out. As a rule she lay about in a Mother Hubbard, barefoot, with a flower in her dark hair; but now, in white silk stockings and high-heeled shoes, she was doing up a pink muslin dress which was the newest she had.

'You're making yourself very smart,' he said. 'Where are you going?'

'I'm going to the Crossleys.'

'I'll come with you.'

'Why?' she asked coolly.

'I don't want you to gad about by yourself all the time.'

'You're not asked.'

'I don't care a damn about that. You're not going without me.'

'You'd better lie down till I'm ready.'

She thought he was drunk and if he once settled himself on the bed would quickly drop off to sleep. He sat down on a chair and began to smoke a cigarette. She watched him with increasing irritation. When she was ready he got up. It happened by an unusual chance that there was no one in the bungalow. Brevald was working on the plantation and his wife had gone into Apia. Ethel faced him.

'I'm not going with you. You're drunk.'

'That's a lie. You're not going without me.'

She shrugged her shoulders and tried to pass him, but he caught her by the arm and held her.

'Let me go, you devil,' she said, breaking into Samoan.

'Why do you want to go without me? Haven't I told you I'm not going to put up with any monkey tricks?'

She clenched her fist and hit him in the face. He lost all control of himself. All his love, all his hatred, welled up in him and he was beside himself.

'I'll teach you,' he shouted. 'I'll teach you.'

He seized a riding-whip which happened to be under his hand, and struck her with it. She screamed, and the scream maddened him so that he went on striking her, again and again. Her shrieks rang through the bungalow and he cursed her as he hit. Then he flung her on the bed. She lay there sobbing with pain and terror. He threw the whip away from him and rushed out of the room. Ethel heard him go and she stopped crying. She looked round cautiously, then she raised herself. She was sore, but she had not been badly hurt, and she looked at her dress to see if it was damaged. The native women are not unused to blows. What he had done did not outrage her. When she looked at herself in the glass and arranged her hair, her eyes were shining. There was a strange look in them. Perhaps then she was nearer loving him than she had ever been before.

But Lawson, driven forth blindly, stumbled through the plantation and suddenly exhausted, weak as a child, flung himself on the ground at the foot of a tree. He was miserable and ashamed. He thought of Ethel, and in the yielding tenderness of his love all his bones seemed to grow soft within him. He thought of the past, and of his hopes, and he was aghast at what he had done. He wanted her more than ever. He wanted to take her in his arms. He must go to her at once. He got up. He was so weak that he staggered as he walked. He went into the house and she was sitting in their cramped bedroom in front of her looking-glass.

'Oh, Ethel, forgive me. I'm so awfully ashamed of myself. I didn't know what I was doing.'

He fell on his knees before her and timidly stroked the skirt of her dress.

'I can't bear to think of what I did. It's awful. I think I was mad. There's no one in the world I love as I love you. I'd do anything to save you from pain and I've hurt you. I can never forgive myself, but for God's sake say you forgive me.'

He heard her shrieks still. It was unendurable. She looked at him silently. He tried to take her hands and the tears streamed from his eyes. In his humiliation he hid his face in her lap and his frail body shook with sobs. An expression of utter contempt came over her face. She had the native woman's disdain of a man who abased himself before a woman. A weak creature! And for a moment she had been on the point of thinking there was something in him. He grovelled at her feet like a cur. She gave him a little scornful kick.

'Get out,' she said. 'I hate you.'

He tried to hold her, but she pushed him aside. She stood up. She began to take off her dress. She kicked off her shoes and slid the stockings off her feet, then she slipped on her old Mother Hubbard.

'Where are you going?'

'What's that got to do with you? I'm going down to the pool.'

'Let me come too,' he said.

He asked as though he were a child.

'Can't you even leave me that?'

He hid his face in his hands, crying miserably, while she, her eyes hard and cold, stepped past him and went out.

From that time she entirely despised him; and though, herded together in the small bungalow, Lawson and Ethel with her two children, Brevald, his wife and her mother, and the vague relations and hangers-on who were always in and about, they had to live cheek by jowl, Lawson, ceasing to be of any account, was hardly noticed. He left in the morning after breakfast, and came back only to have supper. He gave up the struggle, and when for want of money he could not go to the English Club he spent the evening playing hearts with old Brevald and the natives. Except when he was drunk he was cowed and listless. Ethel treated him like a dog. She submitted at times to his fits of wild passion, and she was frightened by the gusts of hatred with which they were followed; but when, afterwards, he was cringing and lachrymose she had such a contempt for him that she could have spat in his face. Sometimes he was violent, but now she was prepared for him, and when he hit her she kicked and scratched and bit. They had horrible battles in which he had not always the best of it. Very soon it was known all over Apia that they got on badly. There was little sympathy for Lawson, and at the hotel the general surprise was that old Brevald did not kick him out of the place.

'Brevald's a pretty ugly customer,' said one of the men. 'I shouldn't be surprised if he put a bullet into Lawson's carcass one of these days.'

Ethel still went in the evenings to bathe in the silent pool. It seemed to have an attraction for her that was not quite human, just that attraction you might imagine that a mermaid who had won a soul would have for the cool salt waves of the sea; and sometimes Lawson went also. I do not know what urged him to go, for Ethel was obviously irritated by his presence; perhaps it was because in that spot he hoped to regain the clean rapture which had filled his heart when first he saw her; perhaps only, with the madness of those who love them that love them not, from the feeling that his obstinacy could force love. One day he strolled down there with a feeling that was rare with him now. He felt suddenly at peace with the world. The evening was drawing in and the dusk seemed to cling to the leaves of the coconut trees like a little thin cloud. A faint breeze stirred them noiselessly. A crescent moon hung just over their tops. He made his way to the bank. He saw Ethel in the water floating on her back. Her hair streamed out all round her, and she was holding in her hand a large hibiscus. He stopped a moment to admire her; she was like Ophelia.

'Hullo, Ethel,' he cried joyfully.

She made a sudden movement and dropped the red flower. It floated idly away. She swam a stroke or two till she knew there was ground within her depth and then stood up.

'Go away,' she said. 'Go away.'

He laughed.

'Don't be selfish. There's plenty of room for both of us.'

'Why can't you leave me alone? I want to be by myself.'

'Hang it all, I want to bathe,' he answered, good-humouredly.

'Go down to the bridge. I don't want you here.'

'I'm sorry for that,' he said, smiling still.

He was not in the least angry, and he hardly noticed that she was in a passion. He began to take off his coat.

'Go away,' she shrieked. 'I won't have you here. Can't you even leave me this? Go away.'

'Don't be silly, darling.'

She bent down and picked up a sharp stone and flung it quickly at him. He had no time to duck. It hit him on the temple. With a cry he put his hand to his head and when he took it away it was wet with blood. Ethel stood still, panting with rage. He turned very pale, and without a word, taking up his coat, went away. Ethel let herself fall back into the water and the stream carried her slowly down to the ford.

The stone had made a jagged wound and for some days Lawson went about with a bandaged head. He had invented a likely story to account for the accident when the fellows at the club asked him about it, but he had no occasion to use it. No one referred to the matter. He saw them cast surreptitious glances at his head, but not a word was said. The silence could only mean that they knew how he came by his wound. He was certain now that Ethel had a lover, and they all knew who it was. But there was not the smallest indication to guide him. He never saw Ethel with anyone; no one showed a wish to be with her, or treated him in a manner that seemed strange. Wild rage seized him, and having no one to vent it on he drank more and more heavily. A little while before I came to the island he had had another attack of delirium tremens.

I met Ethel at the house of a man called Caster, who lived two or three miles from Apia with a native wife. I had been playing tennis with him and when we were tired he suggested a cup of tea. We went into the house and in the untidy living-room found Ethel chatting with Mrs Caster.

'Hullo, Ethel,' he said, 'I didn't know you were here.'

I could not help looking at her with curiosity. I tried to see what there was in her to have excited in Lawson such a devastating passion. But who can explain these things? It was true that she was lovely; she reminded one of the red hibiscus, the common flower of the hedgerow in Samoa, with its grace and its languor and its passion; but what surprised me most, taking into consideration the story I knew even then a good deal of, was her freshness and simplicity. She was quiet and a little shy. There was nothing coarse or loud about her; she had not the exuberance common to the half-caste; and it was almost impossible to believe that she could be the virago that the horrible scenes between husband and wife, which were now common knowledge, indicated. In her pretty pink frock and high-heeled shoes she looked quite European. You could hardly have guessed at that dark background of native life in which she felt herself so much more at home. I did not imagine that she was at all intelligent, and I should not have been surprised if a man, after living with her for some time, had found the passion which had drawn him to her sink into boredom. It suggested itself to me that in her elusiveness, like a thought that presents itself to consciousness and vanishes before it can be captured by words, lay her peculiar charm; but perhaps that was merely fancy, and if I had known nothing about her I should have seen in her only a pretty little half-caste like another.

She talked to me of the various things which they talk of to the stranger in

Samoa, of the journey, and whether I had slid down the water rock at Papaseea, and if I meant to stay in a native village. She talked to me of Scotland, and perhaps I noticed in her a tendency to enlarge on the sumptuousness of her establishment there. She asked me naïvely if I knew Mrs This and Mrs That, with whom she had been acquainted when she lived in the north.

Then Miller, the fat German–American, came in. He shook hands all round very cordially and sat down, asking in his loud, cheerful voice for a whisky and soda. He was very fat and he sweated profusely. He took off his gold-rimmed spectacles and wiped them; you saw then that his little eyes, benevolent behind the large round glasses, were shrewd and cunning; the party had been somewhat dull till he came, but he was a good story-teller and a jovial fellow. Soon he had the two women, Ethel and my friend's wife, laughing delightedly at his sallies. He had a reputation on the island of a lady's man, and you could see how this fat, gross fellow, old and ugly, had yet the possibility of fascination. His humour was on a level with the understanding of his company, an affair of vitality and assurance, and his Western accent gave a peculiar point to what he said. At last he turned to me:

'Well, if we want to get back for dinner we'd better be getting. I'll take you along in my machine if you like.'

I thanked him and got up. He shook hands with the others, went out of the room, massive and strong in his walk, and climbed into his car.

'Pretty little thing, Lawson's wife,' I said, as we drove along.

'Too bad the way he treats her. Knocks her about. Gets my dander up when I hear of a man hitting a woman.'

We went on a little. Then he said:

'He was a darned fool to marry her. I said so at the time. If he hadn't, he'd have had the whip hand over her. He's yaller, that's what he is, yaller.'

The year was drawing to its end and the time approached when I was to leave Samoa. My boat was scheduled to sail for Sydney on the fourth of January. Christmas Day had been celebrated at the hotel with suitable ceremonies, but it was looked upon as no more than a rehearsal for New Year, and the men who were accustomed to foregather in the lounge determined on New Year's Eve to make a night of it. There was an uproarious dinner, after which the party sauntered down to the English Club, a simple little frame house, to play pool. There was a great deal of talking, laughing, and betting, but some very poor play, except on the part of Miller, who had drunk as much as any of them, all far younger than he, but had kept unimpaired the keenness of his eye and the sureness of his hand. He pocketed the young men's money with humour and urbanity. After an hour of this I grew tired and went out. I crossed the road and came to the beach. Three coconut trees grew there, like three moon maidens waiting for their lovers to ride out of the sea, and I sat at the foot of one of them, watching the lagoon and the nightly assemblage of the stars.

I do not know where Lawson had been during the evening, but between ten and eleven he came along to the club. He shambled down the dusty, empty road, feeling dull and bored, and when he reached the club, before going into the billiard-room, went into the bar to have a drink by himself. He had a shyness now about joining the company of white men when there were a lot of them together and needed a stiff dose of whisky to give him confidence. He was standing with the glass in his hand when Miller came in to him. He was in his shirt-sleeves and still held his cue. He gave the bar-tender a glance.

'Get out, Jack,' he said.

The bar-tender, a native in a white jacket and a red lava-lava, without a word slid out of the small room.

'Look here, I've been wanting to have a few words with you, Lawson,' said the big American.

'Well, that's one of the few things you can have free, gratis, and for nothing on this damned island.'

Miller fixed his gold spectacles more firmly on his nose and held Lawson with his cold determined eyes.

'See here, young fellow, I understand you've been knocking Mrs Lawson about again. I'm not going to stand for that. If you don't stop it right now I'll break every bone of your dirty little body.'

Then Lawson knew what he had been trying to find out so long. It was Miller. The appearance of the man, fat, bald-headed, with his round bare face and double chin and the gold spectacles, his age, his benign, shrewd look, like that of a renegade priest, and the thought of Ethel, so slim and virginal, filled him with a sudden horror. Whatever his faults Lawson was no coward, and without a word he hit out violently at Miller. Miller quickly warded the blow with the hand that held the cue, and then with a great swing of his right arm brought his fist down on Lawson's ear. Lawson was four inches shorter than the American and he was slightly built, frail and weakened not only by illness and the enervating tropics, but by drink. He fell like a log and lay half dazed at the foot of the bar. Miller took off his spectacles and wiped them with his handkerchief.

'I guess you know what to expect now. You've had your warning and you'd better take it.'

He took up his cue and went back into the billiard-room. There was so much noise there that no one knew what had happened. Lawson picked himself up. He put his hand to his ear, which was singing still. Then he slunk out of the club.

I saw a man cross the road, a patch of white against the darkness of the night, but did not know who it was. He came down to the beach, passed me sitting at the foot of the tree, and looked down. I saw then that it was Lawson, but since he was doubtless drunk, did not speak. He went on, walked irresolutely two or three steps, and turned back. He came up to me and bending down stared in my face.

'I thought it was you,' he said.

He sat down and took out his pipe.

'It was hot and noisy in the club,' I volunteered.

'Why are you sitting here?'

'I was waiting about for the midnight mass at the Cathedral.'

'If you like I'll come with you.'

Lawson was quite sober. We sat for a while smoking in silence. Now and then in the lagoon was the splash of some big fish, and a little way out towards the opening in the reef was the light of a schooner.

'You're sailing next week, aren't you?' he said.

'Yes.'

'It would be jolly to go home once more. But I could never stand it now. The cold, you know.'

'It's odd to think that in England now they're shivering round the fire,' I said.

There was not even a breath of wind. The balminess of the night was like a spell. I wore nothing but a thin shirt and a suit of ducks. I enjoyed the exquisite languor of the night, and stretched my limbs voluptuously.

'This isn't the sort of New Year's Eve that persuades one to make good resolutions for the future,' I smiled.

He made no answer, but I do not know what train of thought my casual remark had suggested in him, for presently he began to speak. He spoke in a low voice, without any expression, but his accents were educated, and it was a relief to hear him after the twang and the vulgar intonations which for some time had wounded my ears.

'I've made an awful hash of things. That's obvious, isn't it? I'm right down at the bottom of the pit and there's no getting out for me. "*Black as the pit from pole to pole.*"' I felt him smile as he made the quotation. 'And the strange thing is that I don't see how I went wrong.'

I held my breath, for to me there is nothing more awe-inspiring than when a man discovers to you the nakedness of his soul. Then you see that no one is so trivial or debased but that in him is a spark of something to excite compassion.

'It wouldn't be so rotten if I could see that it was all my own fault. It's true I drink, but I shouldn't have taken to that if things had gone differently. I wasn't really fond of liquor. I suppose I ought not to have married Ethel. If I'd kept her it would be all right. But I did love her so.'

His voice faltered.

'She's not a bad lot, you know, not really. It's just rotten luck. We might have been as happy as lords. When she bolted I suppose I ought to have let her go, but I couldn't do that—I was dead stuck on her then; and there was the kid.'

'Are you fond of the kid?' I asked.

'I was. There are two, you know. But they don't mean so much to me now. You'd take them for natives anywhere. I have to talk to them in Samoan.'

'Is it too late for you to start fresh? Couldn't you make a dash for it and leave the place?'

'I haven't the strength. I'm done for.'

'Are you still in love with your wife?'

'Not now. Not now.' He repeated the two words with a kind of horror in his voice. 'I haven't even got that now. I'm down and out.'

The bells of the Cathedral were ringing.

'If you really want to come to the midnight mass we'd better go along,' I said. 'Come on.'

We got up and walked along the road. The Cathedral, all white, stood facing the sea not without impressiveness, and beside it the Protestant chapels had the look of meeting-houses. In the road were two or three cars, and a great number of traps, and traps were put up against the walls at the side. People had come from all parts of the island for the service, and through the great open doors we saw that the place was crowded. The high altar was all ablaze with light. There were a few whites and a good many half-castes, but the great majority were natives. All the men wore trousers, for the Church had decided that the lava-lava is indecent. We found chairs at the back, near the open door, and sat down. Presently, following Lawson's eyes, I saw Ethel come in with a party of half-castes. They were all very much dressed up, the men in high, stiff collars and shiny boots, the women in large, gay hats. Ethel nodded and smiled to her friends as she passed up the aisle. The service began.

When it was over Lawson and I stood on one side for a while to watch the crowd stream out, then he held out his hand.

'Good night,' he said. 'I hope you'll have a pleasant journey home.'

'Oh, but I shall see you before I go.'

He sniggered.

'The question is if you'll see me drunk or sober.'

He turned and left me. I had a recollection of those very large black eyes, shining wildly under the shaggy brows. I paused irresolutely. I did not feel sleepy and I thought I would at all events go along to the club for an hour before turning in. When I got there I found the billiard-room empty, but half-a-dozen men were sitting round a table in the lounge, playing poker. Miller looked up as I came in.

'Sit down and take a hand,' he said.

'All right.'

I bought some chips and began to play. Of course it is the most fascinating game in the world and my hour lengthened out to two, and then to three. The native bar-tender, cheery and wide-awake notwithstanding the time, was at our elbow to supply us with drinks and from somewhere or other he produced a ham and a loaf of bread. We played on. Most of the party had drunk more than was good for them and the play was high and reckless. I played modestly, neither wishing to win nor anxious to lose, but I watched Miller with a fascinated interest. He drank glass for glass with the rest of the company, but remained cool and level-headed. His pile of chips increased in size and he had a neat little paper in front of him on which he had marked various sums lent to players in distress. He beamed amiably at the young men whose money he was taking. He kept up interminably his stream of jest and anecdotes, but he never missed a draw, he never let an expression of the face pass him. At last the dawn crept into the windows, gently, with a sort of deprecating shyness, as though it had no business there, and then it was day.

'Well,' said Miller. 'I reckon we've seen the old year out in style. Now let's have a round of jackpots and me for my mosquito net. I'm fifty, remember, I can't keep these late hours.'

The morning was beautiful and fresh when we stood on the veranda, and the lagoon was like a sheet of multicoloured glass. Someone suggested a dip before going to bed, but none cared to bathe in the lagoon, sticky and treacherous to the feet. Miller had his car at the door and he offered to take us down to the pool. We jumped in and drove along the deserted road. When we reached the pool it seemed as though the day had hardly risen there yet. Under the trees the water was all in shadow and the night had the effect of lurking still. We were in great spirits. We had no towels or any costume and in my prudence I wondered how we were going to dry ourselves. None of us had much on and it did not take us long to snatch off our clothes. Nelson, the little super-cargo, was stripped first.

'I'm going down to the bottom,' he said.

He dived and in a moment another man dived too, but shallow, and was out of the water before him. Then Nelson came up and scrambled to the side.

'I say, get me out,' he said.

'What's up?'

Something was evidently the matter. His face was terrified. Two fellows gave him their hands and he slithered up.

'I say, there's a man down there.'

'Don't be a fool. You're drunk.'

'Well, if there isn't I'm in for D.T.s. But I tell you there's a man down there. It just scared me out of my wits.'

Miller looked at him for a moment. The little man was all white. He was actually trembling.

'Come on, Caster,' said Miller to the big Australian, 'we'd better go down and see.'

'He was standing up,' said Nelson, 'all dressed. I saw him. He tried to catch hold of me.'

'Hold your row,' said Miller. 'Are you ready?'

They dived in. We waited on the bank, silent. It really seemed as though they were underwater longer than any men could breathe. Then Caster came up, and immediately after him, red in the face as though he were going to have a fit, Miller. They were pulling something behind them. Another man jumped in to help them, and the three together dragged their burden to the side. They shoved it up. Then we saw that it was Lawson, with a great stone tied up in his coat and bound to his feet.

'He was set on making a good job of it,' said Miller, as he wiped the water from his short-sighted eyes.

Mackintosh

◆

He splashed about for a few minutes in the sea; it was too shallow to swim in and for fear of sharks he could not go out of his depth; then he got out and went into the bath-house for a shower. The coldness of the fresh water was grateful after the heavy stickiness of the salt Pacific, so warm, though it was only just after seven, that to bathe in it did not brace you but rather increased your languor; and when he had dried himself, slipping into a bath-gown, he called out to the Chinese cook that he would be ready for breakfast in five minutes. He walked barefoot across the patch of coarse grass which Walker, the administrator, proudly thought was a lawn, to his own quarters and dressed. This did not take long, for he put on nothing but a shirt and a pair of duck trousers and then went over to his chief's house on the other side of the compound. The two men had their meals together, but the Chinese cook told him that Walker had set out on horseback at five and would not be back for another hour.

Mackintosh had slept badly and he looked with distaste at the paw-paw and the eggs and bacon which were set before him. The mosquitoes had been maddening that night; they flew about the net under which he slept in such numbers that their humming, pitiless and menacing, had the effect of a note, infinitely drawn out, played on a distant organ, and whenever he dozed off he awoke with a start in the belief that one had found its way inside his curtains. It was so hot that he lay naked. He turned from side to side. And gradually the dull roar of the breakers on the reef, so unceasing and so regular that generally you did not hear it, grew distinct on his consciousness, its rhythm hammered on his tired nerves and he held himself with clenched hands in the effort to bear it. The thought that nothing could stop that sound, for it would continue to all eternity, was almost impossible to bear, and, as though his strength were a match for the ruthless forces of nature, he had an insane impulse to do some violent thing. He felt he must cling to his self-control or he would go mad. And now, looking out of the window at the lagoon and the strip of foam which marked the reef, he shuddered with hatred of the brilliant scene. The cloudless sky was like an inverted bowl that hemmed it in. He lit his pipe and turned over the pile of Auckland papers that had come over from Apia a few days before. The newest of them was three weeks old. They gave an impression of incredible dullness.

Then he went into the office. It was a large, bare room with two desks in it and a bench along one side. A number of natives were seated on this, and a couple of women. They gossiped while they waited for the administrator, and when Mackintosh came in they greeted him.

'*Talofa-li.*'

He returned their greeting and sat down at his desk. He began to write, working on a report which the governor of Samoa had been clamouring for and which Walker, with his usual dilatoriness, had neglected to prepare. Mackintosh as he made his notes reflected vindictively that Walker was late with his report because he was so illiterate that he had an invincible distaste for anything to do with pens and paper; and now when it was at last ready, concise and neatly official, he would accept his subordinate's work without a word of appreciation, with a sneer rather or a gibe, and send it on to his own superior as though it were his own composition. He could not have written a word of it. Mackintosh thought with rage that if his chief pencilled in some insertion it would be childish in expression and faulty in language. If he remonstrated or sought to put his meaning into an intelligible phrase, Walker would fly into a passion and cry:

'What the hell do I care about grammar? That's what I want to say and that's how I want to say it.'

At last Walker came in. The natives surrounded him as he entered, trying to get his immediate attention, but he turned on them roughly and told them to sit down and hold their tongues. He threatened that if they were not quiet he would have them all turned out and see none of them that day. He nodded to Mackintosh.

'Hullo, Mac; up at last? I don't know how you can waste the best part of the day in bed. You ought to have been up before dawn like me. Lazy beggar.'

He threw himself heavily into his chair and wiped his face with a large bandana.

'By heaven, I've got a thirst.'

He turned to the policeman who stood at the door, a picturesque figure in his white jacket and lava-lava, the loincloth of the Samoan, and told him to bring *kava*. The *kava* bowl stood on the floor in the corner of the room, and the policeman filled a half coconut shell and brought it to Walker. He poured a few drops on the ground, murmured the customary words to the company, and drank with relish. Then he told the policeman to serve the waiting natives, and the shell was handed to each one in order of birth or importance and emptied with the same ceremonies.

Then he set about the day's work. He was a little man, considerably less than of middle height, and enormously stout; he had a large, fleshy face, clean-shaven, with the cheeks hanging on each side in great dew-laps, and three vast chins; his small features were all dissolved in fat; and, but for a crescent of white hair at the back of his head, he was completely bald. He reminded you of Mr Pickwick. He was grotesque, a figure of fun, and yet, strangely enough, not without dignity. His blue eyes, behind large gold-rimmed spectacles, were shrewd and vivacious, and there was a great deal of determination in his face. He was sixty, but his native vitality triumphed over advancing years. Notwithstanding his corpulence his movements were quick, and he walked with a heavy, resolute tread as though he sought to impress his weight upon the earth. He spoke in a loud, gruff voice.

It was two years now since Mackintosh had been appointed Walker's assistant. Walker, who had been for a quarter of a century administrator of Talua, one of the larger islands in the Samoan group, was a man known in person or by report through the length and breadth of the South Seas; and it was with lively curiosity that Mackintosh looked forward to his first meeting with him. For one reason or another he stayed a couple of weeks at Apia before he took up his post and both at Chaplin's hotel and at the English Club he heard innumerable stories about the administrator. He thought now with irony of his interest in them. Since then he had heard them a hundred times from Walker himself. Walker knew that he was a character and, proud of his reputation, deliberately acted up to it. He was jealous of his 'legend' and anxious that you should know the exact details of any of the celebrated stories that were told of him. He was ludicrously angry with anyone who had told them to the stranger incorrectly.

There was a rough cordiality about Walker which Mackintosh at first found not unattractive, and Walker, glad to have a listener to whom all he said was fresh, gave of his best. He was good-humoured, hearty, and considerate. To Mackintosh, who had lived the sheltered life of a government official in London till at the age of thirty-four an attack of pneumonia, leaving him with the threat of tuberculosis, had forced him to seek a post in the Pacific, Walker's existence seemed extraordinarily romantic. The adventure with which he started on his conquest of circumstance was typical of the man. He ran away to sea when he was fifteen and for over a year was employed in shovelling coal on a collier. He was an undersized boy and both men and mates were kind to him, but the captain for some reason conceived a savage dislike of him. He used the lad cruelly so that, beaten and kicked, he often could not sleep for the pain that racked his limbs. He loathed the captain with all his soul. Then he was given a tip for some race and managed to borrow twenty-five pounds from a friend he had picked up in Belfast. He put it on the horse, an outsider, at long odds. He had no means of repaying the money if he lost, but it never occurred to him that he could lose. He felt himself in luck. The horse won and he found himself with something over a thousand pounds in hard cash. Now his chance had come. He found out who was the best solicitor in the town—the collier lay then somewhere on the Irish coast—went to him, and, telling him that he heard the ship was for sale, asked him to arrange the purchase for him. The solicitor was amused at his small client, he was only sixteen and did not look so old, and, moved perhaps by sympathy, promised not only to arrange the matter for him but to see that he made a good bargain. After a little while Walker found himself the owner of the ship. He went back to her and had what he described as the most glorious moment of his life when he gave the skipper notice and told him that he must get off *his* ship in half an hour. He made the mate captain and sailed on the collier for another nine months, at the end of which he sold her at a profit.

He came out to the islands at the age of twenty-six as a planter. He was one of the few white men settled in Talua at the time of the German occupation and had then already some influence with the natives. The Germans made him administrator, a position which he occupied for twenty years, and when the island was seized by the British he was confirmed in his post. He ruled the island despotically, but with complete success. The prestige of this success was another reason for the interest that Mackintosh took in him.

But the two men were not made to get on. Mackintosh was an ugly man, with ungainly gestures, a tall thin fellow, with a narrow chest and bowed shoulders. He had sallow, sunken cheeks, and his eyes were large and sombre. He was a great reader, and when his books arrived and were unpacked Walker came over to his quarters and looked at them. Then he turned to Mackintosh with a coarse laugh.

'What in Hell have you brought all this muck for?' he asked.

Mackintosh flushed darkly.

'I'm sorry you think it muck. I brought my books because I want to read them.'

'When you said you'd got a lot of books coming I thought there'd be something for me to read. Haven't you got any detective stories?'

'Detective stories don't interest me.'

'You're a damned fool then.'

'I'm content that you should think so.'

Every mail brought Walker a mass of periodical literature, papers from New Zealand and magazines from America, and it exasperated him that Mackintosh showed his contempt for these ephemeral publications. He had no patience with the books that absorbed Mackintosh's leisure and thought it only a pose that he read Gibbon's *Decline and Fall* or Burton's *Anatomy of Melancholy*. And since he had never learned to put any restraint on his tongue, he expressed his opinion of his assistant freely. Mackintosh began to see the real man, and under the boisterous good-humour he discerned a vulgar cunning which was hateful; he was vain and domineering, and it was strange that he had notwithstanding a shyness which made him dislike people who were not quite of his kidney. He judged others, naïvely, by their language, and if it was free from the oaths and the obscenity which made up the greater part of his own conversation, he looked upon them with suspicion. In the evening the two men played piquet. He played badly but vaingloriously, crowing over his opponent when he won and losing his temper when he lost. On rare occasions a couple of planters or traders would drive over to play bridge, and then Walker showed himself in what Mackintosh considered a characteristic light. He played regardless of his partner, calling up in his desire to play the hand, and argued interminably, beating down opposition by the loudness of his voice. He constantly revoked, and when he did so said with an ingratiating whine: 'Oh, you wouldn't count it against an old man who can hardly see.' Did he know that his opponents thought it as well to keep on the right side of him and hesitated to insist on the rigour of the game? Mackintosh watched him with an icy contempt. When the game was over, while they smoked their pipes and drank whisky, they would begin telling stories. Walker told with gusto the story of his marriage. He had got so drunk at the wedding feast that the bride had fled and he had never seen her since. He had had numberless adventures, commonplace and sordid, with the women of the island and he described them with a pride in his own prowess which was an offence to Mackintosh's fastidious ears. He was a gross, sensual old man. He thought Mackintosh a poor fellow because he would not share his promiscuous amours and remained sober when the company was drunk.

He despised him also for the orderliness with which he did his official work. Mackintosh liked to do everything just so. His desk was always tidy, his papers were always neatly docketed, he could put his hand on any document that was needed, and he had at his fingers' ends all the regulations that were required for the business of their administration.

'Fudge, fudge,' said Walker. 'I've run this island for twenty years without red tape, and I don't want it now.'

'Does it make it any easier for you that when you want a letter you have to hunt half an hour for it?' answered Mackintosh.

'You're nothing but a damned official. But you're not a bad fellow; when you've been out here a year or two you'll be all right. What's wrong about you is that you won't drink. You wouldn't be a bad sort if you got soused once a week.'

The curious thing was that Walker remained perfectly unconscious of the dislike for him which every month increased in the breast of his subordinate. Although he laughed at him, as he grew accustomed to him, he began almost to like him. He had a certain tolerance for the peculiarities of others, and he accepted Mackintosh as a queer fish. Perhaps he liked him, unconsciously, because he could chaff him. His humour consisted of coarse banter and he wanted a butt. Mackintosh's exactness, his morality, his sobriety, were all fruitful subjects; his Scots name gave an opportunity for the usual jokes about Scotland; he enjoyed himself thoroughly when two or three men were there and he could make them all laugh at the expense of Mackintosh. He would say ridiculous things about him to the natives, and Mackintosh, his knowledge of Samoan still imperfect, would see their unrestrained mirth when Walker had made an obscene reference to him. He smiled good-humouredly.

'I'll say this for you, Mac,' Walker would say in his gruff loud voice, 'you can take a joke.'

'Was it a joke?' smiled Mackintosh. 'I didn't know.'

'Scots wha hae!' shouted Walker, with a bellow of laughter. 'There's only one way to make a Scotchman see a joke and that's by a surgical operation.'

Walker little knew that there was nothing Mackintosh could stand less than chaff. He would wake in the night, the breathless night of the rainy season, and brood sullenly over the gibe that Walker had uttered carelessly days before. It rankled. His heart swelled with rage, and he pictured to himself ways in which he might get even with the bully. He had tried answering him, but Walker had a gift of repartee, coarse and obvious, which gave him an advantage. The dullness of his intellect made him impervious to a delicate shaft. His self-satisfaction made it impossible to wound him. His loud voice, his bellow of laughter, were weapons against which Mackintosh had nothing to counter, and he learned that the wisest thing was never to betray his irritation. He learned to control himself. But his hatred grew till it was a monomania. He watched Walker with an insane vigilance. He fed his own self-esteem by every instance of meanness on Walker's part, by every exhibition of childish vanity, of cunning, and of vulgarity. Walker ate greedily, noisily, filthily, and Mackintosh watched him with satisfaction. He took note of the foolish things he said and of his mistakes in grammar. He knew that Walker held him in small esteem, and he found a bitter satisfaction in his chief's opinion of him; it increased his own contempt for the narrow, complacent old man. And it gave him a singular pleasure to know that Walker was entirely unconscious of the hatred he felt for him. He was a fool who liked popularity, and he blandly fancied that everyone admired him. Once Mackintosh had overheard Walker speaking of him.

'He'll be all right when I've licked him into shape,' he said. 'He's a good dog and he loves his master.'

Mackintosh silently, without a movement of his long, sallow face, laughed long and heartily.

But his hatred was not blind; on the contrary, it was peculiarly clear-sighted, and he judged Walker's capabilities with precision. He ruled his small kingdom with efficiency. He was just and honest. With opportunities to make money he was a poorer man than when he was first appointed to his post, and his only support for his old age was the pension which he expected when at last he retired from official life. His pride was that with an assistant and a half-caste clerk he was able to administer the island more competently than Upolu, the island of which Apia is the chief town, was administered with its army of functionaries. He had a few native policemen to sustain his authority, but he made no use of them. He governed by bluff and his Irish humour.

'They insisted on building a jail for me,' he said. 'What the devil do I want a jail for? I'm not going to put the natives in prison. If they do wrong I know how to deal with them.'

One of his quarrels with the higher authorities at Apia was that he claimed entire jurisdiction over the natives of his island. Whatever their crimes he would not give them up to courts competent to deal with them, and several times an angry correspondence had passed between him and the governor at Upolu. For he looked upon the natives as his children. And that was the amazing thing about this coarse, vulgar, selfish man; he loved the island on which he had lived so long with passion, and he had for the natives a strange rough tenderness which was quite wonderful.

He loved to ride about the island on his old grey mare and he was never tired of its beauty. Sauntering along the grassy roads among the coconut trees he would stop every now and then to admire the loveliness of the scene. Now and then he would come upon a native village and stop while the headman brought him a bowl of *kava*. He would look at the little group of bell-shape huts with their high thatched roofs, like beehives, and a smile would spread over his fat face. His eyes rested happily on the spreading green of the bread-fruit trees.

'By George, it's like the garden of Eden.'

Sometimes his rides took him along the coast and through the trees he had a glimpse of the wide sea, empty, with never a sail to disturb the loneliness; sometimes he climbed a hill so that a great stretch of country, with little villages nestling among the tall trees was spread out before him like the kingdom of the world, and he would sit there for an hour in an ecstasy of delight. But he had no words to express his feelings and to relieve them would utter an obscene jest; it was as though his emotion was so violent that he needed vulgarity to break the tension.

Mackintosh observed this sentiment with an icy disdain. Walker had always been a heavy drinker, he was proud of his capacity to see men half his age under the table when he spent a night in Apia, and he had the sentimentality of the toper. He could cry over the stories he read in his magazines and yet would refuse a loan to some trader in difficulties whom he had known for twenty years. He was close with his money. Once Mackintosh said to him:

'No one could accuse you of giving money away.'

He took it as a compliment. His enthusiasm for nature was but the drivelling sensibility of the drunkard. Nor had Mackintosh any sympathy for his chief's feelings towards the natives. He loved them because they were in his power, as a selfish man loves his dog, and his mentality was on a level with theirs. Their humour was obscene and he was never at a loss for the lewd remark. He understood them and they understood him. He was proud of his influence over them. He looked upon them as his children and he mixed himself in all their affairs. But he was very jealous of his authority; if he ruled them with a rod of iron, brooking no contradiction, he would not suffer any of the white men on the island to take advantage of them. He watched the missionaries suspiciously and, if they did anything of which he disapproved, was able to make life so unendurable to them that if he could not get them removed they were glad to go of their own accord. His power over the natives was so great that on his word they would refuse labour and food to their pastor. On the other hand he showed the traders no favour. He took care that they should not cheat the natives; he saw that they got a fair reward for their work and their copra and that the traders made no extravagant profit on the wares they sold them. He was merciless to a bargain that he thought unfair. Sometimes the traders would complain at Apia that they did not get fair opportunities. They suffered for it. Walker then hesitated at no calumny, at no outrageous lie, to get even with them, and they found that if they wanted not only to live at peace, but to exist at all, they had to accept the situation on his own terms. More than once the store of a trader obnoxious to him had been burned down, and there was only the appositeness of the event to show that the administrator had instigated it. Once a Swedish half-caste, ruined by the burning, had gone to him and roundly accused him of arson. Walker laughed in his face.

'You dirty dog. Your mother was a native and you try to cheat the natives. If your rotten old store is burned down it's a judgement of Providence; that's what it is, a judgement of Providence. Get out.'

And as the man was hustled out by two native policemen the administrator laughed fatly.

'A judgement of Providence.'

And now Mackintosh watched him enter upon the day's work. He began with the sick, for Walker added doctoring to his other activities, and he had a small room behind the office full of drugs. An elderly man came forward, a man with a crop of curly grey hair, in a blue lava-lava, elaborately tattooed, with the skin of his body wrinkled like a wine-skin.

'What have you come for?' Walker asked him abruptly.

In a whining voice the man said that he could not eat without vomiting and that he had pains here and pains there.

'Go to the missionaries,' said Walker. 'You know that I only cure children.'

'I have been to the missionaries and they do me no good.'

'Then go home and prepare yourself to die. Have you lived so long and still want to go on living? You're a fool.'

The man broke into querulous expostulation, but Walker, pointing to a woman with a sick child in her arms, told her to bring it to his desk. He asked her questions and looked at the child.

'I will give you medicine,' he said. He turned to the half-caste clerk. 'Go into the dispensary and bring me some calomel pills.'

He made the child swallow one there and then and gave another to the mother.

'Take the child away and keep it warm. Tomorrow it will be dead or better.'

He leaned back in his chair and lit his pipe.

'Wonderful stuff, calomel. I've saved more lives with it than all the hospital doctors at Apia put together.'

Walker was very proud of his skill, and with the dogmatism of ignorance had no patience with the members of the medical profession.

'The sort of case I like,' he said, 'is the one that all the doctors have given up as hopeless. When the doctors have said they can't cure you, I say to them, "come to me". Did I ever tell you about the fellow who had a cancer?'

'Frequently,' said Mackintosh.

'I got him right in three months.'

'You've never told me about the people you haven't cured.'

He finished this part of the work and went on to the rest. It was a queer medley. There was a woman who could not get on with her husband and a man who complained that his wife had run away from him.

'Lucky dog,' said Walker. 'Most men wish their wives would too.'

There was a long complicated quarrel about the ownership of a few yards of land. There was a dispute about the sharing out of a catch of fish. There was a complaint against a white trader because he had given short measure. Walker listened attentively to every case, made up his mind quickly, and gave his decision. Then he would listen to nothing more; if the complainant went on he was hustled out of the office by a policeman. Mackintosh listened to it all with sullen irritation. On the whole, perhaps, it might be admitted that rough justice was done, but it exasperated the assistant that his chief trusted his instinct rather than the evidence. He would not listen to reason. He browbeat the witnesses and when they did not see what he wished them to called them thieves and liars.

He left to the last a group of men who were sitting in the corner of the room. He had deliberately ignored them. The party consisted of an old chief, a tall, dignified man with short, white hair, in a new lava-lava, bearing a huge fly wisp as a badge of office, his son, and half a dozen of the important men of the village. Walker had had a feud with them and had beaten them. As was characteristic of him he meant now to rub in his victory, and because he had them down to profit by their helplessness. The facts were peculiar. Walker had a passion for building roads. When he had come to Talua there were but a few tracks here and there, but in course of time he had cut roads through the country, joining the villages together, and it was to this that a great part of the island's prosperity was due. Whereas in the old days it had been impossible to get the produce of the land, copra chiefly, down to the coast where it could be put on schooners or motor launches and so taken to Apia, now transport was easy and simple. His ambition was to make a road right round the island and a great part of it was already built.

'In two years I shall have done it, and then I can die or they can fire me, I don't care.'

His roads were the joy of his heart and he made excursions constantly to see that they were kept in order. They were simple enough, wide tracks, grass-covered, cut through the scrub or through the plantations; but trees had to be rooted out, rocks dug up or blasted, and here and there levelling had been necessary. He was proud that he had surmounted by his own skill such difficulties as they presented. He rejoiced in his disposition of them so that they were not only convenient, but showed off the beauties of the island which his soul loved. When he spoke of his roads he was almost a poet. They meandered through those lovely scenes, and Walker had taken care that here and there they should run in a straight line, giving you a green vista through the tall trees, and here and there should turn and curve so that the heart was rested by the diversity. It was amazing that this coarse and sensual man should exercise so subtle an ingenuity to get the effects which his fancy suggested to him. He had used in making his roads all the fantastic skill of a Japanese gardener. He received a grant from headquarters for the work but took a curious pride in using but a small part of it, and the year before had spent only a hundred pounds of the thousand assigned to him.

'What do they want money for?' he boomed. 'They'll only spend it on all kinds of muck they don't want; what the missionaries leave them, that is to say.'

For no particular reason, except perhaps pride in the economy of his administration and the desire to contrast his efficiency with the wasteful methods of the authorities at Apia, he got the natives to do the work he wanted for wages that were almost nominal. It was owing to this that he had lately had difficulty with the village whose chief men now were come to see him. The chief's son had been in Upolu for a year and on coming back had told his people of the large sums that were paid at Apia for the public works. In long, idle talks he had inflamed their hearts with the desire for gain. He held out to them visions of vast wealth and they thought of the whisky they could buy—it was dear, since there was a law that it must not be sold to natives, and so it cost them double what the white man had to pay for it—they thought of the great sandalwood boxes in which they kept their treasures, and the scented soap and potted salmon, the luxuries for which the Kanaka will sell his soul; so that when the administrator sent for them and told them he wanted a road made from their village to a certain point along the coast and offered them twenty pounds, they asked him a hundred. The chief's son was called Manuma. He was a tall, handsome fellow, copper-coloured, with his fuzzy hair dyed red with lime, a wreath of red berries round his neck, and behind his ear a flower like a scarlet flame against his brown face. The upper part of his body was naked, but to show that he was no longer a savage, since he had lived in Apia, he wore a pair of dungarees instead of a lava-lava. He told them that if they held together the administrator would be obliged to accept their terms. His heart was set on building the road and when he found they would not work for less he would give them what they asked. But they must not move; whatever he said they must not abate their claim; they had asked a hundred and that they must keep to. When they mentioned the figure, Walker burst into a shout of his long, deep-voiced laughter. He told them not to make fools of themselves, but to set about the work at once. Because he was in a good humour that day he promised to give them a feast when the road was finished. But when he found that no attempt was made to start work, he went to the village and asked the men what silly game they were playing. Manuma had coached them well. They were quite calm, they did not attempt to argue—and argument is a passion with the Kanaka—they merely shrugged their shoulders: they would do it for a hundred pounds, and if he would not give them that they would do no work. He could please himself. They did not care. Then Walker flew into a passion. He was ugly then. His short fat neck swelled ominously, his red face grew purple, he foamed at the mouth. He set upon the natives with invective. He knew well how to wound and how to humiliate. He was terrifying. The older men grew pale and uneasy. They hesitated. If it had not been for Manuma, with his knowledge of the great world, and their dread of his ridicule, they would have yielded. It was Manuma who answered Walker.

'Pay us a hundred pounds and we will work.'

Walker, shaking his fist at him, called him every name he could think of. He riddled him with scorn. Manuma sat still and smiled. There may have been more bravado than confidence in his smile, but he had to make a good show before the others. He repeated his words.

'Pay us a hundred pounds and we will work.'

They thought that Walker would spring on him. It would not have been the first time that he had thrashed a native with his own hands; they knew his strength, and though Walker was three times the age of the young man and six inches shorter they did not doubt that he was more than a match for Manuma. No one had ever thought of resisting the savage onslaught of the administrator. But Walker said nothing. He chuckled.

'I am not going to waste my time with a pack of fools,' he said. 'Talk it over again. You know what I have offered. If you do not start in a week, take care.'

He turned round and walked out of the chief's hut. He untied his old mare and it was typical of the relations between him and the natives that one of the elder men hung on to the off stirrup while Walker from a convenient boulder hoisted himself heavily into the saddle.

That same night when Walker according to his habit was strolling along the road that ran past his house, he heard something whizz past him and with a thud strike a tree. Something had been thrown at him. He ducked instinctively. With a shout, 'Who's that?' he ran towards the place from which the missile had come and he heard the sound of a man escaping through the bush. He knew it was hopeless to pursue in the darkness, and besides he was soon out of breath, so he stopped and made his way back to the road. He looked about for what had been thrown, but could find nothing. It was quite dark. He went quickly back to the house and called Mackintosh and the Chinese boy.

'One of those devils has thrown something at me. Come along and let's find out what it was.'

He told the boy to bring a lantern and the three of them made their way back to the place. They hunted about the ground, but could not find what they sought. Suddenly the boy gave a guttural cry. They turned to look. He held up the lantern, and there, sinister in the light that cut the surrounding darkness, was a long knife sticking into the trunk of a coconut tree. It had been thrown with such force that it required quite an effort to pull it out.

'By George, if he hadn't missed me I'd have been in a nice state.'

Walker handled the knife. It was one of those knives, made in imitation of the sailor knives brought to the islands a hundred years before by the first white men, used to divide the coconuts in two so that the copra might be dried. It was a murderous weapon, and the blade, twelve inches long, was very sharp. Walker chuckled softly.

'The devil, the impudent devil.'

He had no doubt it was Manuma who had flung the knife. He had escaped death by three inches. He was not angry. On the contrary, he was in high spirits; the adventure exhilarated him, and when they got back to the house, calling for drinks, he rubbed his hands gleefully.

'I'll make them pay for this!'

His little eyes twinkled. He blew himself out like a turkey-cock, and for the second time within half an hour insisted on telling Mackintosh every detail of the affair. Then he asked him to play piquet, and while they played he boasted of his intentions. Mackintosh listened with tightened lips.

'But why should you grind them down like this?' he asked. 'Twenty pounds is precious little for the work you want them to do.'

'They ought to be precious thankful I give them anything.'

'Hang it all, it's not your own money. The government allots you a reasonable sum. They won't complain if you spend it.'

'They're a bunch of fools at Apia.'

Mackintosh saw that Walker's motive was merely vanity. He shrugged his shoulders.

'It won't do you much good to score off the fellows at Apia at the cost of your life.'

'Bless you, they wouldn't hurt me, these people. They couldn't do without me. They worship me. Manuma is a fool. He only threw that knife to frighten me.'

The next day Walker rode over again to the village. It was called Matautu. He did not get off his horse. When he reached the chief's house he saw that the men were sitting round the floor in a circle, talking, and he guessed they were discussing again the question of the road. The Samoan huts are formed in this way: trunks of slender trees are placed in a circle at intervals of perhaps five or six feet; a tall tree is set in the middle and from this downwards slopes the thatched roof. Venetian blinds of coconut leaves can be pulled down at night or when it is raining. Ordinarily the hut is open all round so that the breeze can blow through freely. Walker rode to the edge of the hut and called out to the chief.

'Oh, there, Tangatu, your son left his knife in a tree last night. I have brought it back to you.'

He flung it down on the ground in the midst of the circle, and with a low burst of laughter ambled off.

On Monday he went out to see if they had started work. There was no sign of it. He rode through the village. The inhabitants were about their ordinary avocations. Some were weaving mats of the pandanus leaf, one old man was busy with a *kava* bowl, the children were playing, the women went about their household chores. Walker, a smile on his lips, came to the chief's house.

'*Talofa-li*,' said the chief.

'*Talofa*,' answered Walker.

Manuma was making a net. He sat with a cigarette between his lips and looked up at Walker with a smile of triumph.

'You have decided that you will not make the road?'

The chief answered.

'Not unless you pay us one hundred pounds.'

'You will regret it.' He turned to Manuma. 'And you, my lad, I shouldn't wonder if your back was very sore before you're much older.'

He rode away chuckling. He left the natives vaguely uneasy. They feared the fat sinful old man, and neither the missionaries' abuse of him nor the scorn which Manuma had learnt in Apia made them forget that he had a devilish cunning and that no man had ever braved him without in the long run suffering for it. They found out within twenty-four hours what scheme he had devised. It was characteristic. For next morning a great band of men, women, and children came into the village and the chief men said that they had made a bargain with Walker to build the road. He had offered them twenty pounds and they had accepted. Now, the cunning lay in this, that the Polynesians have rules of hospitality which have all the force of laws; an etiquette of absolute rigidity made it necessary for the people of the village not only to give lodging to the strangers, but to provide them with food and drink as long as they wished to stay. The inhabitants of Matautu were outwitted. Every morning the workers went out in a joyous band, cut down trees, blasted rocks, levelled here and there and then in the evening tramped back again, and ate and drank, ate heartily, danced, sang hymns, and enjoyed life. For them it was a picnic. But soon their hosts began to wear long faces; the strangers had enormous appetites, and the plantains and the bread-fruit vanished before their rapacity; the alligator-pear trees, whose fruit sent to Apia might sell for good money, were stripped bare. Ruin stared them in the face. And then they found that the strangers were working very slowly. Had they received a hint from Walker that they might take their time? At this rate by the time the road was finished there would not be a scrap of food in the village. And worse than this, they were a laughing-stock; when one or other of them went to some distant hamlet on an errand he found that the story had got there before him, and he was met with derisive laughter. There is nothing the Kanaka can endure less than ridicule. It was not long before much angry talk passed among the sufferers. Manuma was no longer a hero; he had to put up with a good deal of plain speaking, and one day what Walker had suggested came to pass: a heated argument turned into a quarrel and half a dozen of the young men set upon the chief's son and gave him such a beating that for a week he lay bruised and sore on the pandanus mats. He turned from side to side and could find no ease. Every day or two the administrator rode over on his old mare and watched the progress of the road. He was not a man to resist the temptation of taunting the fallen foe, and he missed no opportunity to rub into the shamed inhabitants of Matautu the bitterness of their humiliation. He broke their spirit. And one morning, putting their pride in their pockets—a figure of speech, since pockets they had not—they all set out with the strangers and started working on the road. It was urgent to get it done quickly if they wanted to save any food at all, and the whole village joined in. But they worked silently, with rage and mortification in their hearts, and even the children toiled in silence. The women wept as they carried away bundles of brushwood. When Walker saw them he laughed so much that he almost rolled out of his saddle. The news spread quickly and tickled the people of the island to death. This was the greatest joke of all, the crowning triumph of that cunning old white man whom no Kanaka had ever been able to circumvent; and they came from distant villages, with their wives and children, to look at the foolish folk who had refused twenty pounds to make the road and now were forced to work for nothing. But the harder they worked the more easily went the guests. Why should they hurry, when they were getting good food for nothing and the longer they took about the job the better the joke became? At last the wretched villagers could stand it no longer, and they were come this morning to beg the administrator to send the strangers back to their own homes. If he would do this they promised to finish the road themselves for nothing. For him it was a victory complete and unqualified. They were humbled. A look of arrogant complacence spread over his large, naked face, and he seemed to swell in his chair like a great bullfrog. There was something sinister in his appearance, so that Mackintosh shivered with disgust. Then in his booming tones he began to speak.

'Is it for my good that I make the road? What benefit do you think I get out of it? It is for you, so that you can walk in comfort and carry your copra in comfort. I offered to pay you for your work, though it was for your own sake the work was done. I offered to pay you generously. Now *you* must pay. I will send the people of Manua back to their homes if you will finish the road and pay the twenty pounds that I have to pay them.'

There was an outcry. They sought to reason with him. They told him they had not the money. But to everything they said he replied with brutal gibes. Then the clock struck.

'Dinner time,' he said. 'Turn them all out.'

He raised himself heavily from his chair and walked out of the room. When Mackintosh followed him, he found him already seated at table, a napkin tied round his neck, holding his knife and fork in readiness for the meal the Chinese cook was about to bring. He was in high spirits.

'I did 'em down fine,' he said, as Mackintosh sat down. 'I shan't have much trouble with the roads after this.'

'I suppose you were joking,' said Mackintosh icily.

'What do you mean by that?'

'You're not really going to make them pay twenty pounds?'

'You bet your life I am.'

'I'm not sure you've got any right to.'

'Ain't you? I guess I've got the right to do any damned thing I like on this island.'

'I think you've bullied them quite enough.'

Walker laughed fatly. He did not care what Mackintosh thought.

'When I want your opinion I'll ask for it.'

Mackintosh grew very white. He knew by bitter experience that he could do nothing but keep silence, and the violent effort at self-control made him sick and faint. He could not eat the food that was before him and with disgust he watched Walker shovel meat into his vast mouth. He was a dirty feeder, and to sit at table with him needed a strong stomach. Mackintosh shuddered. A tremendous desire seized him to humiliate that gross and cruel man; he would give anything in the world to see him in the dust, suffering as much as he had made others suffer. He had never loathed the bully with such loathing as now.

The day wore on. Mackintosh tried to sleep after dinner, but the passion in his heart prevented him; he tried to read, but the letters swam before his eyes. The sun beat down pitilessly, and he longed for rain; but he knew that rain would bring no coolness; it would only make it hotter and more steamy. He was a native of Aberdeen and his heart yearned suddenly for the icy winds that whistled through the granite streets of that city. Here he was a prisoner, imprisoned not only by that placid sea, but by his hatred for that horrible old man. He pressed his hands to his aching head. He would like to kill him. But he pulled himself together. He must do something to distract his mind, and since he could not read he thought he would set his private papers in order. It was a job which he had long meant to do and which he had constantly put off. He unlocked the drawer of his desk and took out a handful of letters. He caught sight of his revolver. An impulse, no sooner realized than set aside, to put a bullet through his head and so escape from the intolerable bondage of life flashed through his mind. He noticed that in the damp air the revolver was slightly rusted, and he got an oil-rag and began to clean it. It was while he was thus occupied that he grew aware of someone slinking round the door. He looked up and called:

'Who is there?'

There was a moment's pause, then Manuma showed himself.

'What do you want?'

The chief's son stood for a moment, sullen and silent, and when he spoke it was with a strangled voice.

'We can't pay twenty pounds. We haven't the money.'

'What am I to do?' said Mackintosh. 'You heard what Mr Walker said.'

Manuma began to plead, half in Samoan and half in English. It was a sing-song whine, with the quavering intonations of a beggar, and it filled Mackintosh with disgust. It outraged him that the man should let himself be so crushed. He was a pitiful object.

'I can do nothing,' said Mackintosh irritably. 'You know that Mr Walker is master here.'

Manuma was silent again. He still stood in the doorway.

'I am sick,' he said at last. 'Give me some medicine.'

'What is the matter with you?'

'I do not know. I am sick. I have pains in my body.'

'Don't stand there,' said Mackintosh sharply. 'Come in and let me look at you.'

Manuma entered the little room and stood before the desk.

'I have pains here and here.'

He put his hands to his loins and his face assumed an expression of pain. Suddenly Mackintosh grew conscious that the boy's eyes were resting on the revolver which he had laid on the desk when Manuma appeared in the doorway. There was a silence between the two which to Mackintosh was endless. He seemed to read the thoughts which were in the Kanaka's mind. His heart beat violently. And then he felt as though something possessed him so that he acted under the compulsion of a foreign will. Himself did not make the movements of his body, but a power that was strange to him. His throat was suddenly dry, and he put his hand to it mechanically in order to help his speech. He was impelled to avoid Manuma's eyes.

'Just wait here,' he said, his voice sounded as though someone had seized him by the windpipe, 'and I'll fetch you something from the dispensary.'

He got up. Was it his fancy that he staggered a little? Manuma stood silently, and though he kept his eyes averted, Mackintosh knew that he was looking dully out of the door. It was this other person that possessed him that drove him out of the room, but it was himself that took a handful of muddled papers and threw them on the revolver in order to hide it from view. He went to the dispensary. He got a pill and poured out some blue draught into a small bottle, and then came out into the compound. He did not want to go back into his own bungalow, so he called to Manuma.

'Come here.'

He gave him the drugs and instructions how to take them. He did not know what it was that made it impossible for him to look at the Kanaka. While he was speaking to him he kept his eyes on his shoulder. Manuma took the medicine and slunk out of the gate.

Mackintosh went into the dining-room and turned over once more the old newspapers. But he could not read them. The house was very still. Walker was upstairs in his room asleep, the Chinese cook was busy in the kitchen, the two policemen were out fishing. The silence that seemed to brood over the house was unearthly, and there hammered in Mackintosh's head the question whether the revolver still lay where he had placed it. He could not bring himself to look. The uncertainty was horrible, but the certainty would be more horrible still. He sweated. At last he could stand the silence no longer, and he made up his mind to go down the road to the trader's, a man named Jervis, who had a store about a mile away. He was a half-caste, but even that amount of white blood made him possible to talk to. He wanted to get away from his bungalow, with the desk littered with untidy papers, and underneath them something, or nothing. He walked along the road. As he passed the fine hut of a chief a greeting was called out to him. Then he came to the store. Behind the counter sat the trader's daughter, a swarthy broad-featured girl in a pink blouse and a white drill skirt. Jervis hoped he would marry her. He had money, and he had told Mackintosh that his daughter's husband would be well-to-do. She flushed a little when she saw Mackintosh.

'Father's just unpacking some cases that have come in this morning. I'll tell him you're here.'

He sat down and the girl went out behind the shop. In a moment her mother waddled in, a huge old woman, a chiefess, who owned much land in her own right; and gave him her hand. Her monstrous obesity was an offence, but she managed to convey an impression of dignity. She was cordial without obsequiousness; affable, but conscious of her station.

'You're quite a stranger, Mr Mackintosh. Teresa was saying only this morning: "Why, we never see Mr Mackintosh now."'

He shuddered a little as he thought of himself as that old native's son-in-law. It was notorious that she ruled her husband, notwithstanding his white blood, with a firm hand. Hers was the authority and hers the business head. She might be no more than Mrs Jervis to the white people, but her father had been a chief of the blood royal, and his father and his father's father had ruled as kings. The trader came in, small beside his imposing wife, a dark man with a black beard going grey, in ducks, with handsome eyes and flashing teeth. He was very British, and his conversation was slangy, but you felt he spoke English as a foreign tongue; with his family he used the language of his native mother. He was a servile man, cringing and obsequious.

'Ah, Mr Mackintosh, this is a joyful surprise. Get the whisky, Teresa; Mr Mackintosh will have a gargle with us.'

He gave all the latest news of Apia, watching his guest's eyes the while, so that he might know the welcome thing to say.

'And how is Walker? We've not seen him just lately. Mrs Jervis is going to send him a sucking-pig one day this week.'

'I saw him riding home this morning,' said Teresa.

'Here's how,' said Jervis, holding up his whisky.

Mackintosh drank. The two women sat and looked at him, Mrs Jervis in her black Mother Hubbard, placid and haughty, and Teresa anxious to smile whenever she caught his eye, while the trader gossiped insufferably.

'They were saying in Apia it was about time Walker retired. He ain't so young as he was. Things have changed since he first come to the islands and he ain't changed with them.'

'He'll go too far,' said the old chiefess. 'The natives aren't satisfied.'

'That was a good joke about the road,' laughed the trader. 'When I told them about it in Apia they fair split their sides with laughing. Good old Walker.'

Mackintosh looked at him savagely. What did he mean by talking of him in that fashion? To a half-caste trader he was Mr Walker. It was on his tongue to utter a harsh rebuke for the impertinence. He did not know what held him back.

'When he goes I hope you'll take his place, Mr Mackintosh,' said Jervis. 'We all like you on the island. You understand the natives. They're educated now, they must be treated differently to the old days. It wants an educated man to be administrator now. Walker was only a trader same as I am.'

Teresa's eyes glistened.

'When the time comes if there's anything anyone can do here, you bet your bottom dollar we'll do it. I'd get all the chiefs to go over to Apia and make a petition.'

Mackintosh felt horribly sick. It had not struck him that if anything happened to Walker it might be he who would succeed him. It was true that no one in his official position knew the island so well. He got up suddenly and scarcely taking his leave walked back to the compound. And now he went straight to his room. He took a quick look at his desk. He rummaged among the papers.

The revolver was not there.

His heart thumped violently against his ribs. He looked for the revolver everywhere. He hunted in the chairs and in the drawers. He looked desperately, and all the time he knew he would not find it. Suddenly he heard Walker's gruff, hearty voice.

'What the devil are you up to, Mac?'

He started. Walker was standing in the doorway and instinctively he turned round to hide what lay upon his desk.

'Tidying up?' quizzed Walker. 'I've told 'em to put the grey in the trap. I'm going down to Tafoni to bathe. You'd better come along.'

'All right,' said Mackintosh.

So long as he was with Walker nothing could happen. The place they were bound for was about three miles away, and there was a fresh-water pool, separated by a thin barrier of rock from the sea, which the administrator had blasted out for the natives to bathe in. He had done this at spots round the island, wherever there was a spring; and the fresh water, compared with the sticky warmth of the sea, was cool and invigorating. They drove along the silent grassy road, splashing now and then through fords, where the sea had forced its way in, past a couple of native villages, the bell-shaped huts spaced out roomily and the white chapel in the middle, and at the third village they got out of the trap, tied up the horse, and walked down to the pool. They were accompanied by four or five girls and a dozen children. Soon they were all splashing about, shouting and laughing, while Walker, in a lava-lava, swam to and fro like an unwieldy porpoise. He made lewd jokes with the girls, and they amused themselves by diving under him and wriggling away when he tried to catch them. When he was tired he lay down on a rock, while the girls and the children surrounded him; it was a happy family; and the old man, huge, with his crescent of white hair and his shining bald crown, looked like some old sea god. Once Mackintosh caught a queer soft look in his eyes.

'They're dear children,' he said. 'They look upon me as their father.'

And then without a pause he turned to one of the girls and made an obscene remark which sent them all into fits of laughter. Mackintosh started to dress. With his thin legs and thin arms he made a grotesque figure, a sinister Don Quixote, and Walker began to make coarse jokes about him. They were acknowledged with little smothered laughs. Mackintosh struggled with his shirt. He knew he looked absurd, but he hated being laughed at. He stood silent and glowering.

'If you want to get back in time for dinner you ought to come soon.'

'You're not a bad fellow, Mac. Only you're a fool. When you're doing one thing you always want to do another. That's not the way we live.'

But all the same he raised himself slowly to his feet and began to put on his clothes. They sauntered back to the village, drank a bowl of *kava* with the chief, and then, after a joyful farewell from all the lazy villagers, drove home.

After dinner, according to his habit, Walker, lighting his cigar, prepared to go for a stroll. Mackintosh was suddenly seized with fear.

'Don't you think it's rather unwise to go out at night by yourself just now?'

Walker stared at him with his round blue eyes.

'What the devil do you mean?'

'Remember the knife the other night. You've got those fellows' backs up.'

'Pooh! They wouldn't dare.'

'Someone dared before.'

'That was only a bluff. They wouldn't hurt me. They look upon me as a father. They know that whatever I do is for their own good.'

Mackintosh watched him with contempt in his heart. The man's self-complacency outraged him, and yet something, he knew not what, made him insist.

'Remember what happened this morning. It wouldn't hurt you to stay at home just tonight. I'll play piquet with you.'

'I'll play piquet with you when I come back. The Kanaka isn't born yet who can make me alter my plans.'

'You'd better let me come with you.'

'You stay where you are.'

Mackintosh shrugged his shoulders. He had given the man full warning. If he did not heed it that was his own lookout. Walker put on his hat and went out. Mackintosh began to read; but then he thought of something; perhaps it would be as well to have his own whereabouts quite clear. He crossed over to the kitchen and, inventing some pretext, talked for a few minutes with the cook. Then he got out the gramophone and put a record on it, but while it ground out its melancholy tune, some comic song of a London music-hall, his ear was strained for a sound away there in the night. At his elbow the record reeled out its loudness, the words were raucous, but notwithstanding he seemed to be surrounded by an unearthly silence. He heard the dull roar of the breakers against the reef. He heard the breeze sigh, far up, in the leaves of the coconut trees. How long would it be? It was awful.

He heard a hoarse laugh.

'Wonders will never cease. It's not often you play yourself a tune, Mac.'

Walker stood at the window, red-faced, bluff and jovial.

'Well, you see I'm alive and kicking. What were you playing for?'

Walker came in.

'Nerves a bit dicky, eh? Playing a tune to keep your pecker up?'

'I was playing your requiem.'

'What the devil's that?'

''Alf o' bitter an' a pint of stout.'

'A rattling good song too. I don't mind how often I hear it. Now I'm ready to take your money off you at piquet.'

They played and Walker bullied his way to victory, bluffing his opponent, chaffing him, jeering at his mistakes, up to every dodge, browbeating him, exulting. Presently Mackintosh recovered his coolness, and standing outside himself, as it were, he was able to take a detached pleasure in watching the overbearing old man and in his own cold reserve. Somewhere Manuma sat quietly and awaited his opportunity.

Walker won game after game and pocketed his winnings at the end of the evening in high good-humour.

'You'll have to grow a little bit older before you stand much chance against me, Mac. The fact is I have a natural gift for cards.'

'I don't know that there's much gift about it when I happen to deal you fourteen aces.'

'Good cards come to good players,' retorted Walker. 'I'd have won if I'd had your hands.'

He went on to tell long stories of the various occasions on which he had played cards with notorious sharpers and to their consternation had taken all their money from them. He boasted. He praised himself. And Mackintosh listened with absorption. He wanted now to feed his hatred; and everything Walker said, every gesture, made him more detestable. At last Walker got up.

'Well, I'm going to turn in,' he said with a loud yawn. 'I've got a long day tomorrow.'

'What are you going to do?'

'I'm driving over to the other side of the island. I'll start at five, but I don't expect I shall get back to dinner till late.'

They generally dined at seven.

'We'd better make it half past seven then.'

'I guess it would be as well.'

Mackintosh watched him knock the ashes out of his pipe. His vitality was rude and exuberant. It was strange to think that death hung over him. A faint smile flickered in Mackintosh's cold, gloomy eyes.

'Would you like me to come with you?'

'What in God's name should I want that for? I'm using the mare and she'll have enough to do to carry me; she don't want to drag you over thirty miles of road.'

'Perhaps you don't quite realize what the feeling is at Matautu. I think it would be safer if I came with you.'

Walker burst out into contemptuous laughter.

'You'd be a fine lot of use in a scrap. I'm not a great hand at getting the wind up.'

Now the smile passed from Mackintosh's eyes to his lips. It distorted them painfully.

'*Quem deus vult perdere prius dementat.*'

'What the hell is that?' said Walker.

'Latin,' answered Mackintosh as he went out.

And now he chuckled. His mood had changed. He had done all he could and the matter was in the hands of fate. He slept more soundly than he had done for weeks. When he awoke next morning he went out. After a good night he found a pleasant exhilaration in the freshness of the early air. The sea was a more vivid blue, the sky more brilliant, than on most days, the trade wind was fresh, and there was a ripple on the lagoon as the breeze brushed over it like velvet brushed the wrong way. He felt himself stronger and younger. He entered upon the day's work with zest. After luncheon he slept again, and as evening drew on he had the bay saddled and sauntered through the bush. He seemed to see it all with new eyes. He felt more normal. The extraordinary thing was that he was able to put Walker out of his mind altogether. So far as he was concerned he might never have existed.

He returned late, hot after his ride, and bathed again. Then he sat on the veranda, smoking his pipe, and looked at the day declining over the lagoon. In the sunset the lagoon, rosy and purple and green, was very beautiful. He felt at peace with the world and with himself. When the cook came out to say that dinner was ready and to ask whether he should wait, Mackintosh smiled at him with friendly eyes. He looked at his watch.

'It's half past seven. Better not wait. One can't tell when the boss'll be back.'

The boy nodded, and in a moment Mackintosh saw him carry across the yard a bowl of steaming soup. He got up lazily, went into the dining-room, and ate his dinner. Had it happened? The uncertainty was amusing and Mackintosh chuckled in the silence. The food did not seem so monotonous as usual, and even though there was Hamburger steak, the cook's invariable dish when his poor invention failed him, it tasted by some miracle succulent and spiced. After dinner he strolled over lazily to his bungalow to get a book. He liked the intense stillness, and now that the night had fallen the stars were blazing in the sky. He shouted for a lamp and in a moment the Chink pattered over on his bare feet, piercing the darkness with a ray of light. He put the lamp on the desk and noiselessly slipped out of the room. Mackintosh stood rooted to the floor, for there, half hidden by untidy papers, was his revolver. His heart throbbed painfully, and he broke into a sweat. It was done then.

He took up the revolver with a shaking hand. Four of the chambers were empty. He paused a moment and looked suspiciously out into the night, but there was no one there. He quickly slipped four cartridges into the empty chambers and locked the revolver in his drawer.

He sat down to wait.

An hour passed, a second hour passed. There was nothing. He sat at his desk as though he were writing, but he neither wrote nor read. He merely listened. He strained his ears for a sound travelling from a far distance. At last he heard hesitating footsteps and knew it was the Chinese cook.

'Ah-Sung,' he called.

The boy came to the door.

'Boss velly late,' he said. 'Dinner no good.'

Mackintosh stared at him, wondering whether he knew what had happened, and whether, when he knew, he would realize on what terms he and Walker had been. He went about his work, sleek, silent, and smiling, and who could tell his thoughts?

'I expect he's had dinner on the way, but you must keep the soup hot at all events.'

The words were hardly out of his mouth when the silence was suddenly broken into by a confusion, cries, and a rapid patter of naked feet. A number of natives ran into the compound, men and women and children; they crowded round Mackintosh and they all talked at once. They were unintelligible. They were excited and frightened and some of them were crying. Mackintosh pushed his way through them and went to the gateway. Though he had scarcely understood what they said he knew quite well what had happened. And as he reached the gate the dog-cart arrived. The old mare was being led by a tall Kanaka, and in the dog-cart crouched two men, trying to hold Walker up. A little crowd of natives surrounded it.

The mare was led into the yard and the natives surged in after it. Mackintosh shouted to them to stand back and the two policemen, appearing suddenly from God knows where, pushed them violently aside. By now he had managed to understand that some lads, who had been fishing, on their way back to their village had come across the cart on the home side of the ford. The mare was nuzzling about the herbage and in the darkness they could just see the great white bulk of the old man sunk between the seat and the dashboard. At first they thought he was drunk and they peered in, grinning, but then they heard him groan, and guessed that something was amiss. They ran to the village and called for help. It was when they returned, accompanied by half a hundred people, that they discovered Walker had been shot.

With a sudden thrill of horror Mackintosh asked himself whether he was already dead. The first thing at all events was to get him out of the cart, and that, owing to Walker's corpulence, was a difficult job. It took four strong men to lift him. They jolted him and he uttered a dull groan. He was still alive. At last they carried him into the house, up the stairs, and placed him on his bed. Then Mackintosh was able to see him, for in the yard, lit only by half a dozen hurricane lamps, everything had been obscured. Walker's white ducks were stained with blood, and the men who had carried him wiped their hands, red and sticky, on their lava-lavas. Mackintosh held up the lamp. He had not expected the old man to be so pale. His eyes were closed. He was breathing still, his pulse could be just felt but it was obvious that he was dying. Mackintosh had not bargained for the shock of horror that convulsed him. He saw that the native clerk was there, and in a voice hoarse with fear told him to go into the dispensary and get what was necessary for a hypodermic injection. One of the policemen had brought up the whisky, and Mackintosh forced a little into the old man's mouth. The room was crowded with natives. They sat about the floor, speechless now and terrified, and every now and then one wailed aloud. It was very hot, but Mackintosh felt cold, his hands and his feet were like ice, and he had to make a violent effort not to tremble in all his limbs. He did not know what to do. He did not know if Walker was bleeding still, and if he was, how he could stop the bleeding.

The clerk brought the hypodermic needle.

'You give it to him,' said Mackintosh. 'You're more used to that sort of thing than I am.'

His head ached horribly. It felt as though all sorts of little savage things were beating inside it, trying to get out. They watched for the effect of the injection. Presently Walker opened his eyes slowly. He did not seem to know where he was.

'Keep quiet,' said Mackintosh. 'You're at home. You're quite safe.'

Walker's lips outlined a shadowy smile.

'They've got me,' he whispered.

'I'll get Jervis to send his motor-boat to Apia at once. We'll get a doctor out by tomorrow afternoon.'

There was a long pause before the old man answered.

'I shall be dead by then.'

A ghastly expression passed over Mackintosh's pale face. He forced himself to laugh.

'What rot! You keep quiet and you'll be as right as rain.'

'Give me a drink,' said Walker. 'A stiff one.'

With shaking hand Mackintosh poured out whisky and water, half and half, and held the glass while Walker drank greedily. It seemed to restore him. He gave a long sigh and a little colour came into his great fleshy face. Mackintosh felt extraordinarily helpless. He stood and stared at the old man.

'If you'll tell me what to do I'll do it,' he said.

'There's nothing to do. Just leave me alone. I'm done for.'

He looked dreadfully pitiful as he lay on the great bed, a huge, bloated, old man; but so wan, so weak, it was heart-rending. As he rested, his mind seemed to grow clearer.

'You were right, Mac,' he said presently. 'You warned me.'

'I wish to God I'd come with you.'

'You're a good chap, Mac, only you don't drink.'

There was another long silence, and it was clear that Walker was sinking. There was an internal haemorrhage and even Mackintosh in his ignorance could not fail to see that his chief had but an hour or two to live. He stood by the side of the bed stock-still. For half an hour perhaps Walker lay with his eyes closed, then he opened them.

'They'll give you my job,' he said, slowly. 'Last time I was in Apia I told them you were all right. Finish my road. 1 want to think that'll be done. All round the island.'

'I don't want your job. You'll get all right.'

Walker shook his head wearily.

'I've had my day. Treat them fairly, that's the great thing. They're children. You must always remember that. You must be firm with them, but you must be kind. And you must be just. I've never made a bob out of them. I haven't saved a hundred pounds in twenty years. The road's the great thing. Get the road finished.'

Something very like a sob was wrung from Mackintosh.

'You're a good fellow, Mac. I always liked you.'

He closed his eyes, and Mackintosh thought that he would never open them again. His mouth was so dry that he had to get himself something to drink. The Chinese cook silently put a chair for him. He sat down by the side of the bed and waited. He did not know how long a time passed. The night was endless. Suddenly one of the men sitting there broke into uncontrollable sobbing, loudly, like a child, and Mackintosh grew aware that the room was crowded by this time with natives. They sat all over the floor on their haunches, men and women, staring at the bed.

'What are all these people doing here?' said Mackintosh. 'They've got no right. Turn them out, turn them out, all of them.'

His words seemed to rouse Walker, for he opened his eyes once more, and now they were all misty. He wanted to speak, but he was so weak that Mackintosh had to strain his ears to catch what he said.

'Let them stay. They're my children. They ought to be here.'

Mackintosh turned to the natives.

'Stay where you are. He wants you. But be silent.'

A faint smile came over the old man's white face.

'Come nearer,' he said.

Mackintosh bent over him. His eyes were closed and the words he said were like a wind sighing through the fronds of the coconut trees.

'Give me another drink. I've got something to say.'

This time Mackintosh gave him his whisky neat. Walker collected his strength in a final effort of will.

'Don't make a fuss about this. In ninety-five when there were troubles white men were killed, and the fleet came and shelled the villages. A lot of people were killed who'd had nothing to do with it. They're damned fools at Apia. If they make a fuss they'll only punish the wrong people. I don't want anyone punished.'

He paused for a while to rest.

'You must say it was an accident. No one's to blame. Promise me that.'

'I'll do anything you like,' whispered Mackintosh.

'Good chap. One of the best. They're children. I'm their father. A father don't let his children get into trouble if he can help it.'

A ghost of a chuckle came out of his throat. It was astonishingly weird and ghastly.

'You're a religious chap, Mac. What's that about forgiving them? You know.'

For a while Mackintosh did not answer. His lips trembled.

'Forgive them, for they know not what they do?'

'That's right. Forgive them. I've loved them, you know, always loved them.'

He sighed. His lips faintly moved, and now Mackintosh had to put his ears quite close to them in order to hear.

'Hold my hand,' he said.

Mackintosh gave a gasp. His heart seemed wrenched. He took the old man's hand, so cold and weak, a coarse, rough hand, and held it in his own. And thus he sat until he nearly started out of his seat, for the silence was suddenly broken by a long rattle. It was terrible and unearthly. Walker was dead. Then the natives broke out with loud cries. The tears ran down their faces, and they beat their breasts.

Mackintosh disengaged his hand from the dead man's and staggering like one drunk with sleep he went out of the room. He went to the locked drawer in his writing-desk and took out the revolver. He walked down to the sea and walked into the lagoon; he waded out cautiously, so that he should not trip against a coral rock, till the water came to his arm-pits. Then he put a bullet through his head.

An hour later half a dozen slim brown sharks were splashing and struggling at the spot where he fell.

The Three Fat Women of Antibes

◆

One was called Mrs Richman and she was a widow. The second was called Mrs Sutcliffe; she was American and she had divorced two husbands. The third was called Miss Hickson and she was a spinster. They were all in the comfortable forties and they were all well off. Mrs Sutcliffe had the odd first name of Arrow. When she was young and slender she had liked it well enough. It suited her and the jests it occasioned though too often repeated were very flattering; she was not disinclined to believe that it suited her character too: it suggested directness, speed, and purpose. She liked it less now that her delicate features had grown muzzy with fat, that her arms and shoulders were so substantial and her hips so massive. It was increasingly difficult to find dresses to make her look as she liked to look. The jests her name gave rise to now were made behind her back and she very well knew that they were far from obliging. But she was by no means resigned to middle age. She still wore blue to bring out the colour of her eyes and, with the help of art, her fair hair had kept its lustre. What she liked about Beatrice Richman and Frances Hickson was that they were both so much fatter than she, it made her look quite slim; they were both of them older and much inclined to treat her as a little young thing. It was not disagreeable. They were good-natured women and they chaffed her pleasantly about her beaux; they had both given up the thought of that kind of nonsense, indeed Miss Hickson had never given it a moment's consideration, but they were sympathetic to her flirtations. It was understood that one of these days Arrow would make a third man happy.

'Only you mustn't get any heavier, darling,' said Mrs Richman.

'And for goodness' sake make certain of his bridge,' said Miss Hickson.

They saw for her a man of about fifty, but well-preserved and of distinguished carriage, an admiral on the retired list and a good golfer, or a widower without encumbrances, but in any case with a substantial income. Arrow listened to them amiably, and kept to herself the fact that this was not at all her idea. It was true that she would have liked to marry again, but her fancy turned to a dark slim Italian with flashing eyes and a sonorous title or to a Spanish don of noble lineage; and not a day more than thirty. There were times when, looking at herself in her mirror, she was certain she did not look any more than that herself.

They were great friends, Miss Hickson, Mrs Richman, and Arrow Sutcliffe. It was their fat that had brought them together and bridge that had cemented their alliance. They had met first at Carlsbad, where they were staying at the same hotel and were treated by the same doctor who used them with the same ruthlessness. Beatrice Richman was enormous. She was a handsome woman, with fine eyes, rouged cheeks, and painted lips. She was very well content to be a widow with a handsome fortune. She adored her food. She liked bread and butter, cream, potatoes, and suet puddings, and for eleven months of the year ate pretty well everything she had a mind to, and for one month went to Carlsbad to reduce. But every year she grew fatter. She upbraided the doctor, but got no sympathy from him. He pointed out to her various plain and simple facts.

'But if I'm never to eat a thing I like, life isn't worth living,' she expostulated.

He shrugged his disapproving shoulders. Afterwards she told Miss Hickson that she was beginning to suspect he wasn't so clever as she had thought. Miss Hickson gave a great guffaw. She was that sort of woman. She had a deep bass voice, a large flat sallow face from which twinkled little bright eyes; she walked with a slouch, her hands in her pockets, and when she could do so without exciting attention smoked a long cigar. She dressed as like a man as she could.

'What the deuce should I look like in frills and furbelows?' she said. 'When you're as fat as I am you may just as well be comfortable.'

She wore tweeds and heavy boots and whenever she could went about bareheaded. But she was as strong as an ox and boasted that few men could drive a longer ball than she. She was plain of speech, and she could swear more variously than a stevedore. Though her name was Frances she preferred to be called Frank. Masterful, but with tact, it was her jovial strength of character that held the three together. They drank their waters together, had their baths at the same hour, they took their strenuous walks together, pounded about the tennis court with a professional to make them run, and ate at the same table their sparse and regulated meals. Nothing impaired their good humour but the scales, and when one or other of them weighed as much on one day as she had the day before neither Frank's coarse jokes, the *bonhomie* of Beatrice, nor Arrow's pretty kittenish ways sufficed to dispel the gloom. Then drastic measures were resorted to, the culprit went to bed for twenty-four hours and nothing passed her lips but the doctor's famous vegetable soup which tasted like hot water in which a cabbage had been well rinsed.

Never were three women greater friends. They would have been independent of anyone else if they had not needed a fourth at bridge. They were fierce, enthusiastic players and the moment the day's cure was over, they sat down at the bridge table. Arrow, feminine as she was, played the best game of the three, a hard, brilliant game, in which she showed no mercy and never conceded a point or failed to take advantage of a mistake. Beatrice was solid and reliable. Frank was dashing; she was a great theorist, and had all the authorities at the tip of her tongue. They had long arguments over the rival systems. They bombarded one another with Culbertson and Sims. It was obvious that not one of them ever played a card without fifteen good reasons, but it was also obvious from the subsequent conversation that there were fifteen equally good reasons why she should not have played it. Life would have been perfect, even with the prospect of twenty-four hours of that filthy soup when the doctor's rotten (Beatrice) bloody (Frank) lousy (Arrow) scales pretended one hadn't lost an ounce in two days, if only there had not been this constant difficulty of finding someone to play with them who was in their class.

It was for this reason that on the occasion with which this narrative deals Frank invited Lena Finch to come and stay with them at Antibes. They were spending some weeks there on Frank's suggestion. It seemed absurd to her, with her common sense, that immediately the cure was over Beatrice who always lost twenty pounds should be giving way to her ungovernable appetite put it all on again. Beatrice was weak. She needed a person of strong will to watch her diet. She proposed then that on leaving Carlsbad they should take a house at Antibes, where they could get plenty of exercise—everyone knew that nothing slimmed you like swimming—and as far as possible could go on with the cure. With a cook of their own they could at least avoid things that were obviously fattening. There was no reason why they should not all lose several pounds more. It seemed a very good idea. Beatrice knew what was good for her, and she could resist temptation well enough if temptation was not put right under her nose. Besides, she liked gambling, and a flutter at the Casino two or three times a week would pass the time very pleasantly. Arrow adored Antibes, and she would be looking her best after a month at Carlsbad. She could just pick and choose among the young Italians, the passionate Spaniards, the gallant Frenchmen, and the long-limbed English who sauntered about all day in bathing trunks and gay-coloured dressing-gowns. The plan worked very well. They had a grand time. Two days a week they ate nothing but hard-boiled eggs and raw tomatoes and they mounted the scales every morning with light hearts. Arrow got down to eleven stone and felt just like a girl; Beatrice and Frank by standing in a certain way just avoided the thirteen. The machine they had bought registered kilogrammes, and they got extraordinarily clever at translating them in the twinkling of an eye to pounds and ounces.

But the fourth at bridge continued to be the difficulty. This person played like a fool, the other was so slow that it drove you frantic, one was quarrelsome, another was a bad loser, a third was next door to a crook. It was strange how hard it was to find exactly the player you wanted.

One morning when they were sitting in pyjamas on the terrace overlooking the sea, drinking their tea (without milk or sugar) and eating a rusk prepared by Dr Hudebert and guaranteed not to be fattening, Frank looked up from her letters.

'Lena Finch is coming down to the Riviera,' she said.

'Who's she?' asked Arrow.

'She married a cousin of mine. He died a couple of months ago and she's just recovering from a nervous breakdown. What about asking her to come here for a fortnight?'

'Does she play bridge?' asked Beatrice.

'You bet your life she does,' boomed Frank in her deep voice. 'And a damned good game too. We should be absolutely independent of outsiders.'

'How old is she?' asked Arrow.

'Same age as I am.'

'That sounds all right.'

It was settled. Frank, with her usual decisiveness, stalked out as soon as she had finished her breakfast to send a wire, and three days later Lena Finch arrived. Frank met her at the station. She was in deep but not obtrusive mourning for the recent death of her husband. Frank had not seen her for two years. She kissed her warmly and took a good look at her.

'You're very thin, darling,' she said.

Lena smiled bravely.

'I've been through a good deal lately. I've lost a lot of weight.'

Frank sighed, but whether from sympathy with her cousin's sad loss, or from envy, was not obvious.

Lena was not, however, depressed, and after a quick bath was quite ready to accompany Frank to Eden Roc. Frank introduced the stranger to her two friends and they sat down in what was known as the Monkey House. It was an enclosure covered with glass overlooking the sea, with a bar at the back, and it was crowded with chattering people in bathing costumes, pyjamas, or dressing-gowns, who were seated at the tables having drinks. Beatrice's soft heart went out to the lorn window, and Arrow, seeing that she was pale, quite ordinary to look at, and probably forty-eight, was prepared to like her very much. A waiter approached them.

'What will you have, Lena dear?' Frank asked.

'Oh, I don't know, what you all have, a dry Martini or a White Lady.'

Arrow and Beatrice gave her a quick look. Everyone knows how fattening cocktails are.

'I daresay you're tired after your journey,' said Frank kindly.

She ordered a dry Martini for Lena and a mixed lemon and orange juice for herself and her two friends.

'We find alcohol isn't very good in all this heat,' she explained.

'Oh, it never affects me at all,' Lena answered airily. 'I like cocktails.'

Arrow went very slightly pale under her rouge (neither she nor Beatrice ever wet their faces when they bathed and they thought it absurd of Frank, a woman of her size, to pretend she liked diving) but she said nothing. The conversation was gay and easy, they all said the obvious things with gusto, and presently they strolled back to the villa for luncheon.

In each napkin were two little antifat rusks. Lena gave a bright smile as she put them by the side of her plate.

'May I have some bread?' she asked.

The grossest indecency would not have fallen on the ears of those three women with such a shock. Not one of them had eaten bread for ten years. Even Beatrice, greedy as she was, drew the line there. Frank, the good hostess, recovered herself first.

'Of course, darling,' she said and turning to the butler asked him to bring some.

'And some butter,' said Lena in that pleasant easy way of hers.

There was a moment's embarrassed silence.

'I don't know if there's any in the house,' said Frank, 'but I'll inquire. There may be some in the kitchen.'

'I adore bread and butter, don't you?' said Lena, turning to Beatrice.

Beatrice gave a sickly smile and an evasive reply. The butler brought a long crisp roll of French bread. Lena slit it in two and plastered it with the butter which was miraculously produced. A grilled sole was served.

'We eat very simply here,' said Frank. 'I hope you won't mind.'

'Oh, no, I like my food very plain,' said Lena as she took some butter and spread it over her fish. 'As long as I can have bread and butter and potatoes and cream I'm quite happy.'

The three friends exchanged a glance. Frank's great sallow face sagged a little and she looked with distaste at the dry, insipid sole on her plate. Beatrice came to the rescue.

'It's such a bore, we can't get cream here,' she said. 'It's one of the things one has to do without on the Riviera.'

'What a pity,' said Lena.

The rest of the luncheon consisted of lamb cutlets, with the fat carefully removed so that Beatrice should not be led astray, and spinach boiled in water, with stewed pears to end up with. Lena tasted her pears and gave the butler a look of inquiry. That resourceful man understood her at once and though powdered sugar had never been served at that table before handed her without a moment's hesitation a bowl of it. She helped herself liberally. The other three pretended not to notice. Coffee was served and Lena took three lumps of sugar in hers.

'You have a very sweet tooth,' said Arrow in a tone which she struggled to keep friendly.

'We think saccharine so much more sweetening,' said Frank, as she put a tiny tablet of it into her coffee.

'Disgusting stuff,' said Lena.

Beatrice's mouth drooped at the corners, and she gave the lump sugar a yearning look.

'Beatrice,' boomed Frank sternly.

Beatrice stifled a sigh, and reached for the saccharine.

Frank was relieved when they could sit down to the bridge table. It was plain to her that Arrow and Beatrice were upset. She wanted them to like Lena and she was anxious that Lena should enjoy her fortnight with them. For the first rubber Arrow cut with the newcomer.

'Do you play Vanderbilt or Culbertson?' she asked her.

'I have no conventions,' Lena answered in a happy-go-lucky way, 'I play by the light of nature.'

'I play strict Culbertson,' said Arrow acidly.

The three fat women braced themselves to the fray. No conventions indeed! They'd learn her. When it came to bridge even Frank's family feeling was forgotten and she settled down with the same determination as the others to trim the stranger in their midst. But the light of nature served Lena very well. She had a natural gift for the game and great experience. She played with imagination, quickly, boldly, and with assurance. The other players were in too high a class not to realize very soon that Lena knew what she was about, and since they were all thoroughly good-natured, generous women, they were gradually mollified. This was real bridge. They all enjoyed themselves. Arrow and Beatrice began to feel more kindly towards Lena, and Frank, noticing this, heaved a fat sigh of relief. It was going to be a success.

After a couple of hours they parted, Frank and Beatrice to have a round of golf, and Arrow to take a brisk walk with a young Prince Roccamare whose acquaintance she had lately made. He was very sweet and young and good-looking. Lena said she would rest.

They met again just before dinner.

'I hope you've been all right, Lena dear,' said Frank. 'I was rather conscience-stricken at leaving you with nothing to do all this time.'

'Oh, don't apologize. I had a lovely sleep and then I went down to Juan and had a cocktail. And d'you know what I discovered? You'll be so pleased. I found a dear little tea-shop where they've got the most beautiful thick fresh cream. I've ordered half a pint to be sent every day. I thought it would be my little contribution to the household.'

Her eyes were shining. She was evidently expecting them to be delighted.

'How very kind of you,' said Frank, with a look that sought to quell the indignation that she saw on the faces of her two friends. 'But we never eat cream. In this climate it makes one so bilious.'

'I shall have to eat it all myself then,' said Lena cheerfully.

'Don't you ever think of your figure?' Arrow asked with icy deliberation.

'The doctor said I must eat.'

'Did he say you must eat bread and butter and potatoes and cream?'

'Yes. That's what I thought you meant when you said you had simple food.'

'You'll get simply enormous,' said Beatrice.

Lena laughed gaily.

'No, I shan't. You see, nothing ever makes me fat. I've always eaten everything I wanted to and it's never had the slightest effect on me.'

The stony silence that followed this speech was only broken by the entrance of the butler.

'*Mademoiselle est servie*,' he announced.

They talked the matter over late that night, after Lena had gone to bed, in Frank's room. During the evening they had been furiously cheerful, and they had chaffed one another with a friendliness that would have taken in the keenest observer. But now they dropped the mask. Beatrice was sullen, Arrow was spiteful and Frank was unmanned.

'It's not very nice for me to sit there and see her eat all the things I particularly like,' said Beatrice plaintively.

'It's not very nice for any of us,' Frank snapped back.

'You should never have asked her here,' said Arrow.

'How was I to know?' cried Frank.

'I can't help thinking that if she really cared for her husband she would hardly eat so much,' said Beatrice. 'He's only been buried two months. I mean, I think you ought to show some resect for the dead.'

'Why can't she eat the same as we do?' asked Arrow viciously. 'She's a guest.'

'Well, you heard what she said. The doctor told her she must eat.'

'Then she ought to go to a sanatorium.'

'It's more than flesh and blood can stand, Frank,' moaned Beatrice.

'If I can stand it you can stand it.'

'She's your cousin, she's not our cousin,' said Arrow. 'I'm not going to sit there for fourteen days and watch that woman make a hog of herself.'

'It's so vulgar to attach all this importance to food,' Frank boomed, and her voice was deeper than ever. 'After all the only thing that counts really is spirit.'

'Are you calling *me* vulgar, Frank?' asked Arrow with flashing eyes.

'No, of course she isn't,' interrupted Beatrice.

'I wouldn't put it past you to go down in the kitchen when we're all in bed and have a good square meal on the sly.'

Frank sprang to her feet.

'How dare you say that, Arrow! I'd never ask anybody to do what I'm not prepared to do myself. Have you known me all these years and do you think me capable of such a mean thing?'

'How is it you never take off any weight then?'

Frank gave a gasp and burst into a flood of tears.

'What a cruel thing to say! I've lost pounds and pounds.'

She wept like a child. Her vast body shook and great tears splashed on her mountainous bosom.

'Darling, I didn't mean it,' cried Arrow.

She threw herself on her knees and enveloped what she could of Frank in her own plump arms. She wept and the mascara ran down her cheeks.

'D'you mean to say I don't look thinner?' Frank sobbed. 'After all I've gone through.'

'Yes, dear, of course you do,' cried Arrow through her tears. 'Everybody's noticed it.'

Beatrice, though naturally of a placid disposition, began to cry gently. It was very pathetic. Indeed, it would have been a hard heart that failed to be moved by the sight of Frank, that lion-hearted woman, crying her eyes out. Presently, however, they dried their tears and had a little brandy and water, which every doctor had told them was the least fattening thing they could drink, and then they felt much better. They decided that Lena should have the nourishing food that had been ordered her and they made a solemn resolution not to let it disturb their equanimity. She was certainly a first-rate bridge player and after all it was only for a fortnight. They would do whatever they could to make her stay enjoyable. They kissed one another warmly and separated for the night feeling strangely uplifted. Nothing should interfere with the wonderful friendship that had brought so much happiness into their three lives.

But human nature is weak. You must not ask too much of it. They ate grilled fish while Lena ate macaroni sizzling with cheese and butter; they ate grilled cutlets and boiled spinach while Lena ate *pâté de foie gras*; twice a week they ate hard-boiled eggs and raw tomatoes, while Lena ate peas swimming in cream and potatoes cooked in all sorts of delicious ways. The chef was a good chef and he leapt at the opportunity afforded him to send up one dish more rich, tasty and succulent than the other.

'Poor Jim,' sighed Lena, thinking of her husband, 'he loved French cooking.'

The butler disclosed the fact that he could make half a dozen kinds of cocktail and Lena informed them that the doctor had recommended her to drink burgundy at luncheon and champagne at dinner. The three fat women persevered. They were gay, chatty and even hilarious (such is the natural gift that women have for deception) but Beatrice grew limp and forlorn, and Arrow's tender blue eyes acquired a steely glint. Frank's deep voice grew more raucous. It was when they played bridge that the strain showed itself. They had always been fond of talking over their hands, but their discussion had been friendly. Now a distinct bitterness crept in and sometimes one pointed out a mistake to another with quite unnecessary frankness. Discussion turned to argument and argument to altercation. Sometimes the session ended in angry silence. Once Frank accused Arrow of deliberately letting her down. Two or three times Beatrice, the softest of the three, was reduced to tears. On another occasion Arrow flung down her cards and swept out of the room in a pet. Their tempers were getting frayed. Lena was the peacemaker.

'I think it's such a pity to quarrel over bridge,' she said. 'After all, it's only a game.'

It was all very well for her. She had had a square meal and half a bottle of champagne. Besides, she had phenomenal luck. She was winning all their money. The score was put down in a book after each session, and hers mounted up day after day with unfailing regularity. Was there no justice in the world? They began to hate one another. And though they hated her too they could not resist confiding in her. Each of them went to her separately and told her how detestable the others were. Arrow said she was sure it was bad for her to see so much of women so much older than herself. She had a good mind to sacrifice her share of the lease and go to Venice for the rest of the summer. Frank told Lena that with her masculine mind it was too much to expect that she could be satisfied with anyone so frivolous as Arrow and so frankly stupid as Beatrice.

'I must have intellectual conversation,' she boomed. 'When you have a brain like mine you've got to consort with your intellectual equals.'

Beatrice only wanted peace and quiet.

'Really I hate women,' she said. 'They're so unreliable; they're so malicious.'

By the time Lena's fortnight drew to its close the three fat women were barely on speaking terms. They kept up appearances before Lena, but when she was not there made no pretences. They had got past quarrelling. They ignored one another, and when this was not possible treated each other with icy politeness.

Lena was going to stay with friends on the Italian Riviera and Frank saw her off by the same train as that by which she had arrived. She was taking away with her a lot of their money.

'I don't know how to thank you,' she said, as she got into the carriage. 'I've had a wonderful visit.'

If there was one thing that Frank Hickson prided herself on more than on being a match for any man it was that she was a gentlewoman, and her reply was perfect in its combination of majesty and graciousness.

'We've all enjoyed having you here, Lena,' she said. 'It's been a real treat.'

But when she turned away from the departing train she heaved such a vast sigh of relief that the platform shook beneath her. She flung back her massive shoulders and strode home to the villa.

'Ouf!' she roared at intervals. 'Ouf!'

She changed into her one-piece bathing-suit, put on her espadrilles and a man's dressing-gown (no nonsense about it), and went to Eden Roc. There was still time for a bathe before luncheon. She passed through the Monkey House, looking about her to say good morning to anyone she knew, for she felt on a sudden at peace with mankind, and then stopped dead still. She could not believe her eyes. Beatrice was sitting at one of the tables, by herself; she wore the pyjamas she had bought at Molyneux's a day or two before, she had a string of pearls round her neck, and Frank's quick eyes saw that she had just had her hair waved; her cheeks, her eyes, her lips were made up. Fat, nay vast, as she was, none could deny that she was an extremely handsome woman. But what was she doing? With the slouching gait of the Neanderthal man which was Frank's characteristic walk she went up to Beatrice. In her black bathing-dress Frank looked like the huge cetacean which the Japanese catch in the Torres Straits and which the vulgar call a sea-cow.

'Beatrice, what are you doing?' she cried in her deep voice.

It was like the roll of thunder in the distant mountans. Beatrice looked at her coolly.

'Eating,' she answered.

'Damn it, I can see you're eating.'

In front of Beatrice was a plate of *croissants* and a plate of butter, a pot of strawberry jam, coffee, and a jug of cream. Beatrice was spreading butter thick on the delicious hot bread, covering this with jam, and then pouring the thick cream over all.

'You'll kill yourself,' said Frank.

'I don't care,' mumbled Beatrice with her mouth full.

'You'll put on pounds and pounds.'

'Go to hell!'

She actually laughed in Frank's face. My God, how good those *croissants* smelt!

'I'm disappointed in you, Beatrice. I thought you had more character.'

'It's your fault. That blasted woman. You would have her down. For a fortnight I've watched her gorge like a hog. It's more than flesh and blood can stand. I'm going to have one square meal if I bust.'

The tears welled up to Frank's eyes. Suddenly she felt very weak and womanly. She would have liked a strong man to take her on his knee and pet her and cuddle her and call her little baby names. Speechless she sank down on a chair by Beatrice's side. A waiter came up. With a pathetic gesture she waved towards the coffee and *croissants.*

'I'll have the same,' she sighed.

She listlessly reached out her hand to take a roll, but Beatrice snatched away the plate.

'No, you don't,' she said. 'You wait till you get your own.'

Frank called her a name which ladies seldom apply to one another in affection. In a moment the waiter brought her *croissants*, butter, jam, and coffee.

'Where's the cream, you fool?' she roared like a lioness at bay.

She began to eat. She ate gluttonously. The place was beginning to fill up with bathers coming to enjoy a cocktail or two after having done their duty by the sun and the sea. Presently Arrow strolled along with Prince Roccamare. She had on a beautiful silk wrap which she held tightly round her with one hand in order to look as slim as possible and she bore her head high so that he should not see her double chin. She was laughing gaily. She felt like a girl. He had just told her (in Italian) that her eyes made the blue of the Mediterranean look like pea-soup. He left her to go into the men's room to brush his sleek black hair and they arranged to meet in five minutes for a drink. Arrow walked on to the women's room to put a little more rouge on her cheeks and a little more red on her lips. On her way she caught sight of Frank and Beatrice. She stopped. She could hardly believe her eyes.

'My God!' she cried. 'You beasts. You hogs.' She seized a chair. 'Waiter.'

Her appointment went clean out of her head. In the twinkling of an eye the waiter was at her side.

'Bring me what these ladies are having,' she ordered.

Frank lifted her great heavy head from her plate.

'Bring me some *pâté de foie gras,*' she boomed.

'Frank!' cried Beatrice.

'Shut up.'

'All right. I'll have some too.'

The coffee was brought and the hot rolls and cream and the *pâté de foie gras* and they set to. They spread the cream on the *pâté* and they ate it. They devoured great spoonfuls of jam. They crunched the delicious crisp bread voluptuously. What was love to Arrow then? Let the Prince keep his palace in Rome and his castle in the Apennines. They did not speak. What they were about was much too serious. They ate with solemn, ecstatic fervour.

'I haven't eaten potatoes for twenty-five years,' said Frank in a far-off brooding tone.

'Waiter,' cried Beatrice, 'bring fried potatoes for three.'

'*Très bien, Madame.*'

The potatoes were brought. Not all the perfumes of Arabia smelt so sweet. They ate them with their fingers.

'Bring me a dry Martini,' said Arrow.

'You can't have a dry Martini in the middle of a meal, Arrow,' said Frank.

'Can't I? You wait and see.'

'All right then. Bring me a double dry Martini,' said Frank.

'Bring three double dry Martinis,' said Beatrice.

They were brought and drunk at a gulp. The women looked at one another and sighed. The misunderstandings of the last fortnight dissolved and the sincere affection each had for the others welled up again in their hearts. They could hardly believe that they had ever contemplated the possibility of severing a friendship that had brought them so much solid satisfaction. They finished the potatoes.

'I wonder if they've got any chocolate éclairs,' said Beatrice.

'Of course they have.'

And of course they had. Frank thrust one whole into her huge mouth, swallowed it and seized another, but before she ate it she looked at the other two and plunged a vindictive dagger into the heart of the monstrous Lena.

'You can say what you like, but the truth is she played a damned rotten game of bridge, really.'

'Lousy,' agreed Arrow.

But Beatrice suddenly thought she would like a meringue.

The
Facts of Life

◆

It was Henry Garnet's habit on leaving the city of an afternoon to drop in at his club and play bridge before going home to dinner. He was a pleasant man to play with. He knew the game well and you could be sure that he would make the best of his cards. He was a good loser; and when he won was more inclined to ascribe his success to his luck than to his skill. He was indulgent, and if his partner made a mistake could be trusted to find an excuse for him. It was surprising then on this occasion to hear him telling his partner with unnecessary sharpness that he had never seen a hand worse played; and it was more surprising still to see him not only make a grave error himself, an error of which you would never have thought him capable, but when his partner, not unwilling to get a little of his own back, pointed it out, insist against all reason and with considerable heat that he was perfectly right. But they were all old friends, the men he was playing with, and none of them took his ill-humour very seriously. Henry Garnet was a broker, a partner in a firm of repute, and it occurred to one of them that something had gone wrong with some stock he was interested in.

'How's the market today?' he asked.

'Booming. Even the suckers are making money.'

It was evident that stocks and shares had nothing to do with Henry Garnet's vexation; but something was the matter; that was evident too. He was a hearty fellow, who enjoyed excellent health; he had plenty of money; he was fond of his wife, and devoted to his children. As a rule he had high spirits, and he laughed easily at the nonsense they were apt to talk while they played; but today he sat glum and silent. His brows were crossly puckered and there was a sulky look about his mouth. Presently, to ease the tension, one of the others mentioned a subject upon which they all knew Henry Garnet was glad to speak.

'How's your boy, Henry? I see he's done pretty well in the tournament.'
Henry Garnet's frown grew darker.

'He's done no better than I expected him to.'

'When does he come back from Monte?'

'He got back last night.'

'Did he enjoy himself?'

'I suppose so; all I know is that he made a damned fool of himself.'

'Oh. How?'

'I'd rather not talk about it if you don't mind.'

The three men looked at him with curiosity. Henry Garnet scowled at the green baize.

'Sorry, old boy. You call.'

The game proceeded in a strained silence. Garnet got his bid, and when he played his cards so badly that he went three down not a word was said. Another rubber was begun and in the second game Garnet denied a suit.

'Having none?' his partner asked him.

Garnet's irritability was such that he did not even reply, and when at the end of the hand it appeared that he had revoked, and that his revoke cost the rubber, it was not to be expected that his partner should let his carelessness go without remark.

'What's the devil's the matter with you, Henry?' he said. 'You're playing like a fool.'

Garnet was disconcerted. He did not so much mind losing a big rubber himself, but he was sore that his inattention should have made his partner lose too. He pulled himself together.

'I'd better not play any more. I thought a few rubbers would calm me, but the fact is I can't give my mind to the game. To tell you the truth I'm in a hell of a temper.'

They all burst out laughing.

'You don't have to tell us that, old boy. It's obvious.'

Garnet gave them a rueful smile.

'Well, I bet you'd be in a temper if what's happened to me had happened to you. As a matter of fact I'm in a damned awkward situation, and if any of you fellows can give me any advice how to deal with it I'd be grateful.'

'Let's have a drink and you tell us all about it. With a K.C., a Home Office official and an eminent surgeon—if we can't tell you how to deal with a situation, nobody can.'

The K.C. got up and rang the bell for a waiter.

'It's about that damned boy of mine,' said Henry Garnet.

Drinks were ordered and brought. And this is the story that Henry Garnet told them.

The boy of whom he spoke was his only son. His name was Nicholas and of course he was called Nicky. He was eighteen. The Garnets had two daughters besides, one of sixteen and the other of twelve, but however unreasonable it seemed, for a father is generally supposed to like his daughters best, and though he did all he could not to show his preference, there was no doubt that the greater share of Henry Garnet's affection was given to his son. He was kind, in a chaffing, casual way, to his daughters, and gave them handsome presents on their birthdays and at Christmas; but he doted on Nicky. Nothing was too good for him. He thought the world of him. He could hardly take his eyes off him. You could not blame him, for Nicky was a son that any parent might have been proud of. He was six foot two, lithe but muscular, with broad shoulders and a slim waist, and he held himself gallantly erect; he had a charming head, well placed on the shoulders, with pale brown hair that waved slightly, blue eyes with long dark lashes under well-marked eyebrows, a full red mouth, and a tanned, clean skin. When he smiled he showed very regular and very white teeth. He was not shy, but there was a modesty in his demeanour that was attractive. In social intercourse he was easy, polite, and quietly gay. He was the offspring of nice, healthy, decent parents, he had been well brought up in a good home, he had been sent to a good school, and the general result was as engaging a specimen of young manhood as you were likely to find in a long time. You felt that he was as honest, open, and virtuous as he looked. He had never given his parents a moment's uneasiness. As a child he was seldom ill and never naughty. As a boy he did everything that was expected of him. His school reports were excellent. He was wonderfully popular, and he ended his career, with a creditable number of prizes, as head of the school and captain of the football team. But this was not all. At the age of fourteen Nicky had developed an unexpected gift for lawn tennis. This was a game that his father not only was fond of, but played very well, and when he discerned in the boy the promise of a tennis-player he fostered it. During the holidays he had him taught by the best professionals and by the time he was sixteen he had won a number of tournaments for boys of his age. He could beat his father so badly that only parental affection reconciled the older player to the poor show he put up. At eighteen Nicky went to Cambridge and Henry Garnet conceived the ambition that before he was through with the university he should play for it. Nicky had all the qualifications for becoming a great tennis-player. He was tall, he had a long reach, he was quick on his feet, and his timing was perfect. He realized instinctively where the ball was coming and, seemingly without hurry, was there to take it. He had a powerful serve, with a nasty break that made it difficult to return, and his forehand drive, low, long, and accurate, was deadly. He was not so good on the backhand and his volleying was wild, but all through the summer before he went to Cambridge Henry Garnet made him work on these points under the best teacher in England. At the back of his mind, though he did not even mention it to Nicky, he cherished a further ambition, to see his son play at Wimbledon, and who could tell, perhaps be chosen to represent his country in the Davis Cup. A great lump came into Henry Garnet's throat as he saw in fancy his son leap over the net to shake hands with the American champion whom he had just defeated, and walk off the court to the deafening plaudits of the multitude.

As an assiduous frequenter of Wimbledon Henry Garnet had a good many friends in the tennis world, and one evening he found himself at a City dinner sitting next to one of them, a Colonel Brabazon, and in due course began talking to him of Nicky and what chance there might be of his being chosen to play for his university during the following season.

'Why don't you let him go down to Monte Carlo and play in the spring tournament there?' said the Colonel suddenly.

'Oh, I don't think he's good enough for that. He's not nineteen yet, he only went up to Cambridge last October; he wouldn't stand a chance against all those cracks.'

'Of course, Austin and von Cramm and so on would knock spots off him, but he might snatch a game or two; and if he got up against some of the smaller fry there's no reason why he shouldn't win two or three matches. He's never been up against any of the first-rate players and it would be wonderful practice for him. He'd learn a lot more than he'll ever learn in the seaside tournaments you enter him for.'

'I wouldn't dream of it. I'm not going to let him leave Cambridge in the middle of a term. I've always impressed upon him that tennis is only a game and it mustn't interfere with work.'

Colonel Brabazon asked Garnet when the term ended.

'That's all right. He'd only have to cut about three days. Surely that could be arranged. You see, two of the men we were depending on have let us down, and we're in a hole. We want to send as good a team as we can. The Germans are sending their best players and so are the Americans.'

'Nothing doing, old boy. In the first place Nicky's not good enough, and secondly, I don't fancy the idea of sending a kid like that to Monte Carlo without anyone to look after him. If I could get away myself I might think of it, but that's out of the question.'

'I shall be there. I'm going as the non-playing captain of the English team. I'll keep an eye on him.'

'You'll be busy, and besides, it's not a responsibility I'd like to ask you to take. He's never been abroad in his life, and to tell you the truth, I shouldn't have a moment's peace all the time he was there.'

They left it at that and presently Henry Garnet went home. He was so flattered by Colonel Brabazon's suggestion that he could not help telling his wife.

'Fancy his thinking Nicky's as good as that. He told me he'd seen him play and his style was fine. He only wants more practice to get into the first flight. We shall see the kid playing in the semi-finals at Wimbledon yet, old girl.'

To his surprise Mrs Garnet was not so much opposed to the notion as he would have expected.

'After all the boy's eighteen. Nicky's never got into mischief yet and there's no reason to suppose he will now.'

'There's his work to be considered; don't forget that. I think it would be a very bad precedent to let him cut the end of term.'

'But what can three days matter? It seems a shame to rob him of a chance like that. I'm sure he'd jump at it if you asked him.'

'Well, I'm not going to. I haven't sent him to Cambridge just to play tennis. I know he's steady, but it's silly to put temptation in his way. He's much too young to go to Monte Carlo by himself.'

'You say he won't have a chance against these crack players, but you can't tell.'

Henry Garnet sighed a little. On the way home in the car it had struck him that Austin's health was uncertain and that von Cramm had his off-days. Supposing, just for the sake of argument, that Nicky had a bit of luck like that—then there would be no doubt that he would be chosen to play for Cambridge. But of course that was all nonsense.

'Nothing doing, my dear. I've made up my mind and I'm not going to change it.'

Mrs Garnet held her peace. But next day she wrote to Nicky, telling him what had happened, and suggested to him what she would do in his place if, wanting to go, he wished to get his father's consent. A day or two later Henry Garnet received a letter from his son. He was bubbling over with excitement. He had seen his tutor, who was a tennis-player himself, and the Provost of his college, who happened to know Colonel Brabazon, and no objection would be made to his leaving before the end of term; they both thought it an opportunity that shouldn't be missed. He didn't see what harm he could come to, and if only, just this once, his father would stretch a point, well, next term, he promised faithfully, he'd work like blazes. It was a very pretty letter. Mrs Garnet watched her husband read it at the breakfast table; she was undisturbed by the frown on his face. He threw it over to her.

'I don't know why you thought it necessary to tell Nicky something I told you in confidence. It's too bad of you. Now you've thoroughly unsettled him.'

'I'm sorry. I thought it would please him to know that Colonel Brabazon had such a high opinion of him. I don't see why one should only tell people the disagreeable things that are said about them. Of course I made it quite clear that there could be no question of his going.'

'You've put me in an odious position. If there's anything I hate it's for the boy to look upon me as a spoil-sport and a tyrant.'

'Oh, he'll never do that. He may think you rather silly and unreasonable, but I'm sure he'll understand that it's only for his own good that you're being so unkind.'

'Christ,' said Henry Garnet.

His wife had a great inclination to laugh. She knew the battle was won. Dear, oh dear, how easy it was to get men to do what you wanted. For appearance sake Henry Garnet held out for forty-eight hours, but then he yielded, and a fortnight later Nicky came to London. He was to start for Monte Carlo next morning, and after dinner, when Mrs Garnet and her elder daughter had left them, Henry took the opportunity to give his son some good advice.

'I don't feel quite comfortable about letting you go off to a place like Monte Carlo at your age practically by yourself,' he finished, 'but there it is and I can only hope you'll be sensible. I don't want to play the heavy father, but there are three things especially that I want to warn you against: one is gambling, don't gamble; the second is money, don't lend anyone money; and the third is women, don't have anything to do with women. If you don't do any of those three things you can't come to much harm, so remember them well.'

'All right, father,' Nicky smiled.

'That's my last word to you. I know the world pretty well and believe me, my advice is sound.'

'I won't forget it. I promise you.'

'That's a good chap. Now let's go up and join the ladies.'

Nicky beat neither Austin nor von Cramm in the Monte Carlo tournament, but he did not disgrace himself. He snatched an unexpected victory over a Spanish player and gave one of the Austrians a closer match than anyone had thought possible. In the mixed doubles he got into the semi-finals. His charm conquered everyone and he vastly enjoyed himself. It was generally allowed that he showed promise, and Colonel Brabazon told him that when he was a little older and had had more practice with first-class players he would be a credit to his father. The tournament came to an end and the day following he was to fly back to London. Anxious to play his best he had lived very carefully, smoking little and drinking nothing, and going to bed early; but on his last evening he thought he would like to see something of the life in Monte Carlo of which he had heard so much. An official dinner was given to the tennis-players and after dinner with the rest of them he went into the Sporting Club. It was the first time he had been there. Monte Carlo was very full and the rooms were crowded. Nicky had never before seen roulette played except in the pictures; in a maze he stopped at the first table he came to; chips of different sizes were scattered over the green cloth in what looked like a hopeless muddle; the croupier gave the wheel a sharp turn and with a flick threw in the little white ball. After what seemed an endless time the ball stopped and another croupier with a broad, indifferent gesture raked in the chips of those who had lost.

Presently Nicky wandered over to where they were playing *trente et quarante*, but he couldn't understand what it was all about and he thought it dull. He saw a crowd in another room and sauntered in. A big game of baccarat was in progress and he was immediately conscious of the tension. The players were protected from the thronging bystanders by a brass rail; they sat round the table, nine on each side, with the dealer in the middle and the croupier facing him. Big money was changing hands. The dealer was a member of the Greek Syndicate. Nicky looked at his impassive face. His eyes were watchful, but his expression never changed whether he won or lost. It was a terrifying, strangely impressive sight. It gave Nicky, who had been thriftily brought up, a peculiar thrill to see someone risk a thousand pounds on the turn of a card and when he lost make a little joke and laugh. It was all terribly exciting. An acquaintance came up to him.

'Been doing any good?' he asked.

'I haven't been playing.'

'Wise of you. Rotten game. Come and have a drink.'

'All right.'

While they were having it Nicky told his friends that this was the first time he had ever been in the rooms.

'Oh, but you must have one little flutter before you go. It's idiotic to leave Monte without having tried your luck. After all it won't hurt you to lose a hundred francs or so.'

'I don't suppose it will, but my father wasn't any too keen on my coming at all and one of the three things he particularly advised me not to do was to gamble.'

But when Nicky left his companion he strolled back to one of the tables where they were playing roulette. He stood for a while looking at the losers' money being raked-in by the croupier and the money that was won paid out to the winners. It was impossible to deny that it was thrilling. His friend was right, it did seem silly to leave Monte without putting something on the table just once. It would be an experience, and at his age you had to have all the experience you could get. He reflected that he hadn't promised his father not to gamble, he'd promised him not to forget his advice. It wasn't quite the same, was it? He took a hundred-franc note out of his pocket and rather shyly put it on number eighteen. He chose it because that was his age. With a wildly beating heart he watched the wheel turn; the little white ball whizzed about like a small demon of mischief; the wheel went round more slowly, the little white ball hesitated, it seemed about to stop, it went on again; Nicky could hardly believe his eyes when it fell into number eighteen. A lot of chips were passed over to him and his hands trembled as he took them. It seemed to amount to a lot of money. He was so confused that he never thought of putting anything on the following round; in fact he had no intention of playing any more, once was enough; and he was surprised when eighteen again came up. There was only one chip on it.

'By George, you've won again,' said a man who was standing near to him.

'Me? I hadn't got anything on.'

'Yes, you had. Your original stake. They always leave it on unless you ask for it back. Didn't you know?'

Another packet of chips was handed over to him. Nicky's head reeled. He counted his gains: seven thousand francs. A queer sense of power seized him; he felt wonderfully clever. This was the easiest way of making money that he had ever heard of. His frank, charming face was wreathed in smiles. His bright eyes met those of a woman standing by his side. She smiled.

'You're in luck,' she said.

She spoke English, but with a foreign accent.

'I can hardly believe it. It's the first time I've ever played.'

'That explains it. Lend me a thousand francs, will you? I've lost everything I've got. I'll give it you back in half an hour.'

'All right.'

She took a large red chip from his pile and with a word of thanks disappeared. The man who had spoken to him before grunted.

'You'll never see that again.'

Nicky was dashed. His father had particularly advised him not to lend anyone money. What a silly thing to do! And to somebody he'd never seen in his life. But the fact was, he felt at that moment such a love for the human race that it had never occurred to him to refuse. And that big red chip, it was almost impossible to realize that it had any value. Oh well, it didn't matter, he still had six thousand francs, he'd just try his luck once or twice more and if he didn't win he'd go home. He put a chip on sixteen, which was his elder sister's age, but it didn't come up; then on twelve, which was his younger sister's, and that didn't come up either; he tried various numbers at random, but without success. It was funny, he seemed to have lost his knack. He thought he would try just once more and then stop; he won. He had made up all his losses and had something over. At the end of an hour, after various ups and downs, having experienced such thrills as he had never known in his life, he found himself with so many chips that they would hardly go in his pockets. He decided to go. He went to the changers' office and he gasped when twenty thousand-franc notes were spread out before him. He had never had so much money in his life. He put it in his pocket and was turning away when the woman to whom he had lent the thousand francs came up to him.

'I've been looking for you everywhere,' she said. 'I was afraid you'd gone. I was in a fever, I didn't know what you'd think of me. Here's your thousand francs and thank you so much for the loan.'

Nicky, blushing scarlet, stared at her with amazement. How he had misjudged her! His father had said, don't gamble; well, he had, and he'd made twenty thousand francs; and his father had said, don't lend anyone money; well, he had, he'd lent quite a lot to a total stranger, and she'd returned it. The fact was that he wasn't nearly such a fool as his father thought: he'd had an instinct that he could lend her money with safety, and you see, his instinct was right. But he was so obviously taken aback that the little lady was forced to laugh.

'What is the matter with you?' she asked.

'To tell you the truth I never expected to see the money back.'

'What did you take me for? Did you think I was a—cocotte?'

Nicky reddened to the roots of his wavy hair.

'No, of course not.'

'Do I look like one?'

'Not a bit.'

She was dressed very quietly, in black, with a string of gold beads round her neck; her simple frock showed off a neat, slight figure; she had a pretty little face and a trim head. She was made up, but not excessively, and Nicky supposed that she was not more than three or four years older than himself. She gave him a friendly smile.

'My husband is in the administration in Morocco, and I've come to Monte Carlo for a few weeks because he thought I wanted a change.'

'I was just going,' said Nicky because he couldn't think of anything else to say.

'Already!'

'Well, I've got to get up early tomorrow. I'm going back to London by air.'

'Of course. The tournament ended today, didn't it? I saw you play, you know, two or three times.'

'Did you? I don't know why you should have noticed me.'

'You've got a beautiful style. And you looked very sweet in your shorts.'

Nicky was not an immodest youth, but it did cross his mind that perhaps she had borrowed that thousand francs in order to scrape acquaintance with him.

'Do you ever go to the Knickerbocker?' she asked.

'No. I never have.'

'Oh, but you mustn't leave Monte Carlo without having been there. Why don't you come and dance a little? To tell you the truth, I'm starving with hunger and I should adore some bacon and eggs.'

Nicky remembered his father's advice not to have anything to do with women, but this was different; you had only to look at the pretty little thing to know at once that she was perfectly respectable. Her husband was in what corresponded, he supposed, to the Civil Service. His father and mother had friends who were Civil Servants and they and their wives sometimes came to dinner. It was true that the wives were neither so young nor so pretty as this one, but she was just as ladylike as they were. And after winning twenty thousand francs he thought it wouldn't be a bad idea to have a little fun.

'I'd love to go with you,' he said. 'But you won't mind if I don't stay very long. I've left instructions at my hotel that I'm to be called at seven.'

'We'll leave as soon as ever you like.'

Nicky found it very pleasant at the Knickerbocker. He ate his bacon and eggs with appetite. They shared a bottle of champagne. They danced, and the little lady told him he danced beautifully. He knew he danced pretty well, and of course she was easy to dance with. As light as a feather. She laid her cheek against his and when their eyes met there was in hers a smile that made his heart go pit-a-pat. A coloured woman sang in a throaty, sensual voice. The floor was crowded.

'Have you ever been told that you're very good-looking?' she asked.

'I don't think so,' he laughed. 'Gosh,' he thought, 'I believe she's fallen for me.'

Nicky was not such a fool as to be unaware that women often liked him, and when she made that remark he pressed her to him a little more closely. She closed her eyes and a faint sigh escaped her lips.

'I suppose it wouldn't be quite nice if I kissed you before all these people,' he said.

'What do you think they would take me for?'

It began to grow late and Nicky said that really he thought he ought to be going.

'I shall go too,' she said. 'Will you drop me at my hotel on your way?'

Nicky paid the bill. He was rather surprised at its amount, but with all that money he had in his pocket he could afford not to care, and they got into a taxi. She snuggled up to him and he kissed her. She seemed to like it.

'By Jove,' he thought, 'I wonder if there's anything doing.'

It was true that she was a married woman, but her husband was in Morocco, and it certainly did look as if she'd fallen for him. Good and proper. It was true also that his father had warned him to have nothing to do with women, but, he reflected again, he hadn't actually promised he wouldn't, he'd only promised not to forget his advice. Well, he hadn't; he was bearing it in mind that very minute. But circumstances alter cases. She was a sweet little thing; it seemed silly to miss the chance of an adventure when it was handed to you like that on a tray. When they reached the hotel he paid off the taxi.

'I'll walk home,' he said. 'The air will do me good after the stuffy atmosphere of that place.'

'Come up a moment,' she said. 'I'd like to show you the photo of my little boy.'

'Oh, have you got a little boy?' he exclaimed, a trifle dashed.

'Yes, a sweet little boy.'

He walked upstairs after her. He didn't in the least want to see the photograph of her little boy, but he thought it only civil to pretend he did. He was afraid he'd made a fool of himself; it occurred to him that she was taking him up to look at the photograph in order to show him in a nice way that he'd made a mistake. He'd told her he was eighteen.

'I suppose she thinks I'm just a kid.'

He began to wish he hadn't spent all that money on champagne at the night-club.

But she didn't show him the photograph of her little boy after all. They had no sooner got into her room than she turned to him, flung her arms round his neck, and kissed him full on the lips. He had never in all his life been kissed so passionately.

'Darling,' she said.

For a brief moment his father's advice once more crossed Nicky's mind and then he forgot it.

Nicky was a light sleeper and the least sound was apt to wake him. Two or three hours later he awoke and for a moment could not imagine where he was. The room was not quite dark, for the door of the bathroom was ajar, and the light in it had been left on. Suddenly he was conscious that someone was moving about the room. Then he remembered. He saw that it was his little friend, and he was on the point of speaking when something in the way she was behaving stopped him. She was walking very cautiously, as though she were afraid of waking him; she stopped once or twice and looked over at the bed. He wondered what she was after. He soon saw. She went over to the chair on which he had placed his clothes and once more looked in his direction. She waited for what seemed to him an interminable time. The silence was so intense that Nicky thought he could hear his own heart beating. Then, very slowly, very quietly, she took up his coat, slipped her hand into the inside pocket and drew out all those beautiful thousand-franc notes that Nicky had been so proud to win. She put the coat back and placed some other clothes on it so that it should look as though it had not been disturbed, then, with the bundle of notes in her hand, for an appreciable time stood once more stock-still. Nicky had repressed an instinctive impulse to jump up and grab her, it was partly surprise that had kept him quiet, partly the notion that he was in a strange hotel, in a foreign country, and if he made a row he didn't know what might happen. She looked at him. His eyes were partly closed and he was sure that she thought he was asleep. In the silence she could hardly fail to hear his regular breathing. When she had reassured herself that her movements had not disturbed him she stepped, with infinite caution, across the room. On a small table in the window a cineraria was growing in a pot. Nicky watched her now with his eyes wide open. The plant was evidently placed quite loosely in the pot, for taking it by the stalks she lifted it out; she put the banknotes in the bottom of the pot and replaced the plant. It was an excellent hiding-place. No one could have guessed that anything was concealed under that richly-flowering plant. She pressed the earth down with her fingers and then, very slowly, taking care not to make the smallest noise, crept across the room and slipped back into bed.

'*Chèri*,' she said, in a caressing voice.

Nicky breathed steadily, like a man immersed in deep sleep. The little lady turned over on her side and disposed herself to slumber. But though Nicky lay so still his thoughts worked busily. He was extremely indignant at the scene he had just witnessed, and to himself he spoke his thoughts with vigour.

'She's nothing but a damned tart. She and her dear little boy and her husband in Morocco. My eye! She's a rotten thief, that's what she is. Took me for a mug. If she thinks she's going to get away with anything like that, she's mistaken.'

He had already made up his mind what he was going to do with the money he had so cleverly won. He had long wanted a car of his own, and had thought it rather mean of his father not to have given him one. After all, a feller doesn't always want to drive about in the family bus. Well, he'd just teach the old man a lesson and buy one himself. For twenty thousand francs, two hundred pounds roughly, he could get a very decent second-hand car. He meant to get the money back, but just then he didn't quite know how. He didn't like the idea of kicking up a row, he was a stranger, in a hotel he knew nothing of; it might very well be that the beastly woman had friends there, he didn't mind facing anyone in a fair fight, but he'd look pretty foolish if someone pulled a gun on him. He reflected besides, very sensibly, that he had no proof the money was his. If it came to a showdown and she swore it was hers, he might very easily find himself hauled off to a police-station. He really didn't know what to do. Presently by her regular breathing he knew that the little lady was asleep. She must have fallen asleep with an easy mind, for she had done her job without a hitch. It infuriated Nicky that she should rest so peacefully while he lay awake worried to death. Suddenly an idea occurred to him. It was such a good one that it was only by the exercise of all his self-control that he prevented himself from jumping out of bed and carrying it out at once. Two could play at her game. She'd stolen his money; well, he'd steal it back again, and they'd be all square. He made up his mind to wait quite quietly until he was sure that deceitful woman was sound asleep. He waited for what seemed to him a very long time. She did not stir. Her breathing was as regular as a child's.

'Darling,' he said at last.

No answer. No movement. She was dead to the world. Very slowly, pausing after every movement, very silently, he slipped out of bed. He stood still for a while, looking at her to see whether he had disturbed her. Her breathing was as regular as before. During the time he was waiting he had taken note carefully of the furniture in the room so that in crossing it he should not knock against a chair or a table and make a noise. He took a couple of steps and waited, he took a couple of steps more; he was very light on his feet and made no sound as he walked; he took fully five minutes to get to the window, and here he waited again. He started, for the bed slightly creaked, but it was only because the sleeper turned in her sleep. He forced himself to wait till he had counted one hundred. She was sleeping like a log. With infinite care he seized the cineraria by the stalks and gently pulled it out of the pot; he put his other hand in, his heart beat nineteen to the dozen as his fingers touched the notes, his hand closed on them and he slowly drew them out. He replaced the plant and in turn carefully pressed down the earth. While he was doing all this he had kept one eye on the form lying in the bed. It remained still. After another pause he crept softly to the chair on which his clothes were lying. He first put the bundle of notes in his coat pocket and then proceeded to dress. It took him a good quarter of an hour, because he could afford to make no sound. He had been wearing a soft shirt with his dinner jacket, and he congratulated himself on this, because it was easier to put on silently than a stiff one. He had some difficulty in tying his tie without a looking-glass, but he very wisely reflected that it didn't really matter if it wasn't tied very well. His spirits were rising. The whole thing now began to seem rather a lark. At length he was completely dressed except for his shoes, which he took in his hand; he thought he would put them on when he got into the passage. Now he had to cross the room to get to the door. He reached it so quietly that he could not have disturbed the lightest sleeper. But the door had to be unlocked. He turned the key very slowly; it creaked.

'Who's that?'

The little woman suddenly sat up in bed. Nicky's heart jumped to his mouth. He made a great effort to keep his head.

'It's only me. It's six o'clock and I've got to go. I was trying not to wake you.'

'Oh, I forgot.'

She sank back on to the pillow.

'Now that you're awake I'll put on my shoes.'

He sat down on the edge of the bed and did this.

'Don't make a noise when you go out. The hotel people don't like it. Oh, I'm so sleepy.'

'You go right off to sleep again.'

'Kiss me before you go.' He bent down and kissed her. 'You're a sweet boy and a wonderful lover. *Bon voyage.*'

Nicky did not feel quite safe till he got out of the hotel. The dawn had broken. The sky was unclouded, and in the harbour the yachts and the fishing-boats lay motionless on the still water. On the quay fishermen were getting ready to start on their day's work. The streets were deserted. Nicky took a long breath of the sweet morning air. He felt alert and well. He also felt as pleased as Punch. With a swinging stride, his shoulders well thrown back, he walked up the hill and along the gardens in front of the Casino—the flowers in that clear light had a dewy brilliance that was delicious—till he came to his hotel. Here the day had already begun. In the hall porters with mufflers round their necks and berets on their heads were busy sweeping. Nicky went up to his room and had a hot bath. He lay in it and thought with satisfaction that he was not such a mug as some people might think. After his bath he did his exercises, dressed, packed, and went down to breakfast. He had a grand appetite. No continental breakfast for him! He had grapefruit, porridge, bacon and eggs, rolls fresh from the oven, so crisp and delicious they melted in your mouth, marmalade, and three cups of coffee. Though feeling perfectly well before, he felt better after that. He lit the pipe he had recently learnt to smoke, paid his bill and stepped into the car that was waiting to take him to the aerodrome on the other side of Cannes. The road as far as Nice ran over the hills and below him was the blue sea and the coast-line. He couldn't help thinking it damned pretty. They passed through Nice, so gay and friendly in the early morning, and presently they came to a long stretch of straight road that ran by the sea. Nicky had paid his bill, not with the money he had won the night before, but with the money his father had given him; he had changed a thousand francs to pay for supper at the Knickerbocker, but that deceitful little woman had returned him the thousand francs he had lent her, so that he still had twenty thousand-franc notes in his pocket. He thought he would like to have a look at them. He had so nearly lost them that they had a double value for him. He took them out of his hip-pocket into which for safety's sake he had stuffed them when he put on the suit he was travelling in, and counted them one by one. Something very strange had happened to them. Instead of there being twenty notes as there should have been there were twenty-six. He couldn't understand it at all. He counted them twice more. There was no doubt about it; somehow or other he had twenty-six thousand francs instead of the twenty he should have had. He couldn't make it out. He asked himself if it was possible that he had won more at the Sporting Club than he had realized. But no, that was out of the question; he distinctly remembered the man at the desk laying the notes out in four rows of five, and he had counted them himself. Suddenly the explanation occurred to him; when he had put his hand into the flower-pot, after taking out the cineraria, he had grabbed everything he felt there. The flower-pot was the little hussy's money-box and he had taken out not only his own money, but her savings as well. Nicky leant back in the car and burst into a roar of laughter. It was the funniest thing he had ever heard in his life. And when he thought of her going to the flower-pot some time later in the morning when she awoke, expecting to find the money she had so cleverly got away with, and finding, not only that it wasn't there, but that her own had gone too, he laughed more than ever. And so far as he was concerned there was nothing to do about it; he neither knew her name, nor the name of the hotel to which she had taken him. He couldn't return her money even if he wanted to.

'It serves her damned well right,' he said.

This then was the story that Henry Garnet told his friends over the bridge-table, for the night before, after dinner when his wife and daughter had left them to their port, Nicky had narrated it in full.

'And you know what infuriated me is that he's so damned pleased with himself. Talk of a cat swallowing a canary. And d'you know what he said to me when he'd finished? He looked at me with those innocent eyes of his and said: "You know, father, I can't help thinking there was something wrong about the advice you gave me. You said, don't gamble; well, I did, and I made a packet; you said, don't lend money; well, I did, and I got it back; and you said, don't have anything to do with women; well, I did, and made six thousand francs on the deal."'

It didn't make it any better for Henry Garnet that his three companions burst out laughing.

'It's all very well for you fellows to laugh, but you know, I'm in a damned awkward position. The boy looked up to me, he respected me, he took whatever I said as gospel truth, and now, I saw it in his eyes, he just looks upon me as a drivelling old fool. It's no good my saying one swallow doesn't make a summer; he doesn't see that it was just a fluke, he thinks the whole thing was due to his own cleverness. It may ruin him.'

'You do look a bit of a damned fool, old man,' said one of the others. 'There's no denying that, is there?'

'I know I do, and I don't like it. It's so dashed unfair. Fate has no right to play one tricks like that. After all, you must admit that my advice was good.'

'Very good.'

'And the wretched boy ought to have burnt his fingers. Well, he hasn't. You're all men of the world, you tell me how I'm to deal with the situation now.'

But they none of them could.

'Well, Henry, if I were you I wouldn't worry,' said the lawyer. 'My belief is that your boy's born lucky, and in the long run that's better than to be born clever or rich.'

Gigolo and Gigolette

◆

The bar was crowded. Sandy Westcott had had a couple of cocktails and he was beginning to feel hungry. He looked at his watch. He had been asked to dinner at half past nine and it was nearly ten. Eva Barrett was always late and he would be lucky if he got anything to eat by ten-thirty. He turned to the barman to order another cocktail and caught sight of a man who at that moment came up to the bar.

'Hullo, Cotman,' he said. 'Have a drink?'

'I don't mind if I do, sir.'

Cotman was a nice-looking fellow, of thirty perhaps, short, but with so good a figure that he did not look it, very smartly dressed in a double-breasted dinner jacket, a little too much waisted, and a butterfly tie a good deal too large. He had a thick mat of black, wavy hair, very sleek and shiny, brushed straight back from his forehead, and large flashing eyes. He spoke with great refinement, but with a Cockney accent.

'How's Stella?' asked Sandy.

'Oh, she's all right. Likes to have a lay-down before the show, you know. Steadies the old nerves, she says.'

'I wouldn't do that stunt of hers for a thousand pounds.'

'I don't suppose you would. No one can do it but her, not from that height, I mean, and only five foot of water.'

'It's the most sick-making thing I've ever seen.'

Cotman gave a little laugh. He took this as a compliment. Stella was his wife. Of course she did the trick and took the risk, but it was he who had thought of the flames, and it was the flames that had taken the public fancy and made the turn the huge success it was. Stella dived into a tank from the top of a ladder sixty feet high, and as he said, there were only five feet of water in the tank. Just before she dived they poured enough petrol on to cover the surface and he set it alight; the flames soared up and she dived straight into them.

'Paco Espinel tells me it's the biggest draw the Casino has ever had,' said Sandy.

'I know. He told me they'd served as many dinners in July as they generally do in August. And that's you, he says to me.'

'Well, I hope you're making a packet.'

'Well, I can't exactly say that. You see, we've got our contract and naturally we didn't know it was going to be a riot, but Mr Espinel's talking of booking us for next month, and I don't mind telling you he's not going to get us on the same terms or anything like it. Why, had a letter from an agent only this morning saying they wanted us to go to Deauville.'

'Here are my people,' said Sandy.

He nodded to Cotman and left him. Eva Barrett sailed in with the rest of her guests. She had gathered them together downstairs. It was a party of eight.

'I knew we should find you here, Sandy,' she said. 'I'm not late, am I?'

'Only half an hour.'

'Ask them what cocktails they want and then we'll dine.'

While they were standing at the bar, emptying now, for nearly everyone had gone down to the terrace for dinner, Paco Espinel passed through and stopped to shake hands with Eva Barrett. Paco Espinel was a young man who had run through his money and now made his living by arranging the turns with which the Casino sought to attract visitors. It was his duty to be civil to the rich and great. Mrs Chaloner Barrett was an American widow of vast wealth; she not only entertained expensively, but also gambled. And after all, the dinners and suppers and the two cabaret shows that accompanied them were only provided to induce people to lose their money at the tables.

'Got a good table for me, Paco?' said Eva Barrett.

'The best.' His eyes, fine, dark Argentine eyes, expressed his admiration of Mrs Barrett's opulent, ageing charms. This also was business. 'You've seen Stella?'

'Of course. Three times. It's the most terrifying thing I've ever seen.'

'Sandy comes every night.'

'I want to be in at the death. She's bound to kill herself one of these nights and I don't want to miss that if I can help it.'

Paco laughed.

'She's been such a success, we're going to keep her on another month. All I ask is that she shouldn't kill herself till the end of August. After that she can do as she likes.'

'Oh, God, have I got to go on eating trout and roast chicken every night till the end of August?' cried Sandy.

'You brute, Sandy,' said Eva Barrett. 'Come on, let's go in to dinner. I'm starving.'

Paco Espinel asked the barman if he'd seen Cotman. The barman said he'd had a drink with Mr Westcott.

'Oh, well, if he comes in here again, tell him I want a word with him.'

Mrs Barrett paused at the top of the steps that led down to the terrace long enough for the press representative, a little haggard woman with an untidy head, to come up with her note-book. Sandy whispered the names of the guests. It was a representative Riviera party. There was an English Lord and his Lady, long and lean both of them, who were prepared to dine with anyone who would give them a free meal. They were certain to be as tight as drums before midnight. There was a gaunt Scotch woman, with a face like a Peruvian mask that has been battered by the storms of ten centuries, and her English husband. Though a broker by profession, he was bluff, military, and hearty. He gave you an impression of such integrity that you were almost more sorry for him than for yourself when the good thing he had put you on to as a special favour turned out to be a dud. There was an Italian countess who was neither Italian nor a countess, but played a beautiful game of bridge, and there was a Russian prince who was ready to make Mrs Barrett a princess and in the meantime sold champagne, motor-cars, and Old Masters on commission. A dance was in progress, and Mrs Barrett, waiting for it to end, surveyed with a look which her short upper lip made scornful the serried throng on the dance floor. It was a gala night and the dining tables were crowded together. Beyond the terrace the sea was calm and silent. The music stopped and the head waiter, affably smiling, came up to guide her to her table. She swept down the steps with majestic gait.

'We shall have quite a good view of the dive,' she said as she sat down.

'I like to be next door to the tank,' said Sandy, 'so that I can see her face.'

'Is she pretty?' asked the Countess.

'It's not that. It's the expression of her eyes. She's scared to death every time she does it.'

'Oh, I don't believe that,' said the City gentleman, Colonel Goodhart by name, though no one had ever discovered how he came by the title. 'I mean, the whole bally stunt's only a trick. There's no danger really, I mean.'

'You don't know what you're talking about. Diving from that height in as little water as that, she's got to turn like a flash the moment she touches the water. And if she doesn't do it right she's bound to bash her head against the bottom and break her back.'

'That's just what I'm telling you, old boy,' said the Colonel, 'it's a trick. I mean, there's no argument.'

'If there's no danger there's nothing to it, anyway,' said Eva Barrett. 'It's over in a minute. Unless she's risking her life it's the biggest fraud of modern times. Don't say we've come to see this over and over again and it's only a fake.'

'Pretty well everything is. You can take my word for that.'

'Well, you ought to know,' said Sandy.

If it occurred to the Colonel that this might be a nasty dig he admirably concealed it. He laughed.

'I don't mind saying I know a thing or two,' he admitted. 'I mean, I've got my eyes peeled all right. You can't put much over on me.'

The tank was on the far left of the terrace, and behind it, supported by stays, was an immensely tall ladder at the top of which was a tiny platform. After two or three dances more, when Eva Barrett's party were eating asparagus, the music stopped and the lights were lowered. A spot was turned on the tank. Cotman was visible in the brilliance. He ascended half a dozen steps so that he was on a level with the top of the tank.

'Ladies and gentlemen,' he cried out, in a loud clear voice, 'you are now going to see the most marvellous feat of the century. Madam Stella, the greatest diver in the world, is about to dive from a height of sixty feet into a lake of flames five foot deep. This is a feat that has never been performed before, and Madam Stella is prepared to give one hundred pounds to anyone who will attempt it. Ladies and gentlemen, I have the honour to present Madam Stella.'

A little figure appeared at the top of the steps that led on to the terrace, ran quickly up to the tank, and bowed to the applauding audience. She wore a man's silk dressing-gown and on her head a bathing-cap. Her thin face was made up as if for the stage. The Italian countess looked at her through her *face-à-main.*

'Not pretty,' she said.

'Good figure,' said Eva Barrett. 'You'll see.'

Stella slipped out of her dressing-gown and gave it to Cotman. He went down the steps. She stood for a moment and looked at the crowd. They were in darkness and she could only see vague white faces and white shirt-fronts. She was small, beautifully made, with legs long for her body and slim hips. Her bathing costume was very scanty.

'You're quite right about the figure, Eva,' said the Colonel. 'Bit un-developed, of course, but I know you girls think that's quite the thing.'

Stella began to climb the ladder and the spot-light followed her. It seemed an incredible height. An attendant poured petrol on the surface of the water. Cotman was handed a flaming torch. He watched Stella reach the top of the ladder and settle herself on the platform.

'Ready?' he cried.

'Yes.'

'Go,' he shouted.

And as he shouted he seemed to plunge the burning torch into the water. The flames sprang up, leaping high, and really terrifying to look at. At the same moment Stella dived. She came down like a streak of lightning and plunged through the flames, which subsided a moment after she had reached the water. A second later she was at the surface and jumped out to a roar, a storm of applause. Cotman wrapped the dressing-gown round her. She bowed and bowed. The applause went on. Music struck up. With a final wave of the hand she ran down the steps and between the tables to the door. The lights went up and the waiters hurried along with their neglected service.

Sandy Westcott gave a sigh. He did not know whether he was disappointed or relieved.

'Top hole,' said the English peer.

'It's a bally fake,' said the Colonel, with his British pertinacity. 'I bet you anything you like.'

'It's over so quickly,' said her English ladyship. 'I mean, you don't get your money's worth really.'

Anyhow it wasn't her money. That it never was. The Italian countess leaned forward. She spoke fluent English, but with a strong accent.

'Eva, my darling, who are those extraordinary people at the table near the door under the balcony?'

'Packet of fun, aren't they?' said Sandy. 'I simply haven't been able to take my eyes off them.'

Eva Barrett glanced at the table the Countess indicated, and the Prince, who sat with his back to it, turned round to look.

'They can't be true,' cried Eva. 'I must ask Angelo who they are.'

Mrs Barrett was the sort of woman who knew the head waiters of all the principal restaurants in Europe by their first names. She told the waiter who was at that moment filling her glass to send Angelo to her.

It was certainly an odd pair. They were sitting by themselves at a small table. They were very old. The man was big and stout, with a mass of white hair, great bushy white eyebrows, and an enormous white moustache. He looked like the late King Humbert of Italy, but much more like a king. He sat bolt upright. He wore full evening dress, with a white tie and a collar that has been out of fashion for hard on thirty years. His companion was a little old lady in a black satin ball dress, cut very low, and tight at the waist. Round her neck were several chains of coloured beads. She wore what was obviously a wig, and a very ill-fitting one at that; it was very elaborate, all curls and sausages, and raven black. She was outrageously made-up, bright blue under the eyes and on the eyelids, the eyebrows heavily black, a great patch of very pink rouge on each cheek, and the lips a livid scarlet. The skin hung loosely on her face in deep wrinkles. She had large bold eyes and they darted eagerly from table to table. She was taking everything in, and every other minute called the old man's attention to someone or other. The appearance of the couple was so fantastic in that fashionable crowd, the men in dinner jackets, the women in thin, pale-coloured frocks, that many eyes were turned on them. The staring did not seem to incommode the old lady. When she felt certain persons were looking at her she raised her eyebrows archly, smiled and rolled her eyes. She seemed on the point of acknowledging applause.

Angelo hurried up to the good customer that Eva Barrett was.

'You wished to see me, my lady?'

'Oh, Angelo, we're simply dying to know who those absolutely marvellous people are at the next table to the door.'

Angelo gave a look and then assumed a deprecating air. The expression of his face, the movement of his shoulders, the turn of his spine, the gesture of his hands, probably even the twiddle of his toes, all indicated a half-humorous apology.

'You must overlook them, my lady.' He knew of course that Mrs Barrett had no right to be thus addressed, just as he knew that the Italian countess was neither Italian nor a countess and that the English lord never paid for a drink if anyone else would pay for it, but he also knew that to be thus addressed did not displease her. 'They begged me to give them a table because they wanted to see Madam Stella do her dive. They were in the profession themselves once. I know they're not the sort of people one expects to see dining here, but they made such a point of it I simply hadn't the heart to refuse.'

'But I think they're a perfect scream. I adore them.'

'I've known them for many years. The man indeed is a compatriot of mine.' The head waiter gave a condescending little laugh. 'I told them I'd give them a table on the condition that they didn't dance. I wasn't taking any risks, my lady.'

'Oh, but I should have loved to see them dance.'

'One has to draw the line somewhere, my lady,' said Angelo gravely.

He smiled, bowed again and withdrew.

'Look,' cried Sandy, 'they're going.'

The funny old couple were paying their bill. The old man got up and put round his wife's neck a large white, but not too clean, feather boa. She rose. He gave her his arm, holding himself very erect, and she, small in comparison, tripped out beside him. Her black satin dress had a long train, and Eva Barrett (who was well over fifty) screamed with joy.

'Look, I remember my mother wearing a dress like that when I was in the schoolroom.'

The comic pair walked, still arm in arm, through the spacious rooms of the

Casino till they came to the door. The old man addressed a commissionaire.

'Be so good as to direct me to the artistes' dressing-rooms. We wish to pay our respects to Madam Stella.'

The commissionaire gave them a look and summed them up. They were not people with whom it was necessary to be very polite.

'You won't find her there.'

'She has not gone? I thought she gave a second performance at two?'

'That's true. They might be in the bar.'

'It won't 'urt us just to go an' 'ave a look, Carlo,' said the old lady.

'Right-o, my love,' he answered with a great roll of the R.

They walked slowly up the great stairs and entered the bar. It was empty but for the deputy-barman and a couple sitting in two arm-chairs in the corner. The old lady released her husband's arm and tripped up with outstretched hands.

''Ow are you, dear? I felt I just 'ad to come and congratulate you, bein' English same as you are. And in the profession meself. It's a grand turn, my dear, it deserves to be a success.' She turned to Cotman. 'And this is your 'usband?'

Stella got out of her arm-chair and a shy smile broke on her lips as she listened with some confusion to the voluble old lady.

'Yes, that's Syd.'

'Pleased to meet you,' he said.

'And this is mine,' said the old lady, with a little dig of the elbow in the direction of the tall white-haired man. 'Mr Penezzi. 'E's a count really, and I'm the Countess Penezzi by rights, but when we retired from the profession we dropped the title.'

'Will you have a drink?' said Cotman.

'No, you 'ave one with us,' said Mrs Penezzi, sinking into an arm-chair. 'Carlo, you order.'

The barman came, and after some discussion three bottles of beer were ordered. Stella would not have anything.

'She never has anything till after the second show,' explained Cotman.

Stella was slight and small, about twenty-six, with light brown hair, cut short and waved, and grey eyes. She had reddened her lips, but wore little rouge on her face. Her skin was pale. She was not very pretty, but she had a neat little face. She wore a very simple evening frock of white silk. The beer was brought and Mr Penezzi, evidently not very talkative, took a long swig.

'What was your line?' asked Syd Cotman, politely.

Mrs Penezzi gave him a rolling glance of her flashing, made-up eyes and turned to her husband.

'Tell 'em who I am, Carlo,' she said.

'The 'uman cannon-ball,' he announced.

Mrs Penezzi smiled brightly and with a quick, birdlike glance looked from one to the other. They stared at her in dismay.

'Flora,' she said. 'The 'uman cannon-ball.'

She so obviously expected them to be impressed that they did not quite know what to do. Stella gave her Syd a puzzled look. He came to the rescue.

'It must have been before our time.'

'Naturally it was before your time. Why, we retired from the profession definitely the year poor Queen Victoria died. It made quite a sensation when we did too. But you've 'eard of me, of course.' She saw the blank look on their faces; her tone changed a little. 'But I was the biggest draw in London. At the Old Aquarium, that was. All the swells came to see me. The Prince of Wales and I don't know who all. I was the talk of the town. Isn't that true, Carlo?'

'She crowded the Aquarium for a year.'

'It was the most spectacular turn they'd ever 'ad there. Why, only a few years ago I went up and introduced meself to Lady de Bathe. Lily Langtry, you know. She used to live down 'ere. She remembered me perfectly. She told me she'd seen me ten times.'

'What did you do?' asked Stella.

'I was fired out of a cannon. Believe me, it was a sensation. And after London I went all over the world with it. Yes, my dear, I'm an old woman now and I won't deny it. Seventy-eight Mr Penezzi is and I shall never see seventy again, but I've 'ad me portrait on every 'oardin' in London. Lady de Bathe said to me: My dear, you was as celebrated as I was. But you know what the public is, give 'em a good thing and they go mad over it, only they want change; 'owever good it is, they get sick of it and then they won't go and see it any more. It'll 'appen to you, my dear, same as it 'appened to me. It comes to all of us. But Mr Penezzi always 'ad 'is 'ead screwed on 'is shoulders the right way. Been in the business since 'e was so 'igh. Circus, you know. Ringmaster. That's 'ow I first knew 'im. I was in a troupe of acrobacks. Trapeze act, you know. 'E's a fine-lookin' man now, but you should 'ave seen 'im then, in 'is Russian boots, and ridin' breeches, and a tight-fittin' coat with frogs all down the front of it, crackin' 'is long whip as 'is 'orses galloped round the ring, the 'andsomest man I ever see in my life.'

Mr Penezzi did not make any remark, but thoughtfully twisted his immense white moustache.

'Well, as I was tellin' you, 'e was never one to throw money about and when the agents couldn't get us bookin's any more 'e said, let's retire. An 'e was quite right, after 'avin' been the biggest star in London, we couldn't go back to circus work any more, I mean, Mr Penezzi bein' a count really, 'e 'ad 'is dignity to think of, so we come down 'ere and we bought a 'ouse and started a pension. It always 'ad been Mr Penezzi's ambition to do something like that. Thirty-five years we been 'ere now. We 'aven't done so badly not until the last two or three years, and the slump came, though visitors are very different from what they was when we first started, the things they want, electric-light and runnin' water in their bedrooms and I don't know what all. Give them a card, Carlo. Mr Penezzi does the cookin' 'imself, and if ever you want a real 'ome from 'ome, you'll know where to find it. I like professional people and we'd 'ave a rare lot to talk about, you and me, dearie. Once a professional always a professional, I say.'

At that moment the head barman came back from his supper. He caught sight of Syd.

'Oh, Mr Cotman, Mr Espinel was looking for you, wants to see you particularly.'

'Oh, where is he?'

'You'll find him around somewhere.'

'We'll be going,' said Mrs Penezzi, getting up. 'Come and 'ave lunch with us one day, will you? I'd like to show you my old photographs and me press cuttin's. Fancy you not 'avin' 'eard of the 'uman cannon-ball. Why, I was as well known as the Tower of London.'

Mrs Penezzi was not vexed at finding that these young people had never even heard of her. She was simply amused.

They bade one another good-bye, and Stella sank back again into her chair.

'I'll just finish my beer,' said Syd, 'and then I'll go and see what Paco wants. Will you stay here, ducky, or would you like to go to your dressing-room?'

Stella's hands were tightly clenched. She did not answer. Syd gave her a look and then quickly glanced away.

'Perfect riot, that old girl,' he went on, in his hearty way. 'Real figure of fun. I suppose it's true what she said. It's difficult to believe, I must say. Fancy 'er drawing all London, what, forty years ago? And the funny thing is, her thinking anybody remembered. Seemed as though she simply couldn't understand us not having heard of her even.'

He gave Stella another glance, from the corner of his eye so that she should not see he was looking at her, and he saw she was crying. He faltered. The tears were rolling down her pale face. She made no sound.

'What's the matter, darling?'

'Syd, I can't do it again tonight,' she sobbed.

'Why on earth not?'

'I'm afraid.'

He took her hand.

'I know you better than that,' he said. 'You're the bravest little woman in the world. Have a brandy, that'll pull you together.'

'No, that'd only make it worse.'

'You can't disappoint your public like that.'

'That filthy public. Swine who eat too much and drink too much. A pack of chattering fools with more money than they know what to do with. I can't stick them. What do they care if I risk my life?'

'Of course, it's the thrill they come for, there's no denying that,' he replied uneasily. 'But you know and I know, there's no risk, not if you keep your nerve.'

'But I've lost my nerve, Syd. I shall kill myself.'

She had raised her voice a little, and he looked round quickly at the barman. But the barman was reading the *Éclaireur de Nice* and paying no attention.

'You don't know what it looks like from up there, the top of the ladder, when I look down at the tank. I give you my word, tonight I thought I was going to faint. I tell you I can't do it again tonight, you've got to get me out of it, Syd.'

'If you funk it tonight it'll be worse tomorrow.'

'No, it won't. It's having to do it twice kills me. The long wait and all that. You go and see Mr Espinel and tell him I can't give two shows a night. It's more than my nerves'll stand.'

'He'll never stand for that. The whole supper trade depends on you. It's only to see you they come in then at all.'

'I can't help it, I tell you I can't go on.'

He was silent for a moment. The tears still streamed down her pale little face, and he saw that she was quickly losing control of herself. He had felt for some days that something was up and he had been anxious. He had tried not to give her an opportunity to talk. He knew obscurely that it was better for her not to put into words what she felt. But he had been worried. For he loved her.

'Anyhow Espinel wants to see me,' he said.

'What about?'

'I don't know. I'll tell him you can't give the show more than once a night and see what he says. Will you wait here?'

'No, I'll go along to the dressing-room.'

Ten minutes later he found her there. He was in great spirits and his step was jaunty. He burst open the door.

'I've got grand news for you, honey. They're keeping us on next month at twice the money.'

He sprang forward to take her in his arms and kiss her, but she pushed him away.

'Have I got to go on again tonight?'

'I'm afraid you must. I tried to make it only one show a night, but he wouldn't hear of it. He says it's quite essential you should do the supper turn. And after all, for double the money, it's worth it.'

She flung herself down on the floor and this time burst into a storm of tears.

'I can't, Syd, I can't. I shall kill myself.'

He sat down on the floor and raised her head and took her in his arms and petted her.

'Buck up, darling. You can't refuse a sum like that. Why, it'll keep us all the winter and we shan't have to do a thing. After all there are only four more days to the end of July and then it's only August.'

'No, no, no. I'm frightened. I don't want to die, Syd. I love you.'

'I know you do, darling, and I love you. Why, since we married I've never looked at another woman. We've never had money like this before and we shall never get it again. You know what these things are, we're a riot now, but we can't expect it to go on for ever. We've got to strike while the iron's hot.'

'D'you want me to die, Syd?'

'Don't talk so silly. Why, where should I be without you? You mustn't give way like this. You've got your self-respect to think of. You're famous all over the world.'

'Like the human cannon-ball was,' she cried with a laugh of fury.

'That damned old woman,' he thought.

He knew that was the last straw. Bad luck, Stella taking it like that.

'That was an eye-opener to me,' she went on. 'What do they come and see me over and over again for? On the chance they'll see me kill myself. And a week after I'm dead they'll have forgotten even my name. That's what the public is. When I looked at that painted old hag I saw it all. Oh, Syd, I'm so miserable.' She threw her arms round his neck and pressed her face to his. 'Syd, it's no good, I can't do it again.'

'Tonight, d'you mean? If you really feel like that about it, I'll tell Espinel you've had a fainting fit. I daresay it'll be all right just for once.'

'I don't mean tonight, I mean never.'

She felt him stiffen a little.

'Syd dear, don't think I'm being silly. It's not just today, it's been growing on me. I can't sleep at night thinking of it, and when I do drop off I see myself standing at the top of the ladder and looking down. Tonight I could hardly get up it, I was trembling so, and when you lit the flames and said go, something seemed to be holding me back. I didn't even know I'd jumped. My mind was a blank till I found myself on the platform and heard them clapping. Syd, if you loved me you wouldn't want me to go through such torture.'

He sighed. His own eyes were wet with tears. For he loved her devotedly.

'You know what it means,' he said. 'The old life. Marathons and all.'

'Anything's better than this.'

The old life. They both remembered it. Syd had been a dancing gigolo since he was eighteen, he was very good-looking in his dark Spanish way and full of life, old women and middle-aged women were glad to pay to dance with him, and he was never out of work. He had drifted from England to the Continent and there he had stayed, going from hotel to hotel, to the Riviera in the winter, to watering-places in France in the summer. It wasn't a bad life they led, there were generally two or three of them together, the men, and they shared a room in cheap lodgings. They didn't have to get up till late and they only dressed in time to go to the hotel at twelve to dance with stout women who wanted to get their weight down. Then they were free till five, when they went to the hotel again and sat at a table, the three of them together, keeping a sharp eye open for anyone who looked a likely client. They had their regular customers. At night they went to the restaurant and the house provided them with quite a decent meal. Between the courses they danced. It was good money. They generally got fifty or a hundred francs from anyone they danced with. Sometimes a rich woman, after dancing a good deal with one of them for two or three nights, would give him as much as a thousand francs. Sometimes a middle-aged woman would ask one to spend a night with her, and he would get two hundred and fifty francs for that. There was always the chance of a silly old fool losing her head, and then there were platinum and sapphire rings, cigarette-cases, clothes, and a wristwatch to be got. One of Syd's friends had married one of them, who was old enough to be his mother, but she gave him a car and money to gamble with, and they lived in a beautiful villa at Biarritz. Those were the good days when everybody had money to burn. The slump came and hit the gigolos hard. The hotels were empty, and the clients didn't seem to want to pay for the pleasure of dancing with a nice-looking young fellow. Often and often Syd passed a whole day without earning the price of a drink, and more than once a fat old girl who weighed a ton had had the nerve to give him ten francs. His expenses didn't go down, for he had to be smartly dressed or the manager of the hotel made remarks, washing cost a packet, and you'd be surprised the amount of linen he needed; then shoes, those floors were terribly hard on shoes, and they had to look new. He had his room to pay for and his lunch.

It was then he met Stella. It was at Évian, and the season was disastrous. She was a swimming instructress. She was Australian, and a beautiful diver. She gave exhibitions every morning and afternoon. At night she was engaged to dance at the hotel. They dined together at a little table in the restaurant apart from the guests, and when the band began to play they danced together to induce the customers to come on to the floor. But often no one followed them and they danced by themselves. Neither of them got anything much in the way of paying partners. They fell in love with one another, and at the end of the season got married.

They had never regretted it. They had gone through hard times. Even though for business reasons (elderly ladies didn't so much like the idea of dancing with a married man when his wife was there) they concealed their marriage, it was not so easy to get a hotel job for the pair of them, and Syd was far from being able to earn enough to keep Stella, even in the most modest pension, without working. The gigolo business had gone to pot. They went to Paris and learnt a dancing act, but the competition was fearful and cabaret engagements were very hard to get. Stella was a good ballroom dancer, but the rage was for acrobatics, and however much they practised she never managed to do anything startling. The public was sick of the apache turn. They were out of a job for weeks at a time. Syd's wrist-watch, his gold cigarette-case, his platinum ring, all went up the spout. At last they found themselves in Nice reduced to such straits that Syd had to pawn his evening clothes. It was a catastrophe. They were forced to enter for the Marathon that an enterprising manager was starting. Twenty-four hours a day they danced, resting every hour for fifteen minutes. It was frightful. Their legs ached, their feet were numb. For long periods they were unconscious of what they were doing. They just kept time to the music, exerting themselves as little as possible. They made a little money, people gave them sums of a hundred francs, or two hundred, to encourage them, and sometimes to attract attention they roused themselves to give an exhibition dance. If the public was in a good humour this might bring in a decent sum. They grew terribly tired. On the eleventh day Stella fainted and had to give up. Syd went on by himself, moving, moving without pause, grotesquely, without a partner. That was the worst time they had ever had. It was the final degradation. It had left with them a recollection of horror and misery.

But it was then that Syd had his inspiration. It had come to him while he was slowly going round the hall by himself. Stella always said she could dive in a saucer. It was just a trick.

'Funny how ideas come,' he said afterwards. 'Like a flash of lightning.'

He suddenly remembered having seen a boy set fire to some petrol that had been spilt on the pavement, and the sudden blaze-up. For of course it was the flames on the water and the spectacular dive into them that had caught the public fancy. He stopped dancing there and then; he was too excited to go on. He talked it over with Stella, and she was enthusiastic. He wrote to an agent who was a friend of his; everyone liked Syd, he was a nice little man, and the agent put up the money for the apparatus. He got them an engagement at a circus in Paris, and the turn was a success. They were made. Engagements followed here and there, Syd bought himself an entire outfit of new clothes, and the climax came when they got a booking for the summer casino on the coast. It was no exaggeration of Syd's when he said that Stella was a riot.

'All our troubles are over, old girl,' he said fondly. 'We can put a bit by now for a rainy day, and when the public's sick of this I'll just think of something else.'

And now, without warning, at the top of their boom, Stella wanted to chuck it. He didn't know what to say to her. It broke his heart to see her so unhappy. He loved her more now even than when he had married her. He loved her because of all they'd gone through together; after all, for five days once they'd had nothing to eat but a hunk of bread each and a glass of milk, and he loved her because she'd taken him out of all that; he had good clothes to wear again and his three meals a day. He couldn't look at her; the anguish in her dear grey eyes was more than he could bear. Timidly she stretched out her hand and touched his. He gave a deep sigh.

'You know what it means, honey. Our connexion in the hotels has gone west, and the business is finished, anyway. What there is'll go to people younger than us. You know what these old women are as well as I do; it's a boy they want, and besides, I'm not tall enough really. It didn't matter so much when I was a kid. It's no good saying I don't look my age because I do.'

'Perhaps we can get into pictures.'

He shrugged his shoulders. They'd tried that before when they were down and out.

'I wouldn't mind what I did. I'd serve in a shop.'

'D'you think jobs can be had for the asking?'

She began to cry again.

'Don't, honey. It breaks my heart.'

'We've got a bit put by.'

'I know we have. Enough to last us six months. And then it'll mean starvation. First popping the bits and pieces, and then the clothes'll have to go, same as they did before. And then dancing in lowdown joints for our supper and fifty francs a night. Out of a job for weeks together. And Marathons whenever we hear of one. And how long will the public stand for them?'

'I know you think I'm unreasonable, Syd.'

He turned and looked at her now. There were tears in her eyes. He smiled, and the smile he gave her was charming and tender.

'No, I don't, ducky. I want to make you happy. After all, you're all I've got. I love you.'

He took her in his arms and held her. He could feel the beating of her heart. If Stella felt like that about it, well, he must just make the best of it. After all, supposing she were killed? No, no, let her chuck it and be damned to the money. She made a little movement.

'What is it, honey?'

She released herself and stood up. She went over to the dressing-table.

'I expect it's about time for me to be getting ready,' she said.

He started to his feet.

'You're not going to do a show tonight?'

'Tonight, and every night till I kill myself. What else is there? I know you're right, Syd. I can't go back to all that other, stinking rooms in fifth-rate hotels and not enough to eat. Oh, that Marathon. Why did you bring that up? Being tired and dirty for days at a time and then having to give up because flesh and blood just couldn't stand it. Perhaps I can go on another month and then there'll be enough to give you a chance of looking round.'

'No, darling. I can't stand for that. Chuck it. We'll manage somehow. We starved before; we can starve again.'

She slipped out of her clothes, and for a moment stood naked but for her stockings, looking at herself in the glass. She gave her reflection a hard smile.

'I mustn't disappoint my public,' she sniggered.

The
Voice of the Turtle

◆

For some time I could not make up my mind if I liked Peter Melrose or not. He had had a novel published that had caused some stir among the rather dreary but worthy people who are always on the lookout for new talent. Elderly gentlemen with nothing much to do but go to luncheon parties praised it with girlish enthusiasm, and wiry little women who didn't get on with their husbands thought it showed promise. I read a few reviews. They contradicted one another freely. Some of the critics claimed that with this first novel the author had sprung into the front rank of English novelists: others reviled it. I did not read it. I have learnt by experience that when a book makes a sensation it is just as well to wait a year before you read it. It is astonishing how many books then you need not read at all. But it chanced that one day I met Peter Melrose. With some misgiving I had accepted an invitation to a sherry party. It was in the top flat of a converted house in Bloomsbury, and I was a trifle out of breath when I had climbed four flights of stairs. My hostesses were two women, much over life-size, in early middle life, the sort of women who know all about the insides of motor-cars and like a good tramp in the rain, but very feminine for all that, fond of eating out of paper bags. The drawing-room, which they called 'our workshop', though being of independent means neither had ever done a stroke of work in her life, was large and bare, furnished with rustless-steel chairs, which looked as though they could with difficulty support the very substantial weight of their owners, glass-topped tables, and a vast divan covered with zebra-skin. On the walls were book-shelves, and pictures by the better-known English imitators of Cézanne, Braque, and Picasso. In the shelves, besides a number of 'curious' books of the eighteenth century (for pornography is ageless) there were only the works of living authors, mostly first editions, and it was indeed to sign some of my own that I had been asked to the party.

It was quite small. There was but one other woman, who might have been a younger sister of my hostesses, for, though stout, she was not quite so stout, though tall, not quite so tall, and though hearty, not quite so hearty. I did not catch her name, but she answered to that of Boofuls. The only man besides myself was Peter Melrose. He was quite young, twenty-two or twenty-three, of the middle height, but with an ungainly figure that made him look squat. He had a reddish skin that seemed to fit over the bones of his face too tightly, a rather large semitic nose, though he was not a Jew, and alert green eyes under bushy eyebrows. His brown hair, cut very short, was scurfy. He was dressed in the brown Norfolk jacket and grey flannel trousers that are worn by the art students who wander hatless along King's Road, Chelsea. An uncouth young man. Nor was there much to attract in his manner. He was self-assertive, disputatious and intolerant. He had a hearty contempt for his fellow-writers which he expressed with zest. The satisfaction he gave me by his breezy attacks on reputations which for my part I considered exaggerated, but prudently held my tongue about, was only lessened by the conviction that no sooner was my back turned than he would tear my own to shreds. He talked well. He was amusing and sometimes witty. I should have laughed at his sallies more easily if those three ladies had not been so unreasonably convulsed by them. They roared with laughter at what he said, whether it was funny or whether it was inept. He said many silly things, for he talked without stopping, but he also said some very clever ones. He had a point of view, crude and not so original as he thought, but sincere. But the most striking thing about him was his eager, impetuous vitality; it was like a hot flame that burnt him with an unendurable fury. It even shed a glow on those about him. He had something, if only that, and when I left it was with a slight sense of curiosity at what would come of him. I did not know if he had talent; so many young things can write a clever novel—that means nothing; but it seemed to me that as a man he was not quite like everybody else. He was the sort of person who at thirty, when time had softened his asperity and experience had taught him that he was not quite so intelligent as he thought, would turn into an interesting and agreeable fellow. But I never expected to see him again.

It was with surprise that I received two or three days later a copy of his novel with a very flattering dedication. I read it. It was obviously autobiographical. The scene was a small town in Sussex, and the characters of the upper middle class that strives to keep up appearances on an inadequate income. The humour was rather brutal and rather vulgar. It grated on me, for it consisted chiefly cf mockery at people because they were old and poor. Peter Melrose did not know how hard those misfortunes are to bear, and that the efforts made to cope with them are more deserving of sympathy than of derision. But there were descriptions of places, little pictures of a room or impressions of the countryside, which were excellently done. They showed tenderness and a sense of the spiritual beauty of material things. The book was written easily, without affectation, and with a pleasant feeling for the sound of words. But what made it indeed somewhat remarkable, so that I understood why it had attracted attention, was the passion that quivered in the love story of which the plot, such as it was, consisted. It was, as is the modern fashion, more than a trifle coarse and, again in the modern fashion, it tailed off vaguely, without any particular result, so that everything was left in the end pretty much as it had been in the beginning; but you did get the impression of young love, idealistic and yet vehemently sexual; it was so vivid and so deeply felt that it took your breath away. It seemed to throb on the printed page like the pulse of life. It had no reticence. It was absurd, scandalous, and beautiful. It was like a force of nature. That was passion all right. There is nothing, anywhere, so moving and so awe-inspiring.

I wrote to Peter Melrose and told him what I thought of his book, then suggested that we might lunch together. He rang me up next day and we made a date.

I found him unaccountably shy when we sat down opposite one another at a table in a restaurant. I gave him a cocktail. He talked glibly enough, but I could not help seeing that he was ill at ease. I gained the impression that his self-assurance was a pose assumed to conceal, from himself, maybe, a diffidence that tortured him. His manners were brusque and awkward. He would say a rude thing and then laugh nervously to cover his own embarrassment. Though he pretended to be so sure of himself he wanted all the time to be reassured by you. By irritating you, by saying the things he thought would annoy, he tried to force from you some admission, tacit it might be, that he was as wonderful as he longed to think himself. He wanted to despise the opinion of his fellows, and nothing was more important to him. I thought him rather an odious young man, but I did not mind that. It is very natural that clever young men should be rather odious. They are conscious of gifts that they do not know how to use. They are exasperated with the world that will not recognize their merit. They have something to give, and no hand is stretched out to receive it. They are impatient for the fame they regard as their due. No, I do not mind odious young men; it is when they are charming that I button up the pockets of my sympathy.

Peter Melrose was extremely modest about his book. He blushed through his reddish skin when I praised what I liked in it, and accepted my strictures with a humility that was almost embarrassing. He had made very little money out of it, and his publishers were giving him a small monthly allowance in advance of royalties on the next one. This he had just started, but he wanted to get away to write it in peace, and knowing I lived on the Riviera he asked me if I could tell him of a quiet place where he could bathe and live cheaply. I suggested that he should come and spend a few days with me so that he could look about till he found something to suit him. His green eyes sparkled when I proposed this and he flushed.

'Shouldn't I be an awful nuisance?'

'No. I shall be working. All I can offer you is three meals a day and a room to sleep in. It'll be very dull, but you can do exactly what you like.'

'It sounds grand. May I let you know if I decide to come?'

'Of course.'

We separated, and a week or two later I went home. This was in May. Early in June I received a letter from Peter Melrose asking, if I had really meant what I said when I invited him to spend a few days with me, whether he might arrive on such and such a date. Well, at the time I had meant it, but now, a month later, I remembered that he was an arrogant and ill-bred youth, whom I had seen but twice and wasn't in the least interested in, and I didn't mean it any longer. It seemed to me very likely that he would be bored stiff. I lived a very quiet life and saw few people. And I thought it would be a great strain on my nerves if he were as rude as I knew he could be, and I as his host felt it behoved me to keep my temper. I saw myself driven beyond endurance, and ringing the bell to have his clothes packed and the car brought round to take him away within half an hour. But there was nothing to do about it. It would save him the cost of board and lodging to spend a short period with me, and if he was tired and unhappy as he said in his letter it might be that it would do him good. I sent him a wire and shortly afterwards he arrived.

He looked very hot and grubby in his grey flannel trousers and brown tweed coat when I met him at the station, but after a swim in the pool he changed into white shorts and a Cochet shirt. He looked then quite absurdly young. He had never been out of England before. He was excited. It was touching to see his delight. He seemed, amid those unaccustomed surroundings, to lose his sense of himself, and he was simple, boyish and modest. I was agreeably surprised. In the evening, after dinner, sitting in the garden, with only the croaking of the little green frogs to break the silence, he began talking to me of his novel. It was a romantic story about a young writer and a celebrated *prima donna*. The theme was reminiscent of Ouida, the last thing I should have expected this hard-boiled youth to write, and I was tickled; it was odd how the fashion completed the circle and returned generation after generation to the same themes. I had no doubt that Peter Melrose would treat it in a very modern way, but there it was, the same old story as had entranced sentimental readers in the three-volume novels of the eighties. He proposed to set it in the beginning of the Edwardian era, which to the young has already acquired the fantastic, far-away feeling of a past age. He talked and talked. He was not unpleasant to listen to. He had no notion that he was putting into fiction his own day-dreams, the comic and touching day-dreams of a rather unattractive, obscure young man who sees himself beloved, to the admiration of the whole world, by an incredibly beautiful, celebrated, and magnificent woman. I always enjoyed the novels of Ouida, and Peter's idea did not at all displease me. With his charming gift of description, his vivid, ingenuous way of looking at material things, fabrics, pieces of furniture, walls, trees, flowers, and his power of representing the passion of life, the passion of love, that thrilled every fibre of his own uncouth body, I had a notion that he might well produce something exuberant, absurd, and poetical. But I asked him a question.

'Have you ever known a *prima donna*?'

'No, but I've read all the autobiographies and memoirs that I could find. I've gone into it pretty thoroughly. Not only the obvious things, you know, but I've hunted around in all sorts of byways to get the revealing touch or the suggestive anecdote.'

'And have you got what you wanted?'

'I think so.'

He began to describe his heroine to me. She was young and beautiful, wilful it is true and with a quick temper, but magnanimous. A woman on the grand scale. Music was her passion; there was music not only in her voice, but in her gestures and in her inmost thoughts. She was devoid of envy, and her appreciation of art was such that when another singer had done her an injury she forgave her when she heard her sing a role beautifully. She was of a wonderful generosity, and would give away everything she possessed when a story of misfortune touched her soft heart. She was a great lover, prepared to sacrifice the world for the man she loved. She was intelligent and well-read. She was tender, unselfish, and disinterested. In fact she was much too good to be true.

'I think you'd better meet a *prima donna*,' I said at last.

'How can I?'

'Have you ever heard of La Falterona?'

'Of course I have. I've read her memoirs.'

'She lives just along the coast. I'll ring her up and ask her to dinner.'

'Will you really? It would be wonderful.'

'Don't blame me if you don't find her quite what you expect.'

'It's the truth I want.'

Everyone has heard of La Falterona. Not even Melba had a greater reputation. She had ceased now to sing in opera, but her voice was still lovely, and she could fill a concert hall in any part of the world. She went for long tours every winter, and in summer rested in a villa by the sea. On the Riviera people are neighbours if they live thirty miles from one another, and for some years I had seen a good deal of La Falterona. She was a woman of ardent temperament, and she was celebrated not only for her singing, but for her love affairs: she never minded talking about them, and I had often sat entranced for hours while with the humour which to me was her most astonishing characteristic she regaled me with lurid tales of royal or very opulent adorers. I was satisfied that there was at least a measure of truth in them. She had been married, for short periods, three or four times, and in one of these unions had annexed a Neapolitan prince. Thinking that to be known as La Falterona was grander than any title, she did not use his name (to which indeed she had no right, since after divorcing him she had married somebody else) but her silver, her cutlery, and her dinner-service were heavily decorated with a coat of arms and a crown, and her servants invariably addressed her as *madame la princesse*. She claimed to be a Hungarian, but her English was perfect; she spoke it with a slight accent (when she remembered), but with an intonation suggestive, I had been told, of Kansas City. This she explained by saying that her father was a political exile who had fled to America when she was no more than a child; but she did not seem quite sure whether he was a distinguished scientist who had got into trouble for his liberal views, or a Magyar of high rank who had brought down on his head the imperial wrath because he had had a love affair with an Archduchess. It depended on whether she was just an artist among artists, or a great lady among persons of noble birth.

With me she was not natural, for that she could never have been if she had tried, but franker than with anyone else. She had a natural and healthy contempt for the arts. She genuinely looked upon the whole thing as a gigantic bluff, and deep down in her heart was an amused sympathy for all the people who were able to put it over on the public. I will admit that I looked forward to the encounter between Peter Melrose and La Falterona with a good deal of sardonic amusement.

She liked coming to dine with me because she knew the food was good. It was the only meal she ate in the day, for she took great care of her figure, but she liked that one to be succulent and ample. I asked her to come at nine, knowing that was the earliest hour she dreamt of eating, and ordered dinner for half past. She turned up at a quarter to ten. She was dressed in apple-green satin, cut very low in front, with no back at all, and she wore a string of huge pearls, a number of expensive-looking rings, and on her left arm diamond and emerald bracelets from the wrist to the elbow. Two or three of them were certainly real. On her raven-black hair was a thin circlet of diamonds. She could not have looked more splendid if she had been going to a ball at Stafford House in the old days. We were in white ducks.

'How grand you are,' I said. 'I told you it wasn't a party.'

She flashed a look of her magnificent black eyes at Peter.

'Of course it's a party. You told me your friend was a writer of talent. I am only an interpreter.' She ran one finger down her flashing bracelets. 'This is the homage I pay to the creative artist.'

I did not utter the vulgar monosyllable that rose to my lips, but offered her what I knew was her favourite cocktail. I was privileged to call her Maria, and she always called me Master. This she did, first because she knew it made me feel a perfect fool, and secondly because, though she was in point of fact not more than two or three years younger than I, it made it quite clear that we belonged to different generations. Sometimes, however, she also called me you dirty swine. This evening she certainly might very well have passed for thirty-five. She had those rather large features which somehow do not seem to betray age. On the stage she was a beautiful woman, and even in private life, notwithstanding her big nose, large mouth, and fleshy face, a good-looking one. She wore a brown make-up, with dark rouge, and her lips were vividly scarlet. She looked very Spanish and, I suspected, felt it, for her accent at the beginning of dinner was quite Sevillian. I wanted her to talk so that Peter should get his money's worth, and I knew there was but one subject in the world that she could talk about. She was in point of fact a stupid woman who had acquired a line of glib chatter which made people on first meeting her think she was as brilliant as she looked; but it was merely a performance she gave, and you soon discovered that she not only did not know what she was talking about, but was not in the least interested in it. I do not think she had ever read a book in her life. Her knowledge of what was going on in the world was confined to what she was able to gather by looking at the pictures in the illustrated press. Her passion for music was complete bunkum. Once at a concert to which I went with her she slept all through the Fifth Symphony, and I was charmed to hear her during the interval telling people that Beethoven stirred her so much that she hesitated to come and hear him, for with those glorious themes singing through her head, it meant that she wouldn't sleep a wink all night. I could well believe she would lie awake, for she had had so sound a nap during the Symphony that it could not but interfere with her night's rest.

But there was one subject in which her interest never failed. She pursued it with indefatigable energy. No obstacle prevented her from returning to it; no chance word was so remote that she could not use it as a stepping-stone to come back to it, and in effecting this she displayed a cleverness of which one would never have thought her capable. On this subject she could be witty, vivacious, philosophic, tragic and inventive. It enabled her to exhibit all the resources of her ingenuity. There was no end to its ramifications, and no limit to its variety. This subject was herself. I gave her an opening at once and then all I had to do was to make suitable interjections. She was in great form. We were dining on the terrace and a full moon was obligingly shining on the sea in front of us. Nature, as though she knew what was proper to the occasion, had set just the right scene. The view was framed by two tall black cypresses, and all round us on the terrace the orange trees in full flower exhaled their heady perfume. There was no wind, and the candles on the table flamed with a steady softness. It was a light that exactly suited La Falterona. She sat between us, eating heartily and thoroughly appreciating the champagne, and she was enjoying herself. She gave the moon a glance. On the sea was a broad pathway of silver.

'How beautiful nature is,' she said. 'My God, the scenery one has to play in.

How can they expect one to sing? You know, really, the sets at Covent Garden are a disgrace. The last time I sang Juliet I just told them I wouldn't go on unless they did something about the moon.'

Peter listened to her in silence. He ate her words. She was better value than I had dared to hope. She got a little tight not only on the champagne but on her own loquaciousness. To listen to her you would have thought she was a meek and docile creature against whom the whole world was in conspiracy. Her life had been one long bitter struggle against desperate odds. Managers treated her vilely, impresarios played foul tricks on her, singers combined to ruin her, critics bought by the money of her enemies wrote scandalous things about her, lovers for whom she had sacrificed everything used her with base ingratitude; and yet, by the miracle of her genius and her quick wits, she had discomfited them all. With joyous glee, her eyes flashing, she told us how she had defeated their machinations and what disaster had befallen the wretches who stood in her way. I wondered how she had the nerve to tell the disgraceful stories she told. Without the smallest consciousness of what she was doing she showed herself vindictive and envious, hard as nails, incredibly vain, cruel, selfish, scheming, and mercenary. I stole a glance now and then at Peter. I was tickled at the confusion he must be experiencing when he compared his ideal picture of the *prima donna* with the ruthless reality. She was a woman without heart. When at last she left us I turned to Peter with a smile.

'Well,' I said, 'at all events you've got some good material.'

'I know, and it all fits in so beautifully,' he said with enthusiasm.

'Does it?' I exclaimed, taken aback.

'She's exactly like my woman. She'll never believe that I'd sketched out the main lines of the character before I'd ever seen her.'

I stared at him in amazement.

'The passion for art. The disinterestedness. She had that same nobility of soul that I saw in my mind's eye. The small-minded, the curious, the vulgar put every obstacle in her way and she sweeps them all aside by the greatness of her purpose and the purity of her ends.' He gave a little happy laugh. 'Isn't it wonderful how nature copies art? I swear to you, I've got her to the life.'

I was about to speak; I held my tongue; though I shrugged a spiritual shoulder I was touched. Peter had seen in her what he was determined to see. There was something very like beauty in his illusion. In his own way he was a poet. We went to bed, and two or three days later, having found a pension to his liking, he left me.

In course of time his book appeared, and like most second novels by young people it had but a very moderate success. The critics had overpraised his first effort and now were unduly censorious. It is of course a very different thing to write a novel about yourself and the people you have known from childhood and to write one about persons of your own invention. Peter's was too long. He had allowed his gift for word-painting to run away with him, the humour was still rather vulgar; but he had reconstructed the period with skill, and the romantic story had that same thrill of real passion which in his first book had so much impressed me.

After the dinner at my house I did not see La Falterona for more than a year. She went for a long tour in South America and did not come down to the Riviera till late in the summer. One night she asked me to dine with her. We were alone but for her companion-secretary, an Englishwoman, Miss Glaser by name, whom La Falterona bullied and ill-treated, hit and swore at, but whom she could not do without. Miss Glaser was a haggard person of fifty, with grey hair and a sallow, wrinkled face. She was a queer creature. She knew everything there was to be known about La Falterona. She both adored and hated her. Behind her back she could be extremely funny at her expense, and the imitation she gave in secret of the great singer with her admirers was the most richly comic thing I have ever heard. But she watched over her like a mother. It was she who, sometimes by wheedling, sometimes by sheer plainness of speech, caused La Falterona to behave herself something like a human being. It was she who had written the singer's exceedingly inaccurate memoirs.

La Falterona wore pale-blue satin pyjamas (she liked satin) and, presumably to rest her hair, a green silk wig; except for a few rings, a pearl necklace, a couple of bracelets, and a diamond brooch at her waist, she wore no jewellery. She had much to tell me of her triumphs in South America. She talked on and on. She had never been in more superb voice and the ovations she had received were unparalleled. The concert halls were sold out for every performance, and she had made a packet.

'Is it true or is it not true, Glaser?' cried Maria with a strong South American accent.

'Most of it,' said Miss Glaser.

La Falterona had the objectionable habit of addressing her companion by her surname. But it must long since have ceased to annoy the poor woman, so there was not much point in it.

'Who was that man we met in Buenos Aires?'

'Which man?'

'You fool, Glaser. You remember perfectly. The man I was married to once.'

'Pepe Zapata,' Miss Glaser replied without a smile.

'He was broke. He had the impudence to ask me to give him back a diamond necklace he'd given me. He said it had belonged to his mother.'

'It wouldn't have hurt you to give it him,' said Miss Glaser. 'You never wear it.'

'Give it him back?' cried La Falterona, and her astonishment was such that she spoke the purest English. 'Give it him back? You're crazy.'

She looked at Miss Glaser as though she expected her there and then to have an attack of acute mania. She got up from the table, for we had finished our dinner.

'Let us go outside,' she said. 'If I hadn't the patience of an angel I'd have sacked that woman long ago.'

La Falterona and I went out, but Miss Glaser did not come with us. We sat on the veranda. There was a magnificent cedar in the garden, and its dark branches were silhouetted against the starry sky. The sea, almost at our feet, was marvellously still. Suddenly La Falterona gave a start.

'I almost forgot. Glaser, you fool,' she shouted, 'why didn't you remind me?' And then again to me: 'I'm furious with you.'

'I'm glad you didn't remember till after dinner,' I answered.

'That friend of yours and his book.'

I didn't immediately grasp what she was talking about.

'What friend and what book?'

'Don't be so stupid. An ugly little man with a shiny face and a bad figure. He wrote a book about me.'

'Oh! Peter Melrose. But it's not about you.'

'Of course it is. Do you take me for a fool? He had the impudence to send it me.'

'I hope you had the decency to acknowledge it.'

'Do you think I have the time to acknowledge all the books twopenny-halfpenny authors send me? I expect Glaser wrote to him. You had no right to ask me to dinner to meet him. I came to oblige you, because I thought you liked me for myself, I didn't know I was just being made use of. It's awful that one can't trust one's oldest friends to behave like gentlemen. I'll never dine with you again so long as I live. Never, never, never.'

She was working herself into one of her tantrums, so I interrupted her before it was too late.

'Come off it, my dear,' I said. 'In the first place the character of the singer in that book, which I suppose is the one you're referring to . . .'

'You don't suppose I'm referring to the charwoman, do you?'

'Well, the character of the singer was roughed out before he'd even seen you, and besides, it isn't in the least like you.'

'How d'you mean, it's not like me? All my friends have recognized me. I mean, it's the most obvious portrait.'

'Mary,' I expostulated.

'My name is Maria and no one knows it better than you, and if you can't call me Maria you can call me Madame Falterona or Princess.'

I paid no attention to this.

'Did you read the book?'

'Of course I read it. When everyone told me it was about me.'

'But the boy's heroine, the *prima donna*, is twenty-five.'

'A woman like me is ageless.'

'She's musical to her finger-tips, gentle as a dove, and a miracle of unselfishness; she's frank, loyal, and disinterested. Is that the opinion you have of yourself?'

'And what is *your* opinion of me?'

'Hard as nails, absolutely ruthless, a born intriguer, and as self-centred as they make 'em.'

She then called me a name which a lady does not habitually apply to a gentleman who, whatever his faults, has never had his legitimacy called in question. But though her eyes flashed I could see that she was not in the least angry. She accepted my description of her as complimentary.

'And what about the emerald ring? Are you going to deny that I told him that?'

The story of the emerald ring was this: La Falterona was having a passionate love-affair with the Crown Prince of a powerful state and he had made her a present of an emerald of immense value. One night they had a quarrel, high words passed, and some reference being made to the ring she tore it off her finger and flung it in the fire. The Crown Prince, being a man of thrifty habit, with a cry of consternation, threw himself on his knees and began raking out the coals till he recovered the ring. La Falterona watched him scornfully as he grovelled on the floor. She didn't give much away herself, but she could not bear economy in others. She finished the story with these splendid words:

'After that I *couldn't* love him.'

The incident was picturesque and had taken Peter's fancy. He had used it very neatly.

'I told you both about that in the greatest confidence and I've never told it to a soul before. It's a scandalous breach of confidence to have to put it into a book. There are no excuses either for him or for you.'

'But I've heard you tell the story dozens of times. And it was told me by Florence Montgomerie about herself and the Crown Prince Rudolf. It was one of her favourite stories too. Lola Montez used to tell it about herself and the King of Bavaria. I have little doubt that Nell Gwyn told it about herself and Charles II. It's one of the oldest stories in the world.'

She was taken aback, but only for an instant.

'I don't see anything strange in its having happened more than once. Everyone knows that women are passionate and that men are as mean as cat's-meat. I could show you the emerald if you liked. I had to have it reset, of course.'

'With Lola Montez it was pearls,' I said ironically. 'I believe they were considerably damaged.'

'Pearls?' She gave that brilliant smile of hers. 'Have I ever told you about Benjy Riesenbaum and the pearls? You might make a story out of it.'

Benjy Riesenbaum was a person of great wealth, but it was common knowledge that for a long time he had been the Falterona's lover. In fact it was he who had bought her the luxurious little villa in which we were now sitting.

'He'd given me a very handsome string in New York. I was singing at the Metropolitan, and at the end of the season we travelled back to Europe together. You never knew him, did you?'

'No.'

'Well, he wasn't bad in some ways, but he was insanely jealous. We had a row on the boat because a young Italian officer was paying me a good deal of attention. Heaven knows, I'm the easiest woman in the world to get on with, but I will not be bullied by any man. After all, I have my self-respect to think of. I told him where he got off, if you understand what I mean, and he slapped my face. On deck if you please. I don't mind telling you I was mad. I tore the string of pearls off my neck and flung it in the sea. "They cost fifty thousand dollars," he gasped. He went white. I drew myself up to my full height. "I only valued them because I loved you," I said. And I turned on my heel.'

'You were a fool,' I said.

'I wouldn't speak to him for twenty-four hours. At the end of that time I had him eating out of my hand. When we got to Paris the first thing he did was to go to Cartier's and buy me another just as good.'

She began to giggle.

'Did you say I was a fool? I'd left the real string in the bank in New York, because I knew I was going back next season. It was an imitation one that I threw in the sea.'

She started to laugh, and her laugh was rich and joyous and like a child's. That was the sort of trick that thoroughly appealed to her. She chortled with glee.

'What fools men are,' she gasped. 'And you, you thought I'd throw a real string into the sea.'

She laughed and laughed. At last she stopped. She was excited.

'I want to sing. Glaser, play an accompaniment.'

A voice came from the drawing-room.

'You can't sing after all that food you walloped down.'

'Shut up, you old cow. Play something, I tell you.'

There was no reply, but in a moment Miss Glaser began to play the opening bars of one of Schumann's songs. It was no strain on the voice, and I guessed that Miss Glaser knew what she was doing when she chose it. La Falterona began to sing, in an undertone, but as she heard the sounds come from her lips and found that they were clear and pure she let herself go. The song finished. There was silence. Miss Glaser had heard that La Falterona was in magnificent voice, and she sensed that she wished to sing again. The *prima donna* was standing in the window, with her back to the lighted room, and she looked out at the darkly shining sea. The cedar made a lovely pattern against the sky. The night was soft and balmy. Miss Glaser played a couple of bars. A cold shiver ran down my spine. La Falterona gave a little start as she recognized the music, and I felt her gather herself together:

> *Mild und leise wie er lächelt*
> *Wie das Auge er öffnet.*

It was Isolde's death song. She had never sung in Wagner, fearing the strain on her voice, but this, I suppose, she had often sung in concerts. It did not matter now that instead of an orchestral accompaniment she had only the thin tinkle of a piano. The notes of the heavenly melody fell upon the still air and travelled over the water. In that too romantic scene, in that starry night, the effect was shattering. La Falterona's voice, even now, was exquisite in its quality, mellow and crystalline; and she sang with wonderful emotion, so tenderly, with such tragic, beautiful anguish that my heart melted within me. I had a most awkward lump in my throat when she finished, and looking at her I saw that tears were streaming down her face. I did not want to speak. She stood quite still looking out at that ageless sea.

What a strange woman! I thought then that I would sooner have her as she was, with her monstrous faults, than as Peter Melrose saw her, a pattern of all the virtues. But then people blame me because I rather like people who are a little worse than is reasonable. She was hateful, of course, but she was irresistible.

The Unconquered

◆

He came back into the kitchen. The man was still on the floor, lying where he had hit him, and his face was bloody. He was moaning. The woman had backed against the wall and was staring with terrified eyes at Willi, his friend, and when he came in she gave a gasp and broke into loud sobbing. Willi was sitting at the table, his revolver in his hand, with a half empty glass of wine beside him. Hans went up to the table, filled his glass and emptied it at a gulp.

'You look as though you'd had trouble, young fellow,' said Willi with a grin.

Hans's face was blood-stained and you could see the gashes of five sharp finger-nails. He put his hand gingerly to his cheek.

'She'd have scratched my eyes out if she could, the bitch. I shall have to put some iodine on. But she's all right now. You go along.'

'I don't know. Shall I? It's getting late.'

'Don't be a fool. You're a man, aren't you? What if it is getting late? We lost our way.'

It was still light and the westering sun streamed into the kitchen windows of the farm-house. Willi hesitated a moment. He was a little fellow, dark and thin-faced, a dress designer in civil life, and he didn't want Hans to think him a cissy. He got up and went towards the door through which Hans had come. When the woman saw what he was going to do she gave a shriek and sprang forwards.

'*Non, non,*' she cried.

With one step Hans was in front of her. He seized her by the shoulders and flung her violently back. She tottered and fell. He took Willi's revolver.

'Stop still, both of you,' he rasped in French, but with his guttural German accent. He nodded his head towards the door. 'Go on. I'll look after them.'

Willi went out, but in a moment was back again.

'She's unconscious.'

'Well, what of it?'

'I can't. It's no good.'

'Stupid, that's what you are. *Ein Weibchen*. A woman.'

Willi flushed.

'We'd better be getting on our way.'

Hans shrugged a scornful shoulder.

'I'll just finish the bottle of wine and then we'll go.'

He was feeling at ease and it would have been pleasant to linger. He had been on the job since morning and after so many hours on his motor-cycle his limbs ached. Luckily they hadn't far to go, only to Soissons—ten or fifteen kilometres. He wondered if he'd have the luck to get a bed to sleep in. Of course all this wouldn't have happened if the girl hadn't been a fool. They had lost their way, he and Willi, they had stopped a peasant working in a field and he had deliberately misled them, and they found themselves on a side road. When they came to the farm they stopped to ask for a direction. They'd asked very politely, for orders were to treat the French population well as long as they behaved themselves. The door was opened for them by the girl and she said she didn't know the way to Soissons, so they pushed in; then the woman, her mother, Hans guessed, told them. The three of them, the farmer, his wife and daughter, had just finished supper and there was a bottle of wine on the table. It reminded Hans that he was as thirsty as the devil. The day had been sweltering and he hadn't had a drink since noon. He asked them for a bottle of wine and Willi had added that they would pay them well for it. Willi was a good little chap, but soft. After all, they were the victors. Where was the French army? In headlong flight. And the English, leaving everything behind, had scuttled like rabbits back to their island. The conquerors took what they wanted, didn't they? But Willi had worked at a Paris dressmaker's for two years. It's true he spoke French well, that's why he had his present job, but it had done something to him. A decadent people. It did a German no good to live among them.

The farmer's wife put a couple of bottles of wine on the table and Willi took twenty francs out of his pocket and gave it to her. She didn't even say thank you. Hans's French wasn't as good as Willi's, but he could make himself understood, and he and Willi spoke it together all the time. Willi corrected his mistakes. It was because Willi was so useful to him in this way that he had made him his friend, and he knew that Willi admired him. He admired him because he was so tall, slim, and broad-shouldered, because his curly hair was so fair and his eyes so blue. He never lost an opportunity to practise his French, and he tried to talk now, but those three French people wouldn't meet him half-way. He told them that he was a farmer's son himself and when the war was over was going back to the farm. He had been sent to school in Munich because his mother wanted him to go into business, but his heart wasn't in it, and so after matriculating he had gone to an agricultural college.

'You came here to ask your way and now you know it,' said the girl. 'Drink up your wine and go.'

He had hardly looked at her before. She wasn't pretty, but she had fine dark eyes and a straight nose. Her face was very pale. She was plainly dressed, but somehow she didn't look quite like what she evidently was. There was a sort of distinction about her. Ever since the war started he'd heard fellows talk about the French girls. They had something the German girls hadn't. Chic, Willi said it was, but when he asked him just what he meant by that Willi could only say that you had to see it to understand. Of course he'd heard others say that they were mercenary and hard as nails. Well, they'd be in Paris in a week and he'd find out for himself. They said the High Command had already arranged for houses for the men to go to.

'Finish your wine and let's go,' said Willi.

But Hans was feeling comfortable and didn't want to be hurried.

'You don't look like a farmer's daughter,' he said to the girl.

'And so what?' she answered.

'She's a teacher,' said her mother.

'Then you've had a good education.' She shrugged her shoulders, but he went on good-humouredly in his bad French. 'You ought to understand that this is the best thing that has ever happened to the French people. We didn't declare war. You declared war. And now we're going to make France a decent country. We're going to put order into it. We're going to teach you to work. You'll learn obedience and discipline.'

She clenched her fists and looked at him, her eyes black with hatred. But she did not speak.

'You're drunk, Hans,' said Willi.

'I'm as sober as a judge. I'm only telling them the truth and they may just as well know it at once.'

'He's right,' she cried out, unable any longer to contain herself. 'You're drunk. Now go. Go.'

'Oh, you understand German, do you? All right, I'll go. But you must give me a kiss first.'

She took a step back to avoid him, but he seized her wrist.

'Father,' she cried. 'Father.'

The farmer flung himself on the German. Hans let go of her and with all his might hit him in the face. He crumpled up on the floor. Then, before she could escape him, he caught the girl in his arms. She gave him a swinging blow on the cheek. . . . He chuckled grimly.

'Is that how you take it when a German soldier wants to kiss you? You'll pay for this.'

With his great strength he pinioned her arms and was dragging her out of the door, but her mother rushed at him and catching him by the clothes tried to pull him away. With one arm holding the girl close to him, with the flat of his other hand he gave the woman a great push and she staggered back to the wall.

'Hans, Hans,' cried Willi.

'Shut up, damn you.'

He put his hands over the girl's mouth to stop her shrieking and carried her out of the room. That was how it had happened and you had to admit that she'd brought it on herself. She shouldn't have slapped him. If she'd given him the kiss he'd asked for he'd have gone away. He gave a glance at the farmer still lying where he had fallen and he could hardly help laughing at his funny face. There was a smile in his eyes when he looked at the woman cowering against the wall. Was she afraid it was her turn next? Not likely. He remembered a French proverb.

'*C'est le premier pas qui coûte.* There's nothing to cry about, old woman. It had to come sooner or later.' He put his hand to his hip pocket and pulled out a wallet. 'Look, here's a hundred francs so that mademoiselle can buy herself a new dress. There's not much left of that one.' He placed the note on the table and put his helmet back on his head. 'Let's go.'

They slammed the door behind them and got on their motor-cycles. The woman went into the parlour. Her daughter was lying on the divan. She was lying as he had left her and she was weeping bitterly.

Three months later Hans found himself in Soissons again. He had been in Paris with the conquering army and had ridden through the Arc de Triomphe on his motor-cycle. He had advanced with the army first to Tours and then to Bordeaux. He'd seen very little fighting. The only French soldiers he'd seen were prisoners. The campaign had been the greatest spree he could ever have imagined. After the armistice he had spent a month in Paris. He'd sent picture postcards to his family in Bavaria and bought them all presents. Willi, because he knew the city like the palm of his hand, had stayed on, but he and the rest of his unit were sent to Soissons to join the force that was holding it. It was a nice little town and he was comfortably billeted. Plenty to eat and champagne for less than a mark a bottle in German money. When he was ordered to proceed there it had occurred to him that it would be fun to go and have a look at the girl he'd had. He'd take her a pair of silk stockings to show there was no ill-feeling. He had a good bump of locality and he thought he would be able to find the farm without difficulty. So one afternoon, when he had nothing to do, he put the silk stockings in his pocket and got on his machine. It was a lovely autumn day, with hardly a cloud in the sky, and it was pretty, undulating country that he rode through. It had been fine and dry for so long that, though it was September, not èven the restless poplars gave sign that the summer was drawing to an end. He took one wrong turning, which delayed him, but for all that he got to the place he sought in less than half an hour. A mongrel dog barked at him as he walked up to the door. He did not knock, but turned the handle and stepped in. The girl was sitting at the table peeling potatoes. She sprang to her feet when she saw the uniformed man.

'What d'you want?' Then she recognized him. She backed to the wall, clutching the knife in her hands. 'It's you. *Cochon*.'

'Don't get excited. I'm not going to hurt you. Look. I've brought you some silk stockings.'

'Take them away and take yourself off with them.'

'Don't be silly. Drop that knife. You'll only get hurt if you try to be nasty. You needn't be afraid of me.'

'I'm not afraid of you,' she said.

She let the knife fall to the floor. He took off his helmet and sat down. He reached out with his foot and drew the knife towards him.

'Shall I peel some of your potatoes for you?' She did not answer. He bent down for the knife and then took a potato out of the bowl and went to work on it. Her face hard, her eyes hostile, she stood against the wall and watched him. He smiled at her disarmingly. 'Why do you look so cross? I didn't do you much harm, you know. I was excited, we all were, they'd talked of the invincible French army and the Maginot line . . .' he finished the sentence with a chuckle. 'And the wine went to my head. You might have fared worse. Women have told me that I'm not a bad-looking fellow.'

She looked him up and down scornfully.

'Get out of here.'

'Not until I choose.'

'If you don't go my father will go to Soissons and complain to the general.'

'Much he'll care. Our orders are to make friends with the population. What's your name?'

'That's not your business.'

There was a flush in her cheeks now and her angry eyes were blazing. She was prettier than he remembered her. He hadn't done so badly. She had a refinement that suggested the city-dweller rather than the peasant. He remembered her mother saying she was a teacher. Because she was almost a lady it amused him to torment her. He felt strong and healthy. He passed his hand through his curly blond hair, and giggled when he thought that many girls would have jumped at the chance she had had. His face was so deeply tanned by the summer that his eyes were startlingly blue.

'Where are your father and mother?'

'Working in the fields.'

'I'm hungry. Give me a bit of bread and cheese and a glass of wine. I'll pay.'

She gave a harsh laugh.

'We haven't seen cheese for three months. We haven't enough bread to stay our hunger. The French took our horses a year ago and now the Boches have taken our cows, our pigs, our chickens, everything.'

'Well, they paid you for them.'

'Can we eat the worthless paper they gave us?'

She began to cry.

'Are you hungry?'

'Oh, no,' she answered bitterly, 'we can eat like kings on potatoes and bread and turnips and lettuce. Tomorrow my father's going to Soissons to see if he can buy some horse meat.'

'Listen, Miss. I'm not a bad fellow. I'll bring you a cheese, and I think I can get hold of a bit of ham.'

'I don't want your presents. I'll starve before I touch the food you swine have stolen from us.'

'We'll see,' he said good-humouredly.

He put on his hat, got up, and with an *Au revoir, mademoiselle*, walked out.

He wasn't supposed to go joy-riding round the country and he had to wait to be sent on an errand before he was able to get to the farm again. It was ten days later. He walked in as unceremoniously as before and this time he found the farmer and his wife in the kitchen. It was round about noon and the woman was stirring a pot on the stove. The man was seated at table. They gave him a glance when he came in, but there was no surprise in it. Their daughter had evidently told them of his visit. They did not speak. The woman went on with her cooking, and the man, a surly look on his face, stared at the oil-cloth on the table. But it required more than this to disconcert the good-humoured Hans.

'*Bonjour, la compagnie,*' he said cheerfully. 'I've brought you a present.'

He undid the package he had with him and set out a sizeable piece of Gruyère cheese, a piece of pork, and a couple of tins of sardines. The woman turned round and he smiled when he saw the light of greed in her eyes. The man looked at the foodstuff sullenly. Hans gave him his sunny grin.

'I'm sorry we had a misunderstanding the first time I came here. But you shouldn't have interfered.'

At that moment the girl came in.

'What are you doing here?' she cried harshly. Then her eyes fell on the things he had brought. She swept them together and flung them at him. 'Take them away. Take them.'

But her mother sprang forward.

'Annette, you're crazy.'

'I won't take his presents.'

'It's our own food that they've stolen from us. Look at the sardines. They're Bordeaux sardines.'

She picked the things up. Hans looked at the girl with a mocking smile in his light blue eyes.

'Annette's your name, is it? A pretty name. Do you grudge your parents a little food? You said you hadn't had cheese for three months. I couldn't get any ham; I did the best I could.'

The farmer's wife took the lump of meat in her hands and pressed it to her bosom. You felt that she could have kissed it. Tears ran down Annette's cheeks.

'The shame of it,' she groaned.

'Oh, come now, there's no shame in a bit of Gruyère and a piece of pork.'

Hans sat down and lit a cigarette. Then he passed the packet over to the old man. The farmer hesitated for a moment, but the temptation was too strong for him; he took one and handed back the packet.

'Keep it,' said Hans. 'I can get plenty more.' He inhaled the smoke and blew a cloud of it from his nostrils. 'Why can't we be friends? What's done can't be undone. War is war, and, well, you know what I mean. I know Annette's an educated girl and I want her to think well of me. I expect we shall be in Soissons for quite a while and I can bring you something now and then to help out. You know, we do all we can to make friends with the townspeople, but they won't let us. They won't even look at us when we pass them in the street. After all, it was an accident, what happened that time I came here with Willi. You needn't be afraid of me. I'll respect Annette as if she was my own sister.'

'Why do you want to come here? Why can't you leave us alone?' asked Annette.

He really didn't know. He didn't like to say that he wanted a little human friendship. The silent hostility that surrounded them all at Soissons got on his nerves so that sometimes he wanted to go up to a Frenchman who looked at him as if he wasn't there and knock him down, and sometimes it affected him so that he was almost inclined to cry. It would be nice if he had some place to go where he was welcome. He spoke the truth when he said he had no desire for Annette. She wasn't the sort of woman he fancied. He liked women to be tall and full-breasted, blue-eyed, and fair-haired like himself; he liked them to be strong and hefty and well-covered. That refinement which he couldn't account for, that thin fine nose and those dark eyes, the long pale face—there was something intimidating about the girl, so that if he hadn't been excited by the great victories of the German armies, if he hadn't been so tired and yet so elated, if he hadn't drunk all that wine on an empty stomach, it would never have crossed his mind that he could have anything to do with her.

For a fortnight after that Hans couldn't get away. He'd left the food at the farm and he had no doubt that the old people had wolfed it. He wondered if Annette had eaten it too; he wouldn't have been surprised to discover that the moment his back was turned she had set to with the others. These French people, they couldn't resist getting something for nothing. They were weak and decadent. She hated him, yes, God, how she hated him, but pork was pork, and cheese was cheese. He thought of her quite a lot. It tantalized him that she should have such a loathing for him. He was used to being liked by women. It would be funny if one of these days she fell in love with him. He'd been her first lover and he'd heard the students at Munich over their beer saying that it was her first lover a woman loved, after that it was love. When he'd set his mind on getting a girl he'd never failed yet. Hans laughed to himself and a sly look came into his eyes.

At last he got his chance to go to the farm. He got hold of cheese and butter, sugar, a tin of sausages, and some coffee, and set off on his motor-cycle. But that time he didn't see Annette. She and her father were at work in the fields. The old woman was in the yard and her face lit up when she saw the parcel he was bringing. She led him into the kitchen. Her hands trembled a little as she untied the string and when she saw what he had brought her eyes filled with tears.

'You're very good,' she said.

'May I sit down?' he asked politely.

'Of course.' She looked out of the window and Hans guessed that she wanted to make sure that Annette was not coming. 'Can I offer you a glass of wine.'

'I'd be glad of it.'

He was sharp enough to see that her greed for food had made her, if not friendly to him, at least willing to come to terms with him. That look out of the window made them almost fellow conspirators.

'Did you like the pork?' he asked.

'It was a treat.'

'I'll try to bring you some more next time I come. Did Annette like it?'

'She wouldn't touch a thing you'd left. She said she'd rather starve.'

'Silly.'

'That's what I said to her. As long as the food is there, I said, there's nothing to be gained by not eating it.'

They chatted quite amicably while Hans sipped his wine. He discovered that she was called Madame Périer. He asked her whether there were any other members of the family. She sighed. No, they'd had a son, but he'd been mobilized at the beginning of the war and he'd died. He hadn't been killed, he'd got pneumonia and died in the hospital at Nancy.

'I'm sorry,' said Hans.

'Perhaps he's better off than if he'd lived. He was like Annette in many ways. He could never have borne the shame of defeat.' She sighed again. 'Oh, my poor friend, we've been betrayed.'

'Why did you want to fight for the Poles? What were they to you?'

'You're right. If we had let your Hitler take Poland he would have left us alone.'

When Hans got up to go he said he would come again soon.

'I shan't forget the pork.'

Then Hans had a lucky break; he was given a job that took him twice a week to a town in the vicinity so that he was able to get to the farm much oftener. He took care never to come without bringing something. But he made no headway with Annette. Seeking to ingratiate himself with her, he used the simple wiles that he had discovered went down with women; but they only excited her derision. Thin-lipped and hard, she looked at him as though he were dirt. On more than one occasion she made him so angry that he would have liked to take her by the shoulders and shake the life out of her. Once he found her alone, and when she got up to go he barred her passage.

'Stop where you are. I want to talk to you.'

'Talk. I am a woman and defenceless.'

'What I want to say is this: for all I know I may be here for a long time. Things aren't going to get easier for you French, they're going to get harder. I can be useful to you. Why don't you be reasonable like your father and mother?'

It was true that old Périer had come round. You couldn't say that he was cordial, he was indeed cold and gruff, but he was civil. He had even asked Hans to bring him some tobacco, and when he wouldn't accept payment for it had thanked him. He was pleased to hear the news of Soissons and grabbed the paper that Hans brought him. Hans, a farmer's son, could talk about the farm as one who knew. It was a good farm, not too big and not too small, well watered, for a sizeable brook ran through it, and well wooded, with arable land and pasture. Hans listened with understanding sympathy when the old man bewailed himself because without labour, without fertilizers, his stock taken from him, it was all going to rack and ruin.

'You ask me why I can't be reasonable like my father and mother,' said Annette.

She pulled her dress tight and showed herself to him. He couldn't believe his eyes. What he saw caused such a convulsion in his soul as he had never known. The blood rushed to his cheeks.

'You're pregnant.'

She sank back on her chair and leaning her head on her hands began to weep as though her heart would break.

'The shame of it. The shame.'

He sprang towards her to take her in his arms.

'My sweet,' he cried.

But she sprang to her feet and pushed him away.

'Don't touch me. Go away. Go away. Haven't you done me enough harm already?'

She flung out of the room. He waited by himself for a few minutes. He was bewildered. His thoughts in a whirl, he rode slowly back to Soissons, and when he went to bed he couldn't get to sleep for hours. He could think of nothing but Annette and her swollen body. She had been unbearably pathetic as she sat there at the table crying her eyes out. It was his child she bore in her womb. He began to feel drowsy, and then with a start he was once more wide awake, for suddenly it came to him, it came to him with the shattering suddenness of gunfire: he was in love with her. It was such a surprise, such a shock that he couldn't cope with it. Of course he'd thought of her a lot, but never in that way, he'd thought it would be a great joke if he made her fall in love with him, it would be a triumph if the time came when she offered what he had taken by force; but not for a moment had it occurred to him that she was anything to him but a woman like another. She wasn't his type. She wasn't very pretty. There was nothing to her. Why should he have all of a sudden this funny feeling for her? It wasn't a pleasant feeling either, it was a pain. But he knew what it was all right; it was love, and it made him feel happier than he had ever felt in his life. He wanted to take her in his arms, he wanted to pet her, he wanted to kiss those tear-stained eyes of hers. He didn't desire her, he thought, as a man desires a woman, he wanted to comfort her, wanted her to smile at him—strange, he had never seen her smile, he wanted to see her eyes—fine eyes they were, beautiful eyes—soft with tenderness.

For three days he could not leave Soissons and for three days, three days and three nights, he thought of Annette and the child she would bear. Then he was able to go to the farm. He wanted to see Madame Périer by herself, and luck was with him, for he met her on the road some way from the house. She had been gathering sticks in the wood and was going home with a great bundle on her back. He stopped his motor-cycle. He knew that the friendliness she showed him was due only to the provisions he brought with him, but he didn't care; it was enough that she was mannerly, and that she was prepared to be so as long as she could get something out of him. He told her he wanted to talk to her and asked her to put her bundle down. She did as he bade. It was a grey, cloudy day, but not cold.

'I know about Annette,' he said.

She started.

'How did you find out? She was set on your not knowing.'

'She told me.'

'That was a pretty job of work you did that evening.'

'I didn't know. Why didn't you tell me sooner?'

She began to talk, not bitterly, not blaming him even, but as though it were a misfortune of nature, like a cow dying in giving birth to a calf or a sharp spring frost nipping the fruit trees and ruining the crop, a misfortune that human kind must accept with resignation and humility. After that dreadful night Annette had been in bed for days with a high fever. They thought she was going out of her mind. She would scream for hours on end. There were no doctors to be got. The village doctor had been called to the colours. Even in Soissons there were only two doctors left, old men both of them, and how could they get to the farm even if it had been possible to send for them? They weren't allowed to leave the town. Even when the fever went down Annette was too ill to leave her bed, and when she got up she was so weak, so pale, it was pitiful. The shock had been terrible, and when a month went by, and another month, without her being unwell she paid no attention. She had always been irregular. It was Madame Périer who first suspected that something was wrong. She questioned Annette. They were terrified, both of them, but they weren't certain and they said nothing to Périer. When the third month came it was impossible to doubt any longer. Annette was pregnant.

They had an old Citroën in which before the war Madame Périer had taken the farm produce into the market at Soissons two mornings a week, but since the German occupation they had had nothing to sell that made the journey worth while. Petrol was almost unobtainable. But now they got it out and drove into town. The only cars to be seen were the military cars of the Germans. German soldiers lounged about. There were German signs in the streets, and on public buildings proclamations in French signed by the Officer Commanding. Many shops were closed. They went to the old doctor they knew, and he confirmed their suspicions. But he was a devout Catholic and would not help them. When they wept he shrugged his shoulders.

'You're not the only one,' he said. '*Il faut souffrir.*'

They knew about the other doctor too and went to see him. They rang the bell and for a long time no one answered. At last the door was opened by a sad-faced woman in black, but when they asked to see the doctor she began to cry. He had been arrested by the Germans because he was a freemason, and was held as a hostage. A bomb had exploded in a café frequented by German officers and two had been killed and several wounded. If the guilty were not handed over before a certain date he was to be shot. The woman seemed kindly and Madame Périer told her of their trouble.

'The brutes,' she said. She looked at Annette with compassion 'My poor child.'

She gave them the address of a midwife in the town and told them to say that they had come from her. The midwife gave them some medicine. It made Annette so ill that she thought she was going to die, but it had no further effect. Annette was still pregnant.

That was the story that Madame Périer told Hans. For a while he was silent.

'It's Sunday tomorrow,' he said then. 'I shall have nothing to do. I'll come and we'll talk. I'll bring something nice.'

'We have no needles. Can you bring some?'

'I'll try.'

She hoisted the bundle of sticks on her back and trudged down the road. Hans went back to Soissons. He dared not use his motor-cycle, so next day he hired a push-bike. He tied his parcel of food on the carrier. It was a larger parcel than usual because he had put a bottle of champagne into it. He got to the farm when the gathering darkness made it certain that they would all be home from work. It was warm and cosy in the kitchen when he walked in. Madame Périer was cooking and her husband was reading a *Paris-Soir*. Annette was darning stockings.

'Look, I've brought you some needles,' he said, as he undid his parcel. 'And here's some material for you, Annette.'

'I don't want it.'

'Don't you?' he grinned. 'You'll have to begin making things for the baby.'

'That's true, Annette,' said her mother, 'and we have nothing.' Annette did not look up from her sewing. Madame Périer's greedy eyes ran over the contents of the parcel. 'A bottle of champagne.'

Hans chuckled.

'I'll tell you what that's for presently. I've had an idea.' He hesitated for a moment, then drew up a chair and sat down facing Annette. 'I don't know quite how to begin. I'm sorry for what I did that night, Annette. It wasn't my fault, it was the circumstances. Can't you forgive me?'

She threw him a look of hatred.

'Never. Why don't you leave me alone? Isn't it enough that you've ruined my life?'

'Well, that's just it. Perhaps I haven't. When I knew you were going to have a baby it had a funny effect on me. It's all different now. It's made me so proud.'

'Proud?' she flung at him viciously.

'I want you to have the baby, Annette. I'm glad you couldn't get rid of it.'

'How dare you say that?'

'But listen to me. I've been thinking of nothing else since I knew. The war will be over in six months. We shall bring the English to their knees in the spring. They haven't got a chance. And then I shall be demobilized and I'll marry you.'

'You? Why?'

He blushed under his tan. He could not bring himself to say it in French, so he said it in German. He knew she understood it.

'*Ich liebe dich.*'

'What does he say?' asked Madame Périer.

'He says he loves me.'

Annette threw back her head and broke into a peal of harsh laughter. She laughed louder and louder and she couldn't stop and tears streamed from her eyes. Madame Périer slapped her sharply on both cheeks.

'Don't pay any attention,' she said to Hans. 'It's hysteria. Her condition, you know.'

Annette gasped. She gained control over herself.

'I brought the bottle of champagne to celebrate our engagement,' said Hans.

'That's the bitterest thing of all,' said Annette, 'that we were beaten by fools, by such fools.'

Hans went on speaking in German.

'I didn't know I loved you till that day when I found out that you were going to have a baby. It came like a clap of thunder, but I think I've loved you all the time.'

'What does he say?' asked Madame Périer.

'Nothing of importance.'

He fell back into French. He wanted Annette's parents to hear what he had to say.

'I'd marry you now, only they wouldn't let me. And don't think I'm nothing at all. My father's well-to-do and we're well thought of in our commune. I'm the eldest son and you'd want for nothing.'

'Are you a Catholic?' asked Madame Périer.

'Yes, I'm a Catholic.'

'That's something.'

'It's pretty, the country where we live and the soil's good. There's not better farming land between Munich and Innsbruck, and it's our own. My grandfather bought it after the war of '70. And we've got a car and a radio, and we're on the telephone.'

Annette turned to her father.

'He has all the tact in the world, this gentleman,' she cried ironically. She eyed Hans. 'It would be a nice position for me, the foreigner from the conquered country with a child born out of wedlock. It offers me a chance of happiness, doesn't it? A fine chance.'

Périer, a man of few words, spoke for the first time.

'No. I don't deny that it's a fine gesture you're making. I went through the last war and we all did things we wouldn't have done in peace time. Human nature is human nature. But now that our son is dead, Annette is all we have. We can't let her go.'

'I thought you might feel that way,' said Hans, 'and I've got my answer to that. I'll stay here.'

Annette gave him a quick look.

'What do you mean?' asked Madame Périer.

'I've got another brother. He can stay and help my father. I like this country. With energy and initiative a man could make a good thing of your farm. When the war's over a lot of Germans will be settling here. It's well known that you haven't got enough men in France to work the land you've got. A fellow gave us a lecture the other day at Soissons. He said that a third of the farms were left uncultivated because there aren't the men to work them.'

Périer and his wife exchanged glances and Annette saw that they were wavering. That was what they'd wanted since their son had died, a son-in-law who was strong and hefty and could take over when they grew too old to do more than potter about.

'That changes the case,' said Madame Périer. 'It's a proposition to consider.'

'Hold your tongue,' cried Annette roughly. She leant forward and fixed her burning eyes on the German. 'I'm engaged to a teacher who worked in the boys' school in the town where I taught, we were to be married after the war. He's not strong and big like you, or handsome; he's small and frail. His only beauty is the intelligence that shines in his face, his only strength is the greatness of his soul. He's not a barbarian, he's civilized; he has a thousand years of civilization behind him. I love him. I love him with all my heart and soul.'

Hans's face grew sullen. It had never occurred to him that Annette might care for anyone else.

'Where is he now?'

'Where do you suppose he is? In Germany. A prisoner and starving. While you eat the fat of our land. How many times have I got to tell you that I hate you? You ask me to forgive you. Never. You want to make reparation. You fool.' She threw her head back and there was a look of intolerable anguish on her face. 'Ruined. Oh, he'll forgive me. He's tender. But I'm tortured by the thought that one day the suspicion may come to him that perhaps I hadn't been forced—that perhaps I'd given myself to you for butter and cheese and silk stockings. I shouldn't be the only one. And what would our life be with that child between us, your child, a German child? Big like you, and blond like you, and blue-eyed like you. Oh, my God, why do I have to suffer this?'

She got up and went swiftly out of the kitchen. For a minute the three were left in silence. Hans looked ruefully at his bottle of champagne. He sighed and rose to his feet. When he went out Madame Périer accompanied him.

'Did you mean it when you said you would marry her?' she asked him, speaking in a low voice.

'Yes. Every word. I love her.'

'And you wouldn't take her away? You'd stay here and work on the farm?'

'I promise you.'

'Evidently my old man can't last for ever. At home you'd have to share with your brother. Here you'd share with nobody.'

'There's that too.'

'We never were in favour of Annette marrying that teacher, but our son was alive then and he said, if she wants to marry him, why shouldn't she? Annette was crazy about him. But now that our son's dead, poor boy, it's different. Even if she wanted to, how could she work the farm alone?'

'It would be a shame if it was sold. I know how one feels about one's own land.'

They had reached the road. She took his hand and gave it a little squeeze.

'Come again soon.'

Hans knew that she was on his side. It was a comfort to him to think that as he rode back to Soissons. It was a bother that Annette was in love with somebody else. Fortunately he was a prisoner; long before he was likely to be released the baby would be born. That might change her: you could never tell with a woman. Why, in his village there'd been a woman who was so much in love with her husband that it had been a joke, and then she had a baby and after that she couldn't bear the sight of him. Well, why shouldn't the contrary happen too? And now that he'd offered to marry her she must see that he was a decent sort of fellow. God, how pathetic she'd looked with her head flung back, and how well she'd spoken! What language! An actress on the stage couldn't have expressed herself better, and yet it had all sounded so natural. You had to admit that, these French people knew how to talk. Oh, she was clever. Even when she lashed him with that bitter tongue it was a joy to listen to her. He hadn't had a bad education himself, but he couldn't hold a candle to her. Culture, that's what she had.

'I'm a donkey,' he said out loud as he rode along. She'd said he was big and strong and handsome. Would she have said that if it hadn't meant something to her? And she'd talked of the baby having fair hair and blue eyes like his own. If that didn't mean that his colouring had made an impression on her he was a Dutchman. He chuckled. 'Give me time. Patience, and let nature go to work.'

The weeks went by. The C.O. at Soissons was an elderly, easy-going fellow and in view of what the spring had in store for them he was content not to drive his men too hard. The German papers told them that England was being wrecked by the Luftwaffe and the people were in a panic. Submarines were sinking British ships by the score and the country was starving. Revolution was imminent. Before summer it would be all over and the Germans would be masters of the world. Hans wrote home and told his parents that he was going to marry a French girl and with her a fine farm. He proposed that his brother should borrow money to buy him out of his share of the family property so that he could increase the size of his own holding while land, owing to the war and the exchange, could still be bought for a song. He went over the farm with Périer. The old man listened quietly when Hans told him his ideas: the farm would have to be restocked and as a German he would have a pull; the motor tractor was old, he would get a fine new one from Germany, and a motor plough. To make a farm pay you had to take advantage of modern inventions. Madame Périer told him afterwards that her husband had said he wasn't a bad lad and seemed to know a lot. She was very friendly with him now and insisted that he should share their midday meal with them on Sundays. She translated his name into French and called him Jean. He was always ready to give a hand, and as time went on and Annette could do less and less it was useful to have a man about who didn't mind doing a job of work.

Annette remained fiercely hostile. She never spoke to him except to answer his direct questions and as soon as it was possible went to her own room. When it was so cold that she couldn't stay there she sat by the side of the kitchen stove, sewing or reading, and took no more notice of him than if he hadn't been there. She was in radiant health. There was colour in her cheeks and in Hans's eyes she was beautiful. Her approaching maternity had given her a strange dignity and he was filled with exultation when he gazed upon her. Then one day when he was on his way to the farm he saw Madame Périer in the road waving to him to stop. He put his brakes on hard.

'I've been waiting for an hour. I thought you'd never come. You must go back. Pierre is dead.'

'Who's Pierre?'

'Pierre Gavin. The teacher Annette was going to marry.'

Hans's heart leapt. What luck! Now he'd have his chance.

'Is she upset?'

'She's not crying. When I tried to say something she bit my head off. If she saw you today she's capable of sticking a knife into you.'

'It's not my fault if he died. How did you hear?'

'A prisoner, a friend of his, escaped through Switzerland and he wrote to Annette. We got the letter this morning. There was a mutiny in the camp because they weren't given enough to eat, and the ringleaders were shot. Pierre was one of them.'

Hans was silent. He could only think it served the man right. What did they think that a prison camp was—the Ritz?

'Give her time to get over the shock,' said Madame Périer. 'When she's calmer I'll talk to her. I'll write you a letter when you can come again.'

'All right. You will help me, won't you?'

'You can be sure of that. My husband and I, we're agreed. We talked it over and we came to the conclusion that the only thing to do was to accept the situation. He's no fool, my husband, and he says the best chance for France now is to collaborate. And take it all in all I don't dislike you. I shouldn't wonder if you didn't make Annette a better husband than that teacher. And with the baby coming and all.'

'I want it to be a boy,' said Hans.

'It's going to be a boy. I know for certain. I've seen it in the coffee grounds and I've put out the cards. The answer is a boy every time.'

'I almost forgot, here are some papers for you,' said Hans, as he turned his cycle and prepared to mount.

He handed her three numbers of *Paris-Soir*. Old Périer read every evening. He read that the French must be realistic and accept the new order that Hitler was going to create in Europe. He read that the German submarines were sweeping the sea. He read that the General Staff had organized to the last detail the campaign that would bring England to her knees and that the Americans were too unprepared, too soft and too divided to come to her help. He read that France must take the heaven-sent opportunity and by loyal collaboration with the Reich regain her honoured position in the new Europe. And it wasn't Germans who wrote it all; it was Frenchmen. He nodded his head with approval when he read that the plutocrats and the Jews would be destroyed and the poor man in France would at last come into his own. They were quite right, the clever fellows who said that France was essentially an agricultural country and its backbone was its industrious farmers. Good sense, that was.

One evening, when they were finishing their supper, ten days after the news had come of Pierre Gavin's death, Madame Périer, by arrangement with her husband, said to Annette:

'I wrote a letter to Hans a few days ago telling him to come here tomorrow.'

'Thank you for the warning. I shall stay in my room.'

'Oh, come, daughter, the time has passed for foolishness. You must be realistic. Pierre is dead. Hans loves you and wants to marry you. He's a fine-looking fellow. Any girl would be proud of him as a husband. How can we restock the farm without his help? He's going to buy a tractor and a plough with his own money. You must let bygones be bygones.'

'You're wasting your breath, Mother. I earned my living before, I can earn my living again. I hate him. I hate his vanity and his arrogance. I could kill him: his death wouldn't satisfy me. I should like to torture him as he's tortured me. I think I should die happy if I could find a way to wound him as he's wounded me.'

'You're being very silly, my poor child.'

'Your mother's right, my girl,' said Périer. 'We've been defeated and we must accept the consequences. We're got to make the best arrangement we can with the conquerors. We're cleverer than they are and if we play our cards well we shall come out on top. France was rotten. It's the Jews and the plutocrats who ruined the country. Read the papers and you'll see for yourself!'

'Do you think I believe a word in that paper? Why do you think he brings it to you except that it's sold to the Germans? The men who write in it—traitors, traitors. Oh God, may I live to see them torn to pieces by the mob. Bought, bought every one of them—bought with German money. The swine.'

Madame Périer was getting exasperated.

'What have you got against the boy? He took you by force—yes, he was drunk at the time. It's not the first time that's happened to a woman and it won't be the last time. He hit your father and he bled like a pig, but does your father bear him malice?'

'It was an unpleasant incident, but I've forgotten it,' said Périer.

Annette burst into harsh laughter.

'You should have been a priest. You forgive injuries with a spirit truly Christian.'

'And what is there wrong about that?' asked Madame Périer angrily. 'Hasn't he done everything he could to make amends? Where would your father have got his tobacco all these months if it hadn't been for him? If we haven't gone hungry it's owing to him.'

'If you'd had any pride, if you'd had any sense of decency, you'd have thrown his presents in his face.'

'You've profited by them, haven't you?'

'Never. Never.'

'It's a lie and you know it. You've refused to eat the cheese he brought and the butter and the sardines. But the soup you've eaten, you know I put the meat in it that he brought; and the salad you ate tonight, if you didn't have to eat it dry, it's because he brought me oil.'

Annette sighed deeply. She passed her hand over her eyes.

'I know. I tried not to, I couldn't help myself, I was so hungry. Yes, I knew his meat went into the soup and I ate it. I knew the salad was made with his oil. I wanted to refuse it; I had such a longing for it, it wasn't I that ate it, it was a ravenous beast within me.'

'That's neither here nor there. You ate it.'

'With shame. With despair. They broke our strength first with their tanks and their planes, and now when we're defenceless they're breaking our spirit by starving us.'

'You get nowhere by being theatrical, my girl. For an educated woman you have really no sense. Forget the past and give a father to your child, to say nothing of a good workman for the farm who'll be worth two hired men. That is sense.'

Annette shrugged her shoulders wearily and they lapsed into silence. Next day Hans came. Annette gave him a sullen look, but neither spoke nor moved. Hans smiled.

'Thank you for not running away,' he said.

'My parents asked you to come and they've gone down to the village. It suits me because I want to have a definite talk with you. Sit down.'

He took off his coat and his helmet and drew a chair to the table.

'My parents want me to marry you. You've been clever; with your presents, with your promises, you've got round them. They believe all they read in the papers you bring them. I want to tell you that I will never marry you. I wouldn't have thought it possible that I could hate a human being as I hate you.'

'Let me speak in German. You understand enough to know what I'm saying.'

'I ought to. I taught it. For two years I was governess to two little girls in Stuttgart.'

He broke into German, but she went on speaking French.

'It's not only that I love you, I admire you. I admire your distinction and your grace. There's something about you I don't understand. I respect you. Oh, I can see that you don't want to marry me now even if it were possible. But Pierre is dead.'

'Don't speak of him,' she cried violently. 'That would be the last straw.'

'I only want to tell you that for your sake I'm sorry he died.'

'Shot in cold blood by his German jailers.'

'Perhaps in time you'll grieve for him less. You know, when someone you love dies, you think you'll never get over it, but you do. Won't it be better then to have a father for your child?'

'Even if there were nothing else do you think I could ever forget that you are a German and I'm a Frenchwoman? If you weren't as stupid as only a German can be you'd see that that child must be a reproach to me as long as I live. Do you think I have no friends? How could I ever look them in the face with the child I had with a German soldier? There's only one thing I ask you; leave me alone with my disgrace. Go, go—for God's sake go and never come again.'

'But he's my child too. I want him.'

'You?' she cried in astonishment. 'What can a by-blow that you got in a moment of savage drunkenness mean to you?'

'You don't understand. I'm so proud and so happy. It was when I knew you were going to have a baby that I knew I loved you. At first I couldn't believe it; it was such a surprise to me. Don't you see what I mean? That child that's going to be born means everything in the world to me. Oh, I don't know how to put it; it's put feelings in my heart that I don't understand myself.'

She looked at him intently and there was a strange gleam in her eyes. You would have said it was a look of triumph. She gave a short laugh.

'I don't know whether I more loathe the brutality of you Germans or despise your sentimentality.'

He seemed not to have heard what she said.

'I think of him all the time.'

'You've made up your mind it'll be a boy?'

'I know it'll be a boy. I want to hold him in my arms and I want to teach him to walk. And then when he grows older I'll teach him all I know. I'll teach him to ride and I'll teach him to shoot. Are there fish in your brook? I'll teach him to fish. I'm going to be the proudest father in the world.'

She stared at him with hard, hard eyes. Her face was set and stern. An idea, a terrible idea was forming itself in her mind. He gave her a disarming smile.

'Perhaps when you see how much I love our boy, you'll come to love me too. I'll make you a good husband, my pretty.'

She said nothing. She merely kept on gazing at him sullenly.

'Haven't you one kind word for me?' he said.

She flushed. She clasped her hands tightly together.

'Others may despise me. I will never do anything that can make me despise myself. You are my enemy and you will always be my enemy. I only live to see the deliverance of France. It'll come, perhaps not next year or the year after, perhaps not for thirty years, but it'll come. The rest of them can do what they like, I will never come to terms with the invaders of my country. I hate you and I hate this child that you've given me. Yes, we've been defeated. Before the end comes you'll see that we haven't been conquered. Now go. My mind's made up and nothing on God's earth can change it.'

He was silent for a minute or two.

'Have you made arrangements for a doctor? I'll pay all the expenses.'

'Do you suppose we want to spread our shame through the whole countryside? My mother will do all that's necessary.'

'But supposing there's an accident?'

'And supposing you mind your own business!'

He sighed and rose to his feet. When he closed the door behind him she watched him walk down the pathway that led to the road. She realized with rage that some of the things he said had aroused in her heart a feeling that she had never felt for him before.

'O God, give me strength,' she cried.

Then, as he walked along, the dog, an old dog they'd had for years, ran up to him barking angrily. He had tried for months to make friends with the dog, but it had never responded to his advances; when he tried to pat it, it backed away growling and showing its teeth. And now as the dog ran towards him, irritably giving way to his feeling of frustration, Hans gave it a savage brutal kick and the dog was flung into the bushes and limped yelping away.

'The beast,' she cried. 'Lies, lies, lies. And I was weak enough to be almost sorry for him.'

There was a looking-glass hanging by the side of the door and she looked at herself in it. She drew herself up and smiled at her reflection. But rather than a smile it was a fiendish grimace.

It was now March. There was a bustle of activity in the garrison at Soissons. There were inspections and there was intensive training. Rumour was rife. There was no doubt they were going somewhere, but the rank and file could only guess where. Some thought they were being got ready at last for the invasion of England, others were of opinion that they would be sent to the Balkans, and others again talked of the Ukraine. Hans was kept busy. It was not till the second Sunday afternoon that he was able to get out to the farm. It was a cold grey day, with sleet that looked as though it might turn to snow falling in sudden windy flurries. The country was grim and cheerless.

'You!' cried Madame Périer when he went in. 'We thought you were dead.'

'I couldn't come before. We're off any day now. We don't know when.'

'The baby was born this morning. It's a boy.'

Hans's heart gave a great leap in his breast. He hung his arms round the old woman and kissed her on both cheeks.

'A Sunday child, he ought to be lucky. Let's open the bottle of champagne. How's Annette?'

'She's as well as can be expected. She had a very easy time. She began to have pains last night and by five o'clock this morning it was all over.'

Old Périer was smoking his pipe sitting as near the stove as he could get. He smiled quietly at the boy's enthusiasm.

'One's first child, it has an effect on one,' he said.

'He has quite a lot of hair and it's as fair as yours; and blue eyes just like you said he'd have,' said Madame Périer. 'I've never seen a lovelier baby. He'll be just like his papa.'

'Oh, my God, I'm so happy,' cried Hans. 'How beautiful the world is! I want to see Annette.'

'I don't know if she'll see you. I don't want to upset her on account of the milk.'

'No, no, don't upset her on my account. If she doesn't want to see me it doesn't matter. But let me see the baby just for a minute.'

'I'll see what I can do. I'll try to bring it down.'

Madame Périer went out and they heard her heavy tread clumping up the stairs. But in a moment they heard her clattering down again. She burst into the kitchen.

'They're not there. She isn't in her room. The baby's gone.'

Périer and Hans cried out and without thinking what they were doing all three of them scampered upstairs. The harsh light of the winter afternoon cast over the shabby furniture, the iron bed, the cheap wardrobe, the chest of drawers, a dismal squalor. There was no one in the room.

'Where is she?' screamed Madame Périer. She ran into the narrow passage, opening doors, and called the girl's name. 'Annette, Annette. Oh, what madness!'

'Perhaps in the sitting-room.'

They ran downstairs to the unused parlour. An icy air met them as they opened the door. They opened the door of a storeroom.

'She's gone out. Something awful has happened.'

'How could she have got out?' asked Hans sick with anxiety.

'Through the front door, you fool.'

Périer went up to it and looked.

'That's right. The bolt's drawn back.'

'Oh, my God, my God, what madness,' cried Madame Périer. 'It'll kill her.'

'We must look for her,' said Hans. Instinctively, because that was the way he always went in and out, he ran back into the kitchen and the others followed him. 'Which way?'

'The brook,' the old woman gasped.

He stopped as though turned to stone with horror. He stared at the old woman aghast.

'I'm frightened,' she cried. 'I'm frightened.'

Hans flung open the door, and as he did so Annette walked in. She had nothing on but her nightdress and a flimsy rayon dressing-gown. It was pink, with pale blue flowers. She was soaked, and her hair, dishevelled, clung damply to her head and hung down her shoulders in bedraggled wisps. She was deathly white. Madame Périer sprang towards her and took her in her arms.

'Where have you been? Oh, my poor child, you're wet through. What madness!'

But Annette pushed her away. She looked at Hans.

'You've come at the right moment, you.'

'Where's the baby?' cried Madame Périer.

'I had to do it at once. I was afraid if I waited I shouldn't have the courage.'

'Annette, what have you done?'

'I've done what I had to do. I took it down to the brook and held it under water till it was dead.'

Hans gave a great cry, the cry of an animal wounded to death; he covered his face with his hands, and staggering like a drunken man flung out of the door. Annette sank into a chair, and leaning her forehead on her two fists burst into passionate weeping.

The Escape

◆

I have always been convinced that if a woman once made up her mind to marry a man nothing but instant flight could save him. Not always that; for once a friend of mine, seeing the inevitable loom menacingly before him, took ship from a certain port (with a tooth-brush for all his luggage, so conscious was he of his danger and the necessity for immediate action) and spent a year travelling round the world; but when, thinking himself safe (women are fickle, he said, and in twelve months she will have forgotten all about me), he landed at the selfsame port the first person he saw gaily waving to him from the quay was the little lady from whom he had fled. I have only once known a man who in such circumstances managed to extricate himself. His name was Roger Charing. He was no longer young when he fell in love with Ruth Barlow and he had had sufficient experience to make him careful; but Ruth Barlow had a gift (or should I call it a quality?) that renders most men defenceless, and it was this that dispossessed Roger of his commonsense, his prudence, and his worldly wisdom. He went down like a row of ninepins. This was the gift of pathos. Mrs Barlow, for she was twice a widow, had splendid dark eyes and they were the most moving I ever saw; they seemed to be ever on the point of filling with tears; they suggested that the world was too much for her, and you felt that, poor dear, her sufferings had been more than anyone should be asked to bear. If, like Roger Charing, you were a strong, hefty fellow with plenty of money, it was almost inevitable that you should say to yourself: I must stand between the hazards of life and this helpless little thing, oh, how wonderful it would be to take the sadness out of those big and lovely eyes! I gathered from Roger that everyone had treated Mrs Barlow very badly. She was apparently one of those unfortunate persons with whom nothing by any chance goes right. If she married a husband he beat her; if she employed a broker he cheated her; if she engaged a cook she drank. She never had a little lamb but it was sure to die.

When Roger told me that he had at last persuaded her to marry him, I wished him joy.

'I hope you'll be good friends,' he said. 'She's a little afraid of you, you know; she thinks you're callous.'

'Upon my word I don't know why she should think that.'

'You do like her, don't you?'

'Very much.'

'She's had a rotten time, poor dear. I feel so dreadfully sorry for her.'

'Yes,' I said.

I couldn't say less. I knew she was stupid and I thought she was scheming. My own belief was that she was as hard as nails.

The first time I met her we had played bridge together and when she was my partner she twice trumped my best card. I behaved like an angel, but I confess that I thought if the tears were going to well up into anybody's eyes they should have been mine rather than hers. And when, having by the end of the evening lost a good deal of money to me, she said she would send me a cheque and never did, I could not but think that I and not she should have worn a pathetic expression when next we met.

Roger introduced her to his friends. He gave her lovely jewels. He took her here, there, and everywhere. Their marriage was announced for the immediate future. Roger was very happy. He was committing a good action and at the same time doing something he had very much a mind to. It is an uncommon situation and it is not surprising if he was a trifle more pleased with himself than was altogether becoming.

Then, on a sudden, he fell out of love. I do not know why. It could hardly have been that he grew tired of her conversation, for she had never had any conversation. Perhaps it was merely that this pathetic look of hers ceased to wring his heart-strings. His eyes were opened and he was once more the shrewd man of the world he had been. He became acutely conscious that Ruth Barlow had made up her mind to marry him and he swore a solemn oath that nothing would induce him to marry Ruth Barlow. But he was in a quandary. Now that he was in possession of his senses he saw with clearness the sort of woman he had to deal with and he was aware that, if he asked her to release him, she would (in her appealing way) assess her wounded feelings at an immoderately high figure. Besides, it is always awkward for a man to jilt a woman. People are apt to think he has behaved badly.

Roger kept his own counsel. He gave neither by word nor gesture an indication that his feelings towards Ruth Barlow had changed. He remained attentive to all her wishes; he took her to dine at restaurants, they went to the play together, he sent her flowers; he was sympathetic and charming. They had made up their minds that they would be married as soon as they found a house that suited them, for he lived in chambers and she in furnished rooms; and they set about looking at desirable residences. The agents sent Roger orders to view and he took Ruth to see a number of houses. It was very hard to find anything that was quite satisfactory. Roger applied to more agents. They visited house after house. They went over them thoroughly, examining them from the cellars in the basement to the attics under the roof. Sometimes they were too large and sometimes they were too small; sometimes they were too far from the centre of things and sometimes they were too close; sometimes they were too expensive and sometimes they wanted too many repairs; sometimes they were too stuffy and sometimes they were too airy; sometimes they were too dark and sometimes they were too bleak. Roger always found a fault that made the house unsuitable. Of course he was hard to please; he could not bear to ask his dear Ruth to live in any but the perfect house, and the perfect house wanted finding. House-hunting is a tiring and a tiresome business and presently Ruth began to grow peevish. Roger begged her to have patience; somewhere, surely, existed the very house they were looking for, and it only needed a little perseverance and they would find it. They looked at hundreds of houses; they climbed thousands of stairs; they inspected innumerable kitchens. Ruth was exhausted and more than once lost her temper.

'If you don't find a house soon,' she said, 'I shall have to reconsider my position. Why, if you go on like this we shan't be married for years.'

'Don't say that,' he answered, 'I beseech you to have patience. I've just received some entirely new lists from agents I've only just heard of. There must be at least sixty houses on them.'

They set out on the chase again. They looked at more houses and more houses. For two years they looked at houses. Ruth grew silent and scornful: her pathetic, beautiful eyes acquired an expression that was almost sullen. There are limits to human endurance. Mrs Barlow had the patience of an angel, but at last she revolted.

'Do you want to marry me or do you not?' she asked him.

There was an unaccustomed hardness in her voice, but it did not affect the gentleness of his reply.

'Of course I do. We'll be married the very moment we find a house. By the way, I've just heard of something that might suit us.'

'I don't feel well enough to look at any more houses just yet.'

'Poor dear, I was afraid you were looking rather tired.'

Ruth Barlow took to her bed. She would not see Roger and he had to content himself with calling at her lodgings to inquire and sending her flowers. He was as ever assiduous and gallant. Every day he wrote and told her that he had heard of another house for them to look at. A week passed and then he received the following letter:

Roger
    I do not think you really love me. I have found someone who is anxious to take care of me and I am going to be married to him today.

                                                             Ruth

He sent back his reply by special messenger:

Ruth
    Your news shatters me. I shall never get over the blow, but of course your happiness must be my first consideration. I send you herewith seven orders to view; they arrived by this morning's post and I am quite sure you will find among them a house that will exactly suit you.

                                                             Roger

Mr Know-All

◆

I was prepared to dislike Max Kelada even before I knew him. The war had just finished and the passenger traffic in the ocean-going liners was heavy. Accommodation was very hard to get and you had to put up with whatever the agents chose to offer you. You could not hope for a cabin to yourself and I was thankful to be given one in which there were only two berths. But when I was told the name of my companion my heart sank. It suggested closed port-holes and the night air rigidly excluded. It was bad enough to share a cabin for fourteen days with anyone (I was going from San Francisco to Yokohama), but I should have looked upon it with less dismay if my fellow-passenger's name had been Smith or Brown.

When I went on board I found Mr Kelada's luggage already below. I did not like the look of it; there were too many labels on the suitcases, and the wardrobe trunk was too big. He had unpacked his toilet things, and I observed that he was a patron of the excellent Monsieur Coty; for I saw on the washing-stand his scent, his hair-wash, and his brilliantine. Mr Kelada's brushes, ebony with his monogram in gold, would have been all the better for a scrub. I did not at all like Mr Kelada. I made my way into the smoking-room. I called for a pack of cards and began to play patience. I had scarcely started before a man came up to me and asked me if he was right in thinking my name was so-and-so.

'I am Mr Kelada,' he added, with a smile that showed a row of flashing teeth, and sat down.

'Oh, yes, we're sharing a cabin, I think.'

'Bit of luck, I call it. You never know who you're going to be put in with. I was jolly glad when I heard you were English. I'm all for us English sticking together when we're abroad, if you understand what I mean.'

I blinked.

'Are you English?' I asked, perhaps tactlessly.

'Rather. You don't think I look an American, do you? British to the backbone, that's what I am.'

To prove it, Mr Kelada took out of his pocket a passport and airily waved it under my nose.

King George has many strange subjects. Mr Kelada was short and of a sturdy build, clean-shaven and dark-skinned, with a fleshy, hooked nose and very large, lustrous and liquid eyes. His long black hair was sleek and curly. He spoke with a fluency in which there was nothing English and his gestures were exuberant. I felt pretty sure that a closer inspection of that British passport would have betrayed the fact that Mr Kelada was born under a bluer sky than is generally seen in England.

'What will you have?' he asked me.

I looked at him doubtfully. Prohibition was in force and to all appearances the ship was bone-dry. When I am not thirsty I do not know which I dislike more, ginger-ale or lemon-squash. But Mr Kelada flashed an oriental smile at me.

'Whisky and soda or a dry Martini, you have only to say the word.'

From each of his hip-pockets he fished a flask and laid them on the table before me. I chose the Martini, and calling the steward he ordered a tumbler of ice and a couple of glasses.

'A very good cocktail,' I said.

'Well, there are plenty more where that came from, and if you've got any friends on board, you tell them you've got a pal who's got all the liquor in the world.'

Mr Kelada was chatty. He talked of New York and of San Francisco. He discussed plays, pictures, and politics. He was patriotic. The Union Jack is an impressive piece of drapery, but when it is flourished by a gentleman from Alexandria or Beirut, I cannot but feel that it loses somewhat in dignity. Mr Kelada was familiar. I do not wish to put on airs, but I cannot help feeling that it is seemly in a total stranger to put mister before my name when he addresses me. Mr Kelada, doubtless to set me at my ease, used no such formality. I did not like Mr Kelada. I had put aside the cards when he sat down, but now, thinking that for this first occasion our conversation had lasted long enough, I went on with my game.

'The three on the four,' said Mr Kelada.

There is nothing more exasperating when you are playing patience than to be told where to put the card you have turned up before you have had a chance to look for yourself.

'It's coming out, it's coming out,' he cried. 'The ten on the knave.'

With rage and hatred in my heart I finished. Then he seized the pack.

'Do you like card tricks?'

'No, I hate card tricks,' I answered.

'Well, I'll just show you this one.'

He showed me three. Then I said I would go down to the dining-room and get my seat at table.

'Oh, that's all right,' he said. 'I've already taken a seat for you. I thought that as we were in the same state-room we might just as well sit at the same table.'

I did not like Mr Kelada.

I not only shared a cabin with him and ate three meals a day at the same table, but I could not walk round the deck without his joining me. It was impossible to snub him. It never occurred to him that he was not wanted. He was certain that you were as glad to see him as he was to see you. In your own house you might have kicked him downstairs and slammed the door in his face without the suspicion dawning on him that he was not a welcome visitor. He was a good mixer, and in three days knew everyone on board. He ran everything. He managed the sweeps, conducted the auctions, collected money for prizes at the sports, got up quoit and golf matches, organized the concert, and arranged the fancy-dress ball. He was everywhere and always. He was certainly the best-hated man in the ship. We called him Mr Know-All, even to his face. He took it as a compliment. But it was at meal times that he was most intolerable. For the better part of an hour then he had us at his mercy. He was hearty, jovial, loquacious and argumentative. He knew everything better than anybody else, and it was an affront to his overweening vanity that you should disagree with him. He would not drop a subject, however unimportant, till he had brought you round to his way of thinking. The possibility that he could be mistaken never occurred to him. He was the chap who knew. We sat at the doctor's table. Mr Kelada would certainly have had it all his own way, for the doctor was lazy and I was frigidly indifferent, except for a man called Ramsay who sat there also. He was as dogmatic as Mr Kelada and resented bitterly the Levantine's cocksureness. The discussions they had were acrimonious and interminable.

Ramsay was in the American Consular Service, and was stationed at Kobe. He was a great heavy fellow from the Middle West, with loose fat under a tight skin, and he bulged out of his ready-made clothes. He was on his way back to resume his post, having been on a flying visit to New York to fetch his wife, who had been spending a year at home. Mrs Ramsay was a very pretty little thing, with pleasant manners and a sense of humour. The Consular Service is ill paid, and she was dressed always very simply; but she knew how to wear her clothes. She achieved an effect of quiet distinction. I should not have paid any particular attention to her but that she possessed a quality that may be common enough in women, but nowadays is not obvious in their demeanour. You could not look at her without being struck by her modesty. It shone in her like a flower on a coat.

One evening at dinner the conversation by chance drifted to the subject of pearls. There had been in the papers a good deal of talk about the culture pearls which the cunning Japanese were making, and the doctor remarked that they must inevitably diminish the value of real ones. They were very good already; they would soon be perfect. Mr Kelada, as was his habit, rushed the new topic. He told us all that was to be known about pearls. I do not believe Ramsay knew anything about them at all, but he could not resist the opportunity to have a fling at the Levantine, and in five minutes we were in the middle of a heated argument. I had seen Mr Kelada vehement and voluble before, but never so voluble and vehement as now. At last something that Ramsay said stung him, for he thumped the table and shouted:

'Well, I ought to know what I am talking about. I'm going to Japan just to look into this Japanese pearl business. I'm in the trade and there's not a man in it who won't tell you that what I say about pearls goes. I know all the best pearls in the world, and what I don't know about pearls isn't worth knowing.'

Here was news for us, for Mr Kelada, with all his loquacity, had never told anyone what his business was. We only knew vaguely that he was going to Japan on some commercial errand. He looked round the table triumphantly.

'They'll never be able to get a culture pearl that an expert like me can't tell with half an eye.' He pointed to a chain that Mrs Ramsay wore. 'You take my word for it, Mrs Ramsay, that chain you're wearing will never be worth a cent less than it is now.'

Mrs Ramsay in her modest way flushed a little and slipped the chain inside her dress. Ramsay leaned forward. He gave us all a look and a smile flickered in his eyes.

'That's a pretty chain of Mrs Ramsay's, isn't it?'

'I noticed it at once,' answered Mr Kelada. 'Gee, I said to myself, those are pearls all right.'

'I didn't buy it myself, of course. I'd be interested to know how much you think it cost.'

'Oh, in the trade somewhere round fifteen thousand dollars. But if it was bought on Fifth Avenue I shouldn't be surprised to hear that anything up to thirty thousand was paid for it.'

Ramsay smiled grimly.

'You'll be surprised to hear that Mrs Ramsay bought that string at a department store the day before we left New York, for eighteen dollars.'

Mr Kelada flushed.

'Rot. It's not only real, but it's as fine a string for its size as I've ever seen.'

'Will you bet on it? I'll bet you a hundred dollars it's imitation.'

'Done.'

'Oh, Elmer, you can't bet on a certainty,' said Mrs Ramsay.

She had a little smile on her lips and her tone was gently deprecating.

'Can't I? If I get a chance of easy money like that I should be all sorts of a fool not to take it.'

'But how can it be proved?' she continued. 'It's only my word against Mr Kelada's.'

'Let me look at the chain, and if it's imitation I'll tell you quickly enough. I can afford to lose a hundred dollars,' said Mr Kelada.

'Take it off, dear. Let the gentleman look at it as much as he wants.'

Mrs Ramsay hesitated a moment. She put her hands to the clasp.

'I can't undo it,' she said. 'Mr Kelada will just have to take my word for it.'

I had a sudden suspicion that something unfortunate was about to occur, but I could think of nothing to say.

Ramsay jumped up.

'I'll undo it.'

He handed the chain to Mr Kelada. The Levantine took a magnifying glass from his pocket and closely examined it. A smile of triumph spread over his smooth and swarthy face. He handed back the chain. He was about to speak. Suddenly he caught sight of Mrs Ramsay's face. It was so white that she looked as though she were about to faint. She was staring at him with wide and terrified eyes. They held a desperate appeal; it was so clear that I wondered why her husband did not see it.

Mr Kelada stopped with his mouth open. He flushed deeply. You could almost *see* the effort he was making over himself.

'I was mistaken,' he said. 'It's a very good imitation, but of course as soon as I looked through my glass I saw that it wasn't real. I think eighteen dollars is just about as much as the damned thing's worth.'

He took out his pocket-book and from it a hundred-dollar note. He handed it to Ramsay without a word.

'Perhaps that'll teach you not to be so cocksure another time, my young friend,' said Ramsay as he took the note.

I noticed that Mr Kelada's hands were trembling.

The story spread over the ship as stories do, and he had to put up with a good deal of chaff that evening. It was a fine joke that Mr Know-All had been caught out. But Mrs Ramsay retired to her state-room with a headache.

Next morning I got up and began to shave. Mr Kelada lay on his bed smoking a cigarette. Suddenly there was a small scraping sound and I saw a letter pushed under the door. I opened the door and looked out. There was nobody there. I picked up the letter and saw that it was addressed to Max Kelada. The name was written in block letters. I handed it to him.

'Who's this from?' He opened it. 'Oh!'

He took out of the envelope, not a letter, but a hundred-dollar note. He looked at me and again he reddened. He tore the envelope into little bits and gave them to me.

'Do you mind just throwing them out of the port-hole?'

I did as he asked, and then I looked at him with a smile.

'No one likes being made to look a perfect damned fool,' he said.

'Were the pearls real?'

'If I had a pretty little wife I shouldn't let her spend a year in New York while I stayed at Kobe,' said he.

At that moment I did not entirely dislike Mr Kelada. He reached out for his pocket-book and carefully put in it the hundred-dollar note.

The
Romantic
Young Lady

◆

One of the many inconveniences of real life is that it seldom gives you a complete story. Some incident has excited your interest, the people who are concerned in it are in the devil's own muddle, and you wonder what on earth will happen next. Well, generally nothing happens. The inevitable catastrophe you foresaw wasn't inevitable after all, and high tragedy, without any regard to artistic decency, dwindles into drawing-room comedy. Now, growing old has many disadvantages, but it has this compensation (among, let us admit, not a few others), that sometimes it gives you the opportunity of seeing what was the outcome of certain events you had witnessed long ago. You had given up the hope of ever knowing what was the end of the story, and then, when you least expected it, it is handed to you on a platter.

These reflections occurred to me when, having escorted the Marquesa de San Esteban to her car, I went back into the hotel and sat down again in the lounge. I ordered a cocktail, lit a cigarette, and composed myself to order my recollections. The hotel was new and splendid, it was like every other first-class hotel in Europe, and I had been regretting that for the sake of its modern plumbing I had deserted the old-fashioned, picturesque Hotel de Madrid to which I generally went when I stayed in Seville. It was true that from my hotel I had a view of the noble river, the Guadalquivir, but that did not make up for the *thés dansants* that filled the bar-lounge two or three days a week with a fashionable crowd whose exuberant conversation almost drowned the strident din of a jazz orchestra.

I had been out all the afternoon, and coming in found myself in the midst of a seething mob. I went to the desk and asked for my key so that I might go straight up to my room. But the porter, handing it to me, said that a lady had been asking for me.

'For me?'

'She wants to see you very much. It's the Marquesa de San Esteban.'

I knew no one of that name.

'It must be some mistake.'

As I said the words, looking rather vaguely around, a lady came up to me with outstretched hands and a bright smile on her lips. To the best of my knowledge I had never seen her before in my life. She seized my hands, both of them, and shook them warmly. She spoke in fluent French.

'How very nice to see you again after all these years. I saw by the paper that you were staying here and I said to myself: I must look him up. How many years is it since we danced together? I daren't think. Do you still dance? I do. And I'm a grandmother. I'm fat of course, I don't care, and it keeps me from getting fatter.'

She talked with such a rush that it took my breath away to listen to her. She was a stout, more than middle-aged woman, very much made up, with dark red hair, obviously dyed, cut short; and she was dressed in the height of Parisian fashion, which never suits Spanish women very well. But she had a gay, fruity laugh that made you feel you wanted to laugh too. It was quite obvious that she thoroughly enjoyed life. She was a fine figure of a woman and I could well believe that in youth she had been beautiful. But I could not place her.

'Come and drink a glass of champagne with me and we will talk of old times. Or will you have a cocktail? Our dear old Seville had changed, you see. *Thés dansants* and cocktails. It's just like Paris and London now. We've caught up. We're a civilized people.'

She led me to a table near the space where they were dancing and we sat down. I could not go on pretending I was at ease; I thought I should only get into a fearful mess.

'It's terribly stupid of me, I'm afraid,' I said, 'but I don't seem able to remember ever having known anyone of your name in the old days in Seville.'

'San Esteban?' she interrupted before I could go on. 'Naturally. My husband came from Salamanca. He was in the diplomatic service. I'm a widow. You knew me as Pilar Carreon. Of course having my hair red changes me a little, but otherwise I don't think I've altered much.'

'Not at all,' I said quickly. 'It was only the name that bothered me.'

Of course now I remembered her, but I was concerned at the moment only with the effort to conceal from her the mingled consternation and amusement that filled me as I realized that the Pilar Carreon I had danced with at the Countess de Marbella's parties and at the Fair had turned into this stout, flaunting dowager. I could not get over it. But I had to watch my step. I wondered if she knew how well I recollected the story that had shaken Seville to its foundations, and I was glad when after she had finally bidden me an effusive farewell I was able to recall it at ease.

In those days, forty years ago, Seville had not become a prosperous commercial city. It had quiet, white streets, paved with cobbles, with a multitude of churches on the belfries of which storks built their nests. Bull-fighters, students, and loungers sauntered in the Sierpes all day long. Life was easy. This of course, was before the time of motor-cars, and the Sevillan would live in penury, practising every possible economy, in order to have a carriage. For this luxury he was willing to sacrifice the necessities of life. Everyone who had any claim to gentility drove up and down the Delicias, the park-like gardens by the Guadalquivir, every blessed afternoon from five till seven. You saw carriages of all sorts, from fashionable London victorias to old broken-down shays that seemed as though they would fall to pieces, magnificent horses and wretched hacks whose tragic end in the bull-ring was near at hand. But there was one equipage that could not fail to attract the stranger's attention. It was a victoria, very smart and new, drawn by two beautiful mules; and the coachman and the footman wore the national costume of Andalusia in pale grey. It was the most splendid turn-out Seville had ever known, and it belonged to the Countess de Marbella. She was a Frenchwoman married to a Spaniard, who had enthusiastically adopted the manners and customs of her husband's country, but with a Parisian elegance that gave them a peculiar distinction. The rest of the carriages went at a snail's pace so that their occupants could see and be seen, but the countess, behind her mules, dashed up between the two crawling lines at a fast trot, went to the end of the Delicias and back twice and then drove away. The proceeding savoured somewhat of royalty. When you looked at her gracefully seated in that swift victoria, her head handsomely poised, her hair of too brilliant a gold to be natural, you did not wonder that her French vivacity and determination had given her the position she held. She made the fashion. Her decrees were law. But the countess had too many adorers not to have as many enemies, and the most determined of these was the widowed Duchess de Dos Palos, whose birth and social consequence made her claim as a right the first place in Society which the Frenchwoman had won by grace, wit and character.

Now the duchess had an only daughter. This was Doña Pilar. She was twenty when I first knew her and she was very beautiful. She had magnificent eyes and a skin that, however hard you tried to find a less hackneyed way to describe it, you could only call peach-like. She was very slim, rather tall for a Spanish girl, with a red mouth and dazzlingly white teeth. She wore her abundant, shining black hair dressed very elaborately in the Spanish style of the period. She was infinitely alluring. The fire in her black eyes, the warmth of her smile, the seductiveness of her movements suggested so much passion that it really wasn't quite fair. She belonged to the generation which was straining to break the old conventions that had kept the Spanish girl of good family hidden away till it was time for her to be married. I often played tennis with her and I used to dance with her at the Countess de Marbella's parties. The duchess considered the Frenchwoman's parties, with champagne and a sit-down supper, ostentatious, and when she opened her own great house to Society, which was only twice a year, it was to give them lemonade and biscuits. But she bred fighting-bulls, as her husband had done, and on the occasions when the young bulls were tried out, she gave picnic luncheons to which her friends were asked, very gay and informal, but with a sort of feudal state which fascinated my romantic imagination. Once, when the duchess's bulls were to fight at a *corrida* in Seville, I rode in with them at night as one of the men escorting Doña Pilar, dressed in a costume that reminded one of a picture by Goya, who headed the cavalcade. It was a charming experience to ride through the night, on those prancing Andalusian horses, with the six bulls, surrounded by oxen, thundering along behind.

A good many men, rich or noble and sometimes both, had asked Doña Pilar's hand in marriage, but, notwithstanding her mother's remonstrances, she had refused them. The duchess had been married at fifteen and it seemed to her really indecent that her daughter at twenty should be still single. The duchess asked her what she was waiting for; it was absurd to be too difficult. It was her duty to marry. But Pilar was stubborn. She found reasons to reject every one of her suitors.

Then the truth came out.

During the daily drives in the Delicias which the duchess, accompanied by her daughter, took in a great old-fashioned landau, they passed the countess as she was twice swiftly driven up and down the promenade. The ladies were on such bad terms that they pretended not to see one another, but Pilar could not keep her eyes off that smart carriage and the two beautiful grey mules and, not wishing to catch the countess's somewhat ironic glance, her own fell on the coachman who drove her. He was the handsomest man in Seville and in his beautiful uniform he was a sight to see. Of course no one knew exactly what happened, but apparently the more Pilar looked at the coachman the more she liked the look of him, and somehow or other, for all this part of the story remained a mystery, the pair met. In Spain the classes are strangely mingled and the butler may have in his veins much nobler blood than the master. Pilar learnt, not I think without satisfaction, that the coachman belonged to the ancient family of León, than which there is none in Andalusia more distinguished; and really so far as birth went there was little to choose between them. Only her life had been passed in a ducal mansion, while fate had forced him to earn his living on the box of a victoria. Neither could regret this, since only in that exalted place could he have attracted the attention of the most difficult young woman in Seville. They fell madly in love with one another. It so happened that just then a young man called the Marqués de San Esteban, whom they had met at San Sebastian the summer before, wrote to the duchess and asked for Pilar's hand in marriage. He was extremely eligible and the two families had formed alliances from time to time ever since the reign of Philip II. The duchess was determined not to stand any more nonsense, and when she told Pilar of the proposal added that she had shilly-shallied long enough. She must either marry him or she should go into a convent.

'I'm not going to do either the one or the other,' said Pilar.

'What are you going to do then? I have given you a home long enough.'

'I'm going to marry José León.'

'Who is he?'

Pilar hesitated for a moment and it may be, it is indeed to be hoped, that she blushed a little.

'He's the countess's coachman.'

'What countess?'

'The Countess de Marbella.'

I remembered the duchess well and I am sure that when roused she stuck at little. She raged, she implored, she cried, she argued. There was a terrific scene. People said that she slapped her daughter and pulled her hair, but I have an impression that Pilar in such a pass was capable of hitting back. She repeated that she loved José León and he loved her. She was determined to marry him. The duchess called a family council. The matter was put before them and it was decided that to save them all from disgrace Pilar should be taken away to the country and kept there till she had recovered from her infatuation. Pilar got wind of the scheme and put a stop to it by slipping out of the window of her room one night when everyone was asleep and going to live with her lover's parents. They were respectable persons who inhabited a small apartment on the unfashionable side of the Guadalquivir, in the quarter called Triana.

After that no concealment was possible. The fat was in the fire and the clubs along the Sierpes buzzed with the scandal. Waiters were kept busy bringing trays of little glasses of Manzanilla to the members from the neighbouring wine-shops. They gossiped and laughed over the scandal, and Pilar's rejected suitors were the recipients of many congratulations. What an escape! The duchess was in despair. She could think of nothing better to do than go to the Archbishop, her trusted friend and former confessor, and beg him himself to reason with the infatuated girl. Pilar was summoned to the episcopal palace, and the good old man, used to intervening in family quarrels, did his utmost to show her the folly of her course. But she would not be persuaded. Nothing that anyone could say would induce her to forsake the man she loved. The duchess, waiting in an adjoining room, was sent for and made a final appeal to her daughter. In vain. Pilar returned to her humble lodging and the duchess in tears was left alone with the Archbishop. The Archbishop was no less astute than he was pious, and when he saw that the distracted woman was in a fit state to listen to him, advised her as a last resource to go to the Countess de Marbella. She was the cleverest woman in Seville and it might be that she could do something.

At first the duchess indignantly refused. She would never suffer the humiliation of appealing to her greatest enemy. Sooner might the ancient house of Dos Palos fall in ruin. The Archbishop was accustomed to dealing with tiresome women. He set himself with gentle cunning to induce her to change her mind and presently she consented to throw herself on the Frenchwoman's mercy. With rage in her heart she sent a message asking if she might see her, and that afternoon was ushered into her drawing-room. The countess of course had been one of the first to hear the story, but she listened to the unhappy mother as though she had not known a thing about it. She relished the situation enormously. It was the crowning triumph to have the vindictive duchess on her knees before her. But she was at heart a good-natured woman and she had a sense of humour.

'It's a most unfortunate situation,' she said. 'And I'm sorry that one of my servants should be the occasion of it. But I don't exactly see what I can do.'

The duchess would have liked to slap her painted face and her voice trembled a little with the effort she made to control her anger.

'It is not for my own sake I'm asking you to help. It's for Pilar's. I know, we all know, that you are the cleverest woman in the city. It seemed to me, it seemed to the Archbishop, that if there was a way out, your quick wit would find it.'

The countess knew she was being grossly flattered. She did not mind. She liked it.

'You must let me think.'

'Of course, if he'd been a gentleman I could have sent for my son and he would have killed him, but the Duke of Dos Palos cannot fight a duel with the Countess de Marbella's coachman.'

'Perhaps not.'

'In the old days it would have been so simple. I should merely have hired a couple of ruffians and had the brute's throat cut one night in the street. But with all these laws they have nowadays decent people have no way of protecting themselves from insult.'

'I should deplore any method of settling the difficulty that deprived me of the services of an excellent coachman,' murmured the countess.

'But if he married my daughter he cannot continue to be your coachman,' cried the duchess indignantly.

'Are you going to give Pilar an income for them to live on?'

'Me? Not a peseta. I told Pilar at once that she should get nothing from me. They can starve for all I care.'

'Well, I should think rather than do that he will prefer to stay on as my coachman. There are very nice rooms over my stables.'

The duchess went pale. The duchess went red.

'Forget all that has passed between us. Let us be friends. You can't expose me to such a humiliation. If I've ever done things to affront you I ask you on my knees to forgive me.'

The duchess cried.

'Dry your eyes, Duchess,' the Frenchwoman said at last. 'I will do what I can.'

'Is there anything you can do?'

'Perhaps. Is it true that Pilar has and will have no money of her own?'

'Not a penny if she marries without my consent.'

The countess gave her one of her brightest smiles.

'There is a common impression that southern people are romantic and northern people matter-of-fact. The reverse is true. It is the northerners who are incurably romantic. I have lived long enough among you Spaniards to know that you are nothing if not practical.'

The duchess was too broken to resent openly these unpleasant remarks, but, oh, how she hated the woman! The Countess de Marbella rose to her feet.

'You shall hear from me in the course of the day.'

She firmly dismissed her visitor.

The carriage was ordered for five o'clock and at ten minutes to, the countess, dressed for her drive, sent for José. When he came into the drawing-room, wearing his pale grey livery with such an air, she could not deny that he was very good to look upon. If he had not been her own coachman–well, it was not the moment for ideas of that sort. He stood before her, holding himself easily, but with a gallant swagger. There was nothing servile in his bearing.

'A Greek god,' the countess murmured to herself. 'It is only Andalusia that can produce such types.' And then aloud: 'I hear that you are going to marry the daughter of the Duchess of Dos Palos.'

'If the countess does not object.'

She shrugged her shoulders.

'Whoever you marry is a matter of complete indifference to me. You know of course that Doña Pilar will have no fortune.'

'Yes, madam. I have a good place and I can keep my wife. I love her.'

'I can't blame you for that. She is a beautiful girl. But I think it only right to tell you that I have a rooted objection to married coachmen. On your wedding-day you leave my service. That is all I had to say to you. You can go.'

She began to look at the daily paper that had just arrived from Paris, but José, as she expected, did not stir. He stared down at the floor. Presently the countess looked up.

'What are you waiting for?'

'I never knew madam would send me away,' he answered in a troubled tone.

'I have no doubt you'll find another place.'

'Yes, but . . .'

'Well, what is it?' she asked sharply.

He sighed miserably.

'There's not a pair of mules in the whole of Spain to come up to ours. They're almost human beings. They understand every word I say to them.'

The countess gave him a smile that would have turned the head of anyone who was not madly in love already.

'I'm afraid you must choose between me and your betrothed.'

He shifted from one foot to the other. He put his hand to his pocket to get himself a cigarette, but then, remembering where he was, restrained the gesture. He glanced at the countess and that peculiar shrewd smile came over his face which those who have lived in Andalusia know so well.

'In that case, I can't hesitate. Pilar must see that this alters my position entirely. One can get a wife any day of the week, but a place like this is found only once in a lifetime. I should be a fool to throw it up for a woman.'

That was the end of the adventure. José León continued to drive the Countess de Marbella, but she noticed when they sped up and down the Delicias that henceforward as many eyes were turned on her handsome coachman as on her latest hat: and a year later Pilar married the Marqués de San Esteban.

A
Man
From Glasgow

◆

It is not often that anyone entering a great city for the first time has the luck to witness such an incident as engaged Shelley's attention when he drove into Naples. A youth ran out of a shop pursued by a man armed with a knife. The man overtook him and with one blow in the neck laid him dead on the road. Shelley had a tender heart. He didn't look upon it as a bit of local colour; he was seized with horror and indignation. But when he expressed his emotions to a Calabrian priest who was travelling with him, a fellow of gigantic strength and stature, the priest laughed heartily and attempted to quiz him. Shelley says he never felt such an inclination to beat anyone.

I have never seen anything so exciting as that, but the first time I went to Algeciras I had an experience that seemed to me far from ordinary. Algeciras was then an untidy, neglected town. I arrived somewhat late at night and went to an inn on the quay. It was rather shabby, but it had a fine view of Gibraltar, solid and matter-of-fact, across the bay. The moon was full. The office was on the first floor, and a slatternly maid, when I asked for a room, took me upstairs. The landlord was playing cards. He seemed little pleased to see me. He looked me up and down, curtly gave me a number, and then, taking no further notice of me, went on with his game.

When the maid had shown me to my room I asked her what I could have to eat.

'What you like,' she answered.

I knew well enough the unreality of the seeming profusion.

'What have you got in the house?'

'You can have eggs and ham.'

The look of the hotel had led me to guess that I should get little else. The maid led me to a narrow room with white-washed walls and a low ceiling in which was a long table laid already for the next day's luncheon. With his back to the door sat a tall man, huddled over a *brasero*, the round brass dish of hot ashes which is erroneously supposed to give sufficient warmth for the temperate winter of Andalusia. I sat down at table and waited for my scanty meal. I gave the stranger an idle glance. He was looking at me, but meeting my eyes he quickly turned away. I waited for my eggs. When at last the maid brought them he looked up again.

'I want you to wake me in time for the first boat,' he said.

'*Si, señor.*'

His accent told me that English was his native tongue, and the breadth of his build, his strongly marked features, led me to suppose him a northerner. The hardy Scot is far more often found in Spain than the Englishman. Whether you go to the rich mines of Rio Tinto, or to the *bodegas* of Jerez, to Seville or to Cadiz, it is the leisurely speech of beyond the Tweed that you hear. You will meet Scotsmen in the olive groves of Carmona, on the railway between Algeciras and Bobadilla, and even in the remote cork woods of Merida.

I finished eating and went over to the dish of burning ashes. It was midwinter and the windy passage across the bay had chilled my blood. The man pushed his chair away as I drew mine forwards.

'Don't move,' I said. 'There's heaps of room for two.'

I lit a cigar and offered one to him. In Spain the Havana from Gib is never unwelcome.

'I don't mind if I do,' he said, stretching out his hand.

I recognized the singing speech of Glasgow. But the stranger was not talkative, and my efforts at conversation broke down before his monosyllables. We smoked in silence. He was even bigger than I had thought, with great broad shoulders and ungainly limbs; his face was sunburned, his hair short and grizzled. His features were hard; mouth, ears and nose were large and heavy and his skin much wrinkled. His blue eyes were pale. He was constantly pulling his ragged, grey moustache. It was a nervous gesture that I found faintly irritating. Presently I felt that he was looking at me, and the intensity of his stare grew so irksome that I glanced up expecting him, as before, to drop his eyes. He did, indeed, for a moment, but then raised them again. He inspected me from under his long, bushy eyebrows.

'Just come from Gib?' he asked suddenly.

'Yes.'

'I'm going tomorrow—on my way home. Thank God.'

He said the last two words so fiercely that I smiled.

'Don't you like Spain?'

'Oh, Spain's all right.'

'Have you been here long?'

'Too long. Too long.'

He spoke with a kind of gasp. I was surprised at the emotion my casual inquiry seemed to excite in him. He sprang to his feet and walked backwards and forwards. He stamped to and fro like a caged beast pushing aside a chair that stood in his way, and now and again repeated the words in a groan. 'Too long. Too long.' I sat still. I was embarrassed. To give myself countenance I stirred the *brasero* to bring the hotter ashes to the top, and he stood suddenly still, towering over me, as though my movement had brought back my existence to his notice. Then he sat down heavily in his chair.

'D'you think I'm queer?' he asked.

'Not more than most people,' I smiled.

'You don't see anything strange in me?'

He leant forward as he spoke so that I might see him well.

'No.'

'You'd say so if you did, wouldn't you?'

'I would.'

I couldn't quite understand what all this meant. I wondered if he was drunk. For two or three minutes he didn't say anything and I had no wish to interrupt the silence.

'What's your name?' he asked suddenly. I told him.

'Mine's Robert Morrison.'

'Scotch?'

'Glasgow. I've been in this blasted country for years. Got any baccy?'

I gave him my pouch and he filled his pipe. He lit it from a piece of burning charcoal.

'I can't stay any longer. I've stayed too long. Too long.'

He had an impulse to jump up again and walk up and down, but he resisted it, clinging to his chair. I saw on his face the effort he was making. I judged that his restlessness was due to chronic alcoholism. I find drunks very boring, and I made up my mind to take an early opportunity of slipping off to bed.

'I've been managing some olive groves,' he went on. 'I'm here working for the Glasgow and South of Spain Olive Oil Company Limited.'

'Oh, yes.'

'We've got a new process for refining oil, you know. Properly treated, Spanish oil is every bit as good as Lucca. And we can sell it cheaper.'

He spoke in a dry, matter-of-fact, business-like way. He chose his words with Scotch precision. He seemed perfectly sober.

'You know, Ecija is more or less the centre of the olive trade, and we had a Spaniard there to look after the business. But I found he was robbing us right and left, so I had to turn him out. I used to live in Seville; it was more convenient for shipping the oil. However, I found I couldn't get a trustworthy man to be at Ecija, so last year I went there myself. D'you know it?'

'No.'

'The firm has got a big estate two miles from the town, just outside the village of San Lorenzo, and it's got a fine house on it. It's on the crest of a hill, rather pretty to look at, all white, you know, and straggling, with a couple of storks perched on the roof. No one lived there, and I thought it would save the rent of a place in town if I did.'

'It must have been a bit lonely,' I remarked.

'It was.'

Robert Morrison smoked on for a minute or two in silence. I wondered whether there was any point in what he was telling me.

I looked at my watch.

'In a hurry?' he asked sharply.

'Not particularly. It's getting late.'

'Well, what of it?'

'I suppose you didn't see many people?' I said, going back.

'Not many. I lived there with an old man and his wife who looked after me, and sometimes I used to go down to the village and play *tresillo* with Fernández, the chemist, and one or two men who met at his shop. I used to shoot a bit and ride.'

'It doesn't sound such a bad life to me.'

'I'd been there two years last spring. By God, I've never known such heat as we had in May. No one could do a thing. The labourers just lay about in the shade and slept. Sheep died and some of the animals went mad. Even the oxen couldn't work. They stood around with their backs all humped up and gasped for breath. That blasted sun beat down and the glare was so awful, you felt your eyes would shoot out of your head. The earth cracked and crumbled, and the crops frizzled. The olives went to rack and ruin. It was simply hell. One couldn't get a wink of sleep. I went from room to room, trying to get a breath of air. Of course I kept the windows shut and had the floors watered, but that didn't do any good. The nights were just as hot as the days. It was like living in an oven.

'At last I thought I'd have a bed made up for me downstairs on the north side of the house in a room that was never used because in ordinary weather it was damp. I had an idea that I might get a few hours' sleep there at all events. Anyhow it was worth trying. But it was no damned good; it was a washout. I turned and tossed and my bed was so hot that I couldn't stand it. I got up and opened the doors that led to the veranda and walked out. It was a glorious night. The moon was so bright that I swear you could read a book by it. Did I tell you the house was on the crest of a hill? I leant against the parapet and looked at the olive-trees. It was like the sea. I suppose that's what made me think of home. I thought of the cool breeze in the fir-trees and the racket of the streets in Glasgow. Believe it or not, I could smell them, and I could smell the sea. By God, I'd have given every bob I had in the world for an hour of that air. They say it's a foul climate in Glasgow. Don't you believe it. I like the rain and the grey sky and that yellow sea and the waves. I forgot that I was in Spain, in the middle of the olive country, and I opened my mouth and took a long breath as though I were breathing in the sea-fog.

'And then all of a sudden I heard a sound. It was a man's voice. Not loud, you know, low. It seemed to creep through the silence like – well, I don't know what it was like. It surprised me. I couldn't think who could be down there in the olives at that hour. It was past midnight. It was a chap laughing. A funny sort of laugh. I suppose you'd call it a chuckle. It seemed to crawl up the hill–disjointedly.'

Morrison looked at me to see how I took the odd word he used to express a sensation that he didn't know how to describe.

'I mean, it seemed to shoot up in little jerks, something like shooting stones out of a pail. I leant forward and stared. With the full moon it was almost as light as day, but I'm dashed if I could see a thing. The sound stopped, but I kept on looking at where it had come from in case somebody moved. And in a minute it started off again, but louder. You couldn't have called it a chuckle any more, it was a real belly laugh. It just rang through the night. I wondered it didn't wake my servants. It sounded like someone who was roaring drunk.

'"Who's there?" I shouted.

'The only answer I got was a roar of laughter. I don't mind telling you I was getting a bit annoyed. I had half a mind to go down and see what it was all about. I wasn't going to let some drunken swine kick up a row like that on my place in the middle of the night. And then suddenly there was a yell. By God, I was startled. Then cries. The man had laughed with a deep bass voice, but his cries were–shrill, like a pig having his throat cut.

'"My God," I cried.

'I jumped over the parapet and ran down towards the sound. I thought somebody was being killed. There was silence and then one piercing shriek. After that sobbing and moaning. I'll tell you what it sounded like, it sounded like someone at the point of death. There was a long groan and then nothing. Silence. I ran from place to place. I couldn't find anyone. At last I climbed the hill again and went back to my room.

'You can imagine how much sleep I got that night. As soon as it was light, I looked out of the window in the direction from which the row had come and I was surprised to see a little white house in a sort of dale among the olives. The ground on that side didn't belong to us and I'd never been through it. I hardly ever went to that part of the house and so I'd never seen the house before. I asked José who lived there. He told me that a madman had inhabited it, with his brother and a servant.'

'Oh, was that the explanation?' I said. 'Not a very nice neighbour.'

The Scot bent over quickly and seized my wrist. He thrust his face into mine and his eyes were starting out of his head with terror.

'The madman had been dead for twenty years,' he whispered.

He let go my wrist and leant back in his chair panting.

'I went down to the house and walked all round it. The windows were barred and shuttered and the door was locked. I knocked. I shook the handle and rang the bell. I heard it tinkle, but no one came. It was a two-storey house and I looked up. The shutters were tight closed, and there wasn't a sign of life anywhere.'

'Well, what sort of condition was the house in?' I asked.

'Oh, rotten. The whitewash had worn off the walls and there was practically no paint left on the door or the shutters. Some of the tiles off the roof were lying on the ground. They looked as though they'd been blown away in a gale.'

'Queer,' I said.

'I went to my friend Fernández, the chemist, and he told me the same story as José. I asked about the madman and Fernández said that no one ever saw him. He was more or less comatose ordinarily, but now and then he had an attack of acute mania and then he could be heard from ever so far laughing his head off and then crying. It used to scare people. He died in one of his attacks and his keepers cleared out at once. No one had ever dared to live in the house since.

'I didn't tell Fernández what I'd heard. I thought he'd only laugh at me. I stayed up that night and kept watch. But nothing happened. There wasn't a sound. I waited about till dawn and then I went to bed.'

'And you never heard anything more?'

'Not for a month. The drought continued and I went on sleeping in the lumber-room at the back. One night I was fast asleep, when something seemed to happen to me; I don't exactly know how to describe it, it was a funny feeling as though someone had given me a little nudge, to warn me, and suddenly I was wide awake. I lay there in my bed and then in the same way as before I heard a long, low gurgle, like a man enjoying an old joke. It came from away down in the valley and it got louder. It was a great bellow of laughter. I jumped out of bed and went to the window. My legs began to tremble. It was horrible to stand there and listen to the shouts of laughter that rang through the night. Then there was the pause, and after that a shriek of pain and that ghastly sobbing. It didn't sound human. I mean, you might have thought it was an animal being tortured. I don't mind telling you I was scared stiff. I couldn't have moved if I'd wanted to. After a time the sounds stopped, not suddenly, but dying away little by little. I strained my ears, but I couldn't hear a thing. I crept back to bed and hid my face.

'I remembered then that Fernández had told me that the madman's attacks only came at intervals. The rest of the time he was quite quiet. Apathetic, Fernández said. I wondered if the fits of mania came regularly. I reckoned out how long it had been between the two attacks I'd heard. Twenty-eight days. It didn't take me long to put two and two together; it was quite obvious that it was the full moon that set him off. I'm not a nervous man really and I made up my mind to get to the bottom of it, so I looked out in the calendar which day the moon would be full next and that night I didn't go to bed. I cleaned my revolver and loaded it. I prepared a lantern and sat down on the parapet of my house to wait. I felt perfectly cool. To tell you the truth, I was rather pleased with myself because I didn't feel scared. There was a bit of a wind, and it whistled about the roof. It rustled over the leaves of the olive trees like waves swishing on the pebbles of the beach. The moon shone on the white walls of the house in the hollow. I felt particularly cheery.

'At last I heard a little sound, the sound I knew, and I almost laughed. I was right; it was the full moon and the attacks came as regular as clockwork. That was all to the good. I threw myself over the wall into the olive grove and ran straight to the house. The chuckling grew louder as I came near. I got to the house and looked up. There was no light anywhere. I put my ears to the door and listened. I heard the madman simply laughing his bloody head off. I beat on the door with my fist and I pulled the bell. The sound of it seemed to amuse him. He roared with laughter. I knocked again, louder and louder, and the more I knocked the more he laughed. Then I shouted at the top of my voice.

'"Open the blasted door, or I'll break it down."

'I stepped back and kicked the latch with all my might. I flung myself at the door with the whole weight of my body. It cracked. Then I put all my strength into it and the damned thing smashed open.

'I took the revolver out of my pocket and held my lantern in the other hand. The laughter sounded louder now that the door was opened. I stepped in. The stink nearly knocked me down. I mean, just think, the windows hadn't been opened for twenty years. The row was enough to raise the dead, but for a moment I didn't know where it was coming from. The walls seemed to throw the sound backwards and forwards. I pushed open a door by my side and went into a room. It was bare and white and there wasn't a stick of furniture in it. The sound was louder and I followed it. I went into another room, but there was nothing there. I opened a door and found myself at the foot of a staircase. The madman was laughing just over my head. I walked up, cautiously, you know, I wasn't taking any risks, and at the top of the stairs there was a passage. I walked along it, throwing my light ahead of me, and I came to a room at the end. I stopped. He was in there. I was only separated from the sound by a thin door.

'It was awful to hear it. A shiver passed through me and I cursed myself because I began to tremble. It wasn't like a human being at all. By Jove, I very nearly took to my heels and ran. I had to clench my teeth to force myself to stay. But I simply couldn't bring myself to turn the handle. And then the laughter was cut, cut with a knife you'd have said, and I heard a hiss of pain. I hadn't heard that before, it was too low to carry to my place, and then a gasp.

'"Ay!" I heard the man speak in Spanish. "You're killing me. Take it away. O God, help me!"

'He screamed. The brutes were torturing him. I flung open the door and burst in. The draught blew a shutter back and the moon streamed in so bright that it dimmed my lantern. In my ears, as clearly as I hear you speak and as close, I heard the wretched chap's groans. It was awful, moaning and sobbing, and frightful gasps. No one could survive that. He was at the point of death. I tell you I heard his broken, choking cries right in my ears. And the room was empty.'

Robert Morrison sank back in his chair. That huge solid man had strangely the look of a lay figure in a studio. You felt that if you pushed him he would fall over in a heap on to the floor.

'And then?' I asked.

He took a rather dirty handkerchief out of his pocket and wiped his forehead.

'I felt I didn't much want to sleep in that room on the north side, so, heat or no heat, I moved back to my own quarters. Well, exactly four weeks later, about two in the morning, I was waked up by the madman's chuckle. It was almost at my elbow. I don't mind telling you that my nerve was a bit shaken by then, so next time the blighter was due to have an attack, next time the moon was full, I mean, I got Fernández to come and spend the night with me. I didn't tell him anything. I kept him up playing cards till two in the morning, and then I heard it again. I asked him if he heard anything. "Nothing," he said. "There's somebody laughing," I said. "You're drunk, man," he said, and he began laughing too. That was too much. "Shut up, you fool," I said. The laughter grew louder and louder. I cried out. I tried to shut it out by putting my hands to my ears, but it wasn't a damned bit of good. I heard it and I heard the scream of pain. Fernández thought I was mad. He didn't dare say so, because he knew I'd have killed him. He said he'd go to bed, and in the morning I found he'd slunk away. His bed hadn't been slept in. He'd taken himself off when he left me.

'After that I couldn't stop in Ecija. I put a factor there and went back to Seville. I felt myself pretty safe there, but as the time came near I began to get scared. Of course I told myself not to be a damned fool, but, you know, I damned well couldn't help myself. The fact is, I was afraid the sounds had followed me, and I knew if I heard them in Seville I'd go on hearing them all my life. I've got as much courage as any man, but damn it all, there are limits to everything. Flesh and blood couldn't stand it. I knew I'd go stark staring mad. I got in such a state that I began drinking, the suspense was so awful, and I used to lie awake counting the days. And at last I knew it'd come. And it came. I heard those sounds in Seville—sixty miles away from Ecija.'

I didn't know what to say. I was silent for a while.

'When did you hear the sounds last?' I asked.

'Four weeks ago.'

I looked up quickly. I was startled.

'What d'you mean by that? It's not full moon tonight?'

He gave me a dark, angry look. He opened his mouth to speak and then stopped as though he couldn't. You would have said his vocal cords were paralysed, and it was with a strange croak that at last he answered.

'Yes, it is.'

He stared at me and his pale blue eyes seemed to shine red. I have never seen in a man's face a look of such terror. He got up quickly and stalked out of the room, slamming the door behind him.

I must admit that I didn't sleep any too well that night myself.

Before the Party

◆

Mrs Skinner liked to be in good time. She was already dressed, in black silk as befitted her age and the mourning she wore for her son-in-law, and now she put on her toque. She was a little uncertain about it, since the egrets' feathers which adorned it might very well arouse in some of the friends she would certainly meet at the party acid expostulations; and of course it was shocking to kill those beautiful white birds, in the mating season too, for the sake of their feathers; but there they were, so pretty and stylish, and it would have been silly to refuse them, and it would have hurt her son-in-law's feelings. He had brought them all the way from Borneo and he expected her to be so pleased with them. Kathleen had made herself rather unpleasant about them, she must wish she hadn't now, after what had happened, but Kathleen had never really liked Harold. Mrs Skinner, standing at her dressing-table, placed the toque on her head, it was after all the only nice hat she had, and put in a pin with a large jet knob. If anybody spoke to her about the ospreys she had her answer.

'I know it's dreadful,' she would say, 'and I wouldn't dream of buying them, but my poor son-in-law brought them back the last time he was home on leave.'

That would explain her possession of them and excuse their use. Everyone had been very kind. Mrs Skinner took a clean handkerchief from a drawer and sprinkled a little eau de Cologne on it. She never used scent, and she had always thought it rather fast, but eau de Cologne was so refreshing. She was very nearly ready now, and her eyes wandered out of the window behind her looking-glass. Canon Heywood had a beautiful day for his garden-party. It was warm and the sky was blue; the trees had not yet lost the fresh green of the spring. She smiled as she saw her little granddaughter in the strip of garden behind the house busily raking her very own flower-bed. Mrs Skinner wished Joan were not quite so pale, it was a mistake to have kept her so long in the tropics; and she was so grave for her age, you never saw her run about; she played quiet games of her own invention and watered her garden. Mrs Skinner gave the front of her dress a little pat, took up her gloves, and went downstairs.

Kathleen was at the writing-table in the window busy with lists she was making, for she was honorary secretary of the Ladies' Golf Club, and when there were competitions had a good deal to do. But she too was ready for the party.

'I see you've put on your jumper after all,' said Mrs Skinner.

They had discussed at luncheon whether Kathleen should wear her jumper or her black chiffon. The jumper was black and white, and Kathleen thought it rather smart, but it was hardly mourning. Millicent, however, was in favour of it.

'There's no reason why we should all look as if we'd just come from a funeral,' she said. 'Harold's been dead eight months.'

To Mrs Skinner it seemed rather unfeeling to talk like that. Millicent was strange since her return from Borneo.

'You're not going to leave off your weeds yet, darling?' she asked.

Millicent did not give a direct answer.

'People don't wear mourning in the way they used,' she said. She paused a little and when she went on there was a tone in her voice which Mrs Skinner thought quite peculiar. It was plain that Kathleen noticed it too, for she gave her sister a curious look. 'I'm sure Harold wouldn't wish me to wear mourning for him indefinitely.'

'I dressed early because I wanted to say something to Millicent,' said Kathleen in reply to her mother's observation.

'Oh?'

Kathleen did not explain. But she put her lists aside and with knitted brows read for the second time a letter from a lady who complained that the committee had most unfairly marked down her handicap from twenty-four to eighteen. It requires a good deal of tact to be honorary secretary to a ladies' golf club. Mrs Skinner began to put on her new gloves. The sun-blinds kept the room cool and dark. She looked at the great wooden hornbill, gaily painted, which Harold had left in her safekeeping; and it seemed a little odd and barbaric to her, but he had set much store on it. It had some religious significance and Canon Heywood had been greatly struck by it. On the wall, over the sofa, were Malay weapons, she forgot what they were called, and here and there on occasional tables pieces of silver and brass which Harold at various times had sent to them. She had liked Harold and involuntarily her eyes sought his photograph which stood on the piano with photographs of her two daughters, her grandchild, her sister, and her sister's son.

'Why, Kathleen, where's Harold's photograph?' she asked.

Kathleen looked round. It no longer stood in its place.

'Someone's taken it away,' said Kathleen.

Surprised and puzzled, she got up and went over to the piano. The photographs had been rearranged so that no gap should show.

'Perhaps Millicent wanted to have it in her bedroom,' said Mrs Skinner.

'I should have noticed it. Besides, Millicent has several photographs of Harold. She keeps them locked up.'

Mrs Skinner had thought it very peculiar that her daughter should have no photographs of Harold in her room. Indeed she had spoken of it once, but Millicent had made no reply. Millicent had been strangely silent since she came back from Borneo, and had not encouraged the sympathy Mrs Skinner would have been so willing to show her. She seemed unwilling to speak of her great loss. Sorrow took people in different ways. Her husband had said the best thing was to leave her alone. The thought of him turned her ideas to the party they were going to.

'Father asked if I thought he ought to wear a top-hat,' she said. 'I said I thought it was just as well to be on the safe side.'

It was going to be quite a grand affair. They were having ices, strawberry and vanilla, from Boddy, the confectioner, but the Heywoods were making the iced coffee at home. Everyone would be there. They had been asked to meet the Bishop of Hong Kong, who was staying with the Canon, an old college friend of his, and he was going to speak on the Chinese missions. Mrs Skinner, whose daughter had lived in the East for eight years and whose son-in-law had been Resident of a district in Borneo, was in a flutter of interest. Naturally it meant more to her than to people who had never had anything to do with the Colonies and that sort of thing.

'What can they know of England who only England know?' as Mr Skinner said.

He came into the room at that moment. He was a lawyer, as his father had been before him, and he had offices in Lincoln's Inn Fields. He went up to London every morning and came down every evening. He was only able to accompany his wife and daughters to the Canon's garden-party because the Canon had very wisely chosen a Saturday to have it on. Mr Skinner looked very well in his tail-coat and pepper-and-salt trousers. He was not exactly dressy, but he was neat. He looked like a respectable family solicitor, which indeed he was; his firm never touched work that was not perfectly above board, and if a client went to him with some trouble that was not quite nice, Mr Skinner would look grave.

'I don't think this is the sort of case that we very much care to undertake,' he said. 'I think you'd do better to go elsewhere.'

He drew towards him his writing-block and scribbled a name and address on it. He tore off a sheet of paper and handed it to his client.

'If I were you I think I would go and see these people. If you mention my name I believe they'll do anything they can for you.'

Mr Skinner was clean-shaven and very bald. His pale lips were tight and thin, but his blue eyes were shy. He had no colour in his cheeks and his face was much lined.

'I see you've put on your new trousers,' said Mrs Skinner.

'I thought it would be a good opportunity,' he answered. 'I was wondering if I should wear a buttonhole.'

'I wouldn't, father,' said Kathleen. 'I don't think it's awfully good form.'

'A lot of people will be wearing them,' said Mrs Skinner.

'Only clerks and people like that,' said Kathleen. 'The Heywoods have had to ask everybody, you know. And besides, we are in mourning.'

'I wonder if there'll be a collection after the Bishop's address,' said Mr Skinner.

'I should hardly think so,' said Mrs Skinner.

'I think it would be rather bad form,' agreed Kathleen.

'It's as well to be on the safe side,' said Mr Skinner. 'I'll give for all of us. I was wondering if ten shillings would be enough or if I must give a pound.'

'If you give anything I think you ought to give a pound, father,' said Kathleen.

'I'll see when the time comes. I don't want to give less than anyone else, but on the other hand I see no reason to give more than I need.'

Kathleen put away her papers in the drawer of the writing-table and stood up. She looked at her wrist-watch.

'Is Millicent ready?' asked Mrs Skinner.

'There's plenty of time. We're only asked at four, and I don't think we ought to arrive much before half past. I told Davis to bring the car round at four-fifteen.'

Generally Kathleen drove the car, but on grand occasions like this Davis, who was the gardener, put on his uniform and acted as chauffeur. It looked better when you drove up, and naturally Kathleen didn't much want to drive herself when she was wearing her new jumper. The sight of her mother forcing her fingers one by one into her new gloves reminded her that she must put on her own. She smelt them to see if any odour of the cleaning still clung to them. It was very slight. She didn't believe anyone would notice.

At last the door opened and Millicent came in. She wore her widow's weeds. Mrs Skinner never could get used to them, but of course she knew that Millicent must wear them for a year. It was a pity they didn't suit her; they suited some people. She had tried on Millicent's bonnet once, with its white band and long veil, and thought she looked very well in it. Of course she hoped dear Alfred would survive her, but if he didn't she would never go out of weeds. Queen Victoria never had. It was different for Millicent; Millicent was a much younger woman; she was only thirty-six: it was very sad to be a widow at thirty-six. And there wasn't much chance of her marrying again. Kathleen wasn't very likely to marry now, she was thirty-five; last time Millicent and Harold had come home she had suggested that they should have Kathleen to stay with them; Harold had seemed willing enough, but Millicent said it wouldn't do. Mrs Skinner didn't know why not. It would give her a chance. Of course they didn't want to get rid of her, but a girl ought to marry, and somehow all the men they knew at home were married already. Millicent said the climate was trying. It was true she was a bad colour. No one would think now that Millicent had been the prettier of the two. Kathleen had fined down as she grew older, of course some people said she was too thin, but now that she had cut her hair, with her cheeks red from playing golf in all weathers, Mrs Skinner thought her quite pretty. No one could say that of poor Millicent; she had lost her figure completely; she had never been tall, and now that she had filled out she looked stocky. She was a good deal too fat; Mrs Skinner supposed it was due to the tropical heat that prevented her from taking exercise. Her skin was sallow and muddy; and her blue eyes, which had been her best feature, had gone quite pale.

'She ought to do something about her neck,' Mrs Skinner reflected. 'She's becoming dreadfully jowly.'

She had spoken of it once or twice to her husband. He remarked that Millicent wasn't as young as she was; that might be, but she needn't let herself go altogether. Mrs Skinner made up her mind to talk to her daughter seriously, but of course she must respect her grief, and she would wait till the year was up. She was just as glad to have this reason to put off a conversation the thought of which made her slightly nervous. For Millicent was certainly changed. There was something sullen in her face which made her mother not quite at home with her. Mrs Skinner liked to say aloud all the thoughts that passed through her head, but Millicent when you made a remark (just to say something, you know) had an awkward habit of not answering, so that you wondered whether she had heard. Sometimes Mrs Skinner found it so irritating, that not to be quite sharp with Millicent she had to remind herself that poor Harold had only been dead eight months.

The light from the window fell on the widow's heavy face as she advanced silently, but Kathleen stood with her back to it. She watched her sister for a moment.

'Millicent, there's something I want to say to you,' she said. 'I was playing golf with Gladys Heywood this morning.'

'Did you beat her?' asked Millicent.

Gladys Heywood was the Canon's only unmarried daughter.

'She told me something about you which I think you ought to know.'

Millicent's eyes passed beyond her sister to the little girl watering flowers in the garden.

'Have you told Annie to give Joan her tea in the kitchen, mother?' she said.

'Yes, she'll have it when the servants have theirs.'

Kathleen looked at her sister coolly.

'The Bishop spent two or three days at Singapore on his way home,' she went on. 'He's very fond of travelling. He's been to Borneo, and he knows a good many of the people that you know.'

'He'll be interested to see you, dear,' said Mrs Skinner. 'Did he know poor Harold?'

'Yes, he met him at Kuala Solor. He remembers him very well. He says he was shocked to hear of his death.'

Millicent sat down and began to put on her black gloves. It seemed strange to Mrs Skinner that she received these remarks with complete silence.

'Oh, Millicent,' she said, 'Harold's photo has disappeared. Have you taken it?'

'Yes, I put it away.'

'I should have thought you'd like to have it out.'

Once more Millicent said nothing. It really was an exasperating habit.

Kathleen turned slightly in order to face her sister.

'Millicent, why did you tell us that Harold died of fever?'

The widow made no gesture, she looked at Kathleen with steady eyes, but her sallow skin darkened with a flush. She did not reply.

'What *do* you mean, Kathleen?' asked Mr Skinner, with surprise.

'The Bishop says that Harold committed suicide.'

Mrs Skinner gave a startled cry, but her husband put out a deprecating hand.

'Is it true, Millicent?'

'It is.'

'But why didn't you tell us?'

Millicent paused for an instant. She fingered idly a piece of Brunei brass which stood on the table by her side. That too had been a present from Harold.

'I thought it better for Joan that her father should be thought to have died of fever. I didn't want her to know anything about it.'

'You've put us in an awfully awkward position,' said Kathleen, frowning a little. 'Gladys Heywood said she thought it rather nasty of me not to have told her the truth. I had the greatest difficulty in getting her to believe that I knew absolutely nothing about it. She said her father was rather put out. He says, after all the years we've known one another, and considering that he married you, and the terms we've been on, and all that, he does think we might have had confidence in him. And at all events, if we didn't want to tell him the truth we needn't have told him a lie.'

'I must say I sympathize with him there,' said Mr Skinner, acidly.

'Of course I told Gladys that we weren't to blame. We only told them what you told us.'

'I hope it didn't put you off your game,' said Millicent.

'Really, my dear, I think that is a most improper observation,' exclaimed her father.

He rose from his chair, walked over to the empty fireplace, and from force of habit stood in front of it with parted coat-tails.

'It was my business,' said Millicent, 'and if I chose to keep it to myself I didn't see why I shouldn't.'

'It doesn't look as if you had any affection for your mother if you didn't even tell her,' said Mrs Skinner.

Millicent shrugged her shoulders.

'You might have known it was bound to come out,' said Kathleen.

'Why? I didn't expect that two gossiping old parsons would have nothing else to talk about than me.'

'When the Bishop said he'd been to Borneo it's only natural that the Heywoods should ask him if he knew you and Harold.'

'All that's neither here nor there,' said Mr Skinner. 'I think you should certainly have told us the truth, and we could have decided what was the best thing to do. As a solicitor I can tell you that in the long run it only makes things worse if you attempt to hide them.'

'Poor Harold,' said Mrs Skinner, and the tears began to trickle down her raddled cheeks. 'It seems dreadful. He was always a good son-in-law to me. Whatever induced him to do such a dreadful thing?'

'The climate.'

'I think you'd better give us all the facts, Millicent,' said her father.

'Kathleen will tell you.'

Kathleen hesitated. What she had to say really was rather dreadful. It seemed terrible that such things should happen to a family like theirs.

'The Bishop says he cut his throat.'

Mrs Skinner gasped and she went impulsively up to her bereaved daughter. She wanted to fold her in her arms.

'My poor child,' she sobbed.

But Millicent withdrew herself.

'Please don't fuss me, mother. I really can't stand being mauled about.'

'Really, Millicent,' said Mr Skinner, with a frown.

He did not think she was behaving very nicely.

Mrs Skinner dabbed her eyes carefully with her handkerchief and with a sigh and a little shake of the head returned to her chair. Kathleen fidgeted with the long chain she wore round her neck.

'It does seem rather absurd that I should have to be told the details of my brother-in-law's death by a friend. It makes us all look such fools. The Bishop wants very much to see you, Millicent; he wants to tell you how much he feels for you.' She paused, but Millicent did not speak. 'He says that Millicent had been away with Joan and when she came back she found poor Harold lying dead on his bed.'

'It must have been a great shock,' said Mr Skinner.

Mrs Skinner began to cry again, but Kathleen put her hand gently on her shoulder.

'Don't cry, mother,' she said. 'It'll make your eyes red and people will think it so funny.'

They were all silent while Mrs Skinner, drying her eyes, made a successful effort to control herself. It seemed very strange to her that this very moment she should be wearing in her toque the ospreys that poor Harold had given her.

'There's something else I ought to tell you,' said Kathleen.

Millicent looked at her sister again, without haste, and her eyes were steady, but watchful. She had the look of a person who is waiting for a sound which he is afraid of missing.

'I don't want to say anything to wound you, dear,' Kathleen went on, 'but there's something else and I think you ought to know it. The Bishop says that Harold drank.'

'Oh, my dear, how dreadful!' cried Mrs Skinner. 'What a shocking thing to say. Did Gladys Heywood tell you? What did you say?'

'I said it was entirely untrue.'

'This is what comes of making secrets of things,' said Mr Skinner, irritably. 'It's always the same. If you try and hush a thing up all sorts of rumours get about which are ten times worse than the truth.'

'They told the Bishop in Singapore that Harold had killed himself while he was suffering from delirium tremens. I think for all our sakes you ought to deny that, Millicent.'

'It's such a dreadful thing to have said about anyone who's dead,' said Mrs Skinner. 'And it'll be so bad for Joan when she grows up.'

'But what is the foundation of this story, Millicent?' asked her father. 'Harold was always very abstemious.'

'Here,' said the widow.

'Did he drink?'

'Like a fish.'

The answer was so unexpected, and the tone so sardonic, that all three of them were startled.

'Millicent, how can you talk like that of your husband when he's dead?' cried her mother, clasping her neatly gloved hands. 'I can't understand you. You've been so strange since you came back. I could never have believed that a girl of mine could take her husband's death like that.'

'Never mind about that, mother,' said Mr Skinner. 'We can go into all that later.'

He walked to the window and looked out at the sunny little garden, and then walked back into the room. He took his pince-nez out of his pocket, and though he had no intention of putting them on, wiped them with his handkerchief. Millicent looked at him and in her eyes, unmistakably, was a look of irony which was quite cynical. Mr Skinner was vexed. He had finished his week's work and he was a free man till Monday morning. Though he had told his wife that this garden-party was a great nuisance and he would much sooner have tea quietly in his own garden, he had been looking forward to it. He did not care very much about Chinese missions, but it would be interesting to meet the Bishop. And now this! It was not the kind of thing he cared to be mixed up in; it was most unpleasant to be told on a sudden that his son-in-law was a drunkard and a suicide. Millicent was thoughtfully smoothing her white cuffs. Her coolness irritated him; but instead of addressing her he spoke to his younger daughter.

'Why don't you sit down, Kathleen? Surely there are plenty of chairs in the room.'

Kathleen drew forward a chair and without a word seated herself. Mr Skinner stopped in front of Millicent and faced her.

'Of course I see why you told us Harold had died of fever. I think it was a mistake, because that sort of thing is bound to come out sooner or later. I don't know how far what the Bishop has told the Heywoods coincides with the facts, but if you will take my advice you will tell us everything as circumstantially as you can, then we can see. We can't hope that it will go no further now that Canon Heywood and Gladys know. In a place like this people are bound to talk. It will make it easier for all of us if we at all events know the exact truth.'

Mrs Skinner and Kathleen thought he put the matter very well. They waited for Millicent's reply. She had listened with an impassive face; that sudden flush had disappeared and it was once more, as usual, pasty and sallow.

'I don't think you'll much like the truth if I tell it you,' she said.

'You must know that you can count on our sympathy and understanding,' said Kathleen gravely.

Millicent gave her a glance and the shadow of a smile flickered across her set mouth. She looked slowly at the three of them. Mrs Skinner had an uneasy impression that she looked at them as though they were mannequins at a dressmaker's. She seemed to live in a different world from theirs and to have no connexion with them.

'You know, I wasn't in love with Harold when I married him,' she said reflectively.

Mrs Skinner was on the point of making an exclamation when a rapid gesture of her husband, barely indicated, but after so many years of married life perfectly significant, stopped her. Millicent went on. She spoke with a level voice, slowly, and there was little change of expression in her tone.

'I was twenty-seven, and no one else seemed to want to marry me. It's true he was forty-four, and it seemed rather old, but he had a very good position, hadn't he? I wasn't likely to get a better chance.'

Mrs Skinner felt inclined to cry again, but she remembered the party.

'Of course I see now why you took his photograph away,' she said dolefully.

'Don't, mother,' exclaimed Kathleen.

It had been taken when he was engaged to Millicent and was a very good photograph of Harold. Mrs Skinner had always thought him quite a fine man. He was heavily built, tall and perhaps a little too fat, but he held himself well, and his presence was imposing. He was inclined to be bald, even then, but men did go bald very early nowadays, and he said that topees, sun-helmets, you know, were very bad for the hair. He had a small dark moustache, and his face was deeply burned by the sun. Of course his best feature was his eyes; they were brown and large, like Joan's. His conversation was interesting. Kathleen said he was pompous, but Mrs Skinner didn't think him so, she didn't mind it if a man laid down the law; and when she saw, as she very soon did, that he was attracted by Millicent she began to like him very much. He was always very attentive to Mrs Skinner, and she listened as though she were really interested when he spoke of his district, and told her of the big game he had killed. Kathleen said he had a pretty good opinion of himself, but Mrs Skinner came of a generation which accepted without question the good opinion that men had of themselves. Millicent saw very soon which way the wind blew, and though she said nothing to her mother, her mother knew that if Harold asked her she was going to accept him.

Harold was staying with some people who had been thirty years in Borneo and they spoke well of the country. There was no reason why a woman shouldn't live there comfortably; of course the children had to come home when they were seven; but Mrs Skinner thought it unnecessary to trouble about that yet. She asked Harold to dine, and she told him they were always in to tea. He seemed to be at a loose end, and when his visit to his old friends was drawing to a close, she told him they would be very much pleased if he would come and spend a fortnight with them. It was towards the end of this that Harold and Millicent became engaged. They had a very pretty wedding, they went to Venice for their honeymoon, and then they started for the East. Millicent wrote from various ports at which the ship touched. She seemed happy.

'People were very nice to me at Kuala Solor,' she said. Kuala Solor was the chief town of the state of Sembulu. 'We stayed with the Resident and everyone asked us to dinner. Once or twice I heard men ask Harold to have a drink, but he refused; he said he had turned over a new leaf now he was a married man. I didn't know why they laughed. Mrs Gray, the Resident's wife, told me they were all so glad Harold was married. She said it was dreadfully lonely for a bachelor on one of the outstations. When we left Kuala Solor Mrs Gray said good-bye to me so funnily that I was quite surprised. It was as if she was solemnly putting Harold in my charge.'

They listened to her in silence. Kathleen never took her eyes off her sister's impassive face; but Mr Skinner stared straight in front of him at the Malay arms, krises and parangs, which hung on the wall above the sofa on which his wife sat.

'It wasn't till I went back to Kuala Solor a year and a half later, that I found out why their manner had seemed so odd.' Millicent gave a queer little sound like the echo of a scornful laugh. 'I knew then a good deal that I hadn't known before. Harold came to England that time in order to marry. He didn't much mind who it was. Do you remember how we spread ourselves out to catch him, mother? We needn't have taken so much trouble.'

'I don't know what you mean, Millicent,' said Mrs Skinner, not without acerbity, for the insinuation of scheming did not please her. 'I saw he was attracted by you.'

Millicent shrugged her heavy shoulders.

'He was a confirmed drunkard. He used to go to bed every night with a bottle of whisky and empty it before morning. The Chief Secretary told him he'd have to resign unless he stopped drinking. He said he'd give him one more chance. He could take his leave then and go to England. He advised him to marry so that when he got back he'd have someone to look after him. Harold married me because he wanted a keeper. They took bets in Kuala Solor on how long I'd make him stay sober.'

'But he was in love with you,' Mrs Skinner interrupted. 'You don't know how he used to speak to me about you, and at that time you're speaking of, when you went to Kuala Solor to have Joan, he wrote me such a charming letter about you.'

Millicent looked at her mother again and a deep colour dyed her sallow skin. Her hands, lying on her lap, began to tremble a little. She thought of those first months of her married life. The government launch took them to the mouth of the river, and they spent the night at the bungalow which Harold said jokingly was their seaside residence. Next day they went up-stream in a prahu. From the novels she had read she expected the rivers of Borneo to be dark and strangely sinister, but the sky was blue, dappled with little white clouds, and the green of the mangroves and the nipahs, washed by the flowing water, glistened in the sun. On each side stretched the pathless jungle, and in the distance, silhouetted against the sky, was the rugged outline of a mountain. The air in the early morning was fresh and buoyant. She seemed to enter upon a friendly, fertile land, and she had a sense of spacious freedom. They watched the banks for monkeys sitting on the branches of the tangled trees, and once Harold pointed out something that looked like a log and said it was a crocodile. The Assistant Resident, in ducks and a topee, was at the landing-stage to meet them, and a dozen trim little soldiers were lined up to do them honour. The Assistant Resident was introduced to her. His name was Simpson.

'By Jove, sir,' he said to Harold. 'I'm glad to see you back. It's been deuced lonely without you.'

The Resident's bungalow, surrounded by a garden in which grew wildly all manner of gay flowers, stood on the top of a low hill. It was a trifle shabby and the furniture was sparse, but the rooms were cool and of generous size.

'The kampong is down there,' said Harold, pointing.

Her eyes followed his gesture, and from among the coconut trees rose the beating of a gong. It gave her a queer little sensation in the heart.

Though she had nothing much to do the days passed easily enough. At dawn a boy brought them their tea and they lounged about the veranda, enjoying the fragrance of the morning (Harold in a singlet and a sarong, she in a dressing-gown) till it was time to dress for breakfast. Then Harold went to his office and she spent an hour or two learning Malay. After tiffin he went back to his office while she slept. A cup of tea revived them both, and they went for a walk or played golf on the nine-hole links which Harold had made on a level piece of cleared jungle below the bungalow. Night fell at six and Mr Simpson came along to have a drink. They chatted till their late dinner hour, and sometimes Harold and Mr Simpson played chess. The balmy evenings were enchanting. The fireflies turned the bushes just below the veranda into coldly-sparkling, tremulous beacons, and flowering trees scented the air with sweet odours. After dinner they read the papers which had left London six weeks before and presently went to bed. Millicent enjoyed being a married woman, with a house of her own, and she was pleased with the native servants, in their gay sarongs, who went about the bungalow, with bare feet, silent but friendly. It gave her a pleasant sense of importance to be the wife of the Resident. Harold impressed her by the fluency with which he spoke the language, by his air of command, and by his dignity. She went into the court-house now and then to hear him try cases. The multifariousness of his duties and the competent way in which he performed them aroused her respect. Mr Simpson told her that Harold understood the natives as well as any man in the country. He had the combination of firmness, tact, and good-humour which was essential in dealing with that timid, revengeful, and suspicious race. Millicent began to feel a certain admiration for her husband.

They had been married nearly a year when two English naturalists came to stay with them for a few days on their way to the interior. They brought a pressing recommendation from the governor, and Harold said he wanted to do

them proud. Their arrival was an agreeable change. Millicent asked Mr
Simpson to dinner (he lived at the Fort and only dined with them on Sunday
nights) and after dinner the men sat down to play bridge. Millicent left them
presently and went to bed, but they were so noisy that for some time she could
not get to sleep. She did not know at what hour she was awakened by Harold
staggering into the room. She kept silent. He made up his mind to have a bath
before getting into bed; the bath-house was just below their room, and he went
down the steps that led to it. Apparently he slipped, for there was a great clatter,
and he began to swear. Then he was violently sick. She heard him sluice the
buckets of water over himself and in a little while, walking very cautiously this
time, he crawled up the stairs and slipped into bed. Millicent pretended to be
asleep. She was disgusted. Harold was drunk. She made up her mind to speak
about it in the morning. What would the naturalists think of him? But in the
morning Harold was so dignified that she hadn't quite the determination to
refer to the matter. At eight Harold and she, with their two guests, sat down to
breakfast. Harold looked round the table.

'Porridge,' he said. 'Millicent, your guests might manage a little Worcester
sauce for breakfast, but I don't think they'll much fancy anything else.
Personally I shall content myself with a whisky and soda.'

The naturalists laughed, but shamefacedly.

'Your husband's a terror,' said one of them.

'I should not think I had properly performed the duties of hospitality if I sent
you sober to bed on the first night of your visit,' said Harold, with his round,
stately way of putting things.

Millicent, smiling acidly, was relieved to think that her guests had been as
drunk as her husband. The next evening she sat up with them and the party
broke up at a reasonable hour. But she was glad when the strangers went on
with their journey. Their life resumed its placid course. Some months later
Harold went on a tour of inspection of his district and came back with a bad
attack of malaria. This was the first time she had seen the disease of which she
had heard so much, and when he recovered it did not seem strange to her that
Harold was very shaky. She found his manner peculiar. He would come back
from the office and stare at her with glazed eyes; he would stand on the veranda,
swaying slightly, but still dignified, and make long harangues about the
political situation in England; losing the thread of his discourse, he would look
at her with an archness which his natural stateliness made somewhat
disconcerting and say:

'Pulls you down dreadfully, this confounded malaria. Ah, little woman, you
little know the strain it puts upon a man to be an empire builder.'

She thought that Mr Simpson began to look worried, and once or twice,
when they were alone, he seemed on the point of saying something to her which
his shyness at the last moment prevented. The feeling grew so strong that it
made her nervous, and one evening when Harold, she knew not why, had
remained later than usual at the office she tackled him.

'What have you got to say to me, Mr Simpson?' she broke out suddenly.

He blushed and hesitated.

'Nothing. What makes you think I have anything in particular to say to
you?'

Mr Simpson was a thin, weedy youth of four and twenty, with a fine head of
waving hair which he took great pains to plaster down very flat. His wrists were
swollen and scarred with mosquito bites. Millicent looked at him steadily.

'If it's something to do with Harold don't you think it would be kinder to tell me frankly?'

He grew scarlet now. He shuffled uneasily on his rattan chair. She insisted.

'I'm afraid you'll think it awful cheek,' he said at last. 'It's rotten of me to say anything about my chief behind his back. Malaria's a rotten thing, and after one's had a bout of it one feels awfully down and out.'

He hesitated again. The corners of his mouth sagged as if he were going to cry. To Millicent he seemed like a little boy.

'I'll be as silent as the grave,' she said with a smile, trying to conceal her apprehension. 'Do tell me.'

'I think it's a pity your husband keeps a bottle of whisky at the office. He's apt to take a nip more often than he otherwise would.'

Mr Simpson's voice was hoarse with agitation. Millicent felt a sudden coldness shiver through her. She controlled herself, for she knew that she must not frighten the boy if she were to get out of him all there was to tell. He was unwilling to speak. She pressed him, wheedling, appealing to his sense of duty, and at last she began to cry. Then he told her that Harold had been drunk more or less for the last fortnight, the natives were talking about it, and they said that soon he would be as bad as he had been before his marriage. He had been in the habit of drinking a good deal too much then, but details of that time, notwithstanding all her attempts, Mr Simpson resolutely declined to give her.

'Do you think he's drinking now?' she asked.

'I don't know.'

Millicent felt herself on a sudden hot with shame and anger. The Fort, as it was called because the rifles and the ammunition were kept there, was also the court-house. It stood opposite the Resident's bungalow in a garden of its own. The sun was just about to set and she did not need a hat. She got up and walked across. She found Harold sitting in the office behind the large hall in which he administered justice. There was a bottle of whisky in front of him. He was smoking cigarettes and talking to three or four Malays who stood in front of him listening with obsequious and at the same time scornful smiles. His face was red.

The natives vanished.

'I came to see what you were doing,' she said.

He rose, for he always treated her with elaborate politeness, and lurched. Feeling himself unsteady he assumed an elaborate stateliness of demeanour.

'Take a seat, my dear, take a seat. I was detained by press of work.'

She looked at him with angry eyes.

'You're drunk,' she said.

He stared at her, his eyes bulging a little, and a haughty look gradually traversed his large and fleshy face.

'I haven't the remotest idea what you mean,' he said.

She had been ready with a flow of wrathful expostulation, but suddenly she burst into tears. She sank into a chair and hid her face. Harold looked at her for an instant, then the tears began to trickle down his own cheeks; he came towards her with outstretched arms and fell heavily on his knees. Sobbing, he clasped her to him.

'Forgive me, forgive me,' he said. 'I promise you it shall not happen again. It was that damned malaria.'

'It's so humiliating,' she moaned.

He wept like a child. There was something very touching in the self-abasement of that big dignified man. Presently Millicent looked up. His eyes, appealing and contrite, sought hers.

'Will you give me your word of honour that you'll never touch liquor again?'

'Yes, yes. I hate it.'

It was then she told him that she was with child. He was overjoyed.

'That is the one thing I wanted. That'll keep me straight.'

They went back to the bungalow. Harold bathed himself and had a nap. After dinner they talked long and quietly. He admitted that before he married her he had occasionally drunk more than was good for him; in outstations it was easy to fall into bad habits. He agreed to everything that Millicent asked. And during the months before it was necessary for her to go to Kuala Solor for her confinement, Harold was an excellent husband, tender, thoughtful, proud, and affectionate; he was irreproachable. A launch came to fetch her, she was to leave him for six weeks, and he promised faithfully to drink nothing during her absence. He put his hands on her shoulders.

'I never break a promise,' he said in his dignified way. 'But even without it, can you imagine that while you are going through so much, I should do anything to increase your troubles?'

Joan was born. Millicent stayed at the Resident's, and Mrs Gray, his wife, a kindly creature of middle age, was very good to her. The two women had little to do during the long hours they were alone but to talk, and in course of time Millicent learnt everything there was to know of her husband's alcoholic past. The fact which she found most difficult to reconcile herself to was that Harold had been told that the only condition upon which he would be allowed to keep his post was that he should bring back a wife. It caused in her a dull feeling of resentment. And when she discovered what a persistent drunkard he had been, she felt vaguely uneasy. She had a horrid fear that during her absence he would not have been able to resist the craving. She went home with her baby and a nurse. She spent a night at the mouth of the river and sent a messenger in a canoe to announce her arrival. She scanned the landing-stage anxiously as the launch approached it. Harold and Mr Simpson were standing there. The trim little soldiers were lined up. Her heart sank, for Harold was swaying slightly, like a man who seeks to keep his balance on a rolling ship, and she knew he was drunk.

It wasn't a very pleasant home-coming. She had almost forgotten her mother and father and her sister who sat there silently listening to her. Now she roused herself and became once more aware of their presence. All that she spoke of seemed very far away.

'I knew that I hated him then,' she said. 'I could have killed him.'

'Oh, Millicent, don't say that,' cried her mother. 'Don't forget that he's dead, poor man.'

Millicent looked at her mother, and for a moment a scowl darkened her impassive face. Mr Skinner moved uneasily.

'Go on,' said Kathleen.

'When he found out that I knew all about him he didn't bother very much more. In three months he had another attack of D.T.s.'

'Why didn't you leave him?' said Kathleen.

'What would have been the good of that? He would have been dismissed from the service in a fortnight. Who was to keep me and Joan? I had to stay. And when he was sober I had nothing to complain of. He wasn't in the least in love with me, but he was fond of me; I hadn't married him because I was in love with him, but because I wanted to be married. I did everything I could to keep liquor from him; I managed to get Mr Gray to prevent whisky being sent from Kuala Solor, but he got it from the Chinese. I watched him as a cat watches a mouse. He was too cunning for me. In a little while he had another outbreak. He neglected his duties. I was afraid complaints would be made. We were two days from Kuala Solor and that was our safeguard, but I suppose something was said, for Mr Gray wrote a private letter of warning to me. I showed it to Harold. He stormed and blustered, but I saw he was frightened, and for two or three months he was quite sober. Then he began again. And so it went on till our leave became due.

'Before we came to stay here I begged and prayed him to be careful. I didn't want any of you to know what sort of a man I had married. All the time he was in England he was all right and before we sailed I warned him. He'd grown to be very fond of Joan, and very proud of her, and she was devoted to him. She always liked him better than she liked me. I asked him if he wanted to have his child grow up, knowing that he was a drunkard, and I found out that at last I'd got a hold on him. The thought terrified him. I told him that *I* wouldn't allow it, and if he ever let Joan see him drunk I'd take her away from him at once. Do you know, he grew quite pale when I said it. I fell on my knees that night and thanked God, because I'd found a way of saving my husband.

'He told me that if I would stand by him he would have another try. We made up our minds to fight the thing together. And he tried so hard. When he felt as though he *must* drink he came to me. You know he was inclined to be rather pompous; with me he was so humble, he was like a child; he depended on me. Perhaps he didn't love me when he married me, but he loved me then, me and Joan. I'd hated him, because of the humiliation, because when he was drunk and tried to be dignified and impressive he was loathsome; but now I got a strange feeling in my heart. It wasn't love, but it was a queer, shy tenderness. He was something more than my husband, he was like a child that I'd carried under my heart for long and weary months. He was so proud of me and, you know, I was proud too. His long speeches didn't irritate me any more, and I only thought his stately ways rather funny and charming. At last we won. For two years he never touched a drop. He lost his craving entirely. He was even able to joke about it.

'Mr Simpson had left us then and we had another young man called Francis.

'"I'm a reformed drunkard, you know, Francis," Harold said to him once. "If it hadn't been for my wife I'd have been sacked long ago. I've got the best wife in the world, Francis."

'You don't know what it meant to me to hear him say that. I felt that all I'd gone through was worth while. I was so happy.'

She was silent. She thought of the broad, yellow and turbid river on whose banks she had lived so long. The egrets, white and gleaming in the tremulous sunset, flew down the stream in a flock, flew low and swift, and scattered. They were like a ripple of snowy notes, sweet and pure and spring-like, which an unseen hand drew forth, a divine arpeggio, from an unseen harp. They fluttered along between the green banks, wrapped in the shadows of evening, like the happy thoughts of a contented mind.

'Then Joan fell ill. For three weeks we were very anxious. There was no doctor nearer than Kuala Solor and we had to put up with the treatment of a native dispenser. When she grew well again I took her down to the mouth of the river in order to give her a breath of sea air. We stayed there a week. It was the first time I had been separated from Harold since I went away to have Joan. There was a fishing village, on piles, not far from us, but really we were quite alone. I thought a great deal about Harold, so tenderly, and all at once I knew that I loved him. I was so glad when the prahu came to fetch us back, because I wanted to tell him. I thought it would mean a good deal to him. I can't tell you how happy I was. As we rowed up-stream the headman told me that Mr Francis had had to go up-country to arrest a woman who had murdered her husband. He had been gone a couple of days.

'I was surprised that Harold was not on the landing-stage to meet me; he was always very punctilious about that sort of thing; he used to say that husband and wife should treat one another as politely as they treated acquaintances; and I could not imagine what business had prevented him. I walked up the little hill on which the bungalow stood. The ayah brought Joan behind me. The bungalow was strangely silent. There seemed to be no servants about, and I could not make it out; I wondered if Harold hadn't expected me so soon and was out. I went up the steps. Joan was thirsty and the ayah took her to the servants' quarters to give her something to drink. Harold was not in the sitting-room. I called him, but there was no answer. I was disappointed because I should have liked him to be there. I went into our bedroom. Harold wasn't out after all; he was lying on the bed asleep. I was really very much amused, because he always pretended he never slept in the afternoon. He said it was an unnecessary habit that we white people got into. I went up to the bed softly. I thought I would have a joke with him. I opened the mosquito curtains. He was lying on his back, with nothing on but a sarong, and there was an empty whisky bottle by his side. He was drunk.

'It had begun again. All my struggles for so many years were wasted. My dream was shattered. It was all hopeless. I was seized with rage.'

Millicent's face grew once again darkly red and she clenched the arms of the chair she sat in.

'I took him by the shoulders and shook him with all my might. "You beast," I cried, "you beast." I was so angry I don't know what I did, I don't know what I said. I kept on shaking him. You don't know how loathsome he looked, that large fat man, half naked; he hadn't shaved for days, and his face was bloated and purple. He was breathing heavily. I shouted at him, but he took no notice. I tried to drag him out of bed, but he was too heavy. He lay there like a log. "Open your eyes," I screamed. I shook him again. I hated him. I hated him all the more because for a week I'd loved him with all my heart. He'd let me down. He'd let me down. I wanted to tell him what a filthy beast he was. I could make no impression on him. "You shall open your eyes,' I cried. I was determined to make him look at me.'

The widow licked her dry lips. Her breath seemed hurried. She was silent.

'If he was in that state I should have thought it best to have let him go on sleeping,' said Kathleen.

'There was a parang on the wall by the side of the bed. You know how fond Harold was of curios.'

'What's a parang?' said Mrs Skinner.

'Don't be silly, mother,' her husband replied irritably. 'There's one on the wall immediately behind you.'

He pointed to the Malay sword on which for some reason his eyes had been unconsciously resting. Mrs Skinner drew quickly into the corner of the sofa, with a little frightened gesture, as though she had been told that a snake lay curled up beside her.

'Suddenly the blood spurted out from Harold's throat. There was a great red gash right across it.'

'Millicent,' cried Kathleen, springing up and almost leaping towards her, 'what in God's name do you mean?'

Mrs Skinner stood staring at her with wide startled eyes, her mouth open.

'The parang wasn't on the wall any more. It was on the bed. Then Harold opened his eyes. They were just like Joan's.'

'I don't understand,' said Mr Skinner. 'How could he have committed suicide if he was in the state you describe?'

Kathleen took her sister's arm and shook her angrily.

'Millicent, for God's sake explain.'

Millicent released herself.

'The parang was on the wall, I told you. I don't know what happened. There was all the blood, and Harold opened his eyes. He died almost at once. He never spoke, but he gave a sort of gasp.'

At last Mr Skinner found his voice.

'But, you wretched woman, it was murder.'

Millicent, her face mottled with red, gave him such a look of scornful hatred that he shrank back. Mrs Skinner cried out.

'Millicent, you didn't do it, did you?'

Then Millicent did something that made them all feel as though their blood were turned to ice in their veins. She chuckled.

'I don't know who else did,' she said.

'My God,' muttered Mr Skinner.

Kathleen had been standing bolt upright with her hands to her heart, as though its beating were intolerable.

'And what happened then?' she said.

'I screamed. I went to the window and flung it open. I called for the ayah. She came across the compound with Joan. "Not Joan," I cried. "Don't let her come." She called the cook and told him to take the child. I cried to her to hurry. And when she came I showed her Harold. "The Tuan's killed himself!" I cried. She gave a scream and ran out of the house.

'No one would come near. They were all frightened out of their wits. I wrote a letter to Mr Francis, telling him what had happened and asking him to come at once.'

'How do you mean you told him what had happened?'

'I said, on my return from the mouth of the river, I'd found Harold with his throat cut. You know, in the tropics you have to bury people quickly. I got a Chinese coffin, and the soldiers dug a grave behind the Fort. When Mr Francis came, Harold had been buried for nearly two days. He was only a boy. I could do anything I wanted with him. I told him I'd found the parang in Harold's hand and there was no doubt he'd killed himself in an attack of delirium tremens. I showed him the empty bottle. The servants said he'd been drinking hard ever since I left to go to the sea. I told the same story at Kuala Solor. Everyone was very kind to me, and the government granted me a pension.'

For a little while nobody spoke. At last Mr Skinner gathered himself together.

'I am a member of the legal profession. I'm a solicitor. I have certain duties.

We've always had a most respectable practice. You've put me in a monstrous position.'

He fumbled, searching for the phrases that played at hide and seek in his scattered wits. Millicent looked at him with scorn.

'What are you going to do about it?'

'It was murder, that's what it was; do you think I can possibly connive at it?'

'Don't talk nonsense, father,' said Kathleen sharply. 'You can't give up your own daughter.'

'You've put me in a monstrous position,' he repeated.

Millicent shrugged her shoulders again.

'You made me tell you. And I've borne it long enough by myself. It was time that all of you bore it too.'

At that moment the door was opened by the maid.

'Davis has brought the car round, sir,' she said.

Kathleen had the presence of mind to say something, and the maid withdrew.

'We'd better be starting,' said Millicent.

'I can't go to the party now,' cried Mrs Skinner, with horror. 'I'm far too upset. How can we face the Heywoods? And the Bishop will want to be introduced to you.'

Millicent made a gesture of indifference. Her eyes held their ironical expression.

'We must go, mother,' said Kathleen. 'It would look so funny if we stayed away.' She turned on Millicent furiously. 'Oh, I think the whole thing is such frightfully bad form.'

Mrs Skinner looked helplessly at her husband. He went to her and gave her his hand to help her up from the sofa.

'I'm afraid we must go, mother,' he said.

'And me with the ospreys in my toque that Harold gave me with his own hands,' she moaned.

He led her out of the room, Kathleen followed close on their heels, and a step or two behind came Millicent.

'You'll get used to it, you know,' she said quietly. 'At first I thought of it all the time, but now I forget it for two or three days together. It's not as if there was any danger.'

They did not answer. They walked through the hall and out of the front door. The three ladies got into the back of the car and Mr Skinner seated himself beside the driver. They had no self-starter; it was an old car, and Davis went to the bonnet to crank it up. Mr Skinner turned round and looked petulantly at Millicent.

'I ought never to have been told,' he said. 'I think it was most selfish of you.'

Davis took his seat and they drove off to the Canon's garden-party.

The
Vessel
of Wrath

◆

There are few books in the world that contain more meat than the *Sailing Directions* published by the Hydrographic Department by order of the Lords Commissioners of the Admiralty. They are handsome volumes, bound (very flimsily) in cloth of different colours, and the most expensive of them is cheap. For four shillings you can buy the *Yangtse Kiang Pilot*, 'containing a description of, and sailing directions for, the Yangtse Kiang from the Wusung river to the highest navigable point, including the Han Kiang, the Kialing Kiang, and the Min Kiang'; and for three shillings you can get Part III of the *Eastern Archipelago Pilot*, 'comprising the N.E. end of Celebes, Molucca and Gilolo passages, Banda and Arafura Seas, and North, West, and South-West coasts of New Guinea'. But it is not very safe to do so if you are a creature of settled habits that you have no wish to disturb or if you have an occupation that holds you fast to one place. These business-like books take you upon enchanted journeys of the spirit; and their matter-of-fact style, the admirable order, the concision with which the material is set before you, the stern sense or the practical that informs every line, cannot dim the poetry that, like the spice-laden breeze that assails your senses with a more than material languor when you approach some of those magic islands of the Eastern seas, blows with so sweet a fragrance through the printed pages. They tell you the anchorages and the landing places, what supplies you can get at each spot, and where you can get water; they tell you the lights and buoys, tides, winds, and weather that you will find there. They give you brief information about the population and the trade. And it is strange when you think how sedately it is all set down, with no words wasted, that so much else is given you besides. What? Well, mystery and beauty, romance and the glamour of the unknown. It is no common book that offers you casually turning its pages such a paragraph as this: 'Supplies. A few jungle fowl are preserved, the island is also the resort of vast numbers of sea birds. Turtle are found in the lagoon, as well as quantities of various fish, including grey mullet, shark, and dog-fish; the seine cannot be used with any effect; but there is a fish which may be taken on a rod. A small store of tinned provisions and spirits is kept in a hut for the relief of shipwrecked persons. Good water may be obtained from a well near the landing-place.' Can the imagination want more material than this to go on a journey through time and space?

In the volume from which I have copied this passage, the compilers with the same restraint have described the Alas Islands. They are composed of a group or chain of islands, 'for the most part low and wooded, extending about 75 miles east and west, and 40 miles north and south'. The information about them, you are told, is very slight; there are channels between the different groups, and several vessels have passed through them, but the passages have not been thoroughly explored, and the positions of many of the dangers not yet determined; it is therefore advisable to avoid them. The population of the group is estimated at about 8,000, of whom 200 are Chinese and 400 Mohammedans. The rest are heathen. The principal island is called Baru, it is surrounded by a reef, and here lives a Dutch Contrôleur. His white house with its red roof on the top of a little hill is the most prominent object that the vessels of the Royal Netherlands Steam Packet Company see when every other month on their way up to Macassar and every four weeks on their way down to Merauke in Dutch New Guinea they touch at the island.

At a certain moment of the world's history the Contrôleur was Mynheer Evert Gruyter and he ruled the people who inhabited the Alas Islands with firmness tempered by a keen sense of the ridiculous. He had thought it a very good joke to be placed at the age of twenty-seven in a position of such consequence, and at thirty he was still amused by it. There was no cable communication between his islands and Batavia, and the mail arrived after so long a delay that even if he asked advice, by the time he received it, it was useless, and so he equably did what he thought best and trusted to his good fortune to keep out of trouble with the authorities. He was very short, not more than five feet four in height, and extremely fat; he was of a florid complexion. For coolness' sake he kept his head shaved and his face was hairless. It was round and red. His eyebrows were so fair that you hardly saw them; and he had little twinkling blue eyes. He knew that he had no dignity, but for the sake of his position made up for it by dressing very dapperly. He never went to his office, nor sat in court, nor walked abroad but in spotless white. His stengahshifter, with its bright brass buttons, fitted him very tightly and displayed the shocking fact that, young though he was, he had a round and protruding belly. His good-humoured face shone with sweat and he constantly fanned himself with a palm-leaf fan.

But in his house Mr Gruyter preferred to wear nothing but a sarong and then with his white podgy little body he looked like a fat funny boy of sixteen. He was an early riser and his breakfast was always ready for him at six. It never varied. It consisted of a slice of papaia, three cold fried eggs, Edam cheese, sliced thin, and a cup of black coffee. When he had eaten it, he smoked a large Dutch cigar, read the papers if he had not read them through and through already, and then dressed to go down to his office.

One morning while he was thus occupied his head boy came into his bedroom and told him that Tuan Jones wanted to know if he could see him. Mr

Gruyter was standing in front of a looking-glass. He had his trousers on and was admiring his smooth chest. He arched his back in order to throw it out and throw in his belly and with a good deal of satisfaction gave his breast three or four resounding slaps. It was a manly chest. When the boy brought the message he looked at his own eyes in the mirror and exchanged a slightly ironic smile with them. He asked himself what the devil his visitor could want. Evert Gruyter spoke English, Dutch, and Malay with equal facility, but he thought in Dutch. He liked to do this. It seemed to him a pleasantly ribald language.

'Ask the tuan to wait and say I shall come directly.' He put on his tunic, over his naked body, buttoned it up, and strutted into the sitting-room. The Rev. Owen Jones got up.

'Good morning, Mr Jones,' said the Contrôleur. 'Have you come in to have a peg with me before I start my day's work?'

Mr Jones did not smile.

'I've come to see you upon a very distressing matter, Mr Gruyter,' he answered.

The Contrôleur was not disconcerted by his visitor's gravity nor depressed by his words. His little blue eyes beamed amiably.

'Sit down, my dear fellow, and have a cigar.'

Mr Gruyter knew quite well that the Rev. Owen Jones neither drank nor smoked, but it tickled something prankish in his nature to offer him a drink and a smoke whenever they met. Mr Jones shook his head.

Mr Jones was in charge of the Baptist Mission on the Alas Islands. His headquarters were at Baru, the largest of them, with the greatest population, but he had meeting-houses under the care of native helpers in several other islands of the group. He was a tall, thin, melancholy man, with a long face, sallow and drawn, of about forty. His brown hair was already white on the temples and it receded from the forehead. This gave him a look of somewhat vacuous intellectuality. Mr Gruyter both disliked and respected him. He disliked him because he was narrow-minded and dogmatic. Himself a cheerful pagan who liked the good things of the flesh and was determined to get as many of them as his circumstances permitted, he had no patience with a man who disapproved of them all. He thought the customs of the country suited its inhabitants and had no patience with the missionary's energetic efforts to destroy a way of life that for centuries had worked very well. He respected him because he was honest, zealous, and good. Mr Jones, an Australian of Welsh descent, was the only qualified doctor in the group and it was a comfort to know that if you fell ill you need not rely only on a Chinese practitioner, and none knew better than the Contrôleur how useful to all Mr Jones's skill had been and with what charity he had given it. On the occasion of an epidemic of influenza the missionary had done the work of ten men and no storm short of a typhoon could prevent him from crossing to one island or another if his help was needed.

He lived with his sister in a little white house about half a mile from the village, and when the Contrôleur had arrived came on board to meet him and begged him to stay till he could get his own house in order. The Contrôleur had accepted and soon saw for himself with what simplicity the couple lived. It was more than he could stand. Tea at three sparse meals a day, and when he lit his cigar Mr Jones politely but firmly asked him to be good enough not to smoke, since both his sister and he strongly disapproved of it. In twenty-four hours Mr Gruyter moved into his own house. He fled, with panic in his heart, as though from a plague-stricken city. The Contrôleur was fond of a joke and he liked to laugh; to be with a man who took your nonsense in deadly earnest and never even smiled at your best story was more than flesh and blood could stand. The Rev. Owen Jones was a worthy man, but as a companion he was impossible. His sister was worse. Neither had a sense of humour, but whereas the missionary was of a melancholy turn, doing his duty so conscientiously, with the obvious conviction that everything in the world was hopeless, Miss Jones was resolutely cheerful. She grimly looked on the bright side of things. With the ferocity of an avenging angel she sought out the good in her fellow-men. Miss Jones taught in the mission school and helped her brother in his medical work. When he did operations she gave the anaesthetic and was matron, dresser, and nurse of the tiny hospital which on his own initiative Mr Jones had added to the mission. But the Contrôleur was an obstinate little fellow and he never lost his capacity of extracting amusement from the Rev. Owen's dour struggle with the infirmities of human nature, and Miss Jones's ruthless optimism. He had to get his fun where he could. The Dutch boats came in three times in two months for a few hours and then he could have a good old crack with the captain and chief engineer, and once in a blue moon a pearling lugger came in from Thursday Island or Port Darwin and for two or three days he had a grand time. They were rough fellows, the pearlers, for the most part, but they were full of guts, and they had plenty of liquor on board, and good stories to tell, and the Contrôleur had them up to his house and gave them a fine dinner, and the party was only counted a success if they were all too drunk to get back on the lugger again that night. But beside the missionary the only white man who lived on Baru was Ginger Ted, and he, of course, was a disgrace to civilization. There was not a single thing to be said in his favour. He cast discredit on the white race. All the same, but for Ginger Ted the Contrôleur sometimes thought he would find life on the island of Baru almost more than he could bear.

Oddly enough it was on account of this scamp that Mr Jones, when he should have been instructing the pagan young in the mysteries of the Baptist faith, was paying Mr Gruyter this early visit.

'Sit down, Mr Jones,' said the Contrôleur. 'What can I do for you?'

'Well, I've come to see you about the man they call Ginger Ted. What are you going to do now?'

'Why, what's happened?'

'Haven't you heard? I thought the sergeant would have told you.'

'I don't encourage the members of my staff to come to my private house unless the matter is urgent,' said the Contrôleur rather grandly. 'I am unlike you, Mr Jones, I only work in order to have leisure, and I like to enjoy my leisure without disturbance.'

But Mr Jones did not care much for small talk and he was not interested in general reflections.

'There was a disgraceful row in one of the Chinese shops last night. Ginger Ted wrecked the place and half killed a Chinaman.'

'Drunk again, I suppose,' said the Contrôleur placidly.

'Naturally. When is he anything else? They sent for the police and he assaulted the sergeant. They had to have six men to get him to the jail.'

'He's a hefty fellow,' said the Contrôleur.

'I suppose you'll send him to Macassar.'

Evert Gruyter returned the missionary's outraged look with a merry twinkle. He was no fool and he knew already what Mr Jones was up to. It gave him considerable amusement to tease him a little.

'Fortunately my powers are wide enough to enable me to deal with the situation myself,' he answered.

'You have power to deport anyone you like, Mr Gruyter, and I'm sure it would save a lot of trouble if you got rid of the man altogether.'

'I have the power of course, but I am sure you would be the last person to wish me to use it arbitrarily.'

'Mr Gruyter, the man's presence here is a public scandal. He's never sober from morning till night; it's notorious that he has relations with one native woman after another.'

'That is an interesting point, Mr Jones. I had always heard that alcoholic excess, though it stimulated sexual desire, prevented its gratification. What you tell me about Ginger Ted does not seem to bear out this theory.'

The missionary flushed a dull red.

'These are physiological matters which at the moment I have no wish to go into,' he said, frigidly. 'The behaviour of this man does incalculable damage to the prestige of the white race, and his example seriously hampers the efforts that are made in other quarters to induce the people of these islands to lead a less vicious life. He's an out-and-out bad lot.'

'Pardon my asking, but have you made any attempts to reform him?'

'When he first drifted here I did my best to get in touch with him. He repelled all my advances. When there was that first trouble I went to him and talked to him straight from the shoulder. He swore at me.'

'No one has a greater appreciation than I of the excellent work that you and other missionaries do on these islands, but are you sure that you always exercise your calling with all the tact possible?'

The Contrôleur was rather pleased with this phrase. It was extremely courteous and yet contained a reproof that he thought worth administering. The missionary looked at him gravely. His sad brown eyes were full of sincerity.

'Did Jesus exercise tact when he took a whip and drove the money-changers from the Temple? No, Mr Gruyter. Tact is the subterfuge the lax avail themselves of to avoid doing their duty.'

Mr Jones's remark made the Contrôleur feel suddenly that he wanted a bottle of beer. The missionary leaned forward earnestly.

'Mr Gruyter, you know this man's transgressions just as well as I do. It's unnecessary for me to remind you of them. There are no excuses for him. Now he really has overstepped the limit. You'll never have a better chance than this. I beg you to use the power you have and turn him out once for all.'

The Contrôleur's eyes twinkled more brightly than ever. He was having a lot of fun. He reflected that human beings were much more amusing when you did not feel called upon in dealing with them to allot praise or blame.

'But, Mr Jones, do I understand you right? Are you asking me to give you an assurance to deport this man before I've heard the evidence against him and listened to his defence?'

'I don't know what his defence can be.'

The Contrôleur rose from his chair and really he managed to get quite a little dignity into his five feet four inches.

'I am here to administer justice according to the laws of the Dutch Government. Permit me to tell you that I am exceedingly surprised that you should attempt to influence me in my judicial functions.'

The missionary was a trifle flustered. It had never occurred to him that this little whipper-snapper of a boy, ten years younger than himself, would dream of adopting such an attitude. He opened his mouth to explain and apologize, but the Contrôleur raised a podgy little hand.

'It is time for me to go to my office, Mr Jones. I wish you good morning.'

The missionary, taken aback, bowed and without another word walked out of the room. He would have been surprised to see what the Contrôleur did when his back was turned. A broad grin broke on his lips and he put his thumb to his nose and cocked a snook at the Rev. Owen Jones.

A few minutes later he went down to his office. His head clerk, who was a Dutch half-caste, gave him his version of the previous night's row. It agreed pretty well with Mr Jones's. The court was sitting that day.

'Will you take Ginger Ted first, sir?' asked the clerk.

'I see no reason to do that. There are two or three cases held over from the last sitting. I will take him in his proper order.'

'I thought perhaps as he was a white man you would like to see him privately, sir.'

'The majesty of the law knows no difference between white and coloured, my friend,' said Mr Gruyter, somewhat pompously.

The court was a big square room with wooden benches on which, crowded together, sat natives of all kinds, Polynesians, Bugis, Chinese, Malays, and they all rose when a door was opened and a sergeant announced the arrival of the Contrôleur. He entered with his clerk and took his place on a little dais at a table of varnished pitch pine. Behind him was a large engraving of Queen Wilhelmina. He dispatched half a dozen cases and then Ginger Ted was brought in. He stood in the dock, handcuffed, with a warder on either side of him. The Contrôleur looked at him with a grave face, but he could not keep the amusement out of his eyes.

Ginger Ted was suffering from a hang-over. He swayed a little as he stood and his eyes were vacant. He was a man still young, thirty perhaps, of somewhat over the middle height, rather fat, with a bloated red face and a shock of curly red hair. He had not come out of the tussle unscathed. He had a black eye and his mouth was cut and swollen. He wore khaki shorts, very dirty and ragged, and his singlet had been almost torn off his back. A great rent showed the thick mat of red hair with which his chest was covered, but showed also the astonishing whiteness of his skin. The Contrôleur looked at the charge sheet. He called the evidence. When he had heard it, when he had seen the Chinaman whose head Ginger Ted had broken with a bottle, when he had heard the agitated story of the sergeant who had been knocked flat when he tried to arrest him, when he had listened to the tale of the havoc wrought by Ginger Ted who in his drunken fury had smashed everything he could lay hands on, he turned and addressed the accused in English.

'Well, Ginger, what have you got to say for yourself?'

'I was blind. I don't remember a thing about it. If they say I half killed 'im I suppose I did. I'll pay the damage if they'll give me time.'

'You will, Ginger,' said the Contrôleur, 'but it's me who'll give you time.'

He looked at Ginger Ted for a minute in silence. He was an unappetizing object. A man who had gone completely to pieces. He was horrible. It made you shudder to look at him and if Mr Jones had not been so officious, at that moment the Contrôleur would certainly have ordered him to be deported.

'You've been a trouble ever since you came to the islands, Ginger. You're a disgrace. You're incorrigibly idle. You've been picked up in the street dead drunk time and time again. You've kicked up row after row. You're hopeless. I told you the last time you were brought here that if you were arrested again I should deal with you severely. You've gone the limit this time and you're for it. I sentence you to six months' hard labour.'

'Me?'

'You.'

'By God, I'll kill you when I come out.'

He burst into a string of oaths both filthy and blasphemous. Mr Gruyter listened scornfully. You can swear much better in Dutch than in English and there was nothing that Ginger Ted said that he could not have effectively capped.

'Be quiet,' he ordered. 'You make me tired.'

The Contrôleur repeated his sentence in Malay and the prisoner was led struggling away.

Mr Gruyter sat down to tiffin in high good-humour. It was astonishing how amusing life could be if you exercised a little ingenuity. There were people in Amsterdam and even in Batavia and Surabaya, who looked upon his island home as a place of exile. They little knew how agreeable it was and what fun he could extract from unpromising material. They asked him whether he did not miss the club and the races and the cinema, the dances that were held once a week at the Casino and the society of Dutch ladies. Not at all. He liked comfort. The substantial furniture of the room in which he sat had a satisfying solidity. He liked reading French novels of a frivolous nature and he appreciated the sensation of reading one after the other without the uneasiness occasioned by the thought that he was wasting his time. It seemed to him a great luxury to waste time. When his young man's fancy turned to thoughts of love his head boy brought to the house a little dark-skinned bright-eyed creature in a sarong. He took care to form no connexion of a permanent nature. He thought that change kept the heart young. He enjoyed freedom and was not weighed down by a sense of responsibility. He did not mind the heat. It made a sluice over with cold water half a dozen times a day a pleasure that had almost an aesthetic quality. He played the piano. He wrote letters to his friends in Holland. He felt no need for the conversation of intellectual persons. He liked a good laugh, but he could get that out of a fool just as well as out of a professor of philosophy. He had a notion that he was a very wise little man.

Like all good Dutchmen in the Far East he began his lunch with a small glass of Hollands gin. It has a musty acrid flavour, and the taste for it must be acquired, but Mr Gruyter preferred it to any cocktail. When he drank it he felt besides that he was upholding the traditions of his race. Then he had *rijsttafel*. He had it every day. He heaped a soup-plate high with rice, and then, his three boys waiting on him, helped himself to the curry that one handed him, to the fried egg that another brought, and to the condiment presented by the third. Then each one brought another dish, of bacon, or bananas, or pickled fish, and presently his plate was piled high in a huge pyramid. He stirred it all together and began to eat. He ate slowly and with relish. He drank a bottle of beer.

He did not think while he was eating. His attention was applied to the mass in front of him and he consumed it with a happy concentration. It never palled on him. And when he had emptied the great plate it was a compensation to think that next day he would have *rijsttafel* again. He grew tired of it as little as the rest of us grow tired of bread. He finished his beer and lit his cigar. The boy brought him a cup of coffee. He leaned back in his chair then and allowed himself the luxury of reflection.

It tickled him to have sentenced Ginger Ted to the richly deserved punishment of six months' hard labour, and he smiled when he thought of him working on the roads with the other prisoners. It would have been silly to deport from the island the one man with whom he could occasionally have a heart-to-heart talk, and besides, the satisfaction it would have given the missionary would have been bad for that gentleman's character. Ginger Ted was a scamp and a scallywag, but the Contrôleur had a kindly feeling for him. They had drunk many a bottle of beer in one another's company, and when the pearl fishers from Port Darwin came in and they all made a night of it, they had got gloriously tight together. The Contrôleur liked the reckless way in which Ginger Ted squandered the priceless treasure of life.

Ginger Ted had wandered in one day on the ship that was going up from Merauke to Macassar. The captain did not know how he had found his way there, but he had travelled steerage with the natives, and he stopped off at the Alas Islands because he liked the look of them. Mr Gruyter had a suspicion that their attraction consisted perhaps in their being under the Dutch flag and so out of British jurisdiction. But his papers were in order, so there was no reason why he should not stay. He said that he was buying pearl-shell for an Australian firm, but it soon appeared that his commercial undertakings were not serious. Drink, indeed, took up so much of his time that he had little left over for other pursuits. He was in receipt of two pounds a week, paid monthly, which came regularly to him from England. The Contrôleur guessed that this sum was paid only so long as he kept well away from the persons who sent it. It was anyway too small to permit him any liberty of movement. Ginger Ted was reticent. The Contrôleur discovered that he was an Englishman, this he learnt from his passport, which described him as Edward Wilson, and that he had been in Australia. But why he had left England and what he had done in Australia he had no notion. Nor could he ever quite tell to what class Ginger Ted belonged. When you saw him in a filthy singlet and a pair of ragged trousers, a battered topee on his head, with the pearl fishers and heard his conversation, coarse, obscene, and illiterate, you thought he must be a sailor before the mast who had deserted his ship, or a labourer, but when you saw his handwriting you were surprised to find that it was that of a man not without at least some education, and on occasion when you got him alone, if he had had a few drinks but was not yet drunk, he would talk of matters that neither a sailor nor a labourer would have been likely to know anything about. The Contrôleur had a certain sensitiveness and he realized that Ginger Ted did not speak to him as an inferior to a superior but as an equal. Most of his remittance was mortgaged before he received it, and the Chinamen to whom he owed money were standing at his elbow when the monthly letter was delivered to him, but with what was left he proceeded to get drunk. It was then that he made trouble, for when drunk he grew violent and was then likely to commit acts that brought him into the hands of the police. Hitherto Mr Gruyter had contented himself with keeping him in jail till he was sober and giving him a talking to. When he was out of money he cadged what drink he could from anyone who would give it him. Rum, brandy, arak, it was all the same to him. Two or three times Mr Gruyter had got him work on plantations run by Chinese in one or other of the islands, but he could not stick to it, and in a few weeks was back again at Baru on the beach. It was a miracle how he kept body and soul together. He had, of course, a way with him. He picked up the various dialects spoken on the islands, and knew how to make the natives laugh. They despised him, but they respected his physical strength, and they liked his company. He was as a result never at a loss for a meal or a mat to sleep on. The strange thing was, and it was this that chiefly outraged the Rev. Owen Jones, that he could do anything he liked with a woman. The Contrôleur could not imagine what it was they saw in him. He was casual with them and rather brutal. He took what they gave him, but seemed incapable of gratitude. He used them for his pleasure and then flung them indifferently away. Once or twice this had got him into trouble, and Mr Gruyter had had to sentence an angry father for sticking a knife in Ginger Ted's back one night, and a Chinese woman had sought to poison herself by swallowing opium because he had deserted her. Once Mr Jones came to the Contrôleur in a great state because the beachcomber had seduced one of his converts. The Contrôleur agreed that it was very deplorable, but could only advise Mr Jones to keep a sharp eye on these young persons. The Contrôleur liked it less when he discovered that a girl whom he fancied a good deal himself and had been seeing for several weeks had all the time been according her favours also to Ginger Ted. When he thought of this particular incident he smiled again at the thought of Ginger Ted doing six months' hard labour. It is seldom in this life that in the process of doing your bounden duty you can get back on a fellow who has played you a dirty trick.

A few days later Mr Gruyter was taking a walk, partly for exercise and partly to see that some job he wanted done was being duly proceeded with, when he passed a gang of prisoners working under the charge of a warder. Among them he saw Ginger Ted. He wore the prison sarong, a dingy tunic called in Malay a *baju*, and his own battered topee. They were repairing the road, and Ginger Ted was wielding a heavy pick. The way was narrow and the Contrôleur saw that he must pass within a foot of him. He remembered his threats. He knew that Ginger Ted was a man of violent passion, and the language he had used in the dock made it plain that he had not seen what a good joke it was of the Contrôleur's to sentence him to six months' hard labour. If Ginger Ted suddenly attacked him with the pick, nothing on God's earth could save him. It was true that the warder would immediately shoot him down, but meanwhile the Contrôleur's head would be bashed in. It was with a funny little feeling in the pit of his stomach that Mr Gruyter walked through the gang of prisoners. They were working in pairs a few feet from one another. He set his mind on neither hastening his pace nor slackening it. As he passed Ginger Ted, the man swung his pick into the ground and looked up at the Contrôleur and as he caught his eye winked. The Contrôleur checked the smile that rose to his lips and with official dignity strode on. But that wink, so lusciously full of sardonic humour, filled him with satisfaction. If he had been the Caliph of Bagdad instead of a junior official in the Dutch Civil Service, he could forthwith have released Ginger Ted, sent slaves to bath and perfume him, and having clothed him in a golden robe entertained him to a sumptuous repast.

Ginger Ted was an exemplary prisoner and in a month or two the Contrôleur, having occasion to send a gang to do some work on one of the outlying islands, included him in it. There was no jail there, so the ten fellows he sent, under the charge of a warder, were billeted on the natives and after their day's work lived like free men. The job was sufficient to take up the rest of Ginger Ted's sentence. The Contrôleur saw him before he left.

'Look here, Ginger,' he said to him, 'here's ten guilder for you so that you can buy yourself tobacco when you're gone.'

'Couldn't you make it a bit more? There's eight pounds a month coming in regularly.'

'I think that's enough. I'll keep the letters that come for you, and when you get back you'll have a tidy sum. You'll have enough to take you anywhere you want to go.'

'I'm very comfortable here,' said Ginger Ted.

'Well, the day you come back, clean yourself up and come over to my house. We'll have a bottle of beer together.'

'That'll be fine. I guess I'll be ready for a good crack then.'

Now chance steps in. The island to which Ginger Ted had been sent was called Maputiti, and like all the rest of them it was rocky, heavily wooded, and surrounded by a reef. There was a village among coconuts on the sea-shore opposite the opening of the reef and another village on a brackish lake in the middle of the island. Of this some of the inhabitants had been converted to Christianity. Communication with Baru was effected by a launch that touched at the various islands at irregular intervals. It carried passengers and produce. But the villagers were seafaring folk, and if they had to communicate urgently with Baru, manned a prahu and sailed the fifty miles or so that separated them from it. It happened that when Ginger Ted's sentence had but another fortnight to run the Christian headman of the village on the lake was taken suddenly ill. The native remedies availed him nothing and he writhed in agony. Messengers were sent to Baru imploring the missionary's help; but as ill luck would have it Mr Jones was suffering at the moment from an attack of malaria. He was in bed and unable to move. He talked the matter over with his sister.

'It sounds like acute appendicitis,' he told her.

'You can't go, Owen,' she said.

'I can't let the man die.'

Mr Jones had a temperature of a hundred and four. His head was aching like mad. He had been delirious all night. His eyes were shining strangely and his sister felt that he was holding on to his wits by a sheer effort of will.

'You couldn't operate in the state you're in.'

'No, I couldn't. Then Hassan must go.'

Hassan was the dispenser.

'You couldn't trust Hassan. He'd never dare to do an operation on his own responsibility. And they'd never let him. I'll go. Hassan can stay here and look after you.'

'You can't remove an appendix.'

'Why not? I've seen you do it. I've done lots of minor operations.'

Mr Jones felt he didn't quite understand what she was saying.

'Is the launch in?'

'No, it's gone to one of the islands. But I can go in the prahu the men came in.'

'You? I wasn't thinking of you. You can't go.'

'I'm going, Owen.'

'Going where?' he said.

She saw that his mind was wandering already. She put her hand soothingly on his dry forehead. She gave him a dose of medicine. He muttered something and she realized that he did not know where he was. Of course she was anxious about him, but she knew that his illness was not dangerous, and she could leave him safely to the mission boy who was helping her nurse him and to the native dispenser. She slipped out of the room. She put her toilet things, a night-dress, and a change of clothes into a bag. A little chest with surgical instruments, bandages, and antiseptic dressings was kept always ready. She gave them to the two natives who had come over from Maputiti, and telling the dispenser what she was going to do gave him instructions to inform her brother when he was able to listen. Above all he was not to be anxious about her. She put on her topee and sallied forth. The mission was about half a mile from the village. She walked quickly. At the end of the jetty the prahu was waiting. Six men manned it. She took her place in the stern and they set off with a rapid stroke. Within the reef the sea was calm, but when they crossed the bar they came upon a long swell. But this was not the first journey of the sort Miss Jones had taken and she was confident of the seaworthiness of the boat she was in. It was noon and the sun beat down from a sultry sky. The only thing that harassed her was that they could not arrive before dark, and if she found it necessary to operate at once she could count only on the light of hurricane lamps.

Miss Jones was a woman of hard on forty. Nothing in her appearance would have prepared you for such determination as she had just shown. She had an odd drooping gracefulness, which suggested that she might be swayed by every breeze; it was almost an affectation; and it made the strength of character which you soon discovered in her seem positively monstrous. She was flat-chested, tall, and extremely thin. She had a long sallow face and she was much afflicted with prickly heat. Her lank brown hair was drawn back straight from her forehead. She had rather small eyes, grey in colour, and because they were somewhat too close they gave her face a shrewish look. Her nose was long and thin and a trifle red. She suffered a good deal from indigestion. But this infirmity availed nothing against her ruthless determination to look upon the bright side of things. Firmly persuaded that the world was evil and men unspeakably vicious, she extracted any little piece of decency she could find in them with the modest pride with which a conjurer extracts a rabbit from a hat. She was quick, resourceful, and competent. When she arrived on the island she saw that there was not a moment to lose if she was to save the headman's life. Under the greatest difficulties, showing a native how to give the anaesthetic, she operated, and for the next three days nursed the patient with anxious assiduity. Everything went very well and she realized that her brother could not have made a better job of it. She waited long enough to take out the stitches and then prepared to go home. She could flatter herself that she had not wasted her time. She had given medical attention to such as needed it, she had strengthened the small Christian community in its faith, admonished such as were lax, and cast the good seed in places where it might be hoped under divine providence to take root.

The launch, coming from one of the other islands, put in somewhat late in the afternoon, but it was full moon and they expected to reach Baru before midnight. They brought her things down to the wharf and the people who were seeing her off stood about repeating their thanks. Quite a little crowd collected. The launch was loaded with sacks of copra, but Miss Jones was used to its strong smell and it did not incommode her. She made herself as comfortable a place to sit in as she could, and waiting for the launch to start, chatted with her grateful flock. She was the only passenger. Suddenly a group of natives emerged from the trees that embowered the little village on the lagoon and she saw that among them was a white man. He wore a prison sarong and a baju. He had long red hair. She at once recognized Ginger Ted. A policeman was with him. They shook hands and Ginger Ted shook hands with the villagers who accompanied him. They bore bundles of fruit and a jar which Miss Jones guessed contained native spirit, and these they put in the launch. She discovered to her surprise that Ginger Ted was coming with her. His term was up and instructions had arrived that he was to be returned to Baru in the launch. He gave her a glance, but did not nod –indeed Miss Jones turned away her head–and stepped in. The mechanic started his engine and in a moment they were jug-jugging through the channel in the lagoon. Ginger Ted clambered on to a pile of sacks and lit a cigarette.

Miss Jones ignored him. Of course she knew him very well. Her heart sank when she thought that he was going to be once more in Baru, creating a scandal and drinking, a peril to the women and a thorn in the flesh of all decent people. She knew the steps her brother had taken to have him deported and she had no patience with the Contrôleur, who would not see a duty that stared him so plainly in the face. When they had crossed the bar and were in the open sea Ginger Ted took the stopper out of the jar of arak and putting his mouth to it took a long pull. Then he handed the jar to the two mechanics who formed the crew. One was a middle-aged man and the other a youth.

'I do not wish you to drink anything while we are on the journey,' said Miss Jones sternly to the elder one.

He smiled at her and drank.

'A little arak can do no one any harm,' he answered. He passed the jar to his companion, who drank also.

'If you drink again I shall complain to the Contrôleur,' said Miss Jones.

The elder man said something she could not understand, but which she suspected was very rude, and passed the jar back to Ginger Ted. They went along for an hour or more. The sea was like glass and the sun set radiantly. It set behind one of the islands and for a few minutes changed it into a mystic city of the skies. Miss Jones turned round to watch it and her heart was filled with gratitude for the beauty of the world.

'And only man is vile,' she quoted to herself.

They went due east. In the distance was a little island which she knew they passed close by. It was uninhabited. A rocky islet thickly grown with virgin forest. The boatman lit his lamps. The night fell and immediately the sky was thick with stars. The moon had not yet risen. Suddenly there was a slight jar and the launch began to vibrate strangely. The engine rattled. The head mechanic calling to his mate to take the helm, crept under the housing. They seemed to be going more slowly. The engine stopped. She asked the youth what was the matter, but he did not know. Ginger Ted got down from the top of the copra sacks and slipped under the housing. When he reappeared she would have liked to ask him what had happened, but her dignity prevented her. She sat still and occupied herself with her thoughts. There was a long swell and the launch rolled slightly. The mechanic emerged once more into view and started the engine. Though it rattled like mad they began to move. The launch vibrated from stem to stern. They went very slowly. Evidently something was amiss, but Miss Jones was exasperated rather than alarmed. The launch was supposed to do six knots, but now it was just crawling along; at that rate they would not get into Baru till long, long after midnight. The mechanic, still busy under the housing, shouted out something to the man at the helm. They spoke in Bugi, of which Miss Jones knew very little. But after a while she noticed that they had changed their course and seemed to be heading for the little uninhabited island a good deal to the lee of which they should have passed.

'Where are we going?' she asked the helmsman with sudden misgiving.

He pointed to the islet. She got up and went to the housing and called to the man to come out.

'You're not going there? Why? What's the matter?'

'I can't get to Baru,' he said.

'But you must. I insist. I order you to go to Baru.'

The man shrugged his shoulders. He turned his back on her and slipped once more under the housing. Then Ginger Ted addressed her.

'One of the blades of the propeller has broken off. He thinks he can get as far as that island. We shall have to stay the night there and he'll put on a new propeller in the morning when the tide's out.'

'I can't spend the night on an uninhabited island with three men,' she cried.

'A lot of women would jump at it.'

'I insist on going to Baru. Whatever happens we must get there tonight.'

'Don't get excited, old girl. We've got to beach the boat to put a new propeller on, and we shall be all right on the island.'

'How dare you speak to me like that! I think you're very insolent.'

'You'll be O.K. We've got plenty of grub and we'll have a snack when we land. You have a drop of arak and you'll feel like a house on fire.'

'You're an impertinent man. If you don't go to Baru I'll have you all put in prison.'

'We're not going to Baru. We can't. We're going to that island and if you don't like it you can get out and swim.'

'Oh, you'll pay for this.'

'Shut up, you old cow,' said Ginger Ted.

Miss Jones gave a gasp of anger. But she controlled herself. Even out there, in the middle of the ocean, she had too much dignity to bandy words with that vile wretch. The launch, the engine rattling horribly, crawled on. It was pitch dark now, and she could no longer see the island they were making for. Miss Jones, deeply incensed, sat with lips tight shut and a frown on her brow; she was not used to being crossed. Then the moon rose and she could see the bulk of Ginger Ted sprawling on the top of the piled sacks of copra. The glimmer of his cigarette was strangely sinister. Now the island was vaguely outlined against the sky. They reached it and the boatman ran the launch on to the beach. Suddenly Miss Jones gave a gasp. The truth had dawned on her and her anger changed to fear. Her heart beat violently. She shook in every limb. She felt dreadfully faint. She saw it all. Was the broken propeller a put-up job or was it an accident? She could not be certain; anyhow, she knew that Ginger Ted would seize the opportunity. Ginger Ted would rape her. She knew his character. He was mad about women. That was what he had done, practically, to the girl at the mission, such a good little thing she was and an excellent sempstress; they would have prosecuted him for that and he would have been sentenced to years of imprisonment only very unfortunately the innocent child had gone back to him several times and indeed had only complained of his ill usage when he left her for somebody else. They had gone to the Contrôleur about it, but he had refused to take any steps, saying in that coarse way of his that even if what the girl said was true, it didn't look very much as though it had been an altogether unpleasant experience. Ginger Ted was a scoundrel. And she was a white woman. What chance was there that he would spare her? None. She knew men. But she must pull herself together. She must keep her wits about her. She must have courage. She was determined to sell her virtue dearly, and if he killed her – well, she would rather die than yield. And if she died she would rest in the arms of Jesus. For a moment a great light blinded her eyes and she saw the mansions of her Heavenly Father. They were a grand and sumptuous mixture of a picture palace and a railway station. The mechanics and Ginger Ted jumped out of the launch and, waist-deep in water, gathered round the broken propeller. She took advantage of their preoccupation to get her case of surgical instruments out of the box. She took out the four scalpels it contained and secreted them in her clothing. If Ginger Ted touched her she would not hesitate to plunge a scalpel in his heart.

'Now then, miss, you'd better get out,' said Ginger Ted. 'You'll be better off on the beach than in the boat.'

She thought so too. At least here she would have freedom of action. Without a word she clambered over the copra sacks. He offered her his hand.

'I don't want your help,' she said coldly.

'You can go to hell,' he answered.

It was a little difficult to get out of the boat without showing her legs, but by the exercise of considerable ingenuity she managed it.

'Damned lucky we've got something to eat. We'll make a fire and then you'd better have a snack and a nip of arak.'

'I want nothing. I only want to be left alone.'

'It won't hurt me if you go hungry.'

She did not answer. She walked, with head erect, along the beach. She held the largest scalpel in her closed fist. The moon allowed her to see where she was going. She looked for a place to hide. The thick forest came down to the very edge of the beach; but, afraid of its darkness (after all, she was but a woman), she dared not plunge into its depth. She did not know what animals lurked there or what dangerous snakes. Besides, her instinct told her that it was better to keep those three bad men in sight; then if they came towards her she would be prepared. Presently she found a little hollow. She looked round. They seemed to be occupied with their own efforts and they could not see her. She slipped in. There was a rock between them and her so that she was hidden from them and yet could watch them. She saw them go to and from the boat carrying things. She saw them build a fire. It lit them luridly and she saw them sit around it and eat, and she saw the jar of arak passed from one to the other. They were all going to get drunk. What would happen to her then? It might be that she could cope with Ginger Ted, though his strength terrified her, but against three she would be powerless. A mad idea came to her to go to Ginger Ted and fall on her knees before him and beg him to spare her. He must have some spark of decent feeling in him and she had always been so convinced that there was good even in the worst of men. He must have had a mother. Perhaps he had a sister. Ah, but how could you appeal to a man blinded with lust and drunk with arak? She began to feel terribly weak. She was afraid she was going to cry. That would never do. She needed all her self-control. She bit her lip. She watched them, like a tiger watching his prey; no, not like that, like a lamb watching three hungry wolves. She saw them put more wood on the fire, and Ginger Ted, in his sarong, silhouetted by the flames. Perhaps after he had had his will of her he would pass her on to the others. How could she go back to her brother when such a thing had happened to her? Of course he would be sympathetic, but would he ever feel quite the same to her again? It would break his heart. And perhaps he would think that she ought to have resisted more. For his sake perhaps it would be better if she said nothing about it. Naturally the men would say nothing. It would mean twenty years in prison for them. But then supposing she had a baby. Miss Jones instinctively clenched her hands with horror and nearly cut herself with the scalpel. Of course it would only infuriate them if she resisted.

'What shall I do?' she cried. 'What have I done to deserve this?'

She flung herself down on her knees and prayed to God to save her. She prayed long and earnestly. She reminded God that she was a virgin and just mentioned, in case it had slipped the divine memory, how much St Paul had valued that excellent state. And then she peeped round the rock again. The three men appeared to be smoking and the fire was dying down. Now was the time that Ginger Ted's lewd thoughts might be expected to turn to the woman who was at his mercy. She smothered a cry, for suddenly he got up and walked in her direction. She felt all her muscles grow taut, and though her heart was beating furiously she clenched the scalpel firmly in her hand. But it was for another purpose that Ginger Ted had got up. Miss Jones blushed and looked away. He strolled slowly back to the others and sitting down again raised the jar of arak to his lips. Miss Jones, crouching behind the rock, watched with straining eyes. The conversation round the fire grew less and presently she divined, rather than saw, that the two natives wrapped themselves in blankets and composed themselves to slumber. She understood. This was the moment Ginger Ted had been waiting for. When they were fast asleep he would get up cautiously and without a sound, in order not to wake the others, creep stealthily towards her. Was it that he was unwilling to share her with them or did he know that his deed was so dastardly that he did not wish them to know of it? After all, he was a white man and she was a white woman. He could not have sunk so low as to allow her to suffer the violence of natives. But his plan, which was so obvious to her, had given her an idea; when she saw him coming she would scream, she would scream so loudly that it would wake the two mechanics. She remembered now that the elder, though he had only one eye, had a kind face. But Ginger Ted did not move. She was feeling terribly tired. She began to fear that she would not have the strength now to resist him. She had gone through too much. She closed her eyes for a minute.

When she opened them it was broad daylight. She must have fallen asleep and, so shattered was she by emotion, have slept till long after dawn. It gave her quite a turn. She sought to rise, but something caught in her legs. She looked and found that she was covered with two empty copra sacks. Someone had come in the night and put them over her. Ginger Ted! She gave a little scream. The horrible thought flashed through her mind that he had outraged her in her sleep. No. It was impossible. And yet he had had her at his mercy. Defenceless. And he had spared her. She blushed furiously. She raised herself to her feet, feeling a little stiff, and arranged her disordered dress. The scalpel had fallen from her hand and she picked it up. She took the two copra sacks and emerged from her hiding-place. She walked towards the boat. It was floating in the shallow water of the lagoon.

'Come on, Miss Jones,' said Ginger Ted. 'We've finished. I was just going to wake you up.'

She could not look at him, but she felt herself as red as a turkey cock.

'Have a banana?' he said.

Without a word she took it. She was very hungry, and ate it with relish.

'Step on this rock and you'll be able to get in without wetting your feet.'

Miss Jones felt as though she could sink into the ground with shame, but she did as he told her. He took hold of her arm–good heavens his hand was like an iron vice, never, never could she have struggled with him–and helped her into the launch. The mechanic started the engine and they slid out of the lagoon. In three hours they were at Baru.

That evening, having been officially released, Ginger Ted went to the Contrôleur's house. He wore no longer the prison uniform but the ragged singlet and the khaki shorts in which he had been arrested. He had had his hair cut and it fitted his head now like a little curly red cap. He was thinner. He had lost his bloated flabbiness and looked younger and better. Mr Gruyter, a friendly grin on his round face, shook hands with him and asked him to sit down. The boy brought two bottles of beer.

'I'm glad to see you hadn't forgotten my invitation, Ginger,' said the Contrôleur.

'Not likely. I've been looking forward to this for six months.'

'Here's luck, Ginger Ted.'

'Same to you, Contrôleur.'

They emptied their glasses and the Contrôleur clapped his hands. The boy brought two more bottles.

'Well, you don't bear me any malice for the sentence I gave you, I hope.'

'No bloody fear. I was mad for a minute, but I got over it. I didn't have half a bad time, you know. Nice lot of girls on that island, Contrôleur. You ought to give 'em a look over one of these days.'

'You're a bad lot, Ginger.'

'Terrible.'

'Good beer, isn't it?'

'Fine.'

'Let's have some more.'

Ginger Ted's remittance had been arriving every month and the Contrôleur now had fifty pounds for him. When the damage he had done to the Chinaman's shop was paid for there would still be over thirty.

'That's quite a lot of money, Ginger. You ought to do something useful with it.'

'I mean to,' answered Ginger. 'Spend it.'

The Contrôleur sighed.

'Well, that's what money's for, I guess.'

The Contrôleur gave his guest the news. Not much had happened during the last six months. Time on the Alas Islands did not matter very much and the rest of the world did not matter at all.

'Any wars anywhere?' asked Ginger Ted.

'No. Not that I've noticed. Harry Jervis found a pretty big pearl. He says he's going to ask a thousand quid for it.'

'I hope he gets it.'

'And Charlie McCormack's married.'

'He always was a bit soft.'

Suddenly the boy appeared and said Mr Jones wished to know if he might come in. Before the Contrôleur could give an answer Mr Jones walked in.

'I won't detain you long,' he said. 'I've been trying to get hold of this good man all day and when I heard he was here I thought you wouldn't mind my coming.'

'How is Miss Jones?' asked the Contrôleur politely. 'None the worse for her night in the open, I trust.'

'She's naturally a bit shaken. She had a temperature and I've insisted on her going to bed, but I don't think it's serious.'

The two men had got up on the missionary's entrance, and now the missionary went up to Ginger Ted and held out his hand.

'I want to thank you. You did a great and noble thing. My sister is right, one should always look for the good in their fellow-men; I am afraid I misjudged you in the past; I beg your pardon.'

He spoke very solemnly. Ginger Ted looked at him with amazement. He had not been able to prevent the missionary taking his hand. He still held it.

'What the hell are you talking about?'

'You had my sister at your mercy and you spared her. I thought you were all evil and I am ashamed. She was defenceless. She was in your power. You had pity on her. I thank you from the bottom of my heart. Neither my sister nor I will ever forget. God bless and guard you always.'

Mr Jones's voice shook a little and he turned his head away. He released Ginger Ted's hand and strode quickly to the door. Ginger Ted watched him with a blank face.

'What the blazes does he mean?' he asked.

The Contrôleur laughed. He tried to control himself, but the more he did the more he laughed. He shook and you saw the folds of his fat belly ripple under the sarong. He leaned back in his long chair and rolled from side to side. He did not laugh only with his face, he laughed with his whole body, and even the muscles of his podgy legs shook with mirth. He held his aching ribs. Ginger Ted looked at him frowning, and because he did not understand what the joke was he grew angry. He seized one of the empty beer bottles by the neck.

'If you don't stop laughing, I'll break your bloody head open,' he said.

The Contrôleur mopped his face. He swallowed a mouthful of beer. He sighed and groaned because his sides were hurting him.

'He's thanking you for having respected the virtue of Miss Jones,' he spluttered at last.

'Me?' cried Ginger Ted.

The thought took quite a long time to travel through his head, but when at last he got it he flew into a violent rage. There flowed from his mouth such a stream of blasphemous obscenities as would have startled a marine.

'That old cow,' he finished. 'What does he take me for?'

'You have the reputation of being rather hot stuff with the girls, Ginger,' giggled the little Contrôleur.

'I wouldn't touch her with the fag-end of a barge-pole. It never entered my head. The nerve. I'll wring his blasted neck. Look here, give me my money, I'm going to get drunk.'

'I don't blame you,' said the Contrôleur.

'That old cow,' repeated Ginger Ted. 'That old cow.'

He was shocked and outraged. The suggestion really shattered his sense of decency.

The Contrôleur had the money at hand and having got Ginger Ted to sign the necessary papers gave it to him.

'Go and get drunk, Ginger Ted,' he said, 'but I warn you, if you get into mischief it'll be twelve months next time.'

'I shan't get into mischief,' said Ginger Ted sombrely. He was suffering from a sense of injury. 'It's an insult,' he shouted at the Contrôleur. 'That's what it is, it's a bloody insult.'

He lurched out of the house, and as he went he muttered to himself: 'Dirty swine, dirty swine.' Ginger Ted remained drunk for a week. Mr Jones went to see the Contrôleur again.

'I'm very sorry to hear that poor fellow has taken up his evil course again,' he said. 'My sister and I are dreadfully disappointed. I'm afraid it wasn't very wise to give him so much money at once.'

'It was his own money. I had no right to keep it back.'

'Not a legal right, perhaps, but surely a moral right.'

He told the Contrôleur the story of that fearful night on the island. With her feminine instinct, Miss Jones had realized that the man, inflamed with lust, was determined to take advantage of her, and, resolved to defend herself to the last, had armed herself with a scalpel. He told the Contrôleur how she had prayed and wept and how she had hidden herself. Her agony was indescribable, and she knew that she could never have survived the shame. She rocked to and fro and every moment she thought he was coming. And there was no help anywhere and at last she had fallen asleep; she was tired out, poor thing, she had undergone more than any human being could stand, and then when she awoke she found that he had covered her with copra sacks. He had found her asleep, and surely it was her innocence, her very helplessness that had moved him, he hadn't the heart to touch her; he covered her gently with two copra sacks and crept silently away.

'It shows you that deep down in him there is something sterling. My sister feels it's our duty to save him. We must do something for him.'

'Well, in your place I wouldn't try till he's got through all his money,' said the Contrôleur, 'and then if he's not in jail you can do what you like.'

But Ginger Ted didn't want to be saved. About a fortnight after his release from prison he was sitting on a stool outside a Chinaman's shop looking vacantly down the street when he saw Miss Jones coming along. He stared at her for a minute and once more amazement seized him. He muttered to himself and there can be little doubt that his mutterings were disrespectful. But then he noticed that Miss Jones had seen him and he quickly turned his head away; he was conscious, notwithstanding, that she was looking at him. She was walking briskly, but she sensibly diminished her pace as she approached him. He thought she was going to stop and speak to him. He got up quickly and went into the shop. He did not venture to come out for at least five minutes. Half an hour later Mr Jones himself came along and he went straight up to Ginger Ted with outstretched hand.

'How do you do, Mr Edward? My sister told me I should find you here.'

Ginger Ted gave him a surly look and did not take the proffered hand. He made no answer.

'We'd be so very glad if you'd come to dinner with us next Sunday. My sister's a capital cook and she'll make you a real Australian dinner.'

'Go to hell,' said Ginger Ted.

'That's not very gracious,' said the missionary, but with a little laugh to show that he was not affronted. 'You go and see the Contrôleur from time to time, why shouldn't you come and see us? It's pleasant to talk to white people now and then. Won't you let bygones be bygones? I can assure you of a very cordial welcome.'

'I haven't got clothes fit to go out in,' said Ginger Ted sulkily.

'Oh, never mind about that. Come as you are.'

'I won't.'

'Why not? You must have a reason.'

Ginger Ted was a blunt man. He had no hesitation in saying what we should all like to when we receive unwelcome invitations.

'I don't want to.'

'I'm sorry. My sister will be very disappointed.'

Mr Jones, determined to show that he was not in the least offended, gave him a breezy nod and walked on. Forty-eight hours later there mysteriously arrived at the house in which Ginger Ted lodged a parcel containing a suit of ducks, a tennis shirt, a pair of socks, and some shoes. He was unaccustomed to receiving presents and next time he saw the Contrôleur asked him if it was he who had sent the things.

'Not on your life,' replied the Contrôleur. 'I'm perfectly indifferent to the state of your wardrobe.'

'Well, then, who the hell can have?'

'Search me.'

It was necessary from time to time for Miss Jones to see Mr Gruyter on business and shortly after this she came to see him one morning in his office. She was a capable woman and though she generally wanted him to do something he had no mind to, she did not waste his time. He was a little surprised then to discover that she had come on a very trivial errand. When he told her that he could not take cognizance of the matter in question, she did not as was her habit try to convince him, but accepted his refusal as definite. She got up to go and then as though it were an afterthought said:

'Oh, Mr Gruyter, my brother is very anxious that we should have the man they call Ginger Ted to supper with us and I've written him a little note inviting him for the day after tomorrow. I think he's rather shy, and I wonder if you'd come with him.'

'That's very kind of you.'

'My brother feels that we ought to do something for the poor fellow.'

'A woman's influence and all that sort of thing,' said the Contrôleur demurely.

'Will you persuade him to come? I'm sure he will if you make a point of it, and when he knows the way he'll come again. It seems such a pity to let a young man like that go to pieces altogether.'

The Contrôleur looked up at her. She was several inches taller than he. He thought her very unattractive. She reminded him strangely of wet linen hung on a clothes-line to dry. His eyes twinkled, but he kept a straight face.

'I'll do my best,' he said.

'How old is he?' she asked.

'According to his passport he's thirty-one.'

'And what is his real name?'

'Wilson.'

'Edward Wilson,' she said softly.

'It's astonishing that after the life he's led he should be so strong,' murmured the Contrôleur. 'He has the strength of an ox.'

'Those red-headed men sometimes are very powerful,' said Miss Jones, but spoke as though she were choking.

'Quite so,' said the Contrôleur.

Then for no obvious reason Miss Jones blushed. She hurriedly said goodbye to the Contrôleur and left his office.

'*Godverdomme!*' said the Contrôleur.

He knew now who had sent Ginger Ted the new clothes.

He met him during the course of the day and asked him whether he had heard from Miss Jones. Ginger Ted took a crumpled ball of paper out of his pocket and gave it to him. It was the invitation. It ran as follows:

Dear Mr Wilson
My brother and I would be so very glad if you would come and have supper with us next Thursday at 7.30. The Contrôleur has kindly promised to come. We have some new records from Australia which I am sure you will like. I am afraid I was not very nice to you last time we met, but I did not know you so well then, and I am big enough to admit it when I have committed an error. I hope you will forgive me and let me be your friend,

Yours sincerely,
Martha Jones

The Contrôleur noticed that she addressed him as Mr Wilson and referred to his own promise to go, so that when she told him she had already invited Ginger Ted she had a little anticipated the truth.

'What are you going to do?'

'I'm not going, if that's what you mean. Damned nerve.'

'You must answer the letter.'

'Well, I won't.'

'Now look here, Ginger, you put on those new clothes and you come as a favour to me. I've got to go and, damn it all, you can't leave me in the lurch. It won't hurt you just once.'

Ginger Ted looked at the Contrôleur suspiciously, but his face was serious and his manner sincere: he could not guess that within him the Dutchman bubbled with laughter.

'What the devil do they want me for?'

'I don't know. The pleasure of your society, I suppose.'

'Will there be any booze?'

'No, but come up to my house at seven, and we'll have a tiddly before we go.'

'Oh, all right,' said Ginger Ted sulkily.

The Contrôleur rubbed his little fat hands with joy. He was expecting a great deal of amusement from the party. But when Thursday came and seven o'clock, Ginger Ted was dead drunk and Mr Gruyter had to go alone. He told the missionary and his sister the plain truth. Mr Jones shook his head.

'I'm afraid it's no good, Martha, the man's hopeless.'

For a moment Miss Jones was silent and the Contrôleur saw two tears trickle down her long thin nose. She bit her lip.

'No one is hopeless. Everyone has some good in him. I shall pray for him every night. It would be wicked to doubt the power of God.'

Perhaps Miss Jones was right in this, but the divine providence took a very funny way of effecting its ends. Ginger Ted began to drink more heavily than ever. He was so troublesome that even Mr Gruyter lost patience with him. He made up his mind that he could not have the fellow on the island any more and resolved to deport him on the next boat that touched at Baru. Then a man died under mysterious circumstances after having been for a trip to one of the islands and the Contrôleur learnt that there had been several deaths on the same island. He sent the Chinese who was the official doctor of the group to look into the matter, and very soon received intelligence that the deaths were due to cholera. Two more took place at Baru and the certainty was forced upon him that there was an epidemic.

The Contrôleur cursed freely. He cursed in Dutch, he cursed in English, and he cursed in Malay. Then he drank a bottle of beer and smoked a cigar. After that he took thought. He knew the Chinese doctor would be useless. He was a nervous little man from Java and the natives would refuse to obey his orders. The Contrôleur was efficient and knew pretty well what must be done, but he could not do everything single-handed. He did not like Mr Jones, but just then he was thankful that he was at hand, and he sent for him at once. He was accompanied by his sister.

'You know what I want to see you about, Mr Jones,' he said abruptly.

'Yes. I've been expecting a message from you. That is why my sister has come with me. We are ready to put all our resources at your disposal. I need not tell you that my sister is as competent as a man.'

'I know. I shall be very glad of her assistance.'

They set to without further delay to discuss the steps that must be taken. Hospital huts would have to be erected and quarantine stations. The inhabitants of the various villages on the islands must be forced to take proper precautions. In a good many cases the infected villages drew their water from the same well as the uninfected, and in each case this difficulty would have to be dealt with according to circumstances. It was necessary to send round people to give orders and make sure that they were carried out. Negligence must be ruthlessly punished. The worst of it was that the natives would not obey other natives, and orders given by native policemen, themselves unconvinced of their efficacy, would certainly be disregarded. It was advisable for Mr Jones to stay at Baru, where the population was largest and his medical attention most wanted; and what with the official duties that forced him to keep in touch with headquarters, it was impossible for Mr Gruyter to visit all the other islands himself. Miss Jones must go; but the natives of some of the outlying islands were wild and treacherous; the Contrôleur had had a good deal of trouble with them. He did not like the idea of exposing her to danger.

'I'm not afraid,' she said.

'I daresay. But if you have your throat cut I shall get into trouble, and besides, we're so short-handed I don't want to risk losing your help.'

'Then let Mr Wilson come with me. He knows the natives better than anyone and can speak all their dialects.'

'Ginger Ted?' The Contrôleur stared at her. 'He's just getting over an attack of D.T.s.'

'I know,' she answered.

'You know a great deal, Miss Jones.'

Even though the moment was so serious Mr Gruyter could not but smile. He gave her a sharp look, but she met it coolly.

'There's nothing like responsibility for bringing out what there is in a man, and I think something like this may be the making of him.'

'Do you think it would be wise to trust yourself for days at a time to a man of such infamous character?' said the missionary.

'I put my trust in God,' she answered gravely.

'Do you think he'd be any use?' asked the Contrôleur. 'You know what he is.'

'I'm convinced of it.' Then she blushed. 'After all, no one knows better than I that he's capable of self-control.'

The Contrôleur bit his lip.

'Let's send for him.'

He gave a message to the sergeant and in a few minutes Ginger Ted stood before them. He looked ill. He had evidently been much shaken by his recent attack and his nerves were all to pieces. He was in rags and he had not shaved for a week. No one could have looked more disreputable.

'Look here, Ginger,' said the Contrôleur, 'it's about this cholera business. We've got to force the natives to take precautions and we want you to help us.'

'Why the hell should I?'

'No reason at all. Except philanthropy.'

'Nothing doing, Contrôleur. I'm not a philanthropist.'

'That settles that. That was all. You can go.'

But as Ginger Ted turned to the door Miss Jones stopped him.

'It was my suggestion, Mr Wilson. You see, they want me to go to Labobo and Sakunchi, and the natives there are so funny I was afraid to go alone. I thought if you came I should be safer.'

He gave her a look of extreme distaste.

'What do you suppose I care if they cut your throat?'

Miss Jones looked at him and her eyes filled with tears. She began to cry. He stood and watched her stupidly.

'There's no reason why you should.' She pulled herself together and dried her eyes. 'I'm being silly. I shall be all right. I'll go alone.'

'It's damned foolishness for a woman to go to Labobo.'

She gave him a little smile.

'I daresay it is, but you see, it's my job and I can't help myself. I'm sorry if I offended you by asking you. You must forget about it. I daresay it wasn't quite fair to ask you to take such a risk.'

For quite a minute Ginger Ted stood and looked at her. He shifted from one foot to the other. His surly face seemed to grow black.

'Oh, hell, have it your own way,' he said at last. 'I'll come with you. When d'you want to start?'

They set out next day, with drugs and disinfectants, in the Government launch. Mr Gruyter as soon as he had put the necessary work in order was to start off in a prahu in the other direction. For four months the epidemic raged. Though everything possible was done to localize it, one island after another was attacked. The Contrôleur was busy from morning to night. He had no sooner got back to Baru from one or other of the islands to do what was necessary there than he had to set off again. He distributed food and medicine. He cheered the terrified people. He supervised everything. He worked like a dog. He saw nothing of Ginger Ted, but he heard from Mr Jones that the experiment was working out beyond all hopes. The scamp was behaving himself. He had a way with the natives; and by cajolery, firmness, and on occasion the use of his fist, managed to make them take the steps necessary for their own safety. Miss Jones could congratulate herself on the success of the scheme. But the Contrôleur was too tired to be amused. When the epidemic had run its course he rejoiced because out of a population of eight thousand only six hundred had died.

Finally he was able to give the district a clean bill of health.

One evening he was sitting in his sarong on the veranda of his house and he read a French novel with the happy consciousness that once more he could take things easy. His head boy came in and told him that Ginger Ted wished to see him. He got up from his chair and shouted to him to come in. Company was just what he wanted. It had crossed the Contrôleur's mind that it would be pleasant to get drunk that night, but it is dull to get drunk alone, and he had regretfully put the thought aside. And heaven had sent Ginger Ted in the nick of time. By

God, they would make a night of it. After four months they deserved a bit of fun. Ginger Ted entered. He was wearing a clean suit of white ducks. He was shaved. He looked another man.

'Why, Ginger, you look as if you'd been spending a month at a health resort instead of nursing a pack of natives dying of cholera. And look at your clothes. Have you just stepped out of a band-box?'

Ginger Ted smiled rather sheepishly. The head boy brought two bottles of beer and poured them out.

'Help yourself, Ginger,' said the Contrôleur as he took his glass.

'I don't think I'll have any, thank you.'

The Contrôleur put down his glass and looked at Ginger Ted with amazement.

'Why, what's the matter? Aren't you thirsty?'

'I don't mind having a cup of tea.'

'A cup of what?'

'I'm on the wagon. Martha and I are going to be married.'

'Ginger!'

The Contrôleur's eyes popped out of his head. He scratched his shaven pate. 'You can't marry Miss Jones,' he said. 'No one could marry Miss Jones.'

'Well, I'm going to. That's what I've come to see you about. Owen's going to marry us in chapel, but we want to be married by Dutch law as well.'

'A joke's a joke, Ginger. What's the idea?'

'She wanted it. She fell for me that night we spent on the island when the propeller broke. She's not a bad old girl when you get to know her. It's her last chance, if you understand what I mean, and I'd like to do something to oblige her. And she wants someone to take care of her, there's no doubt about that.'

'Ginger, Ginger, before you can say knife she'll make you into a damned missionary.'

'I don't know that I'd mind that so much if we had a little mission of our own. She says I'm a bloody marvel with the natives. She says I can do more with a native in five minutes than Owen can do in a year. She says she's never known anyone with the magnetism I have. It seems a pity to waste a gift like that.'

The Contrôleur looked at him without speaking and slowly nodded his head three or four times. She'd nobbled him all right.

'I've converted seventeen already,' said Ginger Ted.

'You? I didn't know you believed in Christianity.'

'Well, I don't know that I did exactly, but when I talked to 'em and they just came into the fold like a lot of blasted sheep, well, it gave me quite a turn. Blimey, I said, I daresay there's something in it after all.'

'You should have raped her, Ginger. I wouldn't have been hard on you. I wouldn't have given you more than three years and three years is soon over.'

'Look here, Contrôleur, don't you ever let on that the thought never entered my head. Women are touchy, you know, and she'd be as sore as hell if she knew that.'

'I guessed she'd got her eye on you, but I never thought it would come to this.' The Contrôleur in an agitated manner walked up and down the veranda. 'Listen to me, old boy,' he said after an interval of reflection, 'we've had some grand times together and a friend's a friend. I'll tell you what I'll do, I'll lend you the launch and you can go and hide on one of the islands till the next ship comes along and then I'll get 'em to slow down and take you on board. You've only got one chance now and that's to cut and run.'

Ginger Ted shook his head.

'It's no good, Contrôleur, I know you mean well, but I'm going to marry the blasted woman, and that's that. You don't know the joy of bringing all them bleeding sinners to repentance, and Christ! that girl can make a treacle pudding. I haven't eaten a better one since I was a kid.'

The Contrôleur was very much disturbed. The drunken scamp was his only companion on the islands and he did not want to lose him. He discovered that he had even a certain affection for him. Next day he went to see the missionary.

'What's this I hear about your sister marrying Ginger Ted?' he asked him. 'It's the most extraordinary thing I've ever heard in my life.'

'It's true nevertheless.'

'You must do something about it. It's madness.'

'My sister is of full age and entitled to do as she pleases.'

'But you don't mean to tell me you approve of it. You know Ginger Ted. He's a bum and there are no two ways about it. Have you told her the risk she's running? I mean, bringing sinners to repentance and all that sort of thing's all right, but there are limits. And does the leopard ever change his spots?'

Then for the first time in his life the Contrôleur saw a twinkle in the missionary's eye.

'My sister is a very determined woman, Mr Gruyter,' he replied. 'From that night they spent on the island he never had a chance.'

The Contrôleur gasped. He was as surprised as the prophet when the Lord opened the mouth of the ass, and she said unto Balaam, What have I done unto thee, that thou hast smitten me these three times? Perhaps Mr Jones was human after all.

'*Allejezus!*' muttered the Contrôleur.

Before anything more could be said Miss Jones swept into the room. She was radiant. She looked ten years younger. Her cheeks were flushed and her nose was hardly red at all.

'Have you come to congratulate me, Mr Gruyter?' she cried, and her manner was sprightly and girlish. 'You see, I was right after all. Everyone has some good in them. You don't know how splendid Edward has been all through this terrible time. He's a hero. He's a saint. Even I was surprised.'

'I hope you'll be very happy, Miss Jones.'

'I know I shall. Oh, it would be wicked of me to doubt it. For it is the Lord who has brought us together.'

'Do you think so?'

'I know it. Don't you see? Except for the cholera Edward would never have found himself. Except for the cholera we should never have learnt to know one another. I have never seen the hand of God more plainly manifest.'

The Contrôleur could not but think that it was rather a clumsy device to bring those two together that necessitated the death of six hundred innocent persons, but not being well versed in the ways of omnipotence he made no remark.

'You'll never guess where we're going for our honeymoon,' said Miss Jones, perhaps a trifle archly.

'Java.'

'No, if you'll lend us the launch, we're going to that island where we were marooned. It has very tender recollections for both of us. It was there that I first guessed how fine and good Edward was. It's there I want him to have his reward.'

The Contrôleur caught his breath. He left quickly, for he thought that unless he had a bottle of beer at once he would have a fit. He was never so shocked in his life.

Louise

◆

I could never understand why Louise bothered with me. She disliked me and I knew that behind my back, in that gentle way of hers, she seldom lost the opportunity of saying a disagreeable thing about me. She had too much delicacy ever to make a direct statement, but with a hint and a sigh and a little flutter of her beautiful hands she was able to make her meaning plain. She was a mistress of cold praise. It was true that we had known one another almost intimately, for five-and-twenty years, but it was impossible for me to believe that she could be affected by the claims of old association. She thought me a coarse, brutal, cynical, and vulgar fellow. I was puzzled at her not taking the obvious course and dropping me. She did nothing of the kind; indeed, she would not leave me alone; she was constantly asking me to lunch and dine with her and once or twice a year invited me to spend a week-end at her house in the country. At last I thought that I had discovered her motive. She had an uneasy suspicion that I did not believe in her; and if that was why she did not like me, it was also why she sought my acquaintance: it galled her that I alone should look upon her as a comic figure and she could not rest till I acknowledged myself mistaken and defeated. Perhaps she had an inkling that I saw the face behind the mask and because I alone held out was determined that sooner or later I too should take the mask for the face. I was never quite certain that she was a complete humbug. I wondered whether she fooled herself as thoroughly as she fooled the world or whether there was some spark of humour at the bottom of her heart. If there was it might be that she was attracted to me, as a pair of crooks might be attracted to one another, by the knowledge that we shared a secret that was hidden from everybody else.

I knew Louise before she married. She was then a frail, delicate girl with large and melancholy eyes. Her father and mother worshipped her with an anxious adoration, for some illness, scarlet fever I think, had left her with a weak heart and she had to take the greatest care of herself. When Tom Maitland proposed to her they were dismayed, for they were convinced that she was much too delicate for the strenuous state of marriage. But they were not too well off and Tom Maitland was rich. He promised to do everything in the world for Louise and finally they entrusted her to him as a sacred charge. Tom Maitland was a big, husky fellow, very good-looking and a fine athlete. He doted on Louise. With her weak heart he could not hope to keep her with him long and he made up his mind to do everything he could to make her few years on earth happy. He gave up the games he excelled in, not because she wished him to, she was glad that he should play golf and hunt, but because by a coincidence she had a heart attack whenever he proposed to leave her for a day. If they had a difference of opinion she gave in to him at once, for she was the most submissive wife a man could have, but her heart failed her and she would be laid up, sweet and uncomplaining, for a week. He would not be such a brute as to cross her. Then they would have quite a little tussle about which should yield and it was only with difficulty that at last he persuaded her to have her own way. On one occasion seeing her walk eight miles on an expedition that she particularly wanted to make, I suggested to Tom Maitland that she was stronger than one would have thought. He shook his head and sighed.

'No, no, she's dreadfully delicate. She's been to all the best heart specialists in the world and they all say that her life hangs on a thread. But she has an unconquerable spirit.'

He told her that I had remarked on her endurance.

'I shall pay for it tomorrow,' she said to me in her plaintive way. 'I shall be at death's door.'

'I sometimes think that you're quite strong enough to do the things you want to,' I murmured.

I had noticed that if a party was amusing she could dance till five in the morning, but if it was dull she felt very poorly and Tom had to take her home early. I am afraid she did not like my reply, for though she gave me a pathetic little smile I saw no amusement in her large blue eyes.

'You can't very well expect me to fall down dead just to please you,' she answered.

Louise outlived her husband. He caught his death of cold one day when they were sailing and Louise needed all the rugs there were to keep her warm. He left her a comfortable fortune and a daughter. Louise was inconsolable. It was wonderful that she managed to survive the shock. Her friends expected her speedily to follow poor Tom Maitland to the grave. Indeed they already felt dreadfully sorry for Iris, her daughter, who would be left an orphan. They redoubled their attentions towards Louise. They would not let her stir a finger; they insisted on doing everything in the world to save her trouble. They had to, because if she was called upon to do anything tiresome or inconvenient her heart went back on her and there she was at death's door. She was entirely lost without a man to take care of her, she said, and she did not know how, with her delicate health, she was going to bring up her dear Iris. Her friends asked why she did not marry again. Oh, with her heart it was out of the question, though of course she knew that dear Tom would have wished her to, and perhaps it would be the best thing for Iris if she did; but who would want to be bothered with a wretched invalid like herself? Oddly enough more than one young man showed himself quite ready to undertake the charge and a year after Tom's death she allowed George Hobhouse to lead her to the altar. He was a fine, upstanding fellow and he was not at all badly off. I never saw anyone so grateful as he for the privilege of being allowed to take care of this frail little thing.

'I shan't live to trouble you long,' she said.

He was a soldier and an ambitious one, but he resigned his commission. Louise's health forced her to spend the winter at Monte Carlo and the summer at Deauville. He hesitated a little at throwing up his career, and Louise at first would not hear of it; but at last she yielded as she always yielded, and he prepared to make his wife's last few years as happy as might be.

'It can't be very long now,' she said. 'I'll try not to be troublesome.'

For the next two or three years Louise managed, notwithstanding her weak heart, to go beautifully dressed to all the most lively parties, to gamble very heavily, to dance and even to flirt with tall slim young men. But George Hobhouse had not the stamina of Louise's first husband and he had to brace himself now and then with a stiff drink for his day's work as Louise's second husband. It is possible that the habit would have grown on him, which Louise would not have liked at all, but very fortunately (for her) the war broke out. He rejoined his regiment and three months later was killed. It was a great shock to Louise. She felt, however, that in such a crisis she must not give way to a private grief; and if she had a heart attack nobody heard of it. In order to distract her mind she turned her villa at Monte Carlo into a hospital for convalescent officers. Her friends told her that she would never survive the strain.

'Of course it will kill me,' she said, 'I know that. But what does it matter? I must do my bit.'

It didn't kill her. She had the time of her life. There was no convalescent home in France that was more popular. I met her by chance in Paris. She was lunching at the Ritz with a tall and very handsome young Frenchman. She explained that she was there on business connected with the hospital. She told me that the officers were too charming to her. They knew how delicate she was and they wouldn't let her do a single thing. They took care of her, well—as though they were all her husbands. She sighed.

'Poor George, who would ever have thought that I with my heart should survive him?'

'And poor Tom!' I said.

I don't know why she didn't like my saying that. She gave me her plaintive smile and her beautiful eyes filled with tears.

'You always speak as though you grudged me the few years that I can expect to live.'

'By the way, your heart's much better, isn't it?'

'It'll never be better. I saw a specialist this morning and he said I must be prepared for the worst.'

'Oh, well, you've been prepared for that for nearly twenty years now, haven't you?'

When the war came to an end Louise settled in London. She was now a woman of over forty, thin and frail still, with large eyes and pale cheeks, but she did not look a day more than twenty-five. Iris, who had been at school and was now grown up, came to live with her.

'She'll take care of me,' said Louise. 'Of course, it'll be hard on her to live with such a great invalid as I am, but it can only be for such a little while, I'm sure she won't mind.'

Iris was a nice girl. She had been brought up with the knowledge that her mother's health was precarious. As a child she had never been allowed to make a noise. She had always realized that her mother must on no account be upset. And though Louise told her now that she would not hear of her sacrificing herself for a tiresome old woman the girl simply would not listen. It wasn't a question of sacrificing herself, it was a happiness to do what she could for her poor dear mother. With a sigh her mother let her do a great deal.

'It pleases the child to think she's making herself useful,' she said.

'Don't you think she ought to go out and about more?' I asked.

'That's what I'm always telling her. I can't get her to enjoy herself. Heaven knows, I never want anyone to put themselves out on my account.'

And Iris, when I remonstrated with her, said: 'Poor dear mother, she wants me to go and stay with friends and go to parties, but the moment I start off anywhere she has one of her heart attacks, so I much prefer to stay at home.'

But presently she fell in love. A young friend of mine, a very good lad, asked her to marry him and she consented. I liked the child and was glad that she was to be given at last the chance to lead a life of her own. She had never seemed to suspect that such a thing was possible. But one day the young man came to me in great distress and told me that his marriage was indefinitely postponed. Iris felt that she could not desert her mother. Of course it was really no business of mine, but I made the opportunity to go and see Louise. She was always glad to receive her friends at tea-time and now that she was older she cultivated the society of painters and writers.

'Well, I hear that Iris isn't going to be married,' I said after a little.

'I don't know about that. She's not going to be married quite as soon as I could have wished. I've begged her on my bended knees not to consider me, but she absolutely refuses to leave me.'

'Don't you think it's rather hard on her?'

'Dreadfully. Of course it can only be for a few months, but I hate the thought of anyone sacrificing themselves for me.'

'My dear Louise, you've buried two husbands, I can't see the least reason why you shouldn't bury at least two more.'

'Do you think that's funny?' she asked me in a tone that she made as offensive as she could.

'I suppose it's never struck you as strange that you're always strong enough to do anything you want to and that your weak heart only prevents you from doing things that bore you?'

'Oh, I know, I know what you've always thought of me. You've never believed that I had anything the matter with me, have you?'

I looked at her full and square.

'Never. I think you've carried out for twenty-five years a stupendous bluff. I think you're the most selfish and monstrous woman I have ever known. You ruined the lives of those two wretched men you married and now you're going to ruin the life of your daughter.'

I should not have been surprised if Louise had had a heart attack then. I fully expected her to fly into a passion. She merely gave me a gentle smile.

'My poor friend, one of these days you'll be so dreadfully sorry you said this to me.'

'Have you quite determined that Iris shall not marry this boy?'

'I've begged her to marry him. I know it'll kill me, but I don't mind. Nobody cares for me. I'm just a burden to everybody.'

'Did you tell her it would kill you?'

'She made me.'

'As if anyone ever made you do anything that you were not yourself quite determined to do.'

'She can marry her young man tomorrow if she likes. If it kills me, it kills me.'

'Well, let's risk it, shall we?'

'Haven't you got any compassion for me?'

'One can't pity anyone who amuses one as much as you amuse me,' I answered.

A faint spot of colour appeared on Louise's pale cheeks and though she smiled still her eyes were hard and angry.

'Iris shall marry in a month's time,' she said, 'and if anything happens to me I hope you and she will be able to forgive yourselves.'

Louise was as good as her word. A date was fixed, a trousseau of great magnificence was ordered, and invitations were issued. Iris and the very good lad were radiant. On the wedding-day, at ten o'clock in the morning, Louise, that devilish woman, had one of her heart attacks—and died. She died gently forgiving Iris for having killed her.

The Promise

◆

My wife is a very unpunctual woman, so when, having arranged to lunch with her at Claridge's, I arrived there ten minutes late and did not find her I was not surprised. I ordered a cocktail. It was the height of the season and there were but two or three vacant tables in the lounge. Some of the people after an early meal were drinking their coffee, others like myself were toying with a dry Martini; the women in their summer frocks looked gay and charming and the men debonair; but I could see no one whose appearance sufficiently interested me to occupy the quarter of an hour I was expecting to wait. They were slim and pleasant to look upon, well dressed and carelessly at ease, but they were for the most part of a pattern and I observed them with tolerance rather than with curiosity. But it was two o'clock and I felt hungry. My wife tells me that she can wear neither a turquoise nor a watch, for the turquoise turns green and the watch stops; and this she attributes to the malignity of fate. I have nothing to say about the turquoise, but I sometimes think the watch might go if she wound it. I was engaged with these reflections when an attendant came up and with that hushed significance that hotel attendants affect (as though their message held a more sinister meaning than their words suggested) told me that a lady had just telephoned to say that she had been detained and could not lunch with me.

I hesitated. It is not very amusing to eat in a crowded restaurant by oneself, but it was late to go to a club and I decided that I had better stay where I was. I strolled into the dining-room. It has never given me any particular satisfaction (as it appears to do to so many elegant persons) to be known by name to the head waiters of fashionable restaurants, but on this occasion I should certainly have been glad to be greeted by less stony an eye. The *maître d'hôtel* with a set and hostile face told me that every table was occupied. I looked helplessly round the

large and stately room and on a sudden to my pleasure caught sight of someone
I knew. Lady Elizabeth Vermont was an old friend. She smiled and noticing
that she was alone I went up to her.

'Will you take pity on a hungry man and let me sit with you?' I asked.

'Oh, do. But I've nearly finished.'

She was at a little table by the side of a massive column and when I took my
place I found that notwithstanding the crowd we sat almost in privacy.

'This is a bit of luck for me,' I said. 'I was on the point of fainting from
hunger.'

She had a very agreeable smile; it did not light up her face suddenly, but
seemed rather to suffuse it by degrees with charm. It hesitated for a moment
about her lips and then slowly travelled to those great shining eyes of hers and
there softly lingered. No one surely could say that Elizabeth Vermont was cast
in the common mould. I never knew her when she was a girl, but many have
told me that then she was so lovely, it brought the tears to one's eyes, and I
could well believe it; for now, though fifty, she was still incomparable. Her
ravaged beauty made the fresh and blooming comeliness of youth a trifle
insipid. I do not like these painted faces that look all alike; and I think women
are foolish to dull their expression and obscure their personality with powder,
rouge, and lipstick. But Elizabeth Vermont painted not to imitate nature, but to
improve it; you did not question the means but applauded the result. The
flaunting boldness with which she used cosmetics increased rather than
diminished the character of that perfect face. I suppose her hair was dyed; it
was black and sleek and shining. She held herself upright as though she had
never learned to loll and she was very slim. She wore a dress of black satin, the
lines and simplicity of which were admirable, and about her neck was a long
rope of pearls. Her only other jewel was an enormous emerald which guarded
her wedding-ring, and its sombre fire emphasized the whiteness of her hand.
But it was in her hands with their reddened nails that she most clearly betrayed
her age; they had none of a girl's soft and dimpled roundness; and you could not
but look at them with a certain dismay. Before very long they would look like
the talons of a bird of prey.

Elizabeth Vermont was a remarkable woman. Of great birth, for she was the
daughter of the seventh Duke of St Erth, she married at the age of eighteen a
very rich man and started at once upon a career of astounding extravagance,
lewdness, and dissipation. She was too proud to be cautious, too reckless to
think of consequences, and within two years her husband in circumstances of
appalling scandal divorced her. She married then one of the three co-
respondents named in the case and eighteen months later ran away from him.
Then followed a succession of lovers. She became notorious for her profligacy.
Her startling beauty and her scandalous conduct held her in the public eye and
it was never very long but that she gave the gossips something to talk about. Her
name stank in the nostrils of decent people. She was a gambler, a spendthrift,
and a wanton. But though unfaithful to her lovers she was constant to her
friends and there always remained a few who would never allow, whatever she
did, that she was anything but a very nice woman. She had candour, high
spirits, and courage. She was never a hypocrite. She was generous and sincere.
It was at this period of her life that I came to know her; for great ladies, now that
religion is out of fashion, when they are very much blown upon take a flattering
interest in the arts. When they receive the cold shoulder from members of their
own class they condescend sometimes to the society of writers, painters, and

musicians. I found her an agreeable companion. She was one of those blessed persons who say quite fearlessly what they think (thus saving much useful time), and she had a ready wit. She was always willing to talk (with a diverting humour) of her lurid past. Her conversation, though uninstructed, was good, because, notwithstanding everything, she was an honest woman.

Then she did a very surprising thing. At the age of forty, she married a boy of twenty-one. Her friends said it was the maddest act of all her life, and some who had stuck to her through thick and thin, now for the boy's sake, because he was nice and it seemed shameful thus to take advantage of his inexperience, refused to have anything more to do with her. It really was the limit. They prophesied disaster, for Elizabeth Vermont was incapable of sticking to any man for more than six months, nay, they hoped for it, since it seemed the only chance for the wretched youth that his wife should behave so scandalously that he must leave her. They were all wrong. I do not know whether time was responsible for a change of heart in her, or whether Peter Vermont's innocence and simple love touched her, but the fact remains that she made him an admirable wife. They were poor, and she was extravagant, but she became a thrifty housewife; she grew on a sudden so careful of her reputation that the tongue of scandal was silenced. His happiness seemed her only concern. No one could doubt that she loved him devotedly. After being the subject of so much conversation for so long Elizabeth Vermont ceased to be talked about. It looked as though her story were told. She was a changed woman, and I amused myself with the notion that when she was a very old lady, with many years of perfect respectability behind her, the past, the lurid past, would seem to belong not to her but to someone long since dead whom once she had vaguely known. For women have an enviable faculty of forgetting.

But who can tell what the fates have in store? In the twinkling of an eye all was changed. Peter Vermont, after ten years of an ideal marriage, fell madly in love with a girl called Barbara Canton. She was a nice girl, the youngest daughter of Lord Robert Canton who was at one time Under-Secretary for Foreign Affairs, and she was pretty in a fair and fluffy way. Of course she was not for a moment to be compared with Lady Elizabeth. Many people knew what had happened, but no one could tell whether Elizabeth Vermont had any inkling of it, and they wondered how she would meet a situation that was so foreign to her experience. It was always she who had discarded her lovers; none had deserted her. For my part I thought she would make short work of little Miss Canton; I knew her courage and her adroitness. All this was in my mind now while we chatted over our luncheon. There was nothing in her demeanour, as gay, charming, and frank as usual, to suggest that anything troubled her. She talked as she always talked, lightly but with good sense and a lively perception of the ridiculous, of the various topics which the course of conversation brought forward. I enjoyed myself. I came to the conclusion that by some miracle she had no notion of Peter's changed feelings, and I explained this to myself by the supposition that her love for him was so great, she could not conceive that his for her might be less.

We drank our coffee and smoked a couple of cigarettes, and she asked me the time.

'A quarter to three.'

'I must ask for my bill.'

'Won't you let me stand you lunch?'

'Of course,' she smiled.

'Are you in a hurry?'

'I'm meeting Peter at three.'

'Oh, how is he?'

'He's very well.'

She gave a little smile, that tardy and delightful smile of hers, but I seemed to discern in it a certain mockery. For an instant she hesitated and she looked at me with deliberation.

'You like curious situations, don't you?' she said. 'You'd never guess the errand I'm bound on. I rang up Peter this morning and asked him to meet me at three. I'm going to ask him to divorce me.'

'You're not,' I cried. I felt myself flush and did not know what to say. 'I thought you got on so well together.'

'Do you think it's likely that I shouldn't know what all the world knows? I'm really not such a fool as all that.'

She was not a woman to whom it was possible to say what one did not believe and I could not pretend that I did not know what she meant. I remained silent for a second or two.

'Why should you allow yourself to be divorced?'

'Robert Canton is a stuffy old thing. I very much doubt if he'd let Barbara marry Peter if I divorced him. And for me, you know, it isn't of the smallest consequence: one divorce more or less . . .'

She shrugged her pretty shoulders.

'How do you know he wants to marry her?'

'He's head over ears in love with her.'

'Has he told you so?'

'No. He doesn't even know that I know. He's been so wretched, poor darling. He's been trying so hard not to hurt my feelings.'

'Perhaps it's only a momentary infatuation,' I hazarded. 'It may pass.'

'Why should it? Barbara's young and pretty. She's quite nice. They're very well suited to one another. And besides, what good would it do if it did pass? They love each other now and the present in love is all that matters. I'm nineteen years older than Peter. If a man stops loving a woman old enough to be his mother do you think he'll ever come to love her again? You're a novelist, you must know more about human nature than that.'

'Why should you make this sacrifice?'

'When he asked me to marry him ten years ago I promised him that when he wanted his release he should have it. You see there was so great a disproportion between our ages I thought that was only fair.'

'And are you going to keep a promise that he hasn't asked you to keep?'

She gave a little flutter of those long thin hands of hers and now I felt that there was something ominous in the dark glitter of that emerald.

'Oh, I must, you know. One must behave like a gentleman. To tell you the truth, that's why I'm lunching here today. It was at this table that he proposed to me; we were dining together, you know, and I was sitting just where I am now. The nuisance is that I'm just as much in love with him now as I was then.' She paused for a minute and I could see that she clenched her teeth. 'Well, I suppose I ought to go. Peter hates one to keep him waiting.'

She gave me a sort of little helpless look and it struck me that she simply could not bring herself to rise from her chair. But she smiled and with an abrupt gesture sprang to her feet.

'Would you like me to come with you?'

'As far as the hotel door,' she smiled.

We walked through the restaurant and the lounge and when we came to the entrance a porter swung round the revolving doors. I asked if she would like a taxi.

'No, I'd sooner walk, it's such a lovely day.' She gave me her hand. 'It's been so nice to see you. I shall go abroad tomorrow, but I expect to be in London all the autumn. Do ring me up.'

She smiled and nodded and turned away. I watched her walk up Davies Street. The air was still bland and springlike, and above the roofs little white clouds were sailing leisurely in a blue sky. She held herself very erect and the poise of her head was gallant. She was a slim and lovely figure so that people looked at her as they passed. I saw her bow graciously to some acquaintance who raised his hat, and I thought that never in a thousand years would it occur to him that she had a breaking heart. I repeat, she was a very honest woman.

The Yellow Streak

◆

The two prahus were dropping easily down-stream, one a few yards ahead of the other, and in the first sat the two white men. After seven weeks on the rivers they were glad to know that they would lodge that night in a civilized house. To Izzart, who had been in Borneo since the war, the Dyak houses and their feasts were of course an old story; but Campion, though new to the country and at first amused by the strangeness, hankered too now for chairs to sit on and a bed to sleep in. The Dyaks were hospitable, but no one could say that there was much comfort to be found in their houses, and there was a monotony in the entertainment they offered a guest which presently grew somewhat wearisome. Every evening, as the travellers reached the landing-place, the headman, bearing a flag, and the more important members of the household came down to the river to fetch them. They were led up to the long-house–a village really under one roof, built on piles, to which access was obtained by climbing up the trunk of a tree rudely notched into steps—and to the beating of drums and gongs walked up and down the whole length of it in long procession. On both sides serried throngs of brown people sat on their haunches and stared silently as the white men passed. Clean mats were unrolled and the guests seated themselves. The headman brought a live chicken and, holding it by the legs, waved it three times over their heads, called the spirits loudly to witness and uttered an invocation. Then various persons brought eggs. Arak was drunk. A girl, a very small shy thing with the grace of a flower but with something hieratic in her immobile face, held a cup to the white man's lips till it was empty and then a great shout arose. The men began to dance, one after the other, each treading his little measure, with his shield and his parang, to the accompaniment of drum and gong. After this had gone on for some time the visitors were taken into one of the rooms that led off the long platform on which was led the common life of the household and found their supper prepared for them. The girls fed them with Chinese spoons. Then everyone grew a little drunk and they all talked till the early hours of the morning.

But now their journey was done and they were on their way to the coast. They had started at dawn. The river then was very shallow and ran clear and bright over a shingly bottom; the trees leaned over it so that above there was only a strip of blue sky; but now it had broadened out, and the men were poling no longer but paddling. The trees, bamboos, wild sago like huge bunches of ostrich feathers, trees with enormous leaves and trees with feathery foliage like the acacia, coconut trees and areca palms, with their long straight white stems, the trees on the banks were immensely and violently luxuriant. Here and there, gaunt and naked, was the bare skeleton of a tree struck by lightning or dead of old age, and its whiteness against all that green was vivid. Here and there, rival kings of the forest, tall trees soared above the common level of the jungle. Then there were the parasites; in the fork of two branches great tufts of lush green leaves, or flowering creepers that covered the spreading foliage like a bride's veil; sometimes they wound round a tall trunk, a sheath of splendour, and threw long flowering arms from branch to branch. There was something thrilling in the passionate wildness of that eager growth; it had the daring abandon of the maenad rioting in the train of the god.

The day wore on, and now the heat was no longer so oppressive. Campion looked at the shabby silver watch on his wrist. It could not be long now before they reached their destination.

'What sort of a chap is Hutchinson?' he asked.

'I don't know him. I believe he's a very good sort.'

Hutchinson was the Resident in whose house they were to spend the night, and they had sent on a Dyak in a canoe to announce their arrival.

'Well, I hope he's got some whisky. I've drunk enough arak to last me a lifetime.'

Campion was a mining engineer whom the Sultan on his way to England had met at Singapore, and finding him at a loose end had commissioned to go to Sembulu and see whether he could discover any mineral which might be profitably worked. He sent Willis, the Resident at Kuala Solor, instructions to afford him every facility, and Willis had put him in the care of Izzart because Izzart spoke both Malay and Dyak like a native. This was the third trip they had made into the interior, and now Campion was to go home with his reports. They were to catch the *Sultan Ahmed*, which was due to pass the mouth of the river at dawn on the next day but one, and with any luck they should reach Kuala Solor on the same afternoon. They were both glad to get back to it. There was tennis and golf there, and the club with its billiard tables, food which was relatively good, and the comforts of civilization. Izzart was glad, too, that he would have other society than Campion's. He gave him a sidelong glance. He was a little man with a big, bald head, and though certainly fifty, strong and wiry; he had quick, shining blue eyes and a stubbly, grey moustache. He was seldom without an old briar pipe between his broken and discoloured teeth. He was neither clean nor neat, his khaki shorts were ragged and his singlet torn; he was wearing now a battered topee. He had knocked about the world since he was eighteen and had been in South Africa, in China and in Mexico. He was good company; he could tell a story well, and he was prepared to drink and drink again with anyone he met. They had got on very well together, but Izzart had never felt quite at home with him. Though they joked and laughed together, got drunk together, Izzart felt that there was no intimacy between them; for all the cordiality of their relations they remained nothing but acquaintances. He was very sensitive to the impression he made on others, and behind Campion's joviality he had felt a certain coolness; those shining blue eyes had summed him up; and it vaguely irritated Izzart that Campion had formed an opinion of him, and he did not quite know what it was. He was exasperated by the possibility that this common little man did not think entirely well of him. He desired to be liked and admired. He wanted to be popular. He wished the people he met to take an inordinate fancy to him, so that he could either reject them or a trifle condescendingly bestow his friendship on them. His inclination was to be familiar with all and sundry, but he was held back by the fear of a rebuff; sometimes he had been uneasily conscious that his effusiveness surprised the persons he lavished it on.

By some chance he had never met Hutchinson, though of course he knew all about him just as Hutchinson knew all about *him*, and they would have many common friends to talk of. Hutchinson had been at Winchester, and Izzart was glad that he could tell him that he had been at Harrow. . . .

The prahu rounded a bend in the river and suddenly, standing on a slight eminence, they saw the bungalow. In a few minutes they caught sight of the landing-stage and on it, among a little group of natives, a figure in white waving to them.

Hutchinson was a tall, stout man with a red face. His appearance led you to expect that he was breezy and self-confident, so that it was not a little surprising to discover quickly that he was diffident and even a trifle shy. When he shook hands with his guests—Izzart introduced himself and then Campion—and led them up the pathway to the bungalow, though he was plainly anxious to be civil it was not hard to see that he found it difficult to make conversation. He took them out on to the veranda and here they found on the table glasses and whisky and soda. They made themselves comfortable on long chairs. Izzart, conscious of Hutchinson's slight embarrassment with strangers, expanded; he was very hearty and voluble. He began to speak of their common acquaintances at Kuala Solor, and he managed very soon to slip in casually the information that he had been at Harrow.

'You were at Winchester, weren't you?' he asked.

'Yes.'

'I wonder if you knew George Parker. He was in my regiment. He was at Winchester. I daresay he was younger than you.'

Izzart felt that it was a bond between them that they had been at these particular schools, and it excluded Campion, who obviously had enjoyed no such advantage. They drank two or three whiskies. Izzart in half an hour began to call his host Hutchie. He talked a good deal about 'my regiment' in which he had got his company during the war, and what good fellows his brother officers were. He mentioned two or three names which could hardly be unknown to Hutchinson. They were not the sort of people that Campion was likely to have come across, and he was not sorry to administer to him a neat snub when he claimed acquaintance with someone he spoke of.

'Billie Meadows? I knew a fellow called Billie Meadows in Sinaloa many years ago,' said Campion.

'Oh, I shouldn't think it could be the same,' said Izzart, with a smile. 'Billie's by way of being a peer of the realm. He's the Lord Meadows who races. Don't you remember, he owned Spring Carrots?'

Dinner time was approaching, and after a wash and brush-up they drank a couple of gin pahits. They sat down. Hutchinson had not been to Kuala Solor for the best part of a year, and had not seen another white man for three months. He was anxious to make the most of his visitors. He could give them no wine, but there was plenty of whisky and after dinner he brought out a precious bottle of Benedictine. They were very gay. They laughed and talked a great deal. Izzart was getting on famously. He thought he had never liked a fellow more than Hutchinson, and he pressed him to come down to Kuala Solor as soon as he could. They would have a wonderful beano. Campion was left out of the conversation by Izzart with the faintly malicious intention of putting him in his place, and by Hutchinson through shyness; and presently, after yawning a good deal, he said he would go to bed. Hutchinson showed him to his room, and when he returned Izzart said to him:

'You don't want to turn in yet, do you?'

'Not on your life. Let's have another drink.'

They sat and talked. They both grew a little drunk. Presently Hutchinson told Izzart that he lived with a Malay girl, and had a couple of children by her. He had told them to keep out of sight while Campion was there.

'I expect she's asleep now,' said Hutchinson, with a glance at the door which Izzart knew led into his room, 'but I'd like you to see the kiddies in the morning.'

Just then a faint wail was heard and Hutchinson with a 'Hullo, the little devil's awake', went to the door and opened it. In a moment or two he came out of the room with a child in his arms. A woman followed him.

'He's cutting his teeth,' said Hutchinson. 'It makes him restless.'

The woman wore a sarong and a thin white jacket and she was barefoot. She was young, with fine dark eyes, and she gave Izzart when he spoke to her a bright and pleasant smile. She sat down and lit a cigarette. She answered the civil questions Izzart put to her without embarrassment, but also without effusion. Hutchinson asked her if she would have a whisky and soda, but she refused. When the two men began to talk again in English she sat on quite quietly, faintly rocking herself in her chair, and occupied with none could tell what calm thoughts.

'She's a very good girl,' said Hutchinson. 'She looks after the house and she's no trouble. Of course it's the only thing to do in a place like this.'

'I shall never do it myself,' said Izzart. 'After all, one may want to get married and then it means all sorts of botherations.'

'But who wants to get married? What a life for a white woman. I wouldn't ask a white woman to live here for anything in the world.'

'Of course it's a matter of taste. If I have any kiddies I'm going to see that they have a white mother.'

Hutchinson looked down at the little dark-skinned child he held in his arms. He gave a faint smile.

'It's funny how you get to like them,' he said. 'When they're your own it doesn't seem to matter that they've got a touch of the tar-brush.'

The woman gave the child a look, and getting up said she would take it back to bed.

'I should think we'd better all turn in,' said Hutchinson. 'God knows what the time is.'

Izzart went to his room and threw open the shutters which his boy Hassan, whom he was travelling with, had closed. Blowing out the candle so that it should not attract the mosquitoes, he sat down at the window and looked at the soft night. The whisky he had drunk made him feel very wide awake, and he was not inclined to go to bed. He took off his ducks, put on a sarong and lit a cheroot. His good-humour was gone. It was the sight of Hutchinson looking fondly at the half-caste child which had upset him.

'They've got no right to have them,' he said to himself. 'They've got no chance in the world. Ever.'

He passed his hands reflectively along his bare and hairy legs. He shuddered a little. Though he had done everything he could to develop the calves, his legs were like broomsticks. He hated them. He was uneasily conscious of them all the time. They were like a native's. Of course they were the very legs for a top-boot. In his uniform he had looked very well. He was a tall, powerful man, over six feet high, and he had a neat black moustache and neat black hair. His dark eyes were fine and mobile. He was a good-looking fellow and he knew it, and he dressed well, shabbily when shabbiness was good form, and smartly when the occasion demanded. He had loved the army, and it was a bitter blow to him when, at the end of the war, he could not remain in it. His ambitions were simple. He wanted to have two thousand a year, give smart little dinners, go to parties, and wear a uniform. He hankered after London.

Of course his mother lived there, and his mother cramped his style. He wondered how on earth he could produce her if ever he got engaged to the girl of good family (with a little money) whom he was looking for to make his wife. Because his father had been dead so long and during the later part of his career was stationed in the most remote of the Malay States, Izzart felt fairly sure that no one in Sembulu knew anything about her, but he lived in terror lest someone, running across her in London, should write over to tell people that she was a half-caste. She had been a beautiful creature when Izzart's father, an engineer in the government service, had married her; but now she was a fat old woman with grey hair who sat about all day smoking cigarettes. Izzart was twelve years old when his father died and then he could speak Malay much more fluently than English. An aunt offered to pay for his education and Mrs Izzart accompanied her son to England. She lived habitually in furnished apartments, and her rooms with their Oriental draperies and Malay silver were overheated and stuffy. She was for ever in trouble with her landladies because she would leave cigarette-ends about. Izzart hated the way she made friends with them: she would be shockingly familiar with them for a time, then there would be a falling-out, and after a violent scene she would flounce out of the house. Her only amusement was the pictures, and to these she went every day in the week. At home she wore an old and tawdry dressing-gown, but when she went out she dressed herself—but, oh, how untidily—in extravagant colours, so that it was a mortification to her dapper son. He quarrelled with her frequently, she made him impatient and he was ashamed of her; and yet he felt for her a deep tenderness; it was almost a physical bond between them, something stronger than the ordinary feeling of mother and son, so that notwithstanding the failings that exasperated him she was the only person in the world with whom he felt entirely at home.

It was owing to his father's position and his own knowledge of Malay, for his mother always spoke it to him, that after the war, finding himself with nothing to do, he had managed to enter the service of the Sultan of Sembulu. He had been a success. He played games well, he was strong and a good athlete; in the rest-house at Kuala Solor were the cups which he had won at Harrow for running and jumping, and to these he had added since others for golf and tennis. With his abundant fund of small-talk he was an asset at parties and his cheeriness made things go. He ought to have been happy and he was wretched. He wanted so much to be popular, and he had an impression, stronger than ever at this moment, that popularity escaped him. He wondered whether by any chance the men at Kuala Solor with whom he was so hail-fellow-well-met suspected that he had native blood in him. He knew very well what to expect if they ever found out. They wouldn't say he was gay and friendly then, they would say he was damned familiar; and they would say he was inefficient and careless, as the half-castes were, and when he talked of marrying a white woman they would snigger. Oh, it was so unfair! What difference could it make, that drop of native blood in his veins, and yet because of it they would always be on the watch for the expected failure at the critical moment. Everyone knew that you couldn't rely on Eurasians, sooner or later they would let you down; he knew it too, but now he asked himself whether they didn't fail because failure was expected of them. They were never given a chance, poor devils.

But a cock crew loudly. It must be very late and he was beginning to feel chilly. He got into bed. When Hassan brought him his tea next morning he had a racking headache, and when he went into breakfast he could not look at the porridge and the bacon and eggs which were set before him. Hutchinson too was feeling none too well.

'I fancy we made rather a night of it,' said his host, with a smile to conceal his faint embarrassment.

'I feel like hell,' said Izzart.

'I'm going to breakfast off a whisky and soda myself,' added Hutchinson.

Izzart asked for nothing better, and it was with distaste that they watched Campion eat with healthy appetite a substantial meal. Campion chaffed them.

'By God, Izzart, you're looking green about the gills,' he said. 'I never saw such a filthy colour.'

Izzart flushed. His swarthiness was always a sensitive point with him. But he forced himself to give a cheery laugh.

'You see, I had a Spanish grandmother,' he answered, 'and when I'm under the weather it always comes out. I remember at Harrow I fought a boy and licked him, because he called me a damned half-caste.'

'You are dark,' said Hutchinson. 'Do Malays ever ask you if you have any native blood in you?'

'Yes, damn their impudence.'

A boat with their kit had started early in the morning in order to get to the mouth of the river before them, and tell the skipper of the *Sultan Ahmed*, if by chance he arrived before he was due, that they were on their way. Campion and Izzart were to set out immediately after tiffin in order to arrive at the place where they were to spend the night before the Bore passed. A Bore is a tidal wave that, by reason of a peculiarity in the lie of the land, surges up certain rivers, and there happened to be one on the river on which they were travelling. Hutchinson had talked to them of it the night before and Campion, who had never seen such a thing, was much interested.

'This is one of the best in Borneo. It's worth looking at,' said Hutchinson.

He told them how the natives, waiting the moment, rode it and were borne up the river on its crest at a breathless and terrifying speed. He had done it once himself.

'Never no more for me,' he said. 'I was scared out of my wits.'

'I should like to try it once,' said Izzart.

'It's exciting enough, but my word, when you're in a flimsy dug-out and you know that if the native doesn't get the right moment you'll be flung in that seething torrent and you won't have a chance in a million . . . no, it's not my idea of sport.'

'I've shot a good many rapids in my day,' said Campion.

'Rapids be damned. You wait till you see the Bore. It's one of the most terrifying things I know. D'you know that at least a dozen natives are drowned in it in this river alone every year?'

They lounged about on the veranda most of the morning and Hutchinson showed them the court-house. Then gin pahits were served. They drank two or three. Izzart began to feel himself, and when at length tiffin was ready he found that he had an excellent appetite. Hutchinson had boasted of his Malay curry and when the steaming, succulent dishes were placed before them they all set to ravenously. Hutchinson pressed them to drink.

'You've got nothing to do but sleep. Why shouldn't you get drunk?'

He could not bear to let them go so soon, it was good after so long to have white men to talk to, and he lingered over the meal. He urged them to eat. They would have a filthy meal that night at the long-house and nothing to drink but arak. They had better make hay while the sun shone. Campion suggested once or twice that they should start, but Hutchinson, and Izzart too, for now he was feeling very happy and comfortable, assured him there was plenty of time. Hutchinson sent for his precious bottle of Benedictine. They had made a hole in it last night; they might as well finish it before they went.

When at last he walked down with them to the river they were all very merry and none of them was quite steady on his legs. Over the middle of the boat was an attap awning, and under this Hutchinson had had a mattress laid. The crew were prisoners who had been marched down from the jail to row the white men, and they wore dingy sarongs with the prison mark. They waited at their oars. Izzart and Campion shook hands with Hutchinson and threw themselves down on the mattress. The boat pushed off. The turbid river, wide and placid, glistened in the heat of that brilliant afternoon like polished brass. In the distance ahead of them they could see the bank with its tangle of green trees. They felt drowsy, but Izzart at least found a curious enjoyment in resisting for a little while the heaviness that was creeping over him, and he made up his mind that he would not let himself fall asleep till he had finished his cheroot. At last the stub began to burn his fingers and he flung it into the river.

'I'm going to have a wonderful snooze,' he said.

'What about the Bore?' asked Campion.

'Oh, that's all right. We needn't worry about that.'

He gave a long and noisy yawn. His limbs felt like lead. He had one moment in which he was conscious of his delicious drowsiness and then he knew nothing more. Suddenly he was awakened by Campion shaking him.

'I say, what's that?'

'What's what?'

He spoke irritably, for sleep was still heavy upon him, but with his eyes he followed Campion's gesture. He could hear nothing, but a good way off he saw two or three white-crested waves following one another. They did not look very alarming.

'Oh, I suppose that's the Bore.'

'What are we going to do about it?' cried Campion.

Izzart was scarcely yet quite awake. He smiled at the concern in Campion's voice.

'Don't worry. These fellows know all about it. They know exactly what to do. We may get a bit splashed.'

But while they were saying these few words the Bore came nearer, very quickly, with a roar like the roar of an angry sea, and Izzart saw that the waves were much higher than he had thought. He did not like the look of them and he tightened his belt so that his shorts should not slip down if the boat were upset. In a moment the waves were upon them. It was a great wall of water that seemed to tower over them, and it might have been ten or twelve feet high, but you could measure it only with your horror. It was quite plain that no boat could weather it. The first wave dashed over them, drenching them all, half filling the boat with water, and then immediately another wave struck them. The boatman began to shout. They pulled madly at their oars and the steersman yelled an order. But in that surging torrent they were helpless, and it was frightening to see how soon they lost all control of the boat. The force of the water turned it broadside on and it was carried along, helter skelter, upon the crest of the Bore. Another great wave dashed over them and the boat began to sink. Izzart and Campion scrambled out of the covered place in which they had been lying and suddenly the boat gave way under their feet and they found themselves struggling in the water. It surged and stormed around them. Izzart's first impulse was to swim for the shore, but his boy, Hassan, shouted to him to cling to the boat. For a minute or two they all did this.

'Are you all right?' Campion shouted to him.

'Yes, enjoying the bath,' said Izzart.

He imagined that the waves would pass by as the Bore ascended the river, and in a few minutes at the outside they would find themselves in calm water once more. He forgot that they were being carried along on its crest. The waves dashed over them. They clung to the gunwale and the base of the structure which supported the attap awning. Then a larger wave caught the boat as it turned over, falling upon them so that they lost their hold; there seemed nothing but a slippery bottom to cling to and Izzart's hands slithered helplessly on the greasy surface. But the boat continued to turn and he made a desperate grab at the gunwale, only to feel it slip out of his hands as the turn went on, then he caught the framework of the awning, and still it turned, turned slowly right round and once more he sought for a hand-hold on the bottom. The boat went round and round with a horrible regularity. He thought this must be because everyone was clinging to one side of it, and he tried to make the crew go round to the other. He could not make them understand. Everyone was shouting and the waves beat against them with a dull and angry roar. Each time the boat rolled over on them Izzart was pushed under water, only to come up again as the gunwale and the framework of the awning gave him something to cling to. The struggle was awful. Presently he began to get terribly out of breath, and he felt his strength leaving him. He knew that he could not hold on much longer, but he did not feel frightened, for his fatigue by now was so great that he did not very much care what happened. Hassan was by his side and he told him he was growing very tired. He thought the best thing was to make a dash for the shore, it did not look more than sixty yards away, but Hassan begged him not to. Still they were being carried along amid those seething, pounding waves. The boat went round and round and they scrambled over it like squirrels in a cage. Izzart swallowed a lot of water. He felt he was very nearly done. Hassan could not help him, but it was a comfort that he was there, for Izzart knew that his boy, used to the water all his life, was a powerful swimmer. Then, Izzart did not know why, for a minute or two the boat held bottom downwards, so that he was able to hold on to the gunwale. It was a precious thing to be able to get his breath. At that moment two dug-outs, with Malays in them riding the Bore, passed swiftly by them. They shouted for help, but the Malays averted their faces and went on. They saw the white men, and did not want to be concerned in any trouble that might befall them. It was agonizing to see them go past, callous and indifferent in their safety. But on a sudden the boat rolled round again, round and round slowly, and the miserable, exhausting scramble repeated itself. It took the heart out of you. But the short respite had helped Izzart, and he was able to struggle a little longer. Then once more he found himself so terribly out of breath that he thought his chest would burst. His strength was all gone, and he did not know now whether he had enough to try to swim for the shore. Suddenly he heard a cry.

'Izzart, Izzart. Help. Help.'

It was Campion's voice. It was a scream of agony. It sent a shock all through Izzart's nerves. Campion, Campion, what did he care for Campion? Fear seized him, a blind animal fear, and it gave him a new strength. He did not answer.

'Help me, quick, quick,' he said to Hassan.

Hassan understood him at once. By a miracle one of the oars was floating quite close to them and he pushed it into Izzart's reach. He placed a hand under Izzart's arm and they struck away from the boat. Izzart's heart was pounding and his breath came with difficulty. He felt horribly weak. The waves beat in his face. The bank looked dreadfully far away. He did not think he could ever reach it. Suddenly the boy cried that he could touch bottom and Izzart put down his legs; but he could feel nothing; he swam a few more exhausted strokes, his eyes fixed on the bank, and then, trying again, felt his feet sink into thick mud. He was thankful. He floundered on and there was the bank within reach of his hands, black mud in which he sank to his knees; he scrambled up, desperate to get out of the cruel water, and when he came to the top he found a little flat with tall rank grass all about it. He and Hassan sank down on it and lay for a while stretched out like dead men. They were so tired that they could not move. They were covered with black mud from head to foot.

But presently Izzart's mind began to work, and a pang of anguish on a sudden shook him. Campion was drowned. It was awful. He did not know how he was going to explain the disaster when he got back to Kuala Solor. They would blame him for it; he ought to have remembered the Bore and told the steersman to make for the bank and tie up the boat when he saw it coming. It wasn't his fault, it was the steersman's, he knew the river; why in God's name hadn't he had the sense to get into safety? How could he have expected that it was possible to ride that horrible torrent? Izzart's limbs shook as he remembered the wall of seething water that rushed down upon them. He must get the body and take it back to Kuala Solor. He wondered whether any of the crew were drowned too. He felt too weak to move, but Hassan now rose and wrung the water out of his sarong; he looked over the river and quickly turned to Izzart.

'Tuan, a boat is coming.'

The lalang grass prevented Izzart from seeing anything.

'Shout to them,' he said.

Hassan slipped out of view and made his way along the branch of a tree that overhung the water; he cried out and waved. Presently Izzart heard voices. There was a rapid conversation between the boy and the occupants of the boat, and then the boy came back.

'They saw us capsize, Tuan,' he said, 'and they came as soon as the Bore passed. There's a long-house on the other side. If you will cross the river they will give us sarongs and food and we can sleep there.'

Izzart for a moment felt that he could not again trust himself on the face of the treacherous water.

'What about the other tuan?' he asked.

'They do not know.'

'If he's drowned they must find the body.'

'Another boat has gone up-stream.'

Izzart did not know what to do. He was numb. Hassan put his arm round his shoulder and raised him to his feet. He made his way through the thick grass to the edge of the water, and there he saw a dug-out with two Dyaks in it. The river now once more was calm and sluggish; the great wave had passed on and no one would have dreamed that so short a while before the placid surface was like a stormy sea. The Dyaks repeated to him what they had already told the boy. Izzart could not bring himself to speak. He felt that if he said a word he would burst out crying. Hassan helped him to get in, and the Dyaks began to pull across. He fearfully wanted something to smoke, but his cigarettes and his matches, both in a hip-pocket, were soaking. The passage of the river seemed endless. The night fell and when they reached the bank the first stars were shining. He stepped ashore and one of the Dyaks took him up to the long-house. But Hassan seized the paddle he had dropped and with the other pushed out into the stream. Two or three men and some children came down to meet Izzart and he climbed to the house amid a babel of conversation. He went up the ladder and was led with greetings and excited comment to the space where the young men slept. Rattan mats were hurriedly laid to make him a couch and he sank down on them. Someone brought him a jar of arak and he took a long drink; it was rough and fiery, burning his throat, but it warmed his heart. He slipped off his shirt and trousers and put on a dry sarong which someone lent him. By chance he caught sight of the yellow new moon lying on her back, and it gave him a keen, almost a sensual, pleasure. He could not help thinking that he might at that moment be a corpse floating up the river with the tide. The moon had never looked to him more lovely. He began to feel hungry and he asked for rice. One of the women went into a room to prepare it. He was more himself now, and he began to think again of the explanations he would make at Kuala Solor. No one could really blame him because he had gone to sleep; he certainly wasn't drunk, Hutchinson would bear him out there, and how was he to suspect that the steersman would be such a damned fool? It was just rotten luck. But he couldn't think of Campion without a shudder. At last a platter of rice was brought him, and he was just about to start eating when a man ran hurriedly along and came up to him.

'The tuan's come,' he cried.

'What tuan?'

He jumped up. There was a commotion about the doorway and he stepped forward. Hassan was coming quickly towards him out of the darkness, and then he heard a voice.

'Izzart. Are you there?'

Campion advanced towards him.

'Well, here we are again. By God, that was a pretty near thing, wasn't it? You seem to have made yourself nice and comfortable. My heavens, I could do with a drink.'

His dank clothes clung round him, and he was muddy and dishevelled. But he was in excellent spirits.

'I didn't know where the hell they were bringing me. I'd made up my mind that I should have to spend the night on the bank. I thought you were drowned.'

'Here's some arak,' said Izzart.

Campion put his mouth to the jar and drank and spluttered and drank again.

'Muck, but by God it's strong.' He looked at Izzart with a grin of his broken and discoloured teeth. 'I say, old man, you look as though you'd be all the better for a wash.'

'I'll wash later.'

'All right, so will I. Tell them to get me a sarong. How did you get out?' He did not wait for an answer. 'I thought I was done for. I owe my life to these two sportsmen here.' He indicated with a cheery nod two of the Dyak prisoners whom Izzart vaguely recognized as having been part of their crew. 'They were hanging on to that blasted boat on each side of me and somehow they cottoned on to it that I was down and out. I couldn't have lasted another minute. They made signs to me that we could risk having a shot at getting to the bank, but I didn't think I had the strength. By George, I've never been so blown in all my life. I don't know how they managed it, but somehow they got hold of the mattress we'd been lying on, and they made it into a roll. They're sportsmen they are. I don't know why they didn't just save themselves without bothering about me. They gave it me. I thought it a damned poor lifebelt, but I saw the force of the proverb about a drowning man clutching at a straw. I caught hold of the damned thing and between them somehow or other they dragged me ashore.'

The danger from which he had escaped made Campion excited and voluble; but Izzart hardly listened to what he said. He heard once more, as distinctly as though the words rang now through the air, Campion's agonized cry for help, and he felt sick with terror. The blind panic raced down his nerves. Campion was talking still, but was he talking to conceal his thoughts? Izzart looked into those bright blue eyes and sought to read the sense behind the flow of words. Was there a hard glint in them or something of cynical mockery? Did he know that Izzart, leaving him to his fate, had cut and run? He flushed deeply. After all, what was there that he could have done? At such a moment it was each for himself and the devil take the hindmost. But what would they say in Kuala Solor if Campion told them that Izzart had deserted him? He ought to have stayed, he wished now with all his heart that he had, but then, then it was stronger than himself, he couldn't. Could anyone blame him? No one who had seen that fierce and seething torrent. Oh, the water and the exhaustion, so that he could have cried!

'If you're as hungry as I am you'd better have a tuck in at this rice,' he said.

Campion ate voraciously, but when Izzart had taken a mouthful or two he found that he had no appetite. Campion talked and talked. Izzart listened suspiciously. He felt that he must be alert and he drank more arak. He began to feel a little drunk.

'I shall get into the devil of a row at K. S.' he said tentatively.

'I don't know why.'

'I was told off to look after you. They won't think it was very clever of me to let you get nearly drowned.'

'It wasn't your fault. It was the fault of the damned fool of a steersman. After all, the important thing is that we're saved. By George, I thought I was finished once. I shouted out to you. I don't know if you heard me.'

'No, I didn't hear anything. There was such a devil of a row, wasn't there?'

'Perhaps you'd got away before. I don't know exactly when you did get away.'

Izzart looked at him sharply. Was it his fancy that there was an odd look in Campion's eyes?

'There was such an awful confusion,' he said. 'I was just about down and out. My boy threw me over an oar. He gave me to understand you were all right. He told me you'd got ashore.'

The oar! He ought to have given Campion the oar and told Hassan, the strong swimmer, to give *him* his help. Was it his fancy again that Campion gave him a quick and searching glance?

'I wish I could have been of more use to you,' said Izzart.

'Oh, I'm sure you had enough to do to look after yourself,' answered Campion.

The headman brought them cups of arak, and they both drank a great deal. Izzart's head began to spin and he suggested that they should turn in. Beds had been prepared for them and mosquito nets fixed. They were to set out at dawn on the rest of their journey down the river. Campion's bed was next to his, and in a few minutes he heard him snoring. He had fallen asleep the moment he lay down. The young men of the long-house and the prisoners of the boat's crew went on talking late into the night. Izzart's head now was aching horribly and he could not think. When Hassan roused him as day broke it seemed to him that he had not slept at all. Their clothes had been washed and dried, but they were bedraggled objects as they walked along the narrow pathway to the river where the prahu was waiting for them. They rowed leisurely. The morning was lovely and the great stretch of placid water gleamed in the early light.

'By George, it's fine to be alive,' said Campion.

He was grubby and unshaved. He took long breaths, and his twisted mouth was half open with a grin. You could tell that he found the air singularly good to breathe. He was delighted with the blue sky and the sunshine and the greenness of the trees. Izzart hated him. He was sure that this morning there was a difference in his manner. He did not know what to do. He had a mind to throw himself on his mercy. He had behaved like a cad, but he was sorry, he would give anything to have the chance again, but anyone might have done what he did, and if Campion gave him away he was ruined. He could never stay in Sembulu; his name would be mud in Borneo and the Straits Settlements. If he made his confession to Campion he could surely get Campion to promise to hold his tongue. But would he keep his promise? He looked at him, a shifty little man: how could he be relied on? Izzart thought of what he had said the night before. It wasn't the truth, of course, but who could know that? At all events who could prove that he hadn't honestly thought that Campion was safe? Whatever Campion said, it was only his word against Izzart's; he could laugh and shrug his shoulders and say that Campion had lost his head and didn't know what he was talking about. Besides, it wasn't certain that Campion hadn't accepted his story; in that frightful struggle for life he could be very sure of nothing. He had a temptation to go back to the subject, but he was afraid if he did that he would excite suspicion in Campion's mind. He *must* hold his tongue. That was his only chance of safety. And when they got to K.S. he would get in his story first.

'I should be completely happy now,' said Campion, 'if I only had something to smoke.'

'We shall be able to get some stinkers on board.'

Campion gave a little laugh.

'Human beings are very unreasonable,' he said. 'At the first moment I was so glad to be alive that I thought of nothing else, but now I'm beginning to regret the loss of my notes and my photographs and my shaving tackle.'

Izzart formulated the thought which had lurked at the back of his mind, but which all through the night he had refused to admit into his consciousness.

'I wish to God he'd been drowned. Then I'd have been safe.'

'There she is,' cried Campion suddenly.

Izzart looked round. They were at the mouth of the river and there was the *Sultan Ahmed* waiting for them. Izzart's heart sank: he had forgotten that she had an English skipper and that he would have to be told the story of their adventure. What would Campion say? The skipper was called Bredon, and Izzart had met him often at Kuala Solor. He was a little bluff man, with a black moustache, and a breezy manner.

'Hurry up,' he called out to them, as they rowed up, 'I've been waiting for you since dawn.' But when they climbed on board his face fell. 'Hullo, what's the matter with you?'

'Give us a drink and you shall hear all about it,' said Campion, with his crooked grin.

'Come along.'

They sat down under the awning. On a table were glasses, a bottle of whisky and soda-water. The skipper gave an order and in a few minutes they were noisily under way.

'We were caught in the Bore,' said Izzart.

He felt he must say something. His mouth was horribly dry notwithstanding the drink.

'Were you, by Jove? You're lucky not to have been drowned. What happened?'

He addressed himself to Izzart because he knew him, but it was Campion who answered. He related the whole incident, accurately, and Izzart listened with strained attention. Campion spoke in the plural when he told the early part of the story, and then, as he came to the moment when they were thrown into the water, changed to the singular. At first it was what *they* had done and now it was what happened to *him*. He left Izzart out of it. Izzart did not know whether to be relieved or alarmed. Why did he not mention him? Was it because in that mortal struggle for life he had thought of nothing but himself or—did he *know*?

'And what happened to you?' said Captain Bredon, turning to Izzart.

Izzart was about to answer when Campion spoke.

'Until I got over to the other side of the river I thought he was drowned. I don't know how he got out. I expect he hardly knows himself.'

'It was touch and go,' said Izzart with a laugh.

Why had Campion said that? He caught his eye. He was sure now that there was a gleam of amusement in it. It was awful not to be certain. He was frightened. He was ashamed. He wondered if he could not so guide the conversation, either now or later, as to ask Campion whether that was the story he was going to tell in Kuala Solor. There was nothing in it to excite anyone's suspicions. But if nobody else knew, Campion knew. He could have killed him.

'Well, I think you're both of you damned lucky to be alive,' said the skipper.

It was but a short run to Kuala Solor, and as they steamed up the Sembulu river Izzart moodily watched the banks. On each side were the mangroves and the nipahs washed by the water, and behind, the dense green of the jungle; here and there, among fruit trees, were Malay houses on piles. Night fell as they docked. Goring, of the police, came on board and shook hands with them. He was living at the rest-house just then, and as he set about his work of seeing the native passengers he told them they would find another man, Porter by name, staying there too. They would all meet at dinner. The boys took charge of their kit, and Campion and Izzart strolled along. They bathed and changed, and at half past eight the four of them assembled in the common-room for gin pahits.

'I say, what's this Bredon tells me about your being nearly drowned?' said Goring as he came in.

Izzart felt himself flush, but before he could answer Campion broke in, and it seemed certain to Izzart that he spoke in order to give the story as he chose. He felt hot with shame. Not a word was spoken in disparagement of him, not a word was said of him at all; he wondered if those two men who listened, Goring and Porter, thought it strange that he should be left out. He looked at Campion intently as he proceeded with his narration; he told it rather humorously; he did not disguise the danger in which they had been, but he made a joke of it, so that the two listeners laughed at the quandary in which they found themselves.

'A thing that's tickled me since,' said Campion, 'is that when I got over to the other bank I was black with mud from head to foot. I felt I really ought to jump in the river and have a wash, but you know I felt I'd been in that damned river as much as ever I wanted, and I said to myself; No, by George, I'll go dirty. And when I got into the long-house and saw Izzart as black as I was, I knew he'd felt just like I did.'

They laughed and Izzart forced himself to laugh too. He noticed that Campion had told the story in precisely the same words as he had used when he told it to the skipper of the *Sultan Ahmed*. There could be only one explanation of that; he knew, he knew everything, and had made up his mind exactly what story to tell. The ingenuity with which Campion gave the facts and yet left out what must be to Izzart's discredit was devilish. But why was he holding his hand? It wasn't in him not to feel contempt and resentment for the man who had callously deserted him in that moment of dreadful peril. Suddenly, in a flash of inspiration Izzart understood: he was keeping the truth to tell to Willis, the Resident. Izzart had gooseflesh as he thought of confronting Willis. He could deny, but would his denials serve him? Willis was no fool, and he would get at Hassan; Hassan could not be trusted to be silent; Hassan would give him away. Then he would be done for. Willis would suggest that he had better go home.

He had a racking headache, and after dinner he went to his room, for he wanted to be alone so that he could devise a plan of action. And then a thought came to him which made him go hot and cold: he knew that the secret which he had guarded so long was a secret to nobody. He was on a sudden certain of it. Why should he have those bright eyes and that swarthy skin? Why should he speak Malay with such ease and have learned Dyak so quickly? Of course they knew. What a fool he was ever to think that they believed that story of his, about the Spanish grandmother! They must have laughed up their sleeves when he told it, and behind his back they had called him a damned nigger. And now another thought came to him, torturing, and he asked himself whether it was on account of that wretched drop of native blood in him that when he heard Campion cry out his nerve failed him. After all, anyone might at that moment have been seized with panic; and why in God's name should he sacrifice his life to save a man's whom he cared nothing for? It was insane. But of course in K. S. they would say it was only what they expected; they would make no allowances.

At last he went to bed, but when, after tossing about recklessly for God knows how long, he fell asleep, he was awakened by a fearful dream; he seemed to be once more in that raging torrent, with the boat turning, turning; and then there was the desperate clutching at the gunwale, and the agony as it slipped out of his hands, and the water that roared over him. He was wide awake before dawn. His only chance was to see Willis and get his story in first; and he thought over carefully what he was going to say, and chose the very words he meant to use.

He got up early, and in order not to see Campion went out without breakfast. He walked along the high road till such time as he knew the Resident would be in his office, and then walked back again. He sent in his name and was ushered into Willis's room. He was a little elderly man with thin grey hair and a long yellow face.

'I'm glad to see you back safe and sound,' he said shaking hands with Izzart. 'What's this I hear about your being nearly drowned?'

Izzart, in clean ducks, his topee spotless, was a fine figure of a man. His black hair was neatly brushed, and his moustache was trimmed. He had an upright and soldierly bearing.

'I thought I'd better come and tell you at once, sir, as you told me to look after Campion.'

'Fire away.'

Izzart told his story. He made light of the danger. He gave Willis to understand that it had not been very great. They would never have been upset if they had not started so late.

'I tried to get Campion away earlier, but he'd had two or three drinks and the fact is, he didn't want to move.'

'Was he tight?'

'I don't know about that,' smiled Izzart good-humouredly. 'I shouldn't say he was cold sober.'

He went on with his story. He managed to insinuate that Campion had lost his head a little. Of course it was a very frightening business to a man who wasn't a decent swimmer: he, Izzart, had been more concerned for Campion than for himself; he knew the only chance was to keep cool, and the moment they were upset he saw that Campion had got the wind up.

'You can't blame him for that,' said the Resident.

'Of course I did everything I possibly could for him, sir, but the fact is, there wasn't anything much I could do.'

'Well, the great thing is that you both escaped. It would have been very awkward for all of us if he'd been drowned.'

'I thought I'd better come and tell you the facts before you saw Campion, sir. I fancy he's inclined to talk rather wildly about it. There's no use exaggerating.'

'On the whole your stories agree pretty well,' said Willis, with a little smile.

Izzart looked at him blankly.

'Haven't you seen Campion this morning? I heard from Goring that there'd been some trouble, and I looked in last night on my way home from the Fort after dinner. You'd already gone to bed.'

Izzart felt himself trembling, and he made a great effort to preserve his composure.

'By the way, you got away first, didn't you?'

'I don't really know, sir. You see, there was a lot of confusion.'

'You must have if you got over to the other side before he did.'

'I suppose I did then.'

'Well, thanks for coming to tell me,' said Willis, rising from his chair.

As he did so he knocked some books on the floor. They fell with a sudden thud. The unexpected sound made Izzart start violently, and he gave a gasp. The Resident looked at him quickly.

'I say, your nerves are in a pretty state.'

Izzart could not control his trembling.

'I'm very sorry, sir,' he murmured.

'I expect it's been a shock. You'd better take it easy for a few days. Why don't you get the doctor to give you something?'

'I didn't sleep very well last night.'

The Resident nodded as though he understood. Izzart left the room, and as he passed out some man he knew stopped and congratulated him on his escape. They all knew of it. He walked back to the rest-house. And as he walked, he repeated to himself the story he had told the Resident. Was it really the same story that Campion had told? He had never suspected that the Resident had already heard it from Campion. What a fool he had been to go to bed! He should never have let Campion out of his sight. Why had the Resident listened without telling him that he already knew? Now Izzart cursed himself for having suggested that Campion was drunk and had lost his head. He had said this in order to discredit him, but he knew now that it was a stupid thing to do. And why had Willis said that about his having got away first? Perhaps he was holding his hand too; perhaps he was going to make inquiries; Willis was very shrewd. But what exactly had Campion said? He must know that; at whatever cost he must know. Izzart's mind was seething, so that he felt he could hardly keep a hold on his thoughts, but he must keep calm. He felt like a hunted animal. He did not believe that Willis liked him; once or twice in the office he had blamed him because he was careless; perhaps he was just waiting till he got all the facts. Izzart was almost hysterical.

He entered the rest-house and there, sitting on a long chair, with his legs stretched out, was Campion. He was reading the papers which had arrived during their absence in the jungle. Izzart felt a blind rush of hatred well up in him as he looked at the little, shabby man who held him in the hollow of his hand.

'Hullo,' said Campion, looking up. 'Where have you been?'

To Izzart it seemed that there was in his eyes a mocking irony. He clenched his hands, and his breath came fast.

'What have you been saying to Willis about me?' he asked abruptly.

The tone in which he put the unexpected question was so harsh that Campion gave him a glance of faint surprise.

'I don't think I've been saying anything very much about you. Why?'

'He came here last night.'

Izzart looked at him intently. His brows were drawn together in an angry frown as he tried to read Campion's thoughts.

'I told him you'd gone to bed with a headache. He wanted to know about our mishap.'

'I've just seen him.'

Izzart walked up and down the large and shaded room; now, though it was still early, the sun was hot and dazzling. He felt himself in a net. He was blind with rage; he could have seized Campion by the throat and strangled him, and yet, because he did not know what he had to fight against, he felt himself powerless. He was tired and ill, and his nerves were shaken. On a sudden the anger which had given him a sort of strength left him, and he was filled with despondency. It was as though water and not blood ran through his veins; his heart sank and his knees seemed to give way. He felt that if he did not take care, he would begin to cry. He was dreadfully sorry for himself.

'Damn you, I wish to God I'd never set eyes on you,' he cried pitifully.

'What on earth's the matter?' asked Campion, with astonishment.

'Oh, don't pretend. We've been pretending for two days, and I'm fed up with it.' His voice rose shrilly, it sounded odd in that robust and powerful man. 'I'm fed up with it. I cut and run. I left you to drown. I know I behaved like a skunk. I couldn't help it.'

Campion rose slowly from his chair.

'What *are* you talking about?'

His tone was so genuinely surprised that it gave Izzart a start. A cold shiver ran down his spine.

'When you called for help I was panic-stricken. I just caught hold of an oar and got Hassan to help me get away.'

'That was the most sensible thing you could do.'

'I couldn't help you. There wasn't a thing I could do.'

'Of course not. It was damned silly of me to shout. It was waste of breath, and breath was the very thing I wanted.'

'Do you mean to say you didn't know?'

'When those fellows got me the mattress, I thought you were still clinging to the boat. I had an idea that I got away before you did.'

Izzart put both his hands to his head, and gave a hoarse cry of despair.

'My God, what a fool I've been.'

The two men stood for a while staring at one another. The silence seemed endless.

'What are you going to do now?' asked Izzart at last.

'Oh, my dear fellow, don't worry. I've been frightened too often myself to blame anyone who shows the white feather. I'm not going to tell a soul.'

'Yes, but you *know*.'

'I promise you, you can trust me. Besides, my job's done here and I'm going home. I want to catch the next boat to Singapore.' There was a pause, and Campion looked for a while reflectively at Izzart. 'There's only one thing I'd like to ask you: I've made a good many friends here, and there are one or two things I'm a little sensitive about; when you tell the story of our upset, I should be grateful if you wouldn't make out that I had behaved badly. I wouldn't like the fellows here to think that I'd lost my nerve.'

Izzart flushed darkly. He remembered what he had said to the Resident. It almost looked as though Campion had been listening over his shoulder. He cleared his throat.

'I don't know why you think I should do that.'

Campion chuckled good-naturedly, and his blue eyes were gay with amusement.

'The yellow streak,' he replied, and then, with a grin that showed his broken and discoloured teeth: 'Have a cheroot, dear boy.'

The
Force
of Circumstance

◆

She was sitting on the veranda waiting for her husband to come in for luncheon. The Malay boy had drawn the blinds when the morning lost its freshness, but she had partly raised one of them so that she could look at the river. Under the breathless sun of midday it had the white pallor of death. A native was paddling along in a dug-out so small that it hardly showed above the surface of the water. The colours of the day were ashy and wan. They were but the various tones of the heat. (It was like an Eastern melody, in the minor key, which exacerbates the nerves by its ambiguous monotony; and the ear awaits impatiently a resolution, but waits in vain.) The cicadas sang their grating song with a frenzied energy; it was as continual and monotonous as the rustling of a brook over the stones; but on a sudden it was drowned by the loud singing of a bird, mellifluous and rich; and for an instant, with a catch at her heart, she thought of the English blackbird.

Then she heard her husband's step on the gravel path behind the bungalow, the path that led to the court-house in which he had been working, and she rose from her chair to greet him. He ran up the short flight of steps, for the bungalow was built on piles, and at the door the boy was waiting to take his topee. He came into the room which served them as a dining-room and parlour, and his eyes lit up with pleasure as he saw her.

'Hulloa, Doris. Hungry?'

'Ravenous.'

'It'll only take me a minute to have a bath and then I'm ready.'

'Be quick,' she smiled.

He disappeared into his dressing-room and she heard him whistling cheerily while, with the carelessness with which she was always remonstrating, he tore off his clothes and flung them on the floor. He was twenty-nine, but he was still a school-boy; he would never grow up. That was why she had fallen in love with him, perhaps, for no amount of affection could persuade her that he was good-looking. He was a little round man, with a red face like the full moon, and blue eyes. He was rather pimply. She had examined him carefully and had been forced to confess to him that he had not a single feature which she could praise. She had told him often that he wasn't her type at all.

'I never said I was a beauty,' he laughed.

'I can't think what it is I see in you.'

But of course she knew perfectly well. He was a gay, jolly little man, who took nothing very solemnly, and he was constantly laughing. He made her laugh too. He found life an amusing rather than a serious business, and he had a charming smile. When she was with him she felt happy and good-tempered. And the deep affection which she saw in those merry blue eyes of his touched her. It was very satisfactory to be loved like that. Once, sitting on his knees, during their honeymoon she had taken his face in her hands and said to him:

'You're an ugly, little fat man, Guy, but you've got charm. I can't help loving you.'

A wave of emotion swept over her and her eyes filled with tears. She saw his face contorted for a moment with the extremity of his feeling and his voice was a little shaky when he answered.

'It's a terrible thing for me to have married a woman who's mentally deficient,' he said.

She chuckled. It was the characteristic answer which she would have liked him to make.

It was hard to realize that nine months ago she had never even heard of him. She had met him at a small place by the seaside where she was spending a month's holiday with her mother. Doris was a secretary to a Member of Parliament. Guy was home on leave. They were staying at the same hotel, and he quickly told her all about himself. He was born in Sembulu, where his father had served for thirty years under the second Sultan, and on leaving school he had entered the same service. He was devoted to the country.

'After all, England's a foreign land to me,' he told her. 'My home's Sembulu.'

And now it was her home too. He asked her to marry him at the end of the month's holiday. She had known he was going to, and had decided to refuse him. She was her widowed mother's only child and she could not go so far away from her, but when the moment came she did not quite know what happened to her, she was carried off her feet by an unexpected emotion, and she accepted him. They had been settled now for four months in the little outstation of which he was in charge. She was very happy.

She told him once that she had quite made up her mind to refuse him.

'Are you sorry you didn't?' he asked, with a merry smile in his twinkling blue eyes.

'I should have been a perfect fool if I had. What a bit of luck that fate or chance or whatever it was stepped in and took the matter entirely out of my hands!'

Now she heard Guy clatter down the steps to the bath-house. He was a noisy fellow and even with bare feet he could not be quiet. But he uttered an exclamation. He said two or three words in the local dialect and she could not understand. Then she heard someone speaking to him, not aloud, but in a sibilant whisper. Really it was too bad of people to waylay him when he was

going to have his bath. He spoke again and though his voice was low she could
hear that he was vexed. The other voice was raised now; it was a woman's.
Doris supposed it was someone who had a complaint to make. It was like a
Malay woman to come in that surreptitious way. But she was evidently getting
very little from Guy, for she heard him say: Get out. That at all events she
understood, and then she heard him bolt the door. There was a sound of the
water he was throwing over himself (the bathing arrangements still amused
her, the bath-houses were under the bedrooms, on the ground; you had a large
tub of water and you sluiced yourself with a little tin pail) and in a couple of
minutes he was back again in the dining-room. His hair was still wet. They sat
down to luncheon.

'It's lucky I'm not a suspicious or a jealous person,' she laughed. 'I don't
know that I should altogether approve of your having animated conversations
with ladies while you're having your bath.'

His face, usually so cheerful, had borne a sullen look when he came in, but
now it brightened.

'I wasn't exactly pleased to see her.'

'So I judged by the tone of your voice. In fact, I thought you were rather
short with the young person.'

'Damned cheek, waylaying me like that!'

'What did she want?'

'Oh, I don't know. It's a woman from the kampong. She's had a row with her
husband or something.'

'I wonder if it's the same one who was hanging about this morning.'

He frowned a little.

'Was there someone hanging about?'

'Yes, I went into your dressing-room to see that everything was nice and
tidy, and then I went down to the bath-house. I saw someone slink out of the
door as I went down the steps and when I looked out I saw a woman standing
there.'

'Did you speak to her?'

'I asked her what she wanted and she said something, but I couldn't
understand.'

'I'm not going to have all sorts of stray people prowling about here,' he said.
'They've got no right to come.'

He smiled, but Doris, with the quick perception of a woman in love, noticed
that he smiled only with his lips, not as usual with his eyes also, and wondered
what it was that troubled him.

'What have you been doing this morning?' he asked.

'Oh, nothing much. I went for a little walk.'

'Through the kampong?'

'Yes. I saw a man send a chained monkey up a tree to pick coconuts, which
rather thrilled me.'

'It's rather a lark, isn't it?'

'Oh, Guy, there were two little boys watching him who were much whiter
than the others. I wondered if they were half-castes. I spoke to them, but they
didn't know a word of English.'

'There are two or three half-caste children in the kampong,' he answered.

'Who do they belong to?'

'Their mother is one of the village girls.'

'Who is their father?'

'Oh, my dear, that's the sort of question we think it a little dangerous to ask out here.' He paused. 'A lot of fellows have native wives, and then when they go home or marry they pension them off and send them back to their village.'

Doris was silent. The indifference with which he spoke seemed a little callous to her. There was almost a frown on her frank, open, pretty English face when she replied.

'But what about the children?'

'I have no doubt they're properly provided for. Within his means, a man generally sees that there's enough money to have them decently educated. They get jobs as clerks in a government office, you know; they're all right.'

She gave him a slightly rueful smile.

'You can't expect me to think it's a very good system.'

'You mustn't be too hard,' he smiled back.

'I'm not hard. But I'm thankful you never had a Malay wife. I should have hated it. Just think if those two little brats were yours.'

The boy changed their plates. There was never much variety in their menu. They started luncheon with river fish, dull and insipid, so that a good deal of tomato ketchup was needed to make it palatable, and then went on to some kind of stew. Guy poured Worcester Sauce over it.

'The old Sultan didn't think it was a white woman's country,' he said presently. 'He rather encouraged people to—keep house with native girls. Of course things have changed now. The country's perfectly quiet and I suppose we know better how to cope with the climate.'

'But, Guy, the eldest of those boys wasn't more than seven or eight and the other was about five.'

'It's awfully lonely on an outstation. Why, often one doesn't see another white man for six months on end. A fellow comes out here when he's only a boy.' He gave her that charming smile of his which transfigured his round, plain face. 'There are excuses, you know.'

She always found that smile irresistible. It was his best argument. Her eyes grew once more soft and tender.

'I'm sure there are.' She stretched her hand across the little table and put it on his. 'I'm very lucky to have caught you so young. Honestly, it would upset me dreadfully if I were told that you had lived like that.'

He took her hand and pressed it.

'Are you happy here, darling?'

'Desperately.'

She looked very cool and fresh in her linen frock. The heat did not distress her. She had no more than the prettiness of youth, though her brown eyes were fine; but she had a pleasing frankness of expression, and her dark, short hair was neat and glossy. She gave you the impression of a girl of spirit and you felt sure that the Member of Parliament for whom she worked had in her a very competent secretary.

'I loved the country at once,' she said. 'Although I'm alone so much I don't think I've ever once felt lonely.'

Of course she had read novels about the Malay Archipelago and she had formed an impression of a sombre land with great ominous rivers and a silent, impenetrable jungle. When a little coasting steamer set them down at the mouth of the river, where a large boat, manned by a dozen Dyaks, was waiting to take them to the station, her breath was taken away by the beauty, friendly rather than awe-inspiring, of the scene. It had a gaiety, like the joyful singing of birds in the trees, which she had never expected. On each bank of the river were mangroves and nipah palms, and behind them the dense green of the forest. In the distance stretched blue mountains, range upon range, as far as the eye could see. She had no sense of confinement nor of gloom, but rather of openness and wide spaces where the exultant fancy could wander with delight. The green glittered in the sunshine and the sky was blithe and cheerful. The gracious land seemed to offer her a smiling welcome.

They rowed on, hugging a bank, and high overhead flew a pair of doves. A flash of colour, like a living jewel, dashed across their path. It was a kingfisher. Two monkeys, with their dangling tails, sat side by side on a branch. On the horizon, over there on the other side of the broad and turbid river, beyond the jungle, was a row of little white clouds, the only clouds in the sky, and they looked like a row of ballet-girls, dressed in white, waiting at the back of the stage, alert and merry, for the curtain to go up. Her heart was filled with joy; and now, remembering it all, her eyes rested on her husband with a grateful, assured affection.

And what fun it had been to arrange their living-room! It was very big. On the floor, when she arrived, was torn and dirty matting; on the walls of unpainted wood hung (much too high up) photogravures of Academy pictures, Dyak shields, and parangs. The tables were covered with Dyak cloth in sombre colours, and on them stood pieces of Brunei brass-ware, much in need of cleaning, empty cigarette tins, and bits of Malay silver. There was a rough wooden shelf with cheap editions of novels and a number of old travel books in battered leather; and another shelf was crowded with empty bottles. It was a bachelor's room, untidy but stiff; and though it amused her she found it intolerably pathetic. It was a dreary, comfortless life that Guy had led there, and she threw her arms round his neck and kissed him.

'You poor darling,' she laughed.

She had deft hands and she soon made the room habitable. She arranged this and that, and what she could not do with she turned out. Her wedding-presents helped. Now the room was friendly and comfortable. In glass vases were lovely orchids and in great bowls huge masses of flowering shrubs. She felt an inordinate pride because it was her house (she had never in her life lived in anything but a poky flat) and she had made it charming for him.

'Are you pleased with me?' she asked when she had finished.

'Quite,' he smiled.

The deliberate understatement was much to her mind. How jolly it was that they should understand each other so well! They were both of them shy of displaying emotion, and it was only at rare moments that they used with one another anything but ironic banter.

They finished luncheon and he threw himself into a long chair to have a sleep. She went towards her room. She was a little surprised that he drew her to him as she passed and, making her bend down, kissed her lips. They were not in the habit of exchanging embraces at odd hours of the day.

'A full tummy is making you sentimental, my poor lamb,' she chaffed him.

'Get out and don't let me see you again for at least two hours.'

'Don't snore.'

She left him. They had risen at dawn and in five minutes were fast asleep.

Doris was awakened by the sound of her husband's splashing in the bath-house. The walls of the bungalow were like a sounding board and not a thing that one of them did escaped the other. She felt too lazy to move, but she heard the boy bring the tea things in, so she jumped up and ran down into her own bath-house. The water, not cold but cool, was deliciously refreshing. When she came into the sitting-room Guy was taking the rackets out of the press, for they played tennis in the short cool of the evening. The night fell at six.

The tennis-court was two or three hundred yards from the bungalow and after tea, anxious not to lose time, they strolled down to it.

'Oh, look' said Doris, 'there's that girl that I saw this morning.'

Guy turned quickly. His eyes rested for a moment on a native woman, but he did not speak.

'What a pretty sarong she's got,' said Doris. 'I wonder where it comes fom.'

They passed her. She was slight and small, with the large, dark, starry eyes of her race and a mass of raven hair. She did not stir as they went by, but stared at them strangely. Doris saw then that she was not quite so young as she had at first thought. Her features were a trifle heavy and her skin was dark, but she was very pretty. She held a small child in her arms. Doris smiled a little as she saw it, but no answering smile moved the woman's lips. Her face remained impassive. She did not look at Guy, she looked only at Doris, and he walked on as though he did not see her. Doris turned to him.

'Isn't that baby a duck?'

'I didn't notice.'

She was puzzled by the look of his face. It was deathly white, and the pimples which not a little distressed her were more than commonly red.

'Did you notice her hands and feet? She might be a duchess.'

'All natives have good hands and feet,' he answered, but not jovially as was his wont; it was as though he forced himself to speak.

But Doris was intrigued.

'Who is she, d'you know?'

'She's one of the girls in the kampong.'

They had reached the court now. When Guy went up to the net to see that it was taut he looked back. The girl was still standing where they had passed her. Their eyes met.

'Shall I serve?' said Doris.

'Yes, you've got the balls on your side.'

He played very badly. Generally he gave her fifteen and beat her, but today she won easily. And he played silently. Generally he was a noisy player, shouting all the time, cursing his foolishness when he missed a ball and chaffing her when he placed one out of her reach.

'You're off your game, young man,' she cried.

'Not a bit,' he said.

He began to slam the balls, trying to beat her, and sent one after the other into the net. She had never seen him with that set face. Was it possible that he was a little out of temper because he was not playing well? The light fell, and they ceased to play. The woman whom they had passed stood in exactly the same position as when they came and once more, with expressionless face, she watched them go.

The blinds on the veranda were raised now, and on the table between their two long chairs were bottles and soda-water. This was the hour at which they had the first drink of the day and Guy mixed a couple of gin slings. The river stretched widely before them, and on the further bank the jungle was wrapped in the mystery of the approaching night. A native was silently rowing up-stream, standing at the bow of the boat, with two oars.

'I played like a fool,' said Guy, breaking a silence. 'I'm feeling a bit under the weather.'

'I'm sorry. You're not going to have fever, are you?'

'Oh, no. I shall be all right tomorrow.'

Darkness closed in upon them. The frogs croaked loudly and, now and then they heard a few short notes from some singing bird of the night. Fireflies flitted across the veranda and they made the trees that surrounded it look like Christmas trees lit with tiny candles. They sparkled softly. Doris thought she heard a little sigh. It vaguely disturbed her. Guy was always so full of gaiety.

'What is it, old man?' she said gently. 'Tell mother.'

'Nothing. Time for another drink,' he answered breezily.

Next day he was as cheerful as ever and the mail came. The coasting steamer passed the mouth of the river twice a month, once on its way to the coalfields and once on its way back. On the outward journey it brought mail, which Guy sent a boat down to fetch. Its arrival was the excitement of their uneventful lives. For the first day or two they skimmed rapidly all that had come, letters, English papers and papers from Singapore, magazines and books, leaving for the ensuing weeks a more exact perusal. They snatched the illustrated papers from one another. If Doris had not been so absorbed she might have noticed that there was a change in Guy. She would have found it hard to describe and harder still to explain. There was in his eyes a sort of watchfulness and in his mouth a slight droop of anxiety.

Then, perhaps a week later, one morning when she was sitting in the shaded room studying a Malay grammar (for she was industriously learning the language) she heard a commotion in the compound. She heard the house boy's voice, he was speaking angrily, the voice of another man, perhaps it was the water-carrier's, and then a woman's, shrill and vituperative. There was a scuffle. She went to the window and opened the shutters. The water-carrier had hold of a woman's arm and was dragging her along, while the house boy was pushing her from behind with both hands. Doris recognized her at once as the woman she had seen one morning loitering in the compound and later in the day outside the tennis-court. She was holding a baby against her breast. All three were shouting angrily.

'Stop,' cried Doris. 'What are you doing?'

At the sound of her voice the water-carrier let go suddenly and the woman, still pushed from behind, fell to the ground. There was a sudden silence and the house boy looked sullenly into space. The water-carrier hesitated a moment and then slunk away. The woman raised herself slowly to her feet, arranged the baby on her arm, and stood impassive, staring at Doris. The boy said something to her which Doris could not have heard even if she had understood: the woman by no change of face showed that his words meant anything to her; but she slowly strolled away. The boy followed her to the gate of the compound. Doris called to him as he walked back, but he pretended not to hear. She was growing angry now and she called more sharply.

'Come here at once,' she cried.

Suddenly, avoiding her wrathful glance, he came towards the bungalow. He came in and stood at the door. He looked at her sulkily.

'What were you doing with that woman?' she asked abruptly.

'Tuan say she no come here.'

'You mustn't treat a woman like that. I won't have it. I shall tell the tuan exactly what I saw.'

The boy did not answer. He looked away, but she felt that he was watching her through his long eyelashes. She dismissed him.

'That'll do.'

Without a word he turned and went back to the servants' quarters. She was exasperated and she found it impossible to give her attention once more to the Malay exercises. In a little while the boy came in to lay the cloth for luncheon. On a sudden he went to the door.

'What is it?' she asked.

'Tuan just coming.'

He went out to take Guy's hat from him. His quick ears had caught the footsteps before they were audible to her. Guy did not as usual come up the steps immediately; he paused, and Doris at once surmised that the boy had gone down to meet him in order to tell him of the morning's incident. She shrugged her shoulders. The boy evidently wanted to get his story in first. But she was astonished when Guy came in. His face was ashy.

'Guy, what on earth's the matter?'

He flushed a sudden hot red.

'Nothing. Why?'

She was so taken aback that she let him pass into his room without a word of what she had meant to speak of at once. It took him longer than usual to have his bath and change his clothes and luncheon was served when he came in.

'Guy,' she said, as they sat down, 'that woman we saw the other day was here again this morning.'

'So I've heard,' he answered.

'The boys were treating her brutally. I had to stop them. You must really speak to them about it.'

Though the Malay understood every word she said, he made no sign that he heard. He handed her the toast.

'She's been told not to come here. I gave instructions that if she showed herself again she was to be turned out.'

'Were they obliged to be so rough?'

'She refused to go. I don't think they were any rougher than they could help.'

'It was horrible to see a woman treated like that. She had a baby in her arms.'

'Hardly a baby. It's three years old.'

'How d'you know?'

'I know all about her. She hasn't the least right to come here pestering everybody.'

'What does she want?'

'She wants to do exactly what she did. She wants to make a disturbance.'

For a little while Doris did not speak. She was surprised at her husband's tone. He spoke tersely. He spoke as though all this were no concern of hers. She thought him a little unkind. He was nervous and irritable.

'I doubt if we shall be able to play tennis this afternoon,' he said. 'It looks to me as though we were going to have a storm.'

The rain was falling when she awoke and it was impossible to go out. During tea Guy was silent and abstracted. She got her sewing and began to work. Guy sat down to read such of the English papers as he had not yet gone through from cover to cover; but he was restless; he walked up and down the large room and then went out on the veranda. He looked at the steady rain. What was he thinking of? Doris was vaguely uneasy.

It was not till after dinner that he spoke. During the simple meal he had exerted himself to be his usual gay self, but the exertion was apparent. The rain had ceased and the night was starry. They sat on the veranda. In order not to attract insects they had put out the lamp in the sitting-room. At their feet, with a mighty, formidable sluggishness, silent, mysterious, and fatal, flowed the river. It had the terrible deliberation and the relentlessness of destiny.

'Doris, I've got something to say to you,' he said suddenly.

His voice was very strange. Was it her fancy that he had difficulty in keeping it quite steady? She felt a little pang in her heart because he was in distress, and she put her hand gently into his. He drew it away.

'It's rather a long story. I'm afraid it's not a very nice one and I find it rather difficult to tell. I'm going to ask you not to interrupt me, or to say anything, till I've finished.'

In the darkness she could not see his face, but she felt that it was haggard. She did not answer. He spoke in a voice so low that it hardly broke the silence of the night.

'I was only eighteen when I came out here. I came straight from school. I spent three months in Kuala Solor, and then I was sent to a station up the Sembulu river. Of course there was a Resident there and his wife. I lived in the court-house, but I used to have my meals with them and spend the evening with them. I had an awfully good time. Then the fellow who was here fell ill and had to go home. We were short of men on account of the war and I was put in charge of this place. Of course I was very young, but I spoke the language like a native, and they remembered my father. I was as pleased as punch to be on my own.'

He was silent while he knocked the ashes out of his pipe and refilled it. When he lit a match Doris, without looking at him, noticed that his hand was unsteady.

'I'd never been alone before. Of course at home there'd been father and mother and generally an assistant. And then at school naturally there were always fellows about. On the way out on the boat, there were people all the time, and at K.S., and the same at my first post. The people there were almost like my own people. I seemed always to live in a crowd. I like people. I'm a noisy blighter. I like to have a good time. All sorts of things make me laugh and you must have somebody to laugh with. But it was different here. Of course it was all right in the day time; I had my work and I could talk to the Dyaks. Although they were head-hunters in those days and now and then I had a bit of trouble with them, they were an awfully decent lot of fellows. I got on very well with them. Of course I should have liked a white man to gas to, but they were better than nothing, and it was easier for me because they didn't look upon me quite as a stranger. I liked the work too. It was rather lonely in the evening to sit on the veranda and drink a gin and bitters by myself, but I could read. And the boys were about. My own boy was called Abdul. He'd known my father. When I got tired of reading I could give him a shout and have a bit of a jaw with him.

'It was the nights that did for me. After dinner the boys shut up and went away to sleep in the kampong. I was all alone. There wasn't a sound in the bungalow except now and then the croak of the chik-chak. It used to come out of the silence, suddenly, so that it made me jump. Over in the kampong I heard the sound of a gong or fire-crackers. They were having a good time, they weren't so far away, but I had to stay where I was. I was tired of reading. I couldn't have been more of a prisoner if I'd been in jail. Night after night it was the same. I tried drinking three or four whiskies, but it's poor fun drinking alone, and it didn't cheer me up; it only made me feel rather rotten next day. I tried going to bed immediately after dinner, but I couldn't sleep. I used to lie in bed, getting hotter and hotter, and more wide awake, till I didn't know what to do with myself. By George, those nights were long. D'you know, I got so low, I was so sorry for myself that sometimes—it makes me laugh now when I think of it, but I was only nineteen and a half—sometimes I used to cry.

'Then, one evening, after dinner, Abdul had cleared away and was just going off, when he gave a little cough. He said, wasn't I lonely in the house all night by myself? "Oh, no, that's all right," I said. I didn't want him to know what a damned fool I was, but I expect he knew all right. He stood there without speaking, and I knew he wanted to say something to me. "What is it?" I said. "Spit it out." Then he said that if I'd like to have a girl to come and live with me he knew one who was willing. She was a very good girl and he could recommend her. She'd be no trouble and it would be someone to have about the bungalow. She'd mend my things for me. . . . I felt awfully low. It had been raining all day and I hadn't been able to get any exercise. I knew I shouldn't sleep for hours. It wouldn't cost me very much money, he said, her people were poor and they'd be quite satisfied with a small present. Two hundred Straits dollars. "You look," he said. "If you don't like her you send her away." I asked him where she was. "She's here," he said. "I call her." He went to the door. She'd been waiting on the steps with her mother. They came in and sat down on the floor. I gave them some sweets. She was shy, of course, but cool enough, and when I said something to her she gave me a smile. She was very young, hardly more than a child, they said she was fifteen. She was awfully pretty, and she had her best clothes on. We began to talk. She didn't say much, but she laughed a lot when I chaffed her. Abdul said I'd find she had plenty to say for herself when she got to know me. He told her to come and sit by me. She giggled and refused, but her mother told her to come, and I made room for her on the chair. She blushed and laughed, but she came, and then she snuggled up to me. The boy laughed too. "You see, she's taken to you already," he said. "Do you want her to stay?" he asked. "Do you want to?" I said to her. She hid her face, laughing, on my shoulder. She was very soft and small. "Very well," I said, "let her stay."'

Guy leaned forward and helped himself to a whisky and soda.

'May I speak now?' asked Doris.

'Wait a minute, I haven't finished yet. I wasn't in love with her, not even at the beginning. I only took her so as to have somebody about the bungalow. I think I should have gone mad if I hadn't, or else taken to drink. I was at the end of my tether. I was too young to be quite alone. I was never in love with anyone but you.' He hesitated a moment. 'She lived here till I went home last year on leave. It's the woman you've seen hanging about.'

'Yes, I guessed that. She had a baby in her arms. Is that your child?'

'Yes. It's a little girl.'

'Is it the only one?'

'You saw the two small boys the other day in the kampong. You mentioned them.'

'She has three children then?'

'Yes.'

'It's quite a family you've got.'

She felt the sudden gesture which her remark forced from him, but she did not speak.

'Didn't she know that you were married till you suddenly turned up here with a wife?' asked Doris.

'She knew I was going to be married.'

'When?'

'I sent her back to the village before I left here. I told her it was all over. I gave her what I'd promised. She always knew it was only a temporary arrangement. I was fed up with it. I told her I was going to marry a white woman.'

'But you hadn't even seen me then.'

'No, I know. But I'd made up my mind to marry when I was home.' He chuckled in his old manner. 'I don't mind telling you that I was getting rather despondent about it when I met you. I fell in love with you at first sight and then I knew it was either you or nobody.'

'Why didn't you tell me? Don't you think it would have been only fair to give me a chance of judging for myself? It might have occurred to you that it would be rather a shock to a girl to find out that her husband had lived for ten years with another girl and had three children.'

'I couldn't expect you to understand. The circumstances out here are peculiar. It's the regular thing. Five men out of six do it. I thought perhaps it would shock you and I didn't want to lose you. You see, I was most awfully in love with you. I am now, darling. There was no reason that you should ever know. I didn't expect to come back here. One seldom goes back to the same station after home leave. When we came here I offered her money if she'd go to some other village. First she said she would and then she changed her mind.'

'Why have you told me now?'

'She's been making the most awful scenes. I don't know how she found out that you knew nothing about it. As soon as she did she began to blackmail me. I've had to give her an awful lot of money. I gave orders that she wasn't to be allowed in the compound. This morning she made that scene just to attract your attention. She wanted to frighten me. It couldn't go on like that. I thought the only thing was to make a clean breast of it.'

There was a long silence as he finished. At last he put his hand on hers.

'You do understand, Doris, don't you? I know I've been to blame.'

She did not move her hand. He felt it cold beneath his.

'Is she jealous?'

'I daresay there were all sorts of perks when she was living here, and I don't suppose she much likes not getting them any longer. But she was never in love with me any more than I was in love with her. Native women never do really care for white men, you know.'

'And the children?'

'Oh, the children are all right. I've provided for them. As soon as the boys are old enough I shall send them to school at Singapore.'

'Do they mean nothing to you at all?'

He hesitated.

'I want to be quite frank with you. I should be sorry if anything happened to them. When the first one was expected I thought I'd be much fonder of it than I ever had been of its mother. I suppose I should have been if it had been white. Of course, when it was a baby it was rather funny and touching, but I had no particular feeling that it was mine. I think that's what it is; you see, I have no sense of their belonging to me. I've reproached myself sometimes, because it seemed rather unnatural, but the honest truth is that they're no more to me than if they were somebody else's children. Of course a lot of slush is talked about children by people who haven't got any.'

Now she had heard everything. He waited for her to speak, but she said nothing. She sat motionless.

'Is there anything more you want to ask me, Doris?' he said at last.

'No I've got rather a headache. I think I shall go to bed.' Her voice was as steady as ever. 'I don't quite know what to say. Of course it's been all very unexpected. You must give me a little time to think.'

'Are you very angry with me?'

'No. Not at all. Only—only I must be left to myself for a while. Don't move. I'm going to bed.'

She rose from her long chair and put her hand on his shoulder.

'It's so very hot tonight. I wish you'd sleep in your dressing-room. Good night.'

She was gone. He heard her lock the door of her bedroom.

She was pale next day and he could see that she had not slept. There was no bitterness in her manner, she talked as usual, but without ease; she spoke of this and that as though she were making conversation with a stranger. They had never had a quarrel, but it seemed to Guy that so would she talk if they had had a disagreement and the subsequent reconciliation had left her still wounded. The look in her eyes puzzled him; he seemed to read in them a strange fear. Immediately after dinner she said:

'I'm not feeling very well tonight. I think I shall go straight to bed.'

'Oh, my poor darling, I'm so sorry,' he cried.

'It's nothing. I shall be all right in a day or two.'

'I shall come in and say good night to you later.'

'No, don't do that. I shall try and get straight off to sleep.'

'Well, then, kiss me before you go.'

He saw that she flushed. For an instant she seemed to hesitate; then, with averted eyes, she leaned towards him. He took her in his arms and sought her lips, but she turned her face away and he kissed her cheek. She left him quickly and again he heard the key turn softly in the lock of her door. He flung himself heavily on the chair. He tried to read, but his ear was attentive to the smallest sound in his wife's room. She had said she was going to bed, but he did not hear her move. The silence in there made him unaccountably nervous. Shading the lamp with his hand he saw that there was a glimmer under her door; she had not put out her light. What on earth was she doing? He put down his book. It would not have surprised him if she had been angry and had made a scene, or if she had cried; he could have coped with that; but her calmness frightened him. And then what was that fear which he had seen so plainly in her eyes? He thought once more over all he had said to her on the previous night. He didn't know how else he could have put it. After all, the chief point was that he'd done the same as everybody else, and it was all over long before he met her. Of course as things turned out he had been a fool, but anyone could be wise after the event. He put his hand to his heart. Funny how it hurt him there.

'I suppose that's the sort of thing people mean when they say they're heartbroken,' he said to himself. 'I wonder how long it's going on like this?'

Should he knock at the door and tell her he must speak to her? It was better to have it out. He *must* make her understand. But the silence scared him. Not a sound! Perhaps it was better to leave her alone. Of course it had been a shock. He must give her as long as she wanted. After all, she knew how devotedly he loved her. Patience, that was the only thing; perhaps she was fighting it out with herself; he must give her time; he must have patience. Next morning he asked her if she had slept better.

'Yes, much,' she said.

'Are you very angry with me?' he asked piteously.

She looked at him with candid, open eyes.

'Not a bit.'

'Oh my dear, I'm so glad. I've been a brute and a beast. I know it's been hateful for you. But do forgive me. I've been so miserable.'

'I do forgive you. I don't even blame you.'

He gave her a little rueful smile, and there was in his eyes the look of a whipped dog.

'I haven't much liked sleeping by myself the last two nights.'

She glanced away. Her face grew a trifle paler.

'I've had the bed in my room taken away. It took up so much space. I've had a little camp bed put there instead.'

'My dear, what are you talking about?'

Now she looked at him steadily.

'I'm not going to live with you as your wife again.'

'Never?'

She shook her head. He looked at her in a puzzled way. He could hardly believe he had heard aright and his heart began to beat painfully.

'But that's awfully unfair to me, Doris.'

'Don't you think it was a little unfair to me to bring me out here in the circumstances?'

'But you just said you didn't blame me.'

'That's quite true. But the other's different. I can't do it.'

'But how are we going to live together like that?'

She stared at the floor. She seemed to ponder deeply.

'When you wanted to kiss me on the lips last night I – it almost made me sick.'

'Doris.'

She looked at him suddenly and her eyes were cold and hostile.

'That bed I slept on, is that the bed in which she had her children?' She saw him flush deeply. 'Oh, it's horrible. How could you?' She wrung her hands, and her twisting, tortured fingers looked like little writhing snakes. But she made a great effort and controlled herself. 'My mind is quite made up. I don't want to be unkind to you, but there are some things that you can't ask me to do. I've thought it all over. I've been thinking of nothing else since you told me, night and day, till I'm exhausted. My first instinct was to get up and go. At once. The steamer will be here in two or three days.'

'Doesn't it mean anything to you that I love you?'

'Oh, I know you love me. I'm not going to do that. I want to give us both a chance. I have loved you so, Guy.' Her voice broke, but she did not cry. 'I don't want to be unreasonable. Heaven knows, I don't want to be unkind. Guy, will you give me time?'

'I don't know quite what you mean.'

'I just want you to leave me alone. I'm frightened by the feelings that I have.'

He had been right then; she was afraid.

'What feelings?'

'Please don't ask me. I don't want to say anything to wound you. Perhaps I shall get over them. Heaven knows, I want to. I'll try, I promise you. I'll try. Give me six months. I'll do everything in the world for you, but just that one thing.' She made a little gesture of appeal. 'There's no reason why we shouldn't be happy enough together. If you really love me you'll—you'll have patience.'

He sighed deeply.

'Very well,' he said. 'Naturally I don't want to force you to do anything you don't like. It shall be as you say.'

He sat heavily for a little, as though, on a sudden grown old, it was an effort to move; then he got up.

'I'll be getting along to the office.'

He took his topee and went out.

A month passed. Women conceal their feelings better than men and a stranger visiting them would never have guessed that Doris was in any way troubled. But in Guy the strain was obvious; his round, good-natured face was drawn, and in his eyes was a hungry, harassed look. He watched Doris. She was gay and she chaffed him as she had been used to do; they played tennis together; they chatted about one thing and another. But it was evident that she was merely playing a part, and at last, unable to contain himself, he tried to speak again of his connexions with the Malay woman.

'Oh, Guy, there's no object in going back on all that,' she answered breezily. 'We've said all we had to say about it and I don't blame you for anything.'

'Why do you punish me then?'

'My poor boy, I don't want to punish you. It's not my fault if . . .' she shrugged her shoulders. 'Human nature is very odd.'

'I don't understand.'

'Don't try.'

The words might have been harsh, but she softened them with a pleasant, friendly smile. Every night when she went to bed she leaned over Guy and lightly kissed his cheek. Her lips only touched it. It was as though a moth had just brushed his face in its flight.

A second month passed, then a third, and suddenly the six months which had seemed so interminable were over. Guy asked himself whether she remembered. He gave a strained attention now to everything she said, to every look on her face and to every gesture of her hands. She remained impenetrable. She had asked him to give her six months; well, he had.

The coasting steamer passed the mouth of the river, dropped their mail, and went on its way. Guy busily wrote the letters which it would pick up on the return journey. Two or three days passed by. It was a Tuesday and the prahu was to start at dawn on Thursday to await the steamer. Except at meal time when Doris exerted herself to make conversation they had not of late talked very much together; and after dinner as usual they took their books and began to read; but when the boy had finished clearing away and was gone for the night Doris put down hers.

'Guy, I have something I want to say to you,' she murmured.

His heart gave a sudden thud against his ribs and he felt himself change colour.

'Oh, my dear, don't look like that, it's not so very terrible,' she laughed.

But he thought her voice trembled a little.

'Well?'

'I want you to do something for me.'

'My darling, I'll do anything in the world for you.'

He put out his hand to take hers, but she drew it away.

'I want you to let me go home.'

'You?' he cried, aghast. 'When? Why?'

'I've borne it as long as I can. I'm at the end of my tether.'

'How long do you want to go for? For always?'

'I don't know. I think so.' She gathered determination. 'Yes, for always.'

'Oh, my God!'

His voice broke and she thought he was going to cry.

'Oh, Guy, don't blame me. It really is not my fault. I can't help myself.'

'You asked me for six months. I accepted your terms. You can't say I've made a nuisance of myself.'

'No, no.'

'I've tried not to let you see what a rotten time I was having.'

'I know. I'm very grateful to you. You've been awfully kind to me. Listen, Guy, I want to tell you again that I don't blame you for a single thing you did. After all, you were only a boy, and you did no more than the others; I know what the loneliness is here. Oh, my dear, I'm so dreadfully sorry for you. I knew all that from the beginning. That's why I asked you for six months. My common sense tells me that I'm making a mountain out of a molehill. I'm unreasonable; I'm being unfair to you. But, you see, common sense has nothing to do with it; my whole soul is in revolt. When I see the woman and her children in the village I just feel my legs shaking. Everything in this house; when I think of that bed I slept in it gives me goose-flesh. . . . You don't know what I've endured.'

'I think I've persuaded her to go away. And I've applied for a transfer.'

'That wouldn't help. She'll be there always. You belong to them, you don't belong to me. I think perhaps I could have stood it if there'd only been one child, but three; and the boys are quite big boys. For ten years you lived with her.' And now she came out with what she had been working up to. She was desperate. 'It's a physical thing, I can't help it, it's stronger than I am. I think of those thin black arms of hers round you and it fills me with a physical nausea. I think of you holding those little black babies in your arms. Oh, it's loathsome. The touch of you is odious to me. Each night, when I've kissed you, I've had to brace myself up to it. I've had to clench my hands and force myself to touch your cheek.' Now she was clasping and unclasping her fingers in a nervous agony, and her voice was out of control. 'I know it's I who am to blame now. I'm a silly, hysterical woman. I thought I'd get over it. I can't, and now I never shall. I've brought it all on myself; I'm willing to take the consequences; if you say I must stay here, I'll stay, but if I stay I shall die. I beseech you to let me go.'

And now the tears which she had restrained so long overflowed and she wept broken-heartedly. He had never seen her cry before.

'Of course I don't want to keep you here against your will,' he said hoarsely.

Exhausted, she leaned back in her chair. Her features were all twisted and awry. It was horribly painful to see the abandonment of grief on that face which was habitually so placid.

'I'm so sorry, Guy. I've broken your life, but I've broken mine too. And we might have been so happy.'

'When do you want to go? On Thursday?'

'Yes.'

She looked at him piteously. He buried his face in his hands. At last he looked up.

'I'm tired out,' he muttered.

'May I go?'

'Yes.'

For two minutes perhaps they sat there without a word. She started when the chik-chak gave its piercing, hoarse, and strangely human cry. Guy rose and went out on to the veranda. He leaned against the rail and looked at the softly flowing water. He heard Doris go into her room.

Next morning, up earlier than usual, he went to her door and knocked.

'Yes?'

'I have to go up-river today. I shan't be back till late.'

'All right.'

She understood. He had arranged to be away all day in order not to be about while she was packing. It was heartbreaking work. When she had packed her clothes she looked round the sitting-room at the things that belonged to her. It seemed dreadful to take them. She left everything but the photograph of her mother. Guy did not come in till ten o'clock at night.

'I'm sorry I couldn't get back to dinner,' he said. 'The headman at the village I had to go to had a lot of things for me to attend to.'

She saw his eyes wander about the room and notice that her mother's photograph no longer stood in its place.

'Is everything quite ready?' he asked. 'I've ordered the boatman to be at the steps at dawn.'

'I told the boy to wake me at five.'

'I'd better give you some money.' He went to his desk and wrote out a cheque. He took some notes from a drawer. 'Here's some cash to take you as far as Singapore and at Singapore you'll be able to change the cheque.'

'Thank you.'

'Would you like me to come to the mouth of the river with you?'

'Oh, I think it would be better if we said good-bye here.'

'All right. I think I shall turn in. I've had a long day and I'm dead beat.'

He did not even touch her hand. He went into his room. In a few minutes she heard him throw himself on his bed. For a little while she sat looking for the last time round that room in which she had been so happy and so miserable. She sighed deeply. She got up and went into her own room. Everything was packed except the one or two things she needed for the night.

It was dark when the boy awakened them. They dressed hurriedly and when they were ready breakfast was waiting for them. Presently they heard the boat row up to the landing-stage below the bungalow, and then the servants carried down her luggage. It was a poor pretence they made of eating. The darkness thinned away and the river was ghostly. It was not yet day, but it was no longer night. In the silence the voices of the natives at the landing-stage were very clear. Guy glanced at his wife's untouched plate.

'If you've finished we might stroll down. I think you ought to be starting.'

She did not answer. She rose from the table. She went into her room to see that nothing had been forgotten and then side by side with him walked down the steps. A little winding path led them to the river. At the landing-stage the native guards in their smart uniform were lined up and they presented arms as Guy and Doris passed. The head boatman gave her his hand as she stepped into the boat. She turned and looked at Guy. She wanted desperately to say one last word of comfort, once more to ask for his forgiveness, but she seemed to be struck dumb.

He stretched out his hand.

'Well, good-bye, I hope you'll have a jolly journey.'

They shook hands.

Guy nodded to the head boatman and the boat pushed off. The dawn now was creeping along the river mistily, but the night lurked still in the dark trees of the jungle. He stood at the landing-stage till the boat was lost in the shadows of the morning. With a sigh he turned away. He nodded absent-mindedly when the guard once more presented arms. But when he reached the bungalow he called the boy. He went round the room picking out everything that had belonged to Doris.

'Pack all these things up,' he said. 'It's no good leaving them about.'

Then he sat down on the veranda and watched the day advance gradually like a bitter, an unmerited, and an overwhelming sorrow. At last he looked at his watch. It was time for him to go to the office.

In the afternoon he could not sleep, his head ached miserably, so he took his gun and went for a tramp in the jungle. He shot nothing, but he walked in order to tire himself out. Towards sunset he came back and had two or three drinks, and then it was time to dress for dinner. There wasn't much use in dressing now; he might just as well be comfortable; he put on a loose native jacket and a sarong. That was what he had been accustomed to wear before Doris came. He was barefoot. He ate his dinner listlessly and the boy cleared away and went. He sat down to read the *Tatler*. The bungalow was very silent. He could not read and let the paper fall on his knees. He was exhausted. He could not think and his mind was strangely vacant. The chik-chak was noisy that night and its hoarse and sudden cry seemed to mock him. You could hardly believe that this reverberating sound came from so small a throat. Presently he heard a discreet cough.

'Who's there?' he cried.

There was a pause. He looked at the door. The chik-chak laughed harshly. A small boy sidled in and stood on the threshold. It was a little half-caste boy in a tattered singlet and a sarong. It was the elder of his two sons.

'What do you want?' said Guy.

The boy came forward into the room and sat down, tucking his legs away under him.

'Who told you to come here?'

'My mother sent me. She says, do you want anything?'

Guy looked at the boy intently. The boy said nothing more. He sat and waited, his eyes cast down shyly. Then Guy in deep and bitter reflection buried his face in his hands. What was the use? It was finished. Finished! He surrendered. He sat back in his chair and sighed deeply.

'Tell your mother to pack up her things and yours. She can come back.'

'When?' asked the boy, impassively.

Hot tears trickled down Guy's funny, round spotty face.

'Tonight.'

Flotsam and Jetsam

◆

Norman Grange was a rubber-planter. He was up before daybreak to take the roll-call of his labour and then walked over the estate to see that the tapping was properly done. This duty performed, he came home, bathed and changed, and now with his wife opposite him he was eating the substantial meal, half breakfast and half luncheon, which in Borneo is called brunch. He read as he ate. The dining-room was dingy. The worn electro-plate, the shabby cruet, the chipped dishes betokened poverty, but a poverty accepted with apathy. A few flowers would have brightened the table, but there was apparently no one to care how things looked. When Grange had finished he belched, filled his pipe and lit it, rose from the table and went out on to the veranda. He took no more notice of his wife than if she had not been there. He lay down in a long rattan chair and went on reading. Mrs Grange reached over for a tin of cigarettes and smoked while she sipped her tea. Suddenly she looked out, for the house boy came up the steps and accompanied by two men went up to her husband. One was a Dyak and the other Chinese. Strangers seldom came and she could not imagine what they wanted. She got up and went to the door to listen. Though she had lived in Borneo for so many years she knew no more Malay than was necessary to get along with the boys, and she only vaguely understood what was said. She gathered from her husband's tone that something had happened to annoy him. He seemed to be asking questions first of the Chink and then of the Dyak; it looked as though they were pressing him to do something he didn't want to do; at length, however, with a frown on his face he raised himself from his chair and followed by the men walked down the steps. Curious to see where he was going she slipped out on to the veranda. He had taken the path that led down to the river. She shrugged her thin shoulders and went to her room. Presently she gave a violent start, for she heard her husband call her.

'Vesta.'

She came out.

'Get a bed ready. There's a white man in a prahu at the landing-stage. He's damned ill.'

'Who is he?'

'How the hell should I know? They're just bringing him up.'

'We can't have anyone to stay here.'

'Shut up and do as I tell you.'

He left her on that and again went down to the river. Mrs Grange called the boy and told him to put sheets on the bed in the spare room. Then she stood at the top of the steps and waited. In a little while she saw her husband coming back and behind him a huddle of Dyaks carrying a man on a mattress. She stood aside to let them pass and caught a glimpse of a white face.

'What shall I do?' she asked her husband.

'Get out and keep quiet.'

'Polite, aren't you?'

The sick man was taken into the room, and in two or three minutes the Dyaks and Grange came out.

'I'm going to see about his kit. I'll have it brought up. His boy's looking after him and there's no cause for you to butt in!'

'What's the matter with him?'

'Malaria. His boatmen are afraid he's going to die and won't take him on. His name's Skelton.'

'He isn't going to die, is he?'

'If he does we'll bury him.'

But Skelton didn't die. He woke next morning to find himself in a room, in bed and under a mosquito-net. He couldn't think where he was. It was a cheap iron bed and the mattress was hard, but to lie on it was a relief after the discomfort of the prahu. He could see nothing of the room but a chest of drawers, roughly made by a native carpenter, and a wooden chair. Opposite was a doorway, with a blind down, and this he guessed led on to a veranda.

'Kong,' he called.

The blind was drawn aside and his boy came in. The Chinaman's face broke into a grin when he saw that his master was free from fever.

'You more better, Tuan. Velly glad.'

'Where the devil am I?'

Kong explained.

'Luggage all right?' asked Skelton.

'Yes, him all light.'

'What's the name of this fellow—the tuan whose house this is?'

'Mr Norman Grange.'

To confirm what he said he showed Skelton a little book in which the owner's name was written. It was Grange. Skelton noticed that the book was Bacon's *Essays.* It was curious to find it in a planter's house away up a river in Borneo.

'Tell him I'd be glad to see him.'

'Tuan out. Him come presently.'

'What about my having a wash? And by God, I want a shave.'

He tried to get out of bed, but his head swam and with a bewildered cry he sank back. But Kong shaved and washed him, and changed the shorts and singlet in which he had been lying ever since he fell ill for a sarong and a baju. After that he was glad to lie still. But presently Kong came in and said that the tuan of the house was back. There was a knock on the door and a large stoutish man stepped in.

'I hear you're better,' he said.

'Oh, much. It's terribly kind of you to have taken me in like this. It seems awful, planting myself on you.'

Grange answered a trifle harshly.

'That's all right. You were pretty bad, you know. No wonder those Dyaks wanted to get rid of you.'

'I don't want to impose myself on you longer than I need. If I could hire a launch here, or a prahu, I could get off this afternoon.'

'There's no launch to hire. You'd better stay a bit. You must be as weak as a rat.'

'I'm afraid I shall be a frightful bother.'

'I don't see why. You've got your own boy and he'll look after you.'

Grange had just come in from his round of the estate and wore dirty shorts, a khaki shirt open at the neck, and an old, battered terai hat. He looked as shabby as a beachcomber. He took off his hat to wipe his sweating brow; he had close-cropped grey hair; his face was red, a broad, fleshy face, with a large mouth under a stubble of grey moustache, a short, pugnacious nose and small, mean eyes.

'I wonder if you could let me have something to read,' said Skelton.

'What sort of thing?'

'I don't mind so long as it's lightish.'

'I'm not much of a novel reader myself, but I'll send you in two or three books. My wife can provide you with novels. They'll be trash, because that's all she reads. But it may suit you.'

With a nod he withdrew. Not a very likeable man. But he was obviously very poor, the room in which Skelton lay, something in Grange's appearance, indicated that; he was probably manager of an estate on a cut salary, and it was not unlikely that the expense of a guest and his servant was unwelcome. Living in that remote spot, and so seeing white men but seldom, it might be that he was ill at ease with strangers. Some people improve unbelievably on acquaintance. But his hard, shifty little eyes were disconcerting; they gave the lie to the red face and the massive frame which otherwise might have persuaded you that this was a jolly sort of fellow with whom you could quickly make friends.

After a while, the house boy came in with a parcel of books. There were half a dozen novels by authors he had never heard of, and a glance told him they were slop; these must be Mrs Grange's; and then there was a Boswell's *Johnson*, Borrow's *Lavengro*, and Lamb's *Essays.* It was an odd choice. They were not the books you would have expected to find in a planter's house. In most planters' houses there is not more than a shelf or two of books and for the most part they're detective stories. Skelton had a disinterested curiosity in human creatures, and he amused himself now by trying to make out from the books Norman Grange had sent, from the look of him, and from the few words they had exchanged, what sort of a man he could be. Skelton was a little surprised that his host did not come to see him again that day; it looked as though he were going to content himself with giving his uninvited guest board and lodging, but were not sufficiently interested in him to seek his company. Next morning he felt well enough to get up, and with Kong's help settled himself in a long chair on the veranda. It badly needed a coat of paint. The bungalow stood on the brow of a hill, about fifty yards from the river; and on the opposite bank, looking very small across that great stretch of water, you could see native houses on piles nestling among the greenery. Skelton had not yet the activity of mind to read steadily, and after a page or two, his thoughts wandering, he found himself content to watch idly the sluggish flow of the turbid stream. Suddenly he heard a step. He saw the little elderly woman come towards him, and knowing that this must be Mrs Grange tried to get up.

'Don't move,' she said. 'I only came to see if you had everything you wanted.'

She wore a blue cotton dress, simple enough, but more suited to a young girl than to a woman of her age; her short hair was tousled, as though on getting out of bed she had scarcely troubled to pass a comb through it, and dyed a vivid yellow, but badly, and the roots showed white. Her skin was raddled and dry, and there was a great dab of rouge on each cheek-bone, put on however so clumsily that you could not for a moment take it for a natural colour, and a smear of lipstick on her mouth. But the strangest thing about her was a tic she had that made her jerk her head as though she were beckoning you to an inner room. It seemed to come at regular intervals, perhaps three times a minute, and her left hand was in almost constant movement; it was not quite a tremble, it was a rapid twirl as though she wanted to draw your attention to something behind her back. Skelton was startled by her appearance and embarrassed by her tic.

'I hope I'm not making myself too great a nuisance,' he said. 'I think I shall be well enough to make a move tomorrow or the day after.'

'It's not often we see anybody in a place like this, you know. It's a treat to have someone to talk to.'

'Won't you sit down? I'll tell my boy to bring you a chair.'

'Norman said I was to leave you alone.'

'I haven't spoken to a white person for two years. I've been longing for a good old talk.'

Her head twitched violently, more quickly than usual, and her hand gave that queer spasmodic gesture.

'He won't be back for another hour. I'll get a chair.'

Skelton told her who he was and what he had been doing, but he discovered that she had questioned his boy and already knew all about him.

'You must be crazy to get back to England?' she asked.

'I shan't be sorry.'

Suddenly Mrs Grange seemed to be attacked by what one could only describe as a nerve storm. Her head twitched so madly, her hand shook with such fury, that it was disconcerting. You could only look away.

'I haven't been to England for sixteen years,' she said.

'You don't mean that? Why, I thought all you planters went home every five years at the longest.'

'We can't afford it; we're broke to the wide. Norman put all the money he had into this plantation, and it hasn't really paid for years. It only just brings in enough to keep us from starvation. Of course it doesn't matter to Norman. He isn't English really.'

'He looks English enough.'

'He was born in Sarawak. His father was in the government service. If he's anything he's a native of Borneo.'

Then, without warning, she began to cry. It was horribly painful to see the tears running down the raddled, painted cheeks of that woman with the constant tic. Skelton knew neither what to say nor what to do. He did what was probably the best thing, he kept silent. She dried her eyes.

'You must think me a silly old fool. I sometimes wonder that after all these years I can still cry. I suppose it's in my nature. I always could cry very easy when I was on the stage.'

'Oh, were you on the stage?'

'Yes, before I married. That's how I met Norman. We were playing in Singapore and he was there on holiday. I don't suppose I shall ever see England any more. I shall stay here till I die and every day of my life I shall look at that beastly river. I shall never get away now. Never.'

'How did you happen to find yourself in Singapore?'

'Well, it was soon after the war, I couldn't get anything to suit me in London, I'd been on the stage a good many years and I was fed up with playing small parts: the agents told me a fellow called Victor Palace was taking a company out East. His wife was playing lead, but I could play seconds. They'd got half a dozen plays, comedies, you know, and farces. The salary wasn't much, but they were going to Egypt and India, the Malay States and China and then down to Australia. It was a chance to see the world and I accepted. We didn't do badly in Cairo and I think we made money in India, but Burma wasn't much good, and Siam was worse; Penang was a disaster and so were the rest of the Malay States. Well, one day Victor called us together and said he was bust, he hadn't got the money for our fares to Hong Kong, and the tour was a wash-out and he was very sorry but we'd have to get back home as best we could. Of course we told him he couldn't do that to us. You never heard such a row. Well, the long and short of it was that he said we could have the scenery and the props if we thought they was any good to us, but as to money it was no use asking for it because he damned well hadn't got it. And next day we found out that him and his wife, without saying a word to anybody, had got on a French boat and skipped. I was in a rare state, I can tell you. I had a few pounds I'd saved out of me salary, and that was all; somebody told me if we was absolutely stranded the government would have to send us home, but only steerage, and I didn't much fancy that. We got the Press to put our plight before the public and someone came along with the proposition that we should give a benefit performance. Well, we did, but it wasn't much without Victor or his wife, and by the time we'd paid the expenses we weren't any better off than we'd been before. I was at my wits' end, I don't mind telling you. It was then that Norman proposed to me. The funny thing is that I hardly knew him. He'd taken me for a drive round the island and we'd had tea two or three times at the Europe and danced. Men don't often do things for you without wanting something in return, and I thought he expected to get a little bit of fun, but I'd had a good deal of experience and I thought he'd be clever if he got round me. But when he asked me to marry him, well, I was so surprised, I couldn't hardly believe me own ears. He said he'd got his own estate in Borneo and it only wanted a little patience and he'd make a packet. And it was on the banks of a fine river and all round was the jungle. He made it sound very romantic. I was getting on, you know, I was thirty, it wasn't going to be any easier to get work as time went on, and it was tempting to have a house of me own and all that. Never to have to hang around agents' offices no more. Never to have to lay awake no more and wonder how you was going to pay next week's rent. He wasn't a bad-looking chap in those days, brown and big and virile. No one could say I was willing to marry anybody just to . . .' Suddenly she stopped. 'There he is. Don't say you've seen me.'

She picked up the chair she had been sitting in and quickly slipped away with it into the house. Skelton was bewildered. Her grotesque appearance, the painful tears, her story told with that incessant twitching; and then her obvious fear when she heard her husband's voice in the compound, and her hurried escape; he could make nothing of it.

In a few minutes Norman Grange stumped along the veranda.

'I hear you're better,' he said.

'Much, thanks.'

'If you care to join us at brunch I'll have a place laid for you.'

'I'd like it very much.'

'All right. I'm just going to have a bath and a change.'

He walked away. Presently a boy came along and told Skelton his tuan was waiting for him. Skelton followed him into a small sitting-room, with the jalousies drawn to keep out the heat, an uncomfortable, overcrowded room with a medley of furniture, English and Chinese, and occasional tables littered with worthless junk. It was neither cosy nor cool. Grange had changed into a sarong and baju and in the native dress looked coarse but powerful. He introduced Skelton to his wife. She shook hands with him as though she had never seen him before and uttered a few polite words of greeting. The boy announced that their meal was ready and they went into the dining-room.

'I hear that you've been in this bloody country for some time,' said Grange.

'Two years. I'm an anthropologist and I wanted to study the manners and customs of tribes that haven't had any contact with civilization.'

Skelton felt that he should tell his host how it had come about that he had been forced to accept a hospitality which he could not but feel was grudgingly offered. After leaving the village that had been his headquarters he had journeyed by land for ten days till he reached the river. There he had engaged a couple of prahus, one for himself and his luggage and the other for Kong, his Chinese servant, and the camp equipment, to take him to the coast. The long trek across country had been hard going and he found it very comfortable to lie on a mattress under an awning of rattan matting and take his ease. All the time he had been away Skelton had been in perfect health, and as he travelled down the river he could not but think that he was very lucky; but even as the thought passed through his mind, it occurred to him that if he happened just then to congratulate himself on his good fortune in this respect, it was because he did not feel quite so well as usual. It was true that he had been forced to drink a great deal of arak the night before at the long-house where he had put up, but he was used to it and that hardly accounted for his headache. He had a general sense of malaise. He was wearing nothing but shorts and a singlet, and he felt chilly; it was curious because the sun was shining fiercely and when he put his hand on the gunwale of the prahu the heat was hardly bearable. If he had had a coat handy he would have put it on. He grew colder and colder and presently his teeth began to chatter; he huddled up on his mattress, shivering all over in a desperate effort to get warm. He could not fail to guess what was the matter.

'Christ,' he groaned. 'Malaria.'

He called the headman, who was steering the prahu.

'Get Kong.'

The headman shouted to the second prahu and ordered his own paddlers to stop. In a moment the two boats were side by side and Kong stepped in.

'I've got fever, Kong,' gasped Skelton. 'Get me the medicine chest and, for God's sake, blankets. I'm freezing to death.'

Kong gave his master a big dose of quinine and piled on him what coverings they had. They started off again.

Skelton was too ill to be taken ashore when they tied up for the night and so passed it in the prahu. All next day and the day after he was very ill. Sometimes one or other of the crew came and looked at him, and often the headman stayed for quite a long while staring at him thoughtfully.

'How many days to the coast?' Skelton asked the boy.

'Four, five.' He paused for a minute. 'Headman, he no go coast. He say, he wantchee go home.'

'Tell him to go to hell.'

'Headman say, you velly sick, you die. If you die and he go coast he catchee trouble.'

'I'm not thinking of dying,' said Skelton. 'I shall be all right. It's just an ordinary go of malaria.'

Kong did not answer. The silence irritated Skelton. He knew that the Chinese had something in mind that he did not like to say.

'Spit it out, you fool,' he cried.

Skelton's heart sank when Kong told him the truth. When they reached their resting-place that night the headman was going to demand his money and slip away with the two prahus before dawn. He was too frightened to carry a dying man farther. Skelton had no strength to take the determined attitude that might have availed him; he could only hope by the offer of more money to persuade the headman to carry out his agreement. The day passed in long arguments between Kong and the headman, but when they tied up for the night the headman came to Skelton and told him sulkily that he would go no farther. There was a long-house near by where he might get lodging till he grew better. He began to unload the baggage. Skelton refused to move. He got Kong to give him his revolver and swore to shoot anyone who came near him.

Kong, the crew, and the headman went up to the long-house and Skelton was left alone. Hour after hour he lay there, the fever burning his body and his mouth parched, while muddled thoughts hammered away in his brain. Then there were lights and the sound of men talking. The Chinese boy came with the headman and another man, whom Skelton had not yet seen, from the neighbouring long-house. He did his best to understand what Kong was telling him. It appeared that a few hours down-stream there lived a white man, and to his house, if that would satisfy Skelton, the headman was willing to take him.

'More better you say yes,' said Kong. 'Maybe white man has launch, then we go down to coast chop-chop.'

'Who is he?'

'Planter,' said Kong. 'This fellow say, him have rubber estate.'

Skelton was too tired to argue further. All he wanted just then was to sleep. He accepted the compromise.

'To tell you the truth,' he finished, 'I don't remember much more till I woke up yesterday morning to find myself an uninvited guest in your house.'

'I don't blame those Dyaks, you know,' said Grange. 'When I came down to the prahu and saw you, I thought you were for it.'

Mrs Grange sat silent while Skelton told his story, her head and her hand twitching regularly, as though by the action of some invisible clockwork, but when her husband addressed her, asking for the Worcester Sauce, and that was the only time he spoke to her, she was seized with such a paroxysm of involuntary movement that it was horrible to see. She passed him what he asked for without a word. Skelton got an uncomfortable impression that she was terrified of Grange. It was odd, because to all appearance he was not a bad sort. He was knowledgeable and far from stupid; and though you could not have said that his manner was cordial, it was plain that he was ready to be of what service he could.

They finished their meal and separated to rest through the heat of the day.

'See you again at six for a sun-downer,' said Grange.

When Skelton had had a good sleep, a bath, and a read, he went out on to the veranda. Mrs Grange came up to him. It looked as though she had been waiting.

'He's back from the office. Don't think it's funny if I don't speak to you. If he thought I liked having you here he'd turn you out tomorrow.'

She said these words in a whisper and slipped back into the house. Skelton was startled. It was a strange house he had come into in a strange manner. He went into the overcrowded sitting-room and there found his host. He had been worried by the evident poverty of the establishment and he felt that the Granges could ill afford even the small expense he must be putting them to. But he had already formed the impression that Grange was a quick-tempered, susceptible man and he did not know how he would take an offer to help. He made up his mind to risk it.

'Look here,' he said to him, 'it looks as though I might have to inflict myself on you for several days. I'd be so much more comfortable if you'd let me pay for my board and lodging.'

'Oh, that's all right, your lodging costs nothing, the house belongs to the mortgagees, and your board doesn't come to much.'

'Well, there are drinks anyway and I've had to come down on your stores of tobacco and cigarettes.'

'It's not more than once a year that anyone comes up here, and then it's only the D.O. or someone like that—besides, when one's as broke as I am nothing matters much.'

'Well, then, will you take my camp equipment? I shan't be wanting it any more, and if you'd like one of my guns, I'd be only too glad to leave it with you.'

Grange hesitated. There was a glimmer of cupidity in those small, cunning eyes of his.

'If you'd let me have one of your guns you'd pay for your board and lodging over and over again.'

'That's settled, then.'

They began to talk over the whisky and sparkler with which, following the Eastern habit, they celebrated the setting of the sun. Discovering that they both played chess they had a game. Mrs Grange did not join them till dinner. The meal was dull. An insipid soup, a tasteless river fish, a tough piece of steak, and a caramel pudding. Norman Grange and Skelton drank beer; Mrs Grange water. She never of her own will uttered a word. Skelton had again the uncomfortable impression that she was scared to death of her husband. Once or twice, Skelton from common politeness sought to bring her into the conversation, addressing himself to her, telling her a story or asking her a question, but it evidently distressed her so much, her head twitched so violently, her hand was agitated by gestures so spasmodic that he thought it kinder not to insist. When the meal was over she got up. 'I'll leave you gentlemen to your port,' she said.

Both the men got up as she left the room. It was rather absurd, and somehow sinister, to see this social pretence in those poverty-stricken surroundings on a Borneo river.

'I may add that there is no port. There might be a little Benedictine left.'
'Oh, don't bother.'

They talked for a while and Grange began to yawn. He got up every morning before sunrise and by nine o'clock at night could hardly keep his eyes open.

'Well, I'm going to turn in,' he said.

He nodded to Skelton and without further ceremony left him. Skelton went to bed, but he could not sleep. Though the heat was oppressive, it was not the heat that kept him awake. There was something horrible about that house and those two people who lived in it. He didn't know what it was that affected him with this peculiar uneasiness, but this he knew, that he would be heartily thankful to be out of it and away from them. Grange had talked a good deal about himself, but he knew no more of him than he had learned at the first glance. To all appearances he was just the commonplace planter who had fallen upon evil days. He had bought his land immediately after the war and had planted trees; but by the time they were bearing the slump had come and since then it had been a constant struggle to keep going. The estate and the house were heavily mortgaged, and now that rubber was once more selling profitably all he made went to the mortgagees. That was an old story in Malaya. What made Grange somewhat unusual was that he was a man without a country. Born in Borneo, he had lived there with his parents till he was old enough to go to school in England; at seventeen he had come back and had never left it since except to go to Mesopotamia during the war. England meant nothing to him. He had neither relations nor friends there. Most planters, like civil servants, have come from England, go back on leave now and then, and look forward to settling down there when they retire. But what had England to offer Norman Grange?

'I was born here,' he said, 'and I shall die here. I'm a stranger in England. I don't like their ways over there and I don't understand the things they talk about. And yet I'm a stranger here too. To the Malays and the Chinese I'm a white man, though I speak Malay as well as they do, and a white man I shall always be.' Then he said a significant thing. 'Of course if I'd had any sense I'd have married a Malay girl and had half a dozen half-caste kids. That's the only solution really for us chaps who were born and bred here.'

Grange's bitterness was greater than could be explained by his financial embarrassment. He had little good to say of any of the white men in the colony. He seemed to think that they despised him because he was native-born. He was a sour, disappointed fellow, and a conceited one. He had shown Skelton his books. There were not many of them, but they were the best on the whole that English literature can show; he had read them over and over again; but it looked as though he had learnt from them neither charity nor loving-kindness, it looked as though their beauty had left him unmoved; and to know them so well had only made him self-complacent. His exterior, which was so hearty and English, seemed to have little relation to the man within; you could not resist the suspicion that it masked a very sinister being.

Early next morning, to enjoy the cool of the day, Skelton, with his pipe and a book, was sitting on the veranda outside his room. He was still very weak, but felt much better. In a little while Mrs Grange joined him. She held in her hand a large album.

'I thought I'd like to show you some of me old photos and me notices. You mustn't think I always looked like what I do now. He's off on his round and he won't be back for two or three hours yet.'

Mrs Grange, in the same blue dress she had worn the day before, her hair as untidy, appeared strangely excited.

'It's all I have to remind me of the past. Sometimes when I can't bear life any more I look at my album.'

She sat by Skelton's side as he turned the pages. The notices were from provincial papers, and the references to Mrs Grange, whose stage name had been apparently Vesta Blaise, were carefully underlined. From the photographs, you could see that she had been pretty enough in an undistinguished way. She had acted in musical comedy and revue, in farce and comedy, and taking the photographs and the notices together it was easy to tell that here had been the common, dreary, rather vulgar career of the girl with no particular talent who has taken to the stage on the strength of a pretty face and a good figure. Her head twitching, her hand shaking, Mrs Grange looked at the photographs and read the notices with as much interest as if she had never seen them before.

'You've got to have influence on the stage, and I never had any,' she said. 'If I'd only had my chance I know I'd have made good. I had bad luck, there's no doubt about that.'

It was all sordid and somewhat pathetic.

'I daresay you're better off as you are,' said Skelton.

She snatched the book from him and shut it with a bang. She had a paroxysm so violent that it was really frightening to look at her.

'What d'you mean by that? What d'you know about the life I lead here? I'd have killed myself years ago only I know he wants me to die. That's the only way I can get back on him, by living, and I'm going to live; I'm going to live as long as he does. Oh, I hate him. I've often thought I'd poison him, but I was afraid. I didn't know how to do it really, and if he died the Chinks would foreclose and I'd be turned out. And where should I go then? I haven't a friend in the world.'

Skelton was aghast. It flashed through his mind that she was crazy. He hadn't a notion what to say. She gave him a keen look.

'I suppose it surprises you to hear me talk like that. I mean it, you know, every word of it. He'd like to kill me too, but he daren't either. And he knows how to do it all right. He knows how the Malays kill people. He was born here. There's nothing he doesn't know about the country.'

Skelton forced himself to speak.

'You know, Mrs Grange, I'm a total stranger. Don't you think it's rather unwise to tell me all sorts of things there's no need for me to know? After all, you live a very solitary life. I daresay you get on one another's nerves. Now that things are looking up perhaps you'll be able to take a trip to England.'

'I don't want to go to England. I'd be ashamed to let them see me like I am now. D'you know how old I am? Forty-six. I look sixty and I know it. That's why I showed you those photos, so as you might see I wasn't always like what I am now. Oh, my God, how I've wasted my life! They talk of the romance of the East. They can have it. I'd rather be a dresser in a provincial theatre, I'd rather be one of the sweepers that keep it clean, than what I am now. Until I came here I'd never been alone in my life, I'd always lived in a crowd; you don't know what it is to have nobody to talk to from year's end to year's end. To have to keep it all bottled up. How would you like to see no one, week in and week out, day after day for sixteen years, except the man you hate most in the world? How would you like to live for sixteen years with a man who hates you so he can't bear to look at you?'

'Oh, come, it can't be as bad as that.'

'I'm telling you the truth. Why should I tell you a lie? I shall never see you again; what do I care what you think of me? And if you tell them what I've said when you get down to the coast, what's the odds? They'll say: "God, you don't mean to say you stayed with those people? I pity you. He's an outsider and she's crazy; got a tic; they say it looks as if she was always trying to wipe the blood off her dress. They were mixed up in a damned funny business, but no one ever really knew the ins and outs of it; it all happened a long time ago and the country was pretty wild in those days." A damned funny business and no mistake. I'd tell you for two pins. That would be a bit of dirt for them at the club. You wouldn't have to pay for a drink for days. Damn them. Oh, Christ, how I hate this country. I hate that river. I hate this house. I hate that damned rubber. I loathe the filthy natives. And that's all I've got to look forward to till I die—till I die without a doctor to take care of me, without a friend to hold me hand.'

She began to cry hysterically. Mrs Grange had spoken with a dramatic intensity of which Skelton would never have thought her capable. Her coarse irony was as painful as her anguish. Skelton was young, he was not yet thirty, and he did not know how to deal with the difficult situation. But he could not keep silent.

'I'm terribly sorry, Mrs Grange. I wish I could do something to help you.'

'I'm not asking for your help. No one can help me.'

Skelton was distressed. From what she said he could not but suspect that she had been concerned in a mysterious and perhaps dreadful occurrence, and it might be that to tell him about it without fear of consequences was just the relief she needed.

'I don't want to butt into what's no business of mine, but, Mrs Grange, if you think it would ease your mind to tell me—what you were referring to just now, I mean what you said was a damned funny business, I promise you on my word of honour that I'll never repeat it to a living soul.'

She stopped crying quite suddenly and gave him a long, intent look. She hesitated. He had an impression that the desire to speak was almost irresistible. But she shook her head and sighed.

'It wouldn't do any good. Nothing can do me any good.'

She got up and abruptly left him.

The two men sat down to brunch by themselves.

'My wife asks you to excuse her,' said Grange. 'She's got one of her sick headaches and she's staying in bed today.'

'Oh, I'm sorry.'

Skelton had a notion that in the searching look that Grange gave him was mistrust and animosity. It flashed through his mind that somehow he had discovered that Mrs Grange had been talking to him and perhaps had said things that should have been left unsaid. Skelton made an effort at conversation, but his host was taciturn, and they ended the meal in a silence that was only broken by Grange when he got up.

'You seem pretty fit today and I don't suppose you want to stay in this God-forsaken place longer than you must. I've sent over the river to arrange for a couple of prahus to take you down to the coast. They'll be here at six tomorrow morning.'

Skelton felt sure then that he was right; Grange knew or guessed that his wife had spoken too freely, and he wanted to be rid as soon as possible of the dangerous visitor.

'That's terribly kind of you,' Skelton answered, smiling. 'I'm as fit as a fiddle.'

But in Grange's eyes was no answering smile. They were coldly hostile.

'We might have another game of chess later on,' said he.

'All right. When d'you get back from your office?'

'I haven't got much to do there today. I shall be about the house.'

Skelton wondered if it were only his fancy that there was something very like a threat in the tone in which Grange uttered these words. It looked as though he were going to make sure that his wife and Skelton should not again be left alone. Mrs Grange did not come to dinner. They drank their coffee and smoked their cheroots. Then Grange, pushing back his chair, said:

'You've got to make an early start tomorrow. I daresay you'd like to turn in. I shall have started out on my round by the time you go, so I'll say good-bye to you now.'

'Let me get my guns. I want you to take the one you like best.'

'I'll tell the boy to fetch them.'

The guns were brought and Grange made his choice. He gave no sign that he was pleased with the handsome gift.

'You quite understand that this gun's worth a damned sight more than what your food and drink and smoke have run me into?' he said.

'For all I know you saved my life. I don't think an old gun is an over-generous return for that.'

'Oh, well, if you like to look at it that way, I suppose it's your own business. Thank you very much all the same.'

They shook hands and parted.

Next morning, while the baggage was being stowed away in the prahus, Skelton asked the house boy whether, before starting, he could say good-bye to Mrs Grange. The house boy said he would go and see. He waited a little while. Mrs Grange came out of her room on to the veranda. She was wearing a pink dressing-gown, shabby, rumpled, and none too clean, of Japanese silk, heavily trimmed with cheap lace. The powder was thick on her face, her cheeks were rouged and her lips scarlet with lipstick. Her head seemed to twitch more violently than usual and her hand was agitated by that strange gesture. When first Skelton saw it he had thought that it suggested a wish to call attention to something behind her back, but now, after what she had told him yesterday, it did indeed look as though she was constantly trying to brush something off her dress. Blood, she had said.

'I didn't want to go without thanking you for all your kindness to me,' he said.

'Oh, that's all right.'

'Well, good-bye.'

'I'll walk down with you to the landing-stage.'

They hadn't far to go. The boatmen were still arranging the luggage. Skelton looked across the river where you could see some native houses.

'I suppose these men come from over there. It looks quite a village.'

'No, only those few houses. There used to be a rubber estate there, but the company went broke and it was abandoned.'

'D'you ever go over there?'

'Me?' cried Mrs Grange. Her voice rose shrill and her head, her hand, were on a sudden convulsed by a paroxysm of involuntary movement. 'No. Why should I?'

Skelton could not imagine why that simple question, asked merely for something to say, should so greatly upset her. But by now all was in order and he shook hands with her. He stepped into the boat and comfortably settled down. They pushed off. He waved to Mrs Grange. As the boat slid into the current she cried out with a harsh, strident scream:

'Give my regards to Leicester Square.'

Skelton heaved a great sigh of relief as with their powerful strokes the paddlers took him farther and farther away from that dreadful house and from those two unhappy and yet repellent people. He was glad now that Mrs Grange had not told him the story that was on the tip of her tongue to tell. He did not want some tragic tale of sin or folly to connect him with them in a recollection that he could not escape. He wanted to forget them as one forgets a bad dream.

But Mrs Grange watched the two prahus till a bend of the river took them out of sight. She walked slowly up to the house and went into her bedroom. The light was dim because the blinds were drawn to keep out the heat, but she sat down at her dressing-table and stared at herself in the glass. Norman had had the dressing-table made for her soon after they were married. It had been made by a native carpenter, of course, and they had had the mirror sent from Singapore, but it was made to her own design, of the exact size and shape she wanted, with plenty of room for all her toilet things and her make-up. It was the dressing-table she had hankered after for donkey's years and had never had. She remembered still how pleased she was when first she had it. She threw her arms round her husband's neck and kissed him.

'Oh, Norman, you are good to me,' she said. 'I'm a lucky little girl to have caught a chap like you, aren't I?'

But then everything delighted her. She was amused by the river life and the life of the jungle, the teeming growth of the forest, the birds with their gay plumage and the brilliant butterflies. She set about giving the house a woman's touch; she put out all her own photographs and she got vases to put flowers in; she routed around and got a lot of knick-knacks to place here and there. 'They make a room look homey,' she said. She wasn't in love with Norman, but she liked him all right; and it was lovely to be married; it was lovely to have nothing to do from morning till night, except play the gramophone, or patience, and read novels. It was lovely to think one hadn't got to bother about one's future. Of course it was a bit lonely sometimes, but Norman said she'd get used to that, and he'd promised that in a year, or two at the outside, he'd take her to England for three months. It would be a lark to show him off to her friends. She felt that what had caught him was the glamour of the stage and she'd made herself out a good deal more successful than she really had been. She wanted him to realize that she'd made a sacrifice when she'd thrown up her career to become a planter's wife. She'd claimed acquaintance with a good many stars that in point of fact she'd never even spoken to. That would need a bit of handling when they went home, but she'd manage it; after all, poor Norman knew no more about the stage than a babe unborn, if she couldn't cod a simple fellow like that, after twelve years on the stage, well, she'd wasted her time, that's all she could say. Things went all right the first year. At one moment she thought she was going to have a baby. They were both disappointed when it turned out not to be true. Then she began to grow bored. It seemed to her that she'd done the same damned thing day after day for ever and it frightened her to think that she'd have to go on doing the same damned thing day after day for ever more. Norman said he couldn't leave the plantation that year. They had a bit of a scene. It was then that he'd said something that scared her.

'I hate England,' he said. 'If I had my way I'd never set foot in the damned country again.'

Living this lonely life Mrs Grange got into the habit of talking out loud to herself. Shut up in her room she could be heard chattering away hour after hour; and now, dipping the puff in her powder and plastering her face with it, she addressed her reflection in the mirror exactly as though she were talking to another person.

'That ought to have warned me. I should have insisted on going by myself, and who knows, I might have got a job when I got to London. With all the experience I had and everything. Then I'd have written to him and said I wasn't coming back.' Her thoughts turned to Skelton. 'Pity I didn't tell him,' she continued. 'I had half a mind to. P'raps he was right, p'raps it would have eased me mind. I wonder what he'd have said.' She imitated his Oxford accent. 'I'm so terribly sorry, Mrs Grange. I wish I could help you.' She gave a chuckle which was almost a sob. 'I'd have liked to tell him about Jack. Oh, Jack.'

It was when they had been married for two years that they got a neighbour. The price of rubber at that time was so high that new estates were being put under cultivation and one of the big companies had bought a great tract of land on the opposite bank of the river. It was a rich company and everything was done on a lavish scale. The manager they had put in had a launch at his disposal so that it was no trouble for him to pop over and have a drink whenever he felt inclined. Jack Carr his name was. He was quite a different sort of chap from Norman; for one thing he was a gentleman, he'd been to a public school and a university; he was about thirty-five, tall, not beefy like Norman, but slight, he had the sort of figure that looked lovely in evening dress; and he had crisply curling hair and a laughing look in his eyes. Just her type. She took to him at once. It was a treat, having someone you could talk about London to, and the theatre. He was gay and easy. He made the sort of jokes you could understand. In a week or two she felt more at home with him than she did with her husband after two years. There had always been something about Norman that she hadn't quite been able to get to the bottom of. He was crazy about her, of course, and he'd told her a lot about himself, but she had a funny feeling that there was something he kept from her, not because he wanted to, but–well, you couldn't hardly explain it, because it was so alien, you might say, that he couldn't put it into words. Later, when she knew Jack better, she mentioned it to him, and Jack said it was because he was country-born; even though he hadn't a drop of native blood in his veins, something of the country had gone to the making of him so that he wasn't white really; he had an Eastern streak in him. However hard he tried he could never be quite English.

She chattered away aloud, in that empty house, for the two boys, the cook and the house boy, were in their own quarters, and the sound of her voice, ringing along the wooden floors, piercing the wooden walls, was like the uncanny, unhuman gibber of new wine fermenting in a vat. She spoke just as though Skelton were there, but so incoherently that if he had been, he would have had difficulty in following the story she told. It did not take her long to discover that Jack Carr wanted her. She was excited. She'd never been promiscuous, but in all those years she'd been on the stage naturally there'd been episodes. You couldn't hardly have put up with being on tour month after month if you didn't have a bit of fun sometimes. Of course now she wasn't going to give in too easily, she didn't want to make herself cheap, but what with the life she led, she'd be a fool if she missed the chance; and as far as Norman was concerned, well, what the eye didn't see the heart didn't grieve over. They understood one another all right, Jack and her; they knew it was bound to happen sooner or later, it was only a matter of waiting for the opportunity; and the opportunity came. But then something happened that they hadn't bargained for: they fell madly in love with one another. If Mrs Grange really had been telling the story to Skelton it might have seemed as unlikely to him as it did to them. They were two very ordinary people, he a jolly, good-natured, commonplace planter, and she a small-part actress far from clever, not even very young, with nothing to recommend her but a neat figure and a prettyish face. What started as a casual affair turned without warning into a devastating passion, and neither of them was of a texture to sustain its exorbitant compulsion. They longed to be with one another; they were restless and miserable apart. She'd been finding Norman a bore for some time, but she'd put up with him because he was her husband; now he irritated her to frenzy because he stood between her and Jack. There was no question of their going off together, Jack Carr had nothing but his salary, and he couldn't throw up a job he'd been only too glad to get. It was difficult for them to meet. They had to run awful risks. Perhaps the chances they had to take, the obstacles they had to surmount, were fuel to their love; a year passed and it was as overwhelming as at the beginning; it was a year of agony and bliss, of fear and thrill. Then she discovered that she was pregnant. She had no doubt that Jack Carr was the father and she was wildly happy. It was true life was difficult, so difficult sometimes that she felt she just couldn't cope with it, but there'd be a baby, his baby, and that would make everything easy. She was going to Kuching for her confinement. It happened about then that Jack Carr had to go to Singapore on business and was to be away for several weeks; but he promised to get back before she left and he said he'd send word by a native the moment he arrived. When at last the message came she felt sick with the anguish of her joy. She had never wanted him so badly.

'I hear that Jack is back,' she told her husband at dinner. 'I shall go over tomorrow morning and get the things he promised to bring me.'

'I wouldn't do that. He's pretty sure to drop in towards sundown and he'll bring them himself.'

'I can't wait. I'm crazy to have them.'

'All right. Have it your own way.'

She couldn't help talking about him. For some time now they had seemed to have little to say to one another, Norman and she, but that night, in high spirits, she chattered away as she had done during the first months of their marriage. She always rose early, at six, and next morning she went down to the river and had a bathe. There was a little dent in the bank just there, with a tiny sandy beach, and it was delicious to splash about in the cool, transparent water. A kingfisher stood on the branch of a tree overhanging the pool and its reflection was brilliantly blue in the water. Lovely. She had a cup of tea and then stepped into a dug-out. A boy paddled her across the river. It took a good half-hour. As they got near she scanned the bank; Jack knew she would come at the earliest opportunity; he must be on the lookout. Ah, there he was. The delicious pain in her heart was almost unbearable. He came down to the landing-stage and helped her to get out of the boat. They walked hand in hand up the pathway and when they were out of sight of the boy who had paddled her over and of prying eyes from the house, they stopped. He put his arms round her and she yielded with ecstasy to his embrace. She clung to him. His mouth sought hers. In that kiss was all the agony of their separation and all the bliss of their reunion. The miracle of love transfused them so that they were unconscious of time and place. They were not human any more, but two spirits united by a divine fire. No thought passed through their minds. No words issued from their lips. Suddenly there was a brutal shock, like a blow, and immediately, almost simultaneously, a deafening noise. Horrified, not understanding, she clung to Jack more tightly and his grip on her was spasmodic, so that she gasped; then she felt that he was bearing her over.

'Jack.'

She tried to hold him up. His weight was too great for her and as he fell to the ground she fell with him. Then she gave a great cry, for she felt a gush of heat, and his blood sputtered over her. She began to scream. A rough hand seized her and dragged her to her feet. It was Norman. She was distraught. She could not understand.

'Norman, what have you done?'

'I've killed him.'

She stared at him stupidly. She pushed him aside.

'Jack. Jack.'

'Shut up. I'll go and get help. It was an accident.'

He walked quickly up the pathway. She fell to her knees and took Jack's head in her arms.

'Darling,' she moaned. 'Oh, my darling.'

Norman came back with some coolies and they carried him up to the house. That night she had a miscarriage and was so ill that for days it looked as if she would die. When she recovered she had the nervous tic that she'd had ever since. She expected that Norman would send her away; but he didn't, he had to keep her to allay suspicion. There was some talk among the natives, and after a while the District Officer came up and asked a lot of questions; but the natives were frightened of Norman, and the D.O. could get nothing out of them. The Dyak boy who paddled her over had vanished. Norman said something had gone wrong with his gun and Jack was looking at it to see what was the matter and it went off. They bury people quickly in that country and by the time they might have dug him up there wouldn't have been much left to show that Norman's story wasn't true. The D.O. hadn't been satisfied.

'It all looks damned fishy to me,' he said, 'but in the absence of any evidence, I suppose I must accept your version.'

She would have given anything to get away, but with that nervous affliction she had no ghost of a chance any longer of earning a living. She had to stay—or starve; and Norman had to keep her—or hang. Nothing had happened since then and now nothing ever would happen. The endless years one after another dragged out their weary length.

Mrs Grange on a sudden stopped talking. Her sharp ears had caught the sound of a footstep on the path and she knew that Norman was back from his round. Her head twitching furiously, her hand agitated by that sinister, uncontrollable gesture, she looked in the untidy mess of her dressing-table for her precious lipstick. She smeared it on her lips, and then, she didn't know why, on a freakish impulse daubed it all over her nose till she looked like a red-nose comedian in a music-hall. She looked at herself in the glass and burst out laughing.

'To hell with life!' she shouted.

The
Alien Corn

◆

I had known the Blands a long time before I discovered that they had any
connexion with Ferdy Rabenstein. Ferdy must have been nearly fifty when I
first knew him and at the time of which I write he was well over seventy. He had
altered little. His hair, coarse but abundant and curly, was white, but he had
kept his figure and held himself as gallantly as ever. It was not hard to believe
that in youth he had been as beautiful as people said. He had still his fine
Semitic profile and the lustrous black eyes that had caused havoc in so many a
Gentile breast. He was very tall, lean, with an oval face and a clear skin. He
wore his clothes very well and in evening dress, even now, he was one of the
handsomest men I had ever seen. He wore then large black pearls in his shirt-
front and platinum and sapphire rings on his fingers. Perhaps he was rather
flashy, but you felt it was so much in character that it would have ill become him
to be anything else.

'After all, I am an Oriental,' he said. 'I can carry a certain barbaric
magnificence.'

I have often thought that Ferdy Rabenstein would make an admirable
subject for a biography. He was not a great man, but within the limits he set
himself he made of his life a work of art. It was a masterpiece in little, like a
Persian miniature, and derived its interest from its perfection. Unfortunately
the materials are scanty. They would consist of letters that may very well have
been destroyed and the recollections of people who are old now and will soon be
dead. His memory is extraordinary, but he would never write his memoirs, for
he looks upon his past as a source of purely private entertainment; and he is a
man of the most perfect discretion. Nor do I know anyone who could do justice
to the subject but Max Beerbohm. There is no one else in this hard world of
today who can look upon the trivial with such tender sympathy and wring such a

delicate pathos from futility. I wonder that Max, who must have known Ferdy
much better than I, and long before, was never tempted to exercise his
exquisite fancy on such a theme. He was born for Max to write about. And who
should have illustrated the elegant book that I see in my mind's eye but Aubrey
Beardsley? Thus would have been erected a monument of triple brass and the
ephemera imprisoned to succeeding ages in the amber's translucency.

Ferdy's conquests were social and his venue was the great world. He was
born in South Africa and did not come to England till he was twenty. For some
time he was on the Stock Exchange, but on the death of his father he inherited a
considerable fortune, and retiring from business devoted himself to the life of a
man about town. At that period English society was still a closed body and it
was not easy for a Jew to force its barriers, but to Ferdy they fell like the walls of
Jericho. He was handsome, he was rich, he was a sportsman and he was good
company. He had a house in Curzon Street, furnished with the most beautiful
French furniture, and a French chef, and a brougham. It would be interesting
to know the first steps in his wonderful career: they are lost in the dark abysm of
time. When I first met him he had been long established as one of the smartest
men in London: this was at a very grand house in Norfolk to which I had been
asked as a promising young novelist by the hostess who took an interest in
letters, but the company was very distinguished and I was over-awed. We were
sixteen, and I felt shy and alone among these Cabinet Ministers, great ladies,
and peers of the realm who talked of people and things of which I knew
nothing. They were civil to me, but indifferent, and I was conscious that I was
somewhat of a burden to my hostess. Ferdy saved me. He sat with me, walked
with me, and talked with me. He discovered that I was a writer and we
discussed the drama and the novel: he learnt that I had lived much on the
Continent and he talked to me pleasantly of France, Germany, and Spain. He
seemed really to seek my society. He gave me the flattering impression that he
and I stood apart from the other members of the company and by our
conversation upon affairs of the spirit made that of the rest of them, the political
situation, the scandal of somebody's divorce, and the growing disinclination of
pheasants to be killed, seem a little ridiculous. But if Ferdy had at the bottom of
his heart a feeling of ever so faint a contempt for the hearty British gentry that
surrounded us I am sure that it was only to me that he allowed an inkling of it to
appear, and looking back I cannot but wonder whether it was not after all a
suave and very delicate compliment that he paid me. I think of course that he
liked to exercise his charm and I dare say the obvious pleasure his conversation
gave me gratified him, but he could have had no motive for taking so much
trouble over an obscure novelist other than his real interest in art and letters. I
felt that he and I at bottom were equally alien in that company, I because I was a
writer and he because he was a Jew, but I envied the ease with which he bore
himself. He was completely at home. Everyone called him Ferdy. He seemed to
be always in good spirits. He was never at a loss for a quip, a jest, or a repartee.
They liked him in that house because he made them laugh, but never made
them uncomfortable by talking over their heads. He brought a faint savour of
Oriental romance into their lives, but so cleverly that they only felt more
English. You could never be dull when he was by and with him present you
were safe from the fear of the devastating silences that sometimes overwhelm a
British company. A pause looked inevitable and Ferdy Rabenstein had broken
into a topic that interested everyone. An invaluable asset to any party. He had
an inexhaustible fund of Jewish stories. He was a very good mimic and he

assumed the Yiddish accent and reproduced the Jewish gestures to perfection; his head sank into his body, his face grew cunning, his voice oily, and he was a rabbi or an old clothes merchant or a smart commercial traveller or a fat procuress in Frankfort. It was as good as a play. Because he was himself a Jew and insisted on it you laughed without reserve, but for my own part not without an under-current of discomfort. I was not quite sure of a sense of humour that made such cruel fun of his own race. I discovered afterwards that Jewish stories were his speciality and I seldom met him anywhere without hearing him tell sooner or later the last he had heard.

But the best story he told me on this occasion was not a Jewish one. It struck me so that I have never forgotten it, but for one reason or another I have never had occasion to tell it again. I give it here because it is a curious little incident concerning persons whose names at least will live in the social history of the Victorian Era and I think it would be a pity if it were lost. He told me then that once when quite a young man he was staying in the country in a house where Mrs Langtry, at that time at the height of her beauty and astounding reputation, was also a guest. It happened to be within driving distance of that in which lived the Duchess of Somerset, who had been Queen of Beauty at the Eglinton Tournament, and knowing her slightly, it occurred to him that it would be interesting to bring the two women together. He suggested it to Mrs Langtry, who was willing, and forthwith wrote to the Duchess asking if he might bring the celebrated beauty to call on her. It was fitting, he said, that the loveliest women of this generation (this was in the eighties) should pay her respects to the loveliest woman of the last. 'Bring her by all means,' answered the Duchess, 'but I warn you that it will be a shock to her.' They drove over in a carriage and pair, Mrs Langtry in a close-fitting blue bonnet with long satin strings, which showed the fine shape of her head and made her blue eyes even bluer, and were received by a little ugly old hag who looked with irony out of her beady eyes at the radiant beauty who had come to see her. They had tea, they talked, and they drove home again. Mrs Langtry was very silent and when Ferdy looked at her he saw that she was quietly weeping. When they got back to the house she went to her room and would not come down to dinner that night. For the first time she had realized that beauty dies.

Ferdy asked me for my address and a few days after I got back to London invited me to dinner. There were only six of us, an American woman married to an English peer, a Swedish painter, an actress, and a well-known critic. We ate very good food and drank excellent wine. The conversation was easy and intelligent. After dinner Ferdy was persuaded to play the piano. He only played Viennese waltzes, I discovered later that they were his speciality, and the light, tuneful, and sensual music seemed to accord well with his discreet flamboyance. He played without affectation, with a lilt, and he had a graceful touch. This was the first of a good many dinners I had with him, he would ask me two or three times a year, and as time passed I met him more and more frequently at other people's houses. I rose in the world and perhaps he came down a little. Of late years I had sometimes found him at parties where other Jews were and I fancied that I read in his shining liquid eyes, resting for a moment on these members of his race, a certain good-natured amusement at the thought of what the world was coming to. There were people who said he was a snob, but I do not think he was; it just happened that in his early days he had never met any but the great. He had a real passion for art and in his commerce with those that produced it was at his best. With them he had never that faint air of persiflage which when he was with very grand persons made you suspect that he was never quite the dupe of their grandeur. His taste was perfect and many of his friends were glad to avail themselves of his knowledge. He was one of the first to value old furniture and he rescued many a priceless piece from the attics of ancestral mansions and gave it an honourable place in the drawing-room. It amused him to saunter round the auction rooms and he was always willing to give his advice to great ladies who desired at once to acquire a beautiful thing and make a profitable investment. He was rich and good-natured. He liked to patronize the arts and would take a great deal of trouble to get commissions for some young painter whose talent he admired or an engagement to play at a rich man's house for a violinist who could in no other way get a hearing. But he never let his rich man down. His taste was too good to deceive and civil though he might be to the mediocre he would not lift a finger to help them. His own musical parties, very small and carefully chosen, were a treat.

He never married.

'I am a man of the world,' he said, 'and I flatter myself that I have no prejudices, *tous les goûts sont dans la nature*, but I do not think I could bring myself to marry a Gentile. There's no harm in going to the opera in a dinner jacket, but it just would never occur to me to do so.'

'Then why didn't you marry a Jewess?'

(I did not hear this conversation, but the lively and audacious creature who thus tackled him told me of it.)

'Oh, my dear, our women are so prolific. I could not bear the thought of peopling the world with a little Ikey and a little Jacob and a little Rebecca and a little Leah and a little Rachel.'

But he had had affairs of note and the glamour of past romance still clung to him. He was in his youth of an amorous complexion. I have met old ladies who told me that he was irresistible, and when in reminiscent mood they talked to me of this woman and that who had completely lost her head over him, I divined that, such was his beauty, they could not find it in their hearts to blame them. It was interesting to hear of great ladies that I had read of in the memoirs of the day or had met as respectable dowagers garrulous over their grandsons at Eton or making a mess of a hand at bridge and bethink myself that they had been consumed with sinful passion for the handsome Jew. Ferdy's most notorious amour was with the Duchess of Hereford, the loveliest, the most gallant and dashing of the beauties of the end of Queen Victoria's reign. It lasted for twenty years. He had doubtless flirtations meanwhile, but their relations were stable and recognized. It was proof of his marvellous tact that when at last they ended he exchanged an ageing mistress for a loyal friend. I remember meeting the pair not so very long ago at luncheon. She was an old woman, tall and of a commanding presence, but with a mask of paint on a ravaged face. We were lunching at the Carlton and Ferdy, our host, came a few minutes late. He offered us a cocktail and the Duchess told him we had already had one.

'Ah, I wondered why your eyes were so doubly bright,' he said.

The old raddled woman flushed with pleasure.

My youth passed, I grew middle-aged, I wondered how soon I must begin to describe myself as elderly; I wrote books and plays, I travelled, I underwent experiences, I fell in love and out of it; and still I kept meeting Ferdy at parties. War broke out and was waged, millions of men were killed, and the face of the world was changed. Ferdy did not like the war. He was too old to take part in it, and his German name was awkward, but he was discreet and took care not to expose himself to humiliation. His old friends were faithful to him and he lived in a dignified but not too strict seclusion. But then peace came and with courage he set himself to making the best of changed conditions. Society was mixed now, parties were rowdy, but Ferdy fitted himself to the new life. He still told his funny Jewish stories, he still played charmingly the waltzes of Strauss, he still went round auction rooms and told the new rich what they ought to buy. I went to live abroad, but whenever I was in London I saw Ferdy and now there was something a little uncanny in him. He did not give in. He had never known a day's illness. He seemed never to grow tired. He still dressed beautifully. He was interested in everybody. His mind was alert and people asked him to dinner, not for old times' sake, but because he was worth his salt. He still gave charming little concerts at his house in Curzon Street.

It was when he invited me to one of these that I made the discovery that started the recollections of him I have here set down. We were dining at a house in Hill Street, a large party, and the women having gone upstairs Ferdy and I found ourselves side by side. He told me that Lea Makart was coming to play for him on the following Friday evening and he would be glad if I would come.

'I'm awfully sorry,' I said, 'but I'm going down to the Blands.'

'What Blands?'

'They live in Sussex at a place called Tilby.'

'I didn't know you knew them.'

He looked at me rather strangely. He smiled. I didn't know what amused him.

'Oh, yes, I've known them for years. It's a very nice house to stay at.'

'Adolf is my nephew.'

'Sir Adolphus?'

'It suggests one of the bucks of the Regency, doesn't it? But I will not conceal from you that he was named Adolf.'

'Everyone I know calls him Freddy.'

'I know, and I understand that Miriam, his wife, only answers to the name of Muriel.'

'How does he happen to be your nephew?'

'Because Hannah Rabenstein, my sister, married Alfons Bleikogel, who ended life as Sir Alfred Bland, first Baronet, and Adolf, their only son, in due course became Sir Adolphus Bland, second Baronet.'

'Then Freddy Bland's mother, the Lady Bland who lives in Portland Place, is your sister?'

'Yes, my sister Hannah. She was the eldest of the family. She's eighty, but in full possession of her faculties and a remarkable woman.'

'I've never met her.'

'I think your friends the Blands would just as soon you didn't. She has never lost her German accent.'

'Do you never see them?' I asked.

'I haven't spoken to them for twenty years. I am such a Jew and they are so English.' He smiled. 'I could never remember that their names were Freddy and Muriel. I used to come out with an Adolf or a Miriam at awkward moments. And they didn't like my stories. It was better that we should not meet. When the war broke out and I would not change my name it was the last straw. It was too late, I could never have accustomed my friends to think of me as anything but Ferdy Rabenstein; I was quite content. I was not ambitious to be a Smith, a Brown or a Robinson.'

Though he spoke facetiously, there was in his tone the faintest possible derision and I felt, hardly felt even, the sensation was so shadowy, that, as it had often vaguely seemed to me before, there was in the depth of his impenetrable heart a cynical contempt for the Gentiles he had conquered.

'Then you don't know the two boys?' I said.

'No.'

'The eldest is called George, you know. I don't think he's so clever as Harry, the other one, but he's an engaging youth. I think you'd like him.'

'Where is he now?'

'Well, he's just been sent down from Oxford. I suppose he's at home. Harry's still at Eton.'

'Why don't you bring George to lunch with me?'

'I'll ask him. I should think he'd love to come.'

'It has reached my ears that he's been a little troublesome.'

'Oh, I don't know. He wouldn't go into the army, which is what they wanted. They rather fancied the Guards. And so he went to Oxford instead. He didn't work and he spent a great deal of money and he painted the town red. It was all quite normal.'

'What was he sent down for?'

'I don't know. Nothing of any consequence.'

At that moment our host rose and we went upstairs. When Ferdy bade me good night he asked me not to forget about his great-nephew.

'Ring me up,' he said. 'Wednesday would suit me. Or Friday.'

Next day I went down to Tilby. It was an Elizabethan mansion standing in a spacious park, in which roamed fallow deer, and from its windows you had wide views of rolling downs. It seemed to me that as far as the eye could reach the land belonged to the Blands. His tenants must have found Sir Adolphus a wonderful landlord, for I never saw farms kept in such order, the barns and cow-sheds were spick and span and the pigsties were a picture; the public-houses looked like Old English water-colours and the cottages he had built on the estate combined admirably picturesqueness and convenience. It must have cost him a pot of money to run the place on these lines. Fortunately he had it. The park with its grand old trees (and its nine-hole golf course) was tended like a garden, and the wide-stretching gardens were the pride of the neigh-bourhood. The magnificent house, with its steep roofs and mullioned windows, had been restored by the most celebrated architect in England and furnished by Lady Bland, with taste and knowledge, in a style that perfectly fitted it.

'Of course it's very simple,' she said. 'Just an English house in the country.'

The dining-room was adorned with old English sporting pictures and the Chippendale chairs were of incredible value. In the drawing-room were portraits by Reynolds and Gainsborough and landscapes by Old Crome and Richard Wilson. Even in my bedroom with its four-post bed were water-colours by Birket Foster. It was very beautiful and a treat to stay there, but though it would have distressed Muriel Bland beyond anything to know it, it entirely missed oddly enough the effect she had sought. It did not give you for a moment the impression of an English house. You had the feeling that every object had been bought with a careful eye to the general scheme. You missed the full Academy portraits that hung in the dining-room beside a Carlo Dolci that an ancestor had brought back from the Grand Tour, and the water-colours painted by a great-aunt that cluttered up the drawing-room so engagingly. There was no ugly Victorian sofa that had always been there and that it never occurred to anybody to take away and no needlework chairs that an unmarried daughter had so painstakingly worked at about the time of the Great Exhibition. There was beauty but no sentiment.

And yet how comfortable it was and how well looked after you were! And what a cordial greeting the Blands gave you! They seemed really to like people. They were generous and kindly. They were never happier than when they were entertaining the county, and though they had not owned the property for more than twenty years they had established themselves firmly in the favour of their neighbours. Except perhaps in their splendour and the competent way in which the estate was run there was nothing to suggest that they had not been settled there for centuries.

Freddy had been at Eton and Oxford. He was now in the early fifties. He was quiet in manner, courtly, very clever, I imagine, but a trifle reserved. He had great elegance, but it was not an English elegance; he had grey hair and a short pointed grey beard, fine dark eyes and an aquiline nose. He was just above middle height; I don't think you would have taken him for a Jew, but rather for a foreign diplomat of some distinction. He was a man of character, but gave you, strangely enough, notwithstanding the success he had had in life, an impression of faint melancholy. His successes had been financial and political; in the world of sport, for all his perseverance, he had never shone. For many years he had followed hounds, but he was a bad rider and I think it must have been a relief to him when he could persuade himself that middle age and pressure of business forced him to give up hunting. He had excellent shooting and gave grand parties for it, but he was a poor shot; and despite the course in his park he never succeeded in being more than an indifferent golfer. He knew only too well how much these things meant in England and his incapacity was a bitter disappointment to him. However George would make up for it.

George was scratch at golf, and though tennis was not his game he played much better than the average; the Blands had had him taught to shoot as soon as he was old enough to hold a gun and he was a fine shot; they had put him on a pony when he was two, and Freddy, watching him mount his horse, knew that out hunting when the boy came to a fence he felt exhilaration and not that sickening feeling in the pit of his stomach, which, though he had chased the fox with such grim determination, had always made the sport a torture to him. George was so tall and slim, his curly hair, of a palish brown, was so fine, his eyes were so blue, he was the perfect type of the young Englishman. He had the engaging candour of the breed. His nose was straight, though perhaps a trifle fleshy, and his lips were perhaps a little full and sensual, but he had beautiful teeth, and his smooth skin was like ivory. George was the apple of his father's eye. He did not like Harry, his second son, so well. He was rather stocky, broad-shouldered and strong for his age, but his black eyes, shining with cleverness, his coarse dark hair, and his big nose revealed his race. Freddy was severe with him, and often impatient, but with George he was all indulgence. Harry would go into the business, he had brains and push, but George was the heir. George would be an English gentleman.

George had offered to motor me down in the roadster his father had given him as a birthday present. He drove very fast and we arrived before the rest of the guests. The Blands were sitting on the lawn and tea was laid out under a magnificent cedar.

'By the way,' I said presently, 'I saw Ferdy Rabenstein the other day and he wants me to bring George to lunch with him.'

I had not mentioned the invitation to George on the way because I thought that if there had been a family coldness I had better address his parents as well.

'Who in God's name is Ferdy Rabenstein?' said George.

How brief is human glory! A generation back such a question would have seemed grotesque.

'He's by way of being your great-uncle,' I replied.

A glance had passed from father to mother when I first spoke.

'He's a horrid old man,' said Muriel.

'I don't think it's in the least necessary for George to resume relationships that were definitely severed before he was born,' said Freddy with decision.

'Anyhow I've delivered the message,' said I, feeling somewhat snubbed.

'I don't want to see the old blighter,' said George.

The conversation was broken off by the arrival of other guests and in a little while George went off to play golf with one of his Oxford friends.

It was not till next day that the matter was referred to again. I had played an unsatisfactory round with Freddy Bland in the morning and several sets of what is known as country-house tennis in the afternoon and was sitting alone with Muriel on the terrace. In England we have so much bad weather that it is only fair that a beautiful day should be more beautiful than anywhere in the world and this June evening was perfect. The blue sky was cloudless and the air was balmy; before us stretched green rolling downs, and woods, and in the distance you saw the red roofs of a little village church. It was a day when to be alive was sufficient happiness. Detached lines of poetry hovered vaguely in my memory. Muriel and I had been chatting desultorily.

'I hope you didn't think it rather horrid of us to refuse to let George lunch with Ferdy,' she said suddenly. 'He's such a fearful snob, isn't he?'

'D'you think so? He's always been very nice to me.'

'We haven't been on speaking terms for twenty years. Freddy never forgave him for his behaviour during the war. So unpatriotic, I thought, and one really must draw the line somewhere. You know, he absolutely refused to drop his horrible German name. With Freddy in Parliament and running munitions and all that sort of thing it was quite impossible. I don't know why he should want to see George. He can't mean anything to him.'

'He's an old man. George and Harry are his great-nephews. He must leave his money to someone.'

'We'd rather not have his money,' said Muriel coldly.

Of course I didn't care a row of pins whether George went to lunch with Ferdy Rabenstein, and I was quite willing to let the matter drop, but evidently the Blands had talked it over and Muriel felt that some explanation was due to me.

'Of course you know that Freddy has Jewish blood in him,' she said.

She looked at me sharply. Muriel was rather a big blonde woman and she spent a great deal of time trying to keep down the corpulence to which she was predisposed. She had been very pretty when young, and even now was a comely person; but her round blue eyes, slightly prominent, her fleshy nose, the shape of her face and the back of her neck, her exuberant manner, betrayed her race. No Englishwoman, however fair-haired, ever looked like that. And yet her observation was designed to make me take it for granted that she was a Gentile. I answered discreetly:

'So many people have nowadays.'

'I know. But there's no reason to dwell on it, is there? After all, we're absolutely English; no one could be more English than George, in appearance and manner and everything; I mean, he's such a fine sportsman and all that sort of thing, I can't see any object of his knowing Jews just because they happen to be distant connexions of his.'

'It's very difficult in England now not to know Jews, isn't it?'

'Oh, I know, in London one does meet a good many, and I think some of them are very nice. They're so artistic. I don't go so far as to say that Freddy and I deliberately avoid them, of course I wouldn't do that, but it just happens that we don't really know any of them very well. And down here, there simply aren't any to know.'

I could not but admire the convincing manner in which she spoke. It would not have surprised me to be told that she really believed every word she said.

'You say that Ferdy might leave George his money. Well, I don't believe it's so very much anyway; it was quite a comfortable fortune before the war, but that's nothing nowadays. Besides we're hoping that George will go in for politics when he's a little older, and I don't think it would do him any good in the constituency to inherit money from a Mr Rabenstein.'

'Is George interested in politics?' I asked, to change the conversation.

'Oh, I do hope so. After all, there's the family constituency waiting for him. It's a safe Conservative seat and one can't expect Freddy to go on with the grind of the House of Commons indefinitely.'

Muriel was grand. She talked already of the constituency as though twenty generations of Blands had sat for it. Her remark, however, was my first intimation that Freddy's ambition was not satisfied.

'I suppose Freddy would go to the House of Lords when George was old enough to stand.'

'We've done a good deal for the party,' said Muriel.

Muriel was a Catholic and she often told you that she had been educated in a convent—'Such sweet women, those nuns, I always said that if I had a daughter I should have sent her to a convent too'—but she liked her servants to be Church of England, and on Sunday evenings we had what was called supper because the fish was cold and there was ice-cream, so that they could go to church, and we were waited on by two footmen instead of four. It was still light when we finished and Freddy and I, smoking our cigars, walked up and down the terrace in the gloaming. I suppose Muriel had told him of her conversation with me, and it may be that his refusal to let George see his great-uncle still troubled him, but being subtler than she he attacked the question more indirectly. He told me that he had been very much worried about George. It had been a great disappointment that he had refused to go into the army.

'I should have thought he'd have loved the life,' he said.

'And he would certainly have looked marvellous in his Guards uniform.'

'He would, wouldn't he?' returned Freddy, ingenuously. 'I wonder he could resist that.'

He had been completely idle at Oxford; although his father had given him a very large allowance, he had got monstrously into debt; and now he had been sent down. But though he spoke so tartly I could see that he was not a little proud of his scapegrace son, he loved him with oh, such an unEnglish love, and in his heart it flattered him that George had cut such a dash.

'Why should you worry?' I said. 'You don't really care if George has a degree or not.'

Freddy chuckled.

'No, I don't suppose I do really. I always think the only important thing about Oxford is that people know you were there, and I dare say that George isn't any wilder than the other young men in his set. It's the future I'm thinking of. He's so damned idle. He doesn't seem to want to do anything but have a good time.'

'He's young, you know.'

'He's not interested in politics, and though he's so good at games he's not even very keen on sport. He seems to spend most of his time strumming the piano.'

'That's a harmless amusement.'

'Oh, yes, I don't mind that, but he can't go on loafing indefinitely. You see, all this will be his one day.' Freddy gave a sweeping gesture that seemed to embrace the whole county, but I knew that he did not own it all yet. 'I'm very anxious that he should be fit to assume his responsibilities. His mother is very ambitious for him, but I only want him to be an English gentleman.'

Freddy gave me a sidelong glance as though he wanted to say something but hesitated in case I thought it ridiculous; but there is one advantage in being a writer that, since people look upon you as of no account, they will often say things to you that they would not to their equals. He thought he would risk it.

'You know, I've got an idea that nowhere in the world now is the Greek ideal of life so perfectly cultivated as by the English country gentleman living on his estates. I think his life has the beauty of a work of art.'

I could not but smile when I reflected that it was impossible for the English country gentleman in these days to do anything of the sort without a packet of money safely invested in American Bonds, but I smiled with sympathy. I thought it rather touching that this Jewish financier should cherish so romantic a dream.

'I want him to be a good landlord. I want him to take his part in the affairs of the country. I want him to be a thorough sportsman.'

'Poor mutt,' I thought, but said: 'Well, what are your plans for George now?'

'I think he has a fancy for the diplomatic service. He's suggested going to Germany to learn the language.'

'A very good idea, I should have thought.'

'For some reason he's got it into his head that he wants to go to Munich.'

'A nice place.'

Next day I went back to London and shortly after my arrival rang up Ferdy.

'I'm sorry, but George isn't able to come to lunch on Wednesday.'

'What about Friday?'

'Friday's no good either.' I thought it useless to beat about the bush. 'The fact is, his people aren't keen on his lunching with you.'

There was a moment's silence. Then:

'I see. Well, will you come on Wednesday anyway?'

'Yes, I'd like to,' I answered.

So on Wednesday at half past one I strolled round to Curzon Street. Ferdy received me with the somewhat elaborate graciousness that he cultivated. He made no reference to the Blands. We sat in the drawing-room and I could not help reflecting what an eye for beautiful objects that family had. The room was more crowded than the fashion of today approves, and the gold snuff-boxes in vitrines, the French china, appealed to a taste that was not mine; but they were no doubt choice pieces; and the Louise XV suite, with its beautiful *petit point*, must have been worth an enormous lot of money. The pictures on the walls by Lancret, Pater, and Watteau did not greatly interest me, but I recognized their intrinsic excellence. It was a proper setting for this aged man of the world. It fitted his period. Suddenly the door opened and George was announced. Ferdy saw my surprise and gave me a little smile of triumph.

'I'm very glad you were able to come after all,' he said as he shook George's hand.

I saw him in a glance take in his great-nephew whom he saw today for the first time. George was very well dressed. He wore a short black coat, striped trousers, and the grey double-breasted waistcoat which at that time was the mode. You could only wear it with elegance if you were tall and thin and your belly was slightly concave. I felt sure that Ferdy knew exactly who George's tailor was and what haberdasher he went to and approved of them. George, so smart and trim, wearing his clothes so beautifully, certainly looked very handsome. We went down to luncheon. Ferdy had the social graces at his fingers' ends and he put the boy at his ease, but I saw that he was carefully appraising him; then, I do not know why, he began to tell some of his Jewish stories. He told them with gusto and with all his wonderful mimicry. I saw George flush, and though he laughed at them, I could see that it was with embarrassment. I wondered what on earth had induced Ferdy to be so tactless. But he was watching George and he told story after story. It looked as though he would never stop. I wondered if for some reason I could not grasp he was taking a malicious pleasure in the boy's obvious discomfiture. At last we went upstairs and to make things easier I asked Ferdy to play the piano. He played us three or four little waltzes. He had lost none of his exquisite lightness nor his sense of their lilting rhythm. Then he turned to George.

'Do you play?' he asked him.

'A little.'

'Won't you play something?'

'I'm afraid I only play classical music. I don't think it would interest you.'

Ferdy smiled slightly, but did not insist. I said it was time for me to go and George accompanied me.

'What a filthy old Jew,' he said as soon as we were in the street. 'I hated those stories of his.'

'They're his great stunt. He always tells them.'

'Would you if you were a Jew?'

I shrugged my shoulders.

'How is it you came to lunch after all?' I asked George.

He chuckled. He was a light-hearted creature, with a sense of humour, and he shook off the slight irritation his great-uncle had caused him.

'He went to see Granny. You don't know Granny, do you?'

'No.'

'She treats daddy like a kid in Etons. Granny said I was to go to lunch with great-uncle Ferdy and what Granny says goes.'

'I see.'

A week or to later George went to Munich to learn German. I happened then to go on a journey and it was not till the following spring that I was again in London. Soon after my arrival I found myself sitting next to Muriel Bland at dinner. I asked after George.

'He's still in Germany,' she said.

'I see in the papers that you're going to have a great beano at Tilby for his coming of age.'

'We're going to entertain the tenants and they're making George a presentation.'

She was less exuberant than usual, but I did not pay much attention to the fact. She led a strenuous life and it might be that she was tired. I knew she liked to talk of her son, so I continued.

'I suppose George has been having a grand time in Germany,' I said.

She did not answer for a moment and I gave her a glance. I was surprised to see that her eyes were filled with tears.

'I'm afraid George has gone mad,' she said.

'What *do* you mean?'

'We've been so frightfully worried. Freddy's so angry, he won't even discuss it. I don't know what we're going to do.'

Of course it immediately occurred to me that George, who, I supposed, like most young Englishmen sent to learn the language, had been put with a German family, had fallen in love with the daughter of the house and wanted to marry her. I had a pretty strong suspicion that the Blands were intent on his making a very grand marriage.

'Why, what's happened?' I asked.

'He wants to become a pianist.'

'A what?'

'A professional pianist.'

'What on earth put that idea in his head?'

'Heaven knows. We didn't know anything about it. We thought he was working for his exam. I went out to see him. I thought I'd like to know that he was getting on all right. Oh, my dear. He looks like nothing on earth. And he used to be so smart; I could have cried. He told me he wasn't going in for the exam, and had never had any intention of doing so; he'd only suggested the diplomatic service so that we'd let him go to Germany and he'd be able to study music.'

'But has he any talent?'

'Oh, that's neither here nor there. Even if he had the genius of Paderewski we couldn't have George traipsing around the country playing at concerts. No one can deny that I'm very artistic, and so is Freddy, we love music and we've always known a lot of artists, but George will have a very great position, it's out of the question. We've set our hearts on his going into Parliament. He'll be very rich one day. There's nothing he can't aspire to.'

'Did you point all that out to him?'

'Of course I did. He laughed at me. I told him he'd break his father's heart. He said his father could always fall back on Harry. Of course I'm devoted to Harry, and he's as clever as a monkey, but it was always understood that he was to go into the business; even though I am his mother I can see that he hasn't got the advantages that George has. Do you know what he said to me? He said that if his father would settle five pounds a week on him he would resign everything in Harry's favour and Harry could be his father's heir and succeed to the baronetcy and everything. It's too ridiculous. He said that if the Crown Prince of Roumania could abdicate a throne he didn't see why he couldn't abdicate a baronetcy. But you can't do that. Nothing can prevent him from being third baronet and if Freddy should be granted a peerage from succeeding to it at Freddy's death. Do you know, he even wants to drop the name of Bland and take some horrible German name.'

I could not help asking what.

'Bleikogel or something like that,' she answered.

That was a name I recognized. I remembered Ferdy telling me that Hannah Rabenstein had married Alfons Bleikogel who became eventually Sir Alfred Bland, first Baronet. It was all very strange. I wondered what had happened to the charming, so typically English boy I had seen only a few months before.

'Of course when I came home and told Freddy he was furious. I've never seen him so angry. He foamed at the mouth. He wired to George to come back immediately and George wired back to say he couldn't on account of his work.'

'Is he working?'

'From morning till night. That's the maddening part of it. He never did a stroke of work in his life. Freddy used to say he was born idle.'

'H'm.'

'Then Freddy wired to say that if he didn't come he'd stop his allowance and George wired back: "Stop it." That put the lid on. You don't know what Freddy can be when his back is up.'

I knew that Freddy had inherited a large fortune, but I knew also that he had immensely increased it, and I could well imagine that behind the courteous and amiable Squire of Tilby there was a ruthless man of affairs. He had been used to having his own way and I could believe that when crossed he would be hard and cruel.

'We'd been making George a very handsome allowance, but you know how frightfully extravagant he was. We didn't think he'd be able to hold out long and in point of fact within a month he wrote to Ferdy and asked him to lend him a hundred pounds. Ferdy went to my mother-in-law, she's his sister, you know, and asked her what it meant. Though they hadn't spoken for twenty years Freddy went to see him and begged him not to send George a penny, and he promised he wouldn't. I don't know how George has been making both ends meet. I'm sure Freddy's right, but I can't help being rather worried. If I hadn't given Freddy my word of honour that I wouldn't send him anything I think I'd have slipped a few notes in a letter in case of accident. I mean, it's awful to think that perhaps he hasn't got enough to eat.'

'It'll do him no harm to go short for a bit.'

'We were in an awful hole, you know. We'd made all sorts of preparations for his coming of age, and I'd issued hundreds of invitations. Suddenly George said he wouldn't come. I was simply frantic. I wrote and wired. I would have gone over to Germany only Freddy wouldn't let me. I practically went down on my bended knees to George. I begged him not to put us in such a humiliating position. I mean, it's the sort of thing it's so difficult to explain. Then my mother-in-law stepped in. You don't know her, do you? She's an extraordinary old woman. You'd never think she was Freddy's mother. She was German originally, but of very good family.'

'Oh?'

'To tell you the truth I'm rather frightened of her. She tackled Freddy and then she wrote to George herself. She said that if he'd come home for his twenty-first birthday she'd pay any debts he had in Munich and we'd all give a patient hearing to anything he had to say. He agreed to that and we're expecting him one day next week. But I'm not looking forward to it, I can tell you.'

She gave a deep sigh. When we were walking upstairs after dinner Freddy addressed me.

'I see Muriel has been telling you about George. The damned fool! I have no
patience with him. Fancy wanting to be a pianist. It's so ungentlemanly.'

'He's very young, you know,' I said soothingly.

'He's had things too easy for him. I've been much too indulgent. There's
never been a thing he wanted that I haven't given him. I'll learn him.'

The Blands had a discreet apprehension of the uses of advertisement and I
gathered from the papers that the celebrations at Tilby of George's twenty-first
birthday were conducted in accordance with the usage of English county
families. There was a dinner-party and a ball for the gentry and a collation and a
dance in marquees on the lawn for the tenants. Expensive bands were brought
down from London. In the illustrated papers were pictures of George
surrounded by his family being presented with a solid silver tea-set by the
tenantry. They had subscribed to have his portrait painted, but since his
absence from the country had made it impossible for him to sit, the tea-service
had been substituted. I read in the columns of the gossip writers that his father
had given him a hunter, his mother a gramophone that changed its own
records, his grandmother the dowager Lady Bland an *Encyclopaedia
Britannica*, and his great-uncle Ferdinand Rabenstein a *Virgin and Child* by
Pellegrino da Modena. I could not help observing that these gifts were bulky
and not readily convertible into cash. From Ferdy's presence at the festivities I
concluded that George's unaccountable vagary had effected a reconciliation
between uncle and nephew. I was right. Ferdy did not at all like the notion of
his great-nephew becoming a professional pianist. At the first hint of danger to
its prestige the family drew together and a united front was presented to
oppose George's designs. Since I was not there I only know from hearsay what
happened when the birthday celebrations were over. Ferdy told me something
and so did Muriel, and later George gave me his version. The Blands had very
much the impression that when George came home and found himself
occupying the centre of the stage, when, surrounded by splendour, he saw for
himself once more how much it meant to be the heir of a great estate, he would
weaken. They surrounded him with love. They flattered him. They hung on
his words. They counted on the goodness of his heart and thought that if they
were very kind to him he would not have the courage to cause them pain. They
seemed to take it for granted that he had no intention of going back to Germany
and in conversation included him in all their plans. George did not say very
much. He seemed to be enjoying himself. He did not open a piano. Things
looked as though they were going very well. Peace descended on the troubled
house. Then one day at luncheon when they were discussing a garden-party to
which they had all been asked for one day of the following week, George said
pleasantly:

'Don't count on me. I shan't be here.'

'Oh, George, why not?' asked his mother.

'I must get back to my work. I'm leaving for Munich on Monday.'

There was an awful pause. Everyone looked for something to say, but was
afraid of saying the wrong thing, and at last it seemed impossible to break it.
Luncheon was finished in silence. Then George went into the garden and the
others, old Lady Bland and Ferdy, Muriel and Sir Adolphus, into the
morning-room. There was a family council. Muriel wept. Freddy flew into a
temper. Presently from the drawing-room they heard the sound of someone
playing a nocturne of Chopin. It was George. It was as though now he had

announced his decision he had gone for comfort, rest, and strength to the instrument he loved. Freddy sprang to his feet.

'Stop that noise,' he cried. 'I won't have him play the piano in my house.'

Muriel rang for a servant and gave him a message.

'Will you tell Mr Bland that her ladyship has a bad headache and would he mind not playing the piano.'

Ferdy, the man of the world, was deputed to have a talk with George. He was authorized to make him certain promises if he would give up the idea of becoming a pianist. If he did not wish to go into the diplomatic service his father would not insist, but if he would stand for Parliament he was prepared to pay his election expenses, give him a flat in London, and make him an allowance of five thousand a year. I must say it was a handsome offer. I do not know what Ferdy said to the boy. I suppose he painted to him the life that a young man could lead in London on such an income. I am sure he made it very alluring. It availed nothing. All George asked was five pounds a week to be able to continue his studies and to be left alone. He was indifferent to the position that he might some day enjoy. He didn't want to hunt. He didn't want to shoot. He didn't want to be a Member of Parliament. He didn't want to be a millionaire. He didn't want to be a baronet. He didn't want to be a peer. Ferdy left him defeated and in a state of considerable exasperation.

After dinner that evening there was a battle royal. Freddy was a quick-tempered man, unused to opposition, and he gave George the rough side of his tongue. I gather that it was very rough indeed. The women who sought to restrain his violence were sternly silenced. Perhaps for the first time in his life Freddy would not listen to his mother. George was obstinate and sullen. He had made up his mind and if his father didn't like it he could lump it. Freddy was peremptory. He forbade George to go back to Germany. George answered that he was twenty-one and his own master. He would go where he chose. Freddy swore he would not give him a penny.

'All right, I'll earn money.'

'You! You've never done a stroke of work in your life. What do you expect to do to earn money?'

'Sell old clothes,' grinned George.

There was a gasp from all of them. Muriel was so taken aback that she said a stupid thing.

'Like a Jew?'

'Well, aren't I a Jew? And aren't you a Jewess and isn't daddy a Jew? We're all Jews, the whole gang of us, and everyone knows it and what the hell's the good of pretending we're not?'

Then a very dreadful thing happened. Freddy burst suddenly into tears. I'm afraid he didn't behave very much like Sir Adolphus Bland, Bart, M.P., and the good old English gentleman he so much wanted to be, but like an emotional Adolf Bleikogel who loved his son and wept with mortification because the great hopes he had set on him were brought to nothing and the ambition of his life was frustrated. He cried noisily with great loud sobs and pulled his beard and beat his breast and rocked to and fro. Then they all began to cry, old Lady Bland and Muriel, and Ferdy, who sniffed and blew his nose and wiped the tears streaming down his face, and even George cried. Of course it was very painful, but to our rough Anglo-Saxon temperament I am afraid it must seem also a trifle ridiculous. No one tried to console anybody else. They just sobbed and sobbed. It broke up the party.

But it had no result on the situation. George remained obdurate. His father would not speak to him. There were more scenes. Muriel sought to excite his pity; he was deaf to her piteous entreaties, he did not seem to mind if he broke her heart, he did not care two hoots if he killed his father. Ferdy appealed to him as a sportsman and a man of the world. George was flippant and indeed personally offensive. Old Lady Bland with her guttural German accent and strong common sense argued with him, but he would not listen to reason. It was she, however, who at last found a way out. She made George acknowledge that it was no use to throw away all the beautiful things the world laid at his feet unless he had talent. Of course he thought he had, but he might be mistaken. It was not worth while to be a second-rate pianist. His only excuse, his only justification, was genius. If he had genius his family had no right to stand in his way.

'You can't expect me to show genius already,' said George. 'I shall have to work for years.'

'Are you sure you are prepared for that?'

'It's my only wish in the world. I'll work like a dog. I only want to be given my chance.'

This was the proposition she made. His father was determined to give him nothing and obviously they could not let the boy starve. He had mentioned five pounds a week. Well, she was willing to give him that herself. He could go back to Germany and study for two years. At the end of that time he must come back and they would get some competent and disinterested person to hear him play, and if then that person said he showed promise of becoming a first-rate pianist no further obstacles would be placed in his way. He would be given every advantage, help, and encouragement. If on the other hand that person decided that his natural gifts were not such as to ensure ultimate success he must promise faithfully to give up all thoughts of making music his profession and in every way accede to his father's wishes. George could hardly believe his ears.

'Do you mean that, Granny?'

'I do.'

'But will daddy agree?'

'I vill see dat he does,' she answered.

George seized her in his arms and impetuously kissed her on both cheeks.

'Darling,' he cried.

'Ah, but de promise?'

He gave her his solemn word of honour that he would faithfully abide by the terms of the arrangement. Two days later he went back to Germany. Though his father consented unwillingly to his going, and indeed could not help doing so, he would not be reconciled to him and when he left refused to say good-bye to him.

I imagine that in no manner could he have caused himself such pain. I permit myself a trite remark. It is strange that men, inhabitants for so short a while of an alien and inhuman world, should go out of their way to cause themselves so much unhappiness.

George had stipulated that during his two years of study his family should not visit him, so that when Muriel heard some months before he was due to come home that I was passing through Munich on my way to Vienna, whither business called me, it was not unnatural that she should ask me to look him up. She was anxious to have first-hand information about him. She gave me

George's address and I wrote ahead, telling him I was spending a day in Munich, and asked him to lunch with me. His answer awaited me at the hotel. He said he worked all day and could not spare the time to lunch with me, but if I would come to his studio about six he would like to show me that and if I had nothing better to do would love to spend the evening with me. So soon after six I went to the address he gave me. He lived on the second floor of a large block of flats and when I came to his door I heard the sound of piano-playing. It stopped when I rang and George opened the door for me. I hardly recognized him. He had grown very fat. His hair was extremely long, it curled all over his head in picturesque confusion; and he had certainly not shaved for three days. He wore a grimy pair of Oxford bags, a tennis shirt, and slippers. He was not very clean and his finger-nails were rimmed with black. It was a startling change from the spruce, slim youth so elegantly dressed in such beautiful clothes that I had last seen. I could not but think it would be a shock to Ferdy to see him now. The studio was large and bare; on the walls were three or four unframed canvases of a highly cubist nature, there were several arm-chairs much the worse for wear, and a grand piano. Books were littered about and old newspapers and art magazines. It was dirty and untidy and there was a frowzy smell of stale beer and stale smoke.

'Do you live here alone?' I asked.

'Yes, I have a woman who comes in twice a week and cleans up. But I make my own breakfast and lunch.'

'Can you cook?'

'Oh, I only have bread and cheese and a bottle of beer for lunch. I dine at a *Bierstube*.'

It was pleasant to discover that he was very glad to see me. He seemed in great spirits and extremely happy. He asked after his relations and we talked of one thing and another. He had a lesson twice a week and for the rest of the time practised. He told me that he worked ten hours a day.

'That's a change,' I said.

He laughed.

'Daddy said I was born tired. I wasn't really lazy. I didn't see the use of working at things that bored me.'

I asked him how he was getting on with the piano. He seemed to be satisfied with his progress and I begged him to play to me.

'Oh, not now, I'm all in, I've been at it all day. Let's go out and dine and come back here later and then I'll play. I generally go to the same place, there are several students I know there, and it's rather fun.'

Presently we set out. He put on socks and shoes and a very old golf coat, and we walked together through the wide quiet streets. It was a brisk cold day. His step was buoyant. He looked round him with a sigh of delight.

'I love Munich,' he said. 'It's the only city in the world where there's art in the very air you breathe. After all, art is the only thing that matters, isn't it? I loathe the idea of going home.'

'All the same I'm afraid you'll have to.'

'I know. I'll go all right, but I'm not going to think about it till the time comes.'

'When you do, you might do worse than get a haircut. If you don't mind my saying so you look almost too artistic to be convincing.'

'You English, you're such Philistines,' he said.

He took me to a rather large restaurant in a side street, crowded even at that early hour with people dining, and furnished heavily in the German medieval style. A table covered with a red cloth, well away from the air, was reserved for George and his friends and when we went to it four or five youths were at it. There was a Pole studying Oriental languages, a student of philosophy, a painter (I suppose the author of George's cubist pictures), a Swede, and a young man who introduced himself to me, clicking his heels, as Hans Reiting, *Dichter*, namely Hans Reiting, poet. Not one of them was more than twenty-two and I felt a trifle out of it. They all addressed George as *du* and I noticed that his German was extremely fluent. I had not spoken it for some time and mine was rusty, so that I could not take much part in the lively conversation. But nevertheless I thoroughly enjoyed myself. They ate sparingly, but drank a good deal of beer. They talked of art and women. They were very revolutionary and though gay very much in earnest. They were contemptuous of everyone you had ever heard of, and the only point on which they all agreed was that in this topsy-turvy world only the vulgar could hope for success. They argued points of technique with animation, and contradicted one another, and shouted and were obscene. They had a grand time.

At about eleven George and I walked back to his studio. Munich is a city that frolics demurely and except about the Marienplatz the streets were still and empty. When we got in he took off his coat and said:

'Now I'll play to you.'

I sat in one of the dilapidated arm-chairs and a broken spring stuck into my behind, but I made myself as comfortable as I could. George played Chopin. I know very little of music and that is one of the reasons for which I have found this story difficult to write. When I go to a concert at the Queen's Hall and in the intervals read the programme it is all Greek to me. I know nothing of harmony and counterpoint. I shall never forget how humiliated I felt once when, having come to Munich for a Wagner festival, I went to a wonderful performance of *Tristan und Isolde* and never heard a note of it. The first few bars sent me off and I began to think of what I was writing, my characters leapt into life and I heard their long conversations, I suffered their pains and was a party to their joy; the years swept by and all sorts of things happened to me, the spring brought me its rapture and in the winter I was cold and hungry; and I loved and I hated and I died. I suppose there were intervals in which I walked round and round the garden and probably ate *Schinken-Brödchen* and drank beer, but I have no recollection of them. The only thing I know is that when the curtain for the last time fell I woke with a start. I had had a wonderful time, but I could not help thinking it was very stupid of me to come such a long way and spend so much money if I couldn't pay attention to what I heard and saw.

I knew most of the things George played. They were the familiar pieces of concert programmes. He played with a great deal of dash. Then he played Beethoven's *Appassionata*. I used to play it myself when I played the piano (very badly) in my far distant youth and I still knew every note of it. Of course it is a classic and a great work, it would be foolish to deny it, but I confess that at this time of day it leaves me cold. It is like *Paradise Lost*, splendid, but a trifle stolid. This too George played with vigour. He sweated profusely. At first I could not make out what was the matter with his playing, something did not seem to me quite right, and then it struck me that the two hands did not exactly synchronize, so that there was ever so slight an interval between the bass and the treble; but I repeat, I am ignorant of these things; what disconcerted me might have been merely the effect of his having drunk a good deal of beer that evening or indeed only my fancy. I said all I could think of to praise him.

'Of course I know I need a lot more work. I'm only a beginner, but I know I can do it. I feel it in my bones. It'll take me ten years, but then I shall be a pianist.'

He was tired and came away from the piano. It was after midnight and I suggested going, but he would not hear of it. He opened a couple of bottles of beer and lit his pipe. He wanted to talk.

'Are you happy here?' I asked him.

'Very,' he answered gravely. 'I'd like to stay for ever. I've never had such fun in my life. This evening, for instance. Wasn't it grand?'

'It was very jolly. But one can't go on leading the student's life. Your friends here will grow older and go away.'

'Others'll come. There are always students here and people like that.'

'Yes, but you'll grow older too. Is there anything more lamentable than the middle-aged man who tries to go on living the undergraduate's life? The old fellow who wants to be a boy among boys, and tries to persuade himself that they'll accept him as one of themselves—how ridiculous he is. It can't be done.'

'I feel so at home here. My poor father wants me to be an English gentleman. It gives me gooseflesh. I'm not a sportsman. I don't care a damn for hunting and shooting and playing cricket. I was only acting.'

'You gave a very natural performance.'

'It wasn't till I came here that I knew it wasn't real. I loved Eton, and Oxford was a riot, but all the same I knew I didn't belong. I played the part all right, because acting's in my blood, but there was always something in me that wasn't satisfied. The house in Grosvenor Square is a freehold and daddy paid a hundred and eighty thousand pounds for Tilby; I don't know if you understand what I mean, I felt they were just furnished houses we'd taken for the season and one of these days we'd pack up and the real owners would come back.'

I listened to him attentively, but I wondered how much he was describing what he had obscurely felt and how much he imagined now in his changed circumstances that he had felt.

'I used to hate hearing great-uncle Ferdy tell his Jewish stories. I thought it so damned mean. I understand now; it was a safety valve. My God, the strain of being a man about town. It's easier for daddy, he can play the old English squire at Tilby, but in the City he can be himself. He's all right. I've taken the make-up off and my stage clothes and at last I can be my real self too. What a relief! You know, I don't like English people. I never really know where I am with you. You're so dull and conventional. You never let yourselves go. There's no freedom in you, freedom of the soul, and you're such funks. There's nothing in the world you're so frightened of as doing the wrong thing.'

'Don't forget that you're English yourself, George,' I murmured.

He laughed.

'I? I'm not English. I haven't got a drop of English blood in me. I'm a Jew and you know it, and a German Jew into the bargain. I don't want to be English. I want to be a Jew. My friends are Jews. You don't know how much more easy I feel with them. I can be myself. We did everything we could to avoid Jews at home; Mummy, because she was blonde, thought she could get away with it and pretended she was a Gentile. What rot! D'you know, I have a lot of fun wandering about the Jewish parts of Munich and looking at the people. I went to Frankfort once, there are a lot of them there, and I walked

about and looked at the frowzy old men with their hooked noses and the fat
women with their false hair. I felt such a sympathy for them, I felt I belonged to
them, I could have kissed them. When they looked at me I wondered if they
knew that I was one of them. I wish to God I knew Yiddish. I'd like to become
friends with them, and go into their houses and eat Kosher food and all that sort
of thing. I wanted to go to a synagogue, but I was afraid I'd do the wrong thing
and be kicked out. I like the smell of the Ghetto and the sense of life, and the
mystery and the dust and the squalor and the romance. I shall never get the
longing for it out of my head now. That's the real thing. All the rest is only
pretence.'

'You'll break your father's heart,' I said.

'It's his or mine. Why can't he let me go? There's Harry. Harry would love to
be squire of Tilby. He'd be an English gentleman all right. You know,
mummy's set her heart on my marrying a Christian. Harry would love to. He'll
found the good old English family all right. After all, I ask so little. I only want
five pounds a week, and they can keep the title and the park and the
Gainsboroughs and the whole bag of tricks.'

'Well, the fact remains that you gave your solemn word of honour to go back
after two years.'

'I'll go back all right,' he said sullenly. 'Lea Makart has promised to come
and hear me play.'

'What'll you do if she says you're no good?'

'Shoot myself,' he said gaily.

'What nonsense,' I answered in the same tone.

'Do *you* feel at home in England?'

'No,' I said, 'but then I don't feel at home anywhere else.'

But he was quite naturally not interested in me.

'I loathe the idea of going back. Now that I know what life has to offer I
wouldn't be an English country gentleman for anything in the world. My God,
the boredom of it!'

'Money's a very nice thing and I've always understood it's very pleasant to be
an English peer.'

'Money means nothing to me. I want none of the things it can buy, and I
don't happen to be a snob.'

It was growing very late and I had to get up early next day. It seemed
unnecessary for me to pay too much attention to what George said. It was the
sort of nonsense a young man might very well indulge in when thrown
suddenly among painters and poets. Art is strong wine and needs a strong head
to carry it. The divine fire burns most efficiently in those who temper its fury
with horse sense. After all, George was not twenty-three yet. Time teaches.
And when all was said and done his future was no concern of mine. I bade him
good night and walked back to my hotel. The stars were shining in the
indifferent sky. I left Munich in the morning.

I did not tell Muriel on my return to London what George had said to me, or
what he looked like, but contented myself with assuring her that he was well
and happy, working very hard, and seemed to be leading a virtuous and sober
life. Six months later he came home. Muriel asked me to go down to Tilby for
the week-end; Ferdy was bringing Lea Makart to hear George play and he
particularly wished me to be there. I accepted. Muriel met me at the station.

'How did you find George?' I asked.

'He's very fat, but he seems in great spirits. I think he's pleased to be back again. He's been very sweet to his father.'

'I'm glad of that.'

'Oh, my dear, I do hope Lea Makart will say he's no good. It'll be such a relief to all of us.'

'I'm afraid it'll be a terrible disappointment to him.'

'Life is full of disappointments,' said Muriel crisply. 'But one learns to put up with them.'

I gave her a smile of amusement. We were sitting in a Rolls, and there was a footman as well as a chauffeur on the box. She wore a string of pearls that had probably cost forty thousand pounds. I recollected that in the birthday honours Sir Adolphus Bland had not been one of the three gentlemen on whom the King had been pleased to confer a peerage.

Lea Makart was able to make only a flying visit. She was playing that evening at Brighton and would motor over to Tilby on the Sunday morning for luncheon. She was returning to London the same day because she had a concert in Manchester on the Monday. George was to play in the course of the afternoon.

He's practising very hard,' his mother told me. 'That's why he didn't come with me to meet you.'

We turned in at the park gates and drove up the imposing avenue of elms that led to the house. I found that there was no party.

I met the dowager Lady Bland for the first time. I had always been curious to see her. I had had in my mind's eye a somewhat sensational picture of an old, old Jewish woman who lived alone in her grand house in Portland Place, and, with a finger in every pie, ruled her family with a despotic hand. She did not disappoint me. She was of commanding presence, rather tall, and stout without being corpulent. Her countenance was markedly Hebraic. She wore a rather heavy moustache and a wig of a peculiarly metallic brown. Her dress was very grand, of black brocade, and she had a row of large diamond stars on her breast and round her neck a chain of diamonds. Diamond rings gleamed on her wrinkled hands. She spoke in a rather harsh voice and with a strong German accent. When I was introduced to her she fixed me with shining eyes. She summed me up with dispatch and to my fancy at all events made no attempt to conceal from me that the judgement she formed was unfavourable.

'You have known my brother Ferdinand for many years, is it not so?' she said, rolling a guttural R. 'My brother Ferdinand has always moved in very good society. Where is Sir Adolphus, Muriel? Does he know your guest is arrived? And will you not send for George? If he does not know his pieces by now he will not know them by tomorrow.'

Muriel explained that Freddy was finishing a round of golf with his secretary and that she had had George told I was there. Lady Bland looked as though she thought Muriel's replies highly unsatisfactory and turned again to me.

'My daughter-in-law tells me you have been in Italy?'

'Yes, I've only just come back.'

'It is a beautiful country. How is the King?'

I said I did not know.

'I used to know him when he was a little boy. He was not very strong then. His mother, Queen Margherita, was a great friend of mine. They thought he would never marry. The Duchess of Aosta was very angry when he fell in love with that Princess of Montenegro.'

She seemed to belong to some long-past period of history, but she was very alert and I imagine that little escaped her beady eyes. Freddy, very spruce in plus-fours, presently came in. It was amusing and yet a little touching to see this grey-bearded man, as a rule somewhat domineering, so obviously on his best behaviour with the old lady. He called her Mamma. Then George came in. He was as fat as ever, but he had taken my advice and had his hair cut; he was losing his boyish looks, but he was a powerful and well-set-up young man. It was good to see the pleasure he took in his tea. He ate quantities of sandwiches and great hunks of cake. He had still a boy's appetite. His father watched him with a tender smile and as I looked at him I could not be surprised at the attachment which they all so obviously felt for him. He had an ingenuousness, a charm, and an enthusiasm which were certainly very pleasant. There was about him a generosity of demeanour, a frankness, and a natural cordiality which could not but make people take to him. I do not know whether it was owing to a hint from his grandmother or merely of his own good nature, but it was plain that he was going out of his way to be nice to his father; and in his father's soft eyes, in the way he hung upon the boy's words, in his pleased, proud, and happy look, you felt how bitterly the estrangement of the last two years had weighed on him. He adored George.

We played golf in the morning, a three-ball match, since Muriel, having to go to Mass, could not join us, and at one Ferdy arrived in Lea Makart's car. We sat down to luncheon. Of course Lea Makart's reputation was well known to me. She was acknowledged to be the greatest woman pianist in Europe. She was a very old friend of Ferdy's, who with his interest and patronage had greatly helped her at the beginning of her career, and it was he who had arranged for her to come and give her opinion of George's chances. At one time I went as often as I could to hear her play. She had no affectations; she played as a bird sings, without any appearance of effort, very naturally, and the silvery notes dripped from her light fingers in a curiously spontaneous manner, so that it gave you the impression that she was improvising those complicated rhythms. They used to tell me that her technique was wonderful. I could never make up my mind how much the delight her playing gave me was due to her person. In those days she was the most ethereal thing you could imagine, and it was surprising that a creature so sylphlike should be capable of so much power. She was very slight, pale, with enormous eyes and magnificent black hair, and at the piano she had a childlike wistfulness that was most appealing. She was very beautiful in a hardly human way and when she played, a little smile on her closed lips, she seemed to be remembering things she had heard in another world. Now, however, a woman in the early forties, she was sylphlike no more; she was stout and her face had broadened; she had no longer that lovely remoteness, but the authority of her long succession of triumphs. She was brisk, business-like, and somewhat overwhelming. Her vitality lit her with a natural spotlight as his sanctity surrounds the saint with a halo. She was not interested in anything very much but her own affairs, but since she had humour and knew the world she was able to invest them with gaiety. She held the conversation, but did not absorb it. George talked little. Every now and then she gave him a glance, but did not try to draw him in. I was the only Gentile at the table. All but old Lady Bland spoke perfect English, yet I could not help feeling that they did not speak like English people; I think they rounded their vowels more than we do, they certainly spoke louder, and the words seemed not to fall, but to gush from their lips. I think if I had been in another room where I could hear the tone but not the words of their speech I should have thought it was in a foreign language that they were conversing. The effect was slightly disconcerting.

Lea Makart wished to set out for London at about six, so it was arranged that George should play at four. Whatever the result of the audition, I felt that I, a stranger in the circle which her departure must render exclusively domestic, would be in the way and so, pretending an early engagement in town next morning, I asked her if she would take me with her in her car.

At a little before four we all wandered into the drawing-room. Old Lady Bland sat on a sofa with Ferdy; Freddy, Muriel, and I made ourselves comfortable in arm-chairs; and Lea Makart sat by herself. She chose instinctively a high-backed Jacobean chair that had somewhat the air of a throne, and in a yellow dress, with her olive skin, she looked very handsome. She had magnificent eyes. She was very much made up and her mouth was scarlet.

George gave no sign of nervousness. He was already seated at the piano when I went in with his father and mother, and he watched us quietly settling ourselves down. He gave me the shadow of a smile. When he saw that we were all at our ease he began to play. He played Chopin. He played two waltzes that were familiar to me, a polonaise and an *étude*. He played with a great deal of brio. I wish I knew music well enough to give an exact description of his playing. It had strength, and a youthful exuberance, but I felt that he missed what to me is the peculiar charm of Chopin, the tenderness, the nervous melancholy, the wistful gaiety and the slightly faded romance that reminds me always of an Early Victorian keepsake. And again I had the vague sensation, so slight that it almost escaped me, that the two hands did not quite synchronize. I looked at Ferdy and saw him give his sister a look of faint surprise. Muriel's eyes were fixed on the pianist, but presently she dropped them and for the rest of the time stared at the floor. His father looked at him too, and his eyes were steadfast, but unless I was much mistaken he went pale and his face betrayed something like dismay. Music was in the blood of all of them, all their lives they had heard the greatest pianists in the world, and they judged with instinctive precision. The only person whose face betrayed no emotion was Lea Makart. She listened very attentively. She was as still as an image in a niche.

At last he stopped and turning round on his seat faced her. He did not speak.

'What is it you want me to tell you?' she asked.

They looked into one another's eyes.

'I want you to tell me whether I have any chance of becoming in time a pianist in the first rank.'

'Not in a thousand years.'

For a moment there was dead silence. Freddy's head sank and he looked down at the carpet at his feet. His wife put out her hand and took his. But George continued to look steadily at Lea Makart.

'Ferdy has told me the circumstances,' she said at last. 'Don't think I'm influenced by them. Nothing of this is very important.' She made a great sweeping gesture that took in the magnificent room with the beautiful things it contained and all of us. 'If I thought you had in you the makings of an artist I shouldn't hesitate to beseech you to give up everything for art's sake. Art is the only thing that matters. In comparison with art, wealth and rank and power are not worth a straw.' She gave us a look so sincere that it was void of insolence.

'We are the only people who count. We give the world significance. You are only our raw material.'

I was not too pleased to be included with the rest under that heading, but that is neither here nor there.

'Of course I can see that you've worked very hard. Don't think it's been wasted. It will always be a pleasure to you to be able to play the piano and it will enable you to appreciate great playing as no ordinary person can hope to do. Look at your hands. They're not a pianist's hands.'

Involuntarily I glanced at George's hands. I had never noticed them before. I was astounded to see how podgy they were and how short and stumpy the fingers.

'Your ear is not quite perfect. I don't think you can ever hope to be more than a very competent amateur. In art the difference between the amateur and the professional is immeasurable.'

George did not reply. Except for his pallor no one would have known that he was listening to the blasting of all his hopes. The silence that fell was quite awful. Lea Makart's eyes suddenly filled with tears.

'But don't take my opinion alone,' she said. 'After all, I'm not infallible. Ask somebody else. You know how good and generous Paderewski is. I'll write to him about you and you can go down and play to him. I'm sure he'll hear you.'

George now gave a little smile. He had very good manners and whatever he was feeling did not want to make the situation too difficult for others.

'I don't think that's necessary, I am content to accept your verdict. To tell you the truth it's not so very different from my master's in Munich.'

He got up from the piano and lit a cigarette. It eased the strain. The others moved a little in their chairs. Lea Makart smiled at George.

'Shall I play to you?' she said.

'Yes, do.'

She got up and went to the piano. She took off the rings with which her fingers were laden. She played Bach. I do not know the names of the pieces, but I recognized the stiff ceremonial of the frenchified little German courts and the sober, thrifty comfort of the burghers, and the dancing on the village green, the green trees that looked like Christmas trees, and the sunlight on the wide German country, and a tender cosiness; and in my nostrils there was a warm scent of the soil and I was conscious of a sturdy strength that seemed to have its roots deep in mother earth, and of an elemental power that was timeless and had no home in space. She played beautifully, with a soft brilliance that made you think of the full moon shining at dusk in the summer sky. With another part of me I watched the others and I saw how intensely they were conscious of the experience. They were rapt. I wished with all my heart that I could get from music the wonderful exaltation that possessed them. She stopped, a smile hovered on her lips, and she put on her rings. George gave a little chuckle.

'That clinches it, I fancy,' he said.

The servants brought in tea and after tea Lea Makart and I bade the company farewell and got into the car. We drove up to London. She talked all the way, if not brilliantly at all events with immense gusto; she told me of her early years in Manchester and of the struggle of her beginnings. She was very interesting. She never even mentioned George; the episode was of no consequence, it was finished and she thought of it no more.

We little knew what was happening at Tilby. When we left George went out on the terrace and presently his father joined him. Freddy had won the day, but he was not happy. With his more than feminine sensitiveness he felt all that George was feeling, and George's anguish simply broke his heart. He had never loved his son more than then. When he appeared George greeted him with a little smile. Freddy's voice broke. In a sudden and overwhelming emotion he found it in him to surrender the fruits of his victory.

'Look here, old boy,' he said, 'I can't bear to think that you've had such a disappointment. Would you like to go back to Munich for another year and then see?'

George shook his head.

'No, it wouldn't be any good. I've had my chance. Let's call it a day.'

'Try not to take it too hard.'

'You see, the only thing in the world I want is to be a pianist. And there's nothing doing. It's a bit thick if you come to think of it.'

George, trying so hard to be brave, smiled wanly.

'Would you like to go round the world? You can get one of your Oxford pals to go with you and I'll pay all the expenses. You've been working very hard for a long time.'

'Thanks awfully, daddy, we'll talk about it. I'm just going for a stroll now.'

'Shall I come with you?'

'I'd rather go alone.'

Then George did a strange thing. He put his arm round his father's neck, and kissed him on the lips. He gave a funny little moved laugh and walked away. Freddy went back to the drawing-room. His mother, Ferdy, and Muriel were sitting there.

'Freddy, why don't you marry the boy?' said the old lady. 'He is twenty-three. It would take his mind off his troubles and when he is married and has a baby he will soon settle down like everybody else.'

'Whom is he to marry, mamma?' asked Sir Adolphus, smiling.

'That's not so difficult. Lady Frielinghausen came to see me the other day with her daughter Violet. She is a very nice maiden and she will have money of her own. Lady Frielinghausen gave me to understand that her Sir Jacob would come down very handsome if Violet made a good match.'

Muriel flushed.

'I hate Lady Frielinghausen. George is much too young to marry. He can afford to marry anyone he likes.'

Old Lady Bland gave her daughter a strange look.

'You are a very foolish girl, Miriam,' she said, using the name Muriel had long discarded. 'As long as I am here I shall not allow you to commit a foolishness.'

She knew as well as if Muriel had said it in so many words that she wanted George to marry a Gentile, but she knew also that so long as she was alive neither Freddy nor his wife would dare to suggest it.

But George did not go for a walk. Perhaps because the shooting season was about to open he took it into his head to go into the gun-room. He began to clean the gun that his mother had given him on his twentieth birthday. No one had used it since he went to Germany. Suddenly the servants were startled by a report. When they went into the gun-room they found George lying on the floor shot through the heart. Apparently the gun had been loaded and George while playing about with it had accidentally shot himself. One reads of such accidents in the paper often.

The
Creative Impulse

◆

I suppose that very few people know how Mrs Albert Forrester came to write *The Achilles Statue*; and since it has been acclaimed as one of the great novels of our time I cannot but think that a brief account of the circumstances that gave it birth must be of interest to all serious students of literature; and indeed, if, as the critics say, this is a book that will live, the following narrative, serving a better purpose than to divert an idle hour, may be regarded by the historian of the future as a curious footnote to the literary annals of our day.

Everyone of course remembers the success that attended the publication of *The Achilles Statue*. Month after month printers were kept busy printing, binders were kept busy binding, edition after edition; and the publishers, both in England and America, were hard put to it to fulfil the pressing orders of the booksellers. It was promptly translated into every European tongue and it has been recently announced that it will soon be possible to read it in Japanese and in Urdu. But it had previously appeared serially in magazines on both sides of the Atlantic and from the editors of these Mrs Albert Forrester's agent had wrung a sum that can only be described as thumping. A dramatization of the work was made, which ran for a season in New York, and there is little doubt that when the play is produced in London it will have an equal success. The film rights have been sold at a great price. Though the amount that Mrs Albert Forrester is reputed (in literary circles) to have made is probably exaggerated, there can be no doubt that she will have earned enough money from this one book to save her for the rest of her life from any financial anxiety.

It is not often that a book meets with equal favour from the public and the critics, and that she, of all persons, had (if I may so put it) squared the circle must have proved the more gratifying to Mrs Albert Forrester, since, though she had received the commendation of the critics in no grudging terms (and indeed had come to look upon it as her due) the public had always remained strangely insensible to her merit. Each work she published, a slender volume beautifully printed and bound in white buckram, was hailed as a masterpiece, always to the length of a column, and in the weekly reviews which you see only in the dusty library of a very long-established club even to the extent of a page; and well-read persons read and praised it. But well-read persons apparently do not buy books, and she did not sell. It was indeed a scandal that so distinguished an author, with an imagination so delicate and a style so exquisite, should remain neglected of the vulgar. In America she was almost completely unknown; and though Mr Carl van Vechten had written an article berating the public for its obtuseness, the public remained callous. Her agent, a warm admirer of her genius, had blackmailed an American publisher into taking two of her books by refusing, unless he did so, to let him have others (trashy novels doubtless) that he badly wanted, and they had been duly published. The reception they received from the press was flattering and showed that in America the best minds were sensitive to her talent; but when it came to the third book the American publisher (in the coarse way publishers have) told the agent that any money he had to spare he preferred to spend on synthetic gin.

Since *The Achilles Statue* Mrs Albert Forrester's previous books have been republished (and Mr Carl van Vechten has written another article pointing out sadly, but firmly, that he had drawn the attention of the reading world to the merits of this exceptional writer fully fifteen years ago), and they have been so widely advertised that they can scarcely have escaped the cultured reader's attention. It is unnecessary, therefore, for me to give an account of them; and it would certainly be no more than cold potatoes after those two subtle articles by Mr Carl van Vechten. Mrs Albert Forrester began to write early. Her first work (a volume of elegies) appeared when she was a maiden of eighteen; and from then on she published, every two or three years, for she had too exalted a conception of her art to hurry her production, a volume either of verse or prose. When *The Achilles Statue* was written she had reached the respectable age of fifty-seven, so that it will be readily surmised that the number of her works was considerable. She had given the world half a dozen volumes of verse, published under Latin titles, such as *Felicitas, Pax Maris*, and *Aes Triplex*, all of the graver kind, for her muse, disinclined to skip on a light, fantastic toe, trod a somewhat solemn measure. She remained faithful to the Elegy, and the Sonnet claimed much of her attention; but her chief distinction was to revive the Ode, a form of poetry that the poets of the present day somewhat neglect; and it may be asserted with confidence that her *Ode to President Fallières* will find a place in every anthology of English verse. It is admirable not only for the noble sonority of its rhythms, but also for its felicitous description of the pleasant land of France. Mrs Albert Forrester wrote of the valley of the Loire with its memories of du Bellay, of Chartres and the jewelled windows of its cathedral, of the sun-swept cities of Provence, with a sympathy all the more remarkable since she had never penetrated further into France than Boulogne, which she visited shortly after her marriage on an excursion steamer from Margate. But the physical mortification of being extremely seasick and the intellectual humiliation of discovering that the inhabitants of that popular seaside resort could not understand her fluent and idiomatic French made her determine not to expose herself a second time to experiences that were at once undignified and unpleasant; and she never again embarked on the treacherous element which she, however, sang (*Pax Maris*) in numbers both grave and sweet.

There are some fine passages too in the *Ode to Woodrow Wilson*, and I regret that, owing to a change in her sentiments towards that no doubt excellent man, the author decided not to reprint it. But I think it must be admitted that Mrs Albert Forrester's most distinguished work was in prose. She wrote several volumes of brief, but perfectly constructed, essays on such subjects as Autumn in Sussex, Queen Victoria, Death, Spring in Norfolk, Georgian Architecture, Monsieur de Diaghileff, and Dante; she also wrote works, both erudite and whimsical, on the Jesuit Architecture of the Seventeenth Century and on the Literary Aspect of the Hundred Years War. It was her prose that gained her that body of devoted admirers, fit though few, as with her rare gift of phrase she herself put it that proclaimed her the greatest master of the English language that this century has seen. She admitted herself that it was her style, sonorous yet racy, polished yet eloquent, that was her strong point; and it was only in her prose that she had occasion to exhibit the delicious, but restrained, humour that her readers found so irresistible. It was not a humour of ideas, nor even a humour of words; it was much more subtle than that, it was a humour of punctuation: in a flash of inspiration she had discovered the comic possibilities of the semi-colon, and of this she had made abundant and exquisite use. She was able to place it in such a way that if you were a person of culture with a keen sense of humour, you did not exactly laugh through a horse-collar, but you giggled delightedly, and the greater your culture the more delightedly you giggled. Her friends said that it made every other form of humour coarse and exaggerated. Several writers had tried to imitate her; but in vain: whatever else you might say about Mrs Albert Forrester you were bound to admit that she was able to get every ounce of humour out of the semi-colon and no one else could get within a mile of her.

Mrs Albert Forrester lived in a flat not far from the Marble Arch, which combined the advantage of a good address and a moderate rent. It had a handsome drawing-room on the street and a large bedroom for Mrs Albert Forrester, a darkish dining-room at the back, and a small poky bedroom, next door to the kitchen, for Mr Albert Forrester, who paid the rent. It was in the handsome drawing-room that Mrs Albert Forrester every Tuesday afternoon received her friends. It was a severe and chaste apartment. On the walls was a paper designed by William Morris himself, and on this, in plain black frames, mezzotints collected before mezzotints grew expensive; the furniture was of the Chippendale period, but for the roll-top desk, vaguely Louis XVI in character, at which Mrs Albert Forrester wrote her works. This was pointed out to visitors the first time they came to see her, and there were few who looked at it without emotion. The carpet was thick and the lights discreet. Mrs Albert Forrester sat in a straight-backed grandfather's chair covered with red damask. There was nothing ostentatious about it, but since it was the only comfortable chair in the room it set her apart as it were and above her guests. Tea was dispensed by a female of uncertain age, silent and colourless, who was never introduced to anyone but who was known to look upon it as a privilege to be allowed to save Mrs Albert Forrester from the irksome duty of pouring out tea. She was thus able to devote herself entirely to conversation, and it must be admitted that her conversation was excellent. It was not sprightly; and since it is difficult to indicate punctuation in speech it may have seemed to some slightly lacking in humour, but it was of wide range, solid, instructive, and interesting. Mrs Albert Forrester was well acquainted with social science, jurisprudence, and theology. She had read much and her memory was retentive. She had a pretty gift for quotation, which is a serviceable substitute for wit, and having for thirty years known more or less intimately a great many distinguished people she had a great many interesting anecdotes to tell, which she placed with tact and which she did not repeat more than was pardonable. Mrs Albert Forrester had the gift of attracting the most varied persons and you were liable at one and the same time to meet in her drawing-room an ex-Prime Minister, a newspaper proprietor, and the ambassador of a First Class Power. I always imagined that these great people came because they thought that here they rubbed shoulders with Bohemia, but with a Bohemia sufficiently neat and clean for them to be in no danger that the dirt would come off on them. Mrs Albert Forrester was deeply interested in politics and I myself heard a Cabinet Minister tell her frankly that she had a masculine intelligence. She had been opposed to Female Suffrage, but when it was at last granted to women she began to dally with the idea of going into Parliament. Her difficulty was that she did not know which party to choose.

'After all,' she said, with a playful shrug of her somewhat massive shoulders, 'I cannot form a party of one.'

Like many serious patriots, in her inability to know for certain which way the cat would jump she held her political opinions in suspense; but of late she had been definitely turning towards Labour as the best hope of the country, and if a safe seat were offered her it was felt fairly certain that she would not hesitate to come out into the open as a champion of the oppressed proletariat.

Her drawing-room was always open to foreigners, to Czecho-Slovaks, Italians, and Frenchmen, if they were distinguished, and to Americans even if they were obscure. But she was not a snob and you seldom met there a duke unless he was of a peculiarly serious turn and a peeress only if in addition to her rank she had the passport of some small social solecism such as having been divorced, written a novel, or forged a cheque, which might give her claim to Mrs Albert Forrester's catholic sympathies. She did not much care for painters, who were shy and silent; and musicians did not interest her: even if they consented to play, and if they were celebrated they were too often reluctant, their music was a hindrance to conversation: if people wanted music they could go to a concert; for her part she preferred the more subtle music of the soul. But her hospitality to writers, especially if they were promising and little known, was warm and constant. She had an eye for budding talent and there were few of the famous writers who from time to time drank a dish of tea with her whose first efforts she had not encouraged and whose early steps she had not guided. Her own position was too well assured for her to be capable of envy, and she had heard the word genius attached to her name too often to feel a trace of jealousy because the talents of others brought them a material success that was denied to her.

Mrs Albert Forrester, confident in the judgement of posterity, could afford to be disinterested. With these elements then it is no wonder that she had succeeded in creating something as near the French salon of the eighteenth century as our barbarous nation has ever reached. To be invited to 'eat a bun and drink a cup of tea on Tuesday' was a privilege that few failed to recognize; and when you sat on your Chippendale chair in the discreetly lit but austere room, you could not but feel that you were living literary history. The American Ambassador once said to Mrs Albert Forrester:

'A cup of tea with you, Mrs Forrester, is one of the richest intellectual treats which it has ever been my lot to enjoy.'

It was indeed on occasion a trifle overwhelming. Mrs Albert Forrester's taste was so perfect, she so inevitably admired the right thing and made the just observation about it, that sometimes you almost gasped for air. For my part I found it prudent to fortify myself with a cocktail or two before I exposed myself to the rarefied atmosphere of her society. Indeed, I very nearly found myself for ever excluded from it, for one afternoon, presenting myself at the door, instead of asking the maid who opened it: 'Is Mrs Forrester at home?' I asked: 'Is there Divine Service today?'

Of course it was said in pure inadvertence, but it was unfortunate that the maid sniggered, and one of Mrs Albert Forrester's most devoted admirers, Ellen Hannaway, happened to be at the moment in the hall taking off her goloshes. She told my hostess what I had said before I got into the drawing-room, and as I entered Mrs Albert Forrester fixed me with an eagle eye.

'Why did you ask if there was Divine Service today?' she inquired.

I explained that I was absent-minded, but Mrs Albert Forrester held me with a gaze that I can only describe as compelling.

'Do you mean to suggest that my parties are . . .' she searched for a word. 'Sacramental?'

I did not know what she meant, but did not like to show my ignorance before so many clever people, and I decided that the only thing was to seize my trowel and the butter.

'Your parties are like you, dear lady, perfectly beautiful and perfectly divine.'

A little tremor passed through Mrs Albert Forrester's substantial frame. She was like a man who enters suddenly a room filled with hyacinths; the perfume is so intoxicating that he almost staggers. But she relented.

'If you were trying to be facetious,' she said, 'I should prefer you to exercise your facetiousness on my guests rather than on my maids. . . . Miss Warren will give you some tea.'

Mrs Albert Forrester dismissed me with a wave of the hand, but she did not dismiss the subject, since for the next two or three years whenever she introduced me to someone she never failed to add:

'You must make the most of him, he only comes here as a penance. When he comes to the door he always asks: Is there Divine Service today? So amusing, isn't he?'

But Mrs Albert Forrester did not confine herself to weekly tea-parties: every Saturday she gave a luncheon of eight persons; this according to her opinion being the perfect number for general conversation and her dining-room conveniently holding no more. If Mrs Albert Forrester flattered herself upon anything it was not that her knowledge of English prosody was unique, but that her luncheons were celebrated. She chose her guests with care, and an invitation to one of them was more than a compliment, it was a consecration. Over the luncheon-table it was possible to keep the conversation on a higher level than in the mixed company of a tea-party and few can have left her dining-room without taking away with them an enhanced belief in Mrs Albert Forrester's ability and a brighter faith in human nature. She only asked men, since, stout enthusiast for her sex as she was and glad to see women on other occasions, she could not but realize that they were inclined at table to talk exclusively to their next-door neighbours and thus hinder the general exchange of ideas that made her own parties an entertainment not only of the body but of the soul. For it must be said that Mrs Albert Forrester gave you uncommonly good food, excellent wine, and a first-rate cigar. Now to anyone who has partaken of literary hospitality this must appear very remarkable, since literary persons for the most part think highly and live plainly; their minds are occupied with the things of the spirit and they do not notice that the roast mutton is underdone and the potatoes cold: the beer is all right, but the wine has a sobering effect, and it is unwise to touch the coffee. Mrs Albert Forrester was pleased enough to receive compliments on the fare she provided.

'If people do me the honour to break bread with me,' she said, 'it is only fair that I should give them as good food as they can get at home.'

But if the flattery was excessive she deprecated it.

'You really embarrass me when you give me a meed of praise which is not my due. You must praise Mrs Bulfinch.'

'Who is Mrs Bulfinch?'

'My cook.'

'She's a treasure then, but you're not going to ask me to believe that she's responsible for the wine.'

'Is it good? I'm terribly ignorant of such things; I put myself entirely in the hands of my wine merchant.'

But if mention was made of the cigars Mrs Albert Forrester beamed.

'Ah, for them you must compliment Albert. It is Albert who chooses the cigars and I am given to understand that no one knows more about a cigar than Albert.'

She looked at her husband, who sat at the end of the table, with the proud bright eyes of a pedigree hen (a Buff Orpington for choice) looking at her only chick. Then there was a quick flutter of conversation as the guests, anxious to be civil to their host and relieved at length to find an occasion, expressed their appreciation of his peculiar merit.

'You're very kind,' he said. 'I'm glad you like them.'

Then he would give a little discourse on cigars, explaining the excellencies he sought and regretting the deterioration in quality which had followed on the commercialization of the industry. Mrs Albert Forrester listened to him with a complacent smile, and it was plain that she enjoyed this little triumph of his. Of course you cannot go on talking of cigars indefinitely and as soon as she perceived that her guests were growing restive she broached a topic of more general, and it may be of more significant, interest. Albert subsided into silence. But he had had his moment.

It was Albert who made Mrs Forrester's luncheons to some less attractive than her tea-parties, for Albert was a bore; but though without doubt perfectly conscious of the fact, she made a point that he should come to them and in fact had fixed upon Saturdays (for the rest of the week he was busy) in order that he should be able to. Mrs Albert Forrester felt that her husband's presence on these festive occasions was an unavoidable debt that she paid to her own self-respect. She would never by a negligence admit to the world that she had married a man who was not spiritually her equal, and it may be that in the silent watches of the nights she asked herself where indeed such could have been found. Mrs Albert Forrester's friends were troubled by no such reticence and they said it was dreadful that such a woman should be burdened with such a man. They asked each other how she had ever come to marry him and (being mostly celibate) answered despairingly that no one ever knew why anybody married anybody else.

It was not that Albert was a verbose and aggressive bore; he did not button-hole you with interminable stories or pester you with pointless jokes; he did not crucify you on a platitude or hamstring you with a commonplace; he was just dull. A cipher. Clifford Boyleston, for whom the French Romantics had no secrets and who was himself a writer of merit, had said that when you looked into a room into which Albert had just gone there was nobody there. This was thought very clever by Mrs Albert Forrester's friends, and Rose Waterford, the well-known novelist and the most fearless of women, had ventured to repeat it to Mrs Albert Forrester. Though she pretended to be annoyed, she had not been able to prevent the smile that rose to her lips. Her behaviour towards Albert could not but increase the respect in which her friends held her. She insisted that whatever in their secret hearts they thought of him, they should treat him with the decorum that was due to her husband. Her own demeanour was admirable. If he chanced to make an observation she listened to him with a pleasant expression and when he fetched her a book that she wanted or gave her his pencil to make a note of an idea that had occurred to her, she always thanked him. Nor would she allow her friends pointedly to neglect him, and though, being a woman of tact, she saw that it would be asking too much of the world if she took him about with her always, and she went out much alone, yet her friends knew that she expected them to ask him to dinner at least once a year. He always accompanied her to public banquets when she was going to make a speech, and if she delivered a lecture she took care that he should have a seat on the platform.

Albert was, I believe, of average height, but perhaps because you never thought of him except in connexion with his wife (of imposing dimensions) you only thought of him as a little man. He was spare and frail and looked older than his age. This was the same as his wife's. His hair, which he kept very short, was white and meagre, and he wore a stubby white moustache; his was a face, thin and lined, without a noticeable feature; and his blue eyes, which once might have been attractive, were now pale and tired. He was always very neatly dressed in pepper-and-salt trousers, which he chose always of the same pattern, a black coat, and a grey tie with a small pearl pin in it. He was perfectly unobtrusive, and when he stood in Mrs Albert Forrester's drawing-room to receive the guests whom she had asked to luncheon you noticed him as little as you noticed the quiet and gentlemanly furniture. He was well mannered and it was with a pleasant, courteous smile that he shook hands with them.

'How do you do? I'm very glad to see you,' he said if they were friends of some standing. 'Keeping well, I hope?'

But if they were strangers of distinction coming for the first time to the house, he went to the door as they entered the drawing-room, and said:

'I am Mrs Albert Forrester's husband. I will introduce you to my wife.'

Then he led the visitor to where Mrs Albert Forrester stood with her back to the light, and she with a glad and eager gesture advanced to make the stranger welcome.

It was agreeable to see the demure pride he took in his wife's literary reputation and the self-effacement with which he furthered her interests. He was always there when he was wanted and never when he wasn't. His tact, if not deliberate, was instinctive. Mrs Albert Forrester was the first to acknowledge his merits.

'I really don't know what I should do without him,' she said. 'He's invaluable to me. I read him everything I write and his criticisms are often very useful.'

'Molière and his cook,' said Miss Waterford.

'Is that funny, dear Rose?' asked Mrs Forrester, somewhat acidly.

When Mrs Albert Forrester did not approve of a remark, she had a way that put many persons to confusion of asking you whether it was a joke which she was too dense to see. But it was impossible to embarrass Miss Waterford. She was a lady who in the course of a long life had had many affairs, but only one passion, and this was for printer's ink. Mrs Albert Forrester tolerated rather than approved her.

'Come, come, my dear,' she replied, 'you know very well that he wouldn't exist without you. He wouldn't know us. It must be wonderful to him to come in contact with all the best brains and the most distinguished people of our day.'

'It may be that the bee would perish without the hive which shelters it, but the bee nevertheless has a significance of its own.'

And since Mrs Albert Forrester's friends, though they knew all about art and literature, knew little about natural history, they had no reply to this observation. She went on:

'He doesn't interfere with me. He knows subconsciously when I don't want to be disturbed and, indeed, when I am following out a train of thought I find his presence in the room a comfort rather than a hindrance to me.'

'Like a Persian cat,' said Miss Waterford.

'But like a very well-trained, well-bred, and well-mannered Persian cat,' answered Mrs Forrester severely, thus putting Miss Waterford in her place.

But Mrs Albert Forrester had not finished with her husband.

'We who belong to the intelligentsia,' she said, 'are apt to live in a world too exclusively our own. We are interested in the abstract rather than in the concrete, and sometimes I think that we survey the bustling world of human affairs in too detached a manner and from too serene a height. Do you not think that we stand in danger of becoming a little inhuman? I shall always be grateful to Albert because he keeps me in contact with the man in the street.'

It was on account of this remark, to which none of her friends could deny the rare insight and subtlety that characterized so many of her utterances, that for some time Albert was known in her immediate circle as The Man in the Street. But this was only for a while, and it was forgotten. He then became known as The Philatelist. It was Clifford Boyleston, with his wicked wit, who invented the name. One day, his poor brain exhausted by the effort to sustain a conversation with Albert, he had asked in desperation:

'Do you collect stamps?'

'No,' answered Albert mildly. 'I'm afraid I don't.'

But Clifford Boyleston had no sooner asked the question than he saw its possibilities. He had written a book on Baudelaire's aunt by marriage, which had attracted the attention of all who were interested in French literature, and was well known in his exhaustive studies of the French spirit to have absorbed a goodly share of the Gallic quickness and the Gallic brilliancy. He paid no attention to Albert's disclaimer, but at the first opportunity informed Mrs Albert Forrester's friends that he had at last discovered Albert's secret. He collected stamps. He never met him afterwards without asking him:

'Well, Mr Forrester, how is the stamp collection?' Or: 'Have you been buying any stamps since I saw you last?'

It mattered little that Albert continued to deny that he collected stamps, the invention was too apt not to be made the most of; Mrs Albert Forrester's friends insisted that he did, and they seldom spoke to him without asking him how he was getting on. Even Mrs Albert Forrester, when she was in a specially gay humour, would sometimes speak of her husband as The Philatelist. The name really did seem to fit Albert like a glove. Sometimes they spoke of him thus to his face and they could not but appreciate the good nature with which he took it; he smiled unresentfully and presently did not even protest that they were mistaken.

Of course Mrs Albert Forrester had too keen a social sense to jeopardize the success of her luncheons by allowing her more distinguished guests to sit on either side of Albert. She took care that only her older and more intimate friends should do this, and when the appointed victims came in she would say to them:

'I know you won't mind sitting by Albert, will you?'

They could only say that they would be delighted, but if their faces too plainly expressed their dismay she would pat their hands playfully and add:

'Next time you shall sit by me. Albert is so shy with strangers and you know so well how to deal with him.'

They did: they simply ignored him. So far as they were concerned the chair in which he sat might as well have been empty. There was no sign that it annoyed him to be taken no notice of by persons who after all were eating food he paid for, since the earnings of Mrs Forrester could certainly not have provided her guests with spring salmon and forced asparagus. He sat quiet and silent, and if he opened his mouth it was only to give a direction to one of the maids. If a guest were new to him he would let his eyes rest on him in a stare that would have been embarrassing if it had not been so childlike. He seemed to be asking himself what this strange creature was; but what answer his mild scrutiny gave him he never revealed. When the conversation grew animated he would look from one speaker to the other, but again you could not tell from his thin, lined face what he thought of the fantastic notions that were bandied across the table.

Clifford Boyleston said that all the wit and wisdom he heard passed over his head like water over a duck's back. He had given up trying to understand and now only made a semblance of listening. But Harry Oakland, the versatile critic, said that Albert was taking it all in; he found it all too, too marvellous, and with his poor, muddled brain he was trying desperately to make head or tail of the wonderful things he heard. Of course in the City he must boast of the distinguished persons he knew, perhaps there he was a light of learning and letters, an authority on the ideal; it would be perfectly divine to hear what he made of it all. Harry Oakland was one of Mrs Albert Forrester's staunchest admirers, and had written a brilliant and subtle essay on her style. With his refined and even beautiful features he looked like a San Sebastian who had had an accident with a hair-restorer; for he was uncommonly hirsute. He was a very young man, not thirty, but he had been in turn a dramatic critic, and a critic of fiction, a musical critic, and a critic of painting. But he was getting a little tired of art and threatened to devote his talents in future to the criticism of sport.

Albert, I should explain, was in the city and it was a misfortune that Mrs Forrester's friends thought she bore with meritorious fortitude that he was not even rich. There would have been something romantic in it if he had been a merchant prince who held the fate of nations in his hand or sent argosies, laden with rare spices, to those ports of the Levant the names of which have provided many a poet with so rich and rare a rhyme. But Albert was only a currant merchant and was supposed to make no more than just enabled Mrs Albert Forrester to conduct her life with distinction and even with liberality. Since his occupation kept him in his office till six o'clock he never managed to get to Mrs Albert Forrester's Tuesdays till the most important visitors were gone. By the time he arrived, there were seldom more than three or four of her more intimate friends in the drawing-room, discussing with freedom and humour the guests who had departed, and when they heard Albert's key in the front door they realized with one accord that it was late. In a moment he opened the door in his hesitating way and looked mildly in. Mrs Albert Forrester greeted him with a bright smile.

'Come in, Albert, come in. I think you know everybody here.'

Albert entered and shook hands with his wife's friends.

'Have you just come from the City?' she asked eagerly, though she knew there was nowhere else he could have come from. 'Would you like a cup of tea?'

'No, thank you, my dear. I had tea in my office.'

Mrs Albert Forrester smiled still more brightly and the rest of the company thought she was perfectly wonderful with him.

'Ah, but I know you like a second cup. I will pour it out for you myself.'

She went to the tea-table and, forgetting that the tea had been stewing for an hour and a half and was stone cold, poured him out a cup and added milk and sugar. Albert took it with a word of thanks, and meekly stirred it, but when Mrs Forrester resumed the conversation which his appearance had interrupted, without tasting it put it quietly down. His arrival was the signal for the party finally to break up, and one by one the remaining guests took their departure. On one occasion, however, the conversation was so absorbing and the point at issue so important that Mrs Albert Forrester would not hear of their going.

'It must be settled once for all. And after all,' she remarked in a manner that for her was almost arch, 'this is a matter on which Albert may have something to say. Let us have the benefit of his opinion.'

It was when women were beginning to cut their hair and the subject of discussion was whether Mrs Albert Forrester should or should not shingle. Mrs Albert Forrester was a woman of authoritative presence. She was large-boned and her bones were well covered; had she not been so tall and strong it might have suggested itself to you that she was corpulent. But she carried her weight gallantly. Her features were a little larger than life-size and it was this that gave her face doubtless the look of virile intellectuality that it certainly possessed. Her skin was dark and you might have thought that she had in her veins some trace of Levantine blood: she admitted that she could not but think there was in her a gypsy strain and that would account, she felt, for the wild and lawless passion that sometimes characterized her poetry. Her eyes were large and black and bright, her nose like the great Duke of Wellington's, but more fleshy, and her chin square and determined. She had a big mouth, with full red lips, which owed nothing to cosmetics, for of these Mrs Albert Forrester had never deigned to make use; and her hair, thick, solid, and grey, was piled on top of her head in such a manner as to increase her already commanding height. She was in appearance an imposing, not to say an alarming, female.

She was always very suitably dressed in rich materials of sombre hue and she looked every inch a woman of letters; but in her discreet way (being after all human and susceptible to vanity) she followed the fashions and the cut of her gowns was modish. I think for some time she had hankered to shingle her hair, but she thought it more becoming to do it at the solicitation of her friends than on her own initiative.

'Oh, you must, you must,' said Harry Oakland, in his eager, boyish way. 'You'd look too, too wonderful.'

Clifford Boyleston, who was now writing a book on Madame de Maintenon, was doubtful. He thought it a dangerous experiment.

'I think,' he said, wiping his eye-glasses with a cambric handkerchief, 'I think when one has made a type one should stick to it. What would Louis XIV have been without his wig?'

'I'm hesitating,' said Mrs Forrester. 'After all, we must move with the times. I am of my day and I do not wish to lag behind. America, as Wilhelm Meister said, is here and now.' She turned brightly to Albert. 'What does my lord and master say about it? What is your opinion, Albert? To shingle or not to shingle, that is the question.'

'I'm afraid my opinion is not of great importance, my dear,' he answered mildly.

'To me it is of the greatest importance,' answered Mrs Albert Forrester, flatteringly.

She could not but see how beautifully her friends thought she treated The Philatelist.

'I insist,' she proceeded, 'I insist. No one knows me as you do, Albert. Will it suit me?'

'It might,' he answered. 'My only fear is that with your–statuesque appearance short hair would perhaps suggest–well, shall we say, the Isle of Greece where burning Sappho loved and sung.'

There was a moment's embarrassed pause. Rose Waterford smothered a giggle, but the others preserved a stony silence. Mrs Forrester's smile froze on her lips. Albert had dropped a brick.

'I always thought Byron a very mediocre poet,' said Mrs Albert Forrester at last.

The company broke up. Mrs Albert Forrester did not shingle, nor indeed was the matter ever again referred to.

It was towards the end of another of Mrs Albert Forrester's Tuesdays that the event occurred that had so great an influence on her literary career.

It had been one of her most successful parties. The leader of the Labour Party had been there and Mrs Albert Forrester had gone as far as she could without definitely committing herself to intimate to him that she was prepared to throw in her lot with Labour. The time was ripe and if she was ever to adopt a political career she must come to a decision. A member of the French Academy had been brought by Clifford Boyleston and, though she knew he was wholly unacquainted with English, it had gratified her to receive his affable compliment on her ornate and yet pellucid style. The American Ambassador had been there and a young Russian prince whose authentic Romanoff blood alone prevented him from looking a gigolo. A duchess who had recently divorced her duke and married a jockey had been very gracious; and her strawberry leaves, albeit sere and yellow, undoubtedly added tone to the assembly. There had been quite a galaxy of literary lights. But now all, all were gone but Clifford Boyleston, Harry Oakland, Rose Waterford, Oscar Charles, and Simmons. Oscar Charles was a little, gnome-like creature, young but with the wizened face of a cunning monkey, with gold spectacles, who earned his living in a government office but spent his leisure in the pursuit of literature. He wrote little articles for the sixpenny weeklies and had a spirited contempt for the world in general. Mrs Albert Forrester liked him, thinking he had talent, but though he always expressed the keenest admiration for her style (it was indeed he who had named her the mistress of the semi-colon), his acerbity was so general that she also somewhat feared him. Simmons was her agent; a round-faced man who wore glasses so strong that his eyes behind them looked strange and misshapen. They reminded you of the eyes of some uncouth crustacean that you had seen in an aquarium. He came regularly to Mrs Albert Forrester's parties, partly because he had the greatest admiration for her genius and partly because it was convenient for him to meet prospective clients in her drawing-room.

Mrs Albert Forrester, for whom he had long laboured with but a trifling recompense, was not sorry to put him in the way of earning an honest penny, and she took care to introduce him, with warm expressions of gratitude, to anyone who might be supposed to have literary wares to sell. It was not without pride that she remembered that the notorious and vastly lucrative memoirs of Lady St Swithin had been first mooted in her drawing-room.

They sat in a circle of which Mrs Albert Forrester was the centre and discussed brightly and, it must be confessed, somewhat maliciously the various persons who had been that day present. Miss Warren, the pallid female who had stood for two hours at the tea-table, was walking silently round the room collecting cups that had been left here and there. She had some vague employment, but was always able to get off in order to pour out tea for Mrs Albert Forrester, and in the evening she typed Mrs Albert Forrester's manuscripts. Mrs Albert Forrester did not pay her for this, thinking quite rightly that as it was she did a great deal for the poor thing; but she gave her the seats for the cinema that were sent her for nothing and often presented her with articles of clothing for which she had no further use.

Mrs Albert Forrester in her rather deep, full voice was talking in a steady flow and the rest were listening to her with attention. She was in good form and the words that poured from her lips could have gone straight down on paper without alteration. Suddenly there was a noise in the passage as though something heavy had fallen and then the sound of an altercation.

Mrs Albert Forrester stopped and a slight frown darkened her really noble brow.

'I should have thought they knew by now that I will not have this devastating racket in the flat. Would you mind ringing the bell, Miss Warren, and asking what is the reason of this tumult?'

Miss Warren rang the bell and in a moment the maid appeared. Miss Warren at the door, in order not to interrupt Mrs Albert Forrester, spoke to her in undertones. But Mrs Albert Forrester somewhat irritably interrupted herself.

'Well, Carter, what is it? Is the house falling down or has the Red Revolution at last broken out?'

'If you please, ma'am, it's the new cook's box,' answered the maid. 'The porter dropped it as he was bringing it in and the cook got all upset about it.'

'What do you mean by "the new cook"?'

'Mrs Bulfinch went away this afternoon, ma'am,' said the maid.

Mrs Albert Forrester stared at her.

'This is the first I've heard of it. Had Mrs Bulfinch given notice? The moment Mr Forrester comes in tell him that I wish to speak to him.'

'Very good, ma'am.'

The maid went out and Miss Warren slowly returned to the tea-table. Mechanically, though nobody wanted them, she poured out several cups of tea.

'What a catastrophe!' cried Miss Waterford.

'You must get her back,' said Clifford Boyleston. 'She's a treasure, that woman, a remarkable cook, and she gets better and better every day.'

But at that moment the maid came in again with a letter on a small plated salver and handed it to her mistress.

'What is this?' said Mrs Albert Forrester.

'Mr Forrester said I was to give you this letter when you asked for him, ma'am,' said the maid.

'Where is Mr Forrester then?'

'Mr Forrester's gone, ma'am,' answered the maid as though the question surprised her.

'Gone? That'll do. You can go.'

The maid left the room and Mrs Albert Forrester, with a look of perplexity on her large face, opened the letter. Rose Waterford has told me that her first thought was that Albert, fearful of his wife's displeasure at the departure of Mrs Bulfinch, had thrown himself in the Thames. Mrs Albert Forrester read the letter and a look of consternation crossed her face.

'Oh, monstrous,' she cried. 'Monstrous! Monstrous!'

'What is it, Mrs Forrester?'

Mrs Albert Forrester pawed the carpet with her foot like a restive, high-spirited horse pawing the ground, and crossing her arms with a gesture that is indescribable (but that you sometimes see in a fishwife who is going to make the very devil of a scene) bent her looks upon her curious and excessively startled friends.

'Albert has eloped with the cook.'

There was a gasp of dismay. Then something terrible happened. Miss Warren, who was standing behind the tea-table, suddenly choked. Miss Warren, who never opened her mouth and whom no one ever spoke to, Miss Warren, whom not one of them, though he had seen her every week for three years, would have recognized in the street, Miss Warren suddenly burst into uncontrollable laughter. With one accord, aghast, they turned and stared at her. They felt as Balaam must have felt when his ass broke into speech. She positively shrieked with laughter. There was a nameless horror about the sight, as though something had on a sudden gone wrong with a natural phenomenon, and you were just as startled as though the chairs and tables without warning began to skip about the floor in an antic dance. Miss Warren tried to contain herself, but the more she tried the more pitilessly the laughter shook her, and seizing a handkerchief she stuffed it in her mouth and hurried from the room. The door slammed behind her.

'Hysteria,' said Clifford Boyleston.

'Pure hysteria, of course,' said Harry Oakland.

But Mrs Albert Forrester said nothing.

The letter had dropped at her feet and Simmons, the agent, picked it up and handed it to her. She would not take it

'Read it,' she said. 'Read it aloud.'

Mr Simmons pushed his spectacles up on his forehead and holding the letter very close to his eyes read as follows:

My Dear—

Mrs Bulfinch is in need of a change and has decided to leave, and as I do not feel inclined to stay on here without her I am going too. I have had all the literature I can stand and I am fed up with art.

Mrs Bulfinch does not care about marriage, but if you care to divorce me she is willing to marry me. I hope you will find the new cook satisfactory. She has excellent references. It may save you trouble if I inform you that Mrs Bulfinch and I are living at 411 Kennington Road, S.E.

Albert

No one spoke. Mr Simmons slipped his spectacles back on to the bridge of his nose. The fact was that none of them, brilliant as they were and accustomed to find topics of conversation to suit every occasion, could think of an appropriate remark. Mrs Albert Forrester was not the kind of woman to whom you could offer condolences and each was too much afraid of the other's ridicule to venture upon the obvious. At last Clifford Boyleston came bravely to the rescue.

'One doesn't know what to say,' he observed.

There was another silence and then Rose Waterford spoke.

'What does Mrs Bulfinch look like?' she asked.

'How should I know?' answered Mrs Albert Forrester, somewhat peevishly. 'I never looked at her. Albert always engaged the servants, she just came in for a moment so that I could see if her aura was satisfactory.'

'But you must have seen her every morning when you did the housekeeping.'

'Albert did the housekeeping. It was his own wish, so that I might be free to devote myself to my work. In this life one has to limit oneself.'

'Did Albert order your luncheons?' asked Clifford Boyleston.

'Naturally. It was his province.'

Clifford Boyleston slightly raised his eyebrows. What a fool he had been never to guess that it was Albert who was responsible for Mrs Forrester's beautiful food! And of course it was owing to him that the excellent Chablis was always just sufficiently chilled to run coolly over the tongue, but never so cold as to lose its bouquet and its savour.

'He certainly knew good food and good wine.'

'I always told you he had his points,' answered Mrs Albert Forrester, as though he were reproaching her. 'You all laughed at him. You would not believe me when I told you that I owed a great deal to him.'

There was no answer to this and once more silence, heavy and ominous, fell on the party. Suddenly Mr Simmons flung a bombshell.

'You must get him back.'

So great was her surprise that if Mrs Albert Forrester had not been standing against the chimney-piece she would undoubtedly have staggered two paces to the rear.

'What on earth do you mean?' she cried. 'I will never see him again as long as I live. Take him back? Never. Not even if he came and begged me on his bended knees.'

'I didn't say take him back; I said, get him back.'

But Mrs Albert Forrester paid no attention to the misplaced interruption.

'I have done everything for him. What would he be without me? I ask you. I have given him a position which never in his remotest dreams could he have aspired to.'

None could deny that there was something magnificent in the indignation of Mrs Albert Forrester, but it appeared to have little effect on Mr Simmons.

'What are you going to live on?'

Mrs Albert Forrester flung him a glance totally devoid of amiability.

'God will provide,' she answered in freezing tones.

'I think it very unlikely,' he returned.

Mrs Albert Forrester shrugged her shoulders. She wore an outraged expression. But Mr Simmons made himself as comfortable as he could on his chair and lit a cigarette.

'You know you have no warmer admirer of your art than me,' he said.

'Than I,' corrected Clifford Boyleston.

'Or than you,' went on Mr Simmonds blandly. 'We all agree that there is no one writing now whom you need fear comparison with. Both in prose and verse you are absolutely first class. And your style – well, everyone knows your style.'

'The opulence of Sir Thomas Browne with the limpidity of Cardinal Newman,' said Clifford Boyleston. 'The raciness of John Dryden with the precision of Jonathan Swift.'

The only sign that Mrs Albert Forrester heard was the smile that hesitated for a brief moment at the corners of her tragic mouth.

'And you have humour.'

'Is there anyone in the world,' cried Miss Waterford, 'who can put such a wealth of wit and satire and comic observation into a semi-colon?'

'But the fact remains that you don't sell,' pursued Mr Simmons imperturbably. 'I've handled your work for twenty years and I tell you frankly that I shouldn't have grown fat on my commission, but I've handled it because now and again I like to do what I can for good work. I've always believed in you and I've hoped that sooner or later we might get the public to swallow you. But if you think you can make your living by writing the sort of stuff you do I'm bound to tell you that you haven't a chance.'

'I have come into the world too late,' said Mrs Albert Forrester. 'I should have lived in the eighteenth century when the wealthy patron rewarded a dedication with a hundred guineas.'

'What do you suppose the currant business brings in?'

Mrs Albert Forrester gave a little sigh.

'A pittance. Albert always told me he made about twelve hundred a year.'

'He must be a very good manager. But you couldn't expect him on that income to allow you very much. Take my word for it, there's only one thing for you to do and that's to get him back.'

'I would rather live in a garret. Do you think I'm going to submit to the affront he has put upon me? Would you have me battle for his affections with my cook? Do not forget that there is one thing which is more valuable to a woman like me than her ease and that is her dignity.'

'I was just coming to that,' said Mr Simmons coldly.

He glanced at the others and those strange, lopsided eyes of his looked more than ever monstrous and fish-like.

'There is no doubt in my mind,' he went on, 'that you have a very distinguished and almost unique position in the world of letters. You stand for something quite apart. You never prostituted your genius for filthy lucre and you have held high the banner of pure art. You're thinking of going into Parliament. I don't think much of politics myself, but there's no denying that it would be a good advertisement and if you get in I daresay we could get you a lecture tour in America on the strength of it. You have ideals and this I can say, that even the people who've never read a word you've written respect you. But in your position there's one thing you can't afford to be and that's a joke.'

Mrs Albert Forrester gave a distinct start.

'What on earth do you mean by that?'

'I know nothing about Mrs Bulfinch and for all I know she's a very respectable woman, but the fact remains that a man doesn't run away with his cook without making his wife ridiculous. If it had been a dancer or a lady of title I daresay it wouldn't have done you any harm, but a cook would finish you. In a week you'd have all London laughing at you, and if there's one thing that kills an author or a politician it is ridicule. You must get your husband back and you must get him back pretty damned quick.'

A dark flush settled on Mrs Albert Forrester's face, but she did not immediately reply. In her ears there rang on a sudden the outrageous and unaccountable laughter that had sent Miss Warren flying from the room.

'We're all friends here and you can count on our discretion.'

Mrs Forrester looked at her friends and she thought that in Rose Waterford's eyes there was already a malicious gleam. On the wizened face of Oscar Charles was a whimsical look. She wished that in a moment of abandon she had not betrayed her secret. Mr Simmons, however, knew the literary world and allowed his eyes to rest on the company.

'After all you are the centre and head of their set. Your husband has not only run away from you but also from them. It's not too good for them either. The fact is that Albert Forrester has made you all look a lot of damned fools.'

'All,' said Clifford Boyleston. 'We're all in the same boat. He's quite right, Mrs Forrester. The Philatelist must come back.'

'*Et tu, Brute.*'

Mr Simmons did not understand Latin and if he had would probably not have been moved by Mrs Albert Forrester's exclamation. He cleared his throat.

'My suggestion is that Mrs Albert Forrester should go and see him tomorrow, fortunately we have his address, and beg him to reconsider his decision. I don't know what sort of things a woman says on these occasions, but Mrs Forrester has tact and imagination and she must say them. If Mr Forrester makes any conditions she must accept them. She must leave no stone unturned.'

'If you play your cards well there is no reason why you shouldn't bring him back here with you tomorrow evening,' said Rose Waterford lightly.

'Will you do it, Mrs Forrester?'

For two minutes, at least, turned away from them, she stared at the empty fireplace; then, drawing herself to her full height, she faced them.

'For my art's sake, not for mine. I will not allow the ribald laughter of the Philistine to besmirch all that I hold good and true and beautiful.'

'Capital,' said Mr Simmons, rising to his feet. 'I'll look in on my way home tomorrow and I hope to find you and Mr Forrester billing and cooing side by side like a pair of turtle-doves.'

He took his leave, and the others, anxious not to be left alone with Mrs Albert Forrester and her agitation, in a body followed his example.

It was latish in the afternoon next day when Mrs Albert Forrester, imposing in black silk and a velvet toque, set out from her flat in order to get a bus from the Marble Arch that would take her to Victoria Station. Mr Simmons had explained to her by telephone how to reach the Kennington Road with expedition and economy. She neither felt nor looked like Delilah. At Victoria she took the tram that runs down the Vauxhall Bridge Road. When she crossed the river she found herself in a part of London more noisy, sordid, and bustling than that to which she was accustomed, but she was too much occupied with her thoughts to notice the varied scene. She was relieved to find that the tram went along the Kennington Road and asked the conductor to put her down a few doors from the house she sought. When it did and rumbled on leaving her alone in the busy street, she felt strangely lost, like a traveller in an Eastern tale set down by a djinn in an unknown city. She walked slowly, looking to right and left, and notwithstanding the emotions of indignation and embarrassment that fought for the possession of her somewhat opulent bosom, she could not but reflect that here was the material for a very pretty piece of prose. The little houses held about them the feeling of a bygone age when here it was still almost country, and Mrs Albert Forrester registered in her retentive memory a note that she must look into the literary associations of the Kennington Road. Number four hundred and eleven was one of a row of shabby houses that stood some way back from the street; in front of it was a narrow strip of shabby grass, and a paved way led up to a latticed wooden porch that badly needed a coat of paint. This and the straggling, stunted creeper that grew over the front of the house gave it a falsely rural air which was strange and even sinister in that road down which thundered a tumultuous traffic. There was something equivocal about the house that suggested that here lived women to whom a life of pleasure had brought an inadequate reward.

The door was opened by a scraggy girl of fifteen with long legs and a tousled head.

'Does Mrs Bulfinch live here, do you know?'

'You've rung the wrong bell. Second floor.' The girl pointed to the stairs and at the same time screamed shrilly: 'Mrs Bulfinch, a party to see you. Mrs Bulfinch.'

Mrs Albert Forrester walked up the dingy stairs. They were covered with torn carpet. She walked slowly, for she did not wish to get out of breath. A door opened as she reached the second floor and she recognized her cook.

'Good afternoon, Bulfinch,' said Mrs Albert Forrester, with dignity. 'I wish to see your master.'

Mrs Bulfinch hesitated for the shadow of a second, then held the door wide open.

'Come in, ma'am.' She turned her head. 'Albert, here's Mrs Forrester to see you.'

Mrs Forrester stepped by quickly and there was Albert sitting by the fire in a leather-covered, but rather shabby, arm-chair, with his feet in slippers, and in shirtsleeves. He was reading the evening paper and smoking a cigar. He rose to his feet as Mrs Albert Forrester came in. Mrs Bulfinch followed her visitor into the room and closed the door.

'How are you, my dear?' said Albert cheerfully. 'Keeping well, I hope.'

'You'd better put on your coat, Albert,' said Mrs Bulfinch. 'What *will* Mrs Forrester think of you, finding you like that? I never.'

She took the coat, which was hanging on a peg, and helped him into it; and like a woman familiar with the peculiarities of masculine dress pulled down his waistcoat so that it should not ride over his collar.

'I received your letter, Albert,' said Mrs Forrester.

'I supposed you had, or you wouldn't have known my address, would you?'

'Won't you sit down, ma'am?' said Mrs Bulfinch, deftly dusting a chair, part of a suite covered in plum-covered velvet, and pushing it forwards.

Mrs Albert Forrester with a slight bow seated herself.

'I should have preferred to see you alone, Albert,' she said.

His eyes twinkled.

'Since anything you have to say concerns Mrs Bulfinch as much as it concerns me I think it much better that she should be present.'

'As you wish.'

Mrs Bulfinch drew up a chair and sat down. Mrs Albert Forrester had never seen her but with a large apron over a print dress. She was wearing now an open-work blouse of white silk, a black skirt, and high-heeled, patent-leather shoes with silver buckles. She was a woman of about five-and-forty, with reddish hair and a reddish face, not pretty, but with a good-natured look, and buxom. She reminded Mrs Albert Forrester of a serving-wench, somewhat overblown, in a jolly picture by an old Dutch master.

'Well, my dear, what have you to say to me?' asked Albert.

Mrs Albert Forrester gave him her brightest and most affable smile. Her great black eyes shone with tolerant good-humour.

'Of course you know that this is perfectly absurd, Albert. I think you must be out of your mind.'

'Do you, my dear? Fancy that.'

'I'm not angry with you, I'm only amused, but a joke's a joke and should not be carried too far. I've come to take you home.'

'Was my letter not quite clear?'

'Perfectly. I ask no questions and I will make no reproaches. We will look upon this as a momentary aberration and say no more about it.'

'Nothing will induce me ever to live with you again, my dear,' said Albert in, however, a perfectly friendly fashion.

'You're not serious?'

'Quite.'

'Do you love this woman?'

Mrs Albert Forrester still smiled with an eager and somewhat metallic brightness. She was determined to take the matter lightly. With her intimate sense of values she realized that the scene was comic. Albert looked at Mrs Bulfinch and a smile broke out on his withered face.

'We get on very well together, don't we, old girl?'

'Not so bad,' said Mrs Bulfinch.

Mrs Albert Forrester raised her eyebrows; her husband had never in all their married life called *her* 'old girl': nor indeed would she have wished it.

'If Bulfinch has any regard or respect for you she must know that the thing is impossible. After the life you've led and the society you've moved in she can hardly expect to make you permanently happy in miserable furnished lodgings.'

'They're not furnished lodgings, ma'am,' said Mrs Bulfinch. 'It's all me own furniture. You see, I'm very independent-like and I've always liked to have a home of me own. So I keep these rooms on whether I'm in a situation or whether I'm not, and so I always have some place to go back to.'

'And a very nice cosy little place it is,' said Albert.

Mrs Albert Forrester looked about her. There was a kitchen range in the fireplace on which a kettle was simmering and on the mantelshelf was a black marble clock flanked by black marble candelabra. There was a large table covered with a red cloth, a dresser, and a sewing-machine. On the walls were photographs and framed pictures from Christmas supplements. A door at the back, covered with a red plush portière, led into what, considering the size of the house, Mrs Albert Forrester (who in her leisure moments had made a somewhat extensive study of architecture) could not but conclude was the only bedroom. Mrs Bulfinch and Albert lived in a contiguity that allowed no doubt about their relations.

'Have you not been happy with me, Albert?' asked Mrs Forrester in a deeper tone.

'We've been married for thirty-five years, my dear. It's too long. It's a great deal too long. You're a good woman in your way, but you don't suit me. You're literary and I'm not. You're artistic and I'm not.'

'I've always taken care to make you share in all my interests. I've taken great pains that you shouldn't be overshadowed by my success. You can't say that I've ever left you out of things.'

'You're a wonderful writer, I don't deny it for a moment, but the truth is I don't like the books you write.'

'That, if I may be permitted to say so, merely shows that you have very bad taste. All the best critics admit their power and their charm.'

'And I don't like your friends. Let me tell you a secret, my dear. Often at your parties I've had an almost irresistible impulse to take off all my clothes just to see what would happen.'

'Nothing would have happened,' said Mrs Albert Forrester with a slight frown. 'I should merely have sent for the doctor.'

'Besides you haven't the figure for that, Albert,' said Mrs Bulfinch.

Mr Simmons had hinted to Mrs Albert Forrester that if the need arose she must not hesitate to use the allurements of her sex in order to bring back her erring husband to the conjugal roof, but she did not in the least know how to do this. It would have been easier, she could not but reflect, had she been in evening dress.

'Does the fidelity of five-and-thirty years count for nothing? I have never looked at another man, Albert. I'm used to you. I shall be lost without you.'

'I've left all my menus with the new cook, ma'am. You've only got to tell her how many to luncheon and she'll manage,' said Mrs Bulfinch. 'She's very reliable and she has as light a hand with pastry as anyone I ever knew.'

Mrs Albert Forrester began to be discouraged. Mrs Bulfinch's remark, well meant no doubt, made it difficult to bring the conversation on to the plane on which emotion could be natural.

'I'm afraid you're only wasting your time, my dear,' said Albert. 'My decision is irrevocable. I'm not very young any more and I want someone to take care of me. I shall of course make you as good an allowance as I can. Corinne wants me to retire.'

'Who is Corinne?' asked Mrs Forrester with the utmost surprise.

'It's my name,' said Mrs Bulfinch. 'My mother was half French.'

'That explains a great deal,' replied Mrs Forrester, pursing her lips, for though she admired the literature of our neighbours she knew that their morals left much to be desired.

'What I say is, Albert's worked long enough, and it's about time he started enjoying himself. I've got a little bit of property at Clacton-on-Sea. It's a very healthy neighbourhood and the air is wonderful. We could live there very comfortable. And what with the beach and the pier there's always something to do. They're a very nice lot of people down there. If you don't interfere with nobody, nobody'll interfere with you.'

'I discussed the matter with my partners today and they're willing to buy me out. It means a certain sacrifice. When everything is settled I shall have an income of nine hundred pounds a year. There are three of us, so it gives us just three hundred a year apiece.'

'How am I to live on that?' cried Mrs Albert Forrester. 'I have my position to keep up.'

'You have a fluent, a fertile, and a distinguished pen, my dear.'

Mrs Albert Forrester impatiently shrugged her shoulders.

'You know very well that my books don't bring me in anything but reputation. The publishers always say that they lose by them and in fact they only publish them because it gives them prestige.'

It was then that Mrs Bulfinch had the idea that was to have consequences of such magnitude.

'Why don't you write a good thrilling detective story?' she asked.

'Me?' exclaimed Mrs Albert Forrester, for the first time in her life regardless of grammar.

'It's not a bad idea,' said Albert. 'It's not a bad idea at all.'

'I should have the critics down on me like a thousand bricks.'

'I'm not so sure of that. Give the highbrow the chance of being lowbrow without demeaning himself and he'll be so grateful to you, he won't know what to do.'

'For this relief much thanks,' murmured Mrs Albert Forrester reflectively.

'My dear, the critics'll eat it. And written in your beautiful English they won't be afraid to call it a masterpiece.'

'The idea is preposterous. It's absolutely foreign to my genius. I could never hope to please the masses.'

'Why not? The masses want to read good stuff, but they dislike being bored. They all know your name, but they don't read you, because you bore them. The fact is, my dear, you're dull.'

'I don't know how you can say that, Albert,' replied Mrs Albert Forrester, with as little resentment as the equator might feel if someone called it chilly. 'Everyone knows and acknowledges that I have an exquisite sense of humour and there is nobody who can extract so much good wholesome fun from a semi-colon as I can.'

'If you can give the masses a good thrilling story and let them think at the same time that they are improving their minds you'll make a fortune.'

'I've never read a detective story in my life,' said Mrs Albert Forrester. 'I once heard of a Mr Barnes of New York and I was told that he had written a book called *The Mystery of a Hansom Cab*. But I never read it.'

'Of course you have to have the knack,' said Mrs Bulfinch. 'The first thing to remember is that you don't want any lovemaking, it's out of place in a detective story, what you want is murder, and sleuth-hounds, and you don't want to be able to guess who done it till the last page.'

'But you must play fair with your reader, my dear,' said Albert. 'It always annoys me when suspicion has been thrown on the secretary or the lady of the title and it turns out to be the second footman who's never done more than say, "The carriage is at the door." Puzzle your reader as much as you can, but don't make a fool of him.'

'I love a good detective story,' said Mrs Bulfinch. 'Give me a lady in evening dress, just streaming with diamonds, lying on the library floor with a dagger in her heart, and I know I'm going to have a treat.'

'There's no accounting for tastes,' said Albert. 'Personally, I prefer a respectable family solicitor, with side-whiskers, gold watch-chain, and a benign appearance, lying dead in Hyde Park.'

'With his throat cut?' asked Mrs Bulfinch eagerly.

'No, stabbed in the back. There's something peculiarly attractive to the reader in the murder of a middle-aged gentleman of spotless reputation. It is pleasant to think that the most apparently blameless of us have a mystery in our lives.'

'I see what you mean, Albert,' said Mrs Bulfinch. 'He was the repository of a fatal secret.'

'We can give you all the tips, my dear,' said Albert, smiling mildly at Mrs Albert Forrester. 'I've read hundreds of detective stories.'

'You!'

'That's what first brought Corinne and me together. I used to pass them on to her when I'd finished them.'

'Many's the time I've heard him switch off the electric light as the dawn was creeping through the window and I couldn't help smiling to myself as I said: "There, he's finished it at last, now he can have a good sleep."'

Mrs Albert Forrester rose to her feet. She drew herself up.

'Now I see what a gulf separates us,' she said, and her fine contralto shook a little. 'You have been surrounded for thirty years with all that was best in English literature and you read hundreds of detective novels.'

'Hundreds and hundreds,' interrupted Albert with a smile of satisfaction.

'I came here willing to make any reasonable concession so that you should come back to your home, but now I wish it no longer. You have shown me that we have nothing in common and never had. There is an abyss between us.'

'Very well, my dear,' said Albert gently, 'I will submit to your decision. But you think over the detective story.'

'I will arise and go now,' she murmured, 'and go to Innisfree.'

'I'll just show you downstairs,' said Mrs Bulfinch. 'One has to be careful of the carpet if one doesn't exactly know where the holes are.'

With dignity, but not without circumspection, Mrs Albert Forrester walked downstairs and when Mrs Bulfinch opened the door and asked her if she would like a taxi she shook her head.

'I shall take the tram.'

'You need not be afraid that I won't take good care of Mr Forrester, ma'am,' said Mrs Bulfinch pleasantly. 'He shall have every comfort. I nursed Mr Bulfinch for three years during his last illness and there's very little I don't know about invalids. Not that Mr Forrester isn't very strong and active for his years. And of course he'll have a hobby. I always think a man should have a hobby. He's going to collect postage-stamps.'

Mrs Albert Forrester gave a little start of surprise. But just then a tram came in sight and, as a woman (even the greatest of them) will, she hurried at the risk of her life into the middle of the road and waved frantically. It stopped and she climbed in. She did not know how she was going to face Mr Simmons. He would be waiting for her when she got home. Clifford Boyleston would probably be there too. They would all be there and she would have to tell them that she had miserably failed. At that moment she had no warm feeling of friendship for her little group of devoted admirers. Wondering what the time was, she looked up at the man sitting opposite her to see whether he was the kind of person she could modestly ask, and suddenly started; for sitting there was a middle-aged gentleman of the most respectable appearance, with side-whiskers, a benign expression, and a gold watch-chain. It was the very man whom Albert had described lying dead in Hyde Park and she could not but jump to the conclusion that he was a family solicitor. The coincidence was extraordinary and really it looked as though the hand of fate were beckoning to her. He wore a silk hat, a black coat, and pepper-and-salt trousers, he was somewhat corpulent, of a powerful build, and by his side was a despatch-case. When the tram was half-way down the Vauxhall Bridge Road he asked the conductor to stop and she saw him go down a small, mean street. Why? Ah, why? When it reached Victoria, so deeply immersed in thought was she, until the conductor somewhat roughly told her where she was, she did not move. Edgar Allan Poe had written detective stories. She took a bus. She sat inside, buried in reflection, but when it arrived at Hyde Park Corner she suddenly made up her mind to get out. She couldn't sit still any longer. She felt she must walk. She entered the gates, walking slowly, and looked about her with an air that was at once intent and abstracted. Yes, there was Edgar Allan Poe; no one could deny that. After all he had invented the genre, and everyone knew how great his influence had been on the Parnassians. Or was it the Symbolists? Never mind. Baudelaire and all that. As she passed the Achilles Statue she stopped for a minute and looked at it with raised eyebrows.

At length she reached her flat and opening the door saw several hats in the hall. They were all there. She went into the drawing-room.

'Here she is at last,' cried Miss Waterford.

Mrs Albert Forrester advanced, smiling with animation, and shook the proffered hands. Mr Simmons and Clifford Boyleston were there, Harry Oakland and Oscar Charles.

'Oh, you poor things, have you had no tea?' she cried brightly. 'I haven't an idea what the time is, but I know I'm fearfully late.'

'Well?' they said. 'Well?'

'My dears, I've got something quite wonderful to tell you. I've had an inspiration. Why should the devil have all the best tunes?'

'What *do* you mean?'

She paused in order to give full effect to the surprise she was going to spring upon them. Then she flung it at them without preamble.

'I'M GOING TO WRITE A DETECTIVE STORY.'

They stared at her with open mouths. She held up her hand to prevent them from interrupting her, but indeed no one had the smallest intention of doing so.

'I am going to raise the detective story to the dignity of Art. It came to me suddenly in Hyde Park. It's a murder story and I shall give the solution on the very last page. I shall write it in an impeccable English, and since it's occurred to me lately that perhaps I've exhausted the possibilities of the semi-colon, I am going to take up the colon. No one yet has explored its potentialities. Humour and mystery are what I aim at. I shall call it *The Achilles Statue*.'

'What a title!' cried Mr Simmons, recovering himself before any of the others. 'I can sell the serial rights on the title and your name alone.'

'But what about Albert?' asked Clifford Boyleston.

'Albert?' echoed Mrs Forrester. 'Albert?'

She looked at him as though for the life of her she could not think what he was talking about. Then she gave a little cry as if she had suddenly remembered.

'Albert! I knew I'd gone out on some errand and it absolutely slipped my memory. I was walking through Hyde Park and I had this inspiration. What a fool you'll all think me!'

'Then you haven't seen Albert?'

'My dear, I forgot all about him.' She gave an amused laugh. 'Let Albert keep his cook. I can't bother about Albert now. Albert belongs to the semicolon period. I am going to write a detective story.'

'My dear, you're too, too wonderful,' said Harry Oakland.

Virtue

◆

There are few things better than a good Havana. When I was young and very poor and smoked a cigar only when somebody gave me one, I determined that if ever I had money I would smoke a cigar every day after luncheon and after dinner. This is the only resolution of my youth that I have kept. It is the only ambition I have achieved that has never been embittered by disillusion. I like a cigar that is mild, but full-flavoured, neither so small that it is finished before you have become aware of it nor so large as to be irksome, rolled so that it draws without consciousness of effort on your part, with a leaf so firm that it doesn't become messy on your lips, and in such condition that it keeps its savour to the very end. But when you have taken the last pull and put down the shapeless stump and watched the final cloud of smoke dwindle blue in the surrounding air it is impossible, if you have a sensitive nature, not to feel a certain melancholy at the thought of all the labour, the care and pains that have gone, the thought, the trouble, the complicated organization that have been required to provide you with half an hour's delight. For this men have sweltered long years under tropical suns and ships have scoured the seven seas. These reflections become more poignant still when you are eating a dozen oysters (with half a bottle of dry white wine), and they become almost unbearable when it comes to a lamb cutlet. For these are animals and there is something that inspires awe in the thought that since the surface of the earth became capable of supporting life from generation to generation for millions upon millions of years creatures have come into existence to end at last upon a plate of crushed ice or on a silver grill. It may be that a sluggish fancy cannot grasp the dreadful solemnity of eating an oyster and evolution has taught us that the bivalve has through the ages kept itself to itself in a manner that inevitably alienates sympathy. There is an aloofness in it that is offensive to the aspiring spirit of man and a self-complacency that is obnoxious to his vanity. But I do not know how anyone can look upon a lamb cutlet without thoughts too deep for tears: here man himself has taken a hand and the history of the race is bound up with the tender morsel on your plate.

And sometimes even the fate of human beings is curious to consider. It is strange to look upon this man or that, the quiet ordinary persons of every day, the bank clerk, the dustman, the middle-aged girl in the second row of the chorus, and think of the interminable history behind them and of the long, long series of hazards by which from the primeval slime the course of events has brought them at this moment to such and such a place. When such tremendous vicissitudes have been needed to get them here at all one would have thought some huge significance must be attached to them; one would have thought that what befell them must matter a little to the Life Spirit or whatever else it is that has produced them. An accident befalls them. The thread is broken. The story that began with the world is finished abruptly and it looks as though it meant nothing at all. A tale told by an idiot. And is it not odd that this event, of an importance so dramatic, may be brought about by a cause so trivial?

An incident of no moment, that might easily not have happened, has consequences that are incalculable. It looks as though blind chance ruled all things. Our smallest actions may affect profoundly the whole lives of people who have nothing to do with us. The story I have to tell would never have happened if one day I had not walked across the street. Life is really very fantastic and one has to have a peculiar sense of humour to see the fun of it.

I was strolling down Bond Street one spring morning and having nothing much to do till lunch-time thought I would look in at Sotheby's, the auction rooms, to see whether there was anything on show that interested me. There was a block in the traffic and I threaded my way through the cars. When I reached the other side I ran into a man I had known in Borneo coming out of a hatter's.

'Hullo, Morton,' I said. 'When did you come home?'

'I've been back about a week.'

He was a District Officer. The Governor had given me a letter of introduction to him and I wrote and told him I meant to spend a week at the place he lived at and should like to put up at the government rest-house. He met me on the ship when I arrived and asked me to stay with him. I demurred. I did not see how I could spend a week with a total stranger, I did not want to put him to the expense of my board, and besides I thought I should have more freedom if I were on my own. He would not listen to me.

'I've got plenty of room,' he said, 'and the rest-house is beastly. I haven't spoken to a white man for six months and I'm fed to the teeth with my own company.'

But when Morton had got me and his launch had landed us at the bungalow and he had offered me a drink he did not in the least know what to do with me. He was seized on a sudden with shyness, and his conversation, which had been fluent and ready, ran dry. I did my best to make him feel at home (it was the least I could do, considering that it was his own house) and asked him if he had any new records. He turned on the gramophone and the sound of rag-time gave him confidence.

His bungalow overlooked the river and his living-room was a large veranda. It was furnished in the impersonal fashion that characterized the dwellings of government officials who were moved here and there at little notice according to the exigencies of the service. There were native hats as ornaments on the walls and the horns of animals, blow-pipes, and spears. In the book-shelf were detective novels and old magazines. There was a cottage piano with yellow keys. It was very untidy, but not uncomfortable.

Unfortunately I cannot very well remember what he looked like. He was young, twenty-eight, I learnt later, and he had a boyish and attractive smile. I spent an agreeable week with him. We went up and down the river and we climbed a mountain. We had tiffin one day with some planters who lived twenty miles away and every evening we went to the club. The only members were the manager of a kutch factory and his assistants, but they were not on speaking terms with one another and it was only on Morton's representations that they must not let him down when he had a visitor that we could get up a rubber of bridge. The atmosphere was strained. We came back to dinner, listened to the gramophone, and went to bed. Morton had little office work and one would have thought the time hung heavy on his hands, but he had energy and high spirits; it was his first post of the sort and he was happy to be independent. His only anxiety was lest he should be transferred before he had finished a road he was building. This was the joy of his heart. It was his own idea and he had wheedled the government into giving him the money to make it; he had surveyed the country himself and traced the path. He had solved unaided the technical problems that presented themselves. Every morning, before he went to his office, he drove out in a rickety old Ford to where the coolies were working and watched the progress that had been made since the day before. He thought of nothing else. He dreamt of it at night. He reckoned that it would be finished in a year and he did not want to take his leave till then. He could not have worked with more zest if he had been a painter or a sculptor creating a work of art. I think it was this eagerness that made me take a fancy to him. I liked his zeal. I liked his ingenuousness. And I was impressed by the passion for achievement that made him indifferent to the solitariness of his life, to promotion, and even to the thought of going home. I forget how long the road was, fifteen or twenty miles, I think, and I forget what purpose it was to serve. I don't believe Morton cared very much. His passion was the artist's and his triumph was the triumph of man over nature. He learnt as he went along. He had the jungle to contend against, torrential rains that destroyed the labour of weeks, accidents of topography; he had to collect his labour and hold it together; he had inadequate funds. His imagination sustained him. His labours gained a sort of epic quality and the vicissitudes of the work were a great saga that unrolled itself with an infinity of episodes.

His only complaint was that the day was too short. He had office duties, he was judge and tax collector, father and mother (at twenty-eight) of the people in his district; he had now and then to make tours that took him away from home. Unless he was on the spot nothing was done. He would have liked to be there twenty-four hours a day driving the reluctant coolies to further effort. It so happened that shortly before I arrived an incident had occurred that filled him with jubilation. He had offered a contract to a Chinese to make a certain section of the road and the Chinese had asked more than Morton could afford to pay. Notwithstanding interminable discussions they had been unable to arrive at an agreement and Morton with rage in his heart saw his work held up. He was at his wits' end. Then going down to his office one morning, he heard that there had been a row in one of the Chinese gambling houses the night before. A coolie had been badly wounded and his assailant was under arrest. This assailant was the contractor. He was brought into court, the evidence was clear, and Morton sentenced him to eighteen months' hard labour.

'Now he'll have to build the blasted road for nothing,' said Morton, his eyes glistening when he told me the story.

We saw the fellow at work one morning, in the prison sarong, unconcerned. He was taking his misfortune in good part.

'I've told him I'll remit the rest of his sentence when the road's finished,' said Morton, 'and he's as pleased as Punch. Bit of a snip for me, eh, what?'

When I left Morton I asked him to let me know when he came to England and he promised to write to me as soon as he landed. On the spur of the moment one gives these invitations and one is perfectly sincere about them. But when one is taken at one's word a slight dismay seizes one. People are so different at home from what they are abroad. There they are easy, cordial, and natural. They have interesting things to tell you. They are immensely kind. You are anxious when your turn comes to do something in return for the hospitality you have received. But it is not easy. The persons who were so entertaining in their own surroundings are very dull in yours. They are constrained and shy. You introduce them to your friends and your friends find them a crashing bore. They do their best to be civil, but sigh with relief when the strangers go and the conversation can once more run easily in its accustomed channels. I think the residents in far places early in their careers understand the situation pretty well, as the result maybe of bitter and humiliating experiences, for I have found that they seldom take advantage of the invitation which on some outstation on the edge of the jungle has been so cordially extended to them and by them as cordially accepted. But Morton was different. He was a young man and single. It is generally the wives that are the difficulty; other women look at their drab clothes, in a glance take in their provincial air, and freeze them with their indifference. But a man can play bridge and tennis, and dance. Morton had charm. I had had no doubt that in a day or two he would find his feet.

'Why didn't you let me know you were back?' I asked him.

'I thought you wouldn't want to be bothered with me,' he smiled.

'What nonsense!'

Of course now as we stood in Bond Street on the kerb and chatted for a minute he looked strange to me. I had never seen him in anything but khaki shorts and a tennis shirt, except when we got back from the club at night and he put on a pyjama jacket and a sarong for dinner. It is as comfortable a form of evening dress as has ever been devised. He looked a bit awkward in his blue serge suit. His face against a white collar was very brown.

'How about the road?' I asked him.

'Finished. I was afraid I'd have to postpone my leave, we struck one or two snags towards the end, but I made 'em hustle and the day before I left I drove the Ford to the end and back without stopping.'

I laughed. His pleasure was charming.

'What have you been doing with yourself in London?'

'Buying clothes.'

'Been having a good time?'

'Marvellous. A bit lonely, you know, but I don't mind that. I've been to a show every night. The Palmers, you know, I think you met them in Sarawak, were going to be in town and we were going to do the play together, but they had to go to Scotland because her mother's ill.'

His words, said so breezily, cut me to the quick. His was the common experience. It was heartbreaking. For months, for long months before it was due, these people planned their leave, and when they got off the ship they were in such spirits they could hardly contain themselves. London. Shops and clubs and theatres and restaurants. London. They were going to have the time of their lives. London. It swallowed them. A strange turbulent city, not hostile but indifferent, and they were lost in it. They had no friends. They had nothing in common with the acquaintances they made. They were more lonely than in the jungle. It was a relief when at a theatre they ran across someone they had known in the East (and perhaps been bored stiff by or disliked) and they could fix up an evening together and have a good laugh and tell one another what a grand time they were having and talk of common friends and at last confide to one another a little shyly that they would not be sorry when their leave was up and they were once again in harness. They went to see their families and of course they were glad to see them, but it wasn't the same as it had been, they did feel a bit out of it, and when you came down to brass tacks the life people led in England was deadly. It was grand fun to come home, but you couldn't live there any more, and sometimes you thought of your bungalow overlooking the river and your tours of the district and what a lark it was to run over once in a blue moon to Sandakan or Kuching or Singapore.

And because I remembered what Morton had looked forward to when, the road finished and off his chest, he went on leave, I could not but feel a pang when I thought of him dining by himself in a dismal club where he knew nobody or alone in a restaurant in Soho and then going off to see a play with no one by his side with whom he could enjoy it and no one to have a drink with during the interval. And at the same time I reflected that even if I had known he was in London I could have done nothing much for him, for during the last week I had not had a moment free. That very evening I was dining with friends and going to a play, and the next day I was going abroad.

'What are you doing tonight?' I asked him.

'I'm going to the Pavilion. It's packed jammed full, but there's a fellow over the road who's wonderful and he's got me a ticket that had been returned. You can often get one seat, you know, when you can't get two.'

'Why don't you come and have supper with me? I'm taking some people to the Haymarket and we're going on to Ciro's afterwards.'

'I'd love to.'

We arranged to meet at eleven and I left him to keep an engagement.

I was afraid the friends I had asked him to meet would not amuse Morton very much, for they were distinctly middle-aged, but I could not think of anyone young that at this season of the year I should be likely to get hold of at the last moment. None of the girls I knew would thank me for asking her to supper to dance with a shy young man from Malaya. I could trust the Bishops to do their best for him, and after all it must be jollier for him to have supper in a club with a good band where he could see pretty women dancing than to go home to bed at eleven because he had nowhere else in the world to go. I had known Charlie Bishop first when I was a medical student. He was then a thin fellow with sandy hair and blunt features; he had fine eyes, dark and gleaming, but he wore spectacles. He had a round, merry, red face. He was very fond of the girls. I suppose he had a way with him, for, with no money and no looks, he managed to pick up a succession of young persons who gratified his roving desires. He was clever and bumptious, argumentative and quick-tempered. He had a caustic tongue. Looking back, I should say he was a rather disagreeable young man, but I do not think he was a bore. Now, half-way through the fifties, he was inclined to be stout and he was very bald, but his eyes behind the gold-rimmed spectacles were still bright and alert. He was dogmatic and somewhat conceited, argumentative still and caustic, but he was good-natured and amusing. After you have known a person so long his idiosyncrasies cease to trouble you. You accept them as you accept your own physical defects. He was by profession a pathologist and now and then he sent me a slim book he had just published. It was severe and extremely technical and grimly illustrated with photographs of bacteria. I did not read it. I gathered from what I sometimes heard that Charlie's views on the subjects with which he dealt were unsound. I do not believe that he was very popular with the other members of his profession, he made no secret of the fact that he looked upon them as a set of incompetent idiots; but he had his job, it brought him in six or eight hundred a year, I think, and he was completely indifferent to other people's opinion of him.

I liked Charlie Bishop because I had known him for thirty years, but I liked Margery, his wife, because she was very nice. I was extremely surprised when he told me he was going to be married. He was hard on forty at the time and so fickle in his affections that I had made up my mind he would remain single. He was very fond of women, but he was not in the least sentimental, and his aims were loose. His views on the female sex would in these idealistic days be thought crude. He knew what he wanted and he asked for it, and if he couldn't get it for love or money he shrugged his shoulders and went his way. To be brief, he did not look to women to gratify his ideal but to provide him with fornication. It was odd that though small and plain he found so many who were prepared to grant his wishes. For his spiritual needs he found satisfaction in unicellular organisms. He had always been a man who spoke to the point, and when he told me he was going to marry a young woman called Margery Hobson I did not hesitate to ask him why. He grinned.

'Three reasons. First, she won't let me go to bed with her without. Second, she makes me laugh like a hyena. And third, she's alone in the world, without a single relation, and she must have someone to take care of her.'

'The first reason is just swank and the second is eyewash. The third is the real one and it means that she's got you by the short hairs.'

His eyes gleamed softly behind his large spectacles.

'I shouldn't be surprised if you weren't dead right.'

'She's not only got you by the short hairs but you're as pleased as Punch that she has.'

'Come and lunch tomorrow and have a look at her. She's easy on the eye.'

Charlie was a member of a cock-and-hen club which at that time I used a good deal and we arranged to lunch there. I found Margery a very attractive young woman. She was then just under thirty. She was a lady. I noticed the fact with satisfaction, but with a certain astonishment, for it had not escaped my notice that Charlie was attracted as a rule by women whose breeding left something to be desired. She was not beautiful, but comely, with fine dark hair and fine eyes, a good colour and a look of health. She had a pleasant frankness and an air of candour that were very taking. She looked honest, simple, and dependable. I took an immediate liking to her. She was easy to talk to and though she did not say anything very brilliant she understood what other people were talking about; she was quick to see a joke and she was not shy. She gave you the impression of being competent and business-like. She had a happy placidity that suggested a good temper and an excellent digestion.

They seemed extremely pleased with one another. I had asked myself when I first saw her why Margery was marrying this irritable little man, baldish already and by no means young, but I discovered very soon that it was because she was in love with him. They chaffed one another a good deal and laughed a lot and every now and then their eyes met more significantly and they seemed to exchange a little private message. It was really rather touching.

A week later they were married at a registrar's office. It was a very successful marriage. Looking back now after sixteen years I could not but chuckle sympathetically at the thought of the lark they had made of their life together. I had never known a more devoted couple. They had never had very much money. They never seemed to want any. They had no ambitions. Their life was a picnic that never came to an end. They lived in the smallest flat I ever saw, in Panton Street, a small bedroom, a small sitting-room, and a bathroom that served also as a kitchen. But they had no sense of home, they ate their meals in restaurants, and only had breakfast in the flat. It was merely a place to sleep in. It was comfortable, though a third person coming in for a whisky and soda crowded it, and Margery with the help of a charwoman kept it as neat as Charlie's untidiness permitted, but there was not a single thing in it that had a personal note. They had a tiny car and whenever Charlie had a holiday they took it across the Channel and started off, with a bag each for all their luggage, to drive wherever the fancy took them. Breakdowns never disturbed them, bad weather was part of the fun, a puncture was no end of a joke, and if they lost their way and had to sleep out in the open they thought they were having the time of their lives.

Charlie continued to be irascible and contentious, but nothing he did ever disturbed Margery's lovely placidity. She could calm him with a word. She still made him laugh. She typed his monographs on obscure bacteria and corrected the proofs of his articles in the scientific magazines. Once I asked them if they ever quarrelled.

'No,' she said, 'we never seem to have anything to quarrel about. Charlie has the temper of an angel.'

'Nonsense,' I said, 'he's an overbearing, aggressive, and cantankerous fellow. He always has been.'

She looked at him and giggled and I saw that she thought I was being funny.

'Let him rave,' said Charlie. 'He's an ignorant fool and he uses words of whose meaning he hasn't the smallest idea.'

They were sweet together. They were very happy in one another's company and were never apart if they could help it. Even after the long time they had been married Charlie used to get into the car every day at luncheon-time to come west and meet Margery at a restaurant. People used to laugh at them, not unkindly, but perhaps with a little catch in the throat, because when they were asked to go and spend a week-end in the country Margery would write to the hostess and say they would like to come if they could be given a double bed. They had slept together for so many years that neither of them could sleep alone. It was often a trifle awkward. Husbands and wives as a rule not only demanded separate rooms, but were inclined to be peevish if asked to share the same bathroom. Modern houses were not arranged for domestic couples, but among their friends it became an understood thing that if you wanted the Bishops you must give them a room with a double bed. Some people of course thought it a little indecent, and it was never convenient, but they were a pleasant pair to have to stay and it was worth while to put up with their crankiness. Charlie was always full of spirits and in his caustic way extremely amusing, and Margery was peaceful and easy. They were no trouble to entertain. Nothing pleased them more than to be left to go out together for a long ramble in the country.

When a man marries, his wife sooner or later estranges him from his old friends, but Margery on the contrary increased Charlie's intimacy with them. By making him more tolerant she made him a more agreeable companion. They gave you the impression not of a married couple, but, rather amusingly, of two middle-aged bachelors living together; and when Margery, as was the rule, found herself the only woman among half a dozen men, ribald, argumentative, and gay, she was not a bar to good-fellowship but an asset. Whenever I was in England I saw them. They generally dined at the club of which I have spoken and if I happened to be alone I joined them.

When we met that evening for a snack before going to the play I told them I had asked Morton to come to supper.

'I'm afraid you'll find him rather dull,' I said. 'But he's a very decent sort of boy and he was awfully kind to me when I was in Borneo.'

'Why didn't you let me know sooner?' cried Margery. 'I'd have brought a girl along.'

'What do you want a girl for?' said Charlie. 'There'll be you.'

'I don't think it can be much fun for a young man to dance with a woman of my advanced years,' said Margery.

'Rot. What's your age got to do with it?' He turned to me. 'Have you ever danced with anyone who danced better?'

I had, but she certainly danced very well. She was light on her feet and she had a good sense of rhythm.

'Never,' I said heartily.

Morton was waiting for us when we reached Ciro's. He looked very sunburned in his evening clothes. Perhaps it was because I knew that they had been wrapped away in a tin box with mothballs for four years that I felt he did not look quite at home in them. He was certainly more at ease in khaki shorts. Charlie Bishop was a good talker and liked to hear himself speak. Morton was shy. I gave him a cocktail and ordered some champagne. I had a feeling that he would be glad to dance, but was not quite sure whether it would occur to him to ask Margery. I was acutely conscious that we all belonged to another generation.

'I think I should tell you that Mrs Bishop is a beautiful dancer,' I said.

'Is she?' He flushed a little. 'Will you dance with me?'

She got up and they took the floor. She was looking peculiarly nice that evening, not at all smart, and I do not think her plain black dress had cost more than six guineas, but she looked a lady. She had the advantage of having extremely good legs and at that time skirts were still being worn very short. I suppose she had a little make-up on, but in contrast with the other women there she looked very natural. Shingled hair suited her; it was not even touched with white and it had an attractive sheen. She was not a pretty woman, but her kindliness, her wholesome air, her good health gave you, if not the illusion that she was, at least the feeling that it didn't at all matter. When she came back to the table her eyes were bright and she had a heightened colour.

'How does he dance?' asked her husband.

'Divinely.'

'You're very easy to dance with,' said Morton.

Charlie went on with his discourse. He had a sardonic humour and he was interesting because he was himself so interested in what he said. But he spoke of things that Morton knew nothing about and though he listened with a civil show of interest I could see that he was too much excited by the gaiety of the scene, the music, and the champagne to give his attention to conversation. When the music struck up again his eyes immediately sought Margery's. Charlie caught the look and smiled.

'Dance with him, Margery. Good for my figure to see you take exercise.'

They set off again and for a moment Charlie watched her with fond eyes.

'Margery's having the time of her life. She loves dancing and it makes me puff and blow. Not a bad youth.'

My little party was quite a success and when Morton and I, having taken leave of the Bishops, walked together towards Piccadilly Circus he thanked me warmly. He had really enjoyed himself. I said good-bye to him. Next morning I went abroad.

I was sorry not to have been able to do more for Morton and I knew that when I returned he would be on his way back to Borneo. I gave him a passing thought now and then, but by the autumn when I got home he had slipped my memory. After I had been in London a week or so I happened to drop in one night at the club to which Charlie Bishop also belonged. He was sitting with three or four men I knew and I went up. I had not seen any of them since my return. One of them, a man called Bill Marsh, whose wife, Janet, was a great friend of mine, asked me to have a drink.

'Where have you sprung from?' asked Charlie. 'Haven't seen you about lately.'

I noticed at once that he was drunk. I was astonished. Charlie had always liked his liquor, but he carried it well and never exceeded. In years gone by, when we were very young, he got tight occasionally, but probably more than anything to show what a great fellow he was, and it is unfair to bring up against a man the excesses of his youth. But I remembered that Charlie had never been very nice when he was drunk: his natural aggressiveness was exaggerated then and he talked too much and too loud; he was very apt to be quarrelsome. He was very dogmatic now, laying down the law and refusing to listen to any of the objections his rash statements called forth. The others knew he was drunk and were struggling between the irritation his cantankerousness aroused in them and the good-natured tolerance which they felt his condition demanded. He was not an agreeable object. A man of that age, bald and fattish, with spectacles, is disgusting drunk. He was generally rather dapper, but he was untidy now and there was tobacco ash all over him. Charlie called the waiter and ordered another whisky. The waiter had been at the club for thirty years.

'You've got one in front of you, sir.'

'Mind your own damned business,' said Charlie Bishop. 'Bring me a double whisky right away or I'll report you to the secretary for insolence.'

'Very good, sir,' said the waiter.

Charlie emptied his glass at a gulp, but his hand was unsteady and he spilled some of the whisky over himself.

'Well, Charlie, old boy, we'd better be toddling along,' said Bill Marsh. He turned to me. 'Charlie's staying with us for a bit.'

I was more surprised still. But I felt that something was wrong and thought it safer not to say anything.

'I'm ready,' said Charlie. 'I'll just have another drink before I go. I shall have a better night if I do.'

It did not look to me as though the party would break up for some time, so I got up and announced that I meant to stroll home.

'I say,' said Bill, as I was about to go, 'you wouldn't come and dine with us tomorrow night, would you, just me and Janet and Charlie?'

'Yes, I'll come with pleasure,' I said.

It was evident that something was up.

The Marshes lived in a terrace on the East side of Regent's Park. The maid who opened the door for me asked me to go in to Mr Marsh's study. He was waiting for me there.

'I thought I'd better have a word with you before you went upstairs,' he said as he shook hands with me. 'You know Margery's left Charlie?'

'No!'

'He's taken it very hard. Janet thought it was so awful for him alone in that beastly little flat that we asked him to stay here for a bit. We've done everything we could for him. He's been drinking like a fish. He hasn't slept a wink for a fortnight.'

'But she hasn't left him for good?'

I was astounded.

'Yes. She's crazy about a fellow called Morton.'

'Morton. Who's he?'

It never struck me it was my friend from Borneo.

'Damn it all, you introduced him and a pretty piece of work you did. Let's go upstairs. I thought I'd better put you wise.'

He opened the door and we went out. I was thoroughly confused.

'But look here,' I said.

'Ask Janet. She knows the whole thing. It beats me. I've got no patience with Margery, and he must be a mess.'

He preceded me into the drawing-room. Janet Marsh rose as I entered and came forward to greet me. Charlie was sitting at the window, reading the evening paper; he put it aside as I went up to him and shook his hand. He was quite sober and he spoke in his usual rather perky manner, but I noticed that he looked very ill. We had a glass of sherry and went down to dinner. Janet was a woman of spirit. She was tall and fair and good to look at. She kept the conversation going with alertness. When she left us to drink a glass of port it was with instructions not to stay more than ten minutes. Bill, as a rule somewhat taciturn, exerted himself now to talk. I tumbled to the game. I was hampered by my ignorance of what exactly had happened, but it was plain that the Marshes wanted to prevent Charlie from brooding, and I did my best to interest him. He seemed willing to play his part, he was always fond of holding forth, and he discussed, from the pathologist's standpoint, a murder that was just then absorbing the public. But he spoke without life. He was an empty shell, and one had the feeling that though for the sake of his host he forced himself to speak, his thoughts were elsewhere. It was a relief when a knocking on the floor above indicated to us that Janet was getting impatient. This was an occasion when a woman's presence eased the situation. We went upstairs and played family bridge. When it was time for me to go Charlie said he would walk with me as far as the Marylebone Road.

'Oh, Charlie, it's so late, you'd much better go to bed,' said Janet.

'I shall sleep better if I have a stroll before turning in,' he replied.

She gave him a worried look. You cannot forbid a middle-aged professor of pathology from going for a little walk if he wants to. She glanced brightly at her husband.

'I daresay it'll do Bill no harm.'

I think the remark was tactless. Women are often a little too managing. Charlie gave her a sullen look.

'There's absolutely no need to drag Bill out,' he said with some firmness.

'I haven't the smallest intention of coming,' said Bill, smiling. 'I'm tired out and I'm going to hit the hay.'

I fancy we left Bill Marsh and his wife to a little argument.

'They've been frightfully kind to me,' said Charlie, as we walked along by the railings. 'I don't know what I should have done without them. I haven't slept for a fortnight.'

I expressed regret but did not ask the reason, and we walked for a little in silence. I presumed that he had come with me in order to talk to me of what had happened, but I felt that he must take his own time. I was anxious to show my sympathy, but afraid of saying the wrong things; I did not want to seem eager to extract confidences from him. I did not know how to give him a lead. I was sure he did not want one. He was not a man given to beating about the bush. I imagined that he was choosing his words. We reached the corner.

'You'll be able to get a taxi at the church,' he said. 'I'll walk on a bit further. Good night.'

He nodded and slouched off. I was taken aback. There was nothing for me to do but to stroll on till I found a cab. I was having my bath next morning when a telephone call dragged me out of it, and with a towel round my wet body I took up the receiver. It was Janet.

'Well, what do you think of it all?' she said. 'You seem to have kept Charlie up pretty late last night. I heard him come home at three.'

'He left me at the Marylebone Road,' I answered. 'He said nothing to me at all.'

'Didn't he?'

There was something in Janet's voice that suggested that she was prepared to have a long talk with me. I suspected she had a telephone by the side of her bed.

'Look here,' I said quickly. 'I'm having my bath.'

'Oh, have you got a telephone in your bathroom?' she answered eagerly, and I think with envy.

'No, I haven't.' I was abrupt and firm. 'And I'm dripping all over the carpet.'

'Oh!' I felt disappointment in her tone and a trace of irritation. 'Well, when can I see you? Can you come here at twelve?'

It was inconvenient, but I was not prepared to start an argument.

'Yes, good-bye.'

I rang off before she could say anything more. In heaven when the blessed use the telephone they will say what they have to say and not a word beside.

I was devoted to Janet, but I knew that there was nothing that thrilled her more than the misfortunes of her friends. She was only too anxious to help them, but she wanted to be in the thick of their difficulties. She was the friend in adversity. Other people's business was meat and drink to her. You could not enter upon a love affair without finding her somehow your confidante nor be mixed up in a divorce case without discovering that she too had a finger in the pie. Withal she was a very nice woman. I could not help then chuckling in my heart when at noon I was shown into Janet's drawing-room and observed the subdued eagerness with which she received me. She was very much upset by the catastrophe that had befallen the Bishops, but it was exciting, and she was tickled to death to have someone fresh whom she could tell all about it. Janet had just that business-like expectancy that a mother has when she is discussing with the family doctor her married daughter's first confinement. Janet was conscious that the matter was very serious, and she would not for a moment have been thought to regard it flippantly, but she was determined to get every ounce of value out of it.

'I mean, no one could have been more horrified than I was when Margery told me she'd finally made up her mind to leave Charlie,' she said, speaking with the fluency of a person who has said the same thing in the same words a dozen times at least. 'They were the most devoted couple I'd ever known. It was a perfect marriage. They got on like a house on fire. Of course Bill and I are devoted to one another, but we have awful rows now and then. I mean, I could kill him sometimes.'

'I don't care a hang about your relations with Bill,' I said. 'Tell me about the Bishops. That's what I've come here for.'

'I simply felt I must see you. After all you're the only person who can explain it.'

'Oh, God, don't go on like that. Until Bill told me last night I didn't know a thing about it.'

'That was my idea. It suddenly dawned on me that perhaps you didn't know and I thought you might put your foot in it too awfully.'

'Supposing you began at the beginning,' I said.

'Well, you're the beginning. After all you started the trouble. You introduced the young man. That's why I was so crazy to see you. You know all about him. I never saw him. All I know is what Margery has told me about him.'

'At what time are you lunching?' I asked.

'Half past one.'

'So am I. Get on with the story.'

But my remark had given Janet an idea.

'Look here, will you get out of your luncheon if I get out of mine? We could have a snack here. I'm sure there's some cold meat in the house, and then we needn't hurry. I don't have to be at the hairdresser's till three.'

'No, no, no,' I said. 'I hate the notion of that. I shall leave here at twenty minutes past one at the latest.'

'Then I shall just have to race through it. What do *you* think of Gerry?'

'Who's Gerry?'

'Gerry Morton. His name's Gerald.'

'How should I know that?'

'You stayed with him. Weren't there any letters lying about?'

'I daresay, but I didn't happen to read them,' I answered somewhat tartly.

'Oh, don't be so stupid. I meant the envelopes. What's he like?'

'All right. Rather the Kipling type, you know. Very keen on his work. Hearty. Empire-builder and all that sort of thing.'

'I don't mean that,' cried Janet, not without impatience. 'I mean, what does he look like?'

'More or less like everybody else, I think. Of course I should recognize him if I saw him again, but I can't picture him to myself very distinctly. He looks clean.'

'Oh, my God,' said Janet. 'Are you a novelist or are you not? What's the colour of his eyes?'

'I don't know.'

'You must know. You can't spend a week with anyone without knowing if their eyes are blue or brown. Is he fair or dark?'

'Neither.'

'Is he tall or short?'

'Average, I should say.'

'Are you trying to irritate me?'

'No. He's just ordinary. There's nothing in him to attract your attention. He's neither plain nor good-looking. He looks quite decent. He looks a gentleman.'

'Margery says he has a charming smile and a lovely figure.'

'I dare say.'

'He's absolutely crazy about her.'

'What makes you think that?' I asked dryly.

'I've seen his letters.'

'Do you mean to say she's shown them to you?'

'Why, of course.'

It is always difficult for a man to stomach the want of reticence that women betray in their private affairs. They have no shame. They will talk to one another without embarrassment of the most intimate matters. Modesty is a masculine virtue. But though a man may know this theoretically, each time he is confronted with women's lack of reserve he suffers a new shock. I wondered what Morton would think if he knew that not only were his letters read by Janet Marsh as well as by Margery, but that she had been kept posted from day to day with the progress of his infatuation. According to Janet he had fallen in love with Margery at first sight. The morning after they had met at my little supper party at Ciro's he had rung up and asked her to come and have tea with him at some place where they could dance. While I listened to Janet's story I was conscious of course that she was giving me Margery's view of the circumstances and I kept an open mind. I was interested to observe that Janet's sympathies were with Margery. It was true that when Margery left her husband it was her idea that Charlie should come to them for two or three weeks rather than stay on in miserable loneliness in the deserted flat and she had been extraordinarily kind to him. She lunched with him almost every day, because he had been accustomed to lunch every day with Margery; she took him for walks in Regent's Park and made Bill play golf with him on Sundays. She listened with wonderful patience to the story of his unhappiness and did what she could to console him. She was terribly sorry for him. But all the same she was definitely on Margery's side and when I expressed my disapproval of her she came down on me like a thousand of bricks. The affair thrilled her. She had been in it from the beginning when Margery, smiling, flattered, and a little doubtful, came and told her that she had a young man to the final scene when Margery, exasperated and distraught, announced that she could not stand the strain any more and had packed her things and moved out of the flat.

'Of course, at first I couldn't believe my ears,' she said. 'You know how Charlie and Margery were. They simply lived in one another's pockets. One couldn't help laughing at them, they were so devoted to one another. I never thought him a very nice little man and heaven knows he wasn't very attractive physically, but one couldn't help liking him because he was so awfully nice to

Margery. I rather envied her sometimes. They had no money and they lived in a hugger-mugger sort of way, but they were frightfully happy. Of course I never thought anything would come of it. Margery was rather amused. "Naturally I don't take it very seriously," she told me, "but it is rather fun to have a young man at my time of life. I haven't had any flowers sent me for years. I had to tell him not to send any more because Charlie would think it so silly. He doesn't know a soul in London and he loves dancing and he says I dance like a dream. It's miserable for him going to the theatre by himself all the time and we've done two or three matinées together. It's pathetic to see how grateful he is when I say I'll go out with him." "I must say," I said, "he sounds rather a lamb." "He is," she said. "I knew you'd understand. You don't blame me, do you?" "Of course not, darling," I said, "surely you know me better than that. I'd do just the same in your place."'

Margery made no secret of her outings with Morton and her husband chaffed her good-naturedly about her beau. But he thought him a very civil, pleasant-spoken young man and was glad that Margery had someone to play with while he was busy. It never occurred to him to be jealous. The three of them dined together several times and went to a show. But presently Gerry Morton begged Margery to spend an evening with him alone; she said it was impossible, but he was persuasive, he gave her no peace; and at last she went to Janet and asked her to ring up Charlie one day and ask him to come to dinner and make a fourth at bridge. Charlie would never go anywhere without his wife, but the Marshes were old friends, and Janet made a point of it. She invented some cock-and-bull story that made it seem important that he should consent. Next day Margery and she met. The evening had been wonderful. They had dined at Maidenhead and danced there and then had driven home through the summer night.

'He says he's crazy about me,' Margery told her.

'Did he kiss you?' asked Janet.

'Of course,' Margery chuckled. 'Don't be silly, Janet. He is awfully sweet and, you know, he has such a nice nature. Of course I don't believe half the things he says to me.'

'My dear, you're not going to fall in love with him.'

'I have,' said Margery.

'Darling, isn't it going to be rather awkward?'

'Oh, it won't last. After all he's going back to Borneo in the autumn.'

'Well, one can't deny that it's made you look years younger.'

'I know, and I feel years younger.'

Soon they were meeting every day. They met in the morning and walked in the Park together or went to a picture gallery. They separated for Margery to lunch with her husband and after lunch met again and motored into the country or to some place on the river. Margery did not tell her husband. She very naturally thought he would not understand.

'How was it you never met Morton?' I asked Janet.

'Oh, she didn't want me to. You see, we belong to the same generation, Margery and I. I can quite understand that.'

'I see.'

'Of course I did everything I could. When she went out with Gerry she was always supposed to be with me.'

I am a person who likes to cross a 't' and dot an 'i'.

'Were they having an affair?' I asked.

'Oh, no. Margery isn't that sort of woman at all.'

'How do you know?'

'She would have told me.'

'I suppose she would.'

'Of course I asked her. But she denied it point-blank and I'm sure she was telling me the truth. There's never been anything of that sort between them at all.'

'It seems rather odd to me.'

'Well, you see, Margery is a very good woman.'

I shrugged my shoulders.

'She was absolutely loyal to Charlie. She wouldn't have deceived him for anything in the world. She couldn't bear the thought of having any secret from him. As soon as she knew she was in love with Gerry she wanted to tell Charlie. Of course I begged her not to. I told her it wouldn't do any good and it would only make Charlie miserable. And after all, the boy was going away in a couple of months, it didn't seem much good to make a lot of fuss about a thing that couldn't possibly last.'

But Gerry's imminent departure was the cause of the crash. The Bishops had arranged to go abroad as usual and proposed to motor through Belgium, Holland, and the North of Germany. Charlie was busy with maps and guides. He collected information from friends about hotels and roads. He looked forward to his holiday with the bubbling excitement of a schoolboy. Margery listened to him discussing it with a sinking heart. They were to be away four weeks and in September Gerry was sailing. She could not bear to lose so much of the short time that remained to them and the thought of the motor tour filled her with exasperation. As the interval grew shorter and shorter she grew more and more nervous. At last she decided that there was only one thing to do.

'Charlie, I don't want to come on this trip,' she interrupted him suddenly, one day when he was talking to her of some restaurant he had just heard of. 'I wish you'd get someone else to go with you.'

He looked at her blankly. She was startled at what she had said and her lips trembled a little.

'Why, what's the matter?'

'Nothing's the matter. I don't feel like it. I want to be by myself for a bit.'

'Are you ill?'

She saw the sudden fear in his eyes. His concern drove her beyond her endurance.

'No. I've never been better in my life. I'm in love.'

'You? Whom with?'

'Gerry.'

He looked at her in amazement. He could not believe his ears. She mistook his expression.

'It's no good blaming me. I can't help it. He's going away in a few weeks. I'm not going to waste the little time he has left.'

He burst out laughing.

'Margery, how can you make such a damned fool of yourself? You're old enough to be his mother.'

She flushed.

'He's just as much in love with me as I am with him.'

'Has he told you so?'

'A thousand times.'

'He's a bloody liar, that's all.'

He chuckled. His fat stomach rippled with mirth. He thought it a huge joke. I daresay Charlie did not treat his wife in the proper way. Janet seemed to think he should have been tender and compassionate. *He should have understood.* I saw the scene that was in her mind's eye, the stiff upper lip, the silent sorrow, and the final renunciation. Women are always sensitive to the beauty of the self-sacrifice of others. Janet would have sympathized also if he had flown into a violent passion, broken one or two pieces of furniture (which he would have had to replace), or given Margery a sock in the jaw. But to laugh at her was unpardonable. I did not point out that it is very difficult for a rather stout and not very tall professor of pathology, aged fifty-five, to act all of a sudden like a cave-man. Anyhow, the excursion to Holland was given up and the Bishops stayed in London through August. They were not very happy. They lunched and dined together every day because they had been in the habit of doing so for so many years and the rest of the time Margery spent with Gerry. The hours she passed with him made up for all she had to put up with and she had to put up with a good deal. Charlie had a ribald and sarcastic humour and he made himself very funny at her expense and at Gerry's. He persisted in refusing to take the matter seriously. He was vexed with Margery for being so silly, but apparently it never occurred to him that she might have been unfaithful to him. I commented upon this to Janet.

'He never suspected it even,' she said. 'He knew Margery much too well.'

The weeks passed and at last Gerry sailed. He went from Tilbury and Margery saw him off. When she came back she cried for forty-eight hours. Charlie watched her with increasing exasperation. His nerves were much frayed.

'Look here, Margery,' he said at last, 'I've been very patient with you, but now you must pull yourself together. This is getting past a joke.'

'Why can't you leave me alone?' she cried. 'I've lost everything that made life lovely to me.'

'Don't be such a fool,' he said.

I do not know what else he said. But he was unwise enough to tell her what he thought of Gerry and I gather that the picture he drew was virulent. It started the first violent scene they had ever had. She had borne Charlie's jibes when she knew that she would see Gerry in an hour or next day, but now that she had lost him for ever she could bear them no longer. She had held herself in for weeks: now she flung her self-control to the winds. Perhaps she never knew exactly what she said to Charlie. He had always been irascible and at last he hit her. They were both frightened when he had. He seized a hat and flung out of the flat. During all that miserable time they had shared the same bed, but when he came back, in the middle of the night, he found that she had made herself up a shake-down on the sofa in the sitting-room.

'You can't sleep there,' he said. 'Don't be so silly. Come to bed.'

'No, I won't, let me alone.'

For the rest of the night they wrangled, but she had her way and now made up her bed every night on the sofa. But in that tiny flat they could not get away from one another; they could not even get out of sight or out of hearing of one another. They had lived in such intimacy for so many years that it was an instinct for them to be together. He tried to reason with her. He thought her incredibly stupid and argued with her interminably in the effort to show her how wrong-headed she was. He could not leave her alone. He would not let her sleep, and he talked half through the night till they were both exhausted. He thought he could talk her out of love. For two or three days at a time they would not speak to one another. Then one day, coming home, he found her crying bitterly; the sight of her tears distracted him; he told her how much he loved her and sought to move her by the recollection of all the happy years they had spent together. He wanted to let bygones be bygones. He promised never to refer to Gerry again. Could they not forget the nightmare they had been through? But the thought of all that a reconciliation implied revolted her. She told him she had a racking headache and asked him to give her a sleeping draught. She pretended to be still asleep when he went out next morning, but the moment he was gone she packed up her things and left. She had a few trinkets that she had inherited and by selling them she got a little money. She took a room at a cheap boarding-house and kept her address a secret from Charlie.

It was when he found she had left him that he went all to pieces. The shock of her flight broke him. He told Janet that his loneliness was intolerable. He wrote to Margery imploring her to come back, and asked Janet to intercede for him; he was willing to promise anything; he abased himself. Margery was obdurate.

'Do you think she'll ever go back?' I asked Janet.

'She says not.'

I had to leave then, for it was nearly half past one and I was bound for the other end of London.

Two or three days later I got a telephone message from Margery asking if I could see her. She suggested coming to my rooms. I asked her to tea. I tried to be nice to her; her affairs were no business of mine, but in my heart I thought her a very silly woman and I dare say my manner was cold. She had never been handsome and the passing years had changed her little. She had still those fine dark eyes and her face was astonishingly unlined. She was very simply dressed and if she wore make-up it was so cunningly put on that I did not perceive it. She had still the charm she had always had of perfect naturalness and of a kindly humour.

'I want you to do something for me if you will,' she began without beating about the bush.

'What is it?'

'Charlie is leaving the Marshes today and going back to the flat. I'm afraid his first few days there will be rather difficult; it would be awfully nice of you if you'd ask him to dinner or something.'

'I'll have a look at my book.'

'I'm told he's been drinking heavily. It's such a pity. I wish you could give him a hint.'

'I understand he's had some domestic worries of late,' I said, perhaps acidly.

Margery flushed. She gave me a pained look. She winced as though I had struck her.

'Of course you've known him ever so much longer than you've known me. It's natural that you should take his part.'

'My dear, to tell you the truth I've known him all these years chiefly on your account. I have never very much liked him, but I thought you were awfully nice.'

She smiled at me and her smile was very sweet. She knew that I meant what I said.

'Do you think I was a good wife to him?'

'Perfect.'

'He used to put people's backs up. A lot of people didn't like him, but I never found him difficult.'

'He was awfully fond of you.'

'I know. We had a wonderful time together. For sixteen years we were perfectly happy.' She paused and looked down. 'I had to leave him. It became quite impossible. That cat-and-dog life we were leading was too awful.'

'I never see why two persons should go on living together if they don't want to.'

'You see, it was awful for us. We'd always lived in such close intimacy. We could never get away from one another. At the end I hated the sight of him.'

'I don't suppose the situation was easy for either of you.'

'It wasn't my fault that I fell in love. You see, it was quite a different love from the one I'd felt for Charlie. There was always something maternal in that and protective. I was so much more reasonable than he was. He was unmanageable, but I could always manage him. Gerry was different.' Her voice grew soft and her face was transfigured with glory. 'He gave me back my youth. I was a girl to him and I could depend on his strength and be safe in his care.'

'He seemed to me a very nice lad,' I said slowly. 'I imagine he'll do well. He was very young for the job he had when I ran across him. He's only twenty-nine now, isn't he?'

She smiled softly. She knew quite well what I meant.

'I never made any secret of my age to him. He says it doesn't matter.'

I knew this was true. She was not the woman to have lied about her age. She had found a sort of fierce delight in telling him the truth about herself.

'How old are you?'

'Forty-four.'

'What are you going to do now?'

'I've written to Gerry and told him I've left Charlie. As soon as I hear from him I'm going out to join him.'

I was staggered.

'You know, it's a very primitive little colony he's living in. I'm afraid you'll find your position rather awkward.'

'He made me promise that if I found my life impossible after he left I'd go to him.'

'Are you sure you're wise to attach so much importance to the things a young man says when he's in love?'

Again that really beautiful look of exaltation came into her face.

'Yes, when the young man happens to be Gerry.'

My heart sank. I was silent for a moment. Then I told her the story of the road Gerry Morton had built. I dramatized it, and I think I made it rather effective.

'What did you tell me that for?' she asked when I finished.

'I thought it rather a good story.'

She shook her head and smiled.

'No, you wanted to show me that he was very young and enthusiastic, and so keen on his work that he hadn't much time to waste on other interests. I wouldn't interfere with his work. You don't know him as I do. He's incredibly romantic. He looks upon himself as a pioneer. I've caught from him something of his excitement at the idea of taking part in the opening up of a new country. It *is* rather splendid, isn't it? It makes life here seem very humdrum and commonplace. But of course it's very lonely there. Even the companionship of a middle-aged woman may be worth having.'

'Are you proposing to marry him?' I asked.

'I leave myself in his hands. I want to do nothing that he does not wish.'

She spoke with so much simplicity, there was something so touching in her self-surrender, that when she left me I no longer felt angry with her. Of course I thought her very foolish, but if the folly of men made one angry one would pass one's life in a state of chronic ire. I thought all would come right. She said Gerry was romantic. He was, but the romantics in this workaday world only get away with their nonsense because they have at bottom a shrewd sense of reality: the mugs are the people who take their vapourings at their face value. The English are romantic; that is why other nations think them hypocritical; they are not: they set out in all sincerity for the Kingdom of God, but the journey is arduous and they have reason to pick up any gilt-edged investment that offers itself by the way. The British soul, like Wellington's armies, marches on its belly. I supposed that Gerry would go through a bad quarter of an hour when he received Margery's letter. My sympathies were not deeply engaged in the matter and I was only curious to see how he would extricate himself from the pass he was in. I thought Margery would suffer a bitter disappointment; well, that would do her no great harm, and then she would go back to her husband and I had no doubt the pair of them, chastened, would live in peace, quiet, and happiness for the rest of their lives.

The event was different. It happened that it was quite impossible for me to make any sort of engagement with Charlie Bishop for some days, but I wrote to him and asked him to dine with me one evening in the following week. I proposed, though with misgiving, that we should go to a play; I knew he was drinking like a fish, and when tight he was noisy. I hoped he would not make a nuisance of himself in the theatre. We arranged to meet at our club and dine at seven because the piece we were going to began at a quarter past eight. I arrived. I waited. He did not come. I rang up his flat, but could get no reply, so concluded that he was on his way. I hate missing the beginning of a play and I waited impatiently in the hall so that when he came we could go straight upstairs. To save time I had ordered dinner. The clock pointed to half past seven, then a quarter to eight; I did not see why I should wait for him any longer, so walked up to the dining-room and ate my dinner alone. He did not appear. I put a call through from the dining-room to the Marshes and presently was told by a waiter that Bill Marsh was at the end of the wire.

'I say, do you know anything about Charlie Bishop?' I said. 'We were dining together and going to a play and he hasn't turned up.'

'He died this afternoon.'

'What?'

My exclamation was so startled that two or three people within earshot looked up. The dining-room was full and the waiters were hurrying to and fro. The telephone was on the cashier's desk and a wine waiter came up with a bottle of hock and two long-stemmed glasses on a tray and gave the cashier a chit. The portly steward showing two men to a table jostled me.

'Where are you speaking from?' asked Bill.

I suppose he heard the clatter that surrounded me. When I told him he asked me if I could come round as soon as I had finished my dinner. Janet wanted to speak to me.

'I'll come at once,' I said.

I found Janet and Bill sitting in the drawing-room. He was reading the paper and she was playing patience. She came forward swiftly when the maid showed me in. She walked with a sort of spring, crouching a little, on silent feet, like a panther stalking his prey. I saw at once that she was in her element. She gave me her hand and turned her face away to hide her eyes brimming with tears. Her voice was low and tragic.

'I brought Margery here and put her to bed. The doctor has given her a sedative. She's all in. Isn't it awful?' She gave a sound that was something between a gasp and a sob. 'I don't know why these things always happen to me.'

The Bishops had never kept a servant but a charwoman went in every morning, cleaned the flat, and washed up the breakfast things. She had her own key. That morning she had gone in as usual and done the sitting-room. Since his wife had left him Charlie's hours had been irregular and she was not surprised to find him asleep. But the time passed and she knew he had his work to go to. She went to the bedroom door and knocked. There was no answer. She thought she heard him groaning. She opened the door softly. He was lying in bed, on his back, and was breathing stertorously. He did not wake. She called him. Something about him frightened her. She went to the flat on the same landing. It was occupied by a journalist. He was still in bed when she rang, and opened the door to her in pyjamas.

'Beg pardon, sir,' she said, 'but would you just come and 'ave a look at my gentleman. I don't think he's well.'

The journalist walked across the landing and into Charlie's flat. There was an empty bottle of veronal by the bed.

'I think you'd better fetch a policeman,' he said.

A policeman came and rang through to the police station for an ambulance. They took Charlie to Charing Cross Hospital. He never recovered consciousness. Margery was with him at the end.

'Of course there'll have to be an inquest,' said Janet. 'But it's quite obvious what happened. He'd been sleeping awfully badly for the last three or four weeks and I suppose he'd been taking veronal. He must have taken an overdose by accident.'

'Is that what Margery thinks?' I asked.

'She's too upset to think anything, but I told her I was positive he hadn't committed suicide. I mean, he wasn't that sort of a man. Am I right, Bill?'

'Yes, dear,' he answered.

'Did he leave any letter?'

'No, nothing. Oddly enough Margery got a letter from him this morning, well, hardly a letter, just a line. "I'm so lonely without you, darling." That's all. But of course that means nothing and she's promised to say nothing about it at the inquest. I mean, what is the use of putting ideas in people's heads? Everyone knows that you never can tell with veronal, I wouldn't take it myself for anything in the world, and it was quite obviously an accident. Am I right, Bill?'

'Yes, dear,' he answered.

I saw that Janet was quite determined to believe that Charlie Bishop had not committed suicide, but how far in her heart she believed what she wanted to believe I was not sufficiently expert in female psychology to know. And of course it might be that she was right. It is unreasonable to suppose that a middle-aged scientist should kill himself because his middle-aged wife leaves him and it is extremely plausible that, exasperated by sleeplessness, and in all probability far from sober, he took a larger dose of the sleeping-draught than he realized. Anyhow that was the view the coroner took of the matter. It was indicated to him that of late Charles Bishop had given way to habits of intemperance which had caused his wife to leave him, and it was quite obvious that nothing was further from his thoughts than to put an end to himself. The coroner expressed his sympathy with the widow and commented very strongly on the dangers of sleeping-draughts.

I hate funerals, but Janet begged me to go to Charlie's. Several of his colleagues at the hospital had intimated their desire to come, but at Margery's wish they were dissuaded; and Janet and Bill, Margery and I were the only persons who attended it. We were to fetch the hearse from the mortuary and they offered to call for me on their way. I was on the look-out for the car and when I saw it drive up went downstairs, but Bill got out and met me just inside the door.

'Half a minute,' he said. 'I've got something to say to you. Janet wants you to come back afterwards and have tea. She says it's no good Margery moping and after tea we'll play a few rubbers of bridge. Can you come?'

'Like this?' I asked.

I had a tail coat on and a black tie and my evening dress trousers.

'Oh, that's all right. It'll take Margery's mind off.'

'Very well.'

But we did not play bridge after all. Janet, with her fair hair, was very smart in her deep mourning and she played the part of the sympathetic friend with amazing skill. She cried a little, wiping her eyes delicately so as not to disturb the black on her eyelashes, and when Margery sobbed broken-heartedly put her arm tenderly through hers. She was a very present help in trouble. We returned to the house. There was a telegram for Margery. She took it and went upstairs. I presumed it was a message of condolence from one of Charlie's friends who had just heard of his death. Bill went to change and Janet and I went up to the drawing-room and got the bridge table out. She took off her hat and put it on the piano.

'It's no good being hypocritical,' she said. 'Of course Margery has been frightfully upset, but she must pull herself together now. A rubber of bridge will help her to get back to her normal state. Naturally I'm dreadfully sorry about poor Charlie, but as far as he was concerned I don't believe he'd ever have got over Margery's leaving him and one can't deny that it has made things much easier for her. She wired to Gerry this morning.'

'What about?'

'To tell him about poor Charlie.'

At that moment the maid came to the room.

'Will you go up to Mrs Bishop, please, ma'am? She wants to see you.'

'Yes, of course.'

She went out of the room quickly and I was left alone. Bill joined me presently and we had a drink. At last Janet came back. She handed a telegram to me. It read as follows:

For God's sake await letter. Gerry

'What do you think it means?' she asked me.

'What it says,' I replied.

'Idiot! Of course I've told Margery that it doesn't mean anything, but she's rather worried. It must have crossed her cable telling him that Charles was dead. I don't think she feels very much like bridge after all. I mean, it would be rather bad form to play on the very day her husband has been buried.'

'Quite,' I said.

'Of course he may wire in answer to the cable. He's sure to do that, isn't he? The only thing we can do now is to sit tight and wait for his letter.'

I saw no object in continuing the conversation. I left. In a couple of days Janet rang me up to tell me that Margery had received a telegram of condolence from Morton. She repeated it to me:

Dreadfully distressed to hear sad news. Deeply sympathize with your great grief. Love. Gerry

'What do you think of it?' she asked me.

'I think it's very proper.'

'Of course he couldn't say he was as pleased as Punch, could he?'

'Not with any delicacy.'

'And he did put in *love*.'

I imagined how those women had examined the two telegrams from every point of view and scrutinized every word to press from it every possible shade of meaning. I almost heard their interminable conversations.

'I don't know what'll happen to Margery if he lets her down now,' Janet went on. 'Of course it remains to be seen if he's a gentleman.'

'Rot,' I said and rang off quickly.

In the course of the following days I dined with the Marshes a couple of times. Margery looked tired. I guessed that she awaited the letter that was on the way with sickening anxiety. Grief and fear had worn her to a shadow, she seemed very fragile now and she had acquired a spiritual look that I had never seen in her before. She was very gentle, very grateful for every kindness shown her, and in her smile, unsure and a little timid, was an infinite pathos. Her helplessness was very appealing. But Morton was several thousand miles away. Then one morning Janet rang me up.

'The letter has come. Margery says I can show it to you. Will you come round?'

Her tense voice told me everything. When I arrived Janet gave it to me. I read it. It was a very careful letter and I guessed that Morton had written it a good many times. It was very kind and he had evidently taken great pains to avoid saying anything that could possibly wound Margery; but what transpired was his terror. It was obvious that he was shaking in his shoes. He had felt apparently that the best way to cope with the situation was to be mildly facetious and he made very good fun of the white people in the colony. What would they say if Margery suddenly turned up? He would be given the order of the boot pretty damn quick. People thought the East was free and easy; it wasn't, it was more suburban than Clapham. He loved Margery far too much to bear the thoughts of those horrible women out there turning up their noses at her. And besides he had been sent to a station ten days from anywhere; she couldn't live in his bungalow exactly and of course there wasn't a hotel, and his work took him out into the jungle for days at a time. It was no place for a woman anyhow. He told her how much she meant to him, but she mustn't bother about him and he couldn't help thinking it would be better if she went back to her husband. He would never forgive himself if he thought he had come between her and Charlie. Yes, I am quite sure it had been a difficult letter to write.

'Of course he didn't know then that Charlie was dead. I've told Margery that changes everything.'

'Does she agree with you?'

'I think she's being rather unreasonable. What do you make of the letter?'

'Well, it's quite plain that he doesn't want her.'

'He wanted her badly enough two months ago.'

'It's astonishing what a change of air and a change of scene will do for you. It must seem to him already like a year since he left London. He's back among his old friends and his old interests. My dear, it's no good Margery kidding herself; the life there has taken him back and there's no place for her.'

'I've advised her to ignore the letter and go straight out to him.'

'I hope she's too sensible to expose herself to a very terrible rebuff.'

'But then what's to happen to her? Oh, it's too cruel. She's the best woman in the world. She has real goodness.'

'It's funny if you come to think of it, it's her goodness that has caused all the trouble. Why on earth didn't she have an affair with Morton? Charlie would have known nothing about it and wouldn't have been a penny the worse. She and Morton could have had a grand time and when he went away they could have parted with the consciousness that a pleasant episode had come to a graceful end. It would have been a jolly recollection, and she could have gone back to Charlie satisfied and rested and continued to make him the excellent wife she had always been.'

Janet pursed her lips. She gave me a look of disdain.

'There is such a thing as virtue, you know.'

'Virtue be damned. A virtue that only causes havoc and unhappiness is worth nothing. You can call it virtue if you like. I call it cowardice.'

'The thought of being unfaithful to Charlie while she was living with him revolted her. There are women like that, you know.'

'Good gracious, she could have remained faithful to him in spirit while she was being unfaithful to him in the flesh. That is a feat of legerdemain that women find it easy to accomplish.'

'What an odious cynic you are.'

'If it's cynical to look truth in the face and exercise common sense in the affairs of life, then certainly I'm a cynic and odious if you like. Let's face it, Margery's a middle-aged woman, Charlie was fifty-five and they'd been married for sixteen years. It was natural enough that she should lose her head over a young man who made a fuss of her. But don't call it love. It was physiology. She was a fool to take anything he said seriously. It wasn't himself speaking, it was his starved sex, he'd suffered from sexual starvation, at least as far as white women are concerned, for four years; it's monstrous that she should seek to ruin his life by holding him to the wild promises he made then. It was an accident that Margery took his fancy; he wanted her, and because he couldn't get her wanted her more. I dare say he thought it love; believe me, it was only letch. If they'd gone to bed together Charlie would be alive today. It's her damned virtue that caused the whole trouble.'

'How stupid you are. Don't you see that she couldn't help herself? She just doesn't happen to be a loose woman.'

'I prefer a loose woman to a selfish one and a wanton to a fool.'

'Oh, shut up. I didn't ask you to come here in order to make yourself absolutely beastly.'

'What did you ask me to come here for?'

'Gerry is your friend. You introduced him to Margery. If she's in the soup it's on his account. But *you* are the cause of the whole trouble. It's your duty to write to him and tell him he must do the right thing by her.'

'I'm damned if I will,' I said.

'Then you'd better go.'

I started to do so.

'Well, at all events it's a mercy that Charlie's life was insured,' said Janet.

Then I turned on her.

'And you have the nerve to call me a cynic.'

I will not repeat the opprobious word I flung at her as I slammed the door behind me. But Janet is all the same a very nice woman. I often think it would be great fun to be married to her.

The
Closed Shop

◆

Nothing would induce me to tell the name of the happy country in which the
incidents occurred that I am constrained to relate; but I see no harm in
admitting that it is a free and independent state on the continent of America.
This is vague enough in all conscience and can give rise to no diplomatic
incident. Now the president of this free and independent state had an eye to a
pretty woman and there came to his capital, a wide and sunny town with a
plaza, a cathedral that was not without dignity, and a few old Spanish houses, a
young person from Michigan of such a pleasing aspect that his heart went out to
her. He lost no time in declaring his passion and was gratified to learn that it was
returned, but he was mortified to discover that the young person regarded his
possession of a wife and her possession of a husband as a bar to their union. She
had a feminine weakness for marriage. Though it seemed unreasonable to the
president, he was not the man to refuse a pretty woman the gratification of her
whim and promised to make such arrangements as would enable him to offer
her wedlock. He called his attorneys together and put the matter before them.
He had long thought, he said, that for a progressive country their marriage laws
were remarkably out of date and he proposed therefore radically to amend
them. The attorneys retired and after a brief interval devised a divorce law that
was satisfactory to the president. But the state of which I write was always
careful to do things in a constitutional way, for it was a highly civilized,
democratic, and reputable country. A president who respects himself and his
oath of office cannot promulgate a law, even if it is to his own interest, without
adhering to certain forms, and these things take time; the president had barely
signed the decree that made the new divorce law valid when a revolution broke
out and he was very unfortunately hanged on a lamp-post in the *plaza* in front
of the cathedral that was not without dignity. The young person of pleasing

aspect left town in a hurry, but the law remained. Its terms were simple. On the payment of one hundred dollars gold and after a residence of thirty days a man could divorce his wife or a wife her husband without even apprising the other party of the intended step. Your wife might tell you that she was going to spend a month with her aged mother and one morning at breakfast when you looked through your mail you might receive a letter from her informing you that she had divorced you and was already married to another.

Now it was not long before the happy news spread here and there that at a reasonable distance from New York was a country, the capital of which had an equable climate and tolerable accommodation, where a woman could release herself, expeditiously and with economy, from the irksome bonds of matrimony. The fact that the operation could be performed without the husband's knowledge saved her from those preliminary and acrimonious discussions that are so wearing to the nerves. Every woman knows that however much a man may argue about a proposition he will generally accept a fact with resignation. Tell him you want a Rolls-Royce and he will say he can't afford it, but buy it and he will sign his cheque like a lamb. So in a very short time beautiful women in considerable numbers began to come down to the pleasant, sunny town; tired business women and women of fashion, women of pleasure and women of leisure; they came from New York, Chicago, and San Francisco, they came from Georgia and they came from Dakota, they came from all the states in the Union. The passenger accommodation on the ships of the United Fruit Line was only just adequate to the demand, and if you wanted a stateroom to yourself you had to engage it six months in advance. Prosperity descended upon the capital of this enterprising state and in a very little while there was not a lawyer in it who did not own a Ford car. Don Agosto, the proprietor of the Grand Hotel, went to the expense of building several bathrooms, but he did not grudge it; he was making a fortune, and he never passed the lamp-post on which the outgoing president had been hanged without giving it a jaunty wave of his hand.

'He was a great man,' he said. 'One day they will erect a statue to him.'

I have spoken as though it were only women who availed themselves of this convenient and reasonable law, and this might indicate that in the United States it is they rather than men who desire release from the impediment of Holy Matrimony. I have no reason to believe that this is so. Though it was women in great majority who travelled to this country to get a divorce, I ascribe this to the fact that it is always easy for them to get away for six weeks (a week there, a week back, and thirty days to establish a domicile) but it is difficult for men to leave their affairs so long. It is true that they could go there during their summer holidays, but then the heat is somewhat oppressive; and besides, there are no golf links; it is reasonable enough to suppose that many a man will hesitate to divorce his wife when he can only do it at the cost of a month's golf. There were of course two or three males spending their thirty days at the Grand Hotel, but they were generally, for a reason that is obscure, commercial travellers. I can but imagine that by the nature of their avocations they were able at one and the same time to pursue freedom and profit.

Be this as it may, the fact remains that the inmates of the Grand Hotel were for the most part women, and very gay it was in the patio at luncheon and at dinner when they sat at little square tables under the arches discussing their matrimonial troubles and drinking champagne. Don Agosto did a roaring trade with the generals and colonels (there were more generals than colonels in the army of this state), the lawyers, bankers, merchants, and the young sparks of the town who came to look at these beautiful creatures. But the perfect is seldom realized in this world. There is always something that is not quite right and women engaged in getting rid of their husbands are very properly in an agitated condition. It makes them at times hard to please. Now it must be confessed that this delightful little city, notwithstanding its manifold advantages, somewhat lacked places of amusement. There was but one cinema and this showed films that had been wandering too long from their happy home in Hollywood. In the daytime you could have consultations with your lawyer, polish your nails, and do a little shopping, but the evenings were intolerable. There were many complaints that thirty days was a long time and more than one impatient young thing asked her lawyer why they didn't put a little pep into their law and do the whole job in eight and forty hours. Don Agosto, however, was a man of resource, and presently he had an inspiration: he engaged a troupe of wandering Guatemalecans who played the marimba. There is no music in the world that sets the toes so irresistibly tingling and in a little while everyone in the patio began dancing. It is of course obvious that twenty-five beautiful women cannot dance with three commercial travellers, but there were all these generals and colonels and there were all the young sparks of the town. They danced divinely and they had great liquid black eyes. The hours flew, the days tripped one upon the heels of the other so quickly that the month passed before you realized it, and more than one of Don Agosto's guests when she bade him farewell confessed that she would willingly have stayed longer. Don Agosto was radiant. He liked to see people enjoy themselves. The marimba band was worth twice the money he paid for it, and it did his heart good to see his ladies dance with the gallant officers and the young men of the town. Since Don Agosto was thrifty he always turned off the electric light on the stairs and in the passages at ten o'clock at night and the gallant officers and the young men of the town improved their English wonderfully.

Everything went as merrily as a marriage bell, if I may use a phrase that, however hackneyed, in this connexion is irresistible, till one day Madame Coralie came to the conclusion that she had had enough of it. For one man's meat is another man's poison. She dressed herself and went to call on her friend Carmencita. After she had in a few voluble words stated the purpose of her visit, Carmencita called a maid and told her to run and fetch La Gorda. They had a matter of importance which they wished to discuss with her. La Gorda, a woman of ample proportions with a heavy moustache, soon joined them, and over a bottle of Malaga the three of them held a momentous conversation. The result of it was that they indited a letter to the president asking for an audience. The new president was a hefty young man in the early thirties who, a few years before, had been a stevedore in the employment of an American firm, and he had risen to his present exalted station by a natural eloquence and an effective use of his gun when he wanted to make a point or emphasize a statement. When one of his secretaries placed the letter before him he laughed.

'What do those three old faggots want with me?'

But he was a good-natured fellow and accessible. He did not forget that he had been elected by the people, as one of the people, to protect the people. He had also during his early youth been employed for some months by Madame Coralie to run errands. He told his secretary that he would see them at ten o'clock next morning. They went at the appointed hour to the palace and were led up a noble stairway to the audience chamber; the official who conducted them knocked softly on the door; a barred judas was opened and a suspicious eye appeared. The president had no intention of suffering the fate of his predecessor if he could help it and no matter who his visitors were did not receive them without precaution. The official gave the three ladies' names, the door was opened, but not too wide, and they slipped in. It was a handsome room and various secretaries at little tables, in their shirtsleeves and with a revolver on each hip, were busy typing. One or two other young men, heavily armed, were lying on sofas reading the papers and smoking cigarettes. The president, also in his shirtsleeves, with a revolver in his belt, was standing with his thumbs in the sleeve-holes of his waistcoat. He was tall and stout, of a handsome and even dignified presence.

'*Qué tal?*' he cried, jovially, with a flash of his white teeth. 'What brings you here, *señoras?*'

'How well you're looking, Don Manuel,' said La Gorda. 'You are a fine figure of a man.'

He shook hands with them, and his staff, ceasing their strenuous activity, leaned back and cordially waved their hands to the three ladies. They were old friends, and the greetings, if a trifle sardonic, were hearty. I must disclose the fact now (which I could without doubt do in a manner so discreet that I might be misunderstood; but if you have to say something you may just as well say it plainly as not) that these three ladies were the Madams of the three principal brothels in the capital of this free and independent state. La Gorda and Carmencita were of Spanish origin and were very decently dressed in black, with black silk shawls over their heads, but Madame Coralie was French and she wore a toque. They were all of mature age and of modest demeanour.

The president made them sit down, and offered them madeira and cigarettes, but they refused.

'No, thank you, Don Manuel,' said Madame Coralie. 'It is on business that we have come to see you.'

'Well, what can I do for you?'

La Gorda and Carmencita looked at Madame Coralie and Madame Coralie looked at La Gorda and Carmencita. They nodded and she saw that they expected her to be their spokeswoman.

'Well, Don Manuel, it is like this. We are three women who have worked hard for many years and not a breath of scandal has ever tarnished our good names. There are not in all the Americas three more distinguished houses than ours and they are a credit to this beautiful city. Why, only last year I spent five hundred dollars to supply my *sala principal* with plate-glass mirrors. We have always been respectable and we have paid our taxes with regularity. It is hard now that the fruits of our labours should be snatched away from us. I do not hesitate to say that after so many years of honest and conscientious attention to business it is unjust that we should have to submit to such treatment.'

The president was astounded.

'But, Coralie, my dear, I do not know what you mean. Has anyone dared to claim money from you that the law does not sanction or that I know nothing about?'

He gave his secretaries a suspicious glance. They tried to look innocent, but though they were, only succeeded in looking uneasy.

'It is the law we complain of. Ruin stares us in the face.'

'Ruin?'

'So long as this new divorce law is in existence we can do no business and we may just as well shut up our beautiful houses.'

Then Madame Coralie explained in a manner so frank that I prefer to paraphrase her speech that owing to this invasion of the town by beautiful ladies from a foreign land the three elegant houses on which she and her two friends paid rates and taxes were utterly deserted. The young men of fashion preferred to spend their evenings at the Grand Hotel where they received for soft words entertainment which at the regular establishments they could only have got for hard cash.

'You cannot blame them,' said the president.

'I don't,' cried Madame Coralie. 'I blame the women. They have no right to come and take the bread out of our mouths. Don Manuel, you are one of the people, you are not one of these aristocrats; what will the country say if you allow us to be driven out of business by blacklegs? I ask you is it just, is it honest?'

'But what can I do?' said the president. 'I cannot lock them up in their rooms for thirty days. How am I to blame if these foreigners have no sense of decency?'

'It's different for a poor girl,' said La Gorda. 'She has her way to make. But that these women do that sort of thing when they're not obliged to, no, that I shall never understand.'

'It is a bad and wicked law,' said Carmencita.

The president sprang to his feet and threw his arms akimbo.

'You are not going to ask me to abrogate a law that has brought peace and plenty to this country. I am of the people and I was elected by the people, and the prosperity of my fatherland is very near my heart. Divorce is our staple industry and the law shall be repealed only over my dead body.'

'Oh, *María Santísima,* that it should come to this,' said Carmencita. 'And me with two daughters in a convent in New Orleans. Ah, in this business one often has unpleasantness, but I always consoled myself by thinking that my daughters would marry well, and when the time came for me to retire they would inherit my business. Do you think I can keep them in a convent in New Orleans for nothing?'

'And who is going to keep my son at Harvard if I have to close my house, Don Manuel?' asked La Gorda.

'As for myself,' said Madame Coralie, 'I do not care. I shall return to France. My dear mother is eighty-seven years of age and she cannot live very much longer. It will be a comfort to her if I spend her last remaining years by her side. But it is the injustice of it that hurts. You have spent many happy evenings in my house, Don Manuel, and I am wounded that you should let us be treated like this. Did you not tell me yourself that it was the proudest day of your life when you entered as an honoured guest the house in which you had once been employed as errand boy?'

'I do not deny it. I stood champagne all round.' Don Manuel walked up and down the large hall, shrugging his shoulders as he went, and now and then, deep in thought, he gesticulated. 'I am of the people, elected by the people,' he cried, 'and the fact is, these women are blacklegs.' He turned to his secretaries with a dramatic gesture. 'It is a stain on my administration. It is against all my principles to allow unskilled foreign labour to take the bread out of the mouths of honest and industrious people. These ladies are quite right to come to me and appeal for my protection. I will not allow the scandal to continue.'

It was of course a pointed and effective speech, but all who heard it knew that it left things exactly where they were. Madame Coralie powdered her nose and gave it, a commanding organ, a brief look in her pocket mirror.

'Of course I know what human nature is,' she said, 'and I can well understand that time hangs heavily on the hands of these creatures.'

'We could build a golf-course,' hazarded one of the secretaries. 'It is true that this would only occupy them by day.'

'If they want men why can't they bring them with them?' said La Gorda.

'*Caramba!*' cried the president, and with that stood on a sudden quite still. 'There is the solution.'

He had not reached his exalted station without being a man of insight and resource. He beamed.

'We will amend the law. Men shall come in as before without let or hindrance, but women only accompanied by their husbands or with their written consent.' He saw the look of consternation which his secretaries gave him, and he waved his hand. 'But the immigration authorities shall receive instructions to interpret the word husband with the widest latitude.'

'*María Santísima!*' cried Madame Coralie. 'If they come with a friend he will take care that no one else interferes with them and our customers will return to the houses where for so long they have been so hospitably entertained. Don Manuel, you are a great man and one of these days they will erect a statue to you.'

It is often the simplest expedients that settle the most formidable difficulties. The law was briefly amended according to the terms of Don Manuel's suggestion and, whereas prosperity continued to pour its blessings on the wide and sunny capital of this free and independent state, Madame Coralie was enabled profitably to pursue her useful avocations, Carmencita's two daughters completed their expensive education in the convent at New Orleans, and La Gorda's son successfully graduated at Harvard.

The Dream

◆

It chanced that in August 1917 the work upon which I was then engaged
obliged me to go from New York to Petrograd, and I was instructed for safety's
sake to travel by way of Vladivostok. I landed there in the morning and passed
an idle day as best I could. The trans-Siberian train was due to start, so far as I
remember, at about nine in the evening. I dined at the station restaurant by
myself. It was crowded and I shared a small table with a man whose appearance
entertained me. He was a Russian, a tall fellow, but amazingly stout, and he had
so vast a paunch that he was obliged to sit well away from the table. His hands,
small for his size, were buried in rolls of fat. His hair, long, dark, and thin, was
brushed carefully across his crown in order to conceal his baldness, and his
huge sallow face, with its enormous double chin, clean-shaven, gave you an
impression of indecent nakedness. His nose was small, a funny little button
upon that mass of flesh, and his black shining eyes were small too. But he had a
large, red, and sensual mouth. He was dressed neatly enough in a black suit. It
was not worn but shabby; it looked as if it had been neither pressed nor brushed
since he had had it.

The service was bad and it was almost impossible to attract the attention of a
waiter. We soon got into conversation. The Russian spoke good and fluent
English. His accent was marked but not tiresome. He asked me many questions
about myself and my plans, which—my occupation at the time making caution
necessary—I answered with a show of frankness but with dissimulation. I told
him I was a journalist. He asked me whether I wrote fiction and when I
confessed that in my leisure moments I did, he began to talk of the later Russian
novelists. He spoke intelligently. It was plain that he was a man of education.

By this time we had persuaded the waiter to bring us some cabbage soup, and
my acquaintance pulled a small bottle of vodka from his pocket which he

invited me to share. I do not know whether it was the vodka or the natural loquaciousness of his race that made him communicative, but presently he told me, unasked, a good deal about himself. He was of noble birth, it appeared, a lawyer by profession, and a radical. Some trouble with the authorities had made it necessary for him to be much abroad, but now he was on his way home. Business had detained him at Vladivostok, but he expected to start for Moscow in a week and if I went there he would be charmed to see me.

'Are you married?' he asked me.

I did not see what business it was of his, but I told him that I was. He sighed a little.

'I am a widower,' he said. 'My wife was a Swiss, a native of Geneva. She was a very cultivated woman. She spoke English, German, and Italian perfectly. French, of course, was her native tongue. Her Russian was much above the average for a foreigner. She had scarcely the trace of an accent.'

He called a waiter who was passing with a tray full of dishes and asked him, I suppose—for then I knew hardly any Russian—how much longer we were going to wait for the next course. The waiter, with a rapid but presumably reassuring exclamation, hurried on, and my friend sighed.

'Since the revolution the waiting in restaurants has become abominable.'

He lighted his twentieth cigarette and I, looking at my watch, wondered whether I should get a square meal before it was time for me to start.

'My wife was a very remarkable woman,' he continued. 'She taught languages at one of the best schools for the daughters of noblemen in Petrograd. For a good many years we lived together on perfectly friendly terms. She was, however, of a jealous temperament and unfortunately she loved me to distraction.'

It was difficult for me to keep a straight face. He was one of the ugliest men I had ever seen. There is sometimes a certain charm in the rubicund and jovial fat man, but this saturnine obesity was repulsive.

'I do not pretend that I was faithful to her. She was not young when I married her and we had been married for ten years. She was small and thin, and she had a bad complexion. She had a bitter tongue. She was a woman who suffered from a fury of possession, and she could not bear me to be attracted to anyone but her. She was jealous not only of the women I knew, but of my friends, my cat, and my books. On one occasion in my absence she gave away a coat of mine merely because I liked none of my coats so well. But I am of an equable temperament. I will not deny that she bored me, but I accepted her acrimonious disposition as an act of God and no more thought of rebelling against it than I would against bad weather or a cold in the head. I denied her accusations as long as it was possible to deny them, and when it was impossible I shrugged my shoulders and smoked a cigarette.

'The constant scenes she made me did not very much affect me. I led my own life. Sometimes, indeed, I wondered whether it was passionate love she felt for me or passionate hate. It seemed to me that love and hate were very near allied.

'So we might have continued to the end of the chapter if one night a very curious thing had not happened. I was awakened by a piercing scream from my wife. Startled, I asked her what was the matter. She told me that she had had a fearful nightmare; she had dreamt that I was trying to kill her. We lived at the top of a large house and the well round which the stairs climbed was broad. She had dreamt that just as we had arrived at our own floor I had caught hold of her and attempted to throw her over the balusters. It was six storeys to the stone floor at the bottom and it meant certain death.

'She was much shaken. I did my best to soothe her. But next morning, and for two or three days after, she referred to the subject again and, notwithstanding my laughter, I saw that it dwelt in her mind. I could not help thinking of it either, for this dream showed me something that I had never suspected. She thought I hated her, she thought I would gladly be rid of her; she knew of course that she was insufferable, and at some time or other the idea had evidently occurred to her that I was capable of murdering her. The thoughts of men are incalculable and ideas enter our minds that we should be ashamed to confess. Sometimes I had wished that she might run away with a lover, sometimes that a painless and sudden death might give me my freedom; but never, never had the idea come to me that I might deliberately rid myself of an intolerable burden.

'The dream made an extraordinary impression upon both of us. It frightened my wife, and she became for a little less bitter and more tolerant. But when I walked up the stairs to our apartment it was impossible for me not to look over the balusters and reflect how easy it would be to do what she had dreamt. The balusters were dangerously low. A quick gesture and the thing was done. It was hard to put the thought out of my mind. Then some months later my wife awakened me one night. I was very tired and I was exasperated. She was white and trembling. She had had the dream again. She burst into tears and asked me if I hated her. I swore by all the saints of the Russian calendar that I loved her. At last she went to sleep again. It was more than I could do. I lay awake. I seemed to see her falling down the well of the stairs, and I heard her shriek and the thud as she struck the stone floor. I could not help shivering.'

The Russian stopped and beads of sweat stood on his forehead. He had told the story well and fluently so that I had listened with attention. There was still some vodka in the bottle; he poured it out and swallowed it at a gulp.

'And how did your wife eventually die?' I asked after a pause.

He took out a dirty handkerchief and wiped his forehead.

'By an extraordinary coincidence she was found late one night at the bottom of the stairs with her neck broken.'

'Who found her?'

'She was found by one of the lodgers who came in shortly after the catastrophe.'

'And where were you?'

I cannot describe the look he gave me of malicious cunning. His little black eyes sparkled.

'I was spending the evening with a friend of mine. I did not come in till an hour later.'

At that moment the waiter brought us the dish of meat that we had ordered, and the Russian fell upon it with good appetite. He shovelled the food into his mouth in enormous mouthfuls.

I was taken aback. Had he really been telling me in this hardly veiled manner that he had murdered his wife? That obese and sluggish man did not look like a murderer; I could not believe that he would have had the courage. Or was he making a sardonic joke at my expense?

In a few minutes it was time for me to go and catch my train. I left him and I have not seen him since. But I have never been able to make up my mind whether he was serious or jesting.

The Colonel's Lady

♦

All this happened two or three years before the outbreak of the war.

The Peregrines were having breakfast. Though they were alone and the table was long they sat at opposite ends of it. From the walls George Peregrine's ancestors, painted by the fashionable painters of the day, looked down upon them. The butler brought in the morning post. There were several letters for the colonel, business letters, *The Times*, and a small parcel for his wife Evie. He looked at his letters and then, opening *The Times*, began to read it. They finished breakfast and rose from the table. He noticed that his wife hadn't opened the parcel.

'What's that?' he asked.

'Only some books.'

'Shall I open it for you?'

'If you like.'

He hated to cut string and so with some difficulty untied the knots.

'But they're all the same,' he said when he had unwrapped the parcel. 'What on earth d'you want six copies of the same book for?' He opened one of them. 'Poetry.' Then he looked at the title-page. *When Pyramids Decay*, he read, by E. K. Hamilton. Eva Katherine Hamilton: that was his wife's maiden name. He looked at her with smiling surprise. 'Have you written a book, Evie? You are a slyboots.'

'I didn't think it would interest you very much. Would you like a copy?'

'Well, you know poetry isn't much in my line, but—yes, I'd like a copy; I'll read it. I'll take it along to my study. I've got a lot to do this morning.'

He gathered up *The Times*, his letters, and the book, and went out. His study was a large and comfortable room, with a big desk, leather arm-chairs, and what he called 'trophies of the chase' on the walls. On the bookshelves were works of reference, books on farming, gardening, fishing, and shooting, and books on the last war, in which he had won an M.C. and a D.S.O. For before his marriage he had been in the Welsh Guards. At the end of the war he retired and settled down to the life of a country gentleman in the spacious house, some twenty miles from Sheffield, which one of his forebears had built in the reign of George III. George Peregrine had an estate of some fifteen hundred acres which he managed with ability; he was a Justice of the Peace and performed his duties conscientiously. During the season he rode to hounds two days a week. He was a good shot, a golfer, and though now a little over fifty could still play a hard game of tennis. He could describe himself with propriety as an all-round sportsman.

He had been putting on weight lately, but was still a fine figure of a man; tall, with grey curly hair, only just beginning to grow thin on the crown, frank blue eyes, good features, and a high colour. He was a public-spirited man, chairman of any number of local organizations and, as became his class and station, a loyal member of the Conservative Party. He looked upon it as his duty to see to the welfare of the people on his estate and it was a satisfaction to him to know that Evie could be trusted to tend the sick and succour the poor. He had built a cottage hospital on the outskirts of the village and paid the wages of a nurse out of his own pocket. All he asked of the recipients of his bounty was that at elections, county or general, they should vote for his candidate. He was a friendly man, affable to his inferiors, considerate with his tenants, and popular with the neighbouring gentry. He would have been pleased and at the same time slightly embarrassed if someone had told him he was a jolly good fellow. That was what he wanted to be. He desired no higher praise.

It was hard luck that he had no children. He would have been an excellent father, kindly but strict, and would have brought up his sons as gentlemen's sons should be brought up, sent them to Eton, you know, taught them to fish, shoot, and ride. As it was, his heir was a nephew, son of his brother killed in a motor accident, not a bad boy, but not a chip off the old block, no, sir, far from it; and would you believe it, his fool of a mother was sending him to a co-educational school. Evie had been a sad disappointment to him. Of course she was a lady, and she had a bit of money of her own; she managed the house uncommonly well and she was a good hostess. The village people adored her. She had been a pretty little thing when he married her, with a creamy skin, light brown hair, and a trim figure, healthy too, and not a bad tennis player; he couldn't understand why she'd had no children; of course she was faded now, she must be getting on for five and forty; her skin was drab, her hair had lost its sheen, and she was as thin as a rail. She was always neat and suitably dressed, but she didn't seem to bother how she looked, she wore no make-up and didn't even use lipstick; sometimes at night when she dolled herself up for a party you could tell that once she'd been quite attractive, but ordinarily she was—well, the sort of woman you simply didn't notice. A nice woman, of course, a good wife, and it wasn't her fault if she was barren, but it was tough on a fellow who wanted an heir of his own loins; she hadn't any vitality, that's what was the matter with her. He supposed he'd been in love with her when he asked her to marry him, at least sufficiently in love for a man who wanted to marry and settle down, but with time he discovered that they had nothing much in common. She didn't care about hunting, and fishing bored her. Naturally they'd drifted apart. He had to do her the justice to admit that she'd never bothered him. There'd been no scenes. They had no quarrels. She seemed to take it for

granted that he should go his own way. When he went up to London now and
then she never wanted to come with him. He had a girl there, well, she wasn't
exactly a girl, she was thirty-five if she was a day, but she was blonde and
luscious and he only had to wire ahead of time and they'd dine, do a show, and
spend the night together. Well, a man, a healthy normal man had to have some
fun in his life. The thought crossed his mind that if Evie hadn't been such a
good woman she'd have been a better wife; but it was not the sort of thought
that he welcomed and he put it away from him.

George Peregrine finished his *Times* and being a considerate fellow rang the
bell and told the butler to take it to Evie. Then he looked at his watch. It was
half past ten and at eleven he had an appointment with one of his tenants. He
had half an hour to spare.

'I'd better have a look at Evie's book,' he said to himself.

He took it up with a smile. Evie had a lot of highbrow books in her sitting-
room, not the sort of books that interested him, but if they amused her he had
no objection to her reading them. He noticed that the volume he now held in his
hand contained no more than ninety pages. That was all to the good. He shared
Edgar Allan Poe's opinion that poems should be short. But as he turned the
pages he noticed that several of Evie's had long lines of irregular length and
didn't rhyme. He didn't like that. At his first school, when he was a little boy, he
remembered learning a poem that began: *The boy stood on the burning deck*, and
later, at Eton, one that started: *Ruin seize thee, ruthless king*; and then there was
Henry V; they'd had to take that, one half. He stared at Evie's pages with
consternation.

'That's not what I call poetry,' he said.

Fortunately it wasn't all like that. Interspersed with the pieces that looked so
odd, lines of three or four words and then a line of ten or fifteen, there were little
poems, quite short, that rhymed, thank God, with the lines all the same length.
Several of the pages were just headed with the word *Sonnet*, and out of curiosity
he counted the lines; there were fourteen of them. He read them. They seemed
all right, but he didn't quite know what they were all about. He repeated to
himself: *Ruin seize thee, ruthless king*.

'Poor Evie,' he sighed.

At that moment the farmer he was expecting was ushered into the study, and
putting the book down he made him welcome. They embarked on their
business.

'I read your book, Evie,' he said as they sat down to lunch. 'Jolly good. Did it
cost you a packet to have it printed?'

'No, I was lucky. I sent it to a publisher and he took it.'

'Not much money in poetry, my dear,' he said in his good-natured, hearty
way.

'No, I don't suppose there is. What did Bannock want to see you about this
morning?'

Bannock was the tenant who had interrupted his reading of Evie's poems.

'He's asked me to advance the money for a pedigree bull he wants to buy.
He's a good man and I've half a mind to do it.'

George Peregrine saw that Evie didn't want to talk about her book and he was
not sorry to change the subject. He was glad she had used her maiden name on
the title-page; he didn't suppose anyone would ever hear about the book, but he
was proud of his own unusual name and he wouldn't have liked it if some
damned penny-a-liner had made fun of Evie's effort in one of the papers.

During the few weeks that followed he thought it tactful not to ask Evie any questions about her venture into verse, and she never referred to it. It might have been a discreditable incident that they had silently agreed not to mention. But then a strange thing happened. He had to go to London on business and he took Daphne out to dinner. That was the name of the girl with whom he was in the habit of passing a few agreeable hours whenever he went to town.

'Oh, George,' she said, 'is that your wife who's written a book they're all talking about?'

'What on earth d'you mean?'

'Well, there's a fellow I know who's a critic. He took me out to dinner the other night and he had a book with him. "Got anything for me to read?" I said. "What's that?" "Oh, I don't think that's your cup of tea," he said. "It's poetry. I've just been reviewing it." "No poetry for me," I said. "It's about the hottest stuff I ever read," he said. "Selling like hot cakes. And it's damned good."'

'Who's the book by?' asked George.

'A woman called Hamilton. My friend told me that wasn't her real name. He said her real name was Peregrine. "Funny," I said, "I know a fellow called Peregrine." "Colonel in the army," he said. "Lives near Sheffield."'

'I'd just as soon you didn't talk about me to your friends,' said George with a frown of vexation.

'Keep your shirt on, dearie. Who d'you take me for? I just said: "It's not the same one."' Daphne giggled. 'My friend said: "They say he's a regular Colonel Blimp."'

George had a keen sense of humour.

'You could tell them better than that,' he laughed. 'If my wife had written a book I'd be the first to know about it, wouldn't I?'

'I suppose you would.'

Anyhow the matter didn't interest her and when the colonel began to talk of other things she forgot about it. He put it out of his mind too. There was nothing to it, he decided, and that silly fool of a critic had just been pulling Daphne's leg. He was amused at the thought of her tackling that book because she had been told it was hot stuff and then finding it just a lot of bosh cut up into unequal lines.

He was a member of several clubs and next day he thought he'd lunch at one in St James's Street. He was catching a train back to Sheffield early in the afternoon. He was sitting in a comfortable arm-chair having a glass of sherry before going into the dining-room when an old friend came up to him.

'Well, old boy, how's life?' he said. 'How d'you like being the husband of a celebrity?'

George Peregrine looked at his friend. He thought he saw an amused twinkle in his eyes.

'I don't know what you're talking about,' he answered.

'Come off it, George. Everyone knows E. K. Hamilton is your wife. Not often a book of verse has a success like that. Look here, Henry Dashwood is lunching with me. He'd like to meet you.'

'Who the devil is Henry Dashwood and why should he want to meet me?'

'Oh, my dear fellow, what do you do with yourself all the time in the country? Henry's about the best critic we've got. He wrote a wonderful review of Evie's book. D'you mean to say she didn't show it you?'

Before George could answer his friend had called a man over. A tall, thin man, with a high forehead, a beard, a long nose, and a stoop, just the sort of man whom George was prepared to dislike at first sight. Introductions were effected. Henry Dashwood sat down.

'Is Mrs Peregrine in London by any chance? I should very much like to meet her,' he said.

'No, my wife doesn't like London. She prefers the country,' said George stiffly.

'She wrote me a very nice letter about my review. I was pleased. You know, we critics get more kicks than halfpence. I was simply bowled over by her book. It's so fresh and original, very modern without being obscure. She seems to be as much at her ease in free verse as in the classical metres.' Then because he was a critic he thought he should criticize. 'Sometimes her ear is a trifle at fault, but you can say the same of Emily Dickinson. There are several of those short lyrics of hers that might have been written by Landor.'

All this was gibberish to George Peregrine. The man was nothing but a disgusting highbrow. But the colonel had good manners and he answered with proper civility: Henry Dashwood went on as though he hadn't spoken.

'But what makes the book so outstanding is the passion that throbs in every line. So many of these young poets are so anaemic, cold, bloodless, dully intellectual, but here you have real naked, earthy passion; of course deep, sincere emotion like that is tragic—ah, my dear Colonel, how right Heine was when he said that the poet makes little songs out of his great sorrows. You know, now and then, as I read and re-read those heart-rending pages I thought of Sappho.'

This was too much for George Peregrine and he got up.

'Well, it's jolly nice of you to say such nice things about my wife's little book. I'm sure she'll be delighted. But I must bolt, I've got to catch a train and I want to get a bite of lunch.'

'Damned fool,' he said irritably to himself as he walked upstairs to the dining-room.

He got home in time for dinner and after Evie had gone to bed he went into his study and looked for her book. He thought he'd just glance through it again to see for himself what they were making such a fuss about, but he couldn't find it. Evie must have taken it away.

'Silly,' he muttered.

He'd told her he thought it jolly good. What more could a fellow be expected to say? Well, it didn't matter. He lit his pipe and read the *Field* till he felt sleepy. But a week or so later it happened that he had to go into Sheffield for the day. He lunched there at his club. He had nearly finished when the Duke of Haverel came in. This was the great local magnate and of course the colonel knew him, but only to say how d'you do to; and he was surprised when the Duke stopped at his table.

'We're so sorry your wife couldn't come to us for the week-end,' he said, with a sort of shy cordiality. 'We're expecting rather a nice lot of people.'

George was taken aback. He guessed that the Haverels had asked him and Evie over for the week-end and Evie, without saying a word to him about it, had refused. He had the presence of mind to say he was sorry too.

'Better luck next time,' said the Duke pleasantly and moved on.

Colonel Peregrine was very angry and when he got home he said to his wife:

'Look here, what's this about our being asked over to Haverel? Why on earth did you say we couldn't go? We've never been asked before and it's the best shooting in the county.'

'I didn't think of that. I thought it would only bore you.'

'Damn it all, you might at least have asked me if I wanted to go.'

'I'm sorry.'

He looked at her closely. There was something in her expression that he didn't quite understand. He frowned.

'I suppose *I* was asked?' he barked.

Evie flushed a little.

'Well, in point of fact you weren't.'

'I call it damned rude of them to ask you without asking me.'

'I suppose they thought it wasn't your sort of party. The Duchess is rather fond of writers and people like that, you know. She's having Henry Dashwood, the critic, and for some reason he wants to meet me.'

'It was damned nice of you to refuse, Evie.'

'It's the least I could do,' she smiled. She hesitated a moment. 'George, my publishers want to give a little dinner party for me one day towards the end of the month and of course they want you to come too.'

'Oh, I don't think that's quite my mark. I'll come up to London with you if you like. I'll find someone to dine with.'

Daphne.

'I expect it'll be very dull, but they're making rather a point of it. And the day after, the American publisher who's taken my book is giving a cocktail party at Claridge's. I'd like you to come to that if you wouldn't mind.'

'Sounds like a crashing bore, but if you really want me to come I'll come.'

'It would be sweet of you.'

George Peregrine was dazed by the cocktail party. There were a lot of people. Some of them didn't look so bad, a few of the women were decently turned out, but the men seemed to him pretty awful. He was introduced to everyone as Colonel Peregrine, E. K. Hamilton's husband, you know. The men didn't seem to have anything to say to him, but the women gushed.

'You *must* be proud of your wife. Isn't it *wonderful*? You know, I read it right through at a sitting, I simply couldn't put it down, and when I'd finished I started again at the beginning and read it right through a second time. I was simply *thrilled.*'

The English publisher said to him:

'We've not had a success like this with a book of verse for twenty years. I've never seen such reviews.'

The American publisher said to him:

'It's swell. It'll be a smash hit in America. You wait and see.'

The American publisher had sent Evie a great spray of orchids. Damned ridiculous, thought George. As they came in, people were taken up to Evie, and it was evident that they said flattering things to her, which she took with a pleasant smile and a word or two of thanks. She was a trifle flushed with the excitement, but seemed quite at her ease. Though he thought the whole thing a lot of stuff and nonsense George noted with approval that his wife was carrying it off in just the right way.

'Well, there's one thing,' he said to himself, 'you can see she's a lady and that's a damned sight more than you can say of anyone else here.'

He drank a good many cocktails. But there was one thing that bothered him. He had a notion that some of the people he was introduced to looked at him in rather a funny sort of way, he couldn't quite make out what it meant, and once when he strolled by two women who were sitting together on a sofa he had the impression that they were talking about him and after he passed he was almost certain they tittered. He was very glad when the party came to an end.

In the taxi on their way back to their hotel Evie said to him:

'You were wonderful, dear. You made quite a hit. The girls simply raved about you: they thought you so handsome.'

'Girls,' he said bitterly. 'Old hags.'

'Were you bored, dear?'

'Stiff.'

She pressed his hand in a gesture of sympathy.

'I hope you won't mind if we wait and go down by the afternoon train. I've got some things to do in the morning.'

'No, that's all right. Shopping?'

'I do want to buy one or two things, but I've got to go and be photographed. I hate the idea, but they think I ought to be. For America, you know.'

He said nothing. But he thought. He thought it would be a shock to the American public when they saw the portrait of the homely, desiccated little women who was his wife. He'd always been under the impression that they liked glamour in America.

He went on thinking, and next morning when Evie had gone out he went to his club and up to the library. There he looked up recent numbers of *The Times Literary Supplement,* the *New Statesman,* and the *Spectator.* Presently he found reviews of Evie's book. He didn't read them very carefully, but enough to see that they were extremely favourable. Then he went to the bookseller's in Piccadilly where he occasionally bought books. He'd made up his mind that he had to read this damned thing of Evie's properly, but he didn't want to ask her what she'd done with the copy she'd given him. He'd buy one for himself. Before going in he looked in the window and the first thing he saw was a display of *When Pyramids Decay.* Damned silly title! He went in. A young man came forward and asked if he could help him.

'No, I'm just having a look round.' It embarrassed him to ask for Evie's book and he thought he'd find it for himself and then take it to the salesman. But he couldn't see it anywhere and at last, finding the young man near him, he said in a carefully casual tone: 'By the way, have you got a book called *When Pyramids Decay?*'

'The new edition came in this morning. I'll get a copy.'

In a moment the young man returned with it. He was a short, rather stout young man, with a shock of untidy carroty hair and spectacles. George Peregrine, tall, upstanding, very military, towered over him.

'Is this a new edition then?' he asked.

'Yes, sir. The fifth. It might be a novel the way it's selling.'

George Peregrine hesitated a moment.

'Why d'you suppose it's such a success? I've always been told no one reads poetry.'

'Well, it's good, you know. I've read it meself.' The young man, though obviously cultured, had a slight Cockney accent, and George quite instinctively adopted a patronizing attitude. 'It's the story they like. Sexy, you know, but tragic.'

George frowned a little. He was coming to the conclusion that the young man was rather impertinent. No one had told him anything about there being a story in the damned book and he had not gathered that from reading the reviews. The young man went on:

'Of course it's only a flash in the pan, if you know what I mean. The way I look at it, she was sort of inspired like by a personal experience, like Housman was with *The Shropshire Lad*. She'll never write anything else.'

'How much is the book?' said George coldly to stop his chatter. 'You needn't wrap it up, I'll just slip it into my pocket.'

The November morning was raw and he was wearing a greatcoat.

At the station he bought the evening papers and magazines and he and Evie settled themselves comfortably in opposite corners of a first-class carriage and read. At five o'clock they went along to the restaurant car to have tea and chatted a little. They arrived. They drove home in the car which was waiting for them. They bathed, dressed for dinner, and after dinner Evie, saying she was tired out, went to bed. She kissed him, as was her habit, on the forehead. Then he went into the hall, took Evie's book out of his greatcoat pocket and going into the study began to read it. He didn't read verse very easily and though he read with attention, every word of it, the impression he received was far from clear. Then he began at the beginning again and read it a second time. He read with increasing malaise, but he was not a stupid man and when he had finished he had a distinct understanding of what it was all about. Part of the book was in free verse, part in conventional metres, but the story it related was coherent and plain to the meanest intelligence. It was the story of a passionate love affair between an older woman, married, and a young man. George Peregrine made out the steps of it as easily as if he had been doing a sum in simple addition.

Written in the first person, it began with the tremulous surprise of the woman, past her youth, when it dawned upon her that the young man was in love with her. She hesitated to believe it. She thought she must be deceiving herself. And she was terrified when on a sudden she discovered that she was passionately in love with him. She told herself it was absurd; with the disparity of age between them nothing but unhappiness could come to her if she yielded to her emotion. She tried to prevent him from speaking but the day came when he told her that he loved her and forced her to tell him that she loved him too. He begged her to run away with him. She couldn't leave her husband, her home; and what life could they look forward to, she an ageing woman, he so young? How could she expect his love to last? She begged him to have mercy on her. But his love was impetuous. He wanted her, he wanted her with all his heart, and at last trembling, afraid, desirous, she yielded to him. Then there was a period of ecstatic happiness. The world, the dull, humdrum world of every day, blazed with glory. Love songs flowed from her pen. The woman worshipped the young, virile body of her lover. George flushed darkly when she praised his broad chest and slim flanks, the beauty of his legs and the flatness of his belly.

Hot stuff, Daphne's friend had said. It was that all right. Disgusting.

There were sad little pieces in which she lamented the emptiness of her life when as must happen he left her, but they ended with a cry that all she had to suffer would be worth it for the bliss that for a while had been hers. She wrote of the long, tremulous nights they passed together and the languor that lulled them to sleep in one another's arms. She wrote of the rapture of brief stolen moments when, braving all danger, their passion overwhelmed them and they surrendered to its call.

She thought it would be an affair of a few weeks, but miraculously it lasted. One of the poems referred to three years having gone by without lessening the love that filled their hearts. It looked as though he continued to press her to go

away with him, far away, to a hill town in Italy, a Greek island, a walled city in
Tunisia, so that they could be together always, for in another of the poems she
besought him to let things be as they were. Their happiness was precarious.
Perhaps it was owing to the difficulties they had to encounter and the rarity of
their meetings that their love had retained for so long its first enchanting
ardour. Then on a sudden the young man died. How, when or where George
could not discover. There followed a long, heartbroken cry of bitter grief, grief
she could not indulge in, grief that had to be hidden. She had to be cheerful,
give dinner-parties and go out to dinner, behave as she had always behaved,
though the light had gone out of her life and she was bowed down with anguish.
The last poem of all was a set of four short stanzas in which the writer, sadly
resigned to her loss, thanked the dark powers that rule man's destiny that she
had been privileged at least for a while to enjoy the greatest happiness that we
poor human beings can ever hope to know.

It was three o'clock in the morning when George Peregrine finally put the
book down. It had seemed to him that he heard Evie's voice in every line, over
and over again he came upon turns of phrase he had heard her use, there were
details that were as familiar to him as to her: there was no doubt about it; it was
her own story she had told, and it was as plain as anything could be that she had
had a lover and her lover had died. It was not anger so much that he felt, nor
horror or dismay, though he was dismayed and he was horrified, but
amazement. It was as inconceivable that Evie should have had a love affair, and
a wildly passionate one at that, as that the trout in a glass case over the chimney-
piece in his study, the finest he had ever caught, should suddenly wag its tail.
He understood now the meaning of the amused look he had seen in the eyes of
that man he had spoken to at the club, he understood why Daphne when she
was talking about the book had seemed to be enjoying a private joke, and why
those two women at the cocktail party had tittered when he strolled past them.

He broke out into a sweat. Then on a sudden he was seized with fury and he
jumped up to go and awake Evie and ask her sternly for an explanation. But he
stopped at the door. After all, what proof had he? A book. He remembered that
he'd told Evie he thought it jolly good. True, he hadn't read it, but he'd
pretended he had. He would look a perfect fool if he had to admit that.

'I must watch my step,' he muttered.

He made up his mind to wait for two or three days and think it all over. Then
he'd decide what to do. He went to bed, but he couldn't sleep for a long time.

'Evie,' he kept on saying to himself. 'Evie, of all people.'

They met at breakfast next morning as usual. Evie was as she always was,
quiet, demure, and self-possessed, a middle-aged woman who made no effort
to look younger than she was, a woman who had nothing of what he still called
It. He looked at her as he hadn't looked at her for years. She had her usual
placid serenity. Her pale blue eyes were untroubled. There was no sign of guilt
on her candid brow. She made the same little casual remarks she always made.

'It's nice to get back to the country again after those two hectic days in
London. What are you going to do this morning?'

It was incomprehensible.

Three days later he went to see his solicitor. Henry Blane was an old friend of
George's as well as his lawyer. He had a place not far from Peregrine's and for
years they had shot over one another's preserves. For two days a week he was a
country gentleman and for the other five a busy lawyer in Sheffield. He was a
tall, robust fellow, with a boisterous manner and a jovial laugh, which

suggested that he liked to be looked upon essentially as a sportsman and a good fellow and only incidentally as a lawyer. But he was shrewd and wordly-wise.

'Well, George, what's brought you here today?' he boomed as the colonel was shown into his office. 'Have a good time in London? I'm taking my missus up for a few days next week. How's Evie?'

'It's about Evie I've come to see you,' said Peregrine, giving him a suspicious look. 'Have you read her book?'

His sensitivity had been sharpened during those last days of troubled thought and he was conscious of a faint change in the lawyer's expression. It was as though he were suddenly on his guard.

'Yes, I've read it. Great success, isn't it? Fancy Evie breaking out into poetry. Wonders will never cease.'

George Peregrine was inclined to lose his temper.

'It's made me look a perfect damned fool.'

'Oh, what nonsense, George! There's no harm in Evie's writing a book. You ought to be jolly proud of her.'

'Don't talk such rot. It's her own story. You know it and everyone else knows it. I suppose I'm the only one who doesn't know who her lover was.'

'There is such a thing as imagination, old boy. There's no reason to suppose the whole thing isn't made up.'

'Look here, Henry, we've known one another all our lives. We've had all sorts of good times together. Be honest with me. Can you look me in the face and tell me you believe it's a made-up story?'

Harry Blane moved uneasily in his chair. He was disturbed by the distress in old George's voice.

'You've got no right to ask me a question like that. Ask Evie.'

'I daren't,' George answered after an anguished pause. 'I'm afraid she'd tell me the truth.'

There was an uncomfortable silence.

'Who was the chap?'

Harry Blane looked at him straight in the eye.

'I don't know, and if I did I wouldn't tell you.'

'You swine. Don't you see what a position I'm in? Do you think it's very pleasant to be made absolutely ridiculous?'

The lawyer lit a cigarette and for some moments silently puffed it.

'I don't see what I can do for you,' he said at last.

'You've got private detectives you employ, I suppose. I want you to put them on the job and let them find everything out.'

'It's not very pretty to put detectives on one's wife, old boy; and besides, taking for granted for a moment that Evie had an affair, it was a good many years ago and I don't suppose it would be possible to find out a thing. They seem to have covered their tracks pretty carefully.'

'I don't care. You put the detectives on. I want to know the truth.'

'I won't, George. If you're determined to do that you'd better consult someone else. And look here, even if you got evidence that Evie had been unfaithful to you what would you do with it? You'd look rather silly divorcing your wife because she'd committed adultery ten years ago.'

'At all events I could have it out with her.'

'You can do that now, but you know just as well as I do that if you do she'll leave you. D'you want her to do that?'

George gave him an unhappy look.

'I don't know. I always thought she'd been a damned good wife to me. She runs the house perfectly, we never have any servant trouble; she's done wonders with the garden and she's splendid with all the village people. But damn it, I have my self-respect to think of. How can I go on living with her when I know that she was grossly unfaithful to me?'

'Have you always been faithful to her?'

'More or less, you know. After all, we've been married for nearly twenty-four years and Evie was never much for bed.'

The solicitor slightly raised his eyebrows, but George was too intent on what he was saying to notice.

'I don't deny that I've had a bit of fun now and then. A man wants it. Women are different.'

'We only have men's word for that,' said Harry Blane, with a faint smile.

'Evie's absolutely the last woman I'd have suspected of kicking over the traces. I mean, she's a very fastidious, reticent woman. What on earth made her write the damned book?'

'I suppose it was a very poignant experience and perhaps it was a relief to her to get it off her chest like that.'

'Well, if she had to write it why the devil didn't she write it under an assumed name?'

'She used her maiden name. I suppose she thought that was enough, and it would have been if the book hadn't had this amazing boom.'

George Peregrine and the lawyer were sitting opposite one another with a desk between them. George, his elbow on the desk, his cheek on his hand, frowned at his thought.

'It's so rotten not to know what sort of a chap he was. One can't even tell if he was by way of being a gentleman. I mean, for all I know he may have been a farm-hand or a clerk in a lawyer's office.'

Harry Blane did not permit himself to smile and when he answered there was in his eyes a kindly, tolerant look.

'Knowing Evie so well I think the probabilities are that he was all right. Anyhow I'm sure he wasn't a clerk in my office.'

'It's been a shock to me,' the colonel sighed. 'I thought she was fond of me. She couldn't have written that book unless she hated me.'

'Oh, I don't believe that. I don't think she's capable of hatred.'

'You're not going to pretend that she loves me.'

'No.'

'Well, what does she feel for me?'

Harry Blane leaned back in his swivel chair and looked at George reflectively.

'Indifference, I should say.'

The colonel gave a little shudder and reddened.

'After all, you're not in love with her, are you?'

George Peregrine did not answer directly.

'It's been a great blow to me not to have any children, but I've never let her see that I think she's let me down. I've always been kind to her. Within reasonable limits I've tried to do my duty by her.'

The lawyer passed a large hand over his mouth to conceal the smile that trembled on his lips.

'It's been such an awful shock to me,' Peregrine went on. 'Damn it all, even ten years ago Evie was no chicken and God knows, she wasn't much to look at. It's so ugly.' He sighed deeply. 'What would *you* do in my place?'

'Nothing.'

George Peregrine drew himself bolt upright in his chair and he looked at Harry with the stern set face that he must have worn when he inspected his regiment.

'I can't overlook a thing like this. I've been made a laughing-stock. I can never hold up my head again.'

'Nonsense,' said the lawyer sharply, and then in a pleasant, kindly manner, 'Listen, old boy: the man's dead; it all happened a long while back. Forget it. Talk to people about Evie's book, rave about it, tell 'em how proud you are of her. Behave as though you had so much confidence in her, you *knew* she could never have been unfaithful to you. The world moves so quickly and people's memories are so short. They'll forget.'

'I shan't forget.'

'You're both middle-aged people. She probably does a great deal more for you than you think and you'd be awfully lonely without her. I don't think it matters if you don't forget. It'll be all to the good if you can get it into that thick head of yours that there's a lot more in Evie than you ever had the gumption to see.'

'Damn it all, you talk as if I was to blame.'

'No, I don't think you were to blame, but I'm not so sure that Evie was either. I don't suppose she wanted to fall in love with this boy. D'you remember those verses right at the end? The impression they gave me was that though she was shattered by his death, in a strange sort of way she welcomed it. All through she'd been aware of the fragility of the tie that bound them. He died in the full flush of his first love and had never known that love so seldom endures; he'd only known its bliss and beauty. In her own bitter grief she found solace in the thought that he'd been spared all sorrow.'

'All that's a bit above my head, old boy. I see more or less what you mean.'

George Peregrine stared unhappily at the inkstand on the desk. He was silent and the lawyer looked at him with curious, yet sympathetic, eyes.

'Do you realize what courage she must have had never by a sign to show how dreadfully unhappy she was?' he said gently.

Colonel Peregrine sighed.

'I'm broken, I suppose you're right; it's no good crying over spilt milk and it would only make things worse if I made a fuss.'

'Well?'

George Peregrine gave a pitiful little smile.

'I'll take your advice. I'll do nothing. Let them think me a damned fool and to hell with them. The truth is, I don't know what I'd do without Evie. But I'll tell you what, there's one thing I shall never understand till my dying day: What in the name of heaven did the fellow ever see in her?'

Miss King

◆

It was not till the beginning of September that Ashenden, a writer by profession, who had been abroad at the outbreak of the war, managed to get back to England. He chanced soon after his arrival to go to a party and was there introduced to a middle-aged colonel whose name he did not catch. He had some talk with him. As he was about to leave, this officer came up to him and asked:

'I say, I wonder if you'd mind coming to see me. I'd rather like to have a chat with you.'

'Certainly,' said Ashenden. 'Whenever you like.'

'What about tomorrow at eleven?'

'All right.'

'I'll just write down my address. Have you a card on you?'

Ashenden gave him one and on this the colonel scribbled in pencil the name of a street and the number of a house. When Ashenden walked along next morning to keep his appointment he found himself in a street of rather vulgar red-brick houses in a part of London that had once been fashionable, but was now fallen in the esteem of the house-hunter who wanted a good address. On the house at which Ashenden had been asked to call there was a board up to announce that it was for sale, the shutters were closed, and there was no sign that anyone lived in it. He rang the bell and the door was opened by a non-commissioned officer so promptly that he was startled. He was not asked his business, but led immediately into a long room at the back, once evidently a dining-room, the florid decoration of which looked oddly out of keeping with the office furniture, shabby and sparse, that was in it. It gave Ashenden the impression of a room in which the brokers had taken possession. The colonel, who was known in the Intelligence Department, as Ashenden later discovered, by the letter R. rose when he came in and shook hands with him. He was a man somewhat above the middle height, lean, with a yellow, deeply lined face, thin grey hair, and a toothbrush moustache. The thing immediately noticeable about him was the closeness with which his blue eyes were set. He only just escaped a squint. They were hard and cruel eyes, and very wary; and they gave him a cunning, shifty look. Here was a man that you could neither like nor trust at first sight. His manner was pleasant and cordial.

He asked Ashenden a good many questions and then, without further to-do, suggested that he had particular qualifications for the secret service. Ashenden was acquainted with several European languages and his profession was excellent cover; on the pretext that he was writing a book he could without attracting attention visit any neutral country. It was while they were discussing this point that R. said:

'You know, you ought to get material that would be very useful to you in your work.'

'I shouldn't mind that,' said Ashenden.

'I'll tell you an incident that occurred only the other day and I can vouch for its truth. I thought at the time it would make a damned good story. One of the French ministers went down to Nice to recover from a cold and he had some very important documents with him that he kept in a dispatch-case. They were very important indeed. Well, a day or two after he arrived he picked up a yellow-haired lady at some restaurant or other where there was dancing, and he got friendly with her. To cut a long story short, he took her back to his hotel—of course it was a very imprudent thing to do—and when he came to himself in the morning the lady and the dispatch-case had disappeared. They had one or two drinks up in his room and his theory is that when his back was turned the woman slipped a drug into his glass.'

R. finished and looked at Ashenden with a gleam in his close-set eyes.

'Dramatic, isn't it?' he asked.

'Do you mean to say that happened the other day?'

'The week before last.'

'Impossible,' cried Ashenden. 'Why, we've been putting that incident on the stage for sixty years, we've written it in a thousand novels. Do you mean to say that life has only just caught up with us?'

R. was a trifle disconcerted.

'Well, if necessary, I could give you names and dates, and believe me, the Allies have been put to no end of trouble by the loss of the documents that the dispatch-case contained.'

'Well, sir, if you can't do better than that in the secret service,' sighed Ashenden, 'I'm afraid that as a source of inspiration to the writer of fiction it's a wash-out. We really *can't* write that story much longer.'

It did not take them long to settle things and when Ashenden rose to go he had already made careful note of his instructions. He was to start for Geneva next day. The last words that R. said to him, with a casualness that made them impressive, were:

'There's just one thing I think you ought to know before you take on this job. And don't forget it. If you do well you'll get no thanks and if you get into trouble you'll get no help. Does that suit you?'

'Perfectly.'

'Then I'll wish you good afternoon.'

Ashenden was on his way back to Geneva. The night was stormy and the wind blew cold from the mountains, but the stodgy little steamer plodded sturdily through the choppy waters of the lake. A scudding rain, just turning into sleet, swept the deck in angry gusts, like a nagging woman who cannot leave a subject alone. Ashenden had been to France in order to write and dispatch a report. A day or two before, about five in the afternoon, an Indian agent of his had come to see him in his rooms; it was only by a lucky chance that he was in, for he had no appointment with him, and the agent's instructions were to come to the hotel only in a case of urgent importance. He told Ashenden that a Bengali in the German service had recently come from Berlin with a black cane trunk in which were a number of documents interesting to the British Government. At that time the Central Powers were doing their best to foment such an agitation in India as would make it necessary for Great Britain to keep her troops in the country and perhaps send others from France. It had been found possible to get the Bengali arrested in Berne on a charge that would keep him out of harm's way for a while, but the black cane trunk could not be found. Ashenden's agent was a very brave and very clever fellow and he mixed freely with such of his countrymen as were disaffected to the interests of Great Britain. He had just discovered that the Bengali before going to Berne had, for greater safety, left the trunk in the cloak-room at Zürich station, and now that he was in gaol, awaiting trial, was unable to get the *bulletin* by which it might be obtained into the hands of any of his confederates. It was a matter of great urgency for the German Intelligence Department to secure the contents of the trunk without delay, and since it was impossible for them to get hold of it by the ordinary official means, they had decided to break into the station that very night and steal it. It was a bold and ingenious scheme and Ashenden felt a pleasant exhilaration (for a great deal of his work was uncommonly dull) when he heard of it. He recognized the dashing and unscrupulous touch of the head of the German secret service at Berne. But the burglary was arranged for two o'clock on the following morning and there was not a moment to lose. He could trust neither the telegraph nor the telephone to communicate with the British officer at Berne, and since the Indian agent could not go (he was taking his life in his hands by coming to see Ashenden and if he were noticed leaving his room it might easily be that he would be found one day floating in the lake with a knife-thrust in his back), there was nothing for it but to go himself.

There was a train to Berne that he could just catch and he put on his hat and coat as he ran downstairs. He jumped into a cab. Four hours later he rang the bell of the headquarters of the Intelligence Department. His name was known there but to one person, and it was for him that Ashenden asked. A tall tired-looking man, whom he had not met before, came out and without a word led him into an office. Ashenden told him his errand. The tall man looked at his watch.

'It's too late for us to do anything ourselves. We couldn't possibly get to Zürich in time.'

He reflected.

'We'll put the Swiss authorities on the job. They can telephone, and when your friends attempt their little burglary, I have no doubt they'll find the station well guarded. Anyhow, you had better get back to Geneva.'

He shook hands with Ashenden and showed him out. Ashenden was well aware that he would never know what happened then. Being no more than a tiny rivet in a vast and complicated machine, he never had the advantage of seeing a completed action. He was concerned with the beginning or the end of it, perhaps, or with some incident in the middle, but what his own doings led to he had seldom a chance of discovering. It was as unsatisfactory as those modern novels that give you a number of unrelated episodes and expect you by piecing them together to construct in your mind a connected narrative.

Notwithstanding his fur coat and his muffler, Ashenden was chilled to the bone. It was warm in the saloon and there were good lights to read by, but he thought it better not to sit there in case some habitual traveller, recognizing him, wondered why he made these constant journeys between Geneva in Switzerland and Thonon in France; and so, making the best of what shelter could be found, he passed the tedious time in the darkness of the deck. He looked in the direction of Geneva, but could see no lights, and the sleet, turning into snow, prevented him from recognizing the landmarks. Lake Leman, on fine days so trim and pretty, artificial like a piece of water in a French garden, in this tempestuous weather was as secret and as menacing as the sea. He made up his mind that, on getting back to his hotel, he would have a fire lit in his sitting-room, a hot bath, and dinner comfortably by the fireside in pyjamas and a dressing-gown. The prospect of spending an evening by himself with his pipe and a book was so agreeable that it made the misery of that journey across the lake positively worth while. Two sailors tramped past him heavily, their heads bent down to save themselves from the sleet that blew in their faces, and one of them shouted to him: *Nous arrivons*; they went to the side and withdrew a bar to allow passage for the gangway, and looking again Ashenden through the howling darkness saw mistily the lights of the quay. A welcome sight. In two or three minutes the steamer was made fast and Ashenden, muffled to the eyes, joined himself to the little knot of passengers that waited to step ashore. Though he made the journey so often—it was his duty to cross the lake into France once a week to deliver his reports and to receive instructions—he had always a faint sense of trepidation when he stood among the crowd at the gangway and waited to land. There was nothing on his passport to show that he had been in France; the steamer went round the lake touching French soil at two places, but going from Switzerland to Switzerland, so that his journey might have been to Vevey or to Lausanne; but he could never be sure that the secret police had not taken note of him, and if he had been followed and seen to land in France, the fact that there was no stamp on his passport would be difficult to explain. Of course he had his story ready, but he well knew that it was not a very convincing one, and though it might be impossible for the Swiss authorities to prove that he was anything but a casual traveller, he might nevertheless spend two or three days in gaol, which would be uncomfortable, and then be firmly conducted to the frontier, which would be mortifying. The Swiss knew well that their country was the scene of all manner of intrigues; agents of the secret service, spies, revolutionaries, and agitators infested the hotels of the principal towns and, jealous of their neutrality, they were determined to prevent conduct that might embroil them with any of the belligerent powers.

There were as usual two police officers on the quay to watch the passengers disembark and Ashenden, walking past them with as unconcerned an air as he could assume, was relieved when he had got safely by. The darkness swallowed him up and he stepped out briskly for his hotel. The wild weather with a scornful gesture had swept all the neatness from the trim promenade. The shops were closed and Ashenden passed only an occasional pedestrian who sidled along, scrunched up, as though he fled from the blind wrath of the unknown. You had a feeling in that black and bitter night that civilization, ashamed of its artificiality, cowered before the fury of elemental things. It was hail now that blew in Ashenden's face, and the pavement was wet and slippery so that he had to walk with caution. The hotel faced the lake. When he reached it and a page-boy opened the door for him, he entered the hall with a flurry of wind that sent the papers on the porter's desk flying into the air. Ashenden was dazzled by the light. He stopped to ask the porter if there were letters for him. There was nothing, and he was about to get into the lift when the porter told him that two gentlemen were waiting in his room to see him. Ashenden had no friends in Geneva.

'Oh?' he answered, not a little surprised. 'Who are they?'

He had taken care to get on friendly terms with the porter and his tips for trifling services had been generous. The porter gave a discreet smile.

'There is no harm in telling you. I think they are members of the police.'

'What do they want?' asked Ashenden.

'They did not say. They asked me where you were, and I told them you had gone for a walk. They said they would wait till you came back.'

'How long have they been there?'

'An hour.'

Ashenden's heart sank, but he took care not to let his face betray his concern.

'I'll go up and see them,' he said. The liftman stood aside to let him step into the lift, but Ashenden shook his head. 'I'm so cold,' he said, 'I'll walk up.'

He wished to give himself a moment to think, but as he ascended the three flights slowly his feet were like lead. There could be small doubt why two police officers were so bent upon seeing him. He felt on a sudden dreadfully tired. He did not feel he could cope with a multitude of questions. And if he were arrested as a secret agent he must spend at least the night in a cell. He longed more than ever for a hot bath and a pleasant dinner by his fireside. He had half a mind to turn tail and walk out of the hotel, leaving everything behind him; he had his passport in his pocket and he knew by heart the hours at which trains started for the frontier: before the Swiss authorities had made up their minds what to do he would be in safety. But he continued to trudge upstairs. He did not like the notion of abandoning his job so easily; he had been sent to Geneva, knowing the risks, to do work of a certain kind, and it seemed to him that he had better go through with it. Of course it would not be very nice to spend two years in a Swiss prison, but the chance of this was, like assassination to kings, one of the inconveniences of his profession. He reached the landing of the third floor and walked to his room. Ashenden had in him, it seems, a strain of flippancy (on account of which, indeed, the critics had often reproached him) and as he stood for a moment outside the door his predicament appeared to him on a sudden rather droll. His spirits went up and he determined to brazen the thing out. It was with a genuine smile on his lips that he turned the handle and entering the room faced his visitors.

'Good evening, gentlemen,' said he.

The room was brightly lit, for all the lights were on, and a fire burned in the hearth. The air was grey with smoke, since the strangers, finding it long to wait for him, had been smoking strong and inexpensive cigars. They sat in their greatcoats and bowler-hats as though they had only just that moment come in; but the ashes in the little tray on the table would alone have suggested that they had been long enough there to make themselves familiar with their surroundings. They were two powerful men, with black moustaches, on the stout side, heavily built, and they reminded Ashenden of Fafner and Fasolt, the giants in *The Rhinegold;* their clumsy boots, the massive way they sat in their chairs, and the ponderous alertness of their expression made it obvious that they were members of the detective force. Ashenden gave his room an enveloping glance. He was a neat creature and saw at once that his things, though not in disorder, were not as he had left them. He guessed that an examination had been made of his effects. That did not disturb him, for he kept in his room no document that would compromise him; his code he had learned by heart and destroyed before leaving England, and such communications as reached him from Germany were handed to him by third parties and transmitted without delay to the proper places. There was nothing he need fear in a search, but the impression that it had been made confirmed his suspicion that he had been denounced to the authorities as a secret agent.

'What can I do for you, gentlemen?' he asked affably. 'It's warm in here, wouldn't you like to take off your coats—and hats?'

It faintly irritated him that they should sit there with their hats on.

'We're only staying a minute,' said one of them. 'We were passing and as the *concierge* said you would be in at once, we thought we would wait.'

He did not remove his hat. Ashenden unwrapped his scarf and disembarrassed himself of his heavy coat.

'Won't you have a cigar?' he asked, offering the box to the two detectives in turn.

'I don't mind if I do,' said the first, Fafner, taking one, upon which the second, Fasolt, helped himself without a word, even of thanks.

The name on the box appeared to have a singular effect on their manners, for both now took off their hats.

'You must have had a very disagreeable walk in this bad weather,' said Fafner, as he bit half an inch off the end of his cigar and spat it in the fire-place.

Now it was Ashenden's principle (a good one in life as well as in the Intelligence Department) always to tell as much of the truth as he conveniently could; so he answered as follows:

'What do you take me for? I wouldn't go out in such weather if I could help it. I had to go to Vevey today to see an invalid friend and I came back by boat. It was bitter on the lake.'

'We come from the police,' said Fafner casually.

Ashenden thought they must consider him a perfect idiot if they imagined he had not guessed that, but it was not a piece of information to which it was discreet to reply with a pleasantry.

'Oh, really,' he said.

'Have you your passport on you?'

'Yes. In these war-times I think a foreigner is wise always to keep his passport on him.'

'Very wise.'

Ashenden handed the man the nice new passport, which gave no information about his movements other than that he had come from London three months before and had since then crossed no frontier. The detective looked at it carefully and passed it on to his colleague.

'It appears to be all in order,' he said.

Ashenden, standing in front of the fire to warm himself, a cigarette between his lips, made no reply. He watched the detectives warily, but with an expression, he flattered himself, of amiable unconcern. Fasolt handed back the passport to Fafner, who tapped it reflectively with a thick forefinger.

'The chief of police told us to come here,' he said, and Ashenden was conscious that both of them now looked at him with attention, 'to make a few inquiries of you.'

Ashenden knew that when you have nothing apposite to say it is better to hold your tongue; and when a man has made a remark that calls to his mind for an answer, he is apt to find silence a trifle disconcerting. Ashenden waited for the detective to proceed. He was not quite sure, but it seemed to him that he hesitated.

'It appears that there have been a good many complaints lately of the noise that people make when they come out of the Casino late at night. We wish to know if you personally have been troubled by the disturbance. It is evident that as your rooms look on the lake and the revellers pass your windows, if the noise is serious, you must have heard it.'

For an instant Ashenden was dumbfounded. What balderdash was this the detective was talking to him (boom, boom, he heard the big drum as the giant lumbered on the scene), and why on earth should the chief of police send to him to find out if his beauty sleep had been disturbed by vociferous gamblers? It looked very like a trap. But nothing is so foolish as to ascribe profundity to what on the surface is merely inept; it is a pitfall into which many an ingenuous reviewer has fallen headlong. Ashenden had a confident belief in the stupidity of the human animal, which in the course of his life had stood him in good stead. It flashed across him that if the detective asked him such a question it was because he had no shadow of proof that he was engaged in any illegal practice. It was clear that he had been denounced, but no evidence had been offered, and the search of his rooms had been fruitless. But what a silly excuse was this to make for a visit and what a poverty of invention it showed! Ashenden immediately thought of three reasons the detectives might have given for seeking an interview with him and he wished that he were on terms sufficiently familiar with them to make the suggestions. This was really an insult to the intelligence. These men were even stupider than he thought; but Ashenden had always a soft corner in his heart for the stupid and now he looked upon them with a feeling of unexpected kindliness. He would have liked to pat them gently. But he answered the question with gravity.

'To tell you the truth, I am a very sound sleeper (the result doubtless of a pure heart and an easy conscience), and I have never heard a thing.'

Ashenden looked at them for the faint smile that he thought his remark deserved, but their countenances remained stolid. Ashenden, as well as an agent of the British Government, was a humorist, and he stifled the beginnings of a sigh. He assumed a slightly imposing air and adopted a more serious tone.

'But even if I had been awakened by noisy people I should not dream of complaining. At a time when there is so much trouble, misery, and unhappiness in the world, I cannot but think it very wrong to disturb the amusement of persons who are lucky enough to be able to amuse themselves.'

'*En effet,*' said the detective. 'But the fact remains that people have been disturbed and the chief of police thought the matter should be inquired into.'

His colleague, who had hitherto preserved a silence that was positively sphinx-like, now broke it.

'I noticed by your passport that you are an author, *monsieur,*' he said.

Ashenden in reaction from his previous perturbation was feeling exceedingly debonair and he answered with good-humour:

'It is true. It is a profession full of tribulation, but it has now and then its compensations.'

'*La gloire,*' said Fafner politely.

'Or shall we say notoriety?' hazarded Ashenden.

'And what are you doing in Geneva?'

The question was put so pleasantly that Ashenden felt it behoved him to be on his guard. A police officer amiable is more dangerous to the wise than a police officer aggressive.

'I am writing a play,' said Ashenden.

He waved his hand to the papers on his table. Four eyes followed his gesture. A casual glance told him that the detectives had looked and taken note of his manuscripts.

'And why should you write a play here rather than in your own country?'

Ashenden smiled upon them with even more affability than before, since this was a question for which he had long been prepared, and it was a relief to give the answer. He was curious to see how it would go down.

'*Mais, monsieur,* there is the war. My country is in turmoil, it would be impossible to sit there quietly and write a play.'

'Is it a comedy or a tragedy?'

'Oh, a comedy, and a light one at that,' replied Ashenden. 'The artist needs peace and quietness. How do you expect him to preserve that detachment of spirit that is demanded by creative work unless he can have perfect tranquillity? Switzerland has the good fortune to be neutral, and it seemed to me that in Geneva I should find the very surroundings I wanted.'

Fafner nodded slightly to Fasolt, but whether to indicate that he thought Ashenden an imbecile or whether in sympathy with his desire for a safe retreat from a turbulent world, Ashenden had no means of knowing. Anyhow the detective evidently came to the conclusion that he could learn nothing more from talking to Ashenden, for his remarks grew now desultory and in a few minutes he rose to go.

When Ashenden, having warmly shaken their hands, closed the door behind the pair he heaved a great sigh of relief. He turned on the water for his bath, as hot as he thought he could possibly bear it, and as he undressed reflected comfortably over his escape.

The day before, an incident had occurred that had left him on his guard There was in his service a Swiss, known in the Intelligence Department as Bernard, who had recently come from Germany, and Ashenden, desiring to see him, had instructed him to go to a certain café at a certain time. Since he had not seen him before, so that there might be no mistake he had informed him through an intermediary what question he himself would ask and what reply he was to give. He chose the luncheon hour for the meeting, since the café was unlikely to be crowded, and it chanced that on entering he saw but one man of about the age he knew Bernard to be. He was by himself, and going up to him Ashenden casually put to him the pre-arranged question. The pre-arranged answer was given, and sitting down beside him, Ashenden ordered himself a Dubonnet. The spy was a stocky little fellow, shabbily dressed, with a bullet-shaped head, close-cropped, fair, with shifty blue eyes and a sallow skin. He did not inspire confidence, and but that Ashenden knew by experience how hard it was to find men willing to go into Germany he would have been surprised that his predecessor had engaged him. He was a German-Swiss and spoke French with a strong accent. He immediately asked for his wages and these Ashenden passed over to him in an envelope. They were in Swiss francs. He gave a general account of his stay in Germany and answered Ashenden's careful questions. He was by calling a waiter and had found a job in a restaurant near one of the Rhine bridges, which gave him good opportunity to get information that was required of him. His reasons for coming to Switzerland for a few days were plausible and there could apparently be no difficulty in his crossing the frontier on his return. Ashenden expressed his satisfaction with his behaviour, gave him his orders and was prepared to finish the interview.

'Very good,' said Bernard. 'But before I go back to Germany I want two thousand francs.'

'Do you?'

'Yes, and I want them now, before you leave this café. It's a sum I have to pay, and I've got to have it.'

'I'm afraid I can't give it to you.'

A scowl made the man's face even more unpleasant to look at than it was before.

'You've got to.'

'What makes you think that?'

The spy leaned forward and, not raising his voice, but speaking so that only Ashenden could hear, burst out angrily:

'Do you think I'm going on risking my life for that beggarly sum you give me? Not ten days ago a man was caught at Mainz and shot. Was that one of your men?'

'We haven't got anyone at Mainz,' said Ashenden, carelessly, and for all he knew it was true. He had been puzzled not to receive his usual communications from that place and Bernard's information might afford the explanation. 'You knew exactly what you were to get when you took on the job, and if you weren't satisfied you needn't have taken it. I have no authority to give you a penny more.'

'Do you see what I've got here?' said Bernard.

He took a small revolver out of his pocket and fingered it significantly.

'What are you going to do with it? Pawn it?'

With an angry shrug of the shoulders he put it back in his pocket. Ashenden reflected that had he known anything of the technique of the theatre Bernard would have been aware that it was useless to make a gesture that had no ulterior meaning.

'You refuse to give me the money?'

'Certainly.'

The spy's manner, which at first had been obsequious, was now somewhat truculent, but he kept his head and never for a moment raised his voice. Ashenden could see that Bernard, however big a ruffian, was a reliable agent, and he made up his mind to suggest to R. that his salary should be raised. The scene diverted him. A little way off two fat citizens of Geneva, with black beards, were playing dominoes, and on the other side a young man with spectacles was with great rapidity writing sheet after sheet of an immensely long letter. A Swiss family (who knows, perhaps Robinson by name), consisting of a father and mother and four children, were sitting round a table making the best of two small cups of coffee. The *caissière* behind the counter, an imposing brunette with a large bust encased in black silk, was reading the local paper. The surroundings made the melodramatic scene in which Ashenden was engaged perfectly grotesque. His own play seemed to him much more real.

Bernard smiled. His smile was not engaging.

'Do you know that I have only to go to the police and tell them about you to have you arrested? Do you know what a Swiss prison is like?'

'No, I've often wondered lately. Do you?'

'Yes, and you wouldn't much like it.'

One of the things that had bothered Ashenden was the possibility that he would be arrested before he finished his play. He disliked the notion of leaving it half done for an indefinite period. He did not know whether he would be treated as a political prisoner or as a common criminal and he had a mind to ask Bernard whether in the latter case (the only one Bernard was likely to know anything about) he would be allowed writing materials. He was afraid Bernard would think the inquiry an attempt to laugh at him. But he was feeling comparatively at ease and was able to answer Bernard's threat without heat.

'You could of course get me sentenced to two years' imprisonment.'

'At least.'

'No, that is the maximum, I understand, and I think it is quite enough. I won't conceal from you that I should find it extremely disagreeable. But not nearly so disagreeable as you would.'

'What could you do?'

'Oh, we'd get you somehow. And after all, the war won't last for ever. You are a waiter, you want your freedom of action. I promise you that if I get into any trouble, you will never be admitted into any of the Allied countries for the rest of your life. I can't help thinking it would cramp your style.'

Bernard did not reply, but looked down sulkily at the marble-topped table. Ashenden thought this was the moment to pay for the drinks and go.

'Think it over, Bernard,' he said. 'If you want to go back to your job, you have your instructions, and your usual wages shall be paid through the usual channels.'

The spy shrugged his shoulders, and Ashenden, though not knowing in the least what was the result of their conversation, felt that it behoved him to walk out with dignity. He did so.

And now as he carefully put one foot into the bath, wondering if he could bear it, he asked himself what Bernard had in the end decided on. The water was just not scalding and he gradually let himself down into it. On the whole it seemed to him that the spy had thought it would be as well to go straight, and the source of his denunciation must be looked for elsewhere. Perhaps in the hotel itself. Ashenden lay back, and as his body grew used to the heat of the water gave a sigh of satisfaction.

'Really,' he reflected, 'there are moments in life when all this to-do that has led from the primeval slime to myself seems almost worth while.'

Ashenden could not but think he was lucky to have wriggled out of the fix he had found himself in that afternoon. Had he been arrested and in due course sentenced, R., shrugging his shoulders, would merely have called him a damned fool and set about looking for someone to take his place. Already Ashenden knew his chief well enough to be aware that when he had told him that if he got into trouble he need look for no help he meant exactly what he said.

Ashenden, lying comfortably in his bath, was glad to think that in all probability he would be able to finish his play in peace. The police had drawn a blank and though they might watch him from now on with some care, it was unlikely that they would take a further step until he had at least roughed out his third act. It behoved him to be prudent (only a fortnight ago his colleague at Lausanne had been sentenced to a term of imprisonment), but it would be foolish to be alarmed: his predecessor in Geneva, seeing himself, with an exaggerated sense of his own importance, shadowed from morning till night, had been so affected by the nervous strain that it had been found necessary to withdraw him. Twice a week Ashenden had to go to the market to receive instructions that were brought to him by an old peasant woman from French Savoy who sold butter and eggs. She came in with the other market-women and the search at the frontier was perfunctory. It was barely dawn when they crossed and the officials were only too glad to have done quickly with these chattering noisy women and get back to their warm fires and their cigars. Indeed this old lady looked so bland and innocent, with her corpulence, her fat red face, and her smiling good-natured mouth, it would have been a very astute detective who could imagine that if he took the trouble to put his hand deep down between those voluminous breasts of hers, he would find a little piece of paper that would land in the dock an honest old woman (who kept her son out of the trenches by taking this risk) and an English writer approaching middle age. Ashenden went to the market about nine when the housewives of Geneva for the most part had done their provisioning, stopped in front of the basket by the side of which, rain or wind, hot or cold, sat that indomitable creature and bought half a pound of butter. She slipped the note into his hand when he was given change for ten francs and he sauntered away. His only moment of risk was when he walked back to his hotel with the paper in his pocket, and after this scare he made up his mind to shorten as much as possible the period during which it could be found on him.

Ashenden sighed, for the water was no longer quite so hot; he could not reach the tap with his hand nor could he turn it with his toes (as every properly regulated tap should turn) and if he got up enough to add more hot water he might just as well get out altogether. On the other hand he could not pull out the plug with his foot in order to empty the bath and so force himself to get out, nor could he find himself the will-power to step out of it like a man. He had often heard people tell him that he possessed character and he reflected that people judge hastily in the affairs of life because they judge on insufficient evidence: they had never seen him in a hot, but diminishingly hot, bath. His mind, however, wandered back to his play, and telling himself jokes and repartees that he knew by bitter experience would never look so neat on paper nor sound so well on the stage as they did then, he abstracted his mind from the fact that his bath was growing almost tepid, when he heard a knock at the door. Since he did not want anyone to enter, he had the presence of mind not to say come in, but the knocking was repeated.

'Who is it?' he cried irascibly.

'A letter.'

'Come in then. Wait a minute.'

Ashenden heard his bedroom door open and getting out of the bath flung a towel round him and went in. A page-boy was waiting with a note. It needed only a verbal answer. It was from a lady staying in the hotel asking him to play bridge after dinner and was signed in the continental fashion Baronne de Higgins. Ashenden, longing for a cosy meal in his own room, in slippers and with a book leaned up against a reading-lamp, was about to refuse when it occurred to him that in the circumstances it might be discreet to show himself in the dining-room that night. It was absurd to suppose that in that hotel the news would not have spread that he had been visited by the police and it would be as well to prove to his fellow guests that he was not disconcerted. It had passed through his mind that it might be someone in the hotel who had denounced him and indeed the name of the sprightly baroness had not failed to suggest itself to him. If it was she who had given him away there would be a certain humour in playing bridge with her. He gave the boy a message that he would be pleased to come and proceeded slowly to don his evening clothes.

The Baroness von Higgins was an Austrian, who on settling in Geneva during the first winter of the war had found it convenient to make her name look as French as possible. She spoke English and French perfectly. Her surname, so far from Teutonic, she owed to her grandfather, a Yorkshire stable-boy, who had been taken over to Austria by a Prince Blankenstein early in the nineteenth century. He had had a charming and romantic career; a very good-looking man, he attracted the attention of one of the archduchesses and then made such good use of his opportunities that he ended his life as a baron and minister plenipotentiary to an Italian court. The baroness, his only descendant, after an unhappy marriage, the particulars of which she was fond of relating to her acquaintance, had resumed her maiden name. She mentioned not infrequently the fact that her grandfather had been an ambassador, but never that he had been a stable-boy and Ashenden had learned this interesting detail from Vienna; for as he grew friendly with her he had thought it necessary to get a few particulars about her past, and he knew among other things that her private income did not permit her to live on the somewhat lavish scale on which she was living in Geneva. Since she had so many advantages for espionage, it was fairly safe to suppose that an alert secret service had enlisted her services and Ashenden took it for granted that she was engaged somehow on the same kind of work as himself. It increased if anything the cordiality of his relations with her.

When he went into the dining-room it was already full. He sat down at his table and feeling jaunty after his adventure ordered himself (at the expense of the British Government) a bottle of champagne. The baroness gave him a flashing, brilliant smile. She was a woman of more than forty, but in a hard and glittering manner extremely beautiful. She was a high-coloured blonde with golden hair of a metallic lustre, lovely no doubt but not attractive, and Ashenden had from the first reflected that it was not the sort of hair you would like to find in your soup. She had fine features, blue eyes, a straight nose, and a pink and white skin, but her skin was stretched over her bones a trifle tightly; she was generously *décolletée* and her white and ample bosom had the quality of marble. There was nothing in her appearance to suggest the yielding tenderness that the susceptible find so alluring. She was magnificently gowned, but scantily bejewelled, so that Ashenden, who knew something of these matters, con-cluded that the superior authority had given her *carte blanche* at a dressmaker's but had not thought it prudent or necessary to provide her with rings or pearls. She was notwithstanding so showy that but for R.'s story of the minister, Ashenden would have thought the sight of her alone must have aroused in any-one on whom she desired to exercise her wiles the sense of prudence.

While he waited for his dinner to be served, Ashenden cast his eyes over the company. Most of the persons gathered were old friends by sight. At that time Geneva was a hot-bed of intrigue and its home was the hotel at which Ashenden was staying. There were Frenchmen there, Italians and Russians, Turks,

Rumanians, Greeks, and Egyptians. Some had fled their country, some doubtless represented it. There was a Bulgarian, an agent of Ashenden, whom for greater safety he had never even spoken to in Geneva; he was dining that night with two fellow countrymen and in a day or so, if he was not killed in the interval, might have a very interesting communication to make. Then there was a little German prostitute, with china-blue eyes and a doll-like face, who made frequent journeys along the lake and up to Berne, and in the exercise of her profession got little titbits of information over which doubtless they pondered with deliberation in Berlin. She was of course of a different class from the baroness and hunted much easier game. But Ashenden was surprised to catch sight of Count von Holzminden and wondered what on earth he was doing there. This was the German agent in Vevey and he came over to Geneva only on occasion. Once Ashenden had seen him in the old quarter of the city, with its silent houses and deserted streets, talking at a corner to a man whose appearance very much suggested the spy and he would have given a great deal to hear what they said to one another. It had amused him to come across the Count, for in London before the war he had known him fairly well. He was of great family and indeed related to the Hohenzollerns. He was fond of England; he danced well, rode well, and shot well; people said he was more English than the English. He was a tall, thin fellow, in well-cut clothes, with a close-cropped Prussian head, and that peculiar bend of the body—as though he were just about to bow to a royalty—that you feel, rather than see, in those who have spent their lives about a court. He had charming manners and was much interested in the Fine Arts. But now Ashenden and he pretended they had never seen one another before. Each of course knew on what work the other was engaged and Ashenden had had a mind to chaff him about it—it seemed absurd when he had dined with a man off and on for years and played cards with him, to act as though he did not know him from Adam—but refrained in case the German looked upon his behaviour as further proof of the British frivolity in face of war. Ashenden was perplexed: Holzminden had never set foot in that hotel before and it was unlikely that he had done so now without good reason.

Ashenden asked himself whether this event had anything to do with the unusual presence in the dining-room of Prince Ali. At that juncture it was imprudent to ascribe any occurrence, however accidental it looked, to the hazard of coincidence. Prince Ali was an Egyptian, a near relation of the Khedive, who had fled his country when the Khedive was deposed. He was a bitter enemy of the English and was known to be actively engaged in stirring up trouble in Egypt. The week before, the Khedive in great secrecy had passed three days at the hotel and the pair of them had held constant meetings in the prince's apartments. He was a little fat man with a heavy black moustache. He was living with his two daughters and a certain pasha, Mustapha by name, who was his secretary and managed his affairs. The four of them were now dining together; they drank a great deal of champagne, but sat in a stolid silence. The two princesses were emancipated young women who spent their nights dancing in restaurants with the bloods of Geneva. They were short and stout, with fine black eyes and heavy sallow faces; and they were dressed with a rich loudness that suggested the Fish-market at Cairo rather than the Rue de la Paix. His Highness usually ate upstairs but the princesses dined every evening in the public dining-room: they were chaperoned vaguely by a little old English-woman, a Miss King, who had been their governess; but she sat at a table by herself and they appeared to pay no attention to her. Once Ashenden, going along a corridor, had come upon the elder of the two fat princesses berating the governess in French with a violence that took his breath away. She was shouting at the top of her voice and suddenly smacked the old woman's face. When she caught sight of Ashenden she gave him a furious look and flinging into her room slammed the door. He walked on as though he had noticed nothing.

On his arrival Ashenden had tried to scrape acquaintance with Miss King, but she had received his advances not merely with frigidity but with churlishness. He had begun by taking off his hat when he met her, and she had given him a stiff bow, then he had addressed her and she had answered with such brevity that it was evident that she wished to have nothing much to do with him. But it was not his business to be discouraged, so with what assurance he could muster he took the first opportunity to enter into conversation with her. She drew herself up and said in French, but with an English accent:

'I don't wish to make acquaintance with strangers.'

She turned her back on him and, next time he saw her, cut him dead.

She was a tiny woman, just a few little bones in a bag of wrinkled skin, and her face was deeply furrowed. It was obvious that she wore a wig, it was of a mousy brown, very elaborate and not always set quite straight, and she was heavily made up, with great patches of scarlet on her withered cheeks and brilliantly red lips. She dressed fantastically in gay clothes that looked as though they had been bought higgledy-piggledy from an old-clothes shop and in the day-time she wore enormous, extravagantly girlish hats. She tripped along in very small smart shoes with very high heels. Her appearance was so grotesque that it created consternation rather than amusement. People turned in the street and stared at her with open mouths.

Ashenden was told that Miss King had not been to England since she was first engaged as governess of the prince's mother and he could not but be amazed to think of all she must have seen during those long years in the harems of Cairo. It was impossible to guess how old she was. How many of those short Eastern lives must have run their course under her eyes and what dark secrets must she have known! Ashenden wondered where she came from; an exile from her own country for so long, she must possess in it neither family nor friends: he knew that her sentiments were anti-English and if she had answered him so rudely he surmised that she had been told to be on her guard against him. She never spoke anything but French. Ashenden wondered what it was she thought of as she sat there, at luncheon and dinner by herself. He wondered if ever she read. After meals she went straight upstairs and was never seen in the public sitting-rooms. He wondered what she thought of those two emancipated princesses who wore garish frocks and danced with strange men in second-rate cafés. But when Miss King passed him on her way out of the dining-room it seemed to Ashenden that her mask of a face scowled. She appeared actively to dislike him. Her gaze met his and the pair of them looked at one another for a moment: he imagined that she tried to put into her stare an unspoken insult. It would have been pleasantly absurd in that painted, withered visage if it had not been for some reason rather oddly pathetic.

But now the Baroness de Higgins, having finished her dinner, gathered up her handkerchief and her bag, and with waiters bowing on either side sailed down the spacious room. She stopped at Ashenden's table. She looked magnificent.

'I'm so glad you can play bridge tonight,' she said in perfect English, with no more than a trace of German accent. 'Will you come to my sitting-room when you are ready and have your coffee?'

'What a lovely dress,' said Ashenden.

'It is frightful. I have nothing to wear, I don't know what I shall do now that I cannot go to Paris. Those horrible Prussians,' and her r's grew guttural as she raised her voice, 'why did they want to drag my poor country into this terrible war?'

She gave a sigh, and a flashing smile, and sailed on. Ashenden was among the last to finish and when he left the dining-room it was almost empty. As he walked past Count Holzminden, Ashenden feeling very gay hazarded the shadow of a wink. The German agent could not be quite sure of it and if he suspected it might rack his brains to discover what mystery it portended. Ashenden walked up to the second floor and knocked at the baroness's door.

'*Entrez, entrez,*' she said and flung it open.

She shook both his hands with cordiality and drew him into the room. He saw that the two persons who were to make the four had already arrived. They were Prince Ali and his secretary. Ashenden was astounded.

'Allow me to introduce Mr Ashenden to Your Highness,' said the baroness, speaking in her fluent French.

Ashenden bowed and took the proffered hand. The prince gave him a quick look, but did not speak. Madame de Higgins went on:

'I do not know if you have met the Pasha.'

'I am delighted to make your acquaintance, Mr Ashenden,' said the prince's secretary, warmly shaking his hand. 'Our beautiful baroness has talked to us of your bridge and His Highness is devoted to the game. *N'est-ce pas, Altesse?*'

'*Oui, oui,*' said the prince.

Mustapha Pasha was a huge fat fellow, of forty-five perhaps, with large mobile eyes and a big black moustache. He wore a dinner jacket with a large diamond in his shirt-front and the *tarboosh* of his country. He was exceedingly voluble, and the words tumbled out of his mouth tumultuously, like marbles out of a bag. He took pains to be extremely civil to Ashenden. The prince sat in silence, looking at Ashenden quietly from under his heavy eyelids. He seemed shy.

'I have not seen you at the club, *Monsieur,*' said the pasha. 'Do you not like baccarat?'

'I play but seldom.'

'The baroness, who has read everything, tells me that you are a remarkable writer. Unfortunately I do not read English.'

The baroness paid Ashenden some very fulsome compliments to which he listened with a proper and grateful politeness, and then, having provided her guests with coffee and liqueurs, she produced the cards. Ashenden could not but wonder why he had been asked to play. He had (he flattered himself) few illusions about himself, and so far as bridge was concerned none. He knew that he was a good player of the second class, but he had played often enough with the best players in the world to know that he was not in the same street with them. The game played now was contract, with which he was not very familiar, and the stakes were high; but the game was obviously but a pretext and Ashenden had no notion what other game was being played under the rose. It might be that knowing he was a British agent the prince and his secretary had desired to see him in order to find out what sort of person he was. Ashenden had felt for a day or two that something was in the air and this meeting confirmed his suspicions, but he had not the faintest notion of what nature this something was. His spies had told him of late nothing that signified. He was now persuaded that he owed that visit of the Swiss police to the kindly intervention of the baroness and it looked as though the bridge-party had been arranged when it was discovered that the detectives had been able to do nothing. The notion was mysterious, but diverting, and as Ashenden played one rubber after another, joining in the incessant conversation, he watched what was said by himself no less closely than what was said by the others. The war was spoken of a good deal and the baroness and the pasha expressed very anti-German sentiments. The baroness's heart was in England whence her family (the stable-boy from Yorkshire) had sprung, and the pasha looked upon Paris as his spiritual home. When the pasha talked of Montmartre and its life by night the prince was roused from his silence.

'*C'est une bien belle ville, Paris,*' he said.

'The Prince has a beautiful apartment there,' said his secretary, 'with beautiful pictures and life-sized statues.'

Ashenden explained that he had the greatest sympathy for the national aspirations of Egypt and that he looked upon Vienna as the most pleasing capital in Europe. He was as friendly to them as they were to him. But if they were under the impression that they would get any information out of him that they had not already seen in the Swiss papers he had a notion that they were mistaken. At one moment he had a suspicion that he was being sounded upon the possibility of selling himself. It was done so discreetly that he could not be quite sure, but he had a feeling that a suggestion floated in the air that a clever writer could do his country a good turn and make a vast amount of money for himself if he cared to enter into an arrangement that would bring to a troubled world the peace that every humane man must so sincerely desire. It was plain that nothing very much would be said that first evening, but Ashenden as evasively as he could, more by general amiability than by words, tried to indicate that he was willing to hear more of the subject. While he talked with the pasha and the beautiful Austrian he was conscious that the watchful eyes of Prince Ali were upon him, and had an uneasy suspicion that they read too much of his thoughts. He felt rather than knew that the prince was an able and astute man. It was possible that after he left them the prince would tell the other two that they were wasting their time and there was nothing to be done with Ashenden.

Soon after midnight, a rubber having been finished, the prince rose from the table.

'It is getting late,' he said, 'and Mr Ashenden has doubtless much to do tomorrow. We must not keep him up.'

Ashenden looked upon this as a signal to take himself off. He left the three together to discuss the situation and retired not a little mystified. He could only trust that they were no less puzzled than he. When he got to his room he suddenly realized that he was dog-tired. He could hardly keep his eyes open while he undressed, and the moment he flung himself into bed he fell asleep.

He would have sworn that he had not been asleep five minutes when he was dragged back to wakefulness by a knocking at the door. He listened for a moment.

'Who is it?'

'It's the maid. Open. I have something to say to you.'

Cursing, Ashenden turned on his light, ran a hand through his thinning and rumpled hair (for like Julius Caesar he disliked exposing an unbecoming baldness) and unlocked and opened the door. Outside it stood a tousled Swiss maid. She wore no apron and looked as though she had thrown on her clothes in a hurry.

'The old English lady, the governess of the Egyptian princesses, is dying and she wants to see you.'

'Me?' said Ashenden. 'It's impossible. I don't know her. She was all right this evening.'

He was confused and spoke his thoughts as they came to him.

'She asks for you. The doctor says, will you come. She cannot last much longer.'

'It must be a mistake. She can't want me.'

'She said your name and the number of your room. She says quick, quick.'

Ashenden shrugged his shoulders. He went back into his room to put on slippers and a dressing-gown, and as an afterthought dropped a small revolver into his pocket. Ashenden believed much more in his acuteness than in a firearm, which is apt to go off at the wrong time and make a noise, but there are moments when it gives you confidence to feel your fingers round its butt, and this sudden summons seemed to him exceedingly mysterious. It was ridiculous to suppose that those two cordial stout Egyptian gentlemen were laying some sort of trap for him, but in the work upon which Ashenden was engaged the dullness of routine was apt now and again to slip quite shamelessly into the melodrama of the sixties. Just as passion will make use brazenly of the hackneyed phrase, so will chance show itself insensitive to the triteness of the literary convention.

Miss King's room was two floors higher than Ashenden's, and as he accompanied the chamber-maid along the corridor and up the stairs he asked her what was the matter with the old governess. She was flurried and stupid.

'I think she has had a stroke. I don't know. The night-porter woke me and said Monsieur Bridet wanted me to get up at once.'

Monsieur Bridet was the assistant-manager.

'What is the time?' asked Ashenden.

'It must be three o'clock.'

They arrived at Miss King's door and the maid knocked. It was opened by Monsieur Bridet. He had evidently been roused from his sleep; he wore slippers on his bare feet, grey trousers and a frock-coat over his pyjamas. He looked absurd. His hair as a rule plastered neatly on his head stood on end. He was extremely apologetic.

'A thousand excuses for disturbing you, Monsieur Ashenden, but she kept asking for you and the doctor said you should be sent for.'

'It doesn't matter at all.'

Ashenden walked in. It was a small back room and all the lights were on. The windows were closed and the curtains drawn. It was intensely hot. The doctor, a bearded, grizzled Swiss, was standing at the bedside. Monsieur Bridet, notwithstanding his costume and his evident harassment, found in himself the presence of mind to remain the attentive manager, and with ceremony effected the proper introduction.

'This is Mr Ashenden, for whom Miss King has been asking. Dr Arbos of the Faculty of Medicine of Geneva.'

Without a word the doctor pointed to the bed. On it lay Miss King. It gave Ashenden a shock to look at her. She wore a large white cotton nightcap (on entering Ashenden had noticed the brown wig on a stand on the dressing-table) tied under the chin, and a white, voluminous nightdress that came high up in the neck. Nightcap and nightdress belonged to a past age and reminded you of Cruikshank's illustrations to the novels of Charles Dickens. Her face was greasy still with the cream she had used before going to bed to remove her make-up, but she had removed it summarily and there were streaks of black on her eyebrows and of red on her cheeks. She looked very small, lying in the bed, no larger than a child, and immensely old.

'She must be well over eighty,' thought Ashenden.

She did not look human, but like a doll, the caricature of an old, old witch that an ironic toymaker had amused himself with modelling. She lay perfectly still on her back, the tiny little body hardly marked under the flatness of the blanket, her face even smaller than usual because she had removed her teeth; and you would have thought she was dead but for the black eyes, strangely large in the shrunken mask, that stared unblinkingly. Ashenden thought their expression changed when she saw him.

'Well, Miss King, I'm sorry to see you like this,' he said with forced cheerfulness.

'She cannot speak,' said the doctor. 'She had another little stroke when the maid went to fetch you. I have just given her an injection. She may partly recover the use of her tongue in a little while. She has something to say to you.'

'I will gladly wait,' said Ashenden.

He fancied that in those dark eyes he saw a look of relief. For a moment or two the four of them stood round the bed and stared at the dying woman.

'Well, if there is nothing I can do I may just as well go back to bed,' said Monsieur Bridet then.

'*Allez, mon ami,*' said the doctor. 'You can do nothing.'

Monsieur Bridet turned to Ashenden.

'May I have a word with you?' he asked.

'Certainly.'

The doctor noticed a sudden fear in Miss King's eyes.

'Do not be alarmed,' he said kindly. 'Monsieur Ashenden is not going. He will stay as long as you wish.'

The assistant-manager took Ashenden to the door and partly closed it so that those within should not hear his undertones.

'I can count on your discretion, Monsieur Ashenden, can I not? It is a very disagreeable thing to have anyone die in a hotel. The other guests do not like it and we must do all we can to prevent their knowing. I shall have the body removed the first possible moment and I shall be extremely obliged if you will not say that there has been a death.'

'You can have every confidence in me,' said Ashenden.

'It is very unfortunate that the manager should be away for the night. I am afraid he will be exceedingly displeased. Of course if it had been possible I would have sent for an ambulance and had her taken to the hospital, but the doctor said she might die before we got her downstairs and absolutely refused to let me. It is not my fault if she dies in the hotel.'

'Death so often chooses its moments without consideration,' murmured Ashenden.

'After all she is an old woman, she should have died years ago. What did this Egyptian prince want to have a governess of that age for? He ought to have sent her back to her own country. These Orientals, they are always giving trouble.'

'Where is the prince now?' asked Ashenden. 'She has been in his service for many years. Ought you not to wake him?'

'He is not in the hotel. He went out with his secretary. He may be playing baccarat. I do not know. Anyhow I cannot send all over Geneva to find him.'

'And the princesses?'

'They have not come in. They seldom return to the hotel till dawn. They are mad about dancing. I do not know where they are; in any case they would not thank me for dragging them away from their diversions because their governess has had a stroke. I know what they are. The night-porter will tell them when they arrive and then they can please themselves. She does not want them. When the night-porter fetched me and I went into her room I asked where His Highness was and she cried with all her strength: no, no.'

'She could talk then?'

'Yes, after a fashion, but the thing that surprised me was that she spoke in English. She always insisted on talking French. You know, she hated the English.'

'What did she want with me?'

'That I cannot tell you. She said she had something that she must say to you at once. It is funny, she knew the number of your room. At first when she asked for you I would not let them send. I cannot have my clients disturbed in the middle of the night because a crazy old woman asks for them. You have the right to your sleep, I imagine. But when the doctor came he insisted. She gave us no peace and when I said she must wait till morning she cried.'

Ashenden looked at the assistant-manager. He seemed to find nothing at all touching in the scene he related.

'The doctor asked who you were and when I told him he said that perhaps she wished to see you because you were a compatriot.'

'Perhaps,' said Ashenden dryly.

'Well, I shall try to get a little sleep. I shall give the night-porter orders to wake me when everything is over. Fortunately the nights are long now and if everything goes well we may be able to get the body away before it is light.'

Ashenden went back into the room and immediately the dark eyes of the dying woman fixed upon him. He felt that it was incumbent upon him to say something, but as he spoke he reflected on the foolish way in which one speaks to the sick.

'I'm afraid you're feeling very ill, Miss King.'

It seemed to him that a flash of anger crossed her eyes and Ashenden could not but imagine that she was exasperated by his futile words.

'You do not mind waiting?' asked the doctor.

'Of course not.'

It appeared that the night-porter had been roused by the ringing of the telephone from Miss King's room, but on listening could get no one to speak. The bell continued to ring, so he went upstairs and knocked at the door. He entered with his pass-key and found Miss King lying on the floor. The telephone had fallen too. It looked as though, feeling ill, she had taken off the receiver to call for help and then collapsed. The night-porter hurried to fetch the assistant-manager and together they had lifted her back into bed. Then the maid was wakened and the doctor sent for. It gave Ashenden a queer feeling to listen to the doctor giving him these facts in Miss King's hearing. He spoke as though she could not understand his French. He spoke as though she were already dead.

Then the doctor said:

'Well, there is really nothing more that I can do. It is useless for me to stay. I can be rung up if there is any change.'

Ashenden, knowing that Miss King might remain in that condition for hours, shrugged his shoulders.

'Very well.'

The doctor patted her raddled cheek as though she were a child.

'You must try to sleep. I will come back in the morning.'

He packed up the dispatch-case in which he had his medical appliances, washed his hands, and shuffled himself into a heavy coat. Ashenden accompanied him to the door and as he shook hands the doctor gave his prognosis in a pout of his bearded mouth. Ashenden, coming back, looked at the maid. She sat on the edge of a chair, uneasily, as though in the presence of death she feared to presume. Her broad, ugly face was bloated with fatigue.

'There's no use in your staying up,' Ashenden said to her. 'Why don't you go to bed?'

'*Monsieur* wouldn't like to remain here alone. Somebody must stay with him.'

'But good heavens, why? You have your day's work to do tomorrow.'

'In any case I have to get up at five.'

'Then try to get a little sleep now. You can give me a look in when you get up. *Allez.*'

She rose heavily to her feet.

'As the gentleman wishes. But I will stay very willingly.'

Ashenden smiled and shook his head.

'*Bonsoir, ma pauvre mademoiselle,*' said the maid.

She went out and Ashenden was left alone. He sat by the bedside and again his eyes met Miss King's. It was embarrassing to encounter that unshrinking stare.

'Don't worry yourself, Miss King. You've had a slight stroke. I'm sure your speech will come back to you in a minute.'

He felt certain then that he saw in those dark eyes a desperate effort to speak. He could not be mistaken. The mind was shaken by desire, but the paralysed body was incapable of obedience. For her disappointment expressed itself quite plainly, tears came to her eyes and ran down her cheeks. Ashenden took out his handkerchief and dried them.

'Don't distress yourself, Miss King. Have a little patience and I'm sure you'll be able to say anything you want.'

He did not know if it was his fancy that he read in her eyes now the despairing thought that she had not the time to wait. Perhaps it was only that he ascribed to her the notions that came to himself. On the dressing-table were the governess's poor little toilet things, silver-backed embossed brushes and a silver mirror, in a corner stood a shabby black trunk, and on the top of the wardrobe a large hat-box in shiny leather. It all looked poor and mean in that trim hotel room, with its suite in highly varnished rosewood. The glare was intolerable.

'Wouldn't you be more comfortable if I turned out some of the lights?' asked Ashenden.

He put out all the lamps but the one by the bedside and then sat down again. He had a longing to smoke. Once more his eyes were held by those other eyes in which was all that remained alive of that old, old woman. He felt certain that she had something that she wanted urgently to say to him. But what was it? What was it? Perhaps she had asked him only because feeling death near, she had had a sudden yearning, she the exile of so many years, to die with someone of her own people, so long forgotten, by her side. That was what the doctor thought. But why should she have sent for him? There were other English people in the hotel. There was an old pair, a retired Indian Civilian and his wife, to whom it seemed more natural that she should turn. No one could be more of a stranger to her than Ashenden.

'Have you got something to say to me, Miss King?'

He tried to read an answer in her eyes. They continued to stare at him meaningly, but what the meaning was he had no notion.

'Don't be afraid I shall go. I will stay as long as you want me.'

Nothing, nothing. The black eyes, and as he looked at them they seemed to glow mysteriously as though there were fire behind them, the eyes continued to hold him with that insistent stare. Then Ashenden asked himself if she had sent for him because she knew that he was a British agent. Was it possible that at that last moment she had had some unexpected revulsion of feeling from everything that had signified to her for so many years? Perhaps at the moment of death a love for her country, a love that had been dead for half a century, awakened again in her–('I'm silly to fancy these idiotic things,' thought Ashenden, 'it's cheap and tawdry fiction')–and she had been seized with a desire to do something for what was after all her own. No one was quite himself just then and patriotism (in peace-time an attitude best left to politicians, publicists, and fools, but in the dark days of war an emotion that can wring the heart-strings), patriotism made one do odd things. It was curious that she had been unwilling to see the prince and his daughters. Did she on a sudden hate them? Did she feel herself a traitor on their account and now at the last hour wish to make amends? ('It's all very improbable, she's just a silly old maid who ought to have died years ago.') But you couldn't ignore the improbable. Ashenden, his common sense protesting, became strangely convinced that she had some secret that she wished to impart to him. She had sent for him knowing who he was because he could make use of it. She was dying and feared nothing. But was it really important? Ashenden leaned forward trying more eagerly to read what her eyes had to say. Perhaps it was only some trivial thing that was important only in her addled old brain. Ashenden was sick of the people who saw spies in every inoffensive passer-by and plots in the most innocent combination of circumstances. It was a hundred to one that if Miss King recovered her speech she would tell him something that could be of no use to anybody.

But how much must that old woman know! With her sharp eyes and sharp ears she must have had the chance to discover matters that were closely hidden from persons that seemed less insignificant. Ashenden thought again how he had the impression that something of real consequence was being prepared round about him. It was curious that Holzminden should have come to the hotel that day; and why had Prince Ali and the pasha, those wild gamblers, wasted an evening in playing contract-bridge with him? It might be that some new plan was in question, it might be that the very greatest affairs were afoot, and perhaps what the old woman had to say might make all the difference in the world. It might mean defeat or victory. It might mean anything. And there she lay powerless to speak. For a long time Ashenden stared at her in silence.

'Has it got anything to do with the war, Miss King?' he said on a sudden, loudly.

Something passed through her eyes and a tremor shot across her little old face. It was a distinct movement. Something strange and horrible was happening and Ashenden held his breath. The tiny frail body was suddenly convulsed and that old woman, as though by a final desperate effort of will, raised herself up in the bed. Ashenden sprang forward to support her.

'England,' she said, just that one word, in a harsh cracked voice, and fell back in his arms.

When he laid her down on the pillow, he saw that she was dead.

The Hairless Mexican

♦

'Do you like macaroni?' said R.

'What do you mean by macaroni?' answered Ashenden. 'It is like asking me if I like poetry. I like Keats and Wordsworth and Verlaine and Goethe. When you say macaroni, do you mean *spaghetti, tagliatelli, vermicelli, fettuccini, tufali, farfalli,* or just macaroni?'

'Macaroni,' replied R., a man of few words.

'I like all simple things, boiled eggs, oysters and caviare, *truite au bleu,* grilled salmon, roast lamb (the saddle by preference), cold grouse, treacle tart, and rice pudding. But of all simple things the only one I can eat day in and day out, not only without disgust but with the eagerness of an appetite unimpaired by excess, is macaroni.'

'I am glad of that because I want you to go down to Italy.'

Ashenden had come from Geneva to meet R. at Lyons and having got there before him had spent the afternoon wandering about the dull, busy and prosaic streets of that thriving city. They were sitting now in a restaurant on the *place* to which Ashenden had taken R. on his arrival because it was reputed to give you the best food in that part of France. But since in so crowded a resort (for the Lyonese like a good dinner) you never knew what inquisitive ears were pricked up to catch any useful piece of information that might fall from your lips, they had contented themselves with talking of indifferent things. They had reached the end of an admirable repast.

'Have another glass of brandy?' said R.

'No, thank you,' answered Ashenden, who was of an abstemious turn.

'One should do what one can to mitigate the rigours of war,' remarked R. as he took the bottle and poured out a glass for himself and another for Ashenden.

Ashenden, thinking it would be affectation to protest, let the gesture pass, but felt bound to remonstrate with his chief on the unseemly manner in which he held the bottle.

'In my youth I was always taught that you should take a woman by the waist and a bottle by the neck,' he murmured.

'I am glad you told me. I shall continue to hold a bottle by the waist and give women a wide berth.'

Ashenden did not know what to reply to this and so remained silent. He sipped his brandy and R. called for his bill. It was true that he was an important person, with power to make or mar quite a large number of his fellows, and his opinions were listened to by those who held in their hands the fate of empires; but he could never face the business of tipping a waiter without an embarrassment that was obvious in his demeanour. He was tortured by the fear of making a fool of himself by giving too much or of exciting the waiter's icy scorn by giving too little. When the bill came he passed some hundred-franc notes over to Ashenden and said:

'Pay him, will you? I can never understand French figures.'

The groom brought them their hats and coats.

'Would you like to go back to the hotel?' asked Ashenden.

'We might as well.'

It was early in the year, but the weather had suddenly turned warm, and they walked with their coats over their arms. Ashenden knowing that R. liked a sitting-room had engaged one for him, and to this, when they reached the hotel, they went. The hotel was old-fashioned and the sitting-room was vast. It was furnished with a heavy mahogany suite upholstered in green velvet and the chairs were set primly round a large table. On the walls, covered with a dingy paper, were large steel engravings of the battles of Napoleon, and from the ceiling hung an enormous chandelier once used for gas, but now fitted with electric bulbs. It flooded the cheerless room with a cold, hard light.

'This is very nice,' said R., as they went in.

'Not exactly cosy,' suggested Ashenden.

'No, but it looks as though it were the best room in the place. It all looks very *good* to me.'

He drew one of the green velvet chairs away from the table and, sitting down, lit a cigar. He loosened his belt and unbuttoned his tunic.

'I always thought I liked a cheroot better than anything,' he said, 'but since the war I've taken quite a fancy to Havanas. Oh well, I suppose it can't last for ever.' The corners of his mouth flickered with the beginning of a smile. 'It's an ill wind that blows nobody any good.'

Ashenden took two chairs, one to sit on and one for his feet, and when R. saw him he said: 'That's not a bad idea,' and swinging another chair out from the table with a sigh of relief put his boots on it.

'What room is that next door?' he asked.

'That's your bedroom.'

'And on the other side?'

'A banqueting hall.'

R. got up and strolled slowly about the room and when he passed the windows, as though in idle curiosity, peeped through the heavy rep curtains that covered them, and then returning to his chair once more comfortably put his feet up.

'It's just as well not to take any more risk than one need,' he said.

He looked at Ashenden reflectively. There was a slight smile on his thin lips, but the pale eyes, too closely set together, remained cold and steely. R.'s stare would have been embarrassing if Ashenden had not been used to it. He knew that R. was considering how he would broach the subject that he had in mind. The silence must have lasted for two or three minutes.

'I'm expecting a fellow to come and see me tonight,' he said at last. 'His train gets in about ten.' He gave his wrist-watch a glance. 'He's known as the Hairless Mexican.'

'Why?'

'Because he's hairless and because he's a Mexican.'

'The explanation seems perfectly satisfactory,' said Ashenden.

'He'll tell you all about himself. He talks nineteen to the dozen. He was on his uppers when I came across him. It appears that he was mixed up in some revolution in Mexico and had to get out with nothing but the clothes he stood up in. They were rather the worse for wear when I found him. If you want to please him you call him General. He claims to have been a general in Huerta's army, at least I think it was Huerta; anyhow he says that if things had gone right he would be Minister of War now and no end of a big bug. I've found him very useful. Not a bad chap. The only thing I really have against him is that he will use scent.'

'And where do I come in?' asked Ashenden.

'He's going down to Italy. I've got rather a ticklish job for him to do and I want you to stand by. I'm not keen on trusting him with a lot of money. He's a gambler and he's a bit too fond of the girls. I suppose you came from Geneva on your Ashenden passport?'

'Yes.'

'I've got another for you, a diplomatic one, by the way, in the name of Somerville with visas for France and Italy. I think you and he had better travel together. He's an amusing cove when he gets going, and I think you ought to know one another.'

'What is the job?'

'I haven't yet quite made up my mind how much it's desirable for you to know about it.'

Ashenden did not reply. They eyed one another in a detached manner, as though they were strangers who sat together in a railway carriage and each wondered who and what the other was.

'In your place I'd leave the General to do most of the talking. I wouldn't tell him more about yourself than you find absolutely necessary. He won't ask you any questions, I can promise you that, I think he's by way of being a gentleman after his own fashion.'

'By the way, what is his real name?'

'I always call him Manuel. I don't know that he likes it very much, his name is Manuel Carmona.'

'I gather by what you have not said that he's an unmitigated scoundrel.'

R. smiled with his pale blue eyes.

'I don't know that I'd go quite as far as that. He hasn't had the advantages of a public-school education. His ideas of playing the game are not quite the same as yours or mine. I don't know that I'd leave a gold cigarette-case about when he was in the neighbourhood, but if he lost money to you at poker and had pinched your cigarette-case he would immediately pawn it to pay you. If he had half a chance he'd seduce your wife, but if you were up against it he'd share his last crust with you. The tears will run down his face when he hears Gounod's *Ave*

Maria on the gramophone, but if you insult his dignity he'll shoot you like a dog. It appears that in Mexico it's an insult to get between a man and his drink and he told me himself that once when a Dutchman who didn't know passed between him and the bar he whipped out his revolver and shot him dead.'

'Did nothing happen to him?'

'No, it appears that he belongs to one of the best families. The matter was hushed up and it was announced in the papers that the Dutchman had committed suicide. He did practically. I don't believe the Hairless Mexican has a great respect for human life.'

Ashenden, who had been looking intently at R., started a little and he watched more carefully than ever his chief's tired, lined, and yellow face. He knew that he did not make this remark for nothing.

'Of course a lot of nonsense is talked about the value of human life. You might just as well say that the counters you use at poker have an intrinsic value. Their value is what you like to make it; for a general giving battle, men are merely counters and he's a fool if he allows himself for sentimental reasons to look upon them as human beings.'

'But, you see, they're counters that feel and think and if they believe they're being squandered they are quite capable of refusing to be used any more.'

'Anyhow, that's neither here nor there. We've had information that a man called Constantine Andreadi is on his way from Constantinople with certain documents that we want to get hold of. He's a Greek. He's an agent of Enver Pasha and Enver has great confidence in him. He's given him verbal messages that are too secret and too important to be put on paper. He's sailing from the Piraeus, on a boat called the *Ithaca*, and will land at Brindisi on his way to Rome. He's to deliver his dispatches at the German Embassy and impart what he has to say personally to the ambassador.'

'I see.'

At this time Italy was still neutral; the Central Powers were straining every nerve to keep her so; the Allies were doing what they could to induce her to declare war on their side.

'We don't want to get into trouble with the Italian authorities, it might be fatal, but we've got to prevent Andreadi from getting to Rome.'

'At any cost?' asked Ashenden.

'Money's no object,' answered R., his lips twisting into a sardonic smile.

'What do you propose to do?'

'I don't think you need bother your head about that.'

'I have a fertile imagination,' said Ashenden.

'I want you to go down to Naples with the Hairless Mexican. He's very keen on getting back to Cuba. It appears that his friends are organizing a show and he wants to be as near at hand as possible so that he can hop over to Mexico when things are ripe. He needs cash. I've brought money down with me, in American dollars, and I shall give it to you tonight. You'd better carry it on your person.'

'Is it much?'

'It's a good deal, but I thought it would be easier for you if it wasn't bulky, so I've got it in thousand-dollar notes. You will give the Hairless Mexican the notes in return for the documents that Andreadi is bringing.'

A question sprang to Ashenden's lips, but he did not ask it. He asked another instead.

'Does this fellow understand what he has to do?'

'Perfectly.'

There was a knock at the door. It opened and the Hairless Mexican stood before them.

'I have arrived. Good evening, Colonel. I am enchanted to see you.'

R. got up.

'Had a nice journey, Manuel? This is Mr Somerville, who's going to Naples with you, General Carmona.'

'Pleased to meet you, sir.'

He shook Ashenden's hand with such force that he winced.

'Your hands are like iron, General,' he murmured.

The Mexican gave them a glance.

'I had them manicured this morning. I do not think they were very well done. I like my nails much more highly polished.'

They were cut to a point, stained bright red, and to Ashenden's mind shone like mirrors. Though it was not cold the General wore a fur coat with an astrakhan collar and with his every movement a wave of perfume was wafted to your nose.

'Take off your coat, General, and have a cigar,' said R.

The Hairless Mexican was a tall man, and though thinnish gave you the impression of being very powerful; he was smartly dressed in a blue serge suit, with a silk handkerchief neatly tucked in the breast pocket of his coat, and he wore a gold bracelet on his wrist. His features were good, but a little larger than life-size, and his eyes were brown and lustrous. He was quite hairless. His yellow skin had the smoothness of a woman's and he had no eyebrows nor eyelashes; he wore a pale brown wig, rather long, and the locks were arranged in artistic disorder. This and the unwrinkled sallow face, combined with his dandified dress, gave him an appearance that was at first glance a trifle horrifying. He was repulsive and ridiculous, but you could not take your eyes from him. There was a sinister fascination in his strangeness.

He sat down and hitched up his trousers so that they should not bag at the knee.

'Well, Manuel, have you been breaking any hearts today?' said R. with his sardonic joviality.

The General turned to Ashenden.

'Our good friend, the Colonel, envies me my successes with the fair sex. I tell him he can have just as many as I if he will only listen to me. Confidence, that is all you need. If you never fear a rebuff you will never have one.'

'Nonsense, Manuel, one has to have your way with the girls. There's something about you that they can't resist.'

The Hairless Mexican laughed with a self-satisfaction that he did not try to disguise. He spoke English very well, with a Spanish accent, but with an American intonation.

'But since you ask me, Colonel, I don't mind telling you that I got into conversation on the train with a little woman who was coming to Lyons to see her mother-in-law. She was not very young and she was thinner than I like a woman to be, but she was possible, and she helped me to pass an agreeable hour.'

'Well, let's get to business,' said R.

'I am at your service, Colonel.' He gave Ashenden a glance. 'Is Mr Somerville a military man?'

'No,' said R., 'he's an author.'

'It takes all sorts to make a world, as you say. I am happy to make your acquaintance, Mr Somerville. I can tell you many stories that will interest you; I am sure that we shall get on well together. You have a sympathetic air. I am very sensitive to that. To tell you the truth I am nothing but a bundle of nerves and if I am with a person who is antipathetic to me I go all to pieces.'

'I hope we shall have a pleasant journey,' said Ashenden.

'When does our friend arrive at Brindisi?' asked the Mexican, turning to R.

'He sails from the Piraeus in the *Ithaca* on the fourteenth. It's probably some old tub, but you'd better get down to Brindisi in good time.'

'I agree with you.'

R. got up and with his hands in his pockets sat on the edge of the table. In his rather shabby uniform, his tunic unbuttoned, he looked a slovenly creature beside the neat and well-dressed Mexican.

'Mr Somerville knows practically nothing of the errand on which you are going and I do not desire to tell him anything. I think you had much better keep your own counsel. He is instructed to give you the funds you need for your work, but your actions are your own affair. If you need his advice of course you can ask for it.'

'I seldom ask other people's advice and never take it.'

'And should you make a mess of things I trust you to keep Mr Somerville out of it. He must on no account be compromised.'

'I am a man of honour, Colonel,' answered the Hairless Mexican with dignity, 'and I would sooner let myself be cut in a thousand pieces than betray my friends.'

'That is what I have already told Mr Somerville. On the other hand, if everything pans out O.K. Mr Somerville is instructed to give you the sum we agreed on in return for the papers I spoke to you about. In what manner you get them is no business of his.'

'That goes without saying. There is only one thing I wish to make quite plain; Mr Somerville understands of course that I have not accepted the mission with which you have entrusted me on account of the money?'

'Quite,' replied R. gravely, looking him straight in the eyes.

'I am with the Allies body and soul, I cannot forgive the Germans for outraging the neutrality of Belgium, and if I accept the money that you have offered me it is because I am first and foremost a patriot. I can trust Mr Somerville implicitly, I suppose?'

R. nodded. The Mexican turned to Ashenden.

'An expedition is being arranged to free my unhappy country from the tyrants that exploit and ruin it and every penny that I receive will go on guns and cartridges. For myself I have no need of money; I am a soldier and I can live on a crust and a few olives. There are only three occupations that befit a gentleman, war, cards, and women; it costs nothing to sling a rifle over your shoulder and take to the mountains—and that is real warfare, not this manoeuvring of battalions and firing of great guns—women love me for myself, and I generally win at cards.'

Ashenden found the flamboyance of this strange creature, with his scented handkerchief and his gold bracelet, very much to his taste. This was far from being just the man in the street (whose tyranny we rail at but in the end submit to) and to the amateur of the baroque in human nature he was a rarity to be considered with delight. He was a purple patch on two legs. Notwithstanding his wig and his hairless big face, he had undoubtedly an air; he was absurd, but he did not give you the impression that he was a man to be trifled with. His self-complacency was magnificent.

'Where is your kit, Manuel?' asked R.

It was possible that a frown for an instant darkened the Mexican's brow at the abrupt question that seemed a little contemptuously to brush to one side his eloquent statement, but he gave no other sign of displeasure. Ashenden suspected that he thought the Colonel a barbarian insensitive to the finer emotions.

'I left it at the station.'

'Mr Somerville has a diplomatic passport so that he can get it through with his own things at the frontier without examination if you like.'

'I have very little, a few suits and some linen, but perhaps it would be as well if Mr Somerville would take charge of it. I bought half a dozen suits of silk pyjamas before I left Paris.'

'And what about you?' asked R., turning to Ashenden.

'I've only got one bag. It's in my room.'

'You'd better have it taken to the station while there's someone about. Your train goes at one ten.'

'Oh?'

This was the first Ashenden had heard that they were to start that night.

'I think you'd better get down to Naples as soon as possible.'

'Very well.'

R. got up.

'I'm going to bed. I don't know what you fellows want to do.'

'I shall take a walk about Lyons,' said the Hairless Mexican. 'I am interested in life. Lend me a hundred francs, Colonel, will you? I have no change on me.'

R. took out his pocket-book and gave the General the note he asked for. Then to Ashenden:

'What are you going to do? Wait here?'

'No,' said Ashenden, 'I shall go to the station and read.'

'You'd both of you better have a whisky and soda before you go, hadn't you? What about it, Manuel?'

'It is very kind of you, but I never drink anything but champagne and brandy.'

'Mixed?' asked R. dryly.

'Not necessarily,' returned the other with gravity.

R. ordered brandy and soda and when it came, whereas he and Ashenden helped themselves to both, the Hairless Mexican poured himself out three parts of a tumbler of neat brandy and swallowed it in two noisy gulps. He rose to his feet and put on his coat with the astrakhan collar, seized in one hand his bold black hat and, with the gesture of a romantic actor giving up the girl he loves to one more worthy of her, held out the other to R.

'Well, Colonel, I will bid you good night and pleasant dreams. I do not expect that we shall meet again so soon.'

'Don't make a hash of things, Manuel, and if you do, keep your mouth shut.'

'They tell me that in one of your colleges where the sons of gentlemen are trained to become naval officers it is written in letters of gold: There is no such word as impossible in the British Navy. I do not know the meaning of the word failure.'

'It has a good many synonyms,' retorted R.

'I will meet you at the station, Mr Somerville,' said the Hairless Mexican, and with a flourish left them.

R. looked at Ashenden with that little smile of his that always made his face look so dangerously shrewd.

'Well, what d'you think of him?'

'You've got me beat,' said Ashenden. 'Is he a mountebank? He seems as vain as a peacock. And with that frightful appearance can he really be the lady's man he pretends? What makes you think you can trust him?'

R. gave a low chuckle and he washed his thin, old hands with imaginary soap.

'I thought you'd like him. He's quite a character, isn't he? I think we can trust him.' R.'s eyes suddenly grew opaque. 'I don't believe it would pay him to double-cross us.' He paused for a moment. 'Anyhow we've got to risk it. I'll give you the tickets and the money and then you can take yourself off; I'm all in and I want to go to bed.'

Ten minutes later Ashenden set out for the station with his bag on a porter's shoulder.

Having nearly two hours to wait he made himself comfortable in the waiting-room. The light was good and he read a novel. When the time drew near for the arrival of the train from Paris that was to take them direct to Rome, and the Hairless Mexican did not appear, Ashenden, beginning to grow a trifle anxious, went out on the platform to look for him. Ashenden suffered from that distressing malady known as train fever: an hour before his train was due he began to have apprehensions lest he should miss it; he was impatient with the porters who would never bring his luggage down from his room in time and he could not understand why the hotel bus cut it so fine; a block in the street would drive him to frenzy and the languid movements of the station porters infuriate him. The whole world seemed in a horrid plot to delay him; people got in his way as he passed through the barriers; others, a long string of them, were at the ticket-office getting tickets for other trains than his and they counted their change with exasperating care; his luggage took an interminable time to register; and then if he was travelling with friends they would go to buy newspapers, or would take a walk along the platform, and he was certain they would be left behind, they would stop to talk to a casual stranger or suddenly be seized with a desire to telephone and disappear at a run. In fact the universe conspired to make him miss every train he wanted to take and he was not happy unless he was settled in his corner, his things on the rack above him, with a good half-hour to spare. Sometimes by arriving at the station too soon he had caught an earlier train than the one he had meant to, but that was nerve-racking and caused him all the anguish of very nearly missing it.

The Rome express was signalled and there was no sign of the Hairless Mexican; it came in and he was not to be seen. Ashenden became more and more harassed. He walked quickly up and down the platform, looked in all the waiting-rooms, went to the *consigne* where the luggage was left; he could not find him. There were no sleeping-cars, but a number of people got out and he took two seats in a first-class carriage. He stood by the door, looking up and down the platform and up at the clock; it was useless to go if his travelling companion did not turn up, and Ashenden made up his mind to take his things out of the carriage as the porter cried *en voiture*; but, by George! he would give the brute hell when he found him. There were three minutes more, then two minutes, then one; at that late hour there were few persons about and all who were travelling had taken their seats. Then he saw the Hairless Mexican, followed by two porters with his luggage and accompanied by a man in a bowler-hat, walk leisurely on to the platform. He caught sight of Ashenden and waved to him.

'Ah, my dear fellow, there you are, I wondered what had become of you.'

'Good God, man, hurry up or we shall miss the train.'

'I never miss a train. Have you got good seats? The *chef de gare* has gone for the night; this is his assistant.'

The man in the bowler-hat took it off when Ashenden nodded to him.

'But this is an ordinary carriage. I am afraid I could not travel in that.' He turned to the stationmaster's assistant with an affable smile. 'You must do better for me than that, *mon cher*.'

'*Certainement, mon général*, I will put you into a *salon-lit*. Of course.'

The assistant stationmaster led them along the train and opened the door of an empty compartment where there were two beds. The Mexican eyed it with satisfaction and watched the porters arrange the luggage.

'That will do very well. I am much obliged to you.' He held out his hand to the man in the bowler-hat. 'I shall not forget you and next time I see the Minister I will tell him with what civility you have treated me.'

'You are too good, General. I shall be very grateful.'

A whistle was blown and the train started.

'This is better than an ordinary first-class carriage, I think, Mr Somerville,' said the Mexican. 'A good traveller should learn how to make the best of things.'

But Ashenden was still extremely cross.

'I don't know why the devil you wanted to cut it so fine. We should have looked a pair of damned fools if we'd missed the train.'

'My dear fellow, there was never the smallest chance of that. When I arrived I told the stationmaster that I was General Carmona, Commander-in-Chief of the Mexican Army, and that I had to stop off in Lyons for a few hours to hold a conference with the British Field-Marshal. I asked him to hold the train for me if I was delayed and suggested that my government might see its way to conferring an order on him. I have been to Lyons before, I like the girls here; they have not the *chic* of the Parisians, but they have something, there is no denying that they have something. Will you have a mouthful of brandy before you go to sleep?'

'No, thank you,' said Ashenden morosely.

'I always drink a glass before going to bed, it settles the nerves.'

He looked in his suit-case and without difficulty found a bottle. He put it to his lips and had a long drink, wiped his mouth with the back of his hand and lit a cigarette. Then he took off his boots and lay down. Ashenden dimmed the light.

'I have never yet made up my mind,' said the Hairless Mexican reflectively, 'whether it is pleasanter to go to sleep with the kisses of a beautiful woman on your mouth or with a cigarette between your lips. Have you ever been to Mexico? I will tell you about Mexico tomorrow. Good night.'

Soon Ashenden heard from his steady breathing that he was asleep and in a little while himself dozed off. Presently he woke. The Mexican, deep in slumber, lay motionless; he had taken off his fur coat and was using it as a blanket; he still wore his wig. Suddenly there was a jolt and the train with a noisy grinding of brakes stopped; in the twinkling of an eye, before Ashenden could realize that anything had happened, the Mexican was on his feet with his hand to his hip.

'What is it?' he cried.

'Nothing. Probably only a signal against us.'

The Mexican sat down heavily on his bed. Ashenden turned on the light.

'You wake quickly for such a sound sleeper,' he said.

'You have to in my profession.'

Ashenden would have liked to ask him whether this was murder, conspiracy, or commanding armies, but was not sure that it would be discreet. The General opened his bag and took out the bottle.

'Will you have a nip?' he asked. 'There is nothing like it when you wake suddenly in the night.'

When Ashenden refused he put the bottle once more to his lips and poured a considerable quantity of liquor down his throat. He sighed and lit a cigarette. Although Ashenden had seen him now drink nearly a bottle of brandy, and it was probable that he had had a good deal more when he was going about the town, he was certainly quite sober. Neither in his manner nor in his speech was there any indication that he had drunk during the evening anything but lemonade.

The train started and Ashenden again fell asleep. When he awoke it was morning and turing round lazily he saw that the Mexican was awake too. He was smoking a cigarette. The floor by his side was strewn with burnt-out butts and the air was thick and grey. He had begged Ashenden not to insist on opening a window, for he said the night air was dangerous.

'I did not get up, because I was afraid of waking you. Will you do your toilet first or shall I?'

'I'm in no hurry,' said Ashenden.

'I am an old campaigner, it will not take me long. Do you wash your teeth every day?'

'Yes,' said Ashenden.

'So do I. It is a habit I learned in New York. I always think that a fine set of teeth are an adornment to a man.'

There was a wash-basin in the compartment and the General scrubbed his teeth, with gurglings and garglings, energetically. Then he got a bottle of eau-de-Cologne from his bag, poured some of it on a towel and rubbed it over his face and hands. He took a comb and carefully arranged his wig; either it had not moved in the night or else he had set it straight before Ashenden awoke. He got another bottle out of his bag, with a spray attached to it, and squeezing a bulb covered his shirt and coat with a fine cloud of scent, did the same to his handkerchief, and then with a beaming face, like a man who has done his duty by the world and is well pleased, turned to Ashenden and said:

'Now I am ready to brave the day. I will leave my things for you, you need not be afraid of the eau-de-Cologne, it is the best you can get in Paris.'

'Thank you very much,' said Ashenden. 'All I want is soap and water.'

'Water? I never use water except when I have a bath. Nothing can be worse for the skin.'

When they approached the frontier, Ashenden, remembering the General's instinctive gesture when he was suddenly awakened in the night, said to him:

'If you've got a revolver on you I think you'd better give it to me. With my diplomatic passport they're not likely to search me, but they might take it into their heads to go through you and we don't want to have any bothers.'

'It is hardly a weapon, it is only a toy,' returned the Mexican, taking out of his hip-pocket a fully loaded revolver of formidable dimensions. 'I do not like parting with it even for an hour, it gives me the feeling that I am not fully dressed. But you are quite right, we do not want to take any risks; I will give you my knife as well. I would always rather use a knife than a revolver; I think it is a more elegant weapon.'

'I dare say it is only a matter of habit,' answered Ashenden. 'Perhaps you are more at home with a knife.'

'Anyone can pull a trigger, but it needs a man to use a knife.'

To Ashenden it looked as though it were in a single movement that he tore open his waistcoat and from his belt snatched and opened a long knife of murderous aspect. He handed it to Ashenden with a pleased smile on his large, ugly, and naked face.

'There's a pretty piece of work for you, Mr Somerville. I've never seen a better bit of steel in my life, it takes an edge like a razor and it's strong; you can cut a cigarette-paper with it and you can hew down an oak. There is nothing to get out of order and when it is closed it might be the knife a schoolboy uses to cut notches in his desk.'

He shut it with a click and Ashenden put it along with the revolver in his pocket.

'Have you anything else?'

'My hands,' replied the Mexican with arrogance, 'but those I dare say the Custom officials will not make trouble about.'

Ashenden remembered the iron grip he had given him when they shook hands and slightly shuddered. They were large and long and smooth; there was not a hair on them or on the wrists, and with the pointed, rosy, manicured nails there was really something sinister about them.

Ashenden and General Carmona went through the formalities at the frontier independently and when they returned to their carriage Ashenden handed back to his companion the revolver and the knife. He sighed.

'Now I feel more comfortable. What do you say to a game of cards?'

'I should like it,' said Ashenden.

The Hairless Mexican opened his bag again and from a corner extracted a greasy pack of French cards. He asked Ashenden whether he played *écarté* and when Ashenden told him that he did not suggested piquet. This was a game that Ashenden was not unfamiliar with, so they settled the stakes and began. Since both were in favour of quick action, they played the game of four hands, doubling the first and last. Ashenden had good enough cards, but the General seemed notwithstanding always to have better. Ashenden kept his eyes open and he was not careless of the possibility that his antagonist might correct the inequalities of chance, but he saw nothing to suggest that everything was not above board. He lost game after game. He was capoted and rubiconed. The score against him mounted up and up till he had lost something like a thousand francs, which at that time was a tidy sum. The General smoked innumerable cigarettes. He made them himself with a twist of the finger, a lick of his tongue and incredible celerity. At last he flung himself against the back of his seat.

'By the way, my friend, does the British Government pay your card losses when you are on a mission?' he asked.

'It certainly doesn't.'

'Well, I think you have lost enough. If it went down on your expense account I would have proposed playing till we reached Rome, but you are sympathetic to me. If it is your own money I do not want to win any more of it.'

He picked up the cards and put them aside. Ashenden somewhat ruefully took out a number of notes and handed them to the Mexican. He counted them and with his usual neatness put them carefully folded into his pocket-book. Then, leaning forward, he patted Ashenden almost affectionately on the knee.

'I like you, you are modest and unassuming, you have not the arrogance of your countrymen, and I am sure that you will take my advice in the spirit in which it is meant. Do not play piquet with people you don't know.'

Ashenden was somewhat mortified and perhaps his face showed it, for the Mexican seized his hand.

'My dear fellow, I have not hurt your feelings? I would not do that for the world. You do not play piquet worse than most piquet players. It is not that. If we were going to be together longer I would teach you how to win at cards. One plays cards to win money and there is no sense in losing.'

'I thought it was only in love and war that all things were fair,' said Ashenden, with a chuckle.

'Ah, I am glad to see you smile. That is the way to take a loss. I see that you have good humour and good sense. You will go far in life. When I get back to Mexico and am in possession of my estates again you must come and stay with me. I will treat you like a king. You shall ride my best horses, we will go to bullfights together, and if there are girls you fancy you have only to say the word and you shall have them.'

He began telling Ashenden of the vast territories, the *haciendas* and the mines in Mexico, of which he had been dispossessed. He told him of the feudal state in which he lived. It did not matter whether what he said was true or not, for those sonorous phrases of his were fruity with the rich-distilled perfumes of romance. He described a spacious life that seemed to belong to another age and his eloquent gestures brought before the mind's eye tawny distances and vast green plantations, great herds of cattle and in the moonlit night the song of the blind singers that melted in the air and the twanging of guitars.

'Everything I lost, everything. In Paris I was driven to earn a pittance by giving Spanish lessons or showing Americans—*Americanos del Norte,* I mean—the night life of the city. I who have flung away a thousand *duros* on a dinner have been forced to beg my bread like a blind Indian. I who have taken pleasure in clasping a diamond bracelet round the wrist of a beautiful woman have been forced to accept a suit of clothes from a hag old enough to be my mother. Patience. Man is born to trouble as the sparks fly upward, but misfortune cannot last for ever. The time is ripe and soon we shall strike our blow.'

He took up the greasy pack of cards and set them out in a number of little piles.

'Let us see what the cards say. They never lie. Ah, if I had only had greater faith in them I should have avoided the only action of my life that has weighed heavily on me. My conscience is at ease. I did what any man would do under the circumstances, but I regret that necessity forced upon me an action that I would willingly have avoided.'

He looked through the cards, set some of them on one side on a system Ashenden did not understand, shuffled the remainder and once more put them in little piles.

'The cards warned me, I will never deny that, their warning was clear and definite. Love and a dark woman, danger, betrayal and death. It was as plain as the nose on your face. Any fool would have known what it meant and I have been using the cards all my life. There is hardly an action that I make without consulting them. There are no excuses. I was besotted. Ah, you of the Northern races do not know what love means, you do not know how it can prevent you from sleeping, how it can take your appetite for food away so that you dwindle as if from a fever, you do not understand what a frenzy it is so that you are like a mad-man and you will stick at nothing to satisfy your desire. A man like me is capable of every folly and every crime when he is in love, *si*, *Señor*, and of heroism. He can scale mountains higher than Everest and swim seas broader than the Atlantic. He is god, he is devil. Women have been my ruin.'

Once more the Hairless Mexican glanced at the cards, took some out of the little piles and left others in. He shuffled them again.

'I have been loved by multitudes of women. I do not say it in vanity. I offer no explanation. It is mere matter of fact. Go to Mexico City and ask them what they know of Manuel Carmona and of his triumphs. Ask them how many women have resisted Manuel Carmona.'

Ashenden, frowning a little, watched him reflectively. He wondered whether R., that shrewd fellow who chose his instruments with such a sure instinct, had not this time made a mistake, and he was uneasy. Did the Hairless Mexican really believe that he was irresistible or was he merely a blatant liar? In the course of his manipulations he had thrown out all the cards in the pack but four, and these now lay in front of him face downwards and side by side. He touched them one by one but did not turn them up.

'There is fate,' he said, 'and no power on earth can change it. I hesitate. This is a moment that ever fills me with apprehension and I have to steel myself to turn over the cards that may tell me that disaster awaits me. I am a brave man, but sometimes I have reached this stage and not had the courage to look at the four vital cards.'

Indeed now he eyed the backs of them with an anxiety he did not try to hide.

'What was I saying to you?'

'You were telling me that women found your fascinations irresistible,' replied Ashenden dryly.

'Once all the same I found a woman who resisted me. I saw her first in a house, a *casa de mujeres* in Mexico City, she was going down the stairs as I went up; she was not very beautiful, I had had a hundred more beautiful, but she had something that took my fancy and I told the old woman who kept the house to send her to me. You will know her when you go to Mexico City; they call her La Marqueza. She said that the girl was not an inmate, but came there only from time to time and had left. I told her to have her there next evening and not to let her go till I came. But I was delayed and when I arrived La Marqueza told me that the girl had said she was not used to being kept waiting and had gone. I am a good-natured fellow and I do not mind if women are capricious and teasing, that is part of their charm, so with a laugh I sent her a note of a hundred *duros* and promised that on the following day I would be punctual. But when I went, on the minute, La Marqueza handed me back my hundred *duros* and told me the girl did not fancy me. I laughed at her impertinence. I took off the diamond ring I was wearing and told the old woman to give her that and see whether it would induce her to change her mind. In the morning La Marqueza brought me in return for my ring—a red carnation. I did not know whether to be amused or angry. I am not used to being thwarted in my passions, I never hesitate to spend money (what is it for but to squander on pretty women?), and I told La Marqueza to go to the girl and say that I would give her a thousand *duros* to dine with me that night. Presently she came back with the answer that the girl would come on the condition that I allowed her to go home immediately after dinner. I accepted with a shrug of the shoulders. I did not think she was serious. I thought that she was saying that only to make herself more desired. She came to dinner at my house. Did I say she was not beautiful? She was the most beautiful, the most exquisite creature I had ever met. I was intoxicated. She had charm and she had wit. She had all the *gracia* of the Andalusian. In one word she was adorable. I asked her why she had treated me so casually and she laughed in my face. I laid myself out to be agreeable. I exercised all my skill. I surpassed myself. But when we finished dinner she rose from her seat and bade me good night. I asked her where she was going. She said I had promised to let her go and she trusted me as a man of honour to keep my word. I expostulated, I reasoned, I raved, I stormed. She held me to my word. All I could induce her to do was to consent to dine with me the following night on the same terms.

'You will think I was a fool, I was the happiest man alive; for seven days I paid her a thousand silver *duros* to dine with me. Every evening I waited for her with my heart in my mouth, as nervous as a *novillero* at his first bull-fight, and every evening she played with me, laughed at me, coquetted with me and drove me frantic. I was madly in love with her. I have never loved anyone so much before or since. I could think of nothing else. I was distracted. I neglected everything. I am a patriot and I love my country. A small band of us had got together and made up our minds that we could no longer put up with the misrule from which we were suffering. All the lucrative posts were given to other people, we were being made to pay taxes as though we were tradesmen, and we were exposed to abominable affronts. We had money and men. Our plans were made and we were ready to strike. I had an infinity of things to do, meetings to go to, ammunition to get, orders to give, I was so besotted over this woman that I could attend to nothing.

'You would have thought that I should be angry with her for making such a fool of me, me who had never known what it was not to gratify my smallest whim; I did not believe that she refused me to inflame my desires, I believed that she told the plain truth when she said that she would not give herself to me until she loved me. She said it was for me to make her love me. I thought her an angel. I was ready to wait. My passion was so consuming that sooner or later, I felt, it must communicate itself to her; it was like a fire on the prairie that devours everything around it; and at last—at last she said she loved me. My emotion was so terrific that I thought I should fall down and die. Oh, what rapture! Oh, what madness! I would have given her everything I possessed in the world, I would have torn down the stars from heaven to deck her hair; I wanted to do something to prove to her the extravagance of my love, I wanted to do the impossible, the incredible, I wanted to give her myself, my soul, my honour, all, all I had and all I was; and that night when she lay in my arms I told her of our plot and who we were that were concerned in it. I felt her body stiffen with attention, I was conscious of a flicker of her eyelids, there was something, I hardly knew what, the hand that stroked my face was dry and cold; a sudden suspicion seized me and all at once I remembered what the cards had told me: love and a dark woman, danger, betrayal, and death. Three times they'd said it and I wouldn't heed. I made no sign that I had noticed anything. She nestled up against my heart and told me that she was frightened to hear such things and asked me if So-and-so was concerned. I answered her. I wanted to make sure. One after the other, with infinite cunning, between her kisses she cajoled me into giving every detail of the plot, and now I was certain, as certain as I am that you sit before me, that she was a spy. She was a spy of the President's and she had been set to allure me with her devilish charm and now she had wormed out of me all our secrets. The lives of all of us were in her hands and I knew that if she left that room in twenty-four hours we should be dead men. And I loved her, I loved her; oh, words cannot tell you the agony of desire that burned my heart; love like that is no pleasure; it is pain, pain, but the exquisite pain that transcends all pleasure. It is that heavenly anguish that the saints speak of when they are seized with a divine ecstasy. I knew that she must not leave the room alive and I feared that if I delayed my courage would fail me.

'"I think I shall sleep," she said.

'"Sleep, my dove," I answered.

'"*Alma de mi corazon*," she called me. "Soul of my heart." They were the last words she spoke. Those heavy lids of hers, dark like a grape and faintly humid, those heavy lids of hers closed over her eyes and in a little while I knew by the regular movement of her breast against mine that she slept. You see, I loved her, I could not bear that she should suffer; she was a spy, yes, but my heart bade me spare her the terror of knowing what must happen. It is strange, I felt no anger because she had betrayed me, I should have hated her because of her vileness; I could not, I only felt that my soul was enveloped in night. Poor thing, poor thing. I could have cried in pity for her. I drew my arm very gently from around her, my left arm that was, my right was free, and raised myself on my hand. But she was so beautiful, I turned my face away when I drew the knife with all my strength across her lovely throat. Without awaking she passed from sleep to death.'

He stopped and stared frowning at the four cards that still lay, their backs upward, waiting to be turned up.

'It was in the cards. Why did I not take their warning? I will not look at them. Damn them. Take them away.'

With a violent gesture he swept the whole pack on to the floor.

'Though I am a free-thinker I had masses said for her soul.' He leaned back and rolled himself a cigarette. He inhaled a long breathful of smoke. He shrugged his shoulders. 'The Colonel said you were a writer. What do you write?'

'Stories,' replied Ashenden.

'Detective stories?'

'No.'

'Why not? They are the only ones I read. If I were a writer I should write detective stories.'

'They are very difficult. You need an incredible amount of invention. I devised a murder story once, but the murder was so ingenious that I could never find a way of bringing it home to the murderer, and, after all, one of the conventions of the detective story is that the mystery should in the end be solved and the criminal brought to justice.'

'If your murder is as ingenious as you think the only means you have of proving the murderer's guilt is by the discovery of his motives. When once you have found a motive the chances are that you will hit upon evidence that till then had escaped you. If there is no motive the most damning evidence will be inconclusive. Imagine for instance that you went up to a man in a lonely street on a moonless night and stabbed him to the heart. Who would ever think of you? But if he was your wife's lover, or your brother, or had cheated or insulted you, then a scrap of paper, a bit of string or a chance remark would be enough to hang you. What were your movements at the time he was killed? Are there not a dozen people who saw you before and after? But if he was a total stranger you would never for a moment be suspected. It was inevitable that Jack the Ripper should escape unless he was caught in the act.'

Ashenden had more than one reason to change the conversation. They were parting at Rome and he thought it necessary to come to an understanding with his companion about their respective movements. The Mexican was going to Brindisi and Ashenden to Naples. He meant to lodge at the Hotel de Belfast, which was a large second-rate hotel near the harbour frequented by commercial travellers and the thriftier kind of tripper. It would be as well to let the General have the number of his room so that he could come up if necessary without inquiring of the porter, and at the next stopping-place Ashenden got an envelope from the station-buffet and made him address it in his own writing to himself at the post-office in Brindisi. All Ashenden had to do then was to scribble a number on a sheet of paper and post it.

The Hairless Mexican shrugged his shoulders.

'To my mind all these precautions are rather childish. There is absolutely no risk. But whatever happens you may be quite sure that I will not compromise you.'

'This is not the sort of job which I'm very familiar with,' said Ashenden. 'I'm content to follow the Colonel's instructions and know no more about it than it's essential I should.'

'Quite so. Should the exigencies of the situation force me to take a drastic step and I get into trouble I shall of course be treated as a political prisoner. Sooner or later Italy is bound to come into the war on the side of the Allies and I shall be released. I have considered everything. But I beg you very seriously to have no more anxiety about the outcome of our mission than if you were going for a picnic on the Thames.'

But when at last they separated and Ashenden found himself alone in a carriage on the way to Naples he heaved a great sigh of relief. He was glad to be rid of that chattering, hideous, and fantastic creature. He was gone to meet Constantine Andreadi at Brindisi and if half of what he had told Ashenden was true, Ashenden could not but congratulate himself that he did not stand in the Greek spy's shoes. He wondered what sort of man he was. There was a grimness in the notion of his coming across the blue Ionian, with his confidential papers and his dangerous secrets, all unconscious of the noose into which he was putting his head. Well, that was war, and only fools thought it could be waged with kid gloves on.

Ashenden arrived in Naples and, having taken a room at the hotel, wrote its number on a sheet of paper in block letters and posted it to the Hairless Mexican. He went to the British Consulate, where R. had arranged to send any instructions he might have for him, and found that they knew about him and everything was in order. Then he put aside these matters and made up his mind to amuse himself. Here in the South the spring was well advanced and in the busy streets the sun was hot. Ashenden knew Naples pretty well. The Piazza di San Ferdinando, with its bustle, the Piazza del Plebiscito, with its handsome church, stirred in his heart pleasant recollections. The Strada di Chiara was as noisy as ever. He stood at corners and looked up the narrow alleys that climbed the hill precipitously, those alleys of high houses with the washing set out to dry on lines across the streets like pennants flying to mark a feast-day: and he sauntered along the shore, looking at the burnished sea with Capri faintly outlined against the bay, till he came to Posilippo, where there was an old, rambling, and bedraggled *palazzo* in which in his youth he had spent many a romantic hour. He observed the curious little pain with which the memories of the past wrung his heart-strings. Then he took a fly drawn by a small and scraggy pony and rattled back over the stones to the Galleria, where he sat in the cool and drank an *americano* and looked at the people who loitered there, talking, for ever talking with vivacious gestures, and, exercising his fancy sought from their appearance to divine their reality.

For three days Ashenden led the idle life that fitted so well the fantastical, untidy, and genial city. He did nothing from morning till night but wander at random, looking, not with the eye of the tourist who seeks for what ought to be seen, nor with the eye of the writer who looks for his own (seeing in a sunset a melodious phrase or in a face the inkling of a character), but with that of the tramp to whom whatever happens is absolute. He went to the museum to look at the statue of Agrippina the Younger, which he had particular reasons for remembering with affection, and took the opportunity to see once more the Titian and the Brueghel in the picture gallery. But he always came back to the church of Santa Chiara. Its grace, its gaiety, the airy persiflage with which it seemed to treat religion and at the back of this its sensual emotion; its extravagance, its elegance of line; to Ashenden it seemed to express, as it were in one absurd and grandiloquent metaphor, the sunny, dusty, lovely city and its bustling inhabitants. It said that life was charming and sad; it's a pity one hadn't any money but money wasn't everything, and anyway why bother when we are here today and gone tomorrow, and it was all very exciting and amusing, and after all we must make the best of things: *facciamo una piccola combinazione.*

But on the fourth morning, when Ashenden, having just stepped out of his bath, was trying to dry himself on a towel that absorbed no moisture, his door was quickly opened and a man slipped into his room.

'What d'you want?' cried Ashenden.

'It's all right. Don't you know me?'

'Good Lord, it's the Mexican. What have you done to yourself?'

He had changed his wig and wore now a black one, close-cropped, that fitted on his head like a cap. It entirely altered the look of him and though this was still odd enough, it was quite different from that which he had borne before. He wore a shabby grey suit.

'I can only stop a minute. He's getting shaved.'

Ashenden felt his cheeks suddenly redden.

'You found him then?'

'That wasn't difficult. He was the only Greek passenger on the ship. I went on board when she got in and asked for a friend who had sailed from the Piraeus. I said I had come to meet a Mr George Diogenidis. I pretended to be much puzzled at his not coming, and I got into conversation with Andreadi. He's travelling under a false name. He calls himself Lombardos. I followed him when he landed and do you know the first thing he did? He went into a barber's and had his beard shaved. What do you think of that?'

'Nothing. Anyone might have his beard shaved.'

'That is not what I think. He wanted to change his appearance. Oh, he's cunning. I admire the Germans, they leave nothing to chance, he's got his whole story pat, but I'll tell you that in a minute.'

'By the way, you've changed your appearance too.'

'Ah, yes, this is a wig I'm wearing; it makes a difference, doesn't it?'

'I should never have known you.'

'One has to take precautions. We are bosom friends. We had to spend the day in Brindisi and he cannot speak Italian. He was glad to have me help him and we travelled up together. I have brought him to this hotel. He says he is going to Rome tomorrow, but I shall not let him out of my sight; I do not want him to give me the slip. He says that he wants to see Naples and I have offered to show him everything there is to see.'

'Why isn't he going to Rome today?'

'That is part of the story. He pretends he is a Greek business man who has made money during the war. He says he was the owner of two coasting steamers and has just sold them. Now he means to go to Paris and have his fling. He says he has wanted to go to Paris all his life and at last has the chance. He is close. I tried to get him to talk. I told him I was a Spaniard and had been to Brindisi to arrange communications with Turkey about war material. He listened to me and I saw he was interested, but he told me nothing and of course I did not think it wise to press him. He has the papers on his person.'

'How do you know?'

'He is not anxious about his grip, but he feels every now and then round his middle. They're either in a belt or in the lining of his vest.'

'Why the devil did you bring him to this hotel?'

'I thought it would be more convenient. We may want to search his luggage.'

'Are you staying here too?'

'No, I am not such a fool as that. I told him I was going to Rome by the night train and would not take a room. But I must go, I promised to meet him outside the barber's in fifteen minutes.'

'All right.'

'Where shall I find you tonight if I want you?'

Ashenden for an instant eyed the Hairless Mexican, then with a slight frown looked away.

'I shall spend the evening in my room.'

'Very well. Will you just see that there's nobody in the passage?'

Ashenden opened the door and looked out. He saw no one. The hotel in point of fact at that season was nearly empty. There were few foreigners in Naples and trade was bad.

'It's all right,' said Ashenden.

The Hairless Mexican walked boldly out. Ashenden closed the door behind him. He shaved and slowly dressed. The sun was shining as brightly as usual on the square and the people who passed, the shabby little carriages with their scrawny horses, had the same air as before, but they did not any longer fill Ashenden with gaiety. He was not comfortable. He went out and called as was his habit at the Consulate to ask if there was a telegram for him. Nothing. Then he went to Cook's and looked out the trains to Rome: there was one soon after midnight and another at five in the morning. He wished he could catch the first. He did not know what were the Mexican's plans; if he really wanted to get to Cuba he would do well to make his way to Spain, and, glancing at the notices in the office, Ashenden saw that next day there was a ship sailing from Naples to Barcelona.

Ashenden was bored with Naples. The glare in the streets tired his eyes, the dust was intolerable, the noise was deafening. He went to the Galleria and had a drink. In the afternoon he went to a cinema. Then, going back to his hotel, he told the clerk that since he was starting so early in the morning he preferred to pay his bill at once, and he took his luggage to the station, leaving in his room only a dispatch-case in which were the printed part of his code and a book or two. He dined. Then returning to the hotel he sat down to wait for the Hairless Mexican. He could not conceal from himself the fact that he was exceedingly nervous. He began to read, but the book was tiresome, and he tried another; his attention wandered and he glanced at his watch. It was desperately early; he took up his book again, making up his mind that he would not look at his watch till he had read thirty pages, but though he ran his eyes conscientiously down one page after another he could not tell more than vaguely what it was he read. He looked at the time again. Good God, it was only half past ten. He wondered where the Hairless Mexican was, and what he was doing; he was afraid he would make a mess of things. It was a horrible business. Then it struck him that he had better shut the window and draw the curtains. He smoked innumerable cigarettes. He looked at his watch and it was a quarter past eleven. A thought struck him and his heart began to beat against his chest; out of curiosity he counted his pulse and was surprised to find that it was normal. Though it was a warm night and the room was stuffy his hands and feet were icy. What a nuisance it was, he reflected irritably, to have an imagination that conjured up pictures of things that you didn't in the least want to see! From his standpoint as a writer he had often considered murder, and his mind went to that fearful description of one in *Crime and Punishment.* He did not want to think of this topic, but it forced itself upon him; his book dropped to his knees and staring at the wall in front of him (it had a brown wall-paper with a pattern of dingy roses) he asked himself how, if one had to, one would commit a murder in Naples. Of course there was the Villa, the great leafy garden facing the bay in which stood the aquarium; that was deserted at night and very dark; things happened there that did not bear the light of day and prudent persons after dusk avoided its sinister paths. Beyond Posilippo the road was very solitary and there were byways that led up the hill in which by night you would never meet a soul, but how would you induce a man who had any nerves to go there? You might suggest a row in the bay, but the boatman who hired the boat would see you; it was doubtful indeed if he would let you go on the water alone; there were disreputable hotels down by the harbour where no questions were asked of persons who arrived late at night without luggage; but here again the waiter who showed you your room had the chance of a good look at you and you had on entering to sign an elaborate questionnaire.

Ashenden looked once more at the time. He was very tired. He sat now not even trying to read, his mind a blank.

Then the door opened softly and he sprang to his feet. His flesh crept. The Hairless Mexican stood before him.

'Did I startle you?' he asked smiling. 'I thought you would prefer me not to knock.'

'Did anyone see you come in?'

'I was let in by the night-watchman; he was asleep when I rang and didn't even look at me. I'm sorry I'm so late, but I had to change.'

The Hairless Mexican wore now the clothes he had travelled down in and his fair wig. It was extraordinary how different he looked. He was bigger and more flamboyant; the very shape of his face was altered. His eyes were shining and he seemed in excellent spirits. He gave Ashenden a glance.

'How white you are, my friend! Surely you're not nervous?'

'Have you got the documents?'

'No. He hadn't got them on him. This is all he had.'

He put down on the table a bulky pocket-book and a passport.

'I don't want them,' said Ashenden quickly. 'Take them.'

With a shrug of the shoulders the Hairless Mexican put the things back in his pocket.

'What was in his belt? You said he kept feeling round his middle.'

'Only money. I've looked through the pocket-book. It contains nothing but private letters and photographs of women. He must have locked the documents in his grip before coming out with me this evening.'

'Damn,' said Ashenden.

'I've got the key of his room. We'd better go and look through his luggage.'

Ashenden felt a sensation of sickness in the pit of his stomach. He hesitated. The Mexican smiled not unkindly.

'There's no risk, *amigo*,' he said, as though he were reassuring a small boy, 'but if you don't feel happy, I'll go alone.'

'No, I'll come with you,' said Ashenden.

'There's no one awake in the hotel and Mr Andreadi won't disturb us. Take off your shoes if you like.'

Ashenden did not answer. He frowned because he noticed that his hands were slightly trembling. He unlaced his shoes and slipped them off. The Mexican did the same.

'You'd better go first,' he said. 'Turn to the left and go straight along the corridor. It's number thirty-eight.'

Ashenden opened the door and stepped out. The passage was dimly lit. It exasperated him to feel so nervous when he could not but be aware that his companion was perfectly at ease. When they reached the door the Hairless Mexican inserted the key, turned the lock, and went in. He switched on the light. Ashenden followed him and closed the door. He noticed that the shutters were shut.

'Now we're all right. We can take our time.'

He took a bunch of keys out of his pocket, tried one or two and at last hit upon the right one. The suitcase was filled with clothes.

'Cheap clothes,' said the Mexican contemptuously as he took them out. 'My own principle is that it's always cheaper in the end to buy the best. After all one is a gentleman or one isn't a gentleman.'

'Are you obliged to talk?' said Ashenden.

'A spice of danger affects people in different ways. It only excites me, but it puts you in a bad temper, *amigo*.'

'You see, I'm scared and you're not,' replied Ashenden with candour.

'It's merely a matter of nerves.'

Meanwhile he felt the clothes, rapidly but with care, as he took them out. There were no papers of any sort in the suitcase. Then he took out his knife and slit the lining. It was a cheap piece and the lining was gummed to the material of which the suitcase was made. There was no possibility of anything being concealed in it.

'They're not here. They must be hidden in the room.'

'Are you sure he didn't deposit them in some office? At one of the consulates, for example?'

'He was never out of my sight for a moment except when he was getting shaved.'

The Hairless Mexican opened the drawers and the cupboard. There was no carpet on the floor. He looked under the bed, in it, and under the mattress. His dark eyes shot up and down the room, looking for a hiding-place, and Ashenden felt that nothing escaped him.

'Perhaps he left them in charge of the clerk downstairs?'

'I should have known it. And he wouldn't dare. They're not here. I can't understand it.'

He looked about the room irresolutely. He frowned in the attempt to guess at a solution of the mystery.

'Let's get out of here,' said Ashenden.

'In a minute.'

The Mexican went down on his knees, quickly and neatly folded the clothes, and packed them up again. He locked the bag and stood up. Then, putting out the light, he slowly opened the door and looked out. He beckoned to Ashenden and slipped into the passage. When Ashenden had followed him he stopped and locked the door, put the key in his pocket, and walked with Ashenden to his room. When they were inside it and the bolt drawn Ashenden wiped his clammy hands and his forehead.

'Thank God, we're out of that!'

'There wasn't really the smallest danger. But what are we to do now? The Colonel will be angry that the papers haven't been found.'

'I'm taking the five o'clock train to Rome. I shall wire for instructions there.'

'Very well, I will come with you.'

'I should have thought it would suit you better to get out of the country more quickly. There's a boat tomorrow that goes to Barcelona. Why don't you take that and if necessary I can come to see you there?'

The Hairless Mexican gave a little smile.

'I see that you are anxious to be rid of me. Well, I won't thwart a wish that your inexperience in these matters excuses. I will go to Barcelona. I have a visa for Spain.'

Ashenden looked at his watch. It was a little after two. He had nearly three hours to wait. His companion comfortably rolled himself a cigarette.

'What do you say to a little supper?' he asked. 'I'm as hungry as a wolf.'

The thought of food sickened Ashenden, but he was terribly thirsty. He did not want to go out with the Hairless Mexican, but neither did he want to stay in that hotel by himself.

'Where could one go at this hour?'

'Come along with me. I'll find you a place.'

Ashenden put on his hat and took his dispatch-case in his hand. They went downstairs. In the hall the porter was sleeping soundly on a mattress on the floor. As they passed the desk, walking softly in order not to wake him, Ashenden noticed in the pigeon-hole belonging to his room a letter. He took it out and saw that it was addressed to him. They tiptoed out of the hotel and shut the door behind them. They then walked quickly away. Stopping after a hundred yards or so under a lamp-post Ashenden took the letter out of his pocket and read; it came from the Consulate and said: *The enclosed telegram arrived tonight and in case it is urgent I am sending it round to your hotel by messenger.* It had apparently been left some time before midnight while Ashenden was sitting in his room. He opened the telegram and saw that it was in code.

'Well, it'll have to wait,' he said, putting it back in his pocket.

The Hairless Mexican walked as though he knew his way through the deserted streets and Ashenden walked by his side. At last they came to a tavern in a blind alley, noisome and evil, and this the Mexican entered.

'It's not the Ritz,' he said, 'but at this hour of the night it's only in a place like this that we stand a chance of getting something to eat.'

Ashenden found himself in a long sordid room at one end of which a wizened young man sat at a piano; there were tables standing out from the wall on each side and against them benches. A number of persons, men and women, were sitting about. They were drinking beer and wine. The women were old, painted, and hideous; and their harsh gaiety was at once noisy and lifeless. When Ashenden and the Hairless Mexican came in they all stared and when they sat down at one of the tables Ashenden looked away in order not to meet the leering eyes, just ready to break into a smile, that sought his insinuatingly. The wizened pianist strummed a tune and several couples got up and began to dance. Since there were not enough men to go round some of the women danced together. The General ordered two plates of spaghetti and a bottle of Capri wine. When the wine was brought he drank a glassful greedily and then waiting for the *pasta* eyed the women who were sitting at the other tables.

'Do you dance?' he asked Ashenden. 'I'm going to ask one of these girls to have a turn with me.'

He got up and Ashenden watched him go up to one who had at least flashing eyes and white teeth to recommend her; she rose and he put his arm round her. He danced well. Ashenden saw him begin talking; the woman laughed and presently the look of indifference with which she had accepted his offer changed to one of interest. Soon they were chatting gaily. The dance came to an end and putting her back at her table he returned to Ashenden and drank another glass of wine.

'What do you think of my girl?' he asked. 'Not bad, is she? It does one good to dance. Why don't you ask one of them? This is a nice place, is it not? You can always trust me to find anything like this. I have an instinct.'

The pianist started again. The woman looked at the Hairless Mexican and when with his thumb he pointed to the floor she jumped up with alacrity. He buttoned up his coat, arched his back, and standing up by the side of the table waited for her to come to him. He swung her off, talking smiling, and already he was on familiar terms with everyone in the room. In fluent Italian, with his Spanish accent, he exchanged badinage with one and the other. They laughed at his sallies. Then the waiter brought two heaped platefuls of macaroni and when the Mexican saw them he stopped dancing without ceremony and, allowing his partner to get back to her table as she chose, hurried to his meal.

'I'm ravenous,' he said. 'And yet I ate a good dinner. Where did you dine? You're going to eat some macaroni, aren't you?'

'I have no appetite,' said Ashenden.

But he began to eat and to his surprise found that he was hungry. The Hairless Mexican ate with huge mouthfuls, enjoying himself vastly; his eyes shone and he was loquacious. The woman he had danced with had in that short time told him all about herself and he repeated now to Ashenden what she had said. He stuffed huge pieces of bread into his mouth. He ordered another bottle of wine.

'Wine?' he cried scornfully. 'Wine is not a drink, only champagne; it does not even quench your thirst. Well, *amigo*, are you feeling better?'

'I'm bound to say I am,' smiled Ashenden.

'Practice, that is all you want, practice.'

He stretched out his hand to pat Ashenden on the arm.

'What's that?' cried Ashenden with a start. 'What's that stain on your cuff?'
The Hairless Mexican gave his sleeve a glance.
'That? Nothing. It's only blood. I had a little accident and cut myself.'
Ashenden was silent. His eyes sought the clock that hung over the door.
'Are you anxious about your train? Let me have one more dance and then I'll
accompany you to the station.'
The Mexican got up and with his sublime self-assurance seized in his arms
the woman who sat nearest to him and danced away with her. Ashenden
watched him moodily. He was a monstrous, terrible figure, with that blond wig
and his hairless face, but he moved with a matchless grace; his feet were small
and seemed to hold the ground like the pads of a cat or a tiger; his rhythm was
wonderful and you could not but see that the bedizened creature he danced
with was intoxicated by his gestures. There was music in his toes and in the
long arms that held her so firmly, and there was music in those long legs that
seemed to move strangely from the hips. Sinister and grotesque though he was,
there was in him now a feline elegance, even something of beauty, and you felt a
secret, shameful fascination. To Ashenden he suggested one of those
sculptures of the pre-Aztec hewers of stone, in which there is barbarism and
vitality, something terrible and cruel, and yet withal a brooding and significant
loveliness. All the same he would gladly have left him to finish the night by
himself in that sordid dance-hall, but he knew that he must have a business
conversation with him. He did not look forward to it without misgiving. He had
been instructed to give Manuel Carmona certain sums in return for certain
documents. Well, the documents were not forthcoming, and as for the
rest—Ashenden knew nothing about that; it was no business of his. The
Hairless Mexican waved gaily as he passed him.
'I will come the moment the music stops. Pay the bill and then I shall be
ready.'
Ashenden wished he could have seen into his mind. He could not even make
a guess at its workings. Then the Mexican, with his scented handkerchief
wiping the sweat from his brow, came back.
'Have you had a good time, General?' Ashenden asked him.
'I always have a good time. Poor white trash, but what do I care? I like to feel
the body of a woman in my arms and see her eyes grow languid and her lips part
as her desire for me melts the marrow in her bones like butter in the sun. Poor
white trash, but women.'
They sallied forth. The Mexican proposed that they should walk and in that
quarter, at that hour, there would have been little chance of finding a cab; but the
sky was starry. It was a summer night and the air was still. The silence walked
beside them like the ghost of a dead man. When they neared the station the
houses seemed on a sudden to take on a greyer, more rigid line, and you felt that
the dawn was at hand. A little shiver trembled through the night. It was a
moment of apprehension and the soul for an instant was anxious; it was as
though, inherited down the years in their countless millions, it felt a witless fear
that perhaps another day would not break. But they entered the station and the
night once more enwrapped them. One or two porters lolled about like stage-
hands after the curtain has rung down and the scene is struck. Two soldiers in
dim uniforms stood motionless.
The waiting-room was empty, but Ashenden and the Hairless Mexican went
to sit in the most retired part of it.
'I still have an hour before my train goes. I'll just see what this cable's about.'